Pat Barr was born in Norwich, Norfolk, and read English at Birmingham University and University College, London.

Her first non-fiction books, *The Coming of the Barbarians* and *The Deer Cry Pavilion*, are about western settlements in Japan, where she once lived for three years. Her other non-fiction books include *A Curious Life for a Lady*, *To China With Love*, *The Memsahibs* and *Taming the Jungle*, all set in the nineteenth-century East. She then turned her hand to fiction with *Jade* (also published by Corgi Books).

Pat Barr makes frequent trips to the East, dividing the rest of her time between Blackheath, London, and the Hebridean Isle of Coll.

Also by Pat Barr

JADE

and published by Corgi Books

KENJIRO

Pat Barr

CORGI BOOKS

KENJIRO
A CORGI BOOK 0 552 12540 7

Originally published in Great Britain by
Martin Secker & Warburg Limited

PRINTING HISTORY
Martin Secker & Warburg edition published 1985
Corgi edition published 1986
Corgi edition reissued 1986

This book is set in 10/11 pt Plantin

Corgi Books are published by Transworld Publishers
Ltd., 61–63 Uxbridge Road, Ealing, London W5 5SA, in
Australia by Transworld Publishers (Aust.) Pty. Ltd.,
4–8 Waters Road, Neutral Bay, Sydney, NSW, and in New
Zealand by Transworld Publishers (N.Z.) Ltd., Cnr. Moselle
and Waipareira Avenues, Henderson, Auckland.

Printed and bound in Great Britain by
Cox & Wyman Ltd., Reading, Berks.

For my dear friends, Valli and Tony Murray,
who once lived on the Bluff

. . . In the land of breakage, who would rate you
for sticking little fingers through a paper screen? –
Since circumstance but rarely spares the rod, and
All at once the screen may fall, the wall, the roof, the world.

And thus you frame the tight and careful carton,
to house an early careworn life –
Tradition's doubtful timber, imported plaster ethics
prone to break and flake away:
Until some war or saké shakes all down – and then
You bathe your head and sober up and quietly build again.

from *Japanese Sandman*
by D. J. Enright; 'Bread rather than Blossoms',
Secker & Warburg, 1956

PART ONE

1862—1869

AUTHOR'S NOTE

I have tried to describe as accurately as possible the actual historical, political, and social conditions of the period. Famous people such as the Emperor Meiji, Sir Harry Parkes, and Saigo Takamori are often referred to, but remain off stage. Some of the fictional characters such as Desmond Hand and Taneo Takahashi are partly based on the records of individuals who lived at the time. Events such as the Imperial Restoration and the First Sino-Japanese War are well known; readers may not be aware that two British officers were indeed assassinated by anti-barbarian swordsmen at Kamakura, that a Consul of Hakodate was convicted for desecrating Ainu graves, that women of the Yoshiwara were displayed to public view in cages. In the realm of fiction, readers of my earlier novel set in nineteenth-century China may recognise the Fortescue family and Captain Hirata of the white gloves. Where practical I have translated Japanese terms, except for words like *tatami* and *saké* that are both familiar and unique to the country. Lastly, I am well aware that the Japanese put family names before our 'first' names, but I have 'westernised' them for clarity. They also use many honorifics and subtle forms of personal address which, I feel, are virtually untranslatable into colloquial English.

FACTUAL PROLOGUE

When Charles Lennox Richardson set sail from Shanghai for Yokohama early in September 1862, he had no premonition that the journey would be his last, or that it would earn him a footnote in history. Mr Richardson had been in business on the China coast for several years and planned to visit Japan briefly before going home to England. In Yokohama, Richardson lodged with his friends, Mr and Mrs William Marshall, for the port had been opened to foreign trade and residence only three years previously and as yet had no decent hotel accommodation.

On the afternoon of Sunday, September 14th, Richardson rode out to see the sights of the vicinity accompanied by William Marshall, Woodthorpe Clarke, another local merchant, and Mrs Borrodail, a relative of Clarke's also on a visit from China. They left Yokohama by boat and landed at Kanagawa, where horses awaited them. They rode off along the Tokaido highway that led towards the capital, Edo, which was still closed to foreigners. Soon they began to pass, at intervals, a number of palanquins each with a retinue of attendants carrying swords and spears. The attendants' uniforms and the palanquins were emblazoned with the crest of a golden cross inside a circle, signifying that the travellers belonged to the Satsuma clan from the southern Japanese island of Kyushu.

The foreigners paid little attention and continued at a leisurely pace, chatting among themselves. Rounding a corner, they suddenly came upon the main body of the procession – palanquins, mounted guards, foot soldiers, and porters – spread right across the road ahead. Mrs Borrodail and Richardson, who were somewhat in advance of their com-

11

panions, edged aside to allow the procession to pass while craning forward curiously to look at an elegantly embossed gold and black palanquin that swung between two rows of mounted guards. Suddenly a man stepped forward, determinedly barring Richardson's way, and he called back, 'We are stopped.'

'Don't go on. We can turn into a side road,' Clarke replied; and the foreigners began wheeling their horses round. As they did so, a man from the centre of the procession loosed his upper garments from his shoulders and, drawing his long sword, swung it in both hands and hurtled forward to attack Richardson. At this the foreigners retreated at a gallop, passing through groups of retainers who aimed sword blows at them as they sped by.

Clearing their assailants, they cantered on until they neared a tea-house at the edge of the village of Namamugi, where Richardson's horse began to flag. Seeing this, Marshall told Clarke to go on with Mrs Borrodail while he turned back. 'Are you badly hurt?' he called. Unable to reply, Richardson swayed in the saddle and fell from his horse, his bowels protruding from a mortal wound in his stomach. Deciding that he could do the wretched man no good and nearly fainting from his own wounds, Marshall galloped off, leaving Richardson for dead at the roadside.

As the survivors fled towards the safety of the American Consulate at Kanagawa, the woman who owned the nearby tea-house crept across to Richardson, who was still just alive. He asked for water in a feeble whisper and she was about to fetch some when she heard the procession approaching and hurried fearfully back indoors. Peeping out, she saw one of the guards approach Richardson who raised his hands in a futile gesture of self-protection. Several men then surrounded him; swords flashed in the sunlight; there was a strangled cry; the men went on their way. Shortly afterwards the gold and black palanquin appeared in the distance and halted while an officer rode forward to examine the bleeding bundle on the roadside. One look was enough to assure him that the foreign barbarian was dead.

CHAPTER ONE

'Good afternoon. Am I speaking to Miss Elinor Mills?' Annette Clarke moved to greet the young lady who had just arrived on the Yokohama quay from Hong Kong on the steamship *Fiery Cross*.

'Yes indeed. But I was expecting my brother . . .'

'Unfortunately the doctor has been delayed and he has sent me to . . . I am Mrs Clarke, my dear. You mustn't be alarmed.'

'Oh, I'm not, only . . .'

'I've brought another chair for you to ride in. We're going to my home first. Pray come along . . .' Mrs Clarke grabbed Elinor's arm and began to positively pull her along the quayside. 'It will soon be dark and we mustn't delay for a moment. Here are the chairs and my bearers will carry us. It's only a short distance and your brother has sent these guards for our extra protection. So please don't be alarmed.'

'But I'm not in the least alarmed, Mrs Clarke,' Elinor began protesting again as the guards, wearing black cloaks and strange, mushroom-shaped hats, stepped forward to bundle her and her hand-luggage into a small, lacquer-wood palanquin.

'My servants will see to the rest of your things in the Customs Shed,' Mrs Clarke promised as she closed the door and jumped into another palanquin with the speed of a rabbit bolting down a hole.

Elinor settled herself as best she might in the stuffy interior, thinking vexedly that this longed-for arrival in Japan was proving very different from her imaginings. And why was this jumpy stranger meeting her instead of Arnold, her dear elder brother? She had only just discovered how to raise the

13

queer little lattice in the chair's side and peep into the gathering dusk when the bearers halted and, lowering the carrying poles, helped her out. Mrs Clarke hurried her through a wicker gate, across a verandah and into a sitting room, where she at last paused to survey the newcomer properly.

'Here we are, Miss Mills. All safe and sound. Now please make yourself at home. My, what a pretty head of hair you have, my dear,' she added, as Elinor removed a velvet-trimmed bonnet to reveal an abundance of braided, tawny-blonde hair that shone in the lamplight. She was scarcely of medium height, Mrs Clarke noted, and only her clear grey eyes suggested her close relationship to large, reddish-haired Dr Mills of the British Legation. 'I'll order tea. You must be tired after the voyage, and then I'll explain . . .'

She darted away, leaving Elinor to look round curiously. There was a lot of flowery chintz and padded cotton about, obviously intended to give more substance to the locally made bamboo furniture, and Chinese rugs were scattered over the native floor-mats of woven straw. Elinor was pleased by the room's rather humble, makeshift air, for she had found Hong Kong, where she had been staying, much too grand and set in its ways.

A Japanese servant appeared with a tray, followed by Mrs Clarke.

'I've opened a tin of Crawford's biscuits specially for you, Miss Mills. They're as scarce as gold dust in this back-of-beyond,' she announced rather accusingly.

'Oh, you really shouldn't have bothered, Mrs Clarke . . .'

'I thought you needed some familiar sustenance to keep you in good heart. You see, I can't conceal from you any longer that something quite dreadful has just happened. Indeed my own husband Woodthorpe was closely involved and it's a great mercy he wasn't killed too.'

'Too? But is my brother . . .?' Elinor gasped, afraid for the first time.

'No, no, he's perfectly well and is coming to fetch you shortly. He went to the scene of the crime yesterday and had

14

to perform a post-mortem on poor Mr Richardson today.' As she poured tea, Mrs Clarke explained briefly, omitting the more violent details, what had occurred the previous day when her husband had gone riding along the Tokaido highway with his cousin Mrs Borrodail, Charles Richardson, and William Marshall, and had encountered the procession of Satsuma clansmen. 'My husband was only slightly injured, praise be, and is giving his account of the affair to our Chargé d'Affaires, Colonel Neale, this very minute, Miss Mills. Mrs Borrodail is still a-bed suffering from shock and Mr Marshall is quite badly cut about. Your brother is attending to him also, I believe. So you can now realise why I was so anxious for your safety when you arrived,' she concluded, offering Elinor another precious biscuit.

'Oh dear, I am sorry! How perfectly dreadful for you all! Is there anything I can do to help?'

'A most kind thought, Miss Mills, but we are assured the immediate danger is past, though we're still in a state of some uproar, as you can imagine. Our menfolk were determined to set off in pursuit of the villains at once last night and exact vengeance on the spot. But Colonel Neale has dissuaded them and is dealing with the matter through normal diplomatic channels.'

Elinor laughed tremulously. 'And my Aunt Clarabella, with whom I was staying in Hong Kong, wouldn't hear of my coming here at first. "Fancy trusting yourself among those little yellow Japs," she said. "Frightful people – liable to slit their own bellies open at the drop of a hat." I thought it such a funny picture at the time – slitting one's belly while dropping one's hat. But now . . .'

'Still I must reassure you . . . some more biscuits, dear? No . . . Then they must go back in the tin before they soften . . . As I was saying . . .' Mrs Clarke settled more comfortably in her chair, '. . . reassure you that yesterday's tragedy was quite the most terrible event since our little settlement was opened as a treaty port three years ago. As a rule we rub along well enough with the natives and they make the most obliging and polite servants. And usually we manage to keep quite jolly among ourselves. There's the Anglo-Saxon hotel where the gentlemen play billiards and we ladies take tea, gossip, and read the Home papers. Our first Episcopal church is just being built, with seating for over three hundred. Though at the moment if every professed Christian in the place attended service − which is far from the case, I fear − there'd still be empty pews.'

'I was told there are about two hundred foreign residents altogether?'

'And so few of them to fly the distaff side of the flag, which is why I'm particularly delighted you've come to stay for a while. That is if . . .' she rushed on without finishing her thought. 'But the place positively swarms with bachelors, the crusty, the confirmed, and those ardently seeking release from their sorry state. So you, as one of the few young un-married ladies, certainly won't lack for escorts . . .'

She glanced covertly at Elinor to see the effect of that, but self-composed Miss Mills only smiled. 'Well, Arnold is still a bachelor, though I'm not sure which category he comes into. He's several years older than I, you see, and has seldom been at home since I grew up.'

'So he told me, and he's been greatly looking forward to your visit. He's counting on you to brighten up his lodgings, where you'll be staying too. Right on the edge of the native town. I hope you won't mind that? Of course, you may not be . . .'

Again she checked herself and hurried on. 'I've done my best with this little bungalow, but it's just blown together. The Japanese simply tie the joint beams, you know, so that in earthquakes they can move a bit instead of collapsing.' She glanced round complacently. 'Chintz works wonders, don't you agree? And I've stuck wallpaper over those wood and paper screens − the natives call them *shoji* − to make them look more home-like. But there's no mantelpiece for orna-ments and no fires to gather cosily round. The natives use portable charcoal stoves called *hibachi* which are very ineffective and dangerous. But here I am rattling on like this without knowing if you . . .'

Elinor had just determined to corner Mrs Clarke into an

explanation of her conditional 'ifs' when they heard steps on the verandah and Arnold hurried in, smothering her in a brotherly hug. 'Elinor, how glad I am to see you! I was so worried about you travelling up alone from Hong Kong without escort.'

She drew herself up against his height. 'But I'm not a child any more, Arnold, and quite capable of getting myself on a ship before it leaves and off when it arrives.'

'And of course in the normal way I'd have met you, only . . . You've told her?' He glanced at Mrs Clarke, who nodded. 'Such a very awful tragedy, and to happen just as you arrive.' He patted her head paternally. 'But in the circumstances I'm afraid I can't possibly allow you to stay in Japan, Elinor. Mrs Borrodail, who's still in a shocked state, is leaving on the *Fiery Cross* when she sails tomorrow and I've suggested you accompany her.'

'What! But I've only just come . . .' Elinor jerked her head away.

'But we aren't safe here, Elinor. These anti-foreign clansmen could strike again at any moment.'

'Then that's simply a risk I shall have to take along with every other foreigner,' she replied. 'I'm certainly not prepared to leave immediately after coming all this way to see you.'

She spoke with quiet determination and he blinked, realising he knew very little about this young sister of his. She had developed very much a mind of her own, his mother had written, and nothing in her home town of Harrogate, or indeed in the whole of England, seemed to satisfy her until eventually she had persuaded her parents to let her visit Hong Kong. Once arrived, however, his Aunt Clarabella had written to say that nothing would satisfy Elinor but to visit Yokohama. Letters had been exchanged on the prudence of this step considering the unsettled state of Japan, but Arnold, who was eager to see his sister, had eventually been persuaded. And now this . . .

Elinor, taking advantage of his irresolution, continued briskly, 'In any case, I feel that a spice of danger is the price we pay for adventure. I've always admired you, Arnold, for

17

taking off to see the world and I think that women who choose to come to outlandish places like this should be as brave as men. Don't you agree, Mrs Clarke?'

Annette Clarke nodded vigorously. 'Yes, yes, Miss Mills. I've been telling myself that very thing since the murder. I keep thinking of a cousin of mine who was killed in the massacre of Cawnpore a few years ago. Compared to what some of our countrywomen have endured in the colonies we are very fortunate here on the whole and the natives are relatively civilised. And I think, if I may say so, Doctor, that your sister is showing the right spirit and should stay. Colonel Neale assured us last night there's no immediate cause for panic, remember.'

Arnold gave in easily to his true inclination. 'Well, all right; we'll see how it goes. But if there's any more trouble you must leave on the next boat, Elinor.'

She nodded vaguely and Mrs Clarke sighed in relief. 'Then that's settled. I'll order more tea and arrange for Miss Mills' luggage to be taken to your lodgings, Doctor. And just think what an asset your pretty sister will be for all our lonely bachelors!'

As she hurried to the kitchen, Mrs Clarke made a quick survey of possible candidates for Elinor's hand. Love-lorn Percival Storey, the Legation's senior interpreter, was the most obvious; but he was an earnest workhorse and she guessed Miss Mills would prefer someone rather more dashing. In any case, she thought with pleasure, the doctor's sister would almost certainly be one of the first Englishwomen to be married in the new church when it opened, and in the meantime she must do her best to help her settle down.

Annette Clark found her self-appointed task easy enough, for Elinor Mills wanted nothing more than to settle down in Yokohama. She took to the settler's life like the proverbial duck to water, everyone said, and whereas in dull Harrogate nothing had been right for her, here nothing seemed wrong.

The fast-growing pioneer settlement was still in the process of being built up, improved upon, and added to and had a rakish, opportunistic air that reminded Elinor of pictures she

18

had seen of frontier towns in the American Wild West.

From the verandah of her room in the Legation, temporarily removed from Edo, Elinor commanded a good view of the low-lying port. Westward was the foreign settlement, with about sixty wooden bungalows, commercial offices, warehouses and two stores that sold imported goods – everything from pickles to sou'westers, from merino-wool underpants to tarpaulins, from tins of anchovies to cigars, anchors, tablecloths, iodine, almanacs, champagne, leather boots, French clocks, Swedish matches and much else beside.

The port's eastern quarter contained the native town, which was similarly unpretentious and temporary-looking. Like the foreigners, its Japanese inhabitants (merchants, servants, customs men, porters) had come to live there during the last three years, for, prior to its opening as one of the country's first treaty ports, in 1859, Yokohama had been no more than a small fishing village. Since then its harbour had become increasingly busy, its waters bordered with a waterfront Bund, two stone jetties and a large Customs House and churned by more and more foreign ships. Traders predominated, their hulls laden with manufactured goods and provisions from China and the West, and carrying away a variety of less sophisticated items, such as raw silk and cotton, vegetable wax, rape-seed and gall nuts. Most of the vessels flew the British flag and were based in Hong Kong, but other nations were well represented also – Dutch corvettes, French frigates, Australian coalers, Russian and American whalers, clippers and paddle steamers from California and Canada.

In spite of the coming and going of foreign vessels, the settlers were jumpily aware of their isolated, precarious position on a confined and swampy fringe of an unknown oriental empire, and had been greatly alarmed by the murderous attack on Richardson. The able-bodied males among them formed a Volunteer Defence Corps soon after and persuaded the Japanese to erect guardhouses along that portion of the Tokaido highway where foreigners were permitted to travel. Colonel Neale, backed by the Foreign

Office, also sent very strong representations to the Shogun's government demanding compensation for the crime and retribution for its perpetrators. However, the rulers of Edo had little control over the clans in the distant south-western provinces, among whom the Satsuma were the strongest and most volatile, as Percival Storey explained to Arnold and Elinor when he called on them one evening.

'We'll have to go down there ourselves and knock some sense into them before they'll comply with our demands, you'll see,' Percival declared, sipping a whisky and soda and wagging his head sagely. Percival was stringily built, with a trim moustache, flat brown hair parted straight in the middle, and a sweeping air of infallibility on the subject of Japanese politics that often infuriated his compatriots. He was a highly ambitious man who had found his right niche and entertained secret dreams of becoming Her Majesty's Minister Plenipotentiary to Japan, if not to China, within the next twenty years.

'Oh, you're always so sure of everything!' Elinor said testily, for she too found his mixture of moony shyness and pomposity trying. Leaving the men to argue, she went to instruct the cook about supper, pausing to lean over the kitchen balcony and watch the evening activities of the neighbouring shopkeepers, whose family quarters overhung the network of canals that dissected the nearby native town. The lively play of people's shadows on the drawn *shoji* screens fascinated her, but the canal's proximity was a mixed blessing for it ran from a salt-water swamp behind the town and stank most offensively during rains and heat. Although Elinor did not yet know it, the notorious Gankiro teahouse stood on the north-eastern part of that swamp. It had been built by the Japanese 'for the amusement of foreigners', as the red banners on its roof proclaimed. Young women and cheap grog were on sale there in a flagrant manner which greatly scandalised visiting clergymen, who wrote to the press complaining that Yokohama's foreign bachelors had been encouraged into dissolute, immoral habits by the money-grubbing, canny Japanese. A principal reason for this lamentable state of affairs, the clerical writers conceded, was the dire shortage of respectable ladies, whose worthy moral influence was sorely needed to civilise and refine the lives of the footloose males.

'Well, here's a bit of good news − another married lady with two daughters coming to live here soon, so writes my Aunt Clarabella from Hong Kong,' Arnold was saying when Elinor returned to the sitting room, where the evening post had just been delivered.

'How old are the daughters?' Percival was ever hopeful.

'She doesn't say, and, knowing her, I think she would if they were at an interesting stage. Beth and Lilian, daughters of Claud and Mary Fortescue. He's in banking, coming out as an agent on spec. from Shanghai. Rather a dull fish, she says, but his wife sounds more promising − "a lively, cheerful little body".' He quoted from his aunt's letter.

'Lilian, what a lovely name!' Percival rolled it wistfully over his tongue, conjuring a vision of a demure, adoring damsel with china-blue eyes perhaps, and cast in quite a different mould from the rather forthright and self-assured Elinor Mills. Why, how much he could tell Lilian about the Japanese and their politics, for a start!

'Aunt says she knew them earlier when they were in Hong Kong,' Arnold continued, and Elinor grinned. 'She would, of course.' Their Aunt Clarabella and her husband Uncle Dickie had first gone to Hong Kong about fifteen years before and had made their mark − he as a successful land agent, she as a generous hostess, a gossip, and a fashion-setter. It was her boast that she knew the names, occupations, marital status, and any relevant scandalous titbits about every British resident along the China coast. Considering this, the information she had given her nephew about the Fortescues was somewhat scant, from which Arnold deduced that they were not especially interesting.

'Any news from your family?' he asked Percival, who was flipping through the *Japan Herald*.

'Nothing much.' Percival's family consisted only of his widowed father and a married sister with whom he had little in common; and this very lack of strong, influential home ties made him the more determined to succeed out here in the East through sheer hard work and perseverance.

Arnold poured a second drink. 'Any whisky on the market, I'm getting short?'

Percival perused the newspaper's back columns. 'Yep. Hansard and Keele have some Long Johns, not to mention Montobellos in pints, Worthington's port wine, Old Q Brandy, Claret, Old Tom Gin, Pyramid Bass in casks of four dozen, and, you'll be glad to hear, copious draughts of Dr Mills' Bitters.'

Arnold groaned; the unfortunate coincidence of his name-sake's manufacture of a particularly noxious brand of tonic bitters was a cross he had long borne. 'Then Elinor can have the last of the port wine.' He handed her a glass. 'Aunt wants to know if you'll be back in Hong Kong in time for the Spring Races.'

'No, I shan't be, shall I, Arnold? Please say no . . . There's these Fortescues for one thing. When are they arriving, does Aunt say?'

'In a few weeks.'

'Then I can be useful helping them to settle in.'

He chuckled. 'Quite the old hand already, hey?'

'Well, I shall be,' she said, 'by the time they arrive.'

'Join us for dinner tonight?' Arnold asked Percival, poking his head round the door of the Yokohama Consulate office a few weeks later. 'The Fortescues are here and staying with us for a while till their bungalow is ready.'

'Oh, rather − I'd love to . . . with daughters, I hope?' He winked.

'Oh, yes.'

'And . . .?'

'You'll see.' Arnold rolled his eyes ardently as he dis-appeared.

Percival dressed with extra care that evening; he had a pre-monition about this Lilian Fortescue − rot, of course. The lack of feminine companionship here made a fellow feel quite soppy sometimes. Now if only Lilian . . . He carried his secret dream intact to the Mills' lodgings and was thus a little disappointed by his first sight of Mrs Fortescue, a small, comely woman with ash-blonde hair and blue eyes; but not really old enough.

'Delighted.' He bowed and shook hands with her husband, long-nosed, long-chinned, and with an expression of such tense sobriety that he could have been a missionary, had he had a different spouse.

Arnold went to an inner door saying, 'And I told Mrs Fortescue that you were specially anxious to meet her daughters, Percy, so they're coming now.' He opened the door with a flourish and Elinor, smiling slyly, ushered in two small girls, the elder with dark ringlets, the younger a whey-faced, bony child with her father's expression.

'Beth is nine, Lilian is seven. Shake hands with the gentleman, dearies. And we have a son, Edgar, who's at school in England.' Mrs Fortescue pushed them forward proudly, while Elinor grinned at Percy.

'Aren't they quite angelic? Mr Storey is devoted to children, Mrs Fortescue. He asked about your daughters several times.'

Percival gave her a venomous look as he shook two small sticky hands, then swallowed a large glass of sherry along with his disappointment. As they went to the dinner table, he resolved to make the best of Mrs Fortescue, who, at least, was positively bubbling with curiosity about Japan.

'Now you old hands must tell me exactly what my daughters and I may and mayn't do here,' she sparkled at them. 'Claud tried hard to dissuade me from coming, didn't you, dear? Far too dangerous, he said, all these murders and such . . . But I simply wouldn't be put off. Shanghai is so very humdrum and full of foreigners these days, while Japan is an absolute Ultima Thule by comparison.'

'That's just what I felt, Mrs Fortescue,' Elinor agreed. 'Japan is much more exciting, and safe enough in my experience so far, providing you stick to the rules.'

'Oh, I've promised to do that, once I know what they are.'

'Well, I suppose you know that foreigners have to keep within the treaty limits, that is about a twenty-four-mile radius of the settlement?' Percival began. 'Except that members of the Legations can go to Edo on official business.'

'And others only by special diplomatic invitation, which isn't a popular measure,' Arnold added.

'Oh dear! Then I shall have to wangle an invitation from someone, shan't I?' She flashed round a brilliant smile and Claud coughed in embarrassment.

'And at sunset the causeway gates leading across the river and swamp are shut and heavily guarded, so we're imprisoned till dawn,' Percival continued.

'There you are, my dear; I told you it would be impossible to really see the country.' Claud liked to have his forebodings proved right.

'Oh, but things are bound to improve. After all, it's been quite peaceful since that dreadful affair of Mr Richardson several months ago, surely? And that was a one in a million chance, really — like the man who was killed by the Rocket engine on the first Manchester to Liverpool run. What was his name, Claud?'

'Mr Huskisson, dear; but that has nothing whatever to do with it. Happened over thirty years ago and I dare say lots of people have been killed by trains since then.'

'Ah yes, but Huskisson was the classic case, the excuse. My mother never would go on a train — dirty and dangerous things, she used to say; look what happened to Huskisson. And I suppose he was just a harmless unfortunate individual like Mr Richardson.'

'Knew Richardson slightly,' Claud interposed to Percival. 'Poor devil — just made his pile in China and was going home. By the way, I gather the matter isn't yet settled?'

'Indeed not. The F.O. instructed our Chief to demand an indemnity of £100,000 from the Shogun for a start, for "allowing an Englishman to be murdered in his territory in open daylight"; I quote. Then the Prince of Satsuma has to pay another £24,000 and "arrange for the execution of Richardson's assassins in the presence of one or more English officers". Quote again.'

'And will they cough up?'

'The Shogun may eventually and we're sending a squadron up from China to help him decide. Even if he gives in I doubt that the stiff-necked Satsumas will.'

'You sound quite pleased about it,' Elinor remarked severely. 'Surely it's preferable to settle things peacefully?'

'Oh, I don't know about that.' Percival began snorting gently, a sure sign that he was about to launch into one of his humorous-dramatic parodies. 'Nothing like a few gunboats to bring the natives to heel, hey Carruthers?' he boomed in his theatrical-military voice. 'We've got the ships, by heaven . . . listen to the ring of their names . . . *Encounter, Rattler, Euryalus, Havoc* . . . *Havoc*, there's a fine name for a British vessel, what? And we've got the men, brave, hearty Jack Tars longing to teach these little yellowskins a lesson . . . No, say I, let's . . .'

Mary laughed, but Arnold reached forward, pretending to take Percival's pulse and stopping him in mid-sentence. 'That's enough now, my lad, calm down. Please excuse him, Mrs Fortescue. He's always doing it. Sometimes the symptoms are even worse than this. We doctors call it *Dramaticus dementia* − chronic among young men not blessed with a normal sense of humour.'

'Oh, I say, that's not fair.' Percival pulled his wrist away angrily.

'No, it's not,' Mary agreed. 'I was quite enjoying Mr Storey's military gentleman.'

'Well, you'll hear lots of repeat performances, madam, don't worry. In our small community every fragment of wit is cherished, buried, and dug up for revaluation many times.'

'Ah, the small community. I wanted to ask you . . . Whom do we have here, Mr Storey?'

'It varies, madam. There's the longer-term stayers such as Legation and consular staffs, established merchants and business people like yourselves, and a few dedicated missionaries. Then there's the floaters − shop-keepers, entrepreneurs, agents, sea-captains, marine riff-raff, treaty port down-and-outs . . . You'll know the sort of thing.'

She nodded. 'Like Shanghai, only writ small. And not

many ladies, I gather?'

'Not nearly enough, which is why I'm so glad you've come,' Elinor confirmed. 'Mrs Clarke is leaving soon because her last baby died here. So that leaves Mrs Marshall, doyenne of the mercantile community, and Mrs Hubbard, our leading light on the missionary side. She wears very tight ringlets at each temple and her husband, Dr Hubbard, labours to compile a much needed Japanese/English dictionary. Only a few others, French mainly, and newcomers like ourselves.'

'Well, I shall just have to make the best of it.' Mary sighed hollowly, for a superabundance of gentlemen never dismayed her.

'And what about the currency situation?' Claud asked. 'I was told it's still in a very fluid state.'

'Gold *cobangs*, silver *ichibu*, Chinese *taels*, Mexican dollars, and pounds sterling; hard to keep track of what equals what. Mex are cut down to size one week, 'bu' the next. Some unscrupulous foreigners have made small fortunes simply through currency dealing between here and Shanghai.'

'And what about food prices?' Mary asked Elinor.

'You can never predict. Buy a tin of imported butter one week and it could halve in price, or double, a week later. Mrs Marshall finds it all a tremendous challenge and always knows where and when to get the best bargains – you should consult her.'

Percival grinned. 'Mrs Hubbard, on the other hand, finds it all a great trial. She'd prefer to keep her mind free for higher things and is much distracted by the need to know the going price of bean-curd and when she should be rushing down to the quay to buy from the ship that's just docked. That's where we get most of our beef, you know. Sheep and pigs come in sometimes too, and there's a very unsavoury little abattoir in the swamp which makes all good Buddhists shudder. As to fleshy imports of the equine variety, that's Arnold's department.'

Mary clapped her hands. 'You have a stable, Doctor? Oh, I simply adore riding and so do the girls.'

Arnold stifled a yawn. 'Hardly worthy of the name stable

yet, ma'am. Just a couple of white Chinese ponies and my thoroughbred beauty, Typhoon, from Australia. But more are coming up soon.'

'Oh, I do hope you'll invite me to . . .'

'Really, my dear,' Claud intervened mildly. 'This is your first night here and you shouldn't keep pestering. Why, you are wearing the good doctor out.'

'Not really, Mr Fortescue; but I am rather tired, I confess, and tomorrow is a busy day so . . .'

Full of apologies Mary jumped up, and she and Elinor left the gentlemen to enjoy a last brandy together.

Yokohama enjoyed a period of relative prosperity in the months following the Fortescues' arrival. Currency stabilised and trade flourished, partly because the American Civil War had caused a world shortage of cotton, and the demand for Japanese raw textiles rose accordingly. The new English church was opened for divine services and the first full calendar of race meetings held – with more foreign residents attending the latter than the former, much to the grief of the newly installed clergyman. The settlers' peace of mind was still overshadowed, however, by disagreements and delays over the Richardson affair.

In June, the government capitulated and 'coughed up' £100,000 – in crates full of Mexican dollars trundled on handcarts from its Treasury to the British Legation. But the Prince of Satsuma remained obdurate, as Percival Storey had forecast; and Colonel Neale soon decided it was time for a spot of gunboat diplomacy. One hot mid-summer afternoon he and his entire staff boarded the ships with the ringing names, under the command of Admiral Kuper, and set sail for the Satsuma capital of Kagoshima on the southern island of Kyushu. Elinor Mills and Mary Fortescue were among a group of citizens standing on the jetty to cheer their departure, the former with considerable anxiety.

'Oh, Mary, I do hope Arnold will be all right! Surely it needn't come to a battle, if only the Satsumas and ourselves will talk it over sensibly?'

27

Mary shrugged. 'Oh, I don't know. We often try to talk sensibly with the Chinese too, but things blow up sometimes. Orientals are very devious and inscrutable.'

'But do we make enough effort to understand them? Percival was telling me that by no means all the Satsuma leaders hate us. Apparently some of them are very eager to learn about the West and do business with foreigners . . . So why did they murder Richardson? And do they regret it now, I wonder? If only one could get to know them better . . .'

'Oh, they're a proud and stiff-necked lot!'

'But so are we,' Elinor protested. 'And I suppose they've as much right to be as we have.'

Mary sniffed. 'I can't think what *they* have to be proud of!'

'Quite a lot, if we only knew the half of it, I'll warrant.'

'Oh, come, Elinor; it's far too hot to stand here arguing. Let's go and have a nice cup of tea on the verandah . . .'

Shading her eyes from the sea's white glare, Elinor took a last look at the British squadron steaming away south, then followed her companion.

CHAPTER TWO

Lord Shimazu Saburo, head of the proud Satsuma clan, sat impassively inside his gold and black palanquin while one of his officers went to examine the bloodied corpse on the roadside in the village of Namamugi. He questioned his men briefly about the circumstances surrounding it, then issued terse commands before continuing on his journey towards Hodogaya, where he was to spend the night. As his palanquin passed the body, Lord Shimazu did not deign to glance outside. He had enough to think about already, for he and his followers were scheming to redress the balance of power between the Shogun and the Emperor, in which cause he had just visited Edo. Nevertheless the incident worried him, for he guessed that the killing of this insufferably insolent barbarian who, according to his men, had refused to give right of way to his procession, might have very serious consequences.

On Lord Shimazu's orders, one Gengoro Miyata, a samurai of middle rank, was then informed that his nephew, Kenjiro Miyata, was to stay behind in Namamugi to observe further developments. Kenjiro, chosen for the assignment because of his knowledge of the foreign tongues, was to conceal himself in the tea-house until the barbarians came to investigate, as they surely would. He was to learn as much as he could about what action they intended taking, and was then to catch up with the Satsuma contingent and report his findings. Gengoro duly passed on these instructions to Kenjiro, an ambitious young samurai, who bowed deferentially, concealing his excitement at being chosen for a mission of such importance.

As the remnants of the procession straggled out of sight, Kenjiro told his servant, Bimyo, to go and keep watch on the outskirts of the village; then he knocked imperiously at the tea-house and demanded to hire the upper room overlooking the street. The proprietor, one Osan, let him in reluctantly, for she wanted nothing to do with these hot-headed southern clansmen who had already created trouble; on the other hand, as she well knew, one didn't argue with a sword-carrying samurai.

Installed in the room, Kenjiro ordered tea and peeped cautiously out of the window. The village street, where all had been clamour and movement a short time before, was now abnormally deserted, though eyes other than his were undoubtedly staring at the heap of black cloth on the roadside from which dark stains were seeping and spreading over the dust. Flies began to gather, and a dog approached it, snuffling and growling. A man rushed from the shop opposite and dragged the animal away still growling. The silence stretched on, spreading ominously over the whole scene like the blood over the dust. No one in the little village of Namamugi knew what to do; the problem was none of their making.

Kenjiro sat back on his heels and swilled tea round his dry mouth; Osan had told him that, just before dying, the foreigner had asked for water. But he was only a barbarian, and one who had flouted the basic rules of respect due to Kenjiro's liege-lord, Shimazu; he had deserved his fate. Kenjiro drank more tea, depressed by the thought that perhaps neither the dead man nor his companions had known the basic rule that all commoners must leave the road to allow clear passage for processions of noblemen, or *daimyo*. Probably the man was just an ordinary Yokohama merchant. But even so there would be a most extraordinary fuss over the manner of his dying, of that Kenjiro was sure. For, in foreigners' eyes, he was a totally innocent victim, and they would seek to revenge his death. Would they send an army against the Satsuma? Were they even now preparing for battle? Kenjiro's heart beat high. Never before in his young life had he been in a position of such anxious responsibility and peril.

How careful he must be to do the correct things in the eyes of his liege-lord, and his uncle, Gengoro.

As the late afternoon shadows lengthened along the roadway the dog returned to the immobile black bundle and began sniffing at the drying blood. The dog's owner reappeared, carrying a tattered mat which he threw over the dead body, arranging it carefully to conceal the gaping wounds. As he was again hauling the dog away, Kenjiro heard the distant thud of horses' hoofs, and his servant, Bimyo, came rushing up the stairs. 'The barbarians are coming,' he gasped, 'legions of them, on horseback, soldiers in uniform. They'll set the whole village ablaze and massacre the lot of us.'

'Who says so?' Kenjiro drew back into the room's shadow, leaving the window screen ajar.

'The boatman from Kanagawa ferry; he was with me.'

Kenjiro snorted, leaning forward as a party of the settlement's foreign guards galloped into view. Seeing the mats on the roadside, they dismounted quickly and went to inspect what lay beneath. Kenjiro strained to understand their exclamations of horror as the mutilated corpse was revealed. They fingered their pistols, glowering uneasily around at the shuttered fronts of the nearby houses. A large man in a black suit rode up and the guards made way as he hastened to examine the body. Expertly he thumbed up the eyelids, then, still kneeling beside the dead man, he looked up and, so it seemed, straight into the window of the tea-house. His hair and bushy beard were reddish-fair, his light-coloured eyes were alarmed and angry. He must be a doctor, Kenjiro thought, as he stood in the shadows not daring to move a muscle.

Now all the barbarians began talking vociferously in two different tongues, but so excited and confused were they that Kenjiro could scarcely comprehend a word. Three soldiers marched up to the tea-house and thumped angrily on the door. Kenjiro heard the frightened maid explain that no one else was there; but the men did not understand her, nor she them. Other guards prowled along the street, revolvers at the ready as if expecting a sudden attack. Darkness was falling, but not a single lamp was lit in any of the village houses. As the last of the light waned, the doctor examined the corpse more thoroughly and made some notes, then the soldiers rolled it in the mat, lifted it on to a horse, and moved off, holding the wet bundle on the saddle between them. The doctor stood for a minute, hands behind his back, staring down at the bloodied patch where the man had lain, then mounted and rode away with the others.

'They're going at last,' whispered Bimyo, who had been crouching near his master.

Kenjiro leaned out of the window again, wondering what on earth to do next. Soon a few lamps flickered behind the house-screens, and the local head man and shopkeepers ventured out and gathered near the tea-house. As Kenjiro strode to join them, they fell silent, bowing low in respect to his rank. But he sensed their resentful hostility towards him, as a stranger with the thick accent of the clan that had brought this sudden trouble into their midst. They knew full well that the men from Satsuma province, original home of the imperial house, were full of stubborn pride and so fiercely independent that even the Lord Shogun in his castle in nearby Edo kept only a tenuous control over their domains. Such provincials, living remote from the recently established western settlements, were given to outbursts of violent xenophobia, whereas during the past three years the villagers of Namamugi had become accustomed to the sight of foreigners riding about in the vicinity and knew that it was foolish to get upset about it.

Some Namamugi merchants had even ventured to Yokohama and made tidy profits selling trinkets to the settlers, who, they had discovered, were a short-tempered bunch, hopelessly ignorant of the common courtesies of behaviour, but not to be trifled with, for they were well protected by armed guards, and warships in the harbour. Now the people quailed at the thought of the retribution that might be exacted from them, even though they were innocent of this bloody deed, and they stared sullenly at Kenjiro, wishing he had gone away with the rest of his proud, outlandish tribe. The three causeway gates leading into Yokohama were always closely guarded, and closed at night, they told him, and, at this crisis, the whole

32

settlement would be on the lookout for any stray samurai, especially one wearing the Satsuma crest. If he valued his skin, he had better make himself scarce.

But, Kenjiro explained, he had orders to find out what the foreigners intended to do next.

The head man snorted. 'We're all wondering that — though it's none of our business. The foreigners must realise we peaceful folk took no part in the deed.'

'That man and his companions grossly insulted our leader,' Kenjiro barked stiffly.

'Probably he didn't mean to,' the head man replied. 'These ignorant barbarians have no notion of the proprieties.'

Not wanting to hear this, Kenjiro turned away, and beckoned to Bimyo. 'You heard what these fellows said. It would be very dangerous for me to try and get into Yokohama. But you're just a nondescript servant, and will be safe. Go to the boatman you met and pay him to guide you — slip into Yokohama as soon as the gates open tomorrow, spy out the land, find out what's going on. I'll have to wait here till you bring me news.'

Bimyo hissed through his teeth; he did not relish the task. He bowed in unquestioning obedience nevertheless, as his father before him had always done to Kenjiro's father. For Bimyo came from generations of servants attached to the households of middle-rank Satsuma samurai, and, though he was only allowed a single name and spent much time with his head lowered before many superiors, he counted himself fortunate to have a reasonable master. So he put on his straw sandals, took up his lantern, and trotted off towards Yokohama while Kenjiro returned disconsolately to the tea-house, where Osan served him supper.

As she ladled the soup he asked, 'Those foreigners in uniforms — have you seen their sort before?'

She nodded. 'They are guards. They escort the barbarian big-wigs when they go to Edo to see our leaders.'

'They seemed to be speaking in different tongues.'

'Yes, the ones in red are British, the blue ones are French. I hear about a lot of things in this house.'

33

'Aren't there any Dutchmen in Yokohama then?'

She shrugged. 'Dutch? I don't know . . . There are a few Americans, but most are British, like the man who was killed.'

He dismissed her curtly, for it irritated him to be seeking information in this fashion − from a lowly tea-house woman who yet knew more about foreign matters than he did.

After his meal, the maid spread his bedding on the mats and lit a low light, wishing him a pleasant sleep; but that, he sensed, would elude him. Wrapping himself in his cloak, for he was chilled with exhaustion, he arranged his head on the wooden pillow − and was immediately wide awake. It seemed several days ago rather than only that morning that the procession had straggled slowly through Shinagawa, Edo's eastern gate onto the Tokaido road. Riding in his allotted position towards the rear, he had had no inkling of the trouble ahead until a halt had been called as they left Kawasaki and a messenger had summoned him forward. Remembering his uncle's commands, he shivered apprehensively at the thought of failure, wishing he had understood more of the foreigners' conversation. The only one whose face Kenjiro distinctly remembered was the doctor, with hair the colour of wet sand and eyes like large grey pebbles. An ocean-crossing man, who must be very skilled in the practices of western medicine, of which his father, Aritomo, used to speak.

Kenjiro's father, a gunnery officer and second son of a castle-town samurai in Kagoshima, had been posted to Fort Nagasaki, where trained men from the nearby provinces served regular terms of guard duty. In Nagasaki, Aritomo, who was blessed or cursed with a restless curiosity, had sought out others of similar rank and inclination who had made contact with the Dutch traders and scholars living in the offshore trading station of Decima. At that time, the late 1840s, such contacts were regarded with grave suspicion by the government officials of the Tokugawa Shoguns, the *bakafu*, who ruled the country. In spite of the dangers, however, close-knit groups of enthusiasts persisted in learning from the Dutch what they could of western science – physical, medical, and military. And the more Aritomo learned, the more he had to acknowledge western superiority in these areas; for instance, as he told his young son, it seemed that European nations had at their command fleets of high-masted sailing ships, their decks bristling with large cannon, and that European doctors had learned how to cut diseased parts from their patients to make them healthy again.

Occasionally, when Kenjiro, his mother Setsu, and sister Ryo were all living in Nagasaki, Aritomo had managed to borrow a few western books for them to see. One, *The Universal Condition of all Countries and Customs*, had astonished, even horrified, Kenjiro when he saw how tiny Japan was on the world map compared with huge countries like China and Russia.

Kenjiro's half-formed realisation of Japan's smallness and vulnerability and the ignorance of the majority of its inhabitants, who had been given no chance to look outward on the world, filled him with uncomfortable foreboding that night as he lay sleepless in Namamugi, where, but a few hours before, the armed foreign soldiers had been striding about furiously. He wished desperately that his wise, open-minded father had been there to advise him; but Aritomo had been killed in an uprising seven years before when Kenjiro was fifteen. Aritomo had still been alive therefore when the American Commodore Perry reached Japan, but had not lived long enough to see the first treaty ports established. His death at such a crucial time had been a tragedy, Kenjiro thought, as his eyes finally closed, for Aritomo would have been so excited by the opening up of his country to the western world.

The next morning, while Kenjiro still slept, government officials arrived in Namamugi asking for eye-witness accounts of the previous day's disturbances. No one told them of Kenjiro's presence in the tea-house; but after they had left, the head man ordered Osan to get rid of her unwanted guest in short order, for any Satsuma samurai hanging about in the neighbourhood might cause trouble. Osan, well practised in the art of easing gentlemen out, diplomatically put it to him that *bakafu* officials were on the prowl and he risked being hauled in for questioning if he did not leave that day; to which Kenjiro replied briskly that he could not decide on his next move until his servant returned.

It was late afternoon before Bimyo came hurrying to the tea-house, knocked his head on the mat and told his tale. Yokohama, he said, was in a veritable state of uproar. According to a friendly customs official, the men of the settlement had met together late the previous evening and demanded that every foreign warship in port set sail at once to launch an attack on the clan responsible for the Englishman's murder.

'Did you learn what manner of man he was?' Kenjiro interrupted.

'Only a common merchant, I was told. Here, a customs interpreter wrote the name for me.' Bimyo handed over a slip of paper. On it in capital letters was the word RICHARDSON.

'His commonness makes no difference in the barbarians' eyes, it seems – they want a whole fleet from China to come and bombard us. And a lot of settlers were riding about this morning waving pistols in the air and ready to set off in pursuit of our liege lord this very day. But then one of their diplomatic big-wigs held another meeting and cooled them down a bit. He told them the whole matter must be dealt with through the proper authorities.'

'Whose authority? How will they deal with it?'

'Their own and the government in Edo, I suppose, sir. But how it will all go on I cannot say.'

'But the barbarians definitely won't attack us immediately?'

'No, though some of them are hot to do so. They give you the dirtiest looks, just for being Japanese. The settlement gates are doubly guarded and no man is allowed to take a sword inside. You'd have been nabbed for sure, sir; they know it's we Satsumas who did it. And if I may respectfully suggest, sir, I think we should take ourselves off at once, catch up with our own men, and give them the news.'

Kenjiro hesitated; it was his duty to do what was best for his clan and his liege-lord; nothing else mattered. But what more could he possibly accomplish here — as a marked man both to government officials and to foreigners? He told Bimyo to settle his account and saddle his horse. Shortly afterwards, to the great relief of the villagers, the two men of Satsuma left.

Darkness had fallen by the time they saw, across the marshes on their left, the distant lights of Yokohama gleaming from low buildings and from the high masts of foreign ships riding at anchor. Kenjiro stared and stared at them, longing to approach nearer, though he knew it would be foolhardy. His father, Kenjiro remembered, had actually been to Yokohama with a clan delegation the year before his death, when the great black ships from America returned for the second time. Their commander was a large man with bristling eyebrows and a fat, melancholy face, who wanted to persuade the Japanese to trade with his country across the ocean.

Aritomo had only seen the Americans' commander from a distance, but he had had a close look at the gifts they brought for the Shogun. The most impressive of them was a metal car on wheels with a miniature engine that ran round a little track by itself. Aritomo had a short ride in it — bumpy and dangerous, fast and exciting, he told his son, who now recalled his chuckle as he described it. He had also been greatly impressed by the modern, business-like foreign weapons compared to the ancient Dutch muskets and matlocks carried by the Japanese and by the smart sailors moving about the ships in practical, close-fitting trousers.

'You'll wear the leg-dividing cloths one day, I'll warrant, even if I never do,' he had told Kenjiro, who thrilled now, believing his father's words.

Late the following afternoon Kenjiro and Bimyo caught up with their clansmen's slow-moving procession. A light rain was falling as they passed the straggling groups of porters, the drops pattering on the oiled covers of the heavy boxes they carried on their backs, each bearing the Satsuma crest. Ahead of them went foot soldiers, their tall banners hanging limp-wet; then the armed rearguard, mounted on shaggy ponies. At length, Kenjiro heard the distant shouts of the advance guards telling the commoners to bow down before the approaching lord, and he straightened self-consciously, feeling an important sense of mission. He sent Bimyo ahead to announce his arrival, and was told to meet his uncle at the next wayside tea-stall, for he was too young and lowly to convey news to his liege-lord directly, even in such an emergency.

Gengoro was waiting under the shelter of the thatch, wiping his damp face with a cloth; nearby, his groom was replacing his horse's straw-shoes with a new set. Kenjiro handed over his horse for similar re-shoeing and bowed before his uncle.

'Well, what's going on?' he barked, then listened keenly to his nephew's report.

'*Ah-so*,' he nodded, as Kenjiro finished. 'And then you left?'

'You instructed me to return quickly with news and not to risk getting caught,' Kenjiro was on the defensive, as so often in his uncle's presence. He leant forward, eyes shining, 'But I have a plan – will the liege-lord allow me to go back again and sneak into Yokohama at night over the marshes? It would be easy. We need to know more – the whole situation is still a powder keg.'

Gengoro raised a warning hand to quench the young man's enthusiasm. The act gave him satisfaction, for, in Gengoro's opinion, Kenjiro possessed too much of his father's wild spirit. It would lead him into trouble as it had Aritomo, for the uprising in which Aritomo had been killed was later found to have been instigated by troublemakers hoping to overthrow the Shogunate. Kenjiro had never been told the whole truth of the matter, though recently Gengoro had been tempted to reveal it in the hope of knocking some sense into him.

Around the time of Aritomo's death, Gengoro had had a recurring dream: he was riding across an open field fully equipped for an archery contest when he came upon his nephew lying spread-eagled on the ground staring up wide-eyed at the sky; Gengoro, spurring his horse, had trampled across his handsome face. Gengoro looked at the face now; the boyish handsomeness had grown manly, the eyes were still unusually wide and alert.

He said, 'No, you won't be going back. The Lord-Chief has already sent two of his trusted spies to enter the settlement in disguise. You are too young and inexperienced for such a task.'

'But they can't understand the barbarians' tongues, so how—?'

'And you? How much did you truly understand yourself? Not much, by the sound of it. A very different kettle of fish reading their twaddle in books as you do and understanding when they spout it out — or so I believe.'

Kenjiro lowered his eyes and Gengoro knew he had scored a bullseye.

'Ah . . . so there. You've done your job, lad. Now return to your companions; I'm going forward to give the Lord-Chief your news. He'll be well satisfied with you, I'm sure.'

The two rose, and Kenjiro bowed in quiet acquiescence, though he was seething with angry disappointment. In his telling of the news to Lord Shimazu, Gengoro would collar as much glory for himself as possible, Kenjiro thought bitterly, for that was his nature — to bolster his position by diminishing lowlier beings. Then it occurred to him for the first time in his life, and like a revelation, that he was frequently guilty of similar behaviour. In the account he had just given of what happened at Namamugi, for instance, had he not minimised the part played by Bimyo — who had actually taken the greatest risk? The system under which they all lived made them behave so, he realised; one survived at the expense of the lower ranks; individual worth and enterprise counted for little. Should he blame his uncle? Should Bimyo blame him? There was no point; no use kicking against the pricks . . .

Nevertheless Kenjiro's mood of irritation and frustration remained as the Satsuma cortège wended its way slowly homeward along the busy, tree-lined Tokaido highway. Riding near the back with other young samurai from branch-families like his own, Kenjiro's spirit chafed at the sleepy scenes of rural life on every side. Glumly, he watched the peasants, who in accordance with government edict had swept their local stretch of road clean before the procession arrived, rise creakily from their knees as Lord Shimazu's splendid retinue passed out of sight. Uncomplainingly they returned to their customary tasks – reaping rice, beating grain from sheaves, collecting winter fuel, picking damsons and persimmons, or collecting nuts and mushrooms from the woods. It all seemed so passive and changeless that Kenjiro felt stifled. It was as if a muffling curtain had fallen, cutting him off from all hope of contact with the foreigners in the treaty ports where the high-masted ships rode at anchor, with their twinkling promises of a more exciting world.

At the ancient imperial capital of Kyoto the party halted while Lord Shimazu attended audiences with the Emperor of Japan and his advisors. The rulers of Satsuma, whose ancestors had been defeated two hundred and sixty years before, when Shogun Tokugawa Ieyasu came to power, had always maintained strong links with the Imperial House and most of them were bitterly critical of the present Shogun's regime. Now, Lord Shimazu had encouraging news to report to the court, for at the great council of *daimyo* which he had just attended in Edo, the Shogun's capital, it was becoming increasingly clear that the Shogun's power was on the decline. Moreover, the traditional restrictions governing the enforced residence of the *daimyo* and their families in Edo for part of each year were soon to be relaxed, which would mean that the pro-Imperial clans like Satsuma would be better placed to muster their forces around the Emperor if required. Compared to this momentous news, the murder of a single foreigner near Yokohama was a minor affair, and the general feeling was that it might further acerbate trouble between the foreigners and the government, which was no bad thing.

Eventually, after much diplomatic manoeuvring, the Satsuma procession resumed its stately course, and by the time its destination was reached the season had grown distinctly chill. Kagoshima, capital of the Satsuma clan, where Lord Shimazu had his private residence and castle, was an ancient, beautiful city built round a bay that was dominated by the magnificent volcano of Sakurajima just offshore. Here the men disbanded, and Kenjiro was free to return to his home in the Imamura valley, a few miles from the city.

For the Miyatas, as for many of their kind, recent times had been hard and it was a struggle for them to retain their position in the hierarchical, overcrowded samurai ranks. Following Aritomo's untimely and (in his relatives' view) inglorious death, his wife Setsu had no choice but to turn to Gengoro for support. Gengoro had meanwhile suffered the misfortune of breeding four daughters in succession and had earlier adopted Aritomo's eldest son, Kentaro, as his heir, in order to perpetuate the male line of the family. This he had done gladly; but it gave him no pleasure to find himself saddled several years later with the additional responsibility for Kentaro's mother, younger brother, and sister. He had allotted them a dwelling in the valley about a mile from his own family compound, for which Setsu expressed deep gratitude, concealing her anger and shame that she, the daughter of a higher-ranking samurai, should be reduced to living in what was little better than a farmhouse.

Dismounting before it now, however, after several months' absence, Kenjiro felt a warm rush of affection for the familiar place where he had spent the last seven years between youth and manhood. For though, as his mother often said, it was a humble abode, yet it was charming. Its mossy thatch (in sore need of repair, he noted worriedly), its walls of mellowed wood, its deep verandah where strings of oranges, onions, and persimmons were hung to dry, all blended harmoniously in colour and texture with the autumnal trees on the hillside that rose steeply behind the house and sheltered it from the prevailing westerlies.

The household sprang to life on his arrival. Two servants unloaded his horse, while Setsu and Ryo bowed, and laughed with pleasure, touched his sleeves, and led him to the seat of honour by the hearth with its painted green and gold draught screen. They begged him to tell them all his adventures and he complied, for, though they were but women, he confided in them more than was customary. Having spent long periods

41

of his boyhood outside the Satsuma domains, he had never become part of the close-knit, fraternal organisation of his district. Most young males of his rank had played wild pranks together from childhood, learned wrestling, jousting, fencing, and, inculcated with the samurai code of etiquette and purity, grown thistle-sharp with the pride and honour of their clan. So, classed as an outsider, Kenjiro, with equal pride, often chose instead the congenial company of his mother and sister, who felt similarly isolated.

As he sipped tea, happily chewed his favourite nut-paste biscuits, and sniffed the familiar home-smell of long-fermenting pickles, he told them about the assassination of the foreigner and about the black-suited doctor who had seemed to look straight into the window where he had stood watching.

Ryo interrupted quietly, 'And was he ancient and wise-looking, this doctor — with a grey beard?'

'Oh no, not old. I can still see his face very clearly. His beard was the colour of sea-sand and his eyes like grey pebbles.'

'Like Mr Moon's eyes?'

'I suppose as wide, but not so blue.' And they both smiled, remembering Mr Moon.

The real name of the man, the first long-nosed barbarian they had ever seen, was Nathaniel Hare, a survivor from an American whaler wrecked off Japan's northern shores. The authorities had sent Hare to Nagasaki for a passage out to China on a Dutch ship and while he was waiting to leave he had made contact with Japanese students of 'western things'. He had met Aritomo, and Kenjiro had been thrilled when he first visited their home. He had tried to explain his name to them by drawing a hare, but hares, as the children knew from legend, lived on the moon. So had this stranger dropped down upon them from that silver mistress of the night sky? In their eyes, he looked sufficiently outlandish. Aritomo soon corrected them, but the name stuck — as a joke, an affectionate tribute to the kind sailor who had spoken English to them, patiently drawing pictures of objects for which they had no words — forks, chimney stacks, gas-lamps.

'Do you remember his pictures of high buildings with floors piled on top of each other? Are the houses in Yokohama like that?' Ryo asked her brother.

'The houses look quite low-down from a distance, but the warships in the harbour were higher and larger than any I have ever seen.'

As Kenjiro concluded his tale his mother sighed, 'Now there'll be more trouble, I suppose. If only your father had been in the procession it probably wouldn't have happened. He could have told those foolish, ignorant foreigners to behave properly.'

Setsu, who had adored her husband and believed implicitly in the rightness of his daring ideas, still felt that not only she but the whole country was worse off without him.

'I suppose it would have been fine tonight, if Aritomo had been alive,' Kono, Gengoro's wife, had mocked her, when at last August's *oban* festival for the dead, unseasonable rain had soaked the dancing, chanting crowds gathered in the temple, and extinguished the ritual bonfires in the cemeteries. Setsu did not rub along easily with Kono or the rest of Gengoro's family, for, though born of higher rank, she was bound in humiliating dependence upon them and they did not allow her to forget it.

Kenjiro smiled indulgently. 'No, mother, the culprits were a few of our maddest barbarian-haters who just attacked wildly. We weren't even there to see and it all happened very fast.'

The mention of Aritomo reminded Kenjiro of his first duty on arrival home, and he went to pay due respect to his dead father while the women prepared supper. In the family altar-room a statue of the Lord Buddha reposed on an alcove shelf; flames of two candles flicked over his gilt surface and Aritomo's memorial tablet. Kenjiro bowed before it, rang the prayer handbell and murmured thanks for his safe return from the longest journey he had ever made. Then he sat back on his heels, staring at his father's name. Had he truly done well in his sight? Suddenly there came to him, with the clarity of a vision, the memory of Aritomo's last hours as he lay dying of the wounds he had received in the uprising.

With the stoic control of a true samurai, the father had imparted his last coherent thoughts to his son. 'You must look outwards,' he had murmured to Kenjiro. 'For too long we Japanese have looked inward on ourselves. You must seek out men who think like me, boy. Learn from them what looking outward means.'

Kenjiro sighed, thinking that, up to now, he had only half-heartedly obeyed his father's last instructions, being pre-occupied with youthful pastimes and the support of his mother and sister. Now, the jolt of his recent journey reminded him forcibly of his father's injunction and he began reproaching himself for not going to Yokohama himself, for not taking the opportunity of a first 'look outward'. Worst of all, if the truth were told, he knew it had been cowardice as well as prudence that had made him send Bimyo instead.

In his heart, Kenjiro was terrified of physical violence, the mortal cuts that the razor-sharp swords he carried could inflict, of the cudgels and madness of battle; afraid even of defending himself to the death – as he might have had to in Yokohama. It was an ignoble trait in one of his samurai kind and in the course of his earlier martial training – spear-throwing, fencing, archery, horsemanship – he had tried desperately to conquer it, but had succeeded only in its con-cealment. Here, before his father's shrine, he bowed his troubled head and admitted his frailty, vowing that neither it nor other trivial concerns would again deflect him from the challenge Aritomo had set.

He rose, and, on the way out, paused to run his fingers appreciatively over the embossed surface of a lacquered set of drawers known as 'mother's chest'. It had been part of Setsu's dowry and its contents – treasured pieces of old crackle-glaze porcelain, red and gold lacquered bowls and caddies, antique censers and preserving jars – were of exceedingly good quality; and even in their present straitened circumstances, Setsu would not part with a single item. Kenjiro wished he could provide her and his sister with more beautiful things, more comfortable surroundings, but, a mere junior samurai with scant personal resources, he could not imagine how this would ever be accomplished. Sighing again, he returned to the hearth-room, where food of unusual extravagance had been prepared in celebration of his home coming.

He ate with relish, seated cross-legged on a cushion at the low lacquer table while the women jumped up and down to serve him, filling his bowl with the most succulent morsels and nibbling almost guiltily at the left-over bits.

'And how has it been with you? Having Kentaro as top dog?' Kenjiro asked when the edge of his hunger was assuaged. The query was sarcastic, for his older brother was a weak-natured man who allowed himself to be ruled by his wife, Fumio, and his Uncle Gengoro instead of taking the initiatives to which his position entitled him. Kenjiro found him both irritating and pitiable, knowing that he would have made much more effective use of similar opportunities. But Setsu, who discouraged open criticism of her first-born, replied simply.

'Oh, things have gone along quietly enough. At least Ofuku's marriage date has been fixed, for early in the new year. The groom is the second Yamaguchi son, and the hand-clasping wine has been accepted. Moreover, the marriage will be officially reported to Lord Shimazu, which pleases Gengoro, of course.'

Gengoro was uneasily aware that his cherished rank of castle-town samurai was precarious in these harsh times, and the marriage-reporting was satisfying reassurance that the Miyata status was secure.

Kenjiro smiled. 'Of course . . . Ofuku, hey? So that's the last of them settled.' He glanced at his sister; Ofuku, the fourth of Gengoro's daughters, was younger than Ryo, whose single state was becoming a family embarrassment. Ryo turned her head as if to avoid hearing his next question. 'And your prospect, sister?'

'Nothing has come of it. The Nakayamas did not consider me fitting.'

There was a long pause as the servant cleared the table and closed the shutters. Darkness had fallen. Outside Kenjiro heard the familiar rush of the rivulet that ran down the wooded hillside behind the house; he imagined the shadow of leaves on the moon-flecked surface and, below it, the long weeds that clung to the stones like tresses of green hair by daylight, now undulating darkly. The women began their usual evening tasks. Setsu was weaving an every-day garment of hemp on a small hand loom; the thread was fragile and broke frequently. Ryo began unpicking a faded summer kimono so that a new pattern could be dyed into the fabric. They worked slowly and patiently, their faces cool and proud in the flickering lamplight.

Kenjiro watched them a while, biting his finger, listening to the click of the loom and the hooting of an owl in the bamboo grove. He did not need to ask why his sister had been rejected as unsuitable by the prosperous, respectable Nakayamas. She had been rejected by others before, and the reasons were always the same. Ryo's father, a second son, had led an irregular life, making contact with foreigners and dying in inauspicious circumstances. As for Ryo herself, she spoke in the outlandish Nagasaki dialect of her childhood and it was rumoured that she had studied foreign tongues. Her bearing was suitably dignified but her features were too long and prominent for real beauty and her skin a little too dark – people said she had eaten too much millet as a child and not enough white rice. Most disturbing were the distinctly wavy kinks in her hair, which suggested that she had been somehow contaminated by barbarian contact, and her straight-haired older cousins, for whom appropriate husbands had easily been found, secretly dubbed her 'the Korean' in reference to the frizzy hair on the heads of a colony of Korean potters who lived in the neighbourhood. Ofuku had always stoutly defended Ryo, however, and it used to be assumed that Kenjiro would marry this sympathetic youngest cousin. He had therefore allowed himself to become quite fond of her; but now Gengoro had decided she should marry into the prestigious Yamaguchi family instead.

'It doesn't matter about the Nakayamas; I didn't much like them,' Ryo remarked, breaking the silence – just as Kenjiro said, 'It's strange to think of little Ofuku becoming a black-

46

toothed married woman and going away.'

They both sounded forlorn, for the coming marriage was another reminder of their own inferior position in the family.

'You must talk to Uncle Gengoro again on Ryo's behalf,' Setsu told her son.

'Oh, leave it until after Ofuku's wedding, I'm in no hurry for a husband,' Ryo protested.

'Come – tell me more about the foreigners you saw, Kenjiro. Did you understand their speech?'

He hesitated, then admitted, 'Very little – that was the difficulty. They were all speaking quickly together in English and French. I was told there are very few Dutchmen in Yokohama and I don't think Holland is as important as we used to think. I'm resolved to learn more English, Mother: I've been too lazy recently.'

'But it's so difficult for you here. We are cut off, and your uncle doesn't approve of foreign learning.' Setsu rose to make sure the shutters had been securely fastened. 'It's chilly tonight,' she murmured. 'When we put some oranges in the loft to dry the other day we noticed how badly the thatch needs repairing. You can see the sky through it. It must be done before the winter, Kenjiro, or we shall be soaked in our beds.'

'Yes, yes, I'll ask Kentaro tomorrow.' He sighed, for he was always having to ask his brother or uncle for jobs to be done and supplies to be provided. In his absence, the women were too proud to plead; they simply tightened their belts, ate yams with rice instead of costly fish, and kept up appearances, as befitted samurai ladies.

He got up restlessly, pressing his hands against several gaps in the weather-warped shutters through which the night breeze blew. 'I suppose he and Fumio are snug as nesting birds in the big house. And how is Fumio?'

'She is expecting another child just before Ofuku's wedding. It is to be a new year of events.' Ryo's tone was gently ironic and Kenjiro felt a return of his earlier irritation.

'Oh such humdrum little events, here in this closed-up valley – births, marriages, deaths, and that is all.'

'But very important events for those concerned,' his

47

mother demurred.

'But I keep thinking of the places beyond here, Mother, where so much is going on − political changes, foreigners arriving, overseas trade increasing, new ideas floating about.' He flung himself on a cushion and stared into the stove's charcoal embers. 'I must learn more. I must find people to help me, as father wished.'

'Ah now, if only your father . . .'

Ryo soothed her mother's familiar lament, as she often did. 'I'm sure his spirit will guide us correctly, Mother. You must go and see Father's old friend, Chomin Komatsu, Kenjiro. I hear he's recently returned to Kagoshima from Nagasaki.'

'Really? Ah, good news at last. Chomin's an honourable man. Yes, yes; why, tomorrow I'll . . .'

'After you've seen about the thatch, please,' his mother interposed.

'Yes, all right.' He prowled about again, impatient to be starting on his various tasks, till Ryo looked up from her work, smiling. 'Why don't you go to bed, brother? You can't mend the thatch or learn English tonight.'

'All right, I will.' He started towards his bedchamber. 'I suppose I am tired.' He paused. 'You understand, I hope, how very glad I am to see you again − and both well?' He smiled and they bowed in grateful acknowledgement of his concern; for he was the most important person in their lives, as they were in his.

Going to his bedroom, he peeped outside through a crack in the rain shutters. A chill, heavy mist shrouded the valley, making the sounds of rushing rivulet and still-hooting owl seem distant and mysterious. It was wonderful to be home; yet he felt his days there were numbered. The premonition made his sleep restless. Once, in his dreams, he again saw the face of the sandy-haired foreign doctor looking straight at him.

Kenjiro's household had to wait its turn for the thatchers, who were always busy just before winter's onset; and he had no time to chivvy them, for he had to resume his normal duties. Because his honourable grandfather had held the post of magistrate at the famous Jokomyoji temple, on a hill overlooking Kagoshima, Kenjiro had inherited the duty of over-seeing the present temple-gate settlement. This meant inspecting and verifying the oblong wooden identification tabs inscribed with the names, ranks, and residence of every inhabitant. The settlement attracted a number of 'floating persons' – religious mendicants and minstrels, footloose priests and soothsayers – who were often without tabs and had either to be sent away or assigned to some lowly position in the community. In the past, Kenjiro had found such people irksome nuisances, but now he regarded them with sneaking sympathy, even admiration. Many had wandered hundreds of miles through every province of the empire, and, though materially poor, were rich in experience. And they possessed that strange quality, freedom, a great rarity in a country where people lived in close-knit groups and could only travel officially within limits prescribed by the authorities.

Prodded by these disquieting thoughts, Kenjiro took an early opportunity to visit Chomin Komatsu, a castle-town samurai who had attended the same western studies school as his father. Chomin gave him a warm welcome, questioned him closely about his experiences in Edo and Kyoto, and when he left, lent him two precious books, published in Shanghai and circulated secretly in Nagasaki: *The Cycle of Knowledge* by Dr Legge of Hong Kong, and Liggin's Japanese – English dictionary.

Thenceforward, every winter's evening Kenjiro studied English with the concentrated dedication of his kind, and Ryo, his helper, learned just as much, for she had an un-common gift for languages. They said nothing of their unusual pursuit; but it did not escape the eyes of the servants, who gathered every evening at the communal bath-house, their tongues relaxing easily into gossip as their warmed limbs sloughed off the dirt of the day's toil. Thus Gengoro was soon informed that Setsu's offspring were studying barbarian tongues; but he said nothing, for, though he found the practice abhorrent, others, more powerful than he in the clan, were increasingly persuaded of the value of western learning. So Gengoro left his nephew alone, as one might leave a half-trained falcon to be directed in due course to whatever prey was seasonally appropriate.

Just before the New Year, in February, Kentaro's wife duly presented Gengoro with a second grandson; and soon after came the marriage of his youngest daughter. Both events pleased Gengoro, for now the family's male line was doubly assured and all his female progeny were off his hands. And thank goodness too for the provision of their dowries had been ruinously expensive, he thought irritably, as he watched Ofuku's possessions and bridal gifts being packed ready for conveyance to the groom's house in Kagoshima, where the actual wedding ceremony would take place.

The marriage day dawned cold but clear, and hairdressers arrived early from Kagoshima to arrange the coiffures of the household's womenfolk – Ofuku's, the most elaborately ornamented, being left till last. In their richly embroidered kimonos with heavily powdered cheeks and brightly painted lips, the women looked both elegant and powerful, as did their menfolk, in stiff, crested jackets and wide trousers, while even the servants wore longer-skirted outfits than usual, for no one would work outside that day.

The groom and his friends came early to escort the bride to the town, and the first of the day's feasts was offered to them. Long-treasured pots of damsons and loquats and chestnut pickles were opened to garnish the dishes of baked and boiled fish, and precious bowls from Setsu's chest were used to display them to best advantage. Seeing these beautiful, little-used receptacles ranged along the festive board, Kenjiro frowned in secret vexation. He had been too occupied to give much thought to his cousin's wedding; but now he saw it as a personal slight. Those bowls of his mother's should have been on display for his own marriage to Ofuku, doubly uniting him with his own family.

Seated with other young men of similar rank, Kenjiro drank liberal quantities of *saké*, ladled from special wedding buckets of red lacquer, and covertly watched Ofuku, who was grouped with her female relatives at the other end of the room. She was young and pretty, as fresh as green persimmons, as the saying went. Her shining oval face, framed by the jewelled bridal headdress, gleamed as she bent to admire a tray of gifts decorated with bows and paper butterflies. Now the Yamaguchi sprig was going to take her away — he mounted on a flower-wreathed horse, she tucked demurely in a palanquin. He would mount his bride that night; she, whimpering but compliant at first, would warm to his caresses during the many nights to come. Kenjiro glanced towards his sister, standing apart from the group of celebrating women, eyes cast down. She too had been rejected, for it was not really fitting that she should be left unwed, even unspoken for, at her younger cousin's marriage. Ryo glanced back at him, her smiling eyes telling him not to worry about it. A servant poured more *saké*; it was only noon, but Kenjiro felt maudlin and outcast, all the old restlessness raging in him.

And so it continued through the coming spring, the last he was ever to spend in his family home. In later years he was to look back on it with nostalgia, remembering the breeze-blown leaf-shadows on his bedroom screen in the early morning; sunlight glistening on the wet paddies in the valley; the smell of manure and fruit blossom as he rode along the well-worn tracks where wild irises and violets blossomed; the everyday country-clatter of peasants working with mattocks, bird-scarers, seed baskets, spade-ploughs, walking on high wooden pattens through the spring mud. At dusk, frogs croaked in the irrigation ditches, while women chopped vegetables for the evening meals, and inevitably, as background to his nightly studies, Kenjiro heard the creak of his mother's loom and the soft surge of the hillside rivulet in the darkness outside. In retrospect that season became a rose-tinted backdrop for a vanished rural past; but during its actual passing Kenjiro seethed with impatience, longing to be released from its peaceful monotony, the constant peasant talk of 'insects, rain, and wind'.

While Kenjiro chafed at the bit, his father's friend, Chomin Komatsu, was sent on a delegation to Nagasaki and, on his return, reported that the killing of the Englishman at

Namamugi the previous autumn had indeed become a matter for international dispute. The Satsuma leaders had completely rejected the British demands, and feelings were running high. Kenjiro was yearning to take part in these exciting developments when, fortunately, a message arrived from Chomin, who was feeling tired and overworked. He had got permission to take on Kenjiro as his assistant, which would give him the opportunity to travel and learn the interpreter's craft properly.

Kenjiro was overjoyed at the appointment and, on an early summer's day when the rice plants sparkled green and peasants, ankle-deep in mud, were patiently weeding them, he straddled his horse, adjusted his conical hat and the stiff girdle that supported his ancestral samurai swords, and rode away to join Chomin in Kagoshima. He scarcely spared a backward glance for his mother and sister, who stood bowing farewell at the wicker gate and for whom his departure was a personal sorrow. Yet they were happy for his happiness, as women of their kind were trained to be. Often it was the nearest they ever came to happiness anyway.

CHAPTER THREE

On August 12th, 1863 the naval force from Yokohama reached the harbour of Kagoshima. Two days of fruitless negotiations followed, then the British seized and burned three of the Satsuma's foreign-built steamers; at noon the next day the Japanese opened retaliatory fire from batteries built on hillsides round the bay. The combatants shelled each other for a few hours, the drama of the conflict being much heightened by typhoon-like winds and rain that hampered the gunners' aim and blew the vessels off course. Late in the afternoon naval fire-rockets were lobbed into the town and the wind, that had earlier favoured the defenders, now whipped the flames into an inferno which reduced part of the city to ashes that night. The following morning the somewhat battered squadron cruised the length of the bay shelling batteries near the harbour entrance as it went. But then, to the amazement of those on shore, it sailed away.

When the British ships were out of range of the Japanese guns anchors were dropped and brief services held by the naval chaplain for those who had died during the bombardment. The flagship *Euryalus* had suffered the greatest damage, and its two chief officers had been killed by shell-fire while standing with Admiral Kuper on the bridge. Now the ship's company stood at stiff attention, bare-headed, while the Admiral read the burial service. Then the sewn-up hammocks containing the bodies were lowered over the side and sank immediately with their weight of shot, as the men sang the hymn customary on such mournful occasion, 'Oh God, our help in ages past'.

'And they shall be turned into seaweed, as the Japanese say,' thought Percival Storey wryly. Covertly he eyed the worried expression on the Admiral's face, thinking he knew the reason for it. The bombardment of Kagoshima had not gone entirely according to plan – what with the adverse weather, the unexpectedly good marksmanship of the Japanese defences, and dissensions between the Admiral and Colonel Neale over the conduct of the battle. Storey guessed that the Admiral was, at this very moment, concocting a version of the affray that would justify to the big-wigs back home the squadron's premature and inconclusive retreat from the scene of action – which had been bitterly opposed by Colonel Neale.

After the service the naval officers gathered together in mutual sympathy while Percival and Arnold withdrew to the shelter of the cabinway.

'Rotten business altogether; and what foul luck, running into weather like this.'

Percival grinned. 'And won't the Satsuma lads make capital out of that! They'll say it was a *kamikaze*, a divine wind of the sort that scuppered the Koreans when they tried to invade in the thirteenth century.'

Arnold chuckled. 'At the first sign of an enemy just call out the wind gods, what? Well old Kuper's going to need some gods on his side to make this affair sound like a good job done. And what will the Japanese make of it, I wonder?'

Percival pondered the question so long and earnestly that Arnold began wishing he had not asked it.

'Always difficult to know how they'll react,' he said at last. 'But I've a hunch this moderate retribution might be about right; though in the heat of battle I wished we'd send in a landing party to shake them up a bit. Still, we demonstrated our strength without humiliating the Satsuma leadership too much, and humiliation would tempt them to take up arms willy-nilly against all barbarians and damn the consequences. That's what the Choshiu leaders are urging them to do, of course.'

'Of course,' Arnold muttered absently.

'We'll hear something about the Satsuma reactions from our friend Desmond Hand soon, I'll warrant,' Percival continued. 'He plays the field in his own peculiar fashion.'

'Well, whatever happens, it was a rotten cause to die for.' Arnold looked at the sea into which the coffins had been lowered. 'If one has to die in battle, the rule is – choose a good one. "He fell in the field of Waterloo" . . . "breathed his last on the walls of Lucknow . . ." – a distinct ring of martial glory there . . . But Kagoshima, I ask you!'

Percival chuckled before launching into one of his humorous parodies. ' "Kago what?" ' he began, in the shrill tone of an earnestly enquiring lady. He became gruffly masculine. ' "Kagoshima, my dear." "And where for pity's sake is that?" "A close reading of the day's *Times* leads me to believe it's in Japan, my dear," ' the husbandly voice explained. ' "That place off the coast of China?" ' Percival went up to a piercing childish treble. ' "Are they the people who wear pigtails and eat puppy dogs, papa?" "No, that's the Chinese, my boy. The Japanese have a big white chief – a big yellow chief, I should say – haw, haw – called the Tycoon. And they cut their pig-tails short and plaster them on top of their heads to look like little brushes. Their warrior classes carry sharp swords about everywhere and if you say 'boo' to one he'll cut off your head before you can cry lawks a-mercy – haw, haw." ' '

Arnold smiled politely. 'As poor old Charlie Richardson found out. Little did we think it would lead to all this bother when we scraped his remains off the road last autumn.'

'Oh, I'm not in the least surprised,' Percival said loftily, 'considering that stiff-necked Brits are confronting equally stiff-necked Sats.'

Arnold yawned. 'Enough of all these politics, let's find ourselves a little pick-me-up before dins. If this weather keeps up we're going to need it.'

As Kenjiro Miyata watched the high masts of the last enemy ship disappear round the headland that morning he felt relieved, elated, worried and angry. Prior to the engagement he had been ordered to help in the civilian evacuation and military defence of the lands around the Jokomyoji temple and had then watched the battle from a vantage point nearby. He had laughed exultantly when two shells landed squarely on the main deck of the British flagship, that was bucking wildly in the waves, for it seemed that even the weather had come to the aid of the Japanese in this crisis. For a while the British then concentrated their fire on the prominent temple itself and Kenjiro had lain quaking on the ground as shot and shell whizzed about him.

Now it was all over and the pride of the Satsuma was intact for the time being. But he realised only too clearly that the foreign squadron had given but a token demonstration of its fighting power and that warships like those, and men armed with modern weapons, could wreak havoc on the town, the province, the whole country. He remained on the hill-top for a while, frowning anxiously at the empty horizon, thinking that such a disaster must not happen, wondering how he could help ensure that it did not. Then he sighed deeply and went to join the townspeople who were already clearing up the battle-rubble.

The Satsuma leadership was also quick to realise the threatening implications of the bombardment, and dispatched officers to Nagasaki to arrange for the purchase of more foreign-built vessels to replace those they had lost. Chomin Komatsu accompanied them and soon after sent for Kenjiro to join him, which he was happy to do, for he had pleasant childhood memories of the picturesque and peaceful port.

In recent months however Nagasaki had been jolted out of its normally peaceful state. Batteries with mud ramparts had been built on the hills overlooking the harbour for fear of attack from foreign ships; others, supplied with thirty-two-pounder guns, menaced the small foreign settlement. Agents of the government and of the south-western clans had gathered there to discuss the tricky situation among themselves and, privately, with foreigners – especially with Desmond Hand, a Yorkshire merchant who had started a business in Nagasaki when it was opened to trade four years previously and who was liked and trusted by the Japanese.

'He's just married one of our women – officially, in the Consul's office, too,' Chomin explained to Kenjiro as they sat at supper in the former's lodgings.

'A night-woman?'

'No, no, a respectable merchant's daughter; and he's building a proper home on the hill. In spite of these disturbances, he's convinced all will turn out well.'

'And do you think so too?' Kenjiro asked, flattered by the older man's confidences.

Chomin put down his chopsticks and leaned forward, lowering his voice. 'This great bother over the death of one stupid Englishman is not the whole story, my lad. We southern clans are using it to embarrass the government. If the anti-barbarian factions carry out their threat and try to drive the barbarians out of the country altogether and close the treaty ports, they will fail, because the barbarians are too strong; and then the government will be finished.'

'Oh, it's even more complicated and exciting than I imagined,' Kenjiro chuckled. 'Thank goodness I'm in the thick of things at last!'

Chomin clapped his shoulder. 'You're your father's son, Kenjiro. It's time we were training more young men like you, as I told the Lord-Chief. We're meeting Mr Hand tomorrow – your first chance to see how foreigners conduct business. I've also arranged for you to meet his assistant, Mr Bell.' Chomin grinned, and sketched the outline of a temple's hand-bell on a paper tissue. 'That's our sign for all foreigners here in Nagasaki. The plan is for you to teach Bell Japanese in return for his helping you with English. But as he's not a very bright sprig you'll gain much more than he from the arrangement.'

The following afternoon Kenjiro, dressed in his finest silks, accompanied Chomin and two Satsuma officials to the western settlement, where stone-masons, carpenters, and tilers were putting the finishing touches to Hand's new house, built on a prominent site overlooking the bay. Watching the scene, Kenjiro marvelled at the boldness of these foreign traders who felt themselves entitled to residences in such commanding positions. Native merchants would never dare to build on hill-tops, where only *daimyo*'s castles dominated the horizons; they kept their treasure chests concealed in huddled, low-roofed houses away from jealous eyes, and were inferior men – servile, vulgar money grabbers and money changers – or so Kenjiro had been taught to believe.

But Mr Desmond Hand was not at all like that, being dapper, confident-looking, with a clipped goatee beard and a clear, incisive manner of speech. The first topic of the afternoon's discussions was Hand's delivery to the Satsuma of a British steamer from Shanghai, which had been progressing smoothly until what both parties termed the 'regrettable recent troubles'. The deal was secret, for the *bakafu*, fearing the growing military strength of the south-western clans, had issued an edict forbidding such transactions. Government fears were justified, for the Satsuma did indeed plan to convert the steamer into a warship and wanted to send agents disguised as coolies and carpenters aboard the vessel to assess its suitability for that purpose. As refreshments were served, the Satsuma officials and Hand waxed quite merry on the problems the disguised agents might encounter, and Kenjiro marvelled again at how relaxed and friendly they seemed with each other. An item of even greater import and secrecy concerning payment of the Richardson indemnity was next on the agenda, and Kenjiro and other junior attendants were curtly dismissed.

Wandering outside, Kenjiro leaned against a verandah pillar and stared at the recently built batteries overlooking the settlement. What would his father have felt about this anti-foreign upsurge? Would he have rebelled against it, warned his superiors that it was dangerous and short-sighted? If only Aritomo . . . He chided himself for thinking exactly like his mother. Yet Aritomo had been a far-seeing man and had understood what his son now perceived for the first time – the necessity for Japan to become a single nation instead of a conglomeration of separate clans. In his mind's eye, Kenjiro saw beyond the harbour of Nagasaki below, to his own city of Kagoshima and further, to the Inland Sea and Osaka, along the tree-lined Tokaido to Yokohama and Edo, and north again to unknown Hokkaido. It was a compact geographical entity, as his father used to say, and this continual internal feuding between clans and ruling factions was absurdly outdated, a stupid waste of the country's energies.

He continued to stand there, trying to work out the full implications of this, until Chomin emerged from the house accompanied by a pale, weedy Englishman, whom he introduced as Mr Timothy Bell.

'You two must learn to talk in both languages to each other,' Chomin said. 'It will be good for you. So why not ask Mr Bell a question, Kenjiro, and see if you can understand his answer in English.'

Kenjiro rose to the challenge. 'It will be a difficult one, but, I've been thinking about we Japanese as one people, a united nation, which is a novel idea to most of us, though you westerners consider us so, surely? But what do you really know about us? Take an average Englishman who's never been to the East – how does he think of us?'

Bell coughed a little apologetically. 'To be honest, I think that to most Englishmen you are an almost unknown race – very strange and quaint and remote. Er . . . rather like the Chinese, only smaller and er . . . yellower, if you'll pardon the expression.'

Kenjiro looked puzzled, thinking he had misunderstood. 'Yellower? Like that?' He indicated a nearby clump of cinquefoil.

'Yes, it's silly, but we learned at school that there are three main races in the world, the white, the black, and the yellow.' (And the first, of course, superior, Chomin inserted in his translation.)

'Of course I know now orientals aren't the colour of those flowers at all . . .' Bell floundered and Kenjiro bowed in cold acknowledgement.

'*Ah-so*, thank you. And one more question if I may, Mr Timothy Bell. Your father, what is his lineage?'

'Oh, he's a merchant in Shanghai – Tinker, Dodsworth and Bell,' he replied enthusiastically, on safer ground. 'We're in tea and silk; quite a large firm, though not one of the top dogs.'

'I see.' Kenjiro smiled stiffly, thinking it strange that he should be considered an equal of this whipper-snapper merchant's son. He wanted to tell Mr Bell of his samurai father, and his magistrate grandfather who had been granted annual audiences with the Lord Shimazu, but when it was Bell's turn to ask questions, he showed no interest in such matters, inquiring instead about the current prices of sugar and copper in Kagoshima.

As they were about to leave, Mr Hand called his wife Misako to be introduced. She looked an ordinary, round-faced merchant's daughter, Kenjiro thought, and was in a considerable fluster about the correct way to behave. If she had not been Hand's wife, she would have performed profound obeisance before men of such high rank.

'Ah, my wife is not yet accustomed to so many strangers at once,' Hand explained, seeing her dilemma, and she gave him a smile of such adoring gratitude that Kenjiro wondered if she could actually love him.

'Do you think she really enjoys doing it, with him?' Kenjiro whispered to Chomin as they rode away.

Chomin grinned. 'Oh, that . . . I suppose it's much the same, though they say barbarian cocks are bigger than ours.'

'And whiter too, I suppose,' Kenjiro snorted.

For the next two months Kenjiro worked extremely hard, attending every meeting between his clansmen and foreigners, until gradually the outlandish English tongue began to form patterns of sense in his head. In the autumnal evenings he and Bell, who was equally diligent but not as quick, pored over their books by dim lamplight, often wearied by their strenuous efforts at mutual communication. In November, Chomin told him they were travelling north with a Satsuma delegation. The reason for the mission was not revealed to one of Kenjiro's junior rank, but he did not care what it was; enough that he would have another chance to visit the Shogun's capital and perhaps even to glimpse the strange foreigners' enclave of Yokohama.

'You'll never guess what's happened — just what I've been

saying all along.' Percival Storey padded into Arnold's sitting room one November evening with papers in one hand and the boots he had forgotten to leave outside in the other.

Arnold adopted a gravely meditative expression. 'Now . . . let me guess . . . I know! The Sats have come to negotiate an indemnity for Richardson's murder.'

'How did you know? It's still a secret.'

'Well, you've been saying it all along, haven't you? If you're intent on becoming a diplomat of consequence, old boy, I should start practising the art of discretion and dissimulation if I were you.'

Percy sniffed vexedly. 'Well, anyway that's it. Oh, and these came in the mails – cuttings from the British press about the Kagoshima fracas. Haven't had a chance to read them . . .' He began doing so, whistling in surprise. 'Lots of criticism of the Chief's decisions . . . "The people of Kagoshima have no more responsibility for the murder of Charles Richardson than the people of Birmingham," ' he quoted. 'True, of course, but nothing new in that when guns and bullets are about.' He began to chortle. 'Oh this is rich . . . listen . . . "The Japanese, with their usual display of cunning, took advantage of the typhoon to launch an attack on our ships." ' He affected his theatrical-colonel voice. ' "Did you hear that, Carruthers? The nasty yellow swine – sneakin' up in a typhoon, what? Not cricket, sir, not cricket at all! Always fight in the open like a man, what? Enemy head on, hey? Charge of the Light Brigade . . . now that was a proper engagement, none of these hole in the corner taking advantage of the elements tricks . . . Darkness is different, mind. Now I remember our fellows creeping towards the ramparts in the depths of the night . . . Sebastopol, was it?" ' Seeing Arnold's lack of amusement, he reverted to his normal tones as he read on . . . 'There, Arnold, you remember that big white building on the hill Kuper would insist on shelling, saying it was the Prince of Satsuma's palace? Well, it was the Jokomyoji temple. I told you it wasn't a palace, didn't I?' He threw the paper down in disgust, shrugging. 'Oh well, I suppose the bombardment did the trick, whatever the cost. Letter to the Chief from Satsuma headquarters in Edo today – they're sending some chaps over tomorrow and it all sounds promising.'

And indeed the ensuing negotiations went extremely smoothly, for the faction in the Satsuma leadership which urged appeasement of the foreigners had triumphed. They had learned the lesson of Kagoshima: without modern military and naval resources, they and their clan allies could neither oust the foreigners from the treaty ports nor dictate their country's future. With impressive politeness the delegates agreed with Colonel Neale on an indemnity payment of £25,000 for Richardson's murder; then asked if they could purchase two made-in-Britain steamships.

On the day of the settlement, Colonel Neale called Arnold to his office, where Percival, also present, gave Arnold a surreptitious wink to reassure him that nothing was amiss.

'Ah, Mills, do sit down. I've a request here . . .' The Colonel searched vaguely through papers on his desk. '. . . somewhere or other . . . from the Satsuma chaps. Storey and I thought it might interest you. They want us to take on and train up one of their interpreters, seems a promising young fellow . . . what's the name, Storey?'

'Miyata, sir; Kenjiro Miyata.'

'Ah, yes. Here's your translation of the letter – they want this Miyata chappy to learn foreign-style methods of conducting diplomatic and general affairs in order that communication between themselves and the honourable British officials may be smoothened in the future.'

' "Smoothened", Storey? That's an odd one, isn't it?'

Percival reddened. 'Sorry, sir. I was in a great hurry, made more smooth, I mean lubricated . . .'

The Colonel puffed. 'Oh, we've got the gist. They want us to take him on the political side, but that's far too risky, even though Storey swears they've changed their spots more quickly and completely than a pack of leopards. But we thought you might like to take him on, Mills? He'll pick up a lot from you undoubtedly, and Storey says you are being constantly pestered by Japanese students asking about western medical techniques, which, naturally, you can't easily explain. Might "smoothen" Japanese–British relations a little more if you can pass on a few tips, hey?'

'It's a capital idea, sir; a good interpreter would be absolutely invaluable.'

'Right. Then let's see the fellow. Try and find out his background and where he learned his English, Storey. See if he seems sound. Of course, he'll pass on everything he learns about us to his clan, but I don't think that need be a worry if it's not political.'

As Kenjiro came in and saw Arnold he started visibly, then made a carefully calculated bow – long enough to show respect for the Colonel's superior age and status, but not as low as for a high-ranking samurai.

Percival, appreciating the subtlety, smiled. 'Please sit down, Mr Miyata.'

Kenjiro perched on a high chair's edge, nervously arranging his wide trousers to suit the unaccustomed posture. The Colonel's questions were briskly to the point and Percival, in translating them, smoothed somewhat the sharp outlines, the habitual military bark. Kenjiro's answers seemed satisfactory, and the Colonel, consulting his pocket watch, soon brought the interview to an end. 'I'm afraid I've some dispatches to read over before the mail boat leaves. Doctor, do you have anything to ask Mr Miyata as he would be working for you?'

'I'm wondering about his medical vocabulary. Parts of the body and all that you are familiar with, Mr Miyata!'

Kenjiro nodded uncertainly.

'This, for instance.' Arnold pointed.

'The ear.'

'And this?' Arnold patted below his belt.

'A tummy.'

Neale gave a snort of laughter and Kenjiro flushed crimson. 'It is wrong?'

'Not wrong exactly,' Percival placated him quickly in Japanese. 'Only that is the child's word, you see. For a doctor "stomach" would usually be more appropriate. You'll soon pick it up.'

'I will read more medical books,' Kenjiro replied stiffly,

remembering he had learned the child's word from Mr Moon, who used to draw labelled stick figures of the human anatomy to amuse him and Ryo. It was pointless trying to explain such things to these strangers.

The Colonel was quizzing Arnold with his eyes. 'All right? Then I'll leave you to settle the details. I think Miyata should be allotted a staff room at the back of the hospital for a start. Thank you, Mr Miyata. I'll write to your clan tomorrow. Good day to you. Now if you'll excuse me, gentlemen.'

Outside the office, Percival took his friend's arm. 'Well, if you ask me you won't do better than Miyata.'

'Seems all right and quite presentable looking for a Japanese.'

'Often are, these Sats – more open-faced, less sly-eyed, but proud as the devil. You saw how he bridled over that tummy business. Don't ever make a fool of him – they don't like it. And I'd clinch the terms straight away if I were you. Give him an advance on his first salary, and tell him he'll have his own pony and groom and a cubby hole somewhere for his servant. Make him feel he's still a samurai and not your lackey. You won't keep him else – and the Frogs or Yanks would be only too glad to get hold of someone with his linguistic capabilities, imperfect though they are.'

So it was settled, and when the Satsuma delegation returned to Kagoshima a few days later, Kenjiro moved into his new quarters, a small room overlooking the hospital's back court-yard and flanked by stables and kitchen quarters. As Kenjiro looked down on the scene on the first evening of his arrival, his eyes sparkled with excitement and triumph. The long years of hard, lonely, much-disparaged studies were bearing fruit at last; and it pleased him mightily that his new employer was the only foreigner in Yokohama whom he had instantly and secretly recognised.

Beside him on a lacquered chest he had carefully laid a row of silver and copper coins. 'To help you with the moving in,' Arnold had said casually, not suspecting that Kenjiro had never in his life before possessed nearly so much money of his own to spend. In his youth, actual currency had been a rarity, handed out frugally by his elders on festive occasions. Such money he had spent on clothes, for he was well aware that he cut an unusually tall and handsome figure in his traditional clan dress, with his broad shoulders and slender waist. He stared at the coins, deciding to get some new clothes made the very next day – wadded-cotton jackets and luxuriously silk-lined over-cloaks for the winter. Even then, he thought with a grin, there would be plenty of money left; he would find a good restaurant tonight, and then a pretty girl. A sharp pang of sexual desire gnawed him and he longed to nuzzle soft female flesh. Yet he didn't really want a casual woman that night, and would have greatly preferred lying with an adoring wife with whom he could not only make love, but share the pleasure of his important new post and his bright hopes for the future. He thought angrily of Gengoro, who had bestowed the sweet Ofuku elsewhere. Well, in time he, Kenjiro, son of Aritomo, would show his uncle a thing or two by finding some higher-ranking, prettier wife for himself. For was he not now a junior interpreter in the service of the British Legation's doctor, with his own horse, groom, servant, and amazingly generous salary? Disbelievingly, he counted the coins again, for the very idea of receiving so many at regular intervals was new to him.

In the courtyard, servants were closing the shutters, padlocking the outside gate against the chilly evening breezes and the treacherous dark. Drawing his shutter also, Kenjiro decided that with his next payment he would buy silken kimonos for his mother and Ryo. The very thought of those two dear familiar faces so far away brought to the surface the underlying tug of melancholy isolation that had been nagging below his excitement. He had never felt so rich before, but he had never felt so alone either. Bereft of relatives and the companionship of his clansmen, what was the point of seeking a night's pleasure by himself? How would he know where to go in this alien place? Bitterly, sadly, he swept the coins into his draw-string purse and called for Bimyo to bring him supper from a noodle vendor's store outside the compound gate. After the meal, he again concentrated on his studies, trying to shut out the loneliness, the awe, the anxiety that verged on panic at the thought of the solitary and difficult path he had chosen.

CHAPTER FOUR

Kenjiro later recalled the first months of his employment in Yokohama as among the most difficult in his life. His status seemed little better than a servant's, and many times he had to conceal his proud rage at the Britishers' peremptory and inconsiderate manner. The casual, self-confident, unpredictable clumsiness of large Arnold also set his nerves on edge; and he was sometimes on the brink of reaching for his short sword in self-protection, imagining that the barbarian might suddenly strike him. He watched anxiously as Arnold lumbered about, threw his bulk on flimsy bamboo chairs that creaked in protest, guffawed loudly, drank fairly copiously, tore at his food with knife and fork, and shouted for his groom or cook – in a manner which, to Arnold's own ears, sounded perfectly affable.

Most of Kenjiro's work was at the medical dispensary; but occasionally he visited settlers' bungalows with Arnold to interpret for ailing servants. There he found the foreign ladies even more alarming than the men, with their brazenly tossing curls, open-mouthed laughter, and voices raised in unchecked arguments with their menfolk, who, astonishingly, held doors open for them to pass through. Yet they fascinated him too – skins pale as spring cherry blossom; bold, sparkling eyes, grey, green or blue; fleshy bosoms visible above low-cut necklines; swirling circular skirts that rustled as they bustled busily about – so totally unlike any women he had ever before seen.

Like a half-wild cat, Kenjiro moved tensely and gingerly in their over-crowded western rooms, with their noxious smells of alien foods like cheese and preserved meats. He felt oppressed and overwhelmed by so much hard-edged furniture, every surface crammed with ornaments, books, photographs, and clocks; and marvelled that the owners of all these material goods often grumbled at the deprivation of their present lot, talking longingly of the spacious, comfortable, solid residences they would build when their 'ships came home'. In addition, Kenjiro was often subject to unpleasant shocks: the tinny rattle of the instrument called an harmonium; the picture of a voluptuous nude on a wall; a negro sailor walking along the Bund, whose black skin and bulging eyes reminded Kenjiro of a demon from some old Buddhist painting. Through all this, however, Mr Miyata maintained his bland expression and his own counsel – self-contained, self-watchful, tight-muscled, and wary as a samurai on an alien battlefield.

He relaxed his guard only during brief visits to Edo, when he stayed at the Satsuma *yashiki*. All the major clans maintained permanent establishments called *yashiki* in the capital, where numbers of samurai, retainers and their families lived for fixed periods at the Shogun's command. Each *yashiki* was a walled enclosure containing a number of residential courtyards, barracks, and weaponry stores, and spacious grounds for the practice of military arts and horsemanship. The Satsuma *yashiki* was one of the grandest, and Kenjiro loved going there, to talk in his own dialect again and hear news of his home province. Sometimes he and a few congenial companions would visit the entertainment quarter of Asakusa, looking for restaurants that served Kyushu delicacies and for pretty, willing girls – who were always available in the nearby Yoshiwara. An adaptable, observant man, he soon ceased to feel like a bumpkin from the sleepy south, and thoroughly enjoyed the colour and verve of this large city, its glad-handed citizenry, its side-shows, shops, and theatres, with their Edo-style songs and jokes. Yokohama was a strange country by comparison; yet it was also a lure and a challenge, the place where he had to make his own mark.

Early in the spring, Arnold and others in British employ

were allotted more palatial quarters in the Consulate's new extension, where Elinor, who had made herself as indispensable as she could to her brother, secured a guest-room on a temporary basis, while Kenjiro was given a room at the back of the premises. The main purpose of the move was to make everyone feel more secure, and it was, therefore, a particularly unpleasant shock when, on the very day it was accomplished, Denshiro, senior interpreter at the nearby French Consulate, was cut down in broad daylight outside its gate by two *ronin*. These were swordsmen of reactionary persuasion who had left, or been dismissed from, the service of their clan lords and had sworn to expel every foreigner from the country at whatever cost. Not even the consulates were safe from such fanatics, it seemed, and Kenjiro felt particularly vulnerable for, in their eyes, he, like Denshiro, was a marked man, a traitor who had sold himself to the barbarians.

Alone in his new quarters that evening he prowled about restlessly, peeping through the shutters occasionally at the dark courtyard below, its menacing shadows only partially dispelled by gable lanterns and fitful moonlight that shone on the waters of the large central well. His skin crawled with the horror of ice-sharp steel and the two swords he laid at his side when he rolled supperless into bed were instruments of fear rather than protection. Stretching his neck to fit his wooden head-rest, he imagined the blade at his throat and lay sleepless for hours watching the flickering shadows of the nightlight, listening to every creak of shutters. When he did eventually sleep, he was beset by the shaming nightmares of his youthful military training – the demoniac yell of the metalled warrior leaping at him from behind a rock, knocking aside his own tentative weapon, pinioning him ready for the final blood-spurting thrust.

He was awakened with a start of alarm by the early morning sounds of servants clattering about the courtyard and drawing water from the well. His first feeling was of gratitude for the bright, morning light, till he remembered that Denshiro had been murdered at noon. Unable to sleep again, he rose, tucked

his short sword into the belt of his loose robe and crept
outside. The consulate servants were now preparing breakfasts
in the kitchen and he went over to the well, remembering the
old superstition: if one's reflection in well-water was clear,
one's life would be long. He stared down into the black,
sparkling depths, and his reflection stared back, comfortingly
apparent. He breathed deeply, and smiled at his mirror image,
relaxing against the plaster parapet. Suddenly a shadow fell
from behind him onto the water and he spun round, drawing
his short sword on the instant.

'Oh, no − please . . . don't!' The young foreign woman
who had been walking across the courtyard halted, raising
her arm in alarm. He lowered his weapon immediately.

'Madam − I beg your pardon, my humble apologies.'
Flushed crimson, he hastily sheathed his sword, bowing as
she recovered herself.

'Oh − you speak good English. May I ask who . . .?'

'Mr Miyata, madam.' He tried ducking his way past her in
confusion.

'Why of course − my brother's interpreter. He's often
spoken highly of you, and naturally you must be nervous at
the moment, considering Denshiro's murder.'

'Not nervous, madam, but on guard,' he corrected with a
haughty bow, hurrying away before she could say more.

Realising she had offended him, Elinor frowned, telling
herself to be more careful of the prickly native temperament
in future. How tall and handsome Mr Miyata was for a
Japanese − something Arnold had never mentioned, but
being male he probably hadn't noticed it. During the next
few weeks Elinor found herself looking out for the intriguing
Mr Miyata, but though they now lived in close proximity
their paths seldom crossed until, one spring evening, she saw
him at a public meeting of the Municipal Council.

The declared aim of the council, most of whose members
were foreign traders, was to transform Yokohama into a solid,
salubrious, and prosperous treaty port like Shanghai, which
meant tackling such thorny matters as 'street repairs,
lighting, jetties, police, nuisances, and cargo boats'. When

the council's attempts to solve these problems reached an impasse, as they often did, public meetings were held to decide future courses of action. They did not accomplish much either, as Arnold warned his sister, adding teasingly that she seemed to be more anxious about the settlement's progress than any councillor.

Still Elinor insisted they go to the meeting, held in the Seamen's Hall, where the audience, crammed on wooden benches, soon began fanning themselves with the agendas, for the weather was warm. Mr Steiner, the Chairman, opened proceedings by listing some of the current difficulties, such as the poor organisation of the Customs House, and an insufficiency of cargo boats and porters to deal with the increasing volume of trade. Moreover, the Japanese authorities, as every settler knew to his cost, charged exorbitant ground rents and had pledged in return to maintain the port's amenities. But what was the result? There was no street-lighting, and every thoroughfare was either a mud-swamp or a dust-heap according to the season.

At this juncture, excitable members of the audience could no longer refrain from airing suggestions for improvement of their own particular grievances, and the Chairman, abandoning his list, let everyone have his say. One vociferous speaker repeatedly drew the meeting's attention to the fact that the imminent and welcome arrival of British and French troops to help protect the settlement would add greatly to the present problems of sanitation and waste disposal. A proper drainage system must be built and a foreign engineer hired for the purpose, as the Japanese were quite incapable of such a feat and, apparently, their flat noses were impervious to public stinks. At this, Elinor glanced anxiously at Mr Miyata and his two Japanese companions, but they, listening to the proceedings with shocked, puzzled concentration, seemed not to notice the insult.

As for the matter of Customs House porters, snarled another man loudly, it was well known their labour was monopolised by coolie masters who demanded ruinous rates of hire. Nor was that the only racket run by the Customs, he added darkly, but, there being ladies present, he would say no more. Arnold glanced guiltily at his sister, for, as he well knew, the speaker was referring to the practice of hiring the services not only of porters but of young women through Customs House officials. He himself had recently acquired the services of one Yasu, a shop-keeper's daughter, in this fashion, and visited her on a regular basis in the native town, thus lessening the prevalent risk of venereal disease.

Eventually the meeting agreed to set up Customs and Sanitation sub-committees and then dispersed with relief. As he moved out, Kenjiro felt somewhat disappointed, for he had gone to watch the processes of popular democracy in action, expecting everything to be well-ordered and clear-cut. Instead he had been bewildered and appalled by the lack of decisions and the raised babble of male voices that sounded as coarse and ignorant as stall-holders yelling the odds in a fish market. He reached the door at the same moment as his employer's sister and was about to push ahead, then, remembering the odd courtesies due to western women, stepped aside to let her pass.

She paused. 'I hope you enjoyed our public meeting, Mr Miyata?'

'There was much shouting,' he replied stiffly.

'Yes – but that's quite customary in public meetings, is it not?' They went outside, standing together to let others pass.

'I didn't know. We Japanese do not have this sort of meeting.'

'Really? Never? But how do you decide things?'

'We are not democracy, ordinary people don't have voice, the leaders decide.'

'Oh yes, of course, I forgot.' She smiled apologetically. 'You must think I'm stupid asking such questions about your country, Mr Miyata. But I find it such an interesting and delightful place that I'm trying to learn as much as I can.'

'I'm very glad you like. You must learn Japanese words, even a few is good for understanding.'

'Yes, I know, and I'd love to, but . . . why now, Mr Miyata, won't you teach me a little? Say twice a week, when you can spare the time? I promise to be a very industrious student . . . please.'

He drew back instinctively from what seemed to him a rather improper proposal. 'But I don't think your brother the doctor . . .'

'Oh, Arnold won't object, I'll soon arrange it with him. So then you will?'

'Maybe, but . . .' Incapable of refusing point blank, he played for time, intending to excuse himself later.

'Oh, I *do* look forward to it. Can I start this very week? There's my brother waiting, I'll tell him. And one last question, if I may, Mr Miyata. Would you like to see public meetings here in Japan? Do you think they're a good idea?'

'I think people need chance to say what they want to authorities, yes. But we Japanese cannot yet conduct matters in such a way. Who would begin? We do not speak, argue, shout, in open place. There is not tradition. It is not polite thing for us.' He smiled with brilliant intensity at her, suddenly willing her to understand the complexities that he could not quite put into words.

'But your people can learn very fast,' she protested earnestly. 'And educated men like yourself could show them the way.'

Flattered by her confidence in his ability, he believed for a minute it could be as easy as that. 'Then I will see what I can do,' he inclined his head obediently as the doctor joined them.

'Oh, Arnold, Mr Miyata is going to give me lessons in Japanese conversation. Isn't that marvellous? So kind of him. You're agreeable, aren't you? I've already said you are!' She drew her arm through his with an affectionate squeeze and, bidding Kenjiro good evening, hurried away.

The arrival of the second battalion of Her Britannic Majesty's XXth Regiment three weeks later was a gala occasion for the settlement. Houses were hung with bright bunting and Union Jacks, and their residents lined the Bund to watch the Red Coats land from HMS *Conqueror*, which had brought them from Hong Kong. Elinor Mills, wearing a new walking-dress of apple-green foulard edged with ruches of white ribbon, found herself standing near Mr Miyata and took the opportunity of trying to increase her Japanese vocabulary.

Kenjiro had found it impossible to delay the conversation lessons, even though they made him most uncomfortable. The behaviour of his student verged on impropriety, he felt, as she leaned eagerly towards him, lips parted and eyes shining with the effort of concentration. 'Please explain again, Mr Miyata', she would plead and, 'Oh, Mr Miyata, can you kindly tell me . . .'

The intensity of her desire to understand quite scared him, compared to the grateful docility with which his own sister Ryo used to pick up what crumbs of knowledge he and his father had thrown to her. But Elinor knew how to get her way, and twice a week the lessons were duly held. He dreaded each one, longing for it to end, yet, afterwards, he sometimes felt it had not been long enough and that he had spent too much time apologising for the lack of Japanese words for things that she took for granted. First there had been the wretched business of public meetings and the broader concepts of democratic political discussion; today, as they waited for the British troops to march past, it was the matter of flags.

'The Japanese have no national flag at all, then? Nothing similar? No national emblem or . . .' Elinor looked quite horrified at this latest deficiency he had just admitted. Percival, standing just behind her as usual, chimed in. 'Each clan has its own crest or *mon*, Miss Mills, and I suppose the Shogun's Tokugawa crest is almost a national symbol. But the situation is more like the primitive Scottish clans in the old days with their divided loyalties and separate tartans.'

Just then a military band struck up and Elinor's heart lifted to the familiar notes as the bandsmen came marching by, brass instruments flashing in the sun, drum-tassels rhythmically swinging. She felt proud and pleased to be British and rather sorry for the Japanese in general and Mr Miyata in particular. It must be most difficult − to have lived unknowingly in a backward condition for so long and now have to learn and

74

adapt so quickly. She glanced at him sympathetically, but Mr Miyata was scowling with irritation – both at the brassy squalling of the tuneless music and at Percival's slighting comparison of his people to primitive Scots.

'Isn't the music grand?' she tried to cheer him, but he merely grunted and edged away.

Elinor shrugged, and as she turned her attention to the smart men of the XXth passing by, one young officer deliberately twisted his head to give her a quick, friendly wink.

'Someone seems to know you?' Percival asked.

'Oh, that's Lieutenant Bradshaw. I met him a few times when I was staying with my aunt in Hong Kong.'

Percival nodded lugubriously, guessing that Lieutenant Bradshaw was the reason for the spanking new and very pretty outfit she was wearing. Percival had been sure there must be someone else. Surely she would have evinced a little more interest in him otherwise? In any case, Elinor Mills would have no lack of attentive swains now, he told himself grimly, as the marching men left the Bund and headed for their temporary barracks on the Bluff.

The presence of about five hundred British troops and three hundred Frenchmen brought a surge of masculine brio to the settlement. Drills, reviews, long marches and firing practices were the order of every day; bugle calls, shouts of command, rifle shots echoed from the Bluff's parade ground; grog shops near the Gankiro sported new names like the 'Army and Navy' and 'Tommy's Tavern'. So much martial effervescence was a source of continuing wonder to the Japanese and of entertainment to the settlers; though a few curmudgeons among them muttered darkly that it would protect no one against the attacks of two-sworded fanatics and that the troops were there only because there was nothing left for them to do in China now the Taipings were finally crushed.

The troops, not given to reason why, simply enjoyed the change of scene and the continual round of mess dinners, riding parties, athletic competitions and drag hunts. And, as Mary Fortescue remarked, even the sensible head of Elinor Mills was a little turned by the extravagance of masculine regard she received that summer. Mrs Fortescue could have been a little jealous, however, for she had always fancied military gentlemen herself, and now felt somewhat encumbered by the presence of pale-cheeked Claud, who abhorred all strenuous outdoor activities.

As for Elinor, any temptation she had to play the coquette was smartly forestalled by Lieutenant Reginald Bradshaw, who called on her the day after his arrival and continued to do so — flattering and escorting her with the confident assiduity of a handsome young man of good background and prospects. Son of a colonel in the Indian army, he looked as virile as a young bull, with strong, thick neck and shoulders, flaring nostrils, ruddy cheeks, brown beard, and a wavy forelock. Only his rather small eyes suggested the uncertain little boy that lurked beneath the manly exterior, but this he did not long conceal from Elinor, who found it touching.

'Had a letter, or rather a lecture, from Father yesterday.' He grinned ruefully at Elinor as they walked up the Bluff track one midsummer evening for a ladies' night supper in the mess. 'More than time I settled down and took life seriously, he says . . . too much of the horses and hounds, my boy. Trouble is, our chief here, Colonel Sutcliffe, is a friend of my old man's and keeps him very well briefed about me. Father's right, of course; he could pull a few strings and get me promoted quickly, once I show I'm worth it.'

'Well, why don't you, then? If it's as easy as that, you should count yourself fortunate,' Elinor reproved.

'Trouble is . . .' He flicked carelessly at a clump of wild roses with his riding whip. 'I need a sensible girl like you to settle me down, Ellie, tell me off when I'm tempted to kick over the traces, keep me on the straight and narrow.'

She puffed. 'You make me sound like a missionary.'

'Oh, I know you're not that, dear, much too pretty and soft.' He encircled her waist with his arm and squeezed. 'But you are level-headed and I'm sure you'd enjoy keeping me in order.'

'Well, perhaps I would — but I'm not devoting all that effort to a mere lieutenant, so you'd better take your father's advice.'

'Oh, I will, if you say so, really I will,' he promised earnestly. 'I'll write tomorrow to say I'm turning over a new leaf entirely, thanks to a certain absolutely stunning young lady I know who wants me to.' He turned in front of her, kissing her lightly, then more forcefully, on the mouth.

'Oh, Reggie, careful; the men will see us.' She drew back.

'And how jealous they'll be if they do,' he chuckled, holding her chin and kissing her again. The warm circle of his arms enclosed her but she forced herself loose. 'Not here, dear, please; it's too public.'

'Later then, after dark,' he whispered as they approached the camp.

She looked at the scene ahead of her – the boarded huts with tin chimneys sticking askew from the roofs, the long barracks with kitchens behind and on the far side the scuffed-dust parade ground – and thought how exciting overseas army life was compared to the dull routine of distant Harrogate. Would it not be mission enough for her life to make Reggie into a son of whom his father could be proud? And one day perhaps she herself would be the colonel's lady? Of course Reggie had not exactly . . . yet . . . but she was sure he would in the near future.

The frolics of what Elinor later remembered as the most carefree summer of her life extended into a pleasantly warm autumn and culminated in the last outdoor event of the season – a grand entertainment held on the main deck of HMS *Perseus*. On a platform strung with coloured lanterns, the men of the *Perseus* performed theatricals supported by the ship's band. The performance – broad skits of military and settlement life, interspersed with songs and dances by a group of golliwog-faced nigger minstrels – was fairly dreadful, but the men cheered lustily and the seated ladies clapped bravely, though everyone was glad when the last curtain was drawn across, signalling a rush for the buffet supper.

Mary Fortescue and Elinor stood against the ship's rail while the men made for the food. 'Oh dear, I do wish these men would stop dressing up as women on stage,' Elinor sighed. 'I can't even pretend to find it funny, can you? It's all so gross and really rather insulting.'

'I suppose they consider it fun; but it wasn't in very good taste tonight, I admit — that midshipman prancing about in bonnet and skirt showing off his hairy legs. I was rather glad the newcomers, Mr and Mrs Rayne, declined to come this evening after all. They arrived today en route for Hakodate, you know; he's to be the Consul there. I certainly don't envy them, going to that God-forsaken place at the onset of a northern winter.'

'How do you think they'll do?'

'Oh, he seems quite genial and good-tempered, but she — I don't know. A very handsome woman, but rather distant and stand-offish. I'm sure she wouldn't have been in the least amused by tonight's antics. Ah, here are the men with the food at last.'

Claud and Percival arrived with one laden tray, Arnold and Reggie with another, and finding a corner out of the wind they set to.

'Fairly appalling show, wasn't it?' Arnold whispered.

'That skit on the Choshiu affair took the biscuit,' Percival agreed.

The men of the *Perseus*, with other British and American troops, had recently been on an expedition to the south-west, where they had bombarded fortifications of the Choshiu clan, which had earlier fired on foreign vessels in the Simonoseki Straits. During the skit, entitled 'How we gave the Josses [i.e., Choshiu] What For', several sailor lads, in crude parodies of Japanese dress, ran screaming in mock terror from a one-armed British marine.

'I saw Miyata nosing around,' Percival continued. 'Must have got aboard with his interpreter's pass. He's bound to report it — which won't please our Satsuma friends.'

'But Mr Miyata isn't a spy; I'm sure he wouldn't,' Elinor protested.

'Don't you believe it,' Arnold cut in. 'Miyata keeps what you might call a watching brief for his clan. No harm in that usually, but as Percy says 'twill be a pity if they hear of tonight's silly charade now we're on much better terms with them.'

Mary groaned. 'Oh, no Japanese politics tonight, please! See, they're clearing a space; I do believe we're getting some hornpipes.'

It was a perfect setting: the sailors' spritely jumping to the music on the rolling deck; the ship's rigging outlined against a starlit sky; lights from portholes and mastheads glinting on the dark sea around. The spirits of the audience rose so high to the lilt of the pipes and the generous libations of champagne accompanying it, that the ship's band was again mustered to play polkas, jigs, and gallops until the few much-in-demand dancing ladies were quite exhausted. It was well after midnight when Reggie escorted Elinor to the Consulate's side gate, and, as Arnold discreetly disappeared inside, kissed her passionately, murmuring that she was the best, sweetest, and only girl he had ever loved. The insistent, exciting warmth of his desire pressing against her roused Elinor, and she caressed him avidly in return, thinking that, if he proposed to her there and then, she would accept. But just then a watchman came round the corner with musket and lantern and Elinor, embarrassed, tore herself from his arms. As she passed across the courtyard to her own quarters, she saw a gleam of light from Mr Miyata's room, and wondered if he really was writing to his superiors about those lamentable theatricals.

Kenjiro was indeed writing to his superiors about his visit to the *Perseus*, but they, intent on strengthening Satsuma sea power, would, he knew, be much more interested in his careful descriptions of the modern cannon he had seen on the quarter deck than in any silly entertainments. Eventually he rolled into his bed-quilt, exhausted as usual, for his daily work was taxing and every evening he studied foreign books, their script so stiff-legged and monotonous compared to the fluid and varied shapes of his own calligraphy. All that summer, while the settlers had revelled, he had worked diligently, and, as autumn came on, continued so to do, for he knew he was perfecting skills that would ensure his future advancement.

One evening, a few weeks after the *Perseus* had returned to its China station, Kenjiro was working late as usual when he was disturbed by a light tap on the outer door. He tensed immediately, reaching for his short sword. There had been no actual assassination since Denshiro's, but several native merchants who dealt with foreigners had been threatened by *ronin* who still lurked in the vicinity. However, the door slid back to reveal the harmless figure of a cloaked female bowing in the entrance way.

'My sister – Ryo, you – can it be?' He jumped up to usher her inside, where she collapsed on a cushion, shielding her face with a sleeve to hide her fatigue and distress.

'Let me sit for a minute, brother. I do not bring good news,' she murmured warningly, not looking up as he came and stood over her.

'But however did you get here? Are you alone?' he asked incredulously, astounded that a young, single woman should travel so far unaccompanied. She nodded but remained silent.

'Tell me.' He began to feel alarmed.

'Kenjiro – brother – you must prepare yourself. Our dearest, most respected mother is dead.' He gave a little moan and fell to his knees beside her, head bowed as she explained that Setsu had caught a chill which turned to fever a few weeks previously. 'I wanted to ask Kentaro to summon a good doctor from Nagasaki, but she wouldn't let me. You know how proud she was. When she got worse I sent for the doctor myself but it was too late.' She rubbed a kerchief against her trembling lips.

'Why didn't you send for me?' Kenjiro asked roughly.

'There was not time, it was all over in a matter of days. She didn't want you worried.'

'Worried . . . worried,' he sighed bitterly. 'She wasn't very old, she always seemed strong.' He glared almost accusingly at his sister.

'Strong – not really, but she kept her weakness from you. She used to cough dreadfully, especially in cold weather.'

He rubbed his fists together in rage. 'And just as I have money that would have helped her. You received what I've sent already?'

'Oh yes, thank you, brother; we were most grateful. You mustn't blame yourself for anything. I'm to blame, if anyone . . .' She paused, voice breaking with fatigue and sadness.

'Why you? Let me call Bimyo for some tea.' He touched her shoulder gently.

'In a minute. He will be distressed also, and there is something else. Nothing important, it seems a minor matter by comparison . . . but . . .' She steadied her voice, 'Just before mother became ill she had a terrible argument with Uncle Gengoro and Kentaro. It upset us both very much and that's why she obstinately refused to ask them for help. So perhaps, if it hadn't been for pride — hers and mine — for we felt the same . . .'

'But what was the trouble? It sounds most unlike her to quarrel openly.'

'Oh it was, but Uncle caused it. He called her to the main house one day and said it was high time I was married and he'd found the right man for me.' She curled her lips contemptuously. 'A man called Otani from the Oade district, a rural-born, low-ranking *goshi*, a mere third son, little better than a common farmer. Mother was furious on my behalf, saying no daughter of Aritomo's would sink so low. Gengoro shouted back that he'd tried, but no higher-ranking man would have me.' Her voice broke again.

'That's a damnable lie, he never made the proper proposals.'

'But my hair is crinkled, it's true; and my skin's too dark, and I was born in the year of the horse and so would probably devour my husband . . .' She sobbed, feeling so much was against her.

The sad tidings and her distress were almost too much for him, and he turned away. 'Oh hush, sister, please.'

She gulped back her tears. 'So we tried to refuse the match, mother and I, but the man Otani was very set on it. He wanted an alliance with our family, of course, and wouldn't take no for an answer. So that's how the matter stood when mother . . .'

He paced about. 'So the matter wasn't closed?'

'No. And then after the first mourning period I begged Uncle to let me to come and tell you myself what had happened. Kentaro was very upset too and pleaded for me, so eventually I was allowed to come. I've brought the maid Ohisa with me, she's waiting outside with my luggage — just as much as I could manage to bring away. You see . . .' Her voice dropped to a whisper, 'I'm not going back, brother. I can't, I won't. If I do they'll force me to marry that low-born clod of earth, and with mother gone there'd be no one to support me. Uncle wants our house for his own men and I can't live there alone. Please, please, let me stay here with you, brother. You are all I have in the world now.' She tugged at his sleeve, and he patted her hand gently, realising she was all he had left too. 'But how can I? How could it be managed?' He looked harassed.

At his hesitation she spat out with a passion that shocked him, 'I'll stay anywhere to be near you. If you send me back I'll take rat poison, I will, I will, rather than marry such a man. Like that poor girl we heard about in Nagasaki, do you remember? Her parents wanted to sell her to a great fat ugly Dutchman and she, she . . .'

'Oh, shush, Ryo, please; you are overwrought.' He touched her hair. 'Yes, yes, of course you must stay here. I'll find a way — at least I have more money now. Neither of us will marry any low-born creature, I promise you.'

'Oh, Kenjiro, thank you, thank you.' She tried to smile. 'That's what mother would want you to say. I'll help you all I can and promise not to be a nuisance. I can sew and weave — don't foreigners want clothes made? And I can keep house for you and make your favourite pickles. And I've brought some of our own bean-curd paste for soup.'

He smiled. 'We'll be all right, the two of us, Ryo. We'll look after each other.' He went to the door to hide another surge of emotion. 'Your luggage can come in here for now. And mother's chest, the pieces she treasured?'

'But I couldn't bring them; it would have aroused suspicion. So there is nothing of hers.'

He sighed. 'Never mind now. I'll go and tell Bimyo, and in

82

the morning I must talk to Dr Mills. There are empty rooms here, if he'll let you have one.'

'Any little space that's decent, or somewhere nearby. Only I simply won't . . . can't . . .'

'No, no, you won't have to,' he reassured her as he went out.

Relaxing at last, she removed her cloak, revealing the creamy-white mourning clothes underneath, then edged nearer to the lighted stove and looked round the room. Its simple familiarity pleased her: dried rushes in a deep blue vase below a calligraphy scroll; her brother's lacquered toilet-cabinet and clothes chest embossed with the Satsuma crest; an old screen with a design of crimson peonies on a golden ground. The only intrusive element was the pile of foreign books in the corner. His knowledge of English would be far in advance of hers now, but she must try and improve so she could help him again. Now that she had arrived safely and seen her brother, she felt a flurry of excitement. 'Yokohama,' she murmured aloud, 'I'm really here and really going to stay.' She imagined the surrounding houses full of strange-faced foreigners and lots of large furniture. The first happiness she had felt since her mother's death began to flow through her as benevolently as the warmth of the stove that began to soothe her cold, tired body.

Sensing that Miss Mills would be more sympathetic, Kenjiro told her rather than the doctor about his sister's plight next morning. Moved by the story, Ellie offered Ryo a spare room at once, saying she was sure her brother would approve. Curious about the new arrival, she called to introduce herself to Ryo that afternoon, expecting to see the feminine equivalent of Mr Miyata's good looks – but the young woman did not quite fit that bill. She also was tall, but rather gawky for a Japanese and her face was too long for beauty; she had an air of sheltered dignity about her that was immediately appealing, and a bruised look of past hurt that Elinor wanted to reassure. Shrinking from Elinor's calm, straight gaze and forgetting every word of English in her shyness, Ryo could only stand blushing darkly with bowed head.

Elinor turned to Kenjiro. 'Please tell your sister she

needn't be in the least nervous, Mr Miyata. She is most welcome here and I hope in due course she may help me a little with my Japanese studies. You yourself are excellent, of course,' she added hastily for fear of giving offence, 'But I always want to learn more than you have time to teach.'

Kenjiro smiled. 'And you are such a diligent student, Miss Mills, that I wish I could spare more time.' He spoke sincerely, for familiarity had dispelled his earlier unease and she had begun to intrigue him. Not that she was in the least beautiful, he told himself; her shoulders did not slope in the proper feminine way, she laughed too loudly and tossed her head. To him, she seemed square-shaped and stiff-backed, bustling noisily about like a little square-sailed junk looking for a harbour. Yet occasionally, when she laughed, he wanted to put his hard narrow tongue in the hole of her mouth to quieten her. The memory of that strange desire now appalled him, and he added coolly, 'You'll find my sister a very satisfactory substitute for me, Miss Mills. She speaks some English and will soon improve once she's settled here.'

'But I meant an addition, not a substitute, Mr Miyata,' she replied quickly, and he bowed, knowing it was futile to oppose any of her decisions.

Ryo did not find settling down easy. She was beset by the same anxieties and insecurities as her brother had been, and these were compounded by her subordinate position and a desperate home-sickness for that tranquil rural life in the Imamuro valley that had gone forever. When she had left Kagoshima it had been red and gold autumn; cheerful peasant women were stacking rice straw along the hill terraces, drying oranges were hung from the cottage eaves like bright bead curtains. But when she reached Yokohama it seemed in the grip of winter – a draughty, ugly place stuck between a colourless swamp and sea where everything was strange and even her compatriots spoke in a harsh provincial dialect quite different from her own soft speech.

Left alone, Ryo would have languished into withdrawal; but Elinor drew her kindly but firmly from her shell. They soon began spending time together, feeling a bond of mutual

84

sympathy that helped to break down the linguistic barriers between them. They were, after all, from similar social backgrounds, Elinor realised – daughters of a country-town doctor and a castle-town samurai. Both had received just sufficient education and training to fit them for their expected futures as wives of equal-ranking men. Elinor's lessons in embroidery, piano-playing, and deportment were paralleled by Ryo's in flower-arranging, learning the *koto*, and the formal etiquette of the tea ceremony, and both had longed to test their mental powers further than was permitted by their class and sex.

Elinor's father wore a top-hat and drove around Harrogate in a smart carriage and pair to visit his patients; her mother spent much time ailing on the drawing room sofa; Elinor's two elder sisters were married and she was five times an aunt. But Elinor could not convey to Ryo that mother considered her youngest daughter to be headstrong and something of a trial to her declining years, nor that she herself found Harrogate depressing and boring. As a child, she had read avidly about distant lands, collected foreign stamps, and yearned to travel. Had Ryo done the same?

During Ryo's childhood, however, such books and stamps had been quite unknown, but she told Elinor of Mr Moon's visits to her home, and the map of the world her father had kept hidden in his 'foreign matters box'. Father, she explained, had encouraged Kenjiro to study the map, for he had high hopes of him seeking wider horizons in the future; that Ryo might also travel eventually had not occurred to him, for women married, stayed at home, and bred children.

For both of them marriage had become a problematic issue, and it was partly because Elinor's father felt she was in danger of perpetual spinsterhood that he had agreed to let her travel East, where, he felt, she might find a husband suitable to her exacting taste. Ryo could scarcely conceive of Elinor's state of mind in this matter; Elinor could not really understand Ryo's humiliation at the marriage proposal suggested by her uncle; so such delicate matters they did not explore.

Reticence was second nature to Ryo in any case, but Elinor, an optimist, hoped to extend their friendship by persuading her of the superior benefits of western civilisation. Foremost among these, Ellie believed, was the message of the Christian gospel, and as Christmas approached, she seized the opportunity to tell Ryo the first Christ story – the shepherds, the angels, the star in the east. Ryo listened politely, thinking it a rather childish legend and quite different from her previous scant knowledge of the faith as handed down by earlier Jesuit missionaries in Nagasaki – the blood of martyrs, the dying man on the cross. Elinor's version of Christianity seemed attractively festive by comparison and much more in keeping with the pre-Christmas preparations going on – the making of pies, cakes, puddings, the painting of cards and pasting of coloured-paper decorations.

Just two days before Christmas, when the masts of every foreign vessel in the harbour were wreathed in evergreens, the fir tree Arnold had ordered from Shanghai arrived, and a carpenter quickly knocked up a wooden tub so that it could stand in the parlour, where Elinor and Ryo were to decorate it. They were thus engaged when Arnold came in with a batch of Christmas mail, including one for Elinor from her mother bemoaning her absence at the festive season. She sighed, thinking resentfully that Arnold never received such self-pitying reprimands – but then he was the apple of his mother's eye. She was about to tell him so, when he diverted her.

'Here's an unexpected one! You remember the Mrs Borrodail who was involved in the Richardson affair? Didn't you meet her briefly? Well, she's written to say that a friend of her husband's, a Mr Felix Coburn, is coming here on a visit.' He read on aloud, ' "You can understand, I'm sure, Doctor, why my husband and I have sworn never again to set foot in Japan and indeed tried to dissuade Mr Coburn; but he's quite set on it. His father is a manufacturer of corsets, would you believe, and he intends looking into Japanese textile exporting. His real enthusiasm is for science, however, and he has a bee in his bonnet about Darwinism that might amuse you. He plans to reach Yokohama in a few weeks' time and any assistance you can give him in the way of accommodation etc. would be greatly appreciated. I hesitate to intrude upon you after such an interval, but my relatives in Yokohama, the Clarkes, have left long ago, and remembering your past kindnesses . . . la di da di da." A Darwinist, hey? what on earth does he expect to find here? Well, we'll find out, I suppose. What does Mother say, Elinor?'

'Oh, the usual headaches and vapours that she explains in great detail to me and spares you. I suppose we should get a sympathy note off to her before the boat sails. Come now, you must dictate something cheerful for me to tell her.'

She bustled him out, and Ryo, left alone, wandered round the tree. It was hung with paper chains, wooden dolls, artificial flowers, and tiny bells, which, she realised, were souvenir miniatures made in Curio Street and modelled on temple-handbells. She tapped one; its ring was thin, shallow, hollow, sad. She suddenly remembered going on a visit with her mother and brother to the Jokomyoji temple of which her grandfather had once been magistrate. She remembered the priest's chanting, gongs beating, bells ringing, people clapping to rouse the gods' attention. That temple was now in ruins; this tinny bell hung in the parlour of foreigners who had been present at its destruction; she, the grand-daughter, had hung it up; the men of Choshiu were even now melting down their temple bells to make modern weapons, her brother had told her. Ryo doubled down on her knees in neat native fashion on the foreign carpet under the bright alien tree and bowed her head low in a mixture of pain, shame and bewilderment.

CHAPTER FIVE

Felix Coburn stood huddled in his greatcoat on the upper deck of the barque-rigged, iron-hulled *Cadiz*, idly watching a pair of errant rope quoits which, used for deck games during more clement weather, had broken loose from their mooring and were slithering wildly about the heaving boards. The quoits seemed to be chasing each other, now the one, now the other in pursuit, touching, enticing, then darting apart tantalisingly like a pair of skittish lovers. Felix thought sourly of Rosalind, the young lady to whom he had been engaged, and how glad he was that he had not married her. His reason, or perhaps excuse, for breaking the engagement had been his mother's recent death. Rosalind had not seemed to mind much. She had cool blue eyes, a tinkling laugh, and a rich father, and had soon found another suitor with whom to play skittish games.

The death of his mother, Marie, was still a black shadow across Felix's mind, a hole in the pit of his stomach. She had been of Huguenot descent and from her he had inherited his dark hair and eyes, a certain tense pallor that set him apart from his father and his two older brothers, Sydney and Stanley, who were unmistakably of ruddy English stock. Mother and youngest son formed a sweet, secret alliance in the family and Marie had poured into him all her own frustrated ambitions and dreams for a broader, more cultivated life than had been possible in provincial Macclesfield, the home of Coburns' Corsetry Manufactory.

Felix's brothers had gone into the family business; he, prompted by Marie, had gone to university, where he had become an enthusiast for the new science of evolution and progress. But he had gained a poor degree, for his cast of mind was discursive, and it was the romance rather than the tough disciplines of science that most appealed to him. In the circumstances, the best course for Felix was to marry a woman of sufficient wealth to support his vague, wide-ranging scientific pursuits, Marie decided, dreaming that one day he might stumble across some universal truth that would make him famous in those academic circles she had always longed to join.

So she had encouraged Rosalind; but on Marie's death such an alliance seemed pointless — pointless as life itself. Only gradually had his scientific interest revived and with it the desire to vindicate his mother's faith in him. That, truly and secretly — for he continued the habit of concealing his thoughts from the rest of the family — was why he stood now on the deck of the *Cadiz* as it steamed slowly into Yokohama harbour.

Almost immediately the vessel was boarded by a group of Japanese customs officers, wearing short black cloaks, baggy trousers, and large lacquered hats like upturned washbowls and followed by squads of porters wearing raincoats made of woven straw so they looked like damp haycocks walking about on skinny bare legs. All the Japanese bowed and smiled courteously to the disembarking foreigners, though Felix reminded himself that this meant nothing, for according to his friends the Borrodails, they customarily bowed, smiled, then stabbed you in the back. Their view was understandable; but Felix was determined to keep an open mind on the subject of the natives, as a good scientist should. Indeed he was predisposed to like them, for he nurtured a vision of Japan as the ultimate in exotic oriental mysteriousness, renowned for its beauty, its hidden violence, and its exotic women.

It was dusk by the time Felix stepped ashore and was approached by a young Japanese, who introduced himself as Mr Miyata and explained that his employer, Dr Mills, had arranged for him to stay with a Mr Fortescue, to whose house he would conduct him. Felix nodded curtly, taking the man for a servant, till he saw the bulging outline of the two swords he wore beneath his cloak. A samurai, then? But one who worked for a doctor and spoke reasonable English? Puzzled already, Felix followed Kenjiro along the Bund to a commodious wooden bungalow just off the main street.

Inside the bungalow, Mary Fortescue was putting the finishing touches to her evening toilette. Her corset strings were pulled a little tighter than usual, for the unknown Mr Coburn was bound to cast a highly critical eye on a lady's shape. She preened her dinner dress of mauve silk before the mirror, wondering if its corsage was a shade too low, pleased with the slimming effect of its gold belt, fastened with a rosette of pink ribbon. She was admittedly a little too plump and short for the perfect hourglass — like that achieved by Mrs Honoria Rayne, for instance. But who would ever dare to put an arm around *that* slim waist and squeeze it? She puffed and chuckled a little, thinking that Mr Rayne was presumably allowed to occasionally, poor man.

Hearing Felix arrive, she dabbed her cheeks with powder and hurried to greet him, while he apologised for the ship's late arrival.

'Oh, but it's Dr Mills who sends apologies for failing to meet you, Mr Coburn,' she smiled, noting that he had not yet appraised her figure. 'But it happens you've come on rather a special night. There's a dance at our Consulate to celebrate the engagement of Elinor Mills, the doctor's sister, to Lieutenant Bradshaw, stationed here with the XXth Regiment. Dr Mills sends you a warm invitation. Do please come or he'll feel even more guilty.'

Having barely found his land-legs, Felix would have preferred to retire early, but was obliged instead hastily to unpack his velvet-trimmed evening dresscoat, eat a quick supper, and hurry to the Consulate with Mary and Claud. The dance had already begun.

Here, he was introduced to genial Arnold and his sister, an attractive young lady with the self-conscious sparkle of one who knows she is, for a night at least, the belle of the ball. Whirling round the crowded floor with Mrs Fortescue, Felix reflected that he had not come to the ultimate Orient to do the polka and gossip, and listened only vaguely to her breathless descriptions of the other guests. There was Mr Powell, the Number One man at Jardine & Mathieson, dancing with Mrs Marshall, the Number One hostess, Percival Storey, the Legation's linguist, was with Mrs Powell, and there now was Reggie Bradshaw, with his new fiancée, of course. Felix watched as they circled by, holding each other close. How besotted with love the handsome officer looked! And he wished, as he often had before, that he could experience a similar state before he grew too old, cynical, and worldly wise. As the music finally ended, Felix indicated a young Japanese woman with beautifully coiled hair standing alone just inside the door.

'Who's that? She doesn't look like a servant.'

'Indeed not. That's Miss Miyata, the interpreter's sister. Very sweet and shy, and a great friend of Miss Mills, which is why she's here, though I doubt that she's enjoying herself. We must go and rescue her once I've got my breath back.' Mary collapsed on a chair, beginning to feel that it had not been worth tying herself in quite so drastically for Felix.

As for Ryo, she certainly was not enjoying herself. Having never been to a dance before, it seemed to her ludicrous and rather indecent that ladies such as Mrs Fortescue, wearing bosom-exposing, tightly contoured dresses, should whirl about in the arms of men they had only just met. The room smelled strongly of heated foreign bodies, strange powders and perfumes, and that fug of dusty upholstery and brocade she now associated with western homes. Suddenly there was a loud report and Ryo jumped in panic. An officer standing on a chair had popped a bottle of champagne that he was splashing liberally in the direction of the engaged couple as he began a slurred speech of congratulation. Ryo turned, as Kenjiro joined her in the doorway.

'It's dreadful to watch, isn't it?' she murmured.

'It's what they do.' He was impassive, looking beyond her, and she followed his gaze.

'Miss Mills does look beautiful, doesn't she?'

'Oh? I know little about the beauty of western women. Shall we slip away? I've something to tell you.'

'Please let's.'

As they crossed the courtyard to their quarters Kenjiro pointed to the well. 'That's where I first saw Miss Mills. I drew a sword on her,' he snorted oddly.

'She told me — she said she was frightened, but only for a second because she didn't believe a man as handsome as you could harm her.'

He smiled in the dark.

Indoors, he slipped into a loose robe and poured himself a small brandy, to which he was becoming quite partial, before breaking the news to his sister. 'I had a letter from Uncle Gengoro today. He's just arrived at the clan *yashiki* in Edo, where he's staying for a while.'

She was instantly alarmed. 'What's he written about?'

'Oh, politics mainly. His barbarian-expelling faction is losing ground, I'm glad to say. The new motto is "enrich the country, strengthen the army, make one nation" — and that's not to his taste. He says we two clans, Satsuma and Choshiu, are drawing closer together; but he abhors the idea of our clan in equal alliance with anyone. He's so prejudiced and proud.'

'And what else?' She guessed his evasiveness.

'Oh, in conclusion he says that he intends coming here on the way back to Kagoshima. He wants to take you away with him.'

'No, no, please, Kenjiro, I won't . . .' Her terror was as immediate as if her uncle had just walked in. 'You must help me defy him, brother, please. I'm reasonably content here, but there — that odious rural boor . . . never.'

'I assumed you'd still feel so and I'll simply write and tell him. Maybe he won't come here at all then; but he's obstinate, as you know, and if he does we can't refuse to see him — our father's brother.'

Kenjiro wrote to Gengoro the following day, but received no reply. During his lengthy, ominous silence Ryo was haunted by his sudden unannounced arrival, and she rehearsed again and again what she would say to him. Staring at her white-socked feet planted firmly on the straw-gold *tatami* of her little room she repeated aloud, 'I won't go back with you,

93

Uncle. I'm sorry, but I'm staying here with my brother.'

And sure enough, one wintry afternoon, Gengoro did indeed strut unannounced into the courtyard, his stocky frame bristling with an outrage that was almost visible. He swaggered indoors leaving his swords, cloak, and shoes in the passageway and bringing with him the familiar smell of his heavily pomaded hair, the thick rustle of his stiff clothes. Without preamble he launched into a tirade about the abominations he had seen on the way: the huge, menacing, iron-clad vessels in the harbour; barbarian men and women strolling about side by side as if they owned the place; shop fronts crammed with ugly, useless foreign gimcracks. That the government could allow such a state to exist on Japanese soil was beyond his comprehension. These Yokohama foreigners, he continued, warming to his theme, were a crew of money-grabbing, exploitative, low-born merchants with no more notions of morality and correct behaviour than the beasts of the field.

At this Kenjiro who, like his sister, had been listening in deferential silence, felt his lips twitch at the thought that if his uncle had seen foreigners behaving as they sometimes did – drinking, dancing, kissing in public – he might actually have exploded in his wrath. And he felt an unexpected quirk of affection for Gengoro, sitting there bolt upright and dignified on the best-stuffed guest-cushion in his wide-shouldered dark blue silk jacket, his bulging eyes flashing furiously. He was rather like an actor on a Kabuki stage – a symbolic figure expressing all the frustration and defeat that hundreds of his samurai generation were feeling at this time. A certain lack of dramatic coherence in his rambling diatribe reminded Kenjiro, however, that this man was actually his own father's brother; and even as he thought so, Gengoro stopped abruptly, saying in a lower, equally stern key, 'But I will not stay a single night in this barbarian dunghill, and the gates shut at dusk, do they not?' He wheeled on Ryo and barked, 'So get your things together, miss, for we must be off.'

Ryo felt her toes curl in panic, her mouth drying; then she raised her head, looked straight at him and said the correct

94

words, the first of such flagrant disobedience she had ever uttered. For a full minute he stared at her unbelieving, then he shouted, 'I said get your things! You are coming with me. No female of my household will stay in this foreign swamp.'

'I am no longer of your household, Uncle. My place is here with my brother to look after his welfare.' She struggled to say the words firmly.

'You are my brother's child,' he ranted at her, 'and I am your master in his place. You will obey me this instant – and marry the man I have chosen for you.'

'I will never, ever in my life lower myself to touch that clodhopping bumpkin,' she spat back at him, her eyes flashing now as wild as his.

He leapt to his feet, whipped his fan from his girdle and rapped her on the head with it. 'And what could be lower than the life you lead here, surrounded by these hairy foreign creatures smelling of cows' butter, with their vulgar manners and lecherous eyes? Heaven only knows to what extent you've been contaminated by them already. Oh, I've heard tales of our women going with these men for money, becoming fat and greedy like blood-sucking leeches. They . . .'

Ryo reeled back in horror, but Kenjiro jumped up to face him shouting in his turn, 'How dare you impute that to my sister? A samurai's daughter! She behaves with the perfect propriety befitting her rank and she always will. As she wishes to stay here with me, then she shall. I, her brother, will look after her; she's my responsibility now, not yours.'

Gengoro glared at them both, his lips working, then stamped towards the door, bellowing, 'Then the devil take the two of you, for you are no more kin of mine. You've sold yourselves to the barbarians, cast aside all the claims of duty and loyalty due to your family and clan. Ah, the seeds of this were there in my own brother – and see what rotten fruit he has begotten.'

'How dare you speak like that of my honourable father!' Kenjiro grabbed him by the sleeve, turning him back. 'You don't understand, have never understood how our world is changing. He was wise enough to see it coming, he tried to explain to us how the future would be – these foreigners coming in, we Japanese going outwards. You can't stop the tide, Uncle, don't you see?'

'See, see? I have seen more than enough for one day. So go your crazy new-fangled ways and much good may it do you. But never ask me or your brother Kentaro to help when you fall flat on your face in the foreigner's manure. Fah! Get my cloak, woman,' he snarled at Ryo, who instinctively stumbled to obey him, trying to hide her tears as she held up the garment.

'Uncle, please can't you try and understand that for us . . .'

He snatched it from her. 'I understand too well what you two are – mealy-mouthed time-servers to barbarian masters, traitors to your proud lineage.'

At the door he jammed his swords in his girdle, bestowed one last venomous glare upon them and thumped off down the passage. They stood together watching him stride across the courtyard and through the gate without a backward glance. Shivering and silent in the wake of his wrath, they could not voice their shared feelings of relief, pain, anger, and sadness. At last Kenjiro went and poured himself a brandy, and sipped, remarking as coolly as he could, 'Once or twice he reminded me of an actor, you know. All that ranting and raving, and the way he sat very dignified and righteous in his wrath, like the samurai of ancient days.'

But Ryo, who had never been to the Kabuki theatre, could not follow his thought. To her, Gengoro was still Uncle, the respected head of the family, who had now completely disowned them both. It was a frightening realisation.

During the time that Ryo had waited with trepidation for the arrival of her uncle, Felix Coburn was waiting impatiently for a ship that would take him to Hokkaido. He had intended going there straight away, but found to his annoyance that the northern island was still totally icebound, and the first mail steamer bound thither for the port of Hakodate did not sail until late March. In the interim, he took little interest in the social life of the settlement or even in its trading potential

– the ostensible object of his visit. Rather, he gained a reputation as something of a solitary – socially charming and detached by turn. He spent much time closeted in his bedroom studying the trunkful of books he had brought with him: the scientific theories of Joseph Hooker, of Cuvier and Sir Richard Owen, Darwin's *Origin of Species*, published six years before, and the recent, even more exciting book by Thomas Huxley, *Man's Place in Nature*. Felix did not divulge the precise reason for his studies beyond saying that he was interested in the manners and customs of the Ainu, the aboriginal tribes that dwelt in Hokkaido.

For most people this reason sufficed, but Dr Mills, who fancied himself something of an anatomist, waited for a chance to probe a little further. It came late one evening as the two of them were sharing a nightcap after a ladies' night supper at the regimental mess on the Bluff. The occasion had been convivial: Felix had found an officer interested in recent scientific developments to whom he could air his views; Arnold had discussed the qualities of the latest equine arrivals from Shanghai with the racing fraternity, while keeping a weather eye on his young sister, whose behaviour had been a little untoward. She had flirted animatedly with every officer except him to whom she was engaged, drunk a little too much wine, and then demanded that Reginald escort her home early. He had done so, returning glumly to say that Ellie had retired with a headache. It was just a young lady's caprice undoubtedly, but she had been out of humour ever since the news of Reggie's probable posting to India later in the year.

'Delhi or Madras if we're lucky, but probably some hot hole in the *mofussil*,' Reggie had explained, joining Arnold and his sister for the previous Sunday's luncheon.

Elinor looked bleak. 'The *mofussil*?'

'Up country, back of beyond, in the sticks.' Reggie grinned. 'Dust and sun, flies and beggars.'

'Oh dear, all those beggars; I've read about them.' She stared gloomily into her soup, wondering how she would ever enjoy food surrounded by so much destitution.

'Mustn't let them worry you. In any case, ladies living in

the cantonments don't see too much of the seamy side.'

'But I'd want to see, I'd want to do something to help all those poor diseased people.'

'My dear little Ernestina' — it was his teasing name for her — 'there's nothing much that even good Queen Victoria can do to change the poverty in India. Still there's always some good works going on — fancy fairs for native charities and so on.'

She sniffed. 'Sounds almost like home, selling embroidered tea-cosies to help the parish poor. There must be more to India than that.'

He squeezed her hand under the table. 'Why, of course there is, darling. There's lots of jolly parties and race-meets and riding picnics beneath the banyans.'

'Lucky old you — sounds a grand life,' Arnold had interposed, but Elinor had replied irritably that she would far rather stay in beautiful, exciting Japan than go to dirty, hopeless old India. To which Arnold had pointed out that the duty of an officer's wife is to make the best of wherever her husband is sent. That had been a few days ago and Elinor's temper had not improved since.

Arnold sighed as he poured Felix a brandy. 'My sister seemed rather rattled tonight, did you notice?'

Felix yawned. 'Can't say I did. She and Bradshaw certainly make a good-looking pair.'

'A sexually selected variety that will flourish à la Darwin, hey?' Arnold quizzed gently.

'Probably. The vigorous, happy, and healthy survive and multiply at the expense of the plain, the dull, and the weak.'

Arnold toyed with his glass. 'So you're going to Hokkaido to look at one of the less favoured racial remnants before they're quite eliminated by the pushy Japs. Is that it?'

Felix hesitated. 'The Ainu — yes, but there's a little more science to it than that, Arnold, only it's not something I want to spread about.'

'Mum's the word if you say so, old man. In any case hardly anyone here knows one end of a scientific theory from t'other.'

Felix stared into his brandy globe, feeling warm and

expansive. 'Ever heard of Professor Tobias Clark? The Edinburgh anatomist? No? Well, I came upon an article of his in a scientific journal a few months ago – just as my father suggested I come out East to look at the textile trade. Clark was discussing the Darwinian missing link, that would prove a continuous line of development between apes and the emergence of intelligent man.'

'Good lord, man, I've heard of that,' Arnold said impatiently. 'Even educated natives have. It's said they used to eat stewed monkeys until Darwin rather put them off the taste!'

'Well, the main burden of Clark's theme was that the Ainu, being one of the hairiest races on earth, of unknown racial origin, and very primitive, might throw some light on the matter. So I got in touch with him saying I was coming out here and would he like me to make a few discreet investigations? He was very enthusiastic and the upshot is that I should send a number of Ainu skeletal remains back to him for examination. If the verdict is promising then we'll publish something rather momentous together when I get back.'

'And if not . . .?'

Felix grimaced. 'Oh, then it's the textile trade, I suppose. I'll have to do something in that line, to keep my father happy anyway. But what do you think, Arnold? By God, man, what wouldn't I give to add my mite to the great search for scientific truth that's going on – the tantalising secrets of the universe being unravelled at last, and in our generation. Doesn't it excite you?'

Arnold pondered. 'It's damned interesting, of course. They've recently discovered a bone in the ear that is common to man and apes, by the way. Did *you* know that? But in my limited experience, Felix, one new discovery like that simply postulates a new missing link, an endless chain, leading the Lord knows where.'

'Ah, the Lord!' Felix finished his brandy with a flourish. 'Surely Darwin's grandest promise is that we'll be able to . . . shall we say, dispense with Him in the near future? That doesn't shock you, I trust?'

99

'No, though it would many. But I think you have a rather romantic idea of science if you imagine it's the cure for all humankind.' Arnold yawned. 'Enough of this philosophising; I'm for bed . . . So that's your secret mission, is it? Well, you won't find Ainu skeletons lying round two a penny. I suggest you take Harold Rayne into your confidence. You'll have to stay at his Consulate; there's simply nowhere else.'

'You met the Raynes when they passed through here earlier, didn't you? How did you find them?'

'He seemed an amiable fellow, not strait-laced; take him a case of brandy and I'll warrant he'll help you and turn a blind eye to any breaking of regulations.'

'And the Mrs?'

'Very different kettle of starch and whalebone.' He gestured a curvaceous hour-glass shape. 'Flatter her beauty and her intellect, but keep her out of it. Take her a book of poems and some perfume,' he grinned. 'And as for the Ainu, I'm told they'll sell their grandmothers for a barrel of *saké*, so grannies' skeletons should go for a couple of bottles apiece, don't you think?'

Felix laughed and went off happily to bed that night, for the very telling of his secret plan convinced him that it was indeed possible to carry out. But by the time, three weeks later, that he actually saw the coast of Hokkaido from the deck of the mail steamer *Pembroke*, he was much less confident. The voyage had been long and cold, the vessel lashed by storms for days on end, during which Felix had buoyed himself up with thoughts of his heroes, Charles Darwin and Thomas Huxley, whose dedication to science had taken them to the perilous ends of the earth. Though his own mission was small fry by comparison, he felt proud to belong in the same glorious traditions. But he was very much an amateur and as the barren, snow-capped mountains of Hokkaido reared over the heavy seas ahead he wondered how on earth he was going to accomplish it.

The arrival of the year's first mail steamer was a momentous event in the monotonous lives of the few foreign residents of Hakodate, and several were waiting on the jetty in anticipation of letters, newspapers, provisions, and the sight of new faces. Felix immediately picked out Harold Rayne, a bulky man of about forty, whose loud English voice was raised in apprehension over some precious cargo. Felix introduced himself and to his relief was immediately invited to stay at the Consulate.

'If you can grace it with the name,' Rayne laughed shortly. 'Blessedly draughty, run down, and uncomfortable; the priests from the temple next door used to live there. Extraordinary place. But please excuse me, Mr Coburn; I must make sure our supplies are intact.'

Rayne hurried off to see the captain while Felix surveyed his new surroundings. They were uncompromisingly northern: streaks of snow covered the grey stone jetty, and gulls screeched around the stinking barrels of fish-oil against the wall. Nearby were a few dreary western-style buildings – Dent & Co., Merchants; a marine insurance agency; a ships' chandlers. The smaller houses behind were bowed under the weight of shingles laid on their low flat roofs to secure them during winter gales. The wind still blew fiercely, and Felix, taking shelter in the Customs shed, watched with some amusement as Rayne fussed anxiously about the barrels, boxes, and crates of brandy coming from the ship's hold.

After a time Rayne joined him. 'Thank goodness, all seems well. And now we must get you up the hill to the Consulate in time for luncheon.'

The Consulate stood inside a large garden bordered with tall, gloomy pines and commanding a good view of the land-locked bay and the volcanic hills to the south. The main room was spacious and chilly, its carved ceilings supported by pillars of much-polished wood; incongruous in the centre stood a few bamboo chairs and a squat dining table set with silver cutlery and starched napkins.

'Honoria, my dear,' Rayne called tentatively. 'We have an unexpected guest. Will you come and meet him?'

A servant took Felix's coat and there was a small, awkward pause during which he felt unaccountably nervous. Then Mrs Rayne came in and was introduced. She was as striking as Yokohama hearsay had suggested, her stately hour-glass form encased in grey poplin, its wide skirt looped with lilac braid. Her light blonde hair was dressed in an elegant coiff, her regular winter-pale features seemed fixed in an expression of detached disdain and her large blue eyes regarded Felix with weary hauteur. Though she was several years her husband's junior, he seemed in some awe of her, reassuring her at once of the safe arrival of the supplies.

At this she turned to Felix with an ironic smile in which real humour lurked. 'You must forgive my excessive concern with a barrel of salt beef, Mr Coburn; but you can scarcely imagine how large such trivialities loom in lives as bereft of incident as ours have been for the past months. Why, to receive some beef, our home letters, and an unknown guest in the same day is almost too much excitement!'

'I've invited Captain MacIntyre of the *Pembroke* to dine with us this evening, my dear.'

She raised her eyes heavenward. 'But what a plethora of events! Come then, we must partake of luncheon straight away lest it run into the delights of dinner.' She rang a handbell. 'Please sit down, Mr Coburn. You see, we've been living almost entirely on salt fish and slabs of dried venison enhanced by the occasional joint of bear's meat.'

'Don't forget the mutton, my dear.' Rayne tried to make light of it all, explaining, 'We brought three sheep here and penned them in the stables. But, oh, what a rumpus there was among the Buddhists next door when we slaughtered the first one for Christmas! You'd have thought we were killing a man at least, if not an entire village. So in the interests of Anglo-Japanese relations we kept the other two alive and they've become objects of great curiosity for the natives, who've never seen their like before.'

Mrs Rayne sighed. 'Thus even the taste of mutton was an unrepeatable Christmas delicacy. I hope I'm not sounding too plaintive, Mr Coburn,' she continued a little archly after the soup was served. 'But the winter just passed has been of unbelievable discomfort and monotony. When we first came the whole place positively reeked of incense and ancient lamp-oil, and the walls were a series of draughty niches where Buddhist statues had been removed or boarded up. One of them still glares out at us in the dark, does he not, Harold? But much worse has been the boredom. No new books or people, and worst of all, no music.'

'My wife is a very talented musician, Mr Coburn,' Rayne explained earnestly. 'And the lack of a good piano is great deprivation for her. Most unfortunately the ship that was bringing her Broadwood from England foundered. I've asked my contacts in Shanghai to look out for something, but pianos of good quality are hard to come by hereabouts.'

Mrs Rayne smiled tartly. 'Well, I've comforted myself with the thought that even had I the piano, there's not a single soul here who'd appreciate my playing. Yokohama is a positive Paris of culture and society by comparison.'

'Well, there are a few other foreigners, my dear,' Rayne interjected mildly.

'Ah yes, so there are – why, we are an extremely lively and cosmopolitan set, really! Let's see.' She counted on her slender ringed fingers. 'There's the German tailor; our energetic compatriot Mr Blakiston, who deals in paint, property, sawmills and salvage from wrecks; the American marine agent who lives on potato brandy, I believe; a whole laundry full of Chinese; two bearded Russian priests at the Greek Orthodox Church, who are very scholarly, I'm told, if only one could converse with them. Then we receive periodic visits from our other American friend, the Reverend Osbert Pepworth, who dwells in the farthest back of beyond – for even Hakodate isn't the Ultima Thule of Hokkaido – trying to turn the poor benighted Ainu into Christians.'

'Really? Then I hope to make the Reverend's acquaintance, Mrs Rayne, for the main purpose of my coming is to study Ainu manners and customs.'

'You are a scientist, Mr Coburn? How exciting!'

'A mere amateur, madam, but science is certainly my chief enthusiasm.'

'Ah, then you must indeed meet the Reverend Mr Pepworth; because he believes scientists to be the very agents of the devil, who will lead us all into perdition.' And she chuckled with a malicious delight that quite surprised Felix.

He grinned at her in return. 'Then we can stage a heated debate – I shall play Thomas Huxley to the Reverend's Bishop Wilberforce.'

She clasped her hands. 'Oh, that would be marvellous – to hear the Reverend's dyed-in-the-wool dogmatism challenged by one qualified to do so!'

Felix began a modest disclaimer; but she was in full flight, her sudden vivacity pleasing her husband and banishing the atmosphere of bored gloom which, Felix sensed, had hung about that cold dining hall for weeks on end.

As soon as the meal was over, Mr Rayne, glad to have something official to do at last, announced he must hurry back to the *Pembroke*, while his wife, eager to read the home mail, also excused herself, and Felix was shown into a bedroom overlooking the garden. It was reminiscent of a priest's cell, but as he arranged his books against the wall, Felix felt absurdly pleased with his new surroundings. This place was truly an outpost, where one could play the pioneer and where everything was waiting to be discovered, analysed, recorded in proper scientific fashion. Moreover he had found the Raynes unexpectedly pleasant and looked forward to knowing them better.

Lacking further occupation, he lay on the bed wrapped in a quilt and began re-reading Darwin's argument that the most useless characteristics of man and animals were yet the most important to classify. This, Felix read, was because they were less affected by natural selection and so 'indicate the distant past of the organism'. But his eyes soon drooped, and he fell into a dozy reverie. He thought of his brothers, Sydney and Stanley, and their devotion to the profitable manufacture of corsets and the raising of large families. They were evidently a 'selected variety', designed to flourish in the new machine age at the expense of less improved forms of life, like himself, who dithered on many brinks and dreamed of scientific miracles. In an oozy state of self-disgusted dreaminess, he vividly recalled a scene from his youth. His elder brother

Sydney had initiated him into the delights of what he called 'slimming and modelling sessions', when the youngest and prettiest of their female factory hands were called upon to try on the latest corset designs. Felix remembered one in particular that took place in the showroom after hours. The 'model's' name was Elsie, and she was laced into whalebone and pink silk from thigh to breast. 'Just a little tighter, dear, there.' Sydney's plump hands pulled the stay-strings while she swayed against him. 'Now, my little rosebud, I'm sure you can still breathe, can't you?' Sydney kissed her pouting lips. 'Oh, sir, please, no more; it's too much,' she gasped as he stroked the curves of the bodice, whispering, 'But you want to be a beautiful little lady, don't you, Elsie, and have all the lads after you?' 'Yes sir,' she whimpered. 'Then let's see,' and again he pulled, examining the eyelets and cords for strength, his fingers brushing the bulging tops of her breasts, the lower reaches of her thighs, his eyes moist and gleaming.

'There now.' He pushed her before a full length mirror and she leaned back against him for support. 'Don't you look beautiful, my little bird? We'll release you from your cage in a minute, just try to breathe naturally while I check the back.' He looked up chuckling, 'A first-class job, this, don't you think, young Felix? What a shape, hey? We'll have to find a little model for you, next time, hey? But just now Elsie and I have . . . ah . . . a little unfinished business.' So saying he swept the small, pinched body into his arms and carried her off to his office. Felix stood in the showroom, helpless with lust and revulsion, listening to Elsie's gasps as Sydney unlaced her corsets. There was a pause, a few whimpers, then the office couch began wheezing rhythmically under Sydney's weight. Felix rushed to the lavatory, pulling at his own swollen organ, imagining it going right up inside a girl until it pressed against the sides of her tiny waist, pushing, pushing her helpless flesh with his hard cock, pushing . . .

Felix woke with a start as the book he had been reading thudded on the floor. He had been indulging what he now called his 'morbid tendency' for tight corsetting and was in a state of high erection. In self-disgust he satisfied himself; but his waking sexual fantasy centred not on the long-ago, long-suffering Elsie, but on the woman he had met for the first time that very day.

CHAPTER SIX

For Honoria Rayne, Felix's coming signalled a beginning of hope after the most desolate period of her life. Her home country was England's mild green south-west, and in Hokkaido she had been perpetually cold for months. Snow drifts like sullen monsters had lain in the temple gardens and wouldn't go away. The building itself, with its cracked walls and warped floors, warmed only by one imported iron stove and charcoal braziers, was whipped through and through by freezing wind. On several occasions, Honoria, heavy with cold and boredom, had gazed at the winter-locked scene outside, imagining she had died and been condemned forever to the freezing inner circle of hell itself, where no music ever penetrated, except the dirge-like heathen chanting from the next-door temple.

But now at long last it was spring; the monsters were dwindling in the garden, the harsh wintry light softening, wild geese flying north. There were letters and papers to read, an attractive stranger to entertain – proofs that the world beyond Hokkaido still existed. Briskly, Honoria brought out some of her lighter-weight clothes and prepared to show Mr Coburn the sights of Hakodate.

These were sparse: the unexpected, onion-shaped domes of the Greek Orthodox church built four years previously; a battery of rusted cannon from a Russian ship stranded there in the 1850s, and the foreign cemetery on the slopes of Observation Hill. 'I find that a rather touching little monument, don't you?' Honoria pointed her grey umbrella at a humble gravestone inscribed to nineteen-year-old Remick, a scullion, who died during Commodore Perry's visit to Hakodate in 1854.

'Such a lonely place to die so young! I wrote a little dirge for him that was partly for myself. I thought I'd be the first foreign lady buried here and on my grave the words, "She died of cold in the winter of 1864".'

He smiled. 'But you didn't, thank goodness.'

'I may yet. I think another winter like the last will kill me.' She laughed lightly, but he sensed her real apprehension of such a fate. It intrigued him – this beautiful, brave, haughty front she put up that concealed her vulnerability, fear, and loneliness. As she stood looking out to sea, very upright in a smart navy-blue walking dress with matching gloves and bonnet, he wanted to call her Honoria, hug her close, and assure her that this dark alien soil on which they stood wouldn't receive her bones. But this he did not dare do, for she was the Consul's wife, whom he had only recently met.

Instead he moved towards the gate. 'Come, enough of these morbid thoughts, Mrs Rayne. You promised to show me the fishing harbour.' They walked in silence down streets of flat-roofed, damp-walled houses where curious children in wooden pattens clattered round pointing at their odd clothes. Honoria ignored them magnificently, but Felix flushed, embarrassed by an uncomfortable childhood memory of himself and nurse-maid walking through the streets of Macclesfield with the local urchins clattering by in clogs, shouting after him, 'Coburn's corsets cause many a pang, and when you squeeze 'em they go bang!' He had not yet told Mrs Rayne of the nature of his family's business; he could imagine her expression of amused disdain when he did so.

The harbour, ice-free at last, was coming back to life, and the quay was stacked with crates of sea-slugs, crabs, seaweed, deer horns, animal hides, and piles of squared timber awaiting shipment. American and Russian whalers were moored along-side, and further out some ramshackle fishing boats rode at anchor, at which Mrs Rayne pointed. 'There are some of your Ainu, Mr Coburn. I must say I wish you joy in your study of their manners and customs.'

He peered eagerly at the thick-set, black-haired men moving slowly about the decks. 'They don't look in the least savage.'

'But they're not – just total ignoramuses. But I imagine the ones that come to Hakodate are relatively civilised, and the Reverend Mr Pepworth will be able to produce some more savage specimens for you.'

He bridled. 'I suppose you consider my scientific mission something of a joke, Mrs Rayne?'

'Not at all. On the contrary, I envy those who pursue an abstract idea, who try and search out a truth, however eccentric. Why, I can even admire the Reverend for his singular devotion to his odd calling. But I'm so used to mixing with commoner clay that I dare say I've developed the habit of a certain . . . scorn.'

She had been twisting the handle of her umbrella as she spoke and now looked up in apologetic appeal. Again he wanted to touch her, feel her starchiness melt under his hands. He confessed, 'And I'm habitually on the defensive. You see, my family think I should concentrate on making money instead of trekking round the world studying the customs of savages.'

'Then I'm glad you have the temerity to defy them, Mr Coburn. Making money as an end in itself is surely the dullest of occupations. And what is your family's business, by the way?'

He dared not look at her as he mumbled, 'Corsets, I'm afraid, madam. They . . . er, we . . . make corsets.'

She laughed at him gaily. 'Why, of course – Coburn's Corsets! I never associated . . . but they are very admirable and necessary garments for ladies, and indeed some gentlemen would be much improved by them. You needn't be ashamed, Mr Coburn.'

'Oh, I've always wished we made something less personal, like biscuits or pickles.'

'Ah!' She wagged a playful finger. 'But anyone can make a biscuit, while there's quite an art to the making of a good corset, I assure you.'

He laughed with relief, wondering if she was a devotee of Coburn's own brand, wondering if he would ever find out. 'Then I'll try not to be so defensive in future – about science or corsets.'

The outing relaxed and pleased them both, and after it they spent much time together while Harold was busily occupied with a burst of consular activity. At the end of the week the Reverend Osbert Pepworth rode into Hakodate, his stringy legs dangling far down over the flanks of a skinny mountain pony also laden with a wicker pannier containing his first translation of the Lord's Prayer into Ainu. This had been a Herculean labour, as he explained to Honoria and Felix, the three of them seated in what Honoria called the parlour. It was the most comfortable room in the uncomfortable dwelling, with its imported iron stove, rugs of brown bear and creamy-coloured Ainu dog on the floor, and a number of gilt and lacquered what-nots, representing Hokkaido's sole contribution to the souvenir trade. To Felix the room was no more than a brave attempt at civilised living, but as Pepworth explained, to him it seemed a luxurious bower, and the tinned ham sandwiches he was steadily munching were ambrosia after life in an Ainu village.

'Nevertheless, these simple and benighted creatures have much to recommend them,' he explained to Felix, delighted to find someone who showed actual interest in his chosen people – who were so lacking in cultural history and picturesque artefacts that it was hard to arouse enthusiasm for them even among his mission brethren. 'And I'll be only too happy to introduce you to my friends at Ubetsu village. Do you have any special line of study?'

'Their folk customs – ceremonies of birth and death, burial rites.'

'Scanty, I fear. Their only deities are shadowy, nameless spirits and they have such a rigid terror of death that they simply carry a corpse off and bury it unceremoniously in some wild spot.'

'Without proper graves, you mean?' Felix concealed his dismay.

'Well, sometimes bodies are marked by an *inrao*, an arrow-shaped shaven stick. Anyway, I'll be happy to show you my monograph on their religious beliefs.'

'But Mr Coburn's interests are chiefly scientific, Reverend,' interrupted Honoria mischievously. 'He has with him several weighty tomes on the subject.'

Pepworth stiffened. 'Oh, really? Well, I can't help you in that direction, sir. I trust you are not one who worships at the modern shrine of science, or labours under the gross illusion that it can cure the world's woes?'

Felix temporised. 'Mm. Not quite, perhaps, but I certainly welcome the clear new light that modern science has thrown on the many dark corners of ignorance and superstition.'

'Mr Coburn and I were discussing the theories of Mr Darwin the other day,' Honoria added with feigned casualness, offering the Reverend the last sandwich. He ate it, sighing so gustily that crumbs blew in all directions.

'Oh, I've read the views of that misguided gentleman in the press. What nonsense! Where is the soul in all that, Mr Coburn? For what is man without his spirit and his faith? What a desolate version of life Darwin offers us – mere victims of mechanistic laws – selection, variation, adaptation, the Lord knows what else. Indeed the Lord *does* know and will in due time show Mr Darwin and his foolish followers the error of their ways in no uncertain fashion.'

Felix, containing his irritation because he badly needed the Reverend's help, smiled falsely. 'Oh come, Reverend, *The Origin of Species* is a wondrous and monumental work; you cannot dismiss it so cavalierly. Darwin's theories are based on very painstaking research and his hypotheses seem to me irrefutable. In the light of them we should surely reconsider the nature of free will, matter versus spirit, and yes, matters of religion?'

Pepworth cracked his raw knuckles in agitation. 'Darwin has nothing to do with religion, sir. He is anti-religion; anti-Christ, I dare say. Does he not contemplate a grotesque link between ourselves and the beasts of the fields? Even make a blasphemous conjecture that we are no more than second cousins to the apes? If you share such views, Mr Coburn, then I shall certainly hesitate to introduce you to my simple Ainu people, whose sense of the spiritual is but fragile and could easily be corrupted by . . .'

Felix pulled him up short and, as Honoria went to fetch some more biscuits, for Pepworth had eaten every one in sight, he tried to placate him. 'I wouldn't go quite that far, Reverend, not being a pure Darwinist. And in any case I promise you that I won't raise such complex issues among the Ainu.'

'Well, in that case, sir . . .' The Reverend was readily mollified, for he hated to miss an opportunity of showing off his very own Ainu village; and it was soon arranged that Felix should return there with the missionary the following week.

'Do I hear you discussing plans to go to Yubetsu, Mr Coburn?' Honoria asked, as she rejoined them. 'Then let us make up a party, may we, Reverend?'

'I'd be delighted, madam. Indeed I would have suggested it earlier, but winter set in soon after your arrival last year – and an Ainu village, I must warn you, is extremely uncomfortable and not very salubrious at the best of times.'

'Oh, I so long for a change of scene – even for the worse! So we'll make what shift we can for one night and return the following day.'

'Then you must bring food supplies and bedding, Mrs Rayne. The Ainu are extremely hospitable, but alas . . .'

She made one of her expansive, joyous gestures. 'Then it shall be a proper little expedition and my husband will adore the arranging of it. But we promise not to intrude too much on your researches, Mr Coburn.'

Felix smiled. 'It will be a pleasure to have your company for the journey, and then I might stay on a while alone.'

At this point the Reverend began to worry that the villagers would be quite overawed by such a large party arriving unheralded, and decided to return first to prepare the way, leaving the others to follow a few days later, guided by his Ainu servant, Benri.

The morning planned for the expedition dawned fair, and

Harold Rayne was up betimes supervising the loading on horseback of a whole 'batterie de haute cuisine', as he termed it. Here at last was something to remind him of earlier, jollier days when he and his Shanghai chums used to hire houseboats and go on snipe-shooting expeditions up the rivers behind the settlement. What a bustle about there used to be – with the dogs, the guns, the hampers of food and the cases of claret! He had been a carefree bachelor in those days, of course, and occasionally during the past winter, and in spite of his deep devotion to Honoria, he wished he had remained one. But on that bright, exciting morning he had no such qualms as he fussed about, checking the balance of the ponies' saddles – high, precarious perches of thick straw-packs connected by wooden arches. Then his wife came down the temple steps, looking magnificent in a tailored outfit of hunting green with a divided skirt.

'I hope you won't find these wretched saddles too uncomfortable, my dear. I've padded them with cotton quilting as best I can.'

She pulled a face. 'Well, there's no alternative, is there, so I shall make the best of it.'

Felix, who had been making a sketch of Benri, glanced up admiringly. 'Why, madam, you look as if you were about to ride to hounds across some lush English pasture.'

She sighed. 'Oh would that I were, how happy I would be this May morning! The larks would be singing, bluebells in the woods, hawthorn white along the hedgerows . . .' She turned and mounted her pony with Harold's assistance, feeling a stab of deep, familiar, painful homesickness.

After a final checking of girths, ropes, and loads, they trotted off down the flagstone path with Benri in the lead. Their route wound steeply up-hill and at the first summit they reined in to enjoy the spectacle of Hakodate Head, looking like an island set in the sparkling sea below. Harold raised his field glasses, 'See those volcanos to the north – that's where the demoniac high and mightiness of the mountains are supposed to dwell.'

'Isn't that a foreign vessel coming into port?' Felix

exclaimed, and Harold realigned his glasses, groaning, 'Oh, Lord, no — I'm sure it is, though — yes, it's the *Basilisk*, up from Nagasaki early, with Admiral Cousins and other bigwigs aboard. Oh damnation, damnation! Excuse me, my dear, but they weren't due for a week.'

Honoria straightened decisively. 'Then you'll simply have to go back, Harold. Considering only a handful of British ships call here, you can scarcely be absent from your Consular post when one does turn up, especially with an Admiral aboard.'

He scowled. 'Oh, it's too bad, too bad . . . just as we were . . .' He looked uncertainly at Honoria, who had moved closer to Felix.

'Now, Harold, when duty calls you must go. I've heard you say that many times. I'll only be away about twenty-four hours and you'll be happily wined and dined on the *Basilisk* and I'm sure Mr Coburn will escort me back.'

'Yes, certainly, of course.'

'So you are not . . .?' Harold began lamely. 'Of course I'm going on,' Honoria said briskly, 'after all these preparations. And think how disappointed the Reverend would be if I didn't. Not to mention his Ainu, who are staging a bear festival for us.'

Harold looked uneasily from one to the other, then, shrugging ill-humouredly, bade them a good trip and rode back down the hill. As he disappeared from sight, his wife drew a quick breath that sounded like excitement. 'Shall we go on, Mr Coburn? I hope you don't mind my coming with you?'

'I'm utterly delighted that you chose to do so, Honoria,' he said quietly.

They rode side by side along a rutted track with Benri leading and, behind, the laden ponies led by two of the Consulate's servants, who wore red belts bearing the Royal coat of arms. There was a brisk sparkle to the morning that suited their mood. Wispy remnants of yesterday's rain clouds raced across the sky and the spring buds were sharp with moisture. The steep slopes beside the track were edged with scrub bamboo, larches, trailing creepers, brush-wood. Occasionally they glimpsed black volcanic peaks to the west, and, opposite, the distant flashes of the sea. They met strings of mountain ponies laden with deer horn, hides, *saké*, and wooden poles. They overtook others carrying cheap manufactured goods to the interior. The travelling peasants stared in wonderment at the foreigners and they stared haughtily back, for they felt bold and free, exhilarated by the risky edge of going into unknown territory and by the pleasure of each other's company.

They spoke seldom and casually. Honoria, who was painfully conscious of her own lack of formal education, had an extreme regard for learning, and hesitated to intrude upon what she imagined were Felix's scientific ponderings. Felix, who was actually thinking about his companion, had soon learned to be cautious of her alternate moods of withdrawal and intense charm that were not unlike his own. In one of her outgoing moods, she had told him she was the eldest daughter of Jameson Tate, a Lymington solicitor, and when he had died in middle age she had become the mainstay of the family – an ailing mother and three young sisters, Lydia, Lavinia, and Sophia. She had smiled, saying, 'such fearfully dignified names and we learned to live up to them. Except Sophia, who called herself Sophie and married a farmer last year.'

The aloof dignity of the 'Tatias', as they were locally nicknamed, froze off many young admirers from Honoria, who passed her spare time playing the piano and reading serious literature. She let it be known that she was waiting for some older, more cultivated man and when she reached the age of twenty-seven without a suitable candidate appearing, she suddenly married the bouncy Harold Rayne, who was on leave and full of tales about glamorous life in China's treaty ports. She soon found out that her husband filled but the first of her requirements and that Eastern glamour was illusive. The Raynes were posted to backwater Foochow, where Honoria lost her first-born child, and nearly died of fever; she returned home to convalesce and had then joined Harold in Japan. Hakodate was his first post as a full Consul, he had written proudly in a letter, omitting to mention that scarcely any consular activity went on there.

But that morning, in spite of it all, Honoria's spirits were as high as the clouds as she jogged along with Felix Coburn, each of them intensely aware of the other's presence. Coming to a particularly steep and slippery slope he helped her dismount; her hand rested on his shoulder for support, then she stood very close, looking at him with her wide blue eyes, beautiful and serious. Behind them a Consulate servant sniggered audibly and they hastily moved apart.

After about four hours' riding they saw ahead an open stretch of grassland and a collection of thatched huts raised above the ground on stilts. Benri, who had been totally silent till then, began speaking volubly.

'We must be here,' Honoria began. 'Why yes – here comes the Reverend to meet us.'

He lolloped towards them, a gangly man with balding hair and long black-jacketed arms extended in welcome. As Honoria explained the reason for her husband's unfortunate absence, they were surrounded by a group of Ainu men. They had long, black, matted hair, wavy moustaches and beards, and wore robes of rough bark-cloth decorated with geometrical patterns in blue and red. They fell back respectfully as Pepworth led Honoria and Felix to the hut of the village chief, Shinondhi, who ushered them graciously into its dim interior, which smelled pungently of woodsmoke, fish oil, and unwashed bodies.

An iron pot was slung from a chain over a fire hole, the reed-woven walls hung about with bows and arrows, nets, fish hooks, traps, and hunting knives. The scantily matted floor was littered with wooden bowls and spoons, dried skins, weaving shuttles, animal bones, and balls of thread. At the chief's bidding, they sat on the raised guest platform nearest the fire, and the women of the house then approached, bowing low to offer bowls of cold *saké* and slivers of dried fish. As he drank and made polite conversation, Felix studied the faces of his hosts. Their high foreheads, straight noses, and full mouths held no hint of prognathism, unfortunately, though he was pleased to observe that their stocky limbs were covered with short, bristling hairs. He had hoped for something more primitive, an animality of the simian kind; but these people, with their low voices, apathetic movement, and sweet melancholy smiles, seemed simply the cowed and resigned remnants of a human race rather than vestiges of an earlier species.

'I see you are studying your subjects, Mr Coburn,' Pepworth remarked. 'You will find them simple folk – without written history or complex numbers, clothed in the bark of trees and skins of beasts, worshipping the bear, the sun, rivers, fire, and I know not what else. Yet they are lovable and kindly in many ways, for God's great mercy illuminates the souls of millions who acknowledge him not.'

Felix gulped more *saké*. He felt vaguely let down by the Ainu already and Pepworth's words irritated him. 'I fail to see that the possession of these qualities by man in his natural state means they must be implanted by the Lord, Reverend. Cannot man create his own virtues as well as his vices?'

'Ah, but man cannot create himself at all, Mr Coburn. That is the crux, though you clever scientists try desperately to produce a piece of living matter in a test tube.'

'I think you gentlemen are greatly bewildering your hosts with your philosophical debate,' Honoria said wearily. She sat surrounded by the chief's female relatives, who were plucking insistently at her clothes and showing her their little girls, whose lips, arms, and hands were heavily marked with deep blue tattoos. 'One thing is sure – whether God created man's virtues or not, women suffer at man's hands. Look at these poor disfigured creatures.'

'They do it for religious reasons, Mrs Rayne,' the Reverend sighed. 'And isn't that one very good reason for trying to introduce them to a more enlightened and merciful doctrine?'

She raised her eyebrows. 'You honestly believe that Christian men are never cruel to their women?'

Felix, who was being presented with a bowl of extremely malodorous stew, chuckled. '*Touché*, Reverend. Come, Mrs Rayne, try some stew; it can't taste worse than it looks and smells.'

117

'It's not at all bad,' Pepworth assured them. 'A concoction of millet seed, salt fish, wild roots, dried venison, seaweed . . .'

'That's quite enough,' Honoria murmured faintly. 'Will you explain that our servants are preparing food for us outside?'

'Oh do try it, just to be polite,' the Reverend pleaded.

She duly sipped; the taste was nauseous; fire smoke was stinging her eyes; she desperately needed a lavatory. If only she and Felix could have carried on riding together through the empty land all day instead of coming to this savage, filthy place. After sipping more stew and *saké*, they finally escaped outside and Honoria was conducted to a hut containing an extremely rudimentary toilet. The villagers gathered round in silent wonderment as they ate their meal, arranged on a starched white tablecloth spread on the grass with cutlery, glasses, and plates. As they finished, Felix suggested visiting some graves to satisfy his scientific curiosity about Ainu burial customs.

'Well, if you really wish; but there's little to see, as I told you, and the people shun such places.' Pepworth was somewhat irritated by Felix's insistence, but as Honoria supported him, he gave in and they set off across reedy grassland towards a distant hill.

'Come now, be honest, Reverend,' Felix challenged as they went, 'you must find your life here extremely lonely, trying, and discouraging in spite of your rock-solid faith?'

Pepworth nodded, his raw-boned, innocent face grave. 'Indeed, yes, Mr Coburn, it tries me to the very marrow of my being every day and every night. But I know it is God's will for me — my hope of redemption. When I was a young missionary, my wife and I — for I was blissfully married then — were sent by our church to the Sandwich Isles. Oh those were halcyon times! Itinerating among the natives, such pleasing people, such lush, beautiful shores, riding for days where our whims took us . . .'

'And what went wrong?' Felix was curious now.

Pepworth sighed deeply. 'My dearly beloved wife, a true Christian woman, died during the birth of our second daughter. I couldn't stay there without her; it was a life of too much ease and temptation. So I asked to be a pilgrim in unopened territory and was sent here.'

'No whims here, Reverend?' Honoria asked slyly.

'No, madam,' he replied shortly, and they fell silent till they reached a low thicket where a number of shaven sticks were stuck negligently in the ground. 'These graves are quite recent, for they are soon quite lost through neglect,' Pepworth explained.

'What a shame.' Honoria looked at Felix, who was staring dismally at the rotting sticks. 'I think it's fine to have a proper stone monument, as if you'd been important in your life. Even a scullion like Remick then has his name still spoken.'

'But much better to make your own monument while you are still alive, surely? A work of art, a grand discovery?' Felix demurred.

'Oh, you and your discoveries,' Pepworth sniffed. 'The grandest discovery a man can make, Mr Coburn, is that of his own spiritual nature, the promise of his soul's salvation.'

'And yours will surely be saved?' Honoria enquired lightly; but he lowered his eyes. 'Of that I have no surety whatsoever, Mrs Rayne, though I pray for it daily. Only God knows the sins of our hearts.'

'Ah, yes – those, the unspeakable ones,' Felix murmured.

Honoria glanced sharply at them both. 'Oh, let's leave this gloomy place. Is there not to be a feast in our honour, Reverend?'

'A bear feast, yes; but to be frank with you it ends cruelly and the people drink far too much *saké* as the night progresses.'

By the time they returned to the village the sun was setting and the feast was well under way, with men and women lounging about together in the open space around a number of high poles topped by fleshless bear skulls. Chief Shinondhi bowed courteously and conducted them to a raised platform before his hut, where fresh *saké* was pressed upon them.

'They are celebrating the strength and bravery of the bear,' Pepworth explained. 'In the manner of many primitive

119

peoples, they both worship the animal and sacrifice him.' He glanced at Honoria. 'We will not stay for that.'

Some of the men began chanting low, sad recitatives accompanied by a guitar-like instrument and short wooden pipes; the women joined in, waving about their tattooed arms ornamented with brass bracelets. As darkness fell, men and women began dancing slowly round the poles by the light of fires, their bodies lurching together as they continued to drink, their gestures broader and voices louder. To Honoria and Felix the scene had become lurid and wild to the point of unreality and Honoria found herself gripping his arm for comfort.

'Do you think it's safe to stay?' she whispered. Felix was about to ask Pepworth the same question when four men rushed to the centre of the space carrying an iron cage with a young bear inside. The people crowded around it yelling and shrieking, and someone shot an arrow that slightly wounded the animal. It snarled and growled furiously, clawing at the bars, its small eyes glittering madly in the firelight. The bars were raised and it sprang out bravely to face its tormentors. 'Oh no,' Honoria jumped up in horror, 'I can't bear it; please take me away this instant.'

Felix, his brain muddled with *saké*, tension, and disgust, burst out laughing. 'Yes, please, Reverend, we can't *bear* it; take us away. There isn't enough of the bestial in us for such spectacles.'

As Pepworth hurried them off a crowd of men fell on the animal armed with stones, sticks, and spears, each determined to inflict a wound before it died. 'The bear's coming took me by surprise and we stayed rather too long – please excuse me.' The Reverend led them to the edge of the village. 'This is your sleeping hut, Mrs Rayne. I thought your husband would be sharing it with you, of course; but I can assure you you'll be perfectly safe alone. And if there is any trouble call for Mr Coburn or your servants, who are just close by. I always stay in the Chief's hut; he considers it a mark of friendship.'

'Thank you, I shall try to sleep.' With shaking fingers, Honoria took from him a saucer of burning fish-oil that did duty for a lamp and went inside. There was an over-powering stench of bodies, both human and animal; her quilts had been laid out on a shelf against the wall. She moaned weakly, exhausted by the long day, and, removing her outer garments, crawled onto the bed.

In the adjoining hut, Felix lay similarly stretched out, but sleep eluded him. The slaughter of the bear had been the climax of the feast and soon the people's voices sank to sodden mumbles as they too sought their beds. In the fetid darkness, Felix heard the rattle and click of insects in the thatch overhead, the skitter of rodent paws. His senses were still alert, sharpened by the excitement of being in such an outlandish spot. He considered creeping off to look at the graves again. How the deuce was he to . . .? A woman's scream pierced his half-sleep and he leapt up. 'Honoria, is that you?' He grabbed his coat and his riding whip and rushed out, bursting into her hut as she screamed again.

'Oh, Felix, thank heaven!' her voice trembled, 'It was a rat – right across my face – I felt it, ugh!' She shuddered deeply, scrubbing at her cheeks. 'And then I heard it just near on the ground. It's still there – ugh!'

'Here, wait for the light.' He felt his way to her bed and managed to light the lamp, peering about and thumping with his whip. The rat seemed to have vanished. 'It probably ran away when I came in.' He sat beside her, taking her trembling hand. 'My poor dear, this place is even worse than I thought. You should have gone back with your husband.'

'Oh, Harold.' She sniffed. 'No, I wanted to come.'

He squeezed her fingers. 'And I must confess I'm glad you did.' His hand stole along her arm. She was wearing a white petticoat; her hair, usually so elegantly upswept, hung loose about her shoulders. He smiled impishly, 'It's so absurd to see a beautiful woman like you in this ghastly hole.' He touched her face. In the flickering light, with her loosened tresses, she looked younger and more vulnerable.

'Oh come, I'm not beautiful,' she whispered.

For answer he began kissing her face, hair, neck, shoulders, and the tops of her soft breasts. His fingers slid over the ribs of her corsets, which she had only loosened, and he half wanted to tighten them again. She pushed him back with a little sigh. 'Oh, Felix, we shouldn't, mustn't . . .'

Her protesting lips parted for him and he pushed gently at the pliant flesh where her corsets ended until it too began to yield. She closed round him in greedy anguish and he felt big enough to go right up inside her soft, dark tunnel to her slim waist. She writhed and moaned as they became oblivious to everything for what was both a few seconds and an entire night. Rats scuttled about unheard, fleas jumped and bit unheeded, moths hovered near the lamp flame till it went out. The man and woman on the bench came together, separated, reunited, making the same sounds and movements as many Ainu couples there before them had made.

At last Felix sat up. 'Oh, my dear, my dear, I've wanted you, so very much, ever since we met.'

'And I you,' she agreed, in a sort of wonderment at the truth of it.

Becoming aware of itchy stickiness, he put a foot gingerly towards the floor, then withdrew quickly hearing a scuttle. Honoria moaned, 'Oh, the rats − oh − in a place like this − it's all too disgusting!' She put a hand over her mouth as if to contain her jarring emotions − revulsion and delight, lust and amazement, tenderness and shame.

'I shall have to go, dearest,' he murmured. 'I've no idea of the time and there's no lamp-oil left to see by.'

'Yes, go, go now before it's daylight.' She almost pushed him away, imagining Ainus leering at them through the wall cracks.

Alone, she lay in a half-awake stupor till dawn revealed the total squalor of the hut − its ceiling smudged with fire-grime and cobwebs, its floor littered with scraps of animal fat, chewed bones, and fish meal. Even between the wholesome marital sheets, Honoria had been appalled by the crudity of sex as she lay, a passive recipient of Harold's grunting animality. But last night in this disgusting place the beast of passion had become two-backed, as she had moved with joy to Felix's rhythms. Now, in spite of herself, she felt a

122

pricking of renewed desire at the memory and covered her face with shame. Soon after a servant came to her with a bowl of water for washing, and in due course she and Felix ate breakfast with the Reverend Mr Pepworth in the chief's hut, feeling spongy with sleeplessness and the hollows of spent lust. All the villagers gathered to see them off, Pepworth in their midst, wispy hair blowing, forlorn and preposterous in his shabby clerical black.

Their ride back to Hakodate seemed far longer than the outward journey and they were grateful for the presence of the Consulate servants that had been such an encumbrance the day before. It was all the same – the sky as bright, the buds as green – but for Honoria all had changed. Now she was an adulteress, her habitual cold poise shaken by shamed disgust and guilty excitement. Felix shared the excitement of their sensual coming together, and he too had misgivings, for it made the accomplishment of his secret scientific quest the more difficult.

Nor was there any immediate chance of pursuing it when they returned to the Consulate and a totally unsuspicious Harold. Admiral Cousins and his entourage from the *Basilisk* were staying there, and riding picnics and festive meals on board were the order of the day. Every occasion was spiced, for Honoria and Felix, with the lovers' secret knowledge of intimacy. One morning Felix slipped off to reconnoitre and discovered some broken burial sticks on a wooded hill a few miles from the town. The deed would have to be done at night, alone. He didn't relish the thought and pushed it from his mind until the *Basilisk* sailed away.

'How quiet it seems, but at least we still have Felix with us,' Harold remarked as they sat down to lunch on the day of the ship's departure. They were now on first-name terms and Felix winced a little at his frank friendliness. 'No time even to read the papers. I've only just discovered that the Foochow Duffers lost again – the old team still can't get along without me, you see, dear.'

Honoria turned to Felix. 'Harold's former cricket team; and their fortunes are his first concern. If they win he's quite upset — "the old team seem to be managing without me," he says.' She repeated each word as if it were a familiar, bitter pill to be ground down and swallowed.

'Come now, Honoria, I'm not so mean-spirited. Of course I want them to keep winning. Honoria never liked Foochow, it was rather small beer,' he explained. 'I'm sure we'll get to Shanghai one day — that'll be more your cup of tea, dear.'

Honoria thought of the indefinite number of exiled years ahead to be spent in Harold's company. Quantities of tea and beer — the tepid brews; no heady wine. She caught Felix's eye, a sympathetic glance. 'There'd be a little more conversation certainly — in the way of treaty port gossip. Harold likes to tell me what everyone in the neighbourhood has been doing since he last saw them. And the field here is so very limited. Why we are sometimes reduced to hearing what Mr Suzuki, his clerk, had for dinner the previous evening!'

Harold, who was painfully aware of how frequently he bored his wife, muttered defensively, 'Well, it's better than nothing.'

'Yes, dear, I'm sure it is,' she replied, implying, nevertheless, that silence was golden by comparison.

Felix, glimpsing again the long tedium of their lives here, past and future, felt a surge of pity for her. 'At least your piano is due to arrive any time, isn't it, Honoria? And that will sweeten the silent hours.'

'Yes — and how I long for it. I've never realised the absolute necessity of music before. My fingers positively tingle in anticipation of the keyboard.'

'Only a few more weeks, dear,' Harold comforted. 'The next ship but one should have it.'

'I pray so,' she sighed.

That afternoon and for several thereafter, when Harold had returned to the office, Felix and Honoria made passionate love in one of the spare rooms. There they re-enacted and embellished the pleasures of their first sexual union, beginning always with the delicious slow ritual of Felix's loosening of Honoria's tightly-laced corsets. It was the time of summer rains and after their love-making they lay entwined, listening to water splashing on the paving stones from the bamboo gutters outside, thinking of nothing beyond the blissful present. At length, reluctantly, they rose together and kissed as Felix pulled her lacings taut against her body — like a flower that he could open and close up at will. And like a flower, a beautiful slender lily, she stood proudly while he sheathed her tight.

When the skies cleared again, Felix, reminded of his mission, bought a spade and pickaxe from the ship's chandlers and the next evening retired early to nerve himself for the task ahead. Soon after midnight, judging everyone to be asleep, he slung the tools in a canvas bag and tiptoed shoeless along the passage. Waiting till the night watchman passed on his usual round, he slipped outside. As he bent to put on his shoes, he saw a lantern approaching up the path and, in panic, crammed on his shoes and started to run. He tripped over his untied lace and fell, twisting an ankle; the tools clattered on the stones.

'Who the devil . . .?' Harold rushed up, his stick raised as the watchman raced back, musket at the ready. 'Felix . . . you . . . It's all right.' Harold waved the watchman away. 'And what's this, a spade? My dear fellow, what on earth?'

Felix rubbed his ankle, feeling foolish. 'I seem to have twisted something . . . er . . . could we go inside? I can explain. I wasn't about to rob a bank.' He grinned feebly.

'No banks here to rob, old man,' Harold said, then put a finger to his lips with a dramatic flourish. 'Mushn't disturb the lady-wife.' It was obvious he had been drinking heavily and, as they crept into the parlour, he made for the what-not where the brandy stood. 'Cheersh . . . have one? Bit of a prank? Was that it, hey, old boy? Might as well come clean.'

Cornered and half relieved, Felix came clean, explaining that he wanted to get the Ainu bones away to England secretly in case his scientific rivals got wind of what could be a momentous discovery. 'So I didn't like to tell you, or anyone official,' he concluded.

Harold, however, was in genial mood, and thought it all a huge joke, chuckling into his brandy and saying he would be delighted to rob a few graves in a strictly unofficial capacity. 'And why not? Those Ainu savages don't give a tinker's cuss about their corpses and we could be helping the illushtrious cause of science. Here's to old Darwin, a grand fellow, puts ush in our place down among the animals, what?' He leaned forward confidentially. 'Know where I've been tonight? For a few drinks at Madame Fleury's — keeps discreet establishment near the harbour. Not a sailor's brothel, no by jove, just a rendezvous for the town's foreign gents. Drinking, playing cards, bit of billiards, and bit of . . . well you know, sometimes. The lady-wife turns a blind eye. I reckon she doesn't much care where I am as long as it's not in her bed, to be honest.' He stared moodily at the floor. 'Difficult for her here — very. Not her short of place, you know. Glad you're here to keep her company a while, talk on a different plane, more intellectual. She likes intellectuals, you know, thin on the ground here. Not many ideas of that kind myself, to be honest. Run out long ago. Bad enough for me — I'm running to seed here after the sporting life in China. Ushed to play for the Foochow Duffers, you know, grand team.' He collapsed into melancholy silence.

'Yes, so you said.' Felix hated feeling sorry for him too.

'But still worsh for Honoria, she's made of finer stuff. How'sh your glass?'

'No more, thanks. I think I'll turn in; my ankle's throbbing. Gave it a bit of a twist.' He limped towards the door, not wanting to hear any more.

'Yes, well, give it a rest and then we'll go for a little quiet digging together, shall we? Leave it for a night or two, can't play hookey too often. We'll fix it up, but not a word to the wife.' He winked. 'Don't think she'd approve of grave robbing.'

Felix was sure she would not; indeed he wasn't too keen on the reality of it himself. He had imagined some moment of scientific illumination of the Darwinian variety — looking into an open grave at a clean-boned skull very similar to the pictures he had seen of the Neander specimen found nine years before. The reality was different: a dark, uncomfortable ride, listening to Harold's reminiscences of the good old days on the China coast; searching for grave sticks in the thorny underbrush; wind blowing out their lanterns; the queasy grubbing about in the damp soil for human remains. The two bodies they eventually unearthed were still in a deep state of decomposition. 'Not long dead, cover 'em up. Ainu pong is bad enough live but dead . . . phew,' Harold snorted.

Felix groaned. 'I suppose I'll have to go back to Pepworth's village and try there. But if he finds out there'll be the devil to pay.'

Harold pulled out a brandy flask, drank, handed it to his companion. Animals rustled in the undergrowth; it was a moonless night and black shadows lurked behind every tree; Felix thought of ghosts, vampires, headless corpses. 'For God's sake let's get out of here.'

As they returned to their waiting horses, Harold said, 'Tell you what, I'll make some discreet enquiries through my interpreter, who speaks Ainu. I'll say you're a scientific expert on burial grounds.'

By this means they were able to locate an older graveyard that became the scene of what Harold termed 'nocturnal diggings'. For him it was all rather a lark; but for Felix each experience was intense and eerie and this, allied to the equally intense experience of his passionate affair, kept him in a state of emotional ferment. Love, death, and their inexplicable conjunctions became a reality to him that summer. Once he uncovered a female skeleton from a shroud of rotten matting, and had a vision of Honoria's sweet slender body revealed as he unlaced her. The proximity of the two pierced him; he wanted to yell, sob, and laugh with the knowledge of it.

In due course Felix thus acquired sufficient skeletal remains for his purpose; but, bound by his own desire and Honoria's pleading, he did not leave on the next mail boat – on which, at long last, was Honoria's piano.

'And we shall have a little musical evening to celebrate, though I'm hopelessly out of practice,' Honoria declared, as they watched the huge crate trundle up the temple path on a creaking cart. The instrument made the parlour look like home at last, its ebonised surface reflecting the vase of wild roses Honoria had picked in its honour. Eagerly, before supper, they gathered round it, Honoria arrayed in a flounced, low-cut dinner dress of peach silk.

'You must forgive me for dressing up, gentlemen,' she had said, making her evening entrance with a flourish of a lace-trimmed train, 'but there are so few excuses to wear anything in the least splendid these days.'

She sat at the piano stool, leaning forward to touch the rose petals. 'You know I envy composers above all people in the world. Do I diminish a sonata by saying it is like the most exquisite bowl of flowers?' She raised the piano lid, leafed through sheaves of music. 'Oh, what shall I try? I don't know – you simply mustn't listen at first. Oh, it's like being able to read again after months of blindness.'

Harold and Felix stood behind her, sipping drinks, both thinking how magnificent she looked, the grandeur of the lily-stem back, the slim waist in its peach sheath, the shining coiff of hair as she bent over the keyboard. She rubbed her knuckles nervously. 'Oh, I don't know, something easy to begin with, I suppose.'

'What about that song Prince Albert wrote – "He is Far From the Land". Appropriate, don't you think?' Harold suggested.

His wife turned witheringly. 'I think we can aspire a little higher than that, dear. But it will be a German composition if you like. Yes, I have it – a Schubert waltz. Such a pity he was German, our dear dead Prince too.' She touched the ivory keys with gentle confidence; then, tentatively, began to play. She faltered, began again; stopped, then, ignoring the music before her, moved from one chord to another, making an increasing dissonance.

Felix's heart began to sink. Harold wandered to the decanter. 'Another, Felix? Just getting the feel of it, hey, darling?'

She did not reply, leaning over the instrument, desperately willing it to produce the right sounds. Felix heard the notes jarring, saw her wince as they did so.

'Is anything wrong?' Harold muttered at last.

She tried once more, then slammed down the lid, burying her face in her hands. 'Can't you hear anything – anything ever? It's hopelessly out of tune – hopelessly, hopelessly – every note just wriggles and jangles – it sets my teeth on edge – can't you even *hear* it?' She turned a tragic face to them and Felix nodded. 'It didn't sound right, certainly.'

'Right – utterly, utterly wrong!' Her wide eyes filled with tears. 'And how can I ever get it put right here in this God-forsaken hole? Oh, it's too much, too much, after all this.' She bit her trembling lips. 'Oh, how I hate this place – hate everything, there's nothing worthwhile here, nothing.'

'Oh, hush, dear, we'll get it seen to somehow.' Harold moved to touch her bare shoulder and she shuddered away.

'And where do you propose to find a piano tuner? Yokohama, Shanghai, London?'

'I'll try my contacts, I'll . . .'

'Your contacts – they don't know black notes from white any more than you do. One of your contacts bought this for us, didn't he? Mr what's his beastly name?'

'Turner.'

'Turner.' She spat the word and stood up, trying to regain her composure. 'I'm sorry, gentlemen, but our musical evening will not take place.'

Harold refilled his glass. 'Please don't distress yourself so, Honoria. Why not have a sherry and then try something simpler – just to give us a tune or two. "Drink To Me Only" or "Robin Adair"?'

She stared at him with such bleak loathing that he recoiled in self-defence. 'You – you oaf,' she choked, and rushed from the room sobbing wildly, her silk train rustling.

The men looked at each other, drinking in silence. Felix trailed his fingers over the piano's polished surface, touched the roses. Harold sighed gustily. 'So that's that. She's a bit of a perfectionist when it comes to music, you know. But I must do something – I really think she'll go mad if she doesn't have a piano she can play before the winter.' He looked at Felix with sudden attention. 'Well, how about it, old man?

You'll be leaving soon, I suppose. Don't mean to hurry you off, but you – we – have accomplished your mission, I think? So perhaps you could look out for another piano in Yokohama – or try and round up a piano tuner and send him up here – whichever is the cheaper? Lord knows if there's a piano tuner in the whole of Japan good enough to suit madam's requirements, though. Here, let me give you another.'

Felix held out his glass; his spirits, that had begun to sink as Honoria played, sank lower. He had to leave her, his whole life seemed suddenly out of tune. 'Yes, of course; I must be off by the next mail boat, I suppose; and I'll certainly see what I can do.'

'About a fortnight from now,' Harold said briskly. 'I'd appreciate it greatly, old chap. And so will Honoria – though don't let's raise her hopes by saying anything yet. In any case, you . . .' He trailed off. Not needing to say what Felix knew full well – that, in more ways than Harold Rayne realised, Felix certainly owed him a good turn.

A fortnight would have been far too short for Honoria and Felix to satiate their mutual passion, but in the event they had less time than that. A few days after the fiasco of the musical evening, Harold drew Felix aside after lunch and told him that a certain Captain Kelly in the trading brig *Colleen* had arrived in port and was Yokohama bound. 'Good chum of mine, Kelly,' he explained. 'Knew him in Foochow – told him you were waiting for a passage south and were also anxious to get a certain wooden chest through the Yokohama customs and away with no questions asked. For a job like that, Felix, Kelly's just your man. "Better tell me what's inside, Harold," he says. "There's certain items, like gold cobangs, are very high risks these days." "Bones," I told him, "old Ainu bones," and we had a good laugh over it. So there you are – and Bob's your uncle.'

'Thank you very much, Harold, and when does she sail?'

'Tomorrow, so why not come to the office later and meet Kelly for a drink, book your berth, and so on?'

Felix nodded numbly; he had no possible excuse for refusing the offer; no alternative but to tell Honoria he was leaving.

He found her in the parlour, where she usually sat sewing in the afternoons, awaiting Felix's arrival. She presented a picture of calm domestic felicity, head bent over her embroidery; but, in fact and in anticipation of the sweet congress she hoped soon to be enjoying with her lover, she was indulging in a fantasy that had often beset her since their affair began. She was walking towards a thicket, and at its edge stood a taller than average Ainu with his back to her, his long black hair shining in the sun. Suddenly he turns, letting his woven skirt drop to reveal a very large, erect member. He beckons her, smiling gently, she tries to run but is immobilised as he walks towards her. Calmly he unlaces her, knowing perfectly how to do it, then picks her up in his strong arms and spreads her open on the grass, still smiling and silent. His body comes down hard and he pushes up inside her, grunting and snorting, hairy and huge like an animal . . .

'Honoria, dear, let's go for a ride; it's a lovely afternoon.'

She started guiltily and blushed. 'Oh, there you are, Felix. I wondered where you'd gone.'

He kissed her forehead. 'Oh, Harold and I were chatting. To our favourite bay, don't you think?'

She rose reluctantly, subduing the desire her fantasy had engendered. 'I'll put on my riding skirt.'

He waited, having decided it would be easier to break the news out of doors than in the seductive embrace of the spare room bed.

They rode northwards out of town to a coastal inlet where they had previously enjoyed picnics. A few Ainu boats were drawn up on the shore, festooned with drying nets; the straight cliff behind the bay was shaded with trees and drooping creepers; two dogs were fighting over fish offal near the boats and crows were pecking their leftovers. At the far end of the beach they dismounted and wandered about aimlessly, picking up shells. Felix could postpone the matter no longer, and told her.

'Tomorrow? . . . Oh no, not that soon.' She grasped his sleeve.

'What can I do? Harold is determined I should see about

your piano before shipping stops for the winter. At least I can do that for you.'

She nodded, looking at him searchingly, then went and leaned against a rock, closing her eyes. Heaps of seaweed drying in the sun emitted a faint hiss like soft rain falling. She imagined herself at home again, walking down a country lane with high hedges on either side, light rain swishing over leaves and grasses. She kept her eyes shut against the unendurable glare and pain of the present.

He said gently, 'Honoria, I'm terribly sorry – for everything. I'll stay in Yokohama for the winter. I came to look into the silk trade, remember; and I haven't done a single thing about it yet.' He twisted his riding crop. 'Truth is, I'm a little financially embarrassed and my money's running out. So one way and another, dearest, I really have to go.'

She opened her eyes and nodded again. During their lovemaking they had never talked of a future together; she could not accuse him of false promises. She said, 'I can't think why I ever agreed to marry Harold, you know. All I really loved in him was his love for me – it was quite inordinate, indiscriminate. To an extent it still is, but I don't love it in him any more. I'm tired of it even before he is. Isn't that a terrible thing to say? But then I'm such an appalling person.'

He touched her cheek. 'No – oh, no, you're not in the least; you're just . . . I mean, it often happens one way or another in a marriage, I'm sure. One partner loves more and it would come naturally to Harold. He's such an amiable man.'

'Oh, I sometimes wish he was wicked – then I'd have something to complain about, some good reason for leaving him . . .' She paused, but Felix said nothing. 'And he deserved an amiable woman, not me. Though I might have been a little more amiable if I hadn't married him. Oh, it's so . . . so . . .' Her voice trembled on the brink of saying how unfair it was that she had not met Felix while she was still single. But would they have come together, at another time, another place? She plucked her white cotton glove. 'Shall we go back?'

For answer he held her gently against the rock, kissing her deep and long, stirred sadly by each other's useless lust. 'We will meet again, in the spring – here or in Yokohama, I promise you, darling,' he breathed.

'Oh, the spring – if I survive the winter.'

'Of course you will; you must.' He reached for her again, longing to fill her with his strength, but then stepped back, hearing voices. Two Ainu lads had come out of the trees and were staring at them, grinning. 'Come – let's go,' Honoria said sharply.

They trotted back along the hard sand to the edge of the town, where Felix left her to go and see Captain Kelly at Harold's office. The three men, who had been drinking rather heavily, returned to the Consulate for a late supper over which Honoria presided in miserable sobriety. And the next morning Felix, who left with Harold, could give her no more than a fleeting farewell kiss. She watched them walk away through the temple garden, followed by the cart loaded with Felix's luggage. At the gate he turned and waved his hat, and she raised an arm in response, feeling an even deeper cold than she was to suffer during the frozen winter that lay ahead.

Returning listlessly to the parlour she leafed through some translations of Ainu songs that Pepworth had left for her to read. One was entitled, 'Song of the Spider Goddess that is Worshipped by Women', and it began,

> 'Doing nothing but needlework
> I remained with my eyes
> focused on a single spot
> and this is the way I continued to live
> on and on . . .'

Honoria's eyes blurred and she began crying quietly.

CHAPTER SEVEN

Yokohama was in its end-of-summer doldrums when Felix returned; and his spirits sank to a similar level. After seeing the chest of bones safely through Customs and off to England with Captain Kelly's help, he sat in his room at the Anglo-Saxon Hotel for two days, drinking beer cooled by the new luxury of chipped ice imported from Tientsin, and thinking his life had reached a sorry pass. At such times, feeling himself faced with basic problems of survival in a blank, pitiless universe, he doubly envied those of strong Christian faith. The godless world he inhabited was a cruel jungle, and promises of progress only hollow, while the mental freedom he had painfully acquired seemed a mockery, for he was still chained – bound by his passion for Honoria, by financial stringency, by his own inadequacies.

His frame of mind hadn't been improved by the letter that awaited him from his elder brother Sydney. It was four-square blunt as was Sydney's wont: unless the family received some return for the outlay of financing his trip, no further allowances would be sent to him. Sydney enclosed a list of questions about silk and cotton exports and the financial and political stability of Japan; there was also a leaflet describing Coburn's latest models – of English leather, lined with muslin, with strong metal eyelets and busk clasps. Underneath Sydney had scrawled 'don't Jap. girls lace themselves tight with those wide kimono belts? Is there a possible market over there?' Felix laughed sourly, thinking of the silken crackle of Honoria's corsets and the crassness of his brother's creed. However, lacking an independent income, he was bound to respect his wishes and bestirred himself accordingly.

First he looked for a piano-tuner, and learned that the one and only had returned to Shanghai two weeks before, after his annual visit to Japan. In an anguish of sympathy for Honoria, he bought the best piano he could find in the settlement and shipped it off north – which took the last of his ready cash. He then sought out his acquaintances, hoping for advice and help. However, Arnold and Elinor Mills were away in Hong Kong, making arrangements for the latter's wedding, planned for the end of the year; the Fortescues were on home leave and due back soon; that left Percival Storey. Percival had not stirred from Yokohama during the long hot summer and looked rather over-tired and peevish, but welcomed Felix at his lodgings cordially enough. 'Come in, Coburn, have a beer. What goes on in the furthest North? I gather the Raynes survived their first winter? But no trade to speak of, judging from Rayne's reports?'

'Very little – sea slugs, seaweed, and sea-otter furs – not very inspiring. Rayne is bored stiff.'

'And the dignified lady-wife?'

'Oh, she manages . . . I suppose. But much more's been going on here, undoubtedly?'

'Socially, commercially, politically? What do you want to know?' Percy settled himself comfortably in his long-armed lounging chair; he liked to conduct his conversation along orderly lines.

'Oh, all three – take them as they come.'

'Well, the social scene is fairly dead, owing to the absence of some of our leading lights. Indeed the Municipal Council hasn't had sufficient members in attendance to make a quorum recently. Mr Black of the *Japan Herald* gave a musical evening in order to capture enough people in one room to listen to his singing. And, oh yes, Charlie Rickerby is about to launch a rival paper, the *Japan Times*, on a waiting world. What else? The usual hectic round at Windsor Castle . . .'

'Where?'

'You know, the Marshall's place – our leading social hosts.

Worthy Mrs Hubbard, the missionary's wife, has started a little school to teach English to Japanese girls of good family, an excellent scheme; and their American missionary friends have brought in pots of geraniums to plant in the public gardens – if ever we get them opened. Worst news is that a Dutch sea captain and three Russian seamen were killed by *ronin* and a French cavalry officer wounded, only the other day.'

'Oh, Lord, I'd hoped that sort of thing was over.'

'So did we all. But these *ronin* are totally reckless. Having lost their samurai status they've nothing else left to lose, and there's a fresh upsurge of the militaristic spirit recently . . . which brings me to politics.'

'Oh, let's have the trade news first, and another beer, if I may,' Felix interrupted. 'Once you get on to politics there's no stopping you.'

Percy went to the row of bottles along the wall. 'Trade isn't my forte, but let's see. General picture quite rosy. Textiles on the up and up – raw silk and cotton exports especially, plus the usual odds and sods – gall nuts, cuttle fish, dried peas. Imports of foreign manufacture are increasing rapidly, especially arms and ammunition, not to mention a few Yankee gun-runners who found that the leaders of Satsuma and Choshui are good customers – which brings me back to politics and the real news.'

'Has anything world-shattering happened, then? Newspapers are weeks out of date when they reach Hakodate.'

'I suppose the world was pretty shattered by the assassination of President Abraham Lincoln last month. Did you hear that?'

'Lincoln – no!'

'Yep. Shot in a theatre by some madman called Booth. Terrible shame, seemed such a decent sort of fellow. However, speaking personally, the world has been more changed by the arrival of Sir Harry Smythe Parkes K.C.B., our new Envoy Extraordinary and Minister Plenipotentiary to the Court of the Shoguns. You've heard of him, I hope?'

'Just about.'

'Old China hand, boyhood spent in Hong Kong, excellent

Chinese linguist, imprisoned and tortured by the Chinese in Peking during the Allies' Expedition of 'sixty. Youngish, thirty-seven − by heaven, I'd like to think I could be in his shoes by that age. He'll never let the grass grow . . . known as P.P.P. − Perpetually Perambulating Parkes. And the Japanese interpreters and I have been perpetually on the trot since he landed. Wants to know abso-bally-lutely everything. Good mind. He's already reaching the right conclusions about this country.'

'Which are?' Felix tried to concentrate, remembering Sydney's letter.

'That the balance of power is shifting inexorably towards the Emperor in Kyoto, and the Shogun and his government − the *bakafu* − are on a very sticky wicket. Didn't I say this to you before? I usually do.'

'Perhaps I wasn't listening, but I am now, so please go on.'

'Priority number one therefore is for us foreigners to get our treaties with the Japanese ratified by the Emperor and his team if we are to develop trade and international relations.'

'Why is it, then, that everyone talks about the Shogun in Edo as the boss?'

'Oriental subtlety, old man, can't beat the Japanese for that; not for nothing is their puppet theatre a national entertainment. Of course the Shogun isn't just a puppet; he's got tremendous power. But the Emperor's been there all along too, holding things together − learning, art, religion; much of the gracious living goes on in Kyoto. And now the Shogun's government is bankrupt, in decline. I've seen it coming and so have the south-western clans − the "Satcho alliance", we call it. If that alliance really works, the Shogunate is doomed.'

Felix sighed, wondering if he should mention all these complexities to Sydney. 'So there could be a civil war which would upset the export trade, presumably?'

'Possibly, depends . . .' Percival wandered to a round table in the corner covered with dictionaries, documents, and correspondence drafts. 'Not that your average trader gives a damn about the state of the nation. Chinese, Japanese − all the same yellow men to them, think of nothing beyond the going price of grey shirtings. But you're not like that? Scientific interests, I believe?' He suddenly faced Felix with one of his disconcerting keen stares.

'Yes − er − manners and customs of the Ainu.'

'Ainu, pah! Pathetic remnants! What about the manners and customs of the Japanese? One of the most fascinating and turbulent periods in their entire history going on right now under your very nose.'

'Yes, I suppose I really ought, really will . . . I say, Percy, do you know of some moderately priced lodgings near here? I've decided to stay for a while, and I'll be looking into textile exports on my family's behalf − which might offend you, of course.'

'Oh, I've nothing against traders *per se*; it's the damn blinkers most of them wear. And, yes, I do happen to know − just next door, the lodgings Mills had before his elevation to the Consulate Extension. Rent's probably gone up − with all these greedy foreign traders arriving, what can you expect? But might suit you. Shall we go and look?'

The lodgings consisted of several draughty, clean rooms furnished with the usual oddments with which foreigners cluttered up empty Japanese living spaces − wash stands, rickety tables, iron bedsteads, a writing desk and chairs, even an umbrella stand and a damp-spotted picture of a Scottish glen askew on a wall. Felix took on the lot and began to pursue the urgent matter of earning his keep.

Silk, for Felix, had simply been one of the materials used in the making of those embarrassing if seductive garments on which the Coburns' prosperity depended. But silk, he now learned, had a mysterious life of its own, that began among the worms rustling and munching the mulberry leaves laid out in trays in the upper storeys of Japanese farmhouses. The cocoons they formed − reward for hours of feeding and caring lavished on them by the farmers' wives − were spun into lengths and twisted together into pale, buff-coloured skeins of raw silk. To strut about in elegant silk was a privilege reserved for the samurai and nobility, and forbidden to the common farmers who produced it. So silk had an intrinsic status, and even a language, of its own.

Silkworm eggs were collected on seed-cards and it took about five hundred cocoons to produce one card of seed; as cocoons could be counted in hundreds of thousands, seed-card supply was almost limitless. This had resulted in a short-lived bonanza in Yokohama. In the mid-'sixties the silk crops of France and Italy had been ruined by disease, and Japanese seed-cards were being sold to Europe at highly inflated prices to replenish stocks. By chance, Felix had chosen a good time to enter the silk trade; and he sent to Shanghai for letters of credit that would provide the necessary capital for investment.

The steamer that brought Felix his letters of credit also returned the Fortescues and Elinor and Arnold Mills to Yokohama. They were all pleased to be back and Arnold was positively ebullient, for he had won considerable sums at the Hong Kong race meetings, with which he had bought a smart phaeton that reposed in the ship's hold and was destined to be among the first wheeled carriages to grace the recently opened road that ran from the settlement towards Mississippi Bay, a picturesque stretch of coast line beyond the Bluff.

Reginald Bradshaw was waiting on the quay to meet them and introduced them to his companion, Major Beale. 'Friend of the family,' Reggie explained as they shook hands. 'An India man and a jolly good vet; he's been sent over to pep up our livestock, Arnold. India and horses – nothing the Major doesn't know about them.'

'And *dawgs*,' chortled the Major.

'And *dawgs*,' agreed Reggie. Reggie had ordered luncheon for them at the recently opened 'Hotel de l'Europe' along the Bund, during which the talk was all of the forthcoming military review and mock battle, and the sad fact that Muffin, Arnold's favourite pony, destined for the new phaeton, was lamed and now on a cure of arnica, cold-water bandages, and bran mash. Elinor, rather left out, stared at the familiar harbour view, trying to feel happier about seeing her fiancé again. Watching the men grow wine-flushed and jolly, she

140

wished suddenly she was of their sex – not to indulge in drink and horsey chat, but so she could choose her own way to live.

Major Beale's skin was freckled and leathery from long years of exposure to the fierce Indian sun; the skins of the Indian memsahibs were the same, she had heard. Ellie wondered how many of them lived as they wished; how long before her skin too became similarly sun-baked and wrinkled. She longed to jump up and shout at them all – for their careless ignorance, their thoughtless masculine selfishness. Instead she got up unobtrusively, saying she really must go and unpack; the men rose too, apologising casually for their manly exclusion of her. She inclined her head. 'Are you coming, Arnold?'

'I'll call on you this evening, dearest.' Reggie squeezed her arm as she went off with her brother.

'Have you seen Ryo?' Elinor asked Arnold, surveying their piles of luggage in the Consulate's passageway. 'I'm sure she'd help me unpack.'

'I think she's gone with her brother.'

'Gone?' Elinor was startled.

'Only to Percival's place. I talked briefly to Miyata on the quay. Apparently the P.P.P. demands so many translations at a rate of knots that the interpreters are working night and day – and Miyata has moved there temporarily for convenience.'

'Then I'll go and see them tomorrow.'

He grimaced. 'Not going to bother with any more Japanese, are you? Won't be much use to you in the *mofussil*.'

'One never knows; we might get posted back here sometime.'

'Please yourself – if you will fill your pretty little head with such linguistic conundrums.'

'I like them,' she returned obstinately, ordering a servant to carry her baggage upstairs.

Ryo herself opened Percival Storey's door when Elinor went to visit the following afternoon; and Elinor hugged her impulsively. 'Oh, you are here! I have missed you, dear. May I come in?' Kenjiro, sitting at the paper-covered table,

141

jumped up as she entered. 'Miss Mills, good afternoon. I heard you are back.'

'Mr Miyata – I am pleased to see you. I believe you're very busy?'

He tutted ruefully. 'It is work, work, work since the new Minister arrives. Ryo, please get tea. And did you enjoy China, Miss Mills?'

'Oh, I suppose so. I was only in Hong Kong and Shanghai. Quite imposing places compared to pioneering little Yokohama.'

'Many stone buildings and wide roads with hard surfaces, I think?'

'Oh yes – and western-style shops and offices; not very interesting.'

'And the Chinese, what are they thinking these days?'

She was nonplussed. 'Er, about what, Mr Miyata?'

'About the foreigners who have come to their country to build up these treaty ports. About the British and French who marched into Peking and burned their Emperor's summer palace a few years ago?' He knew it was improper to ask such searching questions of a woman; but Miss Mills was different from the common run, he was certain.

On this occasion, however, she disappointed him. 'I fear I didn't meet any Chinese socially. We didn't discuss politics. And the situation is quite different in China from here, anyway.'

'I see.' He prepared to resume his work.

'I mean foreigners wouldn't behave so aggressively here.'

He looked at her seriously. 'We Japanese are not so sure of that, Miss Mills. That is why we need modern weapons to defend ourselves if necessary.'

She bit her lip. 'But naturally I can't see foreigners as threats; and I hope you don't personally.'

'No, but many of my compatriots do. As you may know, anti-barbarian extremists killed a Dutch captain only recently. They are very stupid people; but they do it partly because they fear foreign invasion.'

She sighed as he picked up his pen. 'And does our new

142

Minister, your chief, understand this fear?'

'Yes, he's a very clever man. Under his leadership all the diplomatic representatives are going to Osaka soon to persuade the Emperor to ratify earlier treaties made with foreigners. This is a good step because the people greatly revere the Emperor and will accept the rightness of what he does.'

Just then Ryo returned with the tea, followed by Felix. 'Oh, good day, Miss Mills; I heard you and your brother had returned. All ready for the grand wedding?'

'Good day, Mr Coburn. Yes, we are being married in Hong Kong's Christchurch, on December 22nd.'

'A honeymoon for a Christmas present – what could be nicer!' He took some tea. 'Do the Japanese go in for honeymoons, Miss Miyata?'

Ryo, not knowing the word, looked confused till Kenjiro translated it for her, then she reddened. 'It is not Japanese custom, Mr Coburn.'

'Of course, romantic love is not really Japanese custom, is it? Perhaps you're better off without it; though I'm sure Miss Mills wouldn't agree.'

Elinor replied coolly, 'I certainly wouldn't like to have my marriage arranged for me with a man I hadn't even met – which would have been Ryo's fate if she'd stayed at home.'

'Oh, that is *sensei*'s opinion,' Kenjiro remarked. 'He deplores the total lack of freedom of choice for our women.'

'Who is *sensei*?' Felix asked.

'It means "teacher",' Elinor explained, proud of her knowledge. 'Mr Miyata is my Japanese *sensei*; but who is yours?' She turned to him.

'Mr Taneo Takahashi. I met him this summer. He is a very wise man who lives in Edo and writes books about western things. But not only material things – he wants the Japanese to understand the philosophical and political ideas of the West also. It is no use just learning about the machines, he says; it is the spirit behind them that is important. We must learn to think for ourselves, he says, and develop our individual persons.' Kenjiro was quite flushed with the effort of trying to translate such difficult concepts and Elinor smiled

143

at him encouragingly. 'Oh, I'd like to meet your *sensei*; he sounds most interesting.'

'He is fluent in English language also and has a very original mind – I bow at his feet.'

'And has he studied western science too?' Felix asked.

'He has read Mr Darwin's book on origins, also J. S. Mill on liberty, and Mr Samuel Smiles . . .' Kenjiro listed the names reverently.

Felix chuckled. 'Darwin, hey? And what does he think of the grand master?'

'He is very impressed with his ideas, Mr Coburn, as I am myself. The survival of the fittest is very logical but we Japanese, even the fittest of us, are cluttered up and hung about with ancestral traditions, with clans and family obligations and superstitions. Individual fitness is most difficult for us.'

'Yes I see your point and I'd certainly like to meet Mr Takahashi, Miyata.'

Kenjiro bowed. 'I will try to arrange it; but he is an extremely busy man . . .'

'You must be talking about me,' Percival said, coming in with an armful of documents. 'I am the most overworked and underpaid slave in the country and my master is a tyrant.' He dumped the papers on the table. 'More translations to be done before we go to Osaka, Miyata. Is it humanly possible? Shall we not collapse?'

'We have to do it, Mr Storey,' Kenjiro replied quietly.

'Yes, we have to – while you good-for-nothing traders loaf about sipping tea.' He glowered at Felix, who grinned.

'I wish I could help, old man. I agree with you, traders are always loafing about – waiting for ships to come in, letters to arrive, people to make up their grubby little minds; but I can't help it.'

'Well, I'm going to push you all out anyway, Miyata and I will be burning the midnight oil again. Glad to see you back, Elinor, if only for a while. I imagine you'll be cheering your fiancé on tomorrow as he rides heroically into battle?'

'Battle?'

'A mock fight against the French; haven't you heard?'

'Oh yes, he did mention it.'

'Now away with you lotus eaters . . .' He waved them towards the door.

On her way home Elinor wandered along the Bund, thinking how familiar Yokohama had become and how pleasant it was to be friendly with Japanese like the Miyatas. The only natives she had met while in China had been servants or shopkeepers; and it was the same in India apparently, especially if you were with the army. But here it was much more relaxed; and she smiled, remembering Mr Miyata's solemn recital of those familiar household names. She wanted to meet his *sensei*, and wondered sadly if she would have a chance to do so before leaving Japan, perhaps forever.

The next morning was clear and cool as Elinor rode to the parade ground with her brother in the new phaeton. Driving up the Bluff hill they heard the thud of marching feet and horses' hoofs, the thrum of bugle, drum, and fife. The British had mustered a battery of Royal Artillery and a detachment of the XIth and IInd Battalion of the XXth Regiment, among whose ranks Elinor soon spotted Reggie, resplendent in smart, gold-trimmed red and black. Alongside marched sailors from the British, French, and American warships in the harbour, each with its own marine band. On the far side of the ground, a contingent of Japanese soldiers were handling their Enfield rifles and bayonets with great aplomb; though their outfits 'provided a most suggestive indication of the country's state of transition,' as the *Japan Herald* put it, 'varying from outer garments of mediaeval chain-mail through high-collared Western-style jackets worn with loose Chinese-style trousers tied at the ankle, to perfect replicas of European military uniforms made to toy-soldier's size'.

The Japanese Prefectural Governor and Sir Harry Parkes reviewed the lines, the men presenting arms as they passed and performing drills and bayonet exercises before marching off. It was Elinor's first glimpse of the formidable P.P.P. – a slightly built, upright figure on horseback with fair hair and alert blue eyes that took in everyone and everything as he passed. In the afternoon the sham fight was held on the field at the village of Homura, where the men took up positions on either side of a valley and fired blank cartridges at each other – to the astonishment of the villagers, who seemed thoroughly to enjoy the spectacle. Even though, as the *Herald* remarked, '. . . incidental damage was done to the late rice crops and a number of livestock got in the way of the bullets'.

'What did you think of it, then?' Reggie asked Elinor eagerly as he eventually joined her back on the parade ground.

'Oh, it was grand fun!' She beamed at him. 'And you cut quite the most handsome figure in the whole regiment.'

'Oh for the vision of sweet young love,' Arnold chortled, thinking that Reggie Bradshaw quite turned his sensible sister's head. But she looked very pretty and happy for all that, and he was pleased to see her so. As Reginald escorted her to the phaeton, he explained that he and Major Beale had planned an excursion to Kamakura during the coming weekend and so, alas, he wouldn't be able to see her for several days.

'But why can't I come too?' she pouted. 'It's ages since I saw the great Diabutsu.'

'Oh, Diabutsu, is it, Miss? You and your Japanese! Well it's the old statue called Dyeboots we're making for, and I don't really think we can take you, dear. It's not considered very safe for ladies – and not entirely proper either to go off with two military gents, however chivalrous.' He winked at Arnold, who was waiting in the carriage.

'Oh, you're always so worried about what is safe and proper for ladies,' she shrugged petulantly.

'And so he should be, Elinor,' Arnold said with elder-brother firmness. 'And you're certainly not going.'

'Oh well, then – goodbye for now, handsome swain, and enjoy yourself without me.' She put out a gloved hand, coquettishly evading his attempt to kiss her, and climbed into the phaeton, giving him a teasing pout as Arnold drove away.

The weather changed by the weekend and Elinor, looking on a scene of chill autumnal rain, was quite glad she had not gone to Kamakura – slipping over muddy tracks, listening to

146

chat about India, horses, and *dawgs*. There would be plenty of opportunity for that in the near future; for the present she continued to think about Japan and its people – the title of a recent book she was reading by a strait-laced Anglican bishop who had spent just a month in the country. Annoyed by his ill-informed and pompous generalisations, she continued to read, thinking that she might usefully employ her first Indian hot season writing a better book than this about Japan.

The weather remained inclement all day and rain was still falling in the early hours of the next morning when Arnold was awakened by a heavy thudding on the front door. Putting his revolver in his jacket pocket he hurried out, to find a government policeman standing in the passage, rain pouring off his cloak. He handed Arnold a note: 'Mills come at once. Japanese officials report attack on two foreigners at Kamakura. Medical aid urgently required.' It was signed by the British Consul. 'Kamakura; oh, God,' Arnold muttered to himself as he rushed to dress and pick up his medical box.

He long remembered that dismal ride, made in company with the Consul and an army surgeon. The only sounds were of rain falling on trees, horses' hoofs slushing, and the occasional '*hai-hai*' of the grooms who ran ahead holding lanterns aloft. Crossing the low hills between Yokohama and the fishing village of Kanazawa, where the track was steep and more slippery, they entered the temple town of Kamakura as dawn was breaking; and Arnold's heart sank further under its weight of foreboding.

Eventually they saw ahead, at the far end of an avenue of lofty cryptomerias, the immense statue of the Diabutsu silhouetted against a grey half-light. A policeman galloped up and directed them along a path to the left, where a group of men stood, speaking in hushed voices. The foreigners pushed through and were shown two mutilated bodies lying in the mud. They were stretched on their backs; the mangled right hand of one held a revolver and his eyes stared sightlessly upward; the arms and legs of the other were cut to pieces, the head almost severed from the trunk.

'God damn it, it's Beale and Bradshaw,' murmured the

army surgeon; Arnold turned away.

'Is there anything to be done?'

The surgeon dismounted and looked. 'Not a thing.'

In the silence that fell Arnold distinctly heard the ticking of Reggie's watch, which was still attached to his waistcoat; and a great heartsickness washed through him as he thought of the victim's youth and the many hours he had expected to live. As daylight strengthened, the foreigners examined the nearby ground for traces of conflict, and the blood-covered saddles and reins of their two horses, which were tethered to a nearby tree. While they were so engaged, two cavalry officers galloped up and their escort of soldiers made make-shift litters on which the bodies were placed for conveyance to Yokohama.

Arnold watched, uncovering his head to the rain, then step-ped forward impulsively, indicating Reggie's watch. 'May I take that, officer? This man was my sister's fiancé, you see.'

The officer hesitated. 'I'm not really empowered to . . .'

'I'm sure Lieutenant Bradshaw would have wished it,' Arnold said stiffly.

'Then here you are – and please convey my deepest sym-pathies to your sister.'

Arnold put the watch in his pocket and rode slowly back along the path to where he could see the Diabutsu, the Great Buddha, now clearly visible in the morning light. The huge, beautiful face gazed down along the avenue with its usual sightless serenity. He could hardly bear to look at it, such was the tumult of anger and pity in his heart. 'God damn your blasted detachment,' he muttered through his teeth. 'Didn't you see what happened?' The pathetic absurdity of his own question brought a rush of tears to his eyes; he turned and galloped back to his groom, Sam, who was dozing under a tree. Arnold gave him a sharp kick. 'Wake up, Sam, blast you – we're going back.' Sam blinked at him in injured silence before starting off obediently.

On his return, Arnold called first on Mary Fortescue to ask if she would keep Elinor company in the sorrow she must soon experience, as he had to attend the post-mortem at the military hospital. He then went to his surgery and mixed a strong sedative, wondering if he could somehow persuade his sister to drink it before breaking the news. Then he went to find her, wincing with the same sympathetic helplessness he felt for the burden of women's suffering as when attending a birth.

Elinor found it hard to believe at first, asking dry-eyed for details. He handed her Reggie's watch, its scratched face bearing traces of blood. 'It's stopped,' she said quietly.

'It was still going earlier.'

'I'll never wind it again.' Touching the stains she imagined Reggie's strong, thick male neck spurting blood and began crying harshly.

He patted her shoulder. 'Oh, Ellie, dear, please try to be brave. Here, darling — drink this sedative. I've asked Mary to come and be with you. You must go to bed.'

She looked at him, wild-eyed. 'Bed? Sedative? But it's not yet tea-time.'

'I know, dear, but this is a great shock to your nervous system.'

'I shan't be married after all, shall I? Never, never! I'm like a kind of widow, aren't I?' She was weeping fiercely. 'Oh, poor dear Reggie; he was so healthy and heedless. How could they have killed him — just for nothing, like this?'

'We've no idea who did it or why, dear. But we'll catch the devils this time — the whole of the XXth will hunt them out.' He patted her shoulder again. 'It's far better that you hadn't just married him, really it is, Elinor. It would have been even worse for you.'

'I don't see how; at least I'd have been a proper widow, instead of this . . . Oh dear, oh dear, Arnold, it's so awful to bear.'

She was still crying convulsively when Mary Fortescue arrived and persuaded her to swallow the sedative and go to lie down. As Mary helped her undress, Elinor sniffed, 'I shan't go to Hong Kong now, shall I? There's no point — I might as well stay here as anywhere.'

'Well, we'll see, deary; time to think about that later.'

Elinor nodded sleepily, but as she climbed obediently into

149

bed, she sensed a lurking feeling that was akin to relief mixed up with her sadness and anger. And, after Mary had soothed her and gone away, she thought that there would not be India now after all; but there was not any Reggie either – and he had loved her so. As she reached for a handkerchief to dry fresh tears, a gentle knock came on the door and Ryo tiptoed in.

She too held a handkerchief to her eyes, lips trembling. 'Oh, Elinor; poor, poor Elinor!' She flung herself on her knees by the bed. 'We are so shocked; so sad and angry, Kenjiro and I. He told me to come at once and say how ashamed we feel that our countrymen do this terrible thing to your man. Please, please don't blame us. The men who act so are evil, evil, and will be captured and killed. We disown them, as Japanese we despise them. Do you understand, do you, please?'

'Oh, Ryo – yes, of course; I don't blame you or your brother in the least bit. Why, I never thought to do so.' Elinor struggled upright, squeezing Ryo's hand.

'My brother is so raging at them he says his heart could burst, and me too. Oh, but I'm glad you understand – Mrs Fortescue says I mustn't stay two minutes. Come dear, I'll help you to sleep now.'

Ryo bent over, massaging Elinor's neck and back with gentle firmness. 'There, there, rest. Do not cry so any more,' she murmured on softly until she felt Elinor's tense knots of sorrow and pain dissolving as she slid down on the pillow, falling into a deep slumber.

At the funeral of Major Beale and Lieutenant Bradshaw, held two days later, Miss Elinor Mills, the chief mourner, bore herself with great dignity. Dressed in deep mourning, her fair hair hidden under an ugly black bonnet that framed her wan face, she roused the pity and sympathetic anger of all present – and there were many, for it was the most imposing ceremony of its kind yet held in Yokohama. Settlers of various nationalities, men from the visiting foreign ships and from each military corps, a row of high-ranking Japanese officials, all stood to silent attention as the regimental band struck up the funeral march, and mourning salvos boomed from the warships in the harbour. The settlers had been deeply shocked and frightened by the murders and, when even armed officers could be cut down in this brutal, haphazard fashion, it was no wonder they again went about their daily rounds with a prickle of fear down their spines at the thought of the *ronin*'s deadly swords, that could sever head from body in a single stroke.

CHAPTER EIGHT

In the eyes of the foreign diplomatic corps the worst aspect of the murders at Kamakura was that they had happened just before the planned expedition to Osaka to obtain the Emperor's sanction to the trade treaties. To cancel it at such a juncture would be playing into the hands of the anti-barbarian factions responsible; yet to proceed as if nothing of consequence had occurred could be construed as weakness. While the foreigners debated, the Japanese authorities began an extensive hunt for the killers, assuring Sir Harry that they would eventually be captured and brought to justice. Convinced of their good faith, the diplomats eventually departed in a large squadron of vessels – a peaceable but calculated demonstration of western sea power.

Percival and Arnold accompanied Sir Harry on the flagship *Royal Princess*; though Arnold was reluctant to leave, for after the funeral his sister had fallen into a state of what he vaguely diagnosed as nervous collapse. Elinor's misery was indeed acute, heightened as it was by an unacknowledged sense of guilt that her love for Reggie had been somehow wanting, that their engagement had been for her a period of unreality from which his death had released her. Clearly, she thought, huddled listlessly in an armchair on the wintry afternoon when she had been due to leave for Hong Kong and the wedding, she was not meant to marry. She had been seduced by promises of travel, romance, and her desire for children. She frowned at her reflection in the bedroom mirror – how frumpy and haggard she looked. She would wear tight ringlets, large spectacles, and a lace cap; would be the sensible Ellie,

153

the family spinster, her frugal life devoted to good causes . . .

Restlessly she slid back the window shutter and looked out on the street below leading from the Bund. Two scantily clad porters were standing against a hand-cart laden with boxes of provisions for the Consulate. 'Greedy foreign pigs.' The words floated up to her. 'Have you seen their monstrous bellies? They'll gobble this load in a jiffy. Four, five huge meals a day, they have – while we poor sods are lucky to get two bowls of rice and a bit of fish.' He sounded quite cheerful about it, however; and so did his companion, who answered, 'Oh, what does it matter? Let 'em stuff themselves sick while they can. They're all bound for the Hell of Hungry Ghosts eventually.'

The compound gate opened and the men pushed the cart forward, grunting in unison, the veins of their skinny bare legs standing out with effort. Then they stood mopping their faces with clean rags, chatting amiably with the guards. Elinor felt a rush of pure pleasure, at her own understanding of their words, at their cheery, hard-working, frugally-living kind. 'Oh, I must find a way of staying here,' she said aloud, wondering, even as she spoke, how she would persuade her brother of this.

The question did not arise immediately, for Arnold and Percival returned from Osaka in relaxed mood, the expedition having been a great success. 'A long feather in P.P.P.'s diplomatic cap,' Percival explained, when he came to see Elinor the day after their return. 'We were actually risking a showdown between the Shogun and Emperor by forcing them to agree on a united policy towards foreigners. And both sides kept trying to avoid the issue – a positive epidemic of "diplomatic sicknesses" broke out, I can tell you. But we just kept hopping from one ship to another, drinking more than was good for us and waiting for their perfectly sound healths to improve – which they eventually did. And the cream on the cake is that Minister Roches, our swash-buckling French friend, is still backing the Shogun's team, and I bet my Aunt Ada's best Sunday bonnet that he's got the wrong horse. Anyway, eventually the Japanese ran out of excuses, and everything has been signed, sealed, and ratified . . . Ah, excuse me . . .'

There was a knock at the door and Kenjiro Miyata came in with a sheaf of documents. 'I'm sorry to disturb you, Mr Storey, but I heard you were here and these are urgent . . .' He stopped, blushing. 'Miss Mills, I beg your pardon.'

Percy sighed. 'Lord love us, more papers. You should have seen the amount of official twaddle we took with us, Elinor. Foolscap by the ream, quill pens by the cartload, ink by the gallon, and enough red silk tape to tie Mount Fuji in a parcel.'

Elinor smiled, then composed her features, aware of Mr Miyata's keen look. He bowed with unusual deference. 'Miss Mills, I haven't had the chance to express personally my deep humiliation and anger at the terrible deed committed by my countrymen against you.' He spoke formally, but with growing assurance, in English.

'Thank you, Mr Miyata. But as I told your sister I certainly don't hold it against you or your country in general. The murderers were mad fanatics, I know.'

'Yes indeed, and I intend to do all in my power to bring them to justice. I shan't rest until they also are dead.' He stared at her with such fierce intensity that she could only falter, 'Sir Harry tells me they are known to be *ronin*; and the police are doing all they can.'

He bowed again. 'There are times when one determined man can do more than the whole police force.'

'Oh, pray be careful, Mr Miyata. The killers you seek are quite reckless – please don't take any risks on my behalf.'

'In such circumstances, madam, a true samurai doesn't consider risk. I assure you they will be apprehended soon. That is all that matters. Good day to you, Miss Mills.'

As he gave a final stiff bow and left, Percival laughed. 'There – a samurai in shining armour at your service, Elinor! I've never seen young Miyata in such fighting trim. You really should have offered him your glove – or a lock of your golden tresses, perchance.'

'Don't be silly, Percival, it's his national pride at stake, that's all. But I do hope he doesn't come to any harm.'

'So do I. We need him to wield the pen rather than the sword, say I. But the samurai spirit will out. I must look over this wretched stuff, I suppose.' He picked up the papers, and went out, leaving Elinor to her new worry: Mr Miyata was such a pleasant, handsome, intelligent, young man; it would be quite dreadful if he in turn and on her account were to fall victim to the *ronin*'s sword.

But Kenjiro, after seeing Elinor pale-faced and in mourning, did indeed feel imbued with the samurai spirit of his fore-fathers. He enlisted the help of three comrades from the Satsuma *yashiki*, and they spent many evenings prowling about Edo's principal post-stations, where they let it be discreetly known that a reward was offered for information regarding any stranger-*ronin* who were behaving suspiciously. Their luck was in. On a cold December night, as they lingered outside a tea-house in Shinagawa listening to the whine of a *samisen* in the sharp wind, a servant from the nearby Silver Feather Inn hurried up to say an unknown customer was making all sorts of wild threats against foreigners.

The landlord met them at the door, saying that if the hon-ourable gentlemen cared to enter his humble establishment they could hear the troublesome fellow for themselves and decide what to do. Leaving their long swords outside, but with daggers concealed in their sleeves, Kenjiro and his friends slipped unobtrusively into the dining room, crowded with men eating and drinking, cooks shouting, and boys running about with trays of soups and smoked eels held aloft. Dominant over the hubbub rose the voice of a proud-looking young man talking loudly to a circle of drinking companions.

Kenjiro listened for a while, then drew the landlord aside and told him to call the police immediately while they kept an eye on the fellow. His name, as he several times announced, was Shotoku, and, in between tossing back cups of warm *saké*, he was describing his visit to Yokohama several weeks before. There he had actually seen puffed-up foreign soldiers drilling and practising with fire arms alongside the Japanese.

'Even our government forces have sold out to the blasted hairy devils,' he cried. 'And now our only hope is for loyal patriots to band together and drive the barbarians from our sacred soil.'

At this point a pretty singing girl sitting beside Shotoku whispered a warning, and he looked across at the newcomers, his reddened eyes blazing. Kenjiro's throat tightened with fear, knowing he would be an instant target for the man's fury if his identity were known; but Shotoku simply glared, then turned his back on them. In an attempt to calm him down and lighten the atmosphere, the girl called for her *samisen* and offered to sing.

'Then let's have the song of the barbarians coming,' Shotoku shouted at her. 'It's the only one I'll listen to.'

She hesitated, then as he raised his fist at her, plucked the strings and began to sing in a melancholy but powerful falsetto that caused those around to fall silent.

> *'They came from the land of Darkness,*
> *Giants with hooked noses like mountain imps,*
> *Giants with rough hair loose and red.*
> *They stole a promise from our sacred Master,*
> *And danced with joy as they sailed away,*
> *Back to the distant land of Darkness.'*

As she finished, Shotoku laughed and stroked her hair. 'Well done – the song of a true patriot. Get yourself to the bed-chamber now and prepare to feel my weapon up you later. I can wield my cock and my steel as bravely as any man, and better than some, can't I, my sweet-plum?' He leered at her. 'And I've done my share of both, though I've not yet seen twenty-six summers.' The girl shrugged sullenly and slunk away, as Shotoku continued brazenly, 'Oh yes, I'm a samurai who's drawn barbarian blood with my swords and would again in such a righteous cause. I tell you the ancient glory of Japan is at stake – these odious foreign bastards behave like lords of the realm, riding about on horseback, buying up our gold and silks. Come now, who'll join me in taking an oath to hack to pieces any foreigner who crosses our path from this night forward?'

He rose unsteadily and lifted his cup; one man rose reluctantly also, but the others, looking embarrassed, began leaving the table.

'Cowards!' Shotoku spat at them. 'You're too scared of the authorities, aren't you? I'm the only samurai among you, masterless *ronin* though I am.'

As he stood there swaying and shouting, several policemen came rushing into the room and Kenjiro jumped up, pointing. 'Quick, officers, that's your man!' With amazing speed Shotoku drew a short sword from his sleeve and lunged towards Kenjiro, whose companions leaped to his defence just as fast. There was a wild scuffle and Shotoku went down under the combined onslaught of police and samurai, bellowing and fighting madly. As Shotoku's arms were trussed behind his head, Kenjiro showed the officer in charge his interpreter's card and was allowed to go along to the police station, where, in the early morning hours, the prisoner poured out a full confession. Yes, he had killed the two redcoated foreign-devil soldiers, coming up behind them and slashing them down. Right proud of the deed he was, too, asking only that he should now be permitted to die by his own hand like a true warrior.

Shotoku came of good northern samurai stock that had fallen on hard times; his father had been forced to sell all his ancestral heirlooms except his two swords. After his parents' death, he had wandered about the country aimlessly, hearing tales of poverty and hardship, and of the ignoble concessions the government was making to foreign invaders. He had managed to slip into Yokohama unobserved on the day of the military review, and what he had witnessed there fired his resolve. When leaving the settlement, he had fallen in with another young *ronin* who shared his sentiments (but whose name Shotoku refused to give), and the two of them had sworn a covenant unto death to kill as many foreigners as they could. They had lurked in the vicinity for two days; but the foreigners there were well guarded, so the two went to Kamakura to pray for the success of their mission at the temple of Hachiman, the god of warriors. They had come upon Beale

158

and Bradshaw by chance, and Shotoku's ancestral swords had not failed him.

Kenjiro's translation of Shotoku's confession was on Sir Harry Parkes' desk before noon the next day. Shortly thereafter Shotoku was sentenced by a Japanese court to be publicly executed like a common criminal; though the carrying-out of the sentence was delayed, while the search was continued for his accomplice. When this proved unavailing, the execution was ordered for the last day of the Japanese calendar year; and at the appointed hour, Arnold Mills and Percival Storey, in company with many other male settlers, made their way to a flat hill-top above Tobe prison, two miles outside Yokohama.

In due course, a number of government soldiers came riding up, and behind them was Shotoku, tied upright on a pony, looking cool and clean, his top-knot carefully dressed, a board round his neck proclaiming his crime and its punishment. Dismounting, he stared with icy disdain at the foreigners in the fenced enclosure, and the lines of artillery from the XXth Regiment flanking the edges of the execution ground. For a moment he looked above all their heads into the rays of a wintry afternoon sun; then he walked to the pit that had been made to receive his head and knelt on a mat at its brink. The executioner tied his loose sleeves up in readiness and flexed his bared arm muscles at the spectators while Shotoku asked leave to sing his death song.

Contorting his pale face into the threatening glare beloved of heroes and demi-gods, he chanted loudly, 'Now Shotoku must die for having killed the barbarians. It is a bitter day for Japan when a man is executed for such a patriotic deed. But I have no regrets and do not tremble in the face of death.' Then with a strong shrug he loosened his upper garments, revealing his neck and shoulders to the sword. He stretched his neck forward like a cormorant, bared his teeth, and cried loudly to the executioner, '*Yio.*' The blade flashed in the light; the artillery fired a single salvo; the head fell into the pit. By the time the settlers returned to Yokohama in the dusk, they saw, hanging above the bridge at the entrance to the native town, the moist, bleeding head of Shotoku impaled on an iron spike, its vengeful eyes finally closed.

Heavy snow fell during the celebrations of that New Year; skirts of the ladies' best kimonos were bedraggled as they went on customary visits to relatives; and their children screamed with laughter as they batted shuttlecocks through the whirling flakes. It was a time when the Miyatas felt their separation from their own kith and kin most acutely; and Ryo lapsed into a solitary, uncomplaining melancholy. But Kenjiro felt enlivened and unsettled rather than sad; for, in common with most of his countrymen, he loved New Year snow especially, with its clean, uncluttered promises of the future. Having been granted a well-earned week's leave, he indulged the unaccustomed pleasures of sleeping late, reading classical verse, and simply staring outside.

Thus he stood, looking out one wintry morning. Snow had been something of a beauteous rarity in the Kyushu of his childhood, so its very abundance here excited him. Wrapped in a gown of padded brocade, he watched the flakes build a fragile circle on the rim of the courtyard well; as he leaned outside to catch some on his tongue, the cold breeze rinsed his cheeks. He recited a famous *haiku* by the poet Rippo on earth's three loveliest things:

> *'I have seen moon and blossoms;*
> *Now I go to view the loveliest —*
> *The snow.'*

The poet had been on his deathbed, the snow symbolising his imminent departure from the world; but Kenjiro, softly repeating the death verse, gloried in his own pulsating sense of life.

He closed the window, and, looking into a mirror, scrubbed moisture from his cheeks, seeing how the frozen particles had settled on his black top-knot like a frill of lace. What an absurdity the thing was really, he thought as he dabbed it carefully with a towel. In his mind's eye he saw a similar top-knot on the head of the assassin Shotoku, thrown back in defiance, hung bloodied on a spike, a very symbol of old Japan, its

160

stubborn, short-sighted singularity. He began tugging at his own top-knot, gradually at first, then with a growing excitement till he impetuously threw off his house-robe, dressed, and hurried out.

An enterprising barber in Homuro Street had recently started a side-line in what his signboard proclaimed as, 'Random Cropping; Modern Style Hairs for Men'. The barber had removed two top-knots already that morning he told Kenjiro, as he made the decisive chop; it must be the weather. Honourable sir would feel a little naked at first, but he was adept at concealing the shaven part in front so that the transformation did not look so recent. Kenjiro nodded and paid him handsomely, exhilarated by the sight of his brand-new image in the glass. Then he went to Main Street, bought a military-style peaked cap and a pair of kid gloves in the foreign haberdashery, and lunched on tinned ham sandwiches and bottled beer in the recently opened Cosmopolitan Café.

Strolling homewards, feeling very pleased with himself, he saw Miss Mills emerge from the quarters she shared with her brother. She was wearing a blue cloak and ribboned bonnet, he noticed, thinking they suited her much better than the recent mourning garb. He hurried up to her, sweeping off his new cap with a revelatory gesture. 'Good afternoon, Miss Mills'

She turned, and a smile lit her whole face. 'Why, Kenjiro . . . I mean, Mr Miyata . . . surely you have . . . your hair?'

He nodded eagerly. 'Yes . . . You like?'

'It suits you very well indeed.'

He blushed and basked in her admiration. 'But what made you decide suddenly to . . .?'

'I don't know.' He looked at her ruefully. 'The weather, the New Year, another beginning.'

'All good reasons. Let me look at the back.'

He pivoted for her.

'Oh, it is quite fine!' She clapped her hands. 'Why, we must do something to celebrate. I know! I'm going to the dressmaker's this afternoon to get some brighter clothes made – a New Year beginning as you say. Sam's driving me

161

in the carriage. Have you ever ridden in it?'

'I haven't had the pleasure, madam.'

'Then you shall now. We'll take a little drive first. And you see it's stopped snowing, just for us,' she added as Sam drove up.

They sat side by side in the carriage and, on Elinor's directions, went along the Bund, up the Bluff, and along a section of the new road that led towards Mississippi Bay. Kenjiro was rigid with tension, both hoping and fearing that his interpreter colleagues might see him thus – sitting close to a foreign lady in a foreign carriage wearing his new cap. They spoke little; but Elinor, glancing at him, thought how splendidly the haircut had improved him, and how very handsome he would look when it had fully grown. Why, in one stroke he had become a proper young man; whereas before he had always looked a little quaint in her eyes, a figure on an old print, a little droll.

Reaching an open space at the end of the Bluff, they climbed down to look at the well-known view below. Roofs and balconies, arched bridges and jetty walls glittered white in a sudden burst of sunshine; the sea to their right shone also, as did the icy expanse of marshland behind the town where the main creek ran cold and clear.

'How quickly this port will grow, don't you think?' Elinor asked quietly. 'In thirty or forty years I'm sure we won't recognise it – if we're still alive to see.'

He smiled at her. 'In any case I hope your children will.'

'Oh, I don't think I . . .' she halted, realising that her recent decision to put all thoughts of marriage and children behind her would seem quite shocking to a Japanese. Also, she still wanted children; there was no doubt about it. She turned aside, absently flicking snowflakes off the dark green leaves of a camellia bush, wondering suddenly why Mr Miyata was not married either. Japanese males of his age usually were. She changed the subject briskly.

'Do you know the English vocabulary of snow, Mr Miyata? Icicle, snowdrift, snowflake? I admit I don't know the Japanese versions.'

162

'Snowfrake I forget.'

'With an "l", if you don't mind my correcting you. It is important.'

'Yes, the "l's" and "r's" are still very difficult.' He sighed ruefully and tried again: 'Snowfake.' They both laughed and he smote his forehead with his hand. 'Stupid me! Ah . . . a snowfake . . . let me see . . . a piece of white paper drifting down on a Kabuki stage to imitate a winter's night. Yes?'

She beamed at him, 'Why, how very clever, Mr Miyata. You have invented a perfectly good word, it should be added to our vocabulary instantly.'

He rolled his tongue right back. 'Flake – yes?' Scooping some snow from the bush, he took her hand, rolling back her glove, and pressed the damp substance into her warm palm. 'I give you many snowflakes for many happy New Years. We Japanese love them, so beautiful and quick-fading-away, like cherry blossom.'

'Or life.' She stared at her hand where his had briefly rested.

'Of course,' he agreed solemnly. 'That is part of the beauty.'

She smiled into his eyes, drawing her glove back on.

The sky was darkening again and new flakes began drifting slowly down. One settled on a curl of her tawny hair that had escaped from her blue bonnet; others fell on her blue cloak.

'Sometimes I wish I were a snowflake instead of a man. Much more quick and easy,' he said.

She squared her shoulders. 'Oh come, Mr Miyata – much less interesting though, surely? Shall we go; it's beginning to snow again.'

During the short ride downhill they were silent with intense happiness. Kenjiro had re-arranged the rugs so that their legs were covered in one bundle instead of two, and, feeling her thighs warm and close to his under the covers, he imagined her whole body in a detail that was quite shameless. The ride, he thought, had been like the first bud of white cherry-blossom; and beyond that he dare not think.

The day after her ride with Kenjiro, acting on an idea that had been forming for some time, Elinor went to see Mrs

Hubbard to suggest that she and Ryo between them might manage to teach some classes in the school she had recently opened. Mrs Hubbard was delighted, and Elinor, having agreed to work for a small percentage of the students' fees, prepared to start at once. Presented with this *fait accompli*, Arnold huffed and puffed more than a little; for though he was fond of his sister, whose presence added a pleasing feminine charm to his bachelor establishment, it had one distinct drawback. His secret liaison with Yasu had blossomed in the past year, but it was difficult to spend nights away with her without Elinor's knowledge. His sister's questions about his work and whereabouts were prompted, he knew, by a totally innocent interest, but she would have been deeply shocked to discover that he kept a native mistress. So he had continued to lie, assuming she would soon be leaving.

Now she was staying; Yasu was pregnant; it was deuced awkward. But Arnold, who always took the line of least resistance, especially where women were concerned, simply told Elinor he would have to write to their parents, who would probably instruct him to send her home. Elinor accepted the reprieve without protest and threw herself into the process of teaching and earning money of her very own for the first time in her life. For Ryo, trained to a female status of subservience and inferiority, it was very difficult at first to take on the authoritative role of teacher; but with Elinor's help she began learning to be self-confident, and their classes soon became popular and overcrowded.

The rapid growth of the Hubbards' school during the first months of '66 coincided with a general period of expansion of Yokohama. The first Chamber of Commerce was formed by leading gentlemen merchants, while the military gentlemen organised the first Rifle Association – competitions to be held according to Wimbledon rules. Mr George Smith of the Municipal Council opened a market garden to provide settlers with flavour-full vegetables grown from best English and American seeds; he now proposed starting a dairy, for, as he wrote in the *Herald*, 'The native dislike of good fresh milk and the consequent lack of it is deeply felt by foreign residents.'

The first essential for such a venture was obviously cows. And so on a bright spring day, a certain Mr Rolph Risley from California, ex-circus-owner, acrobat, cattle-puncher, billiard champion, and gold-digger, sailed into port on his trading schooner *Ida Rogers* with six cows and their calves aboard. Quite a crowd gathered to watch the momentous arrival. Among them were Elinor and Ryo, and Felix Coburn, who was skulking about in a mood of aimless disappointment. He had recently heard from Professor Tobias Clark that the Ainu remains he had acquired with great difficulty and in great hope were of no discernible scientific value after all. Unfortunately, Clark had written, a thorough examination of the bone structures had shown a disheartening lack of similarities to the Neander skull. Further investigations were under way, but the outlook was not promising. Felix, his dreams of scientific fame dwindling, had passed on the sorry news to Harold Rayne by the season's first mail to Hakodate and was now awaiting a reply from him and, more importantly, a letter from Harold's wife.

Meanwhile there was little to do except deal in the trivia of silkworm-eggs and take what pleasure he might in the events of the small community – such as the spectacle of the sixth large milch cow slung in a net and lowing fearfully as she was lifted from the *Ida Rogers'* deck to the jetty. As her hooves touched *terra firma* and she gazed with mournful reproach through the meshes at the assembled crowd, Rolph Risley came hurrying down the gangplank, a hefty man sucking a cheroot and looking harassed.

Reporters of the port's rival newspapers hurried forward with notebooks at the ready, and Risley, never averse to publicity, stuck his thumbs in his braces and gave them a dramatic account of how the vessel had been blown right off course for ten days in the Pacific and water supplies had run out. The cows, driven mad with thirst, had licked the very deck-boards in search of moisture and, in agony to see the poor dumb creatures suffer so, he had been about to throw them overboard and himself with them, why not? – when the rains came. For twenty-four hours he worked like a drag-horse and collected six thousand gallons of water with his own hands — here he held up his large ham-fists for approval — and the beasts were saved. And a fine herd they were too and, he reckoned, all Yokohama needed now was a few beehives to make it a land flowing with milk and honey.

Several settlers who had gathered to listen clapped Risley's performance, and Elinor, finding herself next to Felix, laughed. 'Well, Mr Coburn, now you know what to venture next!'

'Silk and honey, hey?' he grimaced. 'Sounds like some exotic oriental paradise, doesn't it? Not that it fits Yokohama.'

Disgruntled as usual, Elinor thought irritably. Mary Fortescue had hinted the other day that it was time she bestirred herself to interest Mr Coburn, who was obviously pining for feminine companionship. But he was far too difficult, moody, and airy-fairy, Elinor had protested, and an ordinary down-to-earth mortal like herself would never please him for long. Remembering the conversation, she was about to move away when Kenjiro approached. He was accompanied by a short, wiry man with a pock-marked face who was busily drawing a sketch of the cow in the net. He was dressed in Japanese-style clothes, embellished with a silk muffler and a felt hat of western manufacture.

'A moment, Miss Mills, Mr Coburn . . . Here is someone you both wanted to meet I think? Mr Taneo Takahashi.'

Kenjiro introduced them proudly, adding offhandedly, 'Oh, and this is my sister, Ryo.'

Ryo, quietly in the background, bowed deferentially; she was used to being ignored. The jetty being crowded with spectators, porters and bellowing animals, they decided to go to the Cosmopolitan Café and, as they walked along the Bund, Felix asked, 'I gather from Mr Miyata that you are an expert on "western things", Mr Takahashi? Is that why you've come here today — to see the beginning of Japan's first dairy?'

'Yes and no, Mr Coburn. Yes. No.' He spat his words quickly in a torrent with brief pauses between, and his English, though fluent, was difficult to follow. 'Not the dairy only, but the drinking of milk, eating of beef interests me. To

Japanese such practices are rather disgusting, as you probably know. Yet this may have bad effects on our minds. This is the café, yes?'

'Minds, did you say, Mr Takahashi?' Elinor inquired, puzzled, drawing up a chair inside, next to him.

'Ha, Miss Mills. I miss a thought. It is bad habit of mine. Such a hurry I am always in. Foreign doctors say eating meat and milk helps to make western peoples big and strong, no?' He shot out a skinny arm from his loose-sleeved jacket. 'Now look at me — I am like a dwarf-sparrow beside Mr Coburn here, and most of my countrymen are same. We have to look up at foreigners all the time and we feel physical inferiority with them. And this has bad mental effect . . . we are servile or stiff in your company. I want new generation of Japanese to be taller and stronger, more like Kenjiro here, who is exception, being a Satsuma-born man. Not so we can fight or carry weapons, you understand; this is mere primitive reason. But so our heads are held higher and we feel more comfortable with ourselves. To talk on equal level with western nations. That is important for the mind. You understand now, Miss Mills?' He smiled in a way that lit up his ugly face and brilliant, darting eyes.

'Perfectly, thank you, Mr Takahashi, and I quite agree. It is these secret feelings of inferiority and weakness that sometimes lead to hatred, fear, and outbreaks of violence, is it not?' She sighed as Felix broke in, 'Speaking as a student of Mr Darwin, Mr Takahashi, it seems to me that you Japanese possess a large measure of that valuable quality of adaptability to change which is surely far more important for survival and progress than mere brute strength? Take the Ainu, whom I recently visited — fine muscular figures of men — but what else?'

'Yes, Mr Coburn, that is so. And certainly we educated Japanese are opening our minds very quickly to the wide world and have great potential for power. But it is duty of we few who understand to make sure our national energies are right-directed and not hindered by ignorance and super-stition. Why, I have an old maid-servant in my own household who blames everything that goes wrong on the barbarians – even the weather is worse since you came, she says!' He chuckled and bit into one of the cream buns that Felix had ordered with their coffee, then he pulled a wry face, but continued munching as if in penance.

'It's artificial cream you know; the cows haven't started milk production yet.' Felix was amused. 'And I think you are eating for strength, not pleasure?'

Ryo, seated beside him, whispered, 'Oh, please don't criticise Mr Takahashi; he's a very celebrated man, you know.'

Takahashi, if he heard, ignored her, saying solemnly, 'I try to adapt to new circumstances, Mr Coburn. It is very important, as you say. Perhaps cream buns are good for me and one day may be sold all over Edo. It is more economical to like food that is readily available.' As he continued steadfastly chewing, Kenjiro, who stood in considerable awe of him, ventured, 'Mr Coburn is the man I told you of, who thinks many foreign traders are indeed money-grubbers, scraping about for every tiny coin, *sensei*. He doesn't admire their greedy lust for profit.'

'*Ah-so* . . .' He gave Felix a shrewd glance. 'It may well be so regarding your western people, Mr Coburn; but we Japanese have oppressed and scorned our merchants class for so long that now they need to be lifted up and made to feel their calling is honourable. Then they feel proud to export goods to earn more money. Without wealth a nation can have no self-respect. And I say that, though I am not a materialist at heart. But the attitude of mind is important, is it not?' Swallowing the last lick of cream from his lips as if it were a pill and wiping vestiges from his beard, he smiled at Elinor. 'That was not very nasty. Now you please excuse me, ladies and gents. I have much to do before the gates close this evening. Some new foreign books have arrived at Winterton's store. Your Thomas Huxley's essays I look for. He has written, I believe, on whether there is an absolute connection between the theory of evolution and the inevitability of human progress?' He bowed jerkily without waiting for an answer and hurried off, pulling his faded robe around his skinny frame as he went.

'A real character,' Felix grinned.

'But he is a famous man,' Ryo reproved him. 'His book about western things is selling in thousands.'

'Did you like him, Miss Mills?' Kenjiro asked anxiously.

'Yes, I did, truly – he's lively and clever, and he talks very openly and directly for a Japanese, does he not?'

'It's because he's in such a hurry to express his ideas and learn more. He hasn't time for all the double-meanings and circumlocutions our scholars usually indulge in, and many dislike him for it. They say he's a crude populist, a cheap orator. But we need more like him and I admire greatly what he does.'

'And how is it he has become such an expert on western matters, and speaks so fluently – with such an odd accent?'

'He was a government official until recently and went to America with our very first delegation. The country greatly impressed him – their democratic government, ideas of equality and freedom – and he is in a constant fervour to spread the same gospel here.'

'Such enthusiasm – one forgets how ugly he is when he is talking, no?' Ryo murmured. The three of them had lapsed into the mixture of Japanese and English they often used together, and Felix, feeling excluded, rose to leave. Ryo also rose, saying, 'I hope I do not offend you, Mr Coburn?'

'Hey? Oh, not at all. You were right to chide me for speaking lightly of a famous man. Good-day to you,' he added to Elinor and Kenjiro, who were so deep in conversation that they hardly noticed his departure.

Pity he could not take to Miss Mills rather more, he thought irritably as he paid the bill. A perfectly pleasant young lady, quite pretty. Young Miyata seemed to find her quite fascinating; but then the Japanese thought all western women were wondrous and mysterious, apparently. For Felix though, Elinor held no hint of mystery or melancholy; not in the least like Honoria. His spirits sank again with loneliness and desire. Surely within a week or so the first mailboat of the season must return from Hakodate and then, at last and at least, he would have some news of her?

It was the afternoon of April 14th when a friendly broker mentioned to Felix that the *Northern Star* had arrived from Hakkaido that morning and its cargo. was now being unloaded. Letters from outlying ports were delivered to Yokohama's residents by Customs House runners, and he waited fretfully for the early evening delivery; but nothing came – not even a letter from Harold. Felix could hardly believe it and, after supper, strolled down to the Customs House to see what he could find out. The offices were all shut and he wandered along the deserted quay, staring at the black sea, biting his lips in fury and disappointment. Honoria must have decided to end their liaison without even a word of explanation. He had behaved like a foolish puppy, believing her protestations of affection. She was just a bored, beautiful woman and any man who had happened to turn up at the time would have done as well.

He gripped his cane tensely and marched along the Bund, staring without pleasure at the lively evening scene. The *Oriana*, a passenger steamer on the China-Japan run, was in port, its decks strung with lights, and a group of sailors on the quarter-deck were playing fiddles and singing. The sounds of their merriment grated on his over-wrought nerves and he turned his steps towards the Hotel de l'Europe for a much-needed drink. Approaching the front entrance, he stopped to straighten his collar and heard a familiar voice above him. 'Felix, it is you, isn't it?'

He looked at a woman's vague shape leaning over a first floor balcony. 'Honoria – oh, Honoria, it's you, isn't it?'

'Yes. I happened to see you passing.'

'But are you alone?'

'Ye-es.' She seemed to hesitate. As he stood gazing fervently upward he had a sudden absurd memory of a school play when he had once acted Romeo; Meadows Minor, was it not, had played Juliet? Meadows Minor . . . he grimaced with nostalgic pain for that innocent time – all the boys sniggering behind their hands at lovers' agonies. 'Then I'll come up. Which room?'

'Twelve . . . but . . .'

'No "buts" ', he thought, as he raced through the hotel lobby and up the stairs, afire with a Romeo's desire to hold his beloved in his arms again.

She opened the door at his knock and then stood deliberately back. 'Honoria –' He held out his arms and then faltered. Her features had lost their fine-drawn outline, and so had her figure. The flowing dressing-gown she wore, though loose, could not conceal the large protrusion of her abdomen; compared to the slim hourglass he had often squeezed the previous summer, it looked monstrous, even obscene.

'Honoria . . . you . . .'

'Come in, Felix. Yes, I am, as you see, very pregnant.'

He closed the door and kissed her gently; her lips felt dry and small. He stared at her numbly.

'You are wondering, I expect, when the baby is due?' she asked coolly, though he had not, in fact, had time to formulate anything so precise. 'Would you like some port? I drink it on doctor's orders to keep up my strength.' The bottle stood on a bamboo table beside a large, half-eaten chocolate and cream sponge in a box; crumbs were littered around. She said defensively, 'I haven't tasted real cream for ages and there's little point in worrying about my figure at the moment.'

'The dairy has just opened. The cows came over from California,' he said mechanically, thinking these signs of unleashed greed so unlike her. He raised the glass she handed him. 'Oh, it's wonderful to see you again, Honoria! I've missed you dreadfully.' He looked into her eyes; then away, to avoid seeing below her neckline.

She sat on the bed's edge, a lumpish mass with a pale, care-worn face. 'The voyage was absolutely dreadful,' she whispered. 'I was so flung about – I was utterly terrified of . . . well, you know . . .'

He knelt, taking her limp hands in his. 'Oh Honoria, Honoria, I'm sorry. I'd never dreamed : . . I mean if . . .' He paused, not knowing how to put it.

'. . . if it is yours . . .' She laughed faintly and turned away, speaking to the lamp flickering beside the bed. 'The Russian

171

doctor in Hakodate thinks the child was conceived in early August. That was before you left.' She paused; continued, effortfully. 'But during that time Harold was . . . claiming his usual marital rights. I hated it . . . hated him, but had I refused his suspicions would certainly have been aroused. So . . . I've often remembered recently a newspaper report I once read about some lower-class woman saying in court, "Well I can't rightly be sure who the father is, m'lord judge." ' Bitterly she imitated a Cockney accent, and, taking her hands from his, covered her eyes. 'How shameful, I thought then, little imagining that one day I . . .'

He smoothed her hair. 'Oh, Honoria, please don't think such things, not someone like you.'

She said fiercely, 'I'm sure it's your child, Felix, sure in my bones. I want it to be so much.'

'Then do you want me to . . .? Well, what do you want?' He looked at her beseechingly.

'I honestly don't know at the moment, dearest, beyond having a healthy child. And that may not be easy − after all this buffeting about; and I lost my first, as you know. That's why I came south on the first ship. I saw Dr Mills this afternoon. He isn't very happy about my condition and says I must leave on the *Oriana* tomorrow for the Mission Hospital at Chefoo for the confinement. There are no proper facilities to deal with any complications here.'

'So you weren't going to see me at all?' he blurted.

'Oh, Felix, I longed to see you; but I was so exhausted this evening and the endless winter has pulled me down terribly, as the doctor said. I thought the last one was bad enough . . . but this . . .' She grasped his hands tightly again. 'Thank you, thank you for the piano, dearest. Without that I believe I really would have died.'

'It was the least I could do,' he murmured, raising her tear-stained face. 'So you're going away again at once?'

'Felix, I have to for the baby's sake. I planned to see you in the morning when I'd gained a little strength, but I walked out on the balcony for some air − and there you were. I couldn't resist calling you!' She smiled, stroked his cheek.

172

He kissed the stroking hand and went to pour another port. 'Oh, this is terrible . . . I feel so sorry and helpless. Of course you must get the best possible medical care, darling. I only wish I could come to Chefoo with you, but I suppose Harold assumes . . .?'

'Of course, he's cock-a-hoop. A son at last, he says,' she imitated his jovial tone. Heaving herself from the bed, she added, 'Oh, and he sent you a note, to thank you for the piano, he said.'

He stuffed it carelessly in his pocket and poured her more port, which she drank down like medicine. 'Honoria, what can I do?'

'There's nothing at the moment, Felix; and this reunion, which should have been so joyous, is painful for us both, as I knew it would be. I both longed and dreaded to see you, to tell you everything – honestly.'

'You've been very honourable, Honoria, and always would be.'

She bowed her head at the compliment, 'But now you must go, my dear; this is a small place and someone is bound to have spotted you coming up here.'

'But do you want me to? I'll stay all night and just hold your hand, if you wish, darling.'

She touched his nose with a ringed finger. 'Don't sound like a love-sick puppy, Felix. This is scarcely the time to start a settlement scandal. Yes, go, please.' She sat back wearily on the bed and he kissed her gently. 'I may come in the morning and see you off later?'

'Oh, yes, please do that, dear.' They touched each other like invalids remembering healthier times and then he stole discreetly away.

Felix returned to the hotel fairly early in the morning, but had been forestalled by Arnold, who was at Honoria's bedside mixing a potion. Elinor and Mary Fortescue, who had been told of Honoria's plight, arrived soon thereafter, and the interval before her sailing was devoted to medical attention, feminine concern, and polite conversation. Felix, left on the side-lines, could think of nothing better to do than buy great bunches of flowers and fill Honoria's cabin with them. The *Oriana* sailed at dusk, and Felix and Honoria had opportunity for no more than a surreptitious kiss before the warning departure bells rang. Mary Fortescue, standing with Elinor on the quayside, watched Felix hurry down the gangplank and away without a word to them.

'I wonder?' she said softly, remembering the flower-filled cabin; but Elinor pretended not to understand.

Back in his lodgings, Felix threw himself in an armchair and, digging his hands in his pockets, discovered Harold's note. Harold was extremely sorry to hear the disappointing news, 'on the Ainu front,' as he put it. 'But was it conclusive? Perhaps one should try other avenues? . . . Not give up hope yet?'

'Silly devil,' Felix muttered aloud, flinging the note in the wastepaper basket and going to pour himself a stiff drink, hoping his beloved did not feel as miserable as he did.

But Honoria, feeling the dreaded rise and fall of the sea as the *Oriana* left the bay, was indeed miserable. She sat in her cabin, staring sombrely at the array of flowers stuck in jugs and vases around her, which reminded her forcibly of a funeral parlour and only added to her sense of foreboding about the voyage ahead and the ordeal of birth that awaited her.

CHAPTER NINE

During that same summer of 1866, Sir Harry Parkes, living up to his reputation for energetic diplomacy, arranged a visit to the south-west. Its purpose was primarily political, for Parkes was anxious to cement the friendly relationships that already existed between the British and the Satsuma and Choshiu clans. To preserve the façade of non-interference in the country's internal affairs, Parkes wanted the tour to appear as something of a holiday; and so, in addition to the usual entourage of interpreters, secretaries, and medical attendants, Lady Parkes was of the party. She, protesting at the scarcity of female company, asked Elinor to come; and Elinor, without asking anyone, made room in her cabin for Ryo, who longed to see her home province again.

They sailed in three vessels, the flagship *Corsair* commanded by Admiral Drew, and HMS's *Serpent* and *Salamis*, and reached Kagoshima Bay on a glorious day in late July. The pellucid sea was a-sparkle; wisps of smoke from the Sakurajima volcano puffed harmlessly away in the sunshine; fishermen called cheerily from white-sailed boats as they passed; peasants on the terraced fields stopped work to wave as the ships dropped anchor. A welcoming salute of fifteen guns was then fired from the fort near the town, and the flagship rattled off a suitable response.

Percival Storey, standing next to Arnold on the main deck, grinned. 'Not quite like the last time we were here. Amazing changes that just three years have wrought, ain't it?'

Arnold nodded. 'What a wild day that was – and all because of poor old Charlie Richardson. Must be getting on for four years since he was killed. I hadn't been here long and had never seen a man cut to pieces by swords before. Strange how time slips by.'

Percival wagged a finger. 'Now, Arnold, don't wax too profound on a day like this. See − the sun shines, all is sweetness and jollity, every sword is sheathed. And tomorrow, the Chief says, we are to attend a feast of sumptuous dimensions at the Prince's summer villa.'

Accordingly, the next morning, those invited to the banquet arrayed themselves in their best finery and were carried ashore in the Satsuma state barge, which was bedecked with flowers and coloured banners. Elinor, one of the selected few, was in a fever of excited interest to see the town about which she had heard so much from the Miyatas. Ryo did not rate an invitation; but her brother was one of the interpreters. He was sweating apprehensively as they reached the quay where the Prince of Satsuma and his entourage were waiting.

They were dressed in formal robes of state, wide, loose gowns of blue, black, and golden silks decorated with the Satsuma crest, the whole magnificent ensemble topped with black gauze-winged hats. The British shook hands, the Japanese bowed courteously. Kenjiro, lingering in the rear, felt a sudden paroxysm of sheer panic at the sight of the Prince. His grandfather, the temple magistrate, had been granted an audience with his liege-lord once a year, and this had been a matter for great pride in the family. His father, a mere gunnery officer, had never been admitted into the hallowed presence. Now the Prince, son of the present liege-lord, stood waiting to greet him.

Kenjiro felt his knees buckling and impulsively sank down, touching his cropped head on the stones. 'My lord,' he murmured. 'My lord . . .'

'Ah − old habits die hard, you see.' Percival nudged Elinor as they walked towards the lacquered palanquins that were to carry them in state through the town. She turned; seeing Kenjiro so crumpled she thought, for an alarmed second, that he had collapsed; but then he performed a profound obeisance before moving on. 'Oh yes, they do indeed; how amusing!'

176

she murmured, though she did not find the spectacle of that profoundly feudal posture truly amusing. Rather, it slightly upset her – touching, certainly; but also rather a little . . . pitiable?

However, there was no time to ponder the matter, for Lady Parkes beckoned her over to introduce a dapper-looking westerner with a goatee beard who had been standing on the quay when they arrived.

'Elinor, this is Mr Desmond Hand. I think you'll know of him? It's largely thanks to his powers of organisation and conciliation that we are here.'

'Why, yes indeed – delighted, Mr Hand. You live in Nagasaki, I believe? And you are a friend of the Shimazu family here?' She did not add that Percival dubbed him 'The Hand with Fingers in a Thousand Pies', though she smiled broadly at the recollection.

He doffed his straw hat with a courtly gesture. 'And I am indeed pleased to make your acquaintance, Miss Mills. Everything I've heard about you is good.'

'Really? Then I must congratulate you on your sources of information, though I hesitate to vouch for their accuracy.' She flushed slighty.

'Entirely accurate, madam, I can see. But our attendants are waiting. May I help you into one of these dreadful little carrying-boxes? It may be an honour to ride in one, but a common man's litter is far more comfortable.'

This Elinor quickly proved, as she, her voluminous dress and hooped over-skirt, her broad be-ribboned bonnet and parasol all had to be stuffed somehow into a palanquin. The vehicle smelled unpleasantly of warm lacquer, and, hunched uncomfortably on a velvet cushion, she felt rather like a large animal in a small cage. Peering through the narrow lattice she saw the bearers lift the pole attached to the roof and soon she, in company with the rest of the party, was swinging gently in procession through Kagoshima. Everything she could see was clean, bright, and well maintained – shops, tree-lined streets, bridges, and canals, the tile-topped outer walls of merchants' compounds – and the whole route was lined with silent, orderly citizens in their best going-out clothes, for it was a special occasion, and many had not seen any Europeans before.

The Prince's summer villa was, however, a disappointment. to Elinor. She had expected something rather royal; what she saw was a number of neat, single-storey buildings with tiled roofs, polished-wood pillars and covered verandahs. The surrounding gardens, however, were spacious and beautiful, with flowering shrubs, mossy banks, and ornamental trees clipped flat as table-tops, backed by steep wooded hills overlooking the blue bay with the volcano on its further side. The banquet was laid inside a western-style marquee complete with cutlery, champagne glasses, and white starched napkins, though the food was purely Japanese.

Perched on stools at some distance from the guests of honour, Elinor, Arnold, and the captain of the *Salamis* were served, by a number of deferential but determined servants, a seemingly endless procession of lacquered trays filled with bowls and saucers. There came prawns and mushrooms, cold lampreys, cold bonito with salted plums, wild boar soup, sliced chicken breasts with bamboo pickles, fried trout with green ginger, raw cuttlefish, cooked lobsters with seaweed savouries, cucumbers and *bêche de mer*, vermicelli and beancurd soup, seaweed jellies, preserved red beans, sugared apples, almonds, conserves of chestnuts, yellow and pink sweetmeats and red-berry syrup, all washed down with copious draughts of champagne and bitter green tea. Eventually as Elinor was beginning to feel quite faint with the quantities of food and drink, the heat, and the noise and clatter backed by a *samisen* and pipe band, the diners at the top table rose, and everyone was free to flock into the gardens.

'Phew!' Arnold mopped his brow and, 'Whoops!' he added, nearly crashing on to a diminutive bridge that arched a pond glinting with golden carp and water-lilies. 'Lord, I do feel like Gulliver in Lilliput sometimes. All those twiddly titbits of heaven knows what and nothing for a fellow to get his teeth into. I'd have given anything for a comfortable chair, a mug of beer, and a slab of rump steak!'

His irritation was feigned; but sometimes it was real enough. Flimsy chairs, bedsteads, and chests seemed to collapse at the very sight of him; screens fell out of their grooves in sheer panic as his large fingers touched them. Physically cast in the role of red-haired, huge barbarian, he often guyed it, perversely exaggerating his naturally loud voice and clumsy movements to hide his self-consciousness, in a manner that terrified his servants.

Elinor, guessing this, smiled at him. 'Spoken like a true barbarian, brother mine.'

He snorted. 'It's all very well for you ladies – everything is your size – small, dainty, and feminine.'

'Be careful – the hot-blooded Satsuma samurai might take that for an insult.'

'Well, there's one over there; but I think we'll be safe with him.'

'Oh, Mr Miyata – let's go and talk to him. He must know a lot about this place.' Elinor moved off, but Arnold was waylaid by the *Salamis*' captain bringing a longed-for beer.

Kenjiro was staring tensely at a long, smooth lawn shaded by palms, camphor, and cinnamon trees, where a shining brook bordered with ornamental grasses twisted among a number of flat rocks; a perfectly swept stone path led to a clump of green-grey bamboos on the hill beyond. Elinor began tentatively, 'Isn't it absolutely lovely here? You must have seen it before?'

He looked up with a start. 'Oh, Miss Mills . . . No, I was never permitted before. And yes, it is very beautiful.'

'But you don't look as if you're enjoying the scene, if I may say so, Mr Miyata?'

He evaded her eyes with a little laugh. 'It is a bit difficult for me here, that is all.' He clenched his hands at the difficulty of how awed and discomforted he had felt during the banquet, having to interpret between the Prince and Admiral Drew. The occasion had brought the many conflicts of his life into painful focus, and he had been tongue-tied, searching for words, hardly daring to address the Prince directly. The Prince, for his part, was quite used to meeting foreigners and had been at ease with the Admiral, though impatient with Kenjiro's apparent ineptitude at interpretation.

Now Kenjiro was in an agony of self-recrimination at his poor showing before the Prince, whom he had been so anxious to impress favourably. He yearned to rush back to him, knock his forehead on the ground, explain how it was that he had come to this – a cropped-hair lackey in the westerners' employ, scarcely recognisable as his father's son. He desired the understanding and forgiveness of his Prince more ardently than anything in the world just then; but he could not possibly explain any of this to Miss Elinor Mills, and so stood in stiff silence, wishing she would go away.

But she did not; instead she bent down, trailing a hot hand in the cool water of the brook. 'You must know a lot about this villa, Mr Miyata – its history and so on?'

He made an effort to be civil. 'It has been a summer resort of the Shimazu family for generations. In this part of the garden it is said that the twenty-first Lord of Shimazu, Yoshitake, used to hold poem-creating parties. Guests sat on those flat rocks and had to complete the composition of a *haiku* in the time that a large cup of *saké* came floating to them on the waters of the stream.'

'What a lovely idea! And if they didn't manage it?'

'Oh, I don't know; they probably had to pay a silly forfeit.' He had lost interest in her again, and she was about to give up the conversation when Desmond Hand came briskly across the grass. 'Ah – I see you've found the most delightful spot in the entire grounds, Miss Mills.' He affected surprise, though he had come deliberately in search of her.

'Mr Miyata was just telling me about the poem-creating parties held here in the past.'

'Ah, yes – what civilised pastimes! Though hardly conducive to the good of the common man. The present Lord Shimazu is of a more practical bent. Have you seen the manufactory buildings he's established here?'

'No, there hasn't been time.'

'Then come – we must show her, Miyata.'

The three of them strolled along a gravel path behind the

villa to the other side of the grounds, where there was a smelting furnace built in 1856 by the former Lord of Satsuma after a Dutch model. Agricultural and domestic implements were made there; also gunpowder and cannon – some of which had been turned against the British ships three years before. 'Several of these earlier industrial enterprises were destroyed by us Brits during the Kagoshima bombardment,' Hand explained. 'Though the Japanese are much too polite to mention it now. But the present Lord Shimazu has certainly been persuaded – partly by our example – of the benefits of western technology,' he continued. 'Fourteen of his brightest young samurai are in Europe at this very moment, studying engineering, navigation, and military science; and I've heard they've recently ordered machinery for a cotton-spinning mill to be built here also.'

'We Satsumas are determined to follow a policy of wealth and strength, Miss Mills,' Kenjiro said, forgetting his personal trouble in general pride at his clan's achievements. 'We're increasing our trade with foreign countries and improving our military forces with the profits, quite in the western style!'

Hand winked. 'Which policy is a matter of no small concern to the government, hey, Miyata?'

'Er . . . yes, sir.' Backing away from such a ticklish political subject, Kenjiro suggested they return to the marquee. As they came round the front of the villa, Elinor commented again on the beauty of the place and indeed of everything she had so far seen in Kagoshima. Desmond Hand smiled. 'Miss Mills, I can tell that you, like myself, are a true lover of this country and its delightful people. Nor did you allow the recent tragedy in your life to embitter you. You did not, as many women would, flee the country after your fiancé's assassination with hatred towards all Japanese in your heart. I think that is most admirable, Miss Mills, and I wanted to tell you so personally.'

She stopped, reddening at his praise. 'Why, how kind of you to say such a thing, Mr Hand! No one else has! You are right; yes, I do like Japan and its people very much and I'm glad I didn't run away immediately after Reginald's assassination.

Though how much longer I shall be able to stay I don't quite know.'

'I hope it will be for a very long time; and if you ever need help in that direction, you can count on me. I hope you'll come and meet my wife and child in Nagasaki one day,' he added as they reached the refreshment tent, where the British guests, though still utterly replete, were nibbling valiantly on preserved fruits before returning to their respective ships.

That evening, Kenjiro took advantage of the geniality induced by the day to obtain leave of absence for a brief visit to his relatives, and he and Ryo set off early the next morning. Considering their last meeting with Uncle Gengoro they resolved to avoid him and spend the few available hours with their brother Kentaro and his family. This much at least was their duty, and they were also anxious to procure a few mementoes of their dead mother. They suspected this would not be easy; indeed they feared the encounter would be generally tricky – and they felt anxious as they jolted, in hired chairs, along the hill-tracks that led to the Imamura valley.

Kenjiro had assumed that even the inhabitants of this quiet backwater would know of the visit of the foreign ships to nearby Kagoshima, so that his brother's household might be expecting him. But they had more important matters to think about, and everyone was busy. The older men and women were sitting out in the farm compound, weaving straw sandals, horseshoes, and ropes, mending wooden buckets and tools, while the able-bodied were in the fields spreading about a liquid mixture of fish-oil and vinegar in an effort to check a serious infestation of winged insects. It was threatening the entire crop, Fumio explained, after greeting them on the house-verandah, bowing coldly, concealing her surprise. A servant was sent to fetch Kentaro from the fields, and in the interim they exchanged polite formalities about the family while Fumio handed round tea and chestnut sweetmeats. Ofuku's first-born son was thriving and a second was on the way, she said, her cool glance flickering between Ryo and Kenjiro as she added, 'We expected to hear news of your marriage plans before now?'

'I'm kept too busy to attend to such matters,' Kenjiro replied stiffly, and quickly changed the subject to shield Ryo, whose continuing spinsterhood was a nagging worry.

At that point Kentaro arrived; he was hot and dusty and regaled them with details of the loathsome habits and appetites of the ravenous insects. He evinced neither pleasure at his relatives' appearance nor curiosity about their lives, beyond asking whatever had possessed Kenjiro to have his hair cut in such a barbarous fashion. By the time Fumio summoned them to the midday meal, Kenjiro and Ryo felt extremely depressed, realising how great the gulf had become between them and this once familiar rural life they had left behind.

Nor did Fumio improve their spirits by launching into a tirade about the harshness of the times. They could seldom afford fresh fish these days, she said, doling out with sour satisfaction a soup of vegetable and beancurd, and the insect plague was but the latest in a long series of misfortunes which included unseasonally heavy rains, the illness of Gengoro's wife, the soaring price of animal fodder and, worst of all, the Lord Shimazu's recent drastic reduction of the traditional samurai stipends.

'This is because he spends all our clan's wealth on foreign vessels,' interrupted Kentaro suddenly. 'He doesn't care what happens to simple loyal folk like us as long as he has new-fangled foreign toys and projects.'

'But his plan is to make us strong and rich so we can defend ourselves against our enemies if need be,' Kenjiro protested.

His brother snorted. 'Oh, that's how you'd see it, living in luxury in a distant place without any cares, truckling to the barbarians.'

'Kenjiro works very hard and is much respected for his interpreting skills,' Ryo broke in firmly, 'and we don't live in the least luxuriously.'

Fumio sniffed in patent disbelief as a servant cleared the dishes and Kenjiro, taking a deep breath, said, 'There's the matter of mother's things, Kentaro; the beautiful porcelain and heirlooms she kept in that chest.'

Kentaro lowered his eyes. 'Oh, those – I've sold some of

them.'

'Sold them!' Kenjiro shouted.

'Oh Kentaro, no . . .! Mother promised some to me — as my only dowry,' Ryo wailed at him.

Kentaro shrugged sullenly. 'Times are hard, as we told you. Wife, tell the servant to bring what's left.' They waited in cold silence and Kenjiro felt a deep pang of sorrow as the familiar chest was brought in; he trailed his fingers over its embossed surface as he had many times when a youth. 'Show me,' he commanded, and Fumio ordered the servant to open it, adding sharply, 'Don't speak so to your elder brother.'

Three bowls, a few plates, jars and two vases were laid out on the mats and Ryo cried angrily, 'Is that all? Kentaro, how could you?'

Kenjiro turned furiously on his brother. 'You've already had far more than your portion — what's left is ours.'

Kentaro rose and faced him. 'No! I've had all the expense of mother's illness and funeral — we will divide the remainder and as I'm the elder I should have the largest share.'

'Yes indeed,' confirmed his wife, equally angry. 'And he has a growing family to support — unlike you two — what an unnaturally single and barren pair you are!'

Ryo hid her face in her sleeves as Kenjiro pulled a bag of coins from his girdle and threw them on the floor. 'Here, take that for what's left. At least mother's few treasures will be safe with us and not sold to any passing cheapjack.'

Fumio scooped up the bag, poured out the coins and counted them. 'Let him take them, husband; he can afford such luxuries, unlike us.'

Kentaro agreed with relief, for he was essentially a timid man who hated quarrels. A servant was summoned, who began wrapping each piece in soft cloths ready for transport, and in the uncomfortable silence that fell, Kenjiro heard swarms of insects buzzing in the hot afternoon air — the dreaded plague, he supposed. He glanced pityingly at his brother, wondering how he could begin to bridge the gulfs of upbringing and experience that divided them.

Suddenly they heard the pounding of heavy feet on the

verandah and Gengoro strode in, looking agitated. '*Ah-so* – I was told you were here,' he said sternly. Ryo, overcome with childish panic, trembled and lowered her head to the mats; Kenjiro rose and bowed stiffly. Gengoro gazed fixedly at him, his bulging eyes wide. 'What's that? What in the name of all the demons have you done to your head-hair, boy?' He marched over and twisted Kenjiro's short locks in his hand, puckering his face and staring at it in silence, struggling to keep control of his temper – for he had come that afternoon with conciliatory intent. He and his barbarian-haters were now in very much of a minority within the clan; even his former hero, Saigo Takamori, had come out in favour of strengthening Satsuma power with foreign help and cementing the recent alliance with the Choshiu clan, with the intention of eventually overthrowing the Shogunate. Thus had Gengoro been forced to accept that his clever nephew who spoke the barbarian tongue had a promising future and should not be lightly scorned. But the very sight of him aroused all his impulsive choler and he heard himself roaring, 'Do you recognise this brother of yours, Kentaro? He was once a samurai's son, proud to wear the top-knot of his ancestors. Now he fawns on the mighty foreigner, cropped like an outcast, a common criminal.'

'Oh quiet, leave me be.' Kenjiro jerked his head away from his uncle's grasp. 'You understand nothing, Uncle. You're like an ancient crone crying "woe" in a graveyard. The world is moving on – I've told you before. But you won't listen to me, or your leaders, who've got much more sense than you, thank goodness. I won't stand for these insults any more. There's no place for us here. Come, Ryo . . .'

As Ryo rose obediently, Gengoro tried to recover his temper. 'Wait, boy, I've something to discuss with you.'

'Well?' Kenjiro turned tensely.

'Let us sit down . . .'

'You can tell me standing. We have to return to the foreign ships at Kagoshima.'

Gengoro scowled again, swallowing hard. 'A proposition –

a very generous one. You should come back and live here. I've plans for you. Remember the Okadas, the rich landowners to the east? The elder daughter is now of marriageable age . . . I've begun to sound out the possibilities . . .'

Kenjiro smiled sadly. '*Ah-so*, Uncle, you've realised at last that I could be of some use to you? So you're ready to conceal the hatred in your heart for me and all the other barbarian-lovers in the clan, hey? Well, it's too late. I'm no boy any more, and I won't knuckle under to your commands like my weak-kneed brother here, nor will I marry a woman of your choosing for your aggrandisement. We've gone away from all that, forever, my sister and I − Come . . .' He jerked his head at Ryo and added, 'Goodbye, brother. Is mother's chest ready to go?'

Kentaro nodded and shrilled, 'I'm not weak-kneed. I'm an obedient and grateful son to my adopted father.'

'Yes, I know. I'm sorry.'

Gengoro, thwarted and furious, stood biting his knuckles as Kenjiro and Ryo prepared to depart, thanking Fumio formally for the hospitality of the house.

'Goodbye; may the blessings of a quiet old age be yours,' Kenjiro bowed from the doorway and Gengoro stuttered an inarticulate response.

Leaving the compound, Kenjiro and Ryo passed the humble abode where they used to live with their mother. It was an ordinary farmhouse now and the farmer's babies were tumbling about on the verandah. In the rays of the late afternoon sun, the house, with its time-mellowed thatch and wooden walls, looked like a perfect rural idyll which swam before the moist eyes of the two travellers as they were carried away over the hills.

When they returned they found the British in jolly mood, having just got back from a day's hunting on the Lord of Satsuma's private reserves. 'The setting was quite delightful,' Elinor told Ryo, 'a magnificent park bounded by wooded hills and the seashore. The beaters loosed the dogs on the hill-tops and followed them down with a continuous blowing of conch shells that was weird and magical, like the pipes of Pan must have sounded. But the Commissioner of Woods and Forests, a comical-looking fellow in blue and orange silks armed with a Whitworth carbine, was terribly upset because the total bag was no more than seven deer and two wild boar . . . I really think he might have committed *hara-kiri* on the spot from shame,' she laughed, 'but the Prince told him that such a spectacle really would upset us more than the smallness of the bag!'

The British left the following day, pleased that relations between them and the Satsuma had never been better and that, in the whole course of the visit, not a single mention had been made of the name 'Richardson' or the bombardment just three years before. For the diplomatic staff it was another triumph and, as they sailed out of beautiful Kagoshima Bay, they felt they had cemented an alliance it would be wise to support in the coming, almost inevitable, struggle for power.

That summer, a happy one for some, was not especially so for Felix. In the middle of May Honoria had written to say that she had been safely delivered of a son at the Chefoo Mission hospital, whom she intended to call Oliver. It seemed to her an appropriate name for the musician she fervently hoped the child would one day become. Touching his tiny pink fingers, she imagined them growing supple and sensitive, conjuring magic from a keyboard, an intense youth with dark curls bent over his instrument. Harold, she guessed, might consider the name a little cissy, but this did not worry her, for she did not feel the child to be his, nor indeed Felix's. The very uncertainty of his paternity meant he was thoroughly and completely her own. She did not share these thoughts with either man, however, but simply enjoyed a long, quiet convalescence in Chefoo during the worst of the summer's heat. Felix meanwhile, bound by a sense of duty and unassuaged desire, awaited her return in Yokohama, pleased only with the continuing success of his trading ventures – his exports of silkworm eggs to France and raw silk to the Coburns' factories.

Indeed, letters from home suggested that he was at last in

his family's good books, and it amused him to imagine them all, gathered round the mahogany table for Sunday luncheon, raising a glass to absent Felix, who had once verged on the black sheep, but was now making good – that is, money – at last. The scene was only too clear: the heavily prosperous faces of his father, his brothers, their wives and children. The features of Mildred, Sydney's wife, were quite reminiscent of a horse, while Stanley's Gertrude was round and bosomy like a robin, but not nearly as chirpy. It dismayed Felix to think that, if Honoria's marriage were wrecked and he claimed paternity of the child, whom she felt sure was his, he might have to introduce them all to her one day.

But, early that autumn, such misgivings were forgotten in the joy of actually seeing his beloved. She looked so slim and well at last; the glint of amusement behind the ice-blue eyes entranced him; he would have taken her anywhere – yeah, even to Macclesfield, Cheshire, just for the pleasure of her company. But her feelings were much more ambivalent, and at their first reunion at the Hotel de l'Europe she told him their affair could not be resumed, as she was soon returning to Harold in Hakodate.

'Felix, you must understand; it's no longer just a question of you and me – there's the child to consider. How can I risk blighting his life from his first infancy with the scandal and shame of a discovered adultery? He's too precious and talented, I'm sure, and must have the security of a proper upbringing.'

'But you say that I . . .?'

'Oh, Felix, I don't know it, and that distresses me greatly. But the world believes Harold is the father, which is the most important thing.' She looked at him tenderly. 'Oh, I'm tempted, sorely . . . I might as well confess it . . . but . . .'

'Dearest.' He leaned forward, gazing at her ardently.

She raised a shielding hand. 'Felix, careful, please; don't look like that here.' She had insisted on their meeting in a secluded corner of the hotel lounge, where they were supposed to be having an ordinary tea-time chat.

He murmured, 'Honoria, you cannot so easily forget what

we have shared, surely?'

She raised a teacup, speaking from behind it. 'No, of course. I shall never forget; but there must be nothing more between us. In any case, it's totally impractical. I simply can't afford to stay here in the hotel and Lady Parkes has kindly suggested that I borrow a room in the Consulate while I buy winter clothes and supplies. So how could we possibly?'

'You could come to my lodgings.'

'No, Felix; it mustn't start again, and there's an end to it.' She spoke with a crisp finality that concealed the extent of her misery; so he did not guess that, after he had gone, she paced her bedroom in a passion of frustration, as if his desire had invaded her. Throwing herself on the bed, she bit the sheet angrily, her stomach tense and hard, the place between her legs moistening as she murmured her own name endearingly, imagining the words in his voice. Perhaps, she thought miserably, he, back in his lodgings, was suffering as she was, and the thought of his arousal for her made it all seem worse. How could they bear the long winter ahead without seeing and touching each other again? Oh, the stupidity of it all! Desperately she yearned for him to throw her caution to the winds and come rushing back, cover her face and breasts with kisses. But that Felix did not do, and, shortly after, Honoria moved into the Consulate with Oliver. Which might indeed have meant the end of the affair — had it not been for the addiction of the military fraternity to drag-hunts by moonlight.

The number of troops left in Yokohama had recently been reduced and those left had little to occupy themselves, for there had been no occasion to exercise their prime function of 'protecting the settlers against native attack' since the assassination of Beale and Bradshaw the previous year. So, once the summer crops were cleared from the surrounding countryside, they passed the tedious days organising race-meetings and drag-hunts. The novel frolic of a 'moonlight drag', to be held the following Saturday after guest night at the Officers' Mess, attracted everyone; many settlers arranged their own dinner-parties to coincide, then hurried up the Bluff to watch the fun.

The parade ground was soon crowded with horses, carriages, and merry groups of ladies and gentlemen in evening dress, while the mess band played 'D'ye ken John Peel' and other songs of the hunt. The hunt riders, dressed in 'moonlight regulation' which consisted of night-caps, nightgowns, and knee breeches with bare legs, were enjoying a stirrup cup of champagne before starting. The drag – a bag filled with red herring and aniseed – had already been laid over a two-mile stretch of country, and the camp's beagle pack was quivering in the kennels, eager to follow the scent wherever it led. This much a flirtatious elderly major from the Queen's XIth, who had been Honoria's partner at dinner that evening, explained to her as they stood together near the starting point.

'Oh, what a deliciously absurd spectacle!' Honoria laughed, watching an extremely corpulent man, with a walrus moustache and red-tasselled night-cap, hitching up his gown as he mounted his steed, held by a Japanese groom whose back was tattooed in the manner of his kind with dragons and butterflies. 'Who is that man? I pity his mount!'

Her companion chuckled. 'Oh that's our sporting Captain, yclept Puffles. Rumour has it he's only read two books in his entire life – Ruff's *Racing Calendar* and Bailey's *Guide to the Turf*. That Australian chestnut of his is used to his weight – he was actually second in the Ladies' Purse at the last meeting.' He tried to entertain her further. 'And that pale fellow next to him we call Micawber is riding Pig – devil of a creature who'll snap your finger off given half a chance. And there's Typhoon, quite a goer, ridden by our young aide who hails from the green Isle of Erin – ah, how delicate his lower limbs – and – but they're off . . .'

The released pack of hounds bounded away and with many a crack of the whip and cries of 'Tally-ho', 'Gee-up', and 'Halloa' the riders followed them across the road and up the hill into the dark. 'Would you mind awfully if I take a little canter myself, Mrs Rayne?' The Major looked longingly after them.

'Please do, Major. I've left my baby with the amah and . . .'

190

The Major hurried off and Honoria wandered back to the road, where several carriages were also moving in pursuit of the riders.

'Would you like to come with us, Mrs Rayne? I'm sure we can squeeze you in,' Elinor Mills called from Arnold's phaeton.

'Oh, no thank you, Miss Mills. I must get back to Oliver.' She walked to the grassy edge of the hill and looked down; the sheen of moonlight on the settlement's roofs, the canals and waters of the bay gave the usually mundane scene an air of mysterious enchantment. Honoria smiled to herself; before dinner that evening she had sampled her first American cocktail, a dangerously attractive concoction that had left her feeling a little light-headed and irresponsible. Remembering her maternal obligations, however, she returned to the road and was about to descend when a carriage drew up beside her and Felix said, 'Honoria – at last. I've been looking for you everywhere. Do come for a ride.'

'But I must . . .'

'Please – it's such a beautiful night.' He held out his hand.

'Oh, Felix, I . . .'

'I want to talk to you, Honoria, please.' She glanced around; there was no one to observe just then as she climbed up beside him. Where the new road curved inland he drove off it and towards the wooded valley below.

'Felix,' she protested, 'where are you taking me? I must go back . . . Oliver. What did you want to say to me?'

'I'll tell you in a minute.'

She leaned back, giving herself up to the beauty of the night and the pleasure of riding with him. At the bottom of the hill he reined to a halt, turned to her and began kissing her mouth and neck passionately.

'Felix, no . . . I said you weren't to . . . Felix, please . . . What do you want to say?'

She tried to push him away.

He smiled impishly. 'Nothing – except with my mouth, with my whole soul saying I love you. That's all; isn't it enough?' He began kissing her body gently. 'How beautiful

191

you are, Honoria – your full breasts and shapely waist, this
. . . oh, this everything. Darling, I want you so desperately,
I've wanted you all summer. Please, even if it's only once . . .
we must, we must . . .' Tenderly he began loosening the
fastenings of her evening silks.

'Oh, but we shouldn't . . .' she moaned weakly. But it was
all too much to resist – the spell of the moonlight, the earlier
fire of the cocktails, the pressure of his ardour upon her.
When her whole body lay naked under him he thought that
she was his goddess, his Diana, his huntress, his mistress, his
only love. And when their passion was spent and they lay
together gasping and basking in its aftermath, they still felt
the aching joy of it, glad they had succumbed to the absurd,
bewitching aura of that moonlit night.

Nor were they the only ones affected. Other revellers, like
Honoria, slipped quietly home without explanation at dis-
gracefully late hours; other skirts, like Honoria's, had been
somehow torn and muddied; other bow-ties, like Felix's, had
come adrift and were lost; sundry combs, cuff-links, gloves,
bits of ribbons, and buttons, not to mention champagne
bottles, were found in some odd places by the local peasants
the following day. The peasants kept their finds; no one
admitted to losing anything. But long afterwards, when habits
of decorum and propriety generally prevailed in respectable
Yokohama, residents used to speak of the night of the moonlight drag-hunt with considerable nostalgia. For, in retrospect,
it seemed to mark the end of an era, after which the port
began to change rapidly, its somewhat raffish, risky, flimsy
frontier days disappearing forever.

CHAPTER TEN

The disaster that swept away Yokohama's frontier days most dramatically began on a clear, windy November morning when the inhabitants woke to the sound of bronze bells ringing vigorously from the fire-watching towers in the native town. First to go up in flames were the shack-brothels and tea-houses near the Gankiro and, as the fire began spreading at alarming speed, the streets leading from it became jammed with people fleeing to safety, with their pots and pans, bedding and stores, cricket cages, and babies loaded on carts, wheelbarrows, and backs. Rushing to the rescue came squads of Japanese fire-fighters in leather clothing and highly polished helmets carrying wooden pumps, ladders, and long hooks which they used to pull down burning roofbeams. As watching fires and the fighting of them was a traditional national pastime, they were hampered by crowds of arriving spectators who added to the general confusion, which was worse confounded when an oil merchant's shop blew up with a tremendous explosion, sending sparks flying in the high wind towards the foreign quarter.

Percival Storey, who had coolly watched the distant conflagration while sipping his breakfast tea, found himself two hours later hastily carrying his language books, harmonium, chest of drawers, and best china dinner service to safety just before his lodgings were engulfed in flames. The silver-plated American fire-engine, bedecked with highly polished bells and medallions, then arrived, drawn by horses, and manned by marines and a smart company of matelots from a

French warship. Yokohama's own volunteer fire brigade mustered its forces — only to find two of its engines rusty and leaking and a shortage of water to supply the third. Parties of redcoats and blue-jackets started demolishing the bonded warehouses that lay in the fire's path; but to little avail as pieces of lighted debris then set alight to the American Consulate, leading merchants' houses, and even the so-called fireproof godowns in which valuable goods were stored.

Foreign Consulate buildings, wood-and-paper bungalows, the Japanese Customs House were all reduced to ashes; and, as if in final mockery, flames licked through the shed where stood the ineffective fire-engines. Some of the soldiery, having got hold of liquor from the bonded warehouses, proceeded to get roaring drunk, looting houses and jeering at the civilians as they rushed about hopelessly with buckets of water. During that afternoon '. . . chaos and mayhem reigned supreme,' as the *Herald* later reported and '. . . only the merciful dropping of the wind and rainfall at dusk saved the settlement from complete annihilation'.

Arnold Mills, having sent his sister with the other ladies to the safety of the Bluff, beyond the fire's reach, set up a makeshift surgery in the Yokohama Club to minister to injured Japanese, and called upon Kenjiro to interpret for him. Patients, mostly women and children in great distress who had been trapped by the fire's first onslaught, continued to drift in throughout the day, and by late afternoon both men were exhausted.

'Oh, Lord, that will do . . . I'm in desperate need of a drink. Just go and grab a bottle of whisky from the bar, will you, Kenjiro, old sport? And two glasses. And lock the outer door — we're closed . . . Phew!' Arnold plopped on a chair, holding his aching head in his hands. So much misery in one day — bruised and charred flesh, broken bones, smoke-blinded eyes; he had sent the worst cases to the military hospital and tried to cope with the rest. He sighed, thinking of poor old Percy, who had moved his worldly goods into a 'fireproof godown' only to watch it go up in flames an hour later. He and Elinor had been fortunate; the fire had been contained before it reached the Consulate and other properties nearer the Bluff. Kenjiro returned with the bottle and poured them each a stiff drink.

'Cheers — thanks for your help, Miyata. Quite like the old days, hey? Your English has improved enormously since you worked for me.'

As Kenjiro inclined his head in brief acknowledgement, wishing the doctor would stop addressing him like a good schoolboy, there was a loud knock on the outer door and the sound of a baby screaming.

Arnold groaned. 'No more. I really can't. Tell them to go to their own doctors.'

Kenjiro obeyed; but returned a minute later saying, without looking at Arnold, 'There's a baby with a burned face. The mother says you must see her. The name's Yasu.'

Arnold jumped up. 'Oh, good Lord, I've been wondering about her — bring her here.'

The woman was quite young, her hair and face streaked with fire-smuts. She thrust a bawling bundle at Arnold, crying in her own tongue, 'Help her, Big-san, help her for heaven's sake — she's burned. I was caught near the Gankiro and couldn't get away. I've been looking for you everywhere. You must save your baby — your own flesh and blood.'

Arnold took the baby and carried her to the table in silence; he understood his woman's drift well enough, but did not ask Kenjiro for an exact translation. As he dressed the child's wounds, Yasu sank trembling on the chair, dabbing her smutty face and sipping the whisky Kenjiro gave her. 'All gone,' she whispered, 'all my belongings. It was terrible. Two of my neighbours died and we were all trampled by the crowds as we tried to escape. My poor little Taki! Ask Big-san if she'll live. I'm too tired to remember his horrible language.'

Kenjiro said curtly, 'The woman asks if the baby will survive, doctor.'

'Oh, yes; there's no real danger, providing she keeps infection at bay. There may be skin scars, but she'll be all right.'

Yasu smiled for the first time at the news, and Taki's screams subsided into whimpers. As Arnold went for ointments, Kenjiro glanced at the baby; it was not a pure-bred Japanese, of that there was no doubt. Yasu held out her glass for more whisky, which she gulped down like medicine, and began rocking back and forth, keening to herself in low, piteous tones. 'What can I do now? Where will I take my little one? I've no money and no roof above me. Big-Barbarian is rich but will do nothing for us . . . He should provide my Taki with clothes and food, at least . . .'

Arnold tied the last bandage. 'There, that's better. What's she moaning about, Miyata?'

'She says she's homeless now, and poor, and the baby is . . .' He gulped.

'Yes. Ah, well . . .' Arnold handed Yasu a towel. 'Wipe your face and dry your eyes, woman. And drink that whisky, it'll do you good.' She finished it obediently, then looked up at Arnold. 'Monee – babee.'

Arnold nodded glumly, and she turned to Kenjiro. 'Tell him I want to stay here in this foreigners' place where it's safe and warm. I have nowhere to go and he is a doctor and will cure his baby.'

Reluctantly, in increasing embarrassment, Kenjiro translated the woman's plea, till Arnold broke in, 'Oh, that's ridiculous! This is the Yokohama Club, not a lodging house. There'll be no more room for foreigners after this, much less for . . . I'll give her some money and burn dressings and she must take the baby to her family in Edo.'

Yasu broke into fresh sobs. 'But not now – it's late and cold and bad for the baby.'

Arnold looked hunted. 'I can't do any more. She mustn't be seen here – with my sister about. Go and find Sam, Miyata. Tell him to bring the phaeton at once and she can get out in that before the gates close.'

Kenjiro hurried away leaving Yasu, with the whimpering baby in her arms, still rocking to and fro in distress while Arnold stood with his back to her, washing his hands in a basin. He slammed the outer door. Yasu was only a low-born woman, of course; but she was of his race and it infuriated him to think of her utter powerlessness before the 'Big-san Barbarian.'

The next day, while the embers of the conflagration were still smouldering, the settlers began counting their considerable losses. Over a hundred found themselves homeless and many merchants had lost their entire stocks in the burned-out warehouses; many were under-insured and several went bankrupt as a result. Felix, already sadly missing Honoria, who had returned to Hakodate just a few days before, now felt totally bereft, having lost a valuable consignment of raw silk and most of his personal possessions to boot. It was, he thought sourly, a good time for the testing of Darwinian principles – those endowed with the most resilience and the spirit of competitiveness would best survive the catastrophe, and, having survived, would be judged the fittest. Had his brother Sydney been in his shoes now, he would probably be rolling up his shirt-sleeves and helping to clear away the rubble, as some of the dauntless Japanese were doing that very day. But Felix did not feel equal to any of this; instead he spent the day, like many of his fellow-traders, searching for temporary lodgings and a tailor, for he possessed only the clothes in which he stood.

Hotel prices, house rents, charges for tailoring, hat, shoe- and dress-making, costs of foreign food and alcohol went sky-high at once, and it became incumbent upon the few unscathed to help the many less fortunate. Sir Harry Parkes, acting on this principle, summoned Arnold to his office the following day to tell him his immediate plan of action. Fortunately, the Chief explained, with his usual friendly firmness, the new Legation buildings in Edo were on the verge of completion and, in the light of the present crisis, the whole staff, including Arnold, must be ready to move into them within the week. The Yokohama Consulate could then be used to house some of 'our homeless refugees', as he put it.

As Arnold recounted Sir Harry's plan to his sister over tea, her heart sank in foreboding of his next words. 'And so, my dear Ellie, I'm very much afraid you'll have to leave on the next P & O,' he concluded. 'Sir Harry was quite definite on the point — you cannot be considered eligible for the limited accommodation now available.'

She gave a sharp little cry.

'Come now, sister mine — please be sensible. Why, a whole year has slipped by, somehow, since Reggie's death, and Mother's been pleading with you to go home for months.'

'But I just don't want to go, Arnold, and Mrs Hubbard says my help at the school is invaluable. I could stay with her, or the Fortescues would take me in.'

'Elinor, for heaven's sake!' He didn't conceal his irritation. 'Mrs Hubbard has four children, and a family of American Presbyterians now billeted with her, not to mention her relatives, the Potters. While the hospitable Fortescues are positively bursting at the seams. You've had a very good innings here, Elinor, and it's been delightful; but sometimes others' needs must take priority and that's all about it.' He drained his tea-cup and stood up. 'I must go — there's some pretty severe burn cases in the hospital. You should start counting your blessings, Miss. The *Mongolia* sails in five days and you'll be in Hong Kong in time for a jolly Christmas with Aunt Clarabella. Then home in the New Year.' He stalked out, thinking that Elinor's absence would at least make it easier for him to see more of Yasu, of whom he was carelessly fond.

Elinor sat staring at the leaves in the bottom of her cup, then, with a deep sigh, she walked up to her bedroom and leaned out of the window. Ashes and the smell of smoke still hung in the air and it seemed as if all her dreams had also gone up in flames. Why should she feel so strongly that her future lay in this country that she had grown to love? Other foreigners seemed to arrive and leave again without anguish. Indeed some of them talked as yearningly of Home as if staying here were a prison sentence. What had happened to make her feel so differently?

She sat at her dressing-table, staring in the glass at the misery deep in her eyes. She simply could not bear the thought that she might never return to Japan after next week, never again watch the ocean-going ships arrive in the bay, never ride along the New Road in the clear morning, with dear Mount Fuji-san seeming to float in the blue sky, never again to see . . . She caught herself up short. She toyed with a comb, playing hide-and-seek with her own reflection, catching herself out. I'm quite pretty and still young-ish, she thought. In spite of having lost a fiancé, I'm not yet quite on the shelf; there could be other opportunities. But the trouble was . . . the crux of the matter was . . . She squared herself up in the glass, moistening her lips and stiffening her neck a little in readiness to say it out aloud. She took a deep breath. 'I can't bear never to see Mr Miyata again, because I think I love him.' She paused. 'Kenjiro Miyata,' for the 'Mister' sounded absurdly formal in the context. The saying aloud made it more real; she stared dreamily in the glass. 'Kenjiro . . .' It was the loveliest name in the world.

And then, as if popping at her from a corner of the glass, she saw the image of a Japanese cartoon she had happened upon in a curio shop recently. She had been leafing through an innocent collection of bird and flower prints, and there it was – by mistake, obviously. The picture showed a naked samurai with a sword held aloft above his head, with his penis in a state of large erection. A naked girl bowed before him, her flowing hair covering her face, the nape of her white neck exposed to him. It wasn't clear whether he was about to seduce, murder her, or both, for he was smiling quite tenderly. Elinor had quickly turned the picture over without reading the caption, but now the vision of the picture returned to her vividly – with Kenjiro's face.

Shamed, she rubbed her eyes, then got up, biting her lips. Whatever was she to do? What would happen were she to . . .? One thing was absolutely certain; even if he felt as she did he would never dare declare his love for her. It would be quite impossible in his circumstances. So, unless she acted, she would have to leave with her love undeclared. Then she would never see him again, never even know if he shared her passion, as she truly believed he did. The thought made her ache, but the alternative filled her with panic. What would everyone say? Arnold, her parents, Mrs Fortescue, Mrs Hubbard, Aunt

Clarabella? Kenjiro was a 'native'; proper English ladies simply did not form attachments to them.

She paced the room until darkness fell and eventually reached an interim resolution. She would see Kenjiro alone, tell him she was suddenly obliged to leave the country, and try to judge how he felt. If he appeared utterly unmoved at the news, she would say nothing more. She could, after all, be mistaken about the many signs of his seeming affection: his personal pursuit of Reggie's assassin; the joyous ride in the snow; the number of occasions when he had deliberately sought her company during the past year. But could not her own feelings have led her to misinterpret his? That much at least she had to find out.

Two days, now become precious, slipped by before Elinor managed to see Kenjiro alone, for the ordinary routines of work and social life had been quite disrupted by the fire. He, Pervival, and their assistants were occupied from morn till night packing books and papers for transportation to Edo; even before an office was cleared, merchants arrived with armfuls of ledgers for which they had no houseroom. People were muddled, irritable, and envious of Elinor for her chance to escape the prevailing discontents, and when Arnold produced her ticket for Hong Kong, Elinor accepted it in silence and hopelessly began to pack her trunks.

But she stuck to her intention and, on the third morning, observing Kenjiro going alone into the Consulate's library, she followed him. The room had been emptied, except for a dust-covered oval table covered with old papers and magazines; outside rain poured from a grey sky. It was not a cheery scene and her heart, that was beating fast, gave a small, sad thud.

Kenjiro looked up from the papers he was sorting. 'Ah, Miss Mills. Good morning. Only it is not good, it is wet.'

'Yes, miserable weather, isn't it? Can I help you at all? I don't seem to be much use recently.'

'No, thank you; this is official stuff, mostly to be thrown away.' There was a pause, during which they were both awkwardly aware of the other's presence.

Elinor gulped. 'I . . . I've come to tell you, Mr Miyata, that I have to leave Japan almost immediately and probably for ever. I don't want to go but I've been given no choice.'

He looked up quickly. 'You leave? Now? Forever? That is very dreadful.'

'Yes, isn't it? But Sir Harry insists that there's nowhere for me to stay any more.'

'Oh, I see – the staff going to Edo because of the fire?'

'Yes.'

He edged round the table. 'But you do not wish it?'

'No, no, not in the least. I hate the thought of leaving Japan, and, the Japanese people, especially my friends – like Ryo and you . . .' Her eyes were wide with appeal, willing him to help her out.

'I . . . I . . .' he floundered. 'And I shall hate it if you go. But is it really necessary?'

'But I have nowhere to stay any more.'

'You . . . I . . .' His English was failing him in his crisis. 'You stay with me somewhere – me and Ryo.'

'Oh, yes, yes please, I'd love to. But how can . . . I mean it is not the custom. People would say . . .' She began tracing circles in the dust on the table; rain splashed outside; it seemed as if she had been in the room for a long time; he was standing quite close to her now.

'Not custom for man and woman to live in same house unless they are brother, sister, husband, wife?' He mumbled so she hardly heard.

'Married – yes. Then it's all right, of course.'

'Yes, of course.'

She looked at him despairingly; how could she bring herself to go on; how could he? Yet another little push had to be made. 'Marriage is or can be very wonderful – when two people love each other, that is. But sometimes it's difficult, to know what to say about love.'

'Yes, love is very difficult thing to say about.'

'But sometimes one has to say – the whole course of one's future might depend upon it.'

'On the love?'

201

'Or the saying.'

He hissed through his teeth, his forehead wet with perspiration as he watched the smaller, even more agitated circles she was drawing on the table.

'That day of the snow ride, you remember?' he gasped.

'Oh yes, yes. I enjoyed it so much — the beautiful snow, how we talked, everything about it. I shall never forget.'

'I think so and I remember always, also. That day I begin . . . began . . . to thought . . . think . . .' — again he was whispering so she could scarcely catch the words — 'maybe . . . is that I love you, only I will not ever say.'

Her eyes brimmed with joy. 'And now you say — after all? And you feel the same, still?'

He took a folded cloth and dabbed his damp brow. He said jerkily, 'And I feel — that is just how I felt, on that day, and from then on I knew in my inside-heart, only I didn't want to . . .'

'Oh, Kenjiro, I do, do, do love you much much more than I've ever loved anyone. I never knew about love before, not really, I only imagined I did. Oh, Kenjiro, my darling, my darling . . .' She went into his arms, he holding her awkwardly, brushing her face and damp eyes with his half-closed lips instead of kissing in the western fashion. They were both shuddering with the pleasure of their first, acknowledged physical touching. 'So we have said now about love and we marry? You truly want marrying me, Elinor?' He used her first name with a quiet assurance that pleased her.

'Oh yes, yes, more than anything in the world. Forever.' They touched each other closely again, then he held her arms and looked at her quite fiercely. 'You are sure? Absolute sure? It will be very difficult . . . so many things . . .'

'I know, but I am sure. Utterly, utterly sure.' She met his gaze openly. 'And you? Sure?'

'Sure, yes; for always. Sure. I was sure before, but could not say.' He banged both temples with his hands in an expressive gesture. 'Sometimes you see we Japanese feel all locked up inside here — the high walls we cannot jump over to say feelings.'

'Then let us write them!' she cried impulsively. Reaching across the table, she drew a large heart with an arrow through and the initials 'K' and 'E'. They stood close, regarding it together.

'I will bring you heart-drawing on this day, the last day of November every year of our life,' he vowed solemnly, then reached for a duster from a nearby chair.

'Oh no, you mustn't rub it out,' she protested.

'But someone will see.'

'That doesn't matter now – everyone will soon know. We'll have to tell them at once. I'm supposed to leave in three days; but now I shan't.'

He frowned anxiously. 'Yes, we shall have to say. But how will we say it?'

'We'll simply announce that we are engaged to be married, are we not?'

'Yes, that is so.'

'Then I will tell my brother this evening – get the worst over first.'

'He will hate me.'

She touched his cheek. 'He will hate me too, but I don't care. It is my life, our life together that is important.'

He wiped his moist face again. 'You wish me to come with you – to tell your brother?'

'No . . . I think he'll be so angry, he might . . . no, I'll see him alone first.'

'You are brave with your own heart. Like a lioness, I often think.' He stroked her tawny braids. 'The colour is right,' he grinned suddenly. 'And I will tame you.'

She giggled. 'But not with a whip, like a lion-tamer?'

'No, no, no whip – with love. Love can tame men also. We tame each other for each other's pleasure.'

'Oh, Kenjiro, what a poetic way of putting it! Englishmen are never poetic, they don't say odd and lovely things like you do sometimes. Come, let's go . . .' she dragged on his sleeve as he looked back anxiously at the heart on the table. 'Leave it be, leave it be. Let the whole world see it, Kenjiro – and guess whose initials they are!' Laughingly she pushed him out, shutting the door behind them.

That afternoon, when Kenjiro had returned to work, Elinor rather wished someone would tell her brother about the heart-drawing on the library table – to prepare him somewhat for the shock she had to administer. But no one did and so, after she heard him return from work that evening, she dressed with special care and went to join him as usual.

'You're looking very sweet this evening, Ellie.' He smiled as she came in. 'Will you join me in a sherry?'

'Thank you, Arnold.' Her flushed face and bright eyes suggested to him that she was getting excited about the prospect of her imminent departure at last, which was a blessing, he thought, handing her a glass. 'If only we'd had this amount of rain on the day of the fire a lot of life and property would have been saved,' he remarked. 'But now it's just making everything worse. The burnt-out areas are quagmires and can't even be cleared properly. A fellow nearly drowned in a canal today while carting rubble away – the banks just caved in.'

'Yes, it's awful, won't stop, will it?' Elinor sipped her drink nervously.

'And the foundations of the Aldertons' bungalow just where the fire stopped along Main Street have begun to collapse, so that looks like another family made homeless.'

'The Aldertons? Insurance broker?'

'Yes, and his young wife is expecting her first baby. I imagine they'll be billetted here soon.' He glanced at her, but she avoided him, twirling her glass in her fingers. Arnold frowned; for him too it was a time of stress – what with the fire, the casualties, the problem of Yasu, the sudden move to Edo. The least his sister could do was to go away quietly without any fuss. 'I saw Mrs Hubbard today and she told me her sister and brother-in-law will be on the *Mongolia* – nice company for you. They're leaving early because the Hubbards are so overcrowded.'

Elinor pulled a wry face. 'Nice? Agnes and Archibald Potter – I think they're dreadful people, so very narrow-minded and strait-laced.'

'Oh well, it's only as far as Hong Kong.'

Elinor spun her glass again; she felt like a swimmer about to take a very high dive, and took a deep breath. 'I'm not going on the *Mongolia* to Hong Kong, Arnold.'

'Oh, for heaven's sake, Elinor, of course you are. I'm quite tired of your behaviour over this – and there's simply nowhere . . .'

She jumped in. '. . . because Mr Miyata and I are engaged to be married.'

He stared at her incredulously, thinking he must have mis-heard. Mayer, perhaps, young Willis Mayer, the shipping agent? 'Mr . . . who?'

'Kenjiro Miyata and I are engaged.' She gave a little gasp, coming up for air.

He walked over and shook her shoulder angrily. 'Elinor, you're mad! Utterly mad! What are you talking about? What an absolutely impossible idea. Whatever has possessed you?'

'Love . . . I am deeply in love with him, Arnold, and he with me, only we didn't acknowledge it until now. Your forcing me to leave has brought matters to a head and I'm glad it did. So I'm staying here.'

She felt his fingers dig into her shoulder, willing her to be quiet. 'Elinor, you can't be serious; it's preposterous and I forbid it absolutely.'

'On what grounds, Arnold? Kenjiro is a samurai's son, a clever and able man with very good prospects. I've often heard you say so. Now if he were English . . .'

'But, Ellie, he is not, and there's the world of difference.' He went to pour himself another drink. 'You can't be serious about this – you're still grieving for Reginald, there's the root of it and this is an aberration – a flight of fanciful . . .'

'Arnold, Kenjiro Miyata is worth three Reggie Bradshaws. I was dreadfully sorry about his death, but he was just a boy really and I never truly loved him. That's why I often behaved frivolously in his company. Then I was indeed being rather flighty and silly; but now – why, I've never been so serious about anything in my life.'

He came and stood over her, almost shouting. 'Elinor, for pity's sake. A man of another race, another religion, another culture. No, I say. You must go away from this madness, and you will, if I have to carry you on to the boat . . . I simply won't allow . . .'

'You won't stop me, you're not my gaoler.' She backed away from his fury.

'Elinor, I can and . . . or, at least,' he tried to contain himself, 'I shall insist on your having time to reconsider from a distance. I'll talk to Miyata . . .'

'Mr Miyata. He's not your lackey, he's my fiancé.'

'Goddamn it, Elinor − pardon my language − I won't endure this from you . . . this flagrant disobedience, this shameful . . .'

The calm she had maintained was cracking, but she was resolved not to cry in his presence. 'I'm not listening to your ill-mannered outburst, Arnold. I'm staying here and I'm marrying Kenjiro and there's an end to it.' She hurried out, slamming the door.

After a gloomy, solitary supper, Arnold decided he had to seek advice and comfort, and hurried through the wet streets to the Fortescues, where Percival and Felix were staying since their lodgings had been burnt down. Not wishing to intrude all evening on the Fortescue family circle, they had returned to Percy's bedroom, where they sat reading by a charcoal stove. Arnold had intended breaking the terrible news immediately; but, once inside, the incredible, shaming words stuck in his throat and instead he accepted a whisky and stood in silence warming himself beside the inadequate embers.

'Heard the latest?' Percival asked. 'The Froggies intend opening a School of Three Arms here − Infantry, Cavalry, Artillery. With French instructors to train government forces. Minister Roches is *enchanté* − silly old blighter; he'll lose in the end, of course.'

Neither Felix nor Arnold answered, for they were tired of the petty rivalries between Parkes and the French Minister. 'That's all confidential, mind; I've just been telling Felix, in confidence.'

Arnold grinned. 'Ah, fortunate Felix − to be in such close and constant communication with the all-knowing source.'

Felix grimaced. 'Lucky by name and nature, as they say — burned out of house and home; most of my capital up in smoke; and here I am with Percival. What could be more fortunate! But you look quite harassed, old sport. Anything wrong?'

'My sister has just announced that she intends to marry Kenjiro Miyata.'

'Miyata!' they both exclaimed, and listened with satisfactory incredulity to Arnold's account of what had just passed.

Arnold lowered his large frame into a small chair. 'Perhaps I should have seen it coming? Never would have let her be alone so often in the company of a handsome young Englishman, that's the rub. But Miyata is a native interpreter — never once occurred to me she'd find him attractive in that sort of way.'

Percival coughed to hide a chuckle. 'Well, people do occasionally become attracted to . . . er . . . natives in that sort of way, don't they? It's not entirely unknown even for Englishmen to form attachments to . . .'

Arnold glowered. 'All right; enough of that. Very different kettle of fish, and there's no question of marriage in such cases. God, if only I'd sent her straight home after Reggie's murder. But she pleaded to stay on, felt she could help the Japanese, enlighten them about the ways of the West and so forth. So charitable and full of good intentions. Huh! Now look what's happened. And what the devil do I do?'

He stared solemnly at Felix, who sighed, feeling sorry for him. No good could come of it, of course; just as with him and Honoria, no good. He poured everyone another drink while Percival added a few bits of charcoal to the fire with tweezer-like tongs. 'It's deucedly difficult. Elinor's always struck me as rather headstrong,' Felix volunteered. 'And if you push her too far she might just . . .'

'Do what?'

'Well, run off, elope or something.'

Arnold groaned. 'Damn it, how do I know, and — what's more to the point — how does Elinor know, what Kenjiro Miyata is really like? We rub along on the social surface with

207

the Japs., but deep down they're as unknown and mysterious as Hades. Come, isn't that the truth, Percival? And you know them better than most.'

Percival considered. 'More or less, yes, to be honest. Certainly no one, not even the couple themselves, could possibly predict how such a marriage will turn out. Something of a precedent, actually!'

'Good God, man, don't talk of it as a *fait accompli*. It mustn't be allowed to happen,' Arnold snapped.

'But what can you do to stop it?'

In the silence that followed, Felix considered Elinor Mills in a new light. She'd always seemed rather too commonsensical and, yes, ordinary for his taste. But here she was, prepared to take this dramatically unconventional step – and all for love. He felt almost cheated; apparently she had depths he had not bothered to plumb. Perhaps he should have; now it was too late; she was definitely bespoke.

Percival meanwhile tried to be practical. 'Let Mary talk to her – woman to woman – Arnold. That might do some good. See the Chief first thing tomorrow before he goes to Edo. Get him to take Miyata with him and contrive to see they don't meet again before the *Mongolia* sails. Then persuade Elinor to leave for a holiday – just to think things over. It might cool them down – distance, another country, pause for reflection and reconsideration. See what your aunt can do in Hong Kong.'

Arnold listened moodily. 'Thanks, Percy. You've given me something to work on, at least. Elinor used to be so sensible; I feel this is some kind of temporary insanity and if I can just get her away as you say . . .' He glanced at his watch. 'I'd better see Mary now – though it will be all over the settlement once she knows.'

'Oh, Mary can be discreet if required; and so can we, right, Felix?' Percival assured him as Arnold drained his glass and went off to the Fortescues' sitting room.

Elinor, waiting nervously in her bedroom, heard her brother's late return and dreaded he would send for her; even though he did not, she lay sleepless for hours, and, waking late, was still at breakfast when Ryo came to see her. Ryo perched herself on the edge of a dining chair, legs and feet tight together, and began agitatedly smoothing a kerchief over her knees with the tips of her fingers, head lowered in concentration.

'Has Kenjiro told you?' Elinor asked gently. Ryo looked up, eyes puffy with sleeplessness. 'And you don't approve?'

'Oh, Elinor, how can I approve? It would be much too difficult, too impossible for you both. No, no it cannot be.'

Elinor sighed. All these denials were disappointing, but distant; they did not closely touch her. 'And what did Kenjiro say to that?'

'He said you love each other very much and therefore it would be all right in spite of the difficulties.'

'And that's exactly what I say – so can't *you* at least give us your blessing, Ryo?' She got up, coming to touch Ryo's shoulder. 'We've been such good friends; now we'll be as sisters – won't you like that?'

Ryo remained silent, head still bent.

'Well, wouldn't you? What is so dreadful about it?' Elinor moved away, staring out of the window; it was still raining.

'But do you really love my brother so much? You loved Reginald Bradshaw once, so you told me.' Ryo gulped, finding it highly embarrassing to talk of such intimacies, but driven to it by the urgency of the situation. 'And now my brother – are you sure?'

Elinor turned from the window. 'Ryo, I promise you I've never been more sure of anything in my life. As for poor Reggie – deep down I knew I wasn't suited to him. I'd have been no use as a dried-up Indian memsahib. But here in this country with Kenjiro there'll be so much to do – for years to come.' Her face glowed.

Ryo continued trying to smoothe out the cloth as if it were the surface of life itself. 'It'll be such a great shock to our family. I told Kenjiro that.'

'And?'

'He said he didn't care.' Ryo had been appalled by such reckless bravado and had lain awake beset by visions of Uncle

Gengoro, the terror of her childhood, galloping into Yokohama one day with sword unsheathed, and cutting off her brother's head.

'And my family, they too will be horrified; Arnold is already, and I don't care either,' Elinor said calmly. 'You see, we are so truly in love that these things don't matter to us.'

Ryo crunched the cloth in a tight ball. 'Then I can say nothing else – except a message from Kenjiro. Sir Harry took him off to Edo with him this morning on urgent business. It is an attempt to try and separate you, he says. But you're not to worry. He'll come back this evening and asks you to . . .' – she paused, hating to voice such an impropriety – 'to go to his room about seven o'clock and he'll meet you there.'

Elinor smiled happily. 'I'll be there. And Ryo – stay with me a while.' She held out her hand. But Ryo rose in a fluster. 'Elinor, I'm sorry but I feel it is a grave mistake – for you both. I can say no more.' She hurried from the room, and Elinor returned sadly to the table to drink more tea.

It seemed absurd that in a time of such crisis she did not quite know how to pass the leaden hours and, well before the appointed time, she crept across the courtyard to Kenjiro's room. She closed the shutters, lit the lantern, sat on a cushion by the stove and looked round with loving eyes. The room was uncluttered, exquisite – soft lamplight flickering on the black and gold lacquer chest and the painted screen. She wanted their first home together to look like this, devoid of ugly foreign furniture, expressing the beauty of simplicity and elegant taste.

Engulfed in love as she was, she could imagine no greater happiness just then than spending a life sitting on *tatami*, eating from low tables, lying in bed quilts on the floor with Kenjiro always beside her. At last she heard him coming along the passage; he slid the door back and stood quietly for a moment, looking at the light shining on her hair, her strong, fair face. Then he came towards her and they held each other close, hugging gently. 'So what happened?' he whispered.

'My brother forbids us to marry, as I thought he would.'

He looked at her, agonised. 'And you will obey him?'

'Of course not, Kenjiro.' Her calm, matter-of-fact reply soothed him.

'And why does he forbid it so harshly? I'm a man with good prospects, a samurai's son, a respectable and an honourable person,' he snorted.

'But of another race and culture, he said, so it wouldn't do.'

'He means a native, doesn't he; a yellow-skinned native, not good enough for his sister, that's what he means?' He rubbed his fists together angrily, then began, 'I have to tell you something, my Elinor, even if you do not like it. But you should know.'

Her heart sank with fear that he had some terrible secret to reveal about himself. 'Your brother is a hypocrite.' He pronounced the last word very carefully, so there should be no mistake.

'Arnold? But what makes you say so?'

'He forbids us to marry legally according to honourable custom in the proper manner, while he keeps a native woman for his own pleasure. She has borne him a child, but he won't marry her – oh no, never.'

'A woman? Oh, Kenjiro, are you sure?'

'Sure, sure. After the fire she came to him for help for the baby, who had been burned. I was there in his surgery. She's called Yasu, a shopkeeper's daughter. So much for your honourable and respectable brother.'

'Oh, that's shameful of him! And the baby, what did he do for it?'

'He dressed the burns and sent the woman away with some money. She couldn't stay, he said, in case you found out.'

Elinor sat down on the cushion again, staring into the charcoal embers. She knew it was true, had heard rumours that foreign bachelors behaved in such immoral ways, but had never imagined her beloved Arnold being so cruel and dissolute. Her eyes moistened at the thought of the poor burnt baby and her brother's hypocrisy – yes, that was exactly the word.

'And so,' Kenjiro continued relentlessly, 'he holds up his hands in horror because you want to marry a Japanese man of

211

rank, while he keeps a lower-class woman hidden in a back street.'

She looked up at him. 'It's utterly sickening, and I'll tell him so, Kenjiro, now. It should bring him to his senses about you and me. Surely he must see that in comparison we . . .'

Kenjiro shook his head. 'He won't see, won't change. But go and confront him, yes, shame him if you can – the Big-san Englishman. I'll wait here, he can send for me if he likes.'

'But you're not supposed to be here, Kenjiro; he thinks you're in Edo tonight.'

'Ah yes, and I must hurry back as soon as the causeway gates open. They are trying to keep us apart. I think the assistant interpreter, Kokan Sanjo, is a snake-in-the-grass-man told to watch me. But I gave him the slip.'

'They won't keep us apart, will they, Kenjiro?' She took his hand.

'No,' he replied as they looked at each other in the flickering light.

She squeezed his fingers. 'I'm going to tackle Arnold now, while I'm still so shocked and angry. Some good may come of it. I'll come back and tell you.'

Arnold, tired of waiting for supper, had started eating when his sister came in the dining room and said in a firm voice without preamble, 'So there you are, Arnold – upright citizen of Yokohama, respected doctor, pillar of the community –' she paused for emphasis – 'and hypocrite, deep-dyed hypocrite.'

'Elinor! What the deuce is this all about, now? For mercy's sake . . .' Shocked, he swallowed a fish-bone and began spluttering mightily.

'Drink some water.' She waited coolly for the spasm to pass.

'I could have choked to death – you shouldn't spring things like that on a fellow. Now come and eat your supper and explain yourself.'

She didn't move. 'A hypocrite, Arnold, full of righteous indignation at my intention of marrying a Japanese in a proper legal fashion, while you and a woman called Yasu . . .'

He stumbled into embarrassment. 'Oh, damn Miyata; he's

told you, has he?'

'Do you deny it?'

He slammed down his knife and fork. 'Will you stop trying to put me on trial, Elinor. I refuse to discuss matters of this nature with you.'

'It's perfectly all right then for you to keep a native woman behind the scenes?'

'There's no comparison between my situation and yours, and no question of marriage in my case,' he retorted stiffly.

'Perhaps you'd prefer me to engage in a similar kind of liaison with Kenjiro, would you?'

'Elinor, you must listen to reason.' He came across and took her by the shoulders. 'Surely you know that women differ greatly from men in this regard . . . There is . . er . . . medical evidence to prove . . . the fact is that we frail men have needs that women know little of. More urgent, shall we say?' He was staring over her head. 'Probably you ladies are fortunate in this. For you of course any physical attraction must be based on heartfelt mental affinity — at least in regard to ladies like yourself.'

'Exactly.' She shook herself free. 'And I have a feeling of heartfelt mental affinity with Kenjiro. And as for women's other needs — I'm beginning to understand there's a lot male doctors don't know. We have urgent needs too — for children, for love and for, yes, the physical expression of it.' She looked at him boldly.

'Children — ha!' He fastened on that. 'Of course you want children, my dear, and very naturally too. And it is indeed sad that your maternal desires should have been thwarted. But that doesn't alter the tragedy which would result if you and Miyata . . . Don't you realise that any offspring of yours would be virtually outcasts? To put it bluntly — half-and-halfs?'

Elinor's cheeks flamed. 'Our children will be happy and beloved, Arnold, because they will spring from a deeply loving union between a man and woman.'

'Love, you call it!' He turned away, twisting his mouth.

'Love it is, I know it.' She looked at him keenly. 'My poor

big brother, I don't think you've ever been in love, have you? It's a condition you can't medically diagnose. But Kenjiro and I are in love, and nothing you can do or say will prevent it.'

He walked heavily back to the table, pushing aside his plate. 'Ellie, Ellie, please, I swear you don't realise what difficulties and troubles you're letting yourself in for. If you refuse to break off this engagement, then at least go to Hong Kong on the *Mongolia*, I beg of you. Spend Christmas with Aunt Clarabella, talk it over, let her counsel you, then we'll see. Consider Mother and Father – they have a right to know before you do anything so precipitate, surely? And you simply can't stay here in the meanwhile, as you well know. So please, Elinor, do this much for me – go on Friday, take some time to think it over.' His look was so pleading and harassed she felt a little sorry for him.

She gave a small, tight laugh. 'All right, Arnold; there's no room for me any more, as you say. I'll leave on Friday, the day after tomorrow. I shall be ready.'

He sighed. 'Well, thank you for that much. And I think you'll find . . . but come, let us have the rest of our supper together in peace.'

'I'm afraid I'm not in the least hungry, Arnold, please carry on.' She walked away from him. 'Good-night,' she said, closing the door behind her.

After that there was little left to say; indeed, Arnold, thinking he had won as much of a concession as he could hope for, decided to avoid any further painful confrontations. Mary sought him out the following afternoon to say that her efforts to talk some sense into his sister had been fruitless. Elinor had been sitting quietly in her bedroom crocheting, her trunks already packed for departure; she would say nothing whatever on the subject of Kenjiro Miyata. Whether she was happy or miserable Mary simply could not decide, and worriedly advised Arnold to keep a careful eye on his sister. As for Kenjiro, he told her, the assistant interpreter had been instructed to be secretly on the alert and report any suspicious behaviour to Sir Harry Parkes immediately. It was a wretched shame that things should have reached such a sorry pass, Mary thought, filled with foreboding, as she said goodbye to Arnold.

That evening Elinor ate supper alone in her bedroom and Arnold ate at the Club. The following afternoon, servants carried Elinor's trunks to the phaeton and Arnold drove her to the *Mongolia* in the harbour. 'Please give this letter to Aunt Clarabella,' he said, breaking the icy silence and handing her a sealed envelope. 'I'm sure you'll have a jolly Christmas; wish I could be with you.'

She nodded and put it in her handbag. Rain still poured from a colourless sky, which seemed appropriate. In the painful circumstances, no one else had felt inclined to see Elinor off; her brother led her to her cabin and there took awkward leave. 'Ellie, please . . .'

'Arnold, no. Please go. You have work to do and we won't sail for at least an hour. I'll write to you.'

'Yes. Well, all right. And please find it in yourself to reconsider . . .'

She turned her pale face from him. 'Please go, Arnold. We can't talk here, and anyway, there's no more to be said.'

'Well, if you insist. Give my love to Clarabella and Dickie.' He kissed her cold damp cheek and left, feeling wretched.

As he was leaving the Bluff hospital after work, he saw the *Mongolia* steam slowly past Treaty Point and vanish into the wet, grey dusk. It was a melancholy sight; he would miss her, of course. Tomorrow he would have to confront Miyata, which was a prospect he did not relish. After a gloomy supper, Arnold was just about to pour himself a night-cap when he heard a thunderous knock on the front door and his heart sank with a premonition of disaster. In the porch stood a messenger from the Edo Legation, who handed him a packet covered with Her Majesty's red wax seals. It contained three letters: two addressed to him, the other to Ryo Miyata.

The first, from Sir Harry Parkes, was briskly to the point:

My dear Mills, I'm terribly sorry to say that I fear the birds have flown. Miyata went for lunch at a Shinagawa restaurant today with Kokan Sanjo keeping a weather eye. Apparently they

*met up with a couple of Miyata's clansmen (obviously in cahoots)
and started drinking heavily. Miyata slipped away on some pre-
text and his friends plied Sanjo with liquor till he fell into a
stupor. When he came to he rushed to me − full of remorse,
needless to say − and we found the letters I enclose on the library
table. I'm extremely sorry, but I know you'll realise that I
couldn't keep a constant personal watch, and Sanjo failed us. I
suspect it's too late to do anything, but am sending these through
the diplomatic pouch to reach you tonight.*

The second letter, from his sister, was also brief:

*My dear Arnold, By the time you read this, Kenjiro and I will
have sailed on the* Mongolia *together. We intend to marry as
soon as is legally permissible, but I shall give you no details at
present. It distresses me greatly to have to deceive you in this
manner, but your obstinate attitude left me no choice. I've made
my feelings about my fiancé quite clear and, now you have this
evidence that my intentions are both serious and honourable, I
pray we may soon be reconciled. I send you my love, dear brother,
Kenjiro his regards. And we hope you will attend our wedding, to
which I shall send you an invitation. Love, Elinor*

'Damn, damn, damn . . .' Arnold crumbled the letter in his
fist, ordered a servant to take Ryo's letter to her, then went to
pour himself a very large night-cap.

CHAPTER ELEVEN

The desperate tactics of secrecy and deception to which Elinor had resorted during her last week in Yokohama were quite alien to her, and she had promised herself an immediate return to normality as soon as the *Mongolia* sailed. But this proved impossible, for there were several Yokohama residents aboard, the most intrusive being Archibald and Agnes Potter, who had been asked by Arnold to chaperone his sister during the voyage. Had they learned of Elinor's intention to marry, in defiance of her brother, the Japanese interpreter travelling second class on the same ship, they would undoubtedly have made a most tremendous fuss. So Elinor remained mostly in her cabin, pleading sea-sickness – which was plausible enough, for the seas were stormy and the winds high.

On the second morning the weather cleared, however, as the *Mongolia* steamed into the long estuary of Nagasaki, past the island of Pappenberg. 'Here,' Agnes Potter reminded Elinor with doleful pleasure, 'hundreds of Japanese converted to Christianity by Jesuit missionaries were massacred three hundred years ago, rather than deny their Christian faith.'

'I don't think I'd have the strength for that, do you?' Elinor asked curiously.

'I would trust so, my dear. Indeed I often pray that were I called upon to meet the ultimate challenge of a Christian's life I would not fail.' Agnes gripped the deck-rail, staring with fierce longing at the pale wash of grey rocks and green hill that was Pappenberg. Vividly she imagined the long-ago terror – the screams, brutality, spilled blood. Such dramas were part of many missionaries' imagination; some, like

217

Agnes, secretly yearned for the final violence of martyrdom.

Archibald Potter, who did not, explained that the batteries built on the hill overlooking the harbour were meant to repel foreign invasion and had been refurbished for that reason quite recently. But the foreigners had come and stayed nevertheless, and were now peacefully established in the cluster of houses on the hillside south of the main port.

'And there's the famous islet of Decima,' he added, as they passed a semi-circular row of houses fronting the water. 'That's where the Dutch traders made their fortunes when the country was closed to all other westerners. They paid for it, mind – having to scrape and kowtow before the mighty Shogun in Edo every year.'

As the engines slowed, Elinor said tensely, 'Now, you two please go ashore straight away, and make the most of our short stay. You were anxious to buy some tortoiseshell pieces in Curio Street, remember, Mrs Potter? I still feel a little peaky and I'll probably join you later.' At first they demurred; but, at Elinor's insistence, went ashore with a party of sightseers, while, in her cabin, Elinor finished packing her suitcase and prepared to disembark.

Kenjiro was waiting with two hired litters as she came through the Customs shed, and they smiled at each other in relief. 'So far, so good,' Elinor murmured. 'May I be long protected from people like the Potters.'

'You are sure we should go straight to Mr Hand?' Kenjiro asked anxiously.

'Certain – he's more likely to understand and to help us than anyone else.' Kenjiro hesitated; he was not convinced, but having no better alternative to offer he fell in with the plan she had suggested before they sailed.

Desmond Hand was enjoying a pre-luncheon sherry in the conservatory of his charming hill-top bungalow called Bay View House, when Elinor, Kenjiro and their luggage were carried into the garden. He hurried to meet them. 'Upon my word it's Miss Elinor Mills – and Mr Miyata, isn't it? What a pleasant surprise! You must be off the *Mongolia*? And it looks as if you've come to stay in Nagasaki, Miss Mills? If so,

I shall be delighted to offer you the hospitality of my home.'

'How very kind of you, Mr Hand.' As she greeted him he noted her strained pallor. 'This is not exactly a social visit, but we will explain.'

He ushered her inside with fussy gallantry and Kenjiro, left to trail behind, felt a surge of angry triumph in the knowledge that Mr Hand would not be able to treat him simply as a native interpreter for much longer. 'Please sit down – sherry or some cordial?' Hand went to call his wife while Elinor stood in the centre of the room twisting the velvet ribbon of her bonnet round her finger, and Kenjiro moved uneasily to the window.

'Is anything wrong, Miss Mills?' He came back, closing the door quietly.

'Not wrong, exactly; indeed not wrong at all. Only I . . . we . . . have some particular news that I think we should tell you at once.'

'By all means, please.' His blandly inquiring face was so obviously unprepared for what was to come that she faltered. 'You see, it's just . . . I mean, not just . . . but . . .'

Kenjiro, who was carefully dressed in his best western suit, drew himself up to his full height, saying, 'Miss Mills and I are engaged, Mr Hand. And we have come to Nagasaki to be married because Miss Mills' brother greatly disapproves of the match.'

Misako Hand, coming in at the door, gave a bird-like cry of astonishment and hurried to Elinor's side. 'Miss Mills – you and Mr Miyata. But this is delightful! How pleased we are for you both – aren't we, husband?' She appealed to him shyly.

He hesitated, feeling an instinctive tug of sympathy for the disapproving brother in the case. 'You are quite sure of this, Miss Mills?' He spoke quietly, cutting out Kenjiro. Elinor moved to Kenjiro's side and put her arm through his. 'I've never been more certain of anything in my life, Mr Hand,' she said, as she had several times before.

'Then it is splendid, splendid.' He kissed her on both cheeks and shook Kenjiro's hand warmly. 'Why – sherry is far too everyday for such news! Misako, bring some champagne.

And, Miss Mills, please take off your cloak and make yourself at home.'

She did so and when Misako returned with champagne on a silver tray they stood in a circle and raised their glasses. Desmond Hand, now quite caught up in the sense of occasion, began earnestly, 'Miss Mills, Mr Miyata, may we be among the first to congratulate you. May your union, like mine with Misako, be happy and fruitful. A living proof that the British and Japanese, though separate and different peoples, can live together in love and friendship. For we are both island races, gifted with enterprise, energy, and . . . my dear, what is it?'

For Ellie, having taken a generous gulp of champagne, suddenly burst out crying and collapsed into her chair. 'Oh, please excuse me . . . I'm not miserable at all . . . just so hap . . . hap . . . happy,' she blurted, searching for a handkerchief. 'You see, no one has wished us well till now, Mr Hand. No one has congratulated us as you just have, and it's just too . . . too . . . much. Your kindness and welcome after all the trouble and strain we've been through.' She sniffed. 'I haven't cried once, till now, and it's silly when I'm so . . . so . . . hap . . . hap . . .'

'There, there my dear.' Desmond patted her lowered head. 'Here, drink this.'

'You are really all right?' Kenjiro bent over her anxiously and took her hand.

'Oh, yes, dear.' She looked up smiling. 'Mr Hand, this is the first time we've been able to hold hands openly together. So you see why I'm crying so happily.'

Misako, who was dabbing her eyes with her kimono sleeve in sympathy, brought Elinor a large clean handkerchief. 'Now I'm truly recovered, Mr Hand; and we must explain why we've landed ourselves on you for help and advice. I think we'll have to stay in Nagasaki for a while before we can legally marry, isn't that so?'

'Indeed yes, a residential qualification of at least two months is required.'

'That's as I thought. And to speak plainly, Mr Hand, I want there to be no hint of impropriety in our conduct during that period. Kenjiro and I have been very careful on that point until now and will continue to do so. Society — I mean the tittle-tattles of the foreign settlements — must be given no possible grounds for scandalmongering. Isn't that so, Kenjiro?'

He nodded, finding the conversation embarrassing if necessary. 'That is so, Mr Hand.' He turned to his host. 'And I propose to take lodgings in the town with some of my clansmen until the wedding day. But I am anxious for Miss Mills. Is there some respectable accommodation?'

'But she'll stay here with us, of course — we shall be absolutely delighted!' And Mr Hand extended his arms to Elinor with such generous warmth that she was again on the brink of tears; but, hastily swallowing more champagne, laughed her acceptance of the invitation instead. After a merry and prolonged lunch, during which they concocted a note to be sent to the *Mongolia* saying that, at Mr Hand's pressing invitation, Elinor was staying in Nagasaki for a few days, Kenjiro went to seek lodgings in the town. On the way to show Elinor to her bedroom, Misako beckoned her into the nursery where her first-born, two-year-old Yakumo, was asleep.

'Isn't he beautiful?' Misako stroked his cheek. To Elinor the baby looked almost entirely Japanese except for a rather ruddy complexion. But what of it? He was indeed beautiful and she longed for the day when she might hold Kenjiro's son in her arms. 'Another one, I hope, in the summer.' Misako patted her stomach, and the women smiled at each other.

The wedding date was fixed for February 26th and at first Elinor feared that each steamer might bring her brother storming into port to try to prevent it. But he did not appear and eventually, guessing that his easy-going nature had resigned him to the inevitable, she judged it time to send a wedding invitation to him and Ryo. Neither of them replied. Apart from that cloud, however, Elinor's horizons were serene, and as the days passed, she could scarcely imagine what all the fuss had been about.

She and Kenjiro usually met in the presence of Desmond or his wife; and this was as well for, to Kenjiro, the western

221

style of courtship, the ardent fumblings of the frustrated swain, were incomprehensible. He and his young samurai friends had gained their sexual experience quite openly with women of the pleasure quarters, and he had then expected to marry a woman of his class chosen by his family. Thus, on the few occasions when he was alone with Elinor, he became confused and self-conscious, desperately wanting her but constrained by her rules and propriety. While she, longing to respond wholeheartedly to his passion, parried it with a flirtatious manner that baffled him.

Kenjiro kept these perplexities to himself, however, and told no one except the two clansmen who shared his lodgings, Ando and Watanabe, of his engagement to a foreign woman. To them, such an alliance seemed incomprehensible, not to say shocking, and for the most part they ignored it and were embarrassed by Kenjiro's occasional references to his future wife. One February evening the three of them were eating supper together as usual when a clatter of hooves in the courtyard announced the arrival of Chomin Komatsu, still chief interpreter in the service of Lord Shimazu. He had just returned from a three-month stay in Kyoto and brought momentous news: the Emperor Komnei had died just three weeks before, of smallpox, though his death had been kept secret until the enthronement of his son, Mutsuhito, which had just taken place. Mutsuhito was only fourteen years old, and in consequence the powerful nobles of the court were busily jockeying for positions of influence over him.

'It's a great chance,' Chomin said, as he joined them round the table, 'for us Satsuma to establish our dominance in the Imperial capital. The great Saigo Takamori is there now working for this, and soon he'll go to Kagoshima to persuade our Chief to march to Kyoto himself, supported by an armed force.'

'It will be war against the *bakafu* at last, then?' Watanabe jumped up and postured about excitedly, brandishing an imaginary sword.

'Cool your hot blood, young man; it may come to that, maybe not. If the coalition between our clan, Choshiu and

Tosa holds, the Shogun, seeing our strength, may capitulate without a fight and a peaceful compromise can be reached.'

'Oh, pooh! Not if the great Saigo has his way; he detests compromises.'

'But he's not a man to choose bloodshed for its own sake, either.'

'You've met him, Chomin — what does he really want for this country, do you think?' Kenjiro asked.

Chomin put down his chopsticks, lit his pipe and puffed a little. 'Great Saigo wants many things, because he's a warrior, an idealist, and a statesman. In a nutshell, he wants the reformation of the country, and a forward-looking Imperial government with the young Emperor at its head.'

'And Satsuma as the dominant faction in that government? Isn't that so?' Ando asked eagerly. He was an ambitious young man whose family belonged to Nagasaki's secret Christian community, and he wanted Japan to be Asia's first Christian democracy — though he would have been hard put to explain exactly what that meant.

'Of course we Satsumas want the most power,' Chonin answered him, imperturbably. 'We must still be discreet and try to negotiate a peace. The time for sword-play has not yet arrived, Mr Watanabe, so please stop parading about and order more *saké* instead.'

'But what should we do now, then?' Kenjiro asked. 'Just stay here translating documents when so much is happening elsewhere?'

'There's no immediate call to arms, Kenjiro, and you, like me, are not a warrior by nature. Perhaps Mr Watanabe here should go to Kagoshima and join our forces there.'

'That I will and straightaway . . .' Mr Watanabe looked ready to ride off that very night.

'There's no great urgency, young man. So come now, here's the *saké* — let's relax. I've had a hard journey.' He turned again to Kenjiro. 'So what brings you here, Kenjiro? I heard a rumour that you'd left British employ, but not the reason for it.'

Kenjiro turned bright red, while Watanabe sniggered.

'And you'll never guess the reason, Mr Komatsu – not in ten thousand years, I'll warrant!'

Chomin leaned forward, interested. 'Really? I trust you haven't committed any action of which your late father would be ashamed?'

'No, I have not.' Kenjiro faced him tensely. 'I left of my own accord, because . . .' He stared appealingly at the older man, then lowered his forehead to the mat. 'Please do not condemn me, honourable sir, I have done . . . I am committed to a strange deed, a way that is new and different, but it is not wrong. I'm not being disloyal to our clan, I promise you, though some may view it so. But you – trusted and honourable friend of my late father – try and understand, please.'

In the uncomfortable pause, Chomin looked questioningly at Ando and Watanabe, who averted their eyes. 'Tell me, lad,' he said gently.

'Next week I'm going to marry a foreign young lady of very respectable background. She's the sister of Dr Mills of the British Legation, whom I believe you've met.' Kenjiro glanced imploringly at Chomin, who was drawing loud hisses of amazement through his pipe.

Ando, to relieve the tension, refilled the *saké* cups.

'I think I've met the young lady, too – at Kagoshima three years ago. She's fair-haired, is she not?' Chomin's voice was neutral.

'Yes, sir.'

'And can you explain to me why you are proposing to do this extremely odd thing?'

'I . . . We have known each other for about four years . . . Her fiancé, an army officer, was one of the Kamakura victims.'

'Ah yes, I remember now. And you feel sorry for her? Without a man of her own?' He was teasing to hide his discomfiture at the news.

'No, no, of course not. We spent much time together. I was teaching her our language. She and my sister became good friends. Then after the Yokohama fire her brother said she must leave the country, and she . . . didn't want to,' he stumbled, then continued, 'And I didn't want her to.'

Watanabe grimaced into his *saké* and gave a little belch of disgust.

'Because you had become very fond of her?' Chomin was incredulous.

'Yes, sir,' Kenjiro admitted in a whisper. 'Very, very fond. So we told her brother, who was furious. And then we ran away here to be married. It is all being done correctly – she is staying with the merchant Hand until the wedding.'

'It is an astounding thing. Whatever would your honourable father . . .?' Chomin rubbed his forehead. 'Haven't you thought, Kenjiro, that such a step would probably ruin your chances of high advancement within the clan? And just at a time when there are so many opportunities for young men like yourself?'

Kenjiro turned his head away from the words. 'I can't help that.'

'Are you sure? There is still time to change your mind.'

'It is all arranged and I will marry her. It would break her heart if I didn't do so now.'

'And your heart, Kenjiro?' Chomin leaned forward intently.

'And my heart too.'

Chomin hissed again, long and sadly, then told Watanabe to order more *saké*. Ando, feeling sorry for Kenjiro, asked timidly, 'And will it be a church wedding – when you are not a Christian?'

'We will have two simple ceremonies – a Buddhist and a Christian – as the Hands did.'

Flasks of fresh hot *saké* appeared and they all quaffed deeply in embarrassed silence till Chomin said, 'It is a great shame that this has happened to you, Kenjiro; and I confess I cannot in the least understand it when you are surrounded by so many lovely young ladies of your own race.' He looked discouraged and began to yawn after the long journey and the bad news. 'But I won't turn away from you because of this. Your father was my good friend – we ate rice from the same pot. And you will need all the help you can get along the thorny path you have chosen.' He drained his cup and began to rise from his cushion, muttering crossly, 'Old bones, old bones. We'll talk further of this in the morning, young man, when I'm refreshed.'

They bowed deeply as Chomin moved towards the door, where he paused. 'And will she be a loyal and obedient wife to you, Kenjiro? This straw-haired woman from a distant land?'

'Yes, I know she will,' he replied boldly. 'She is totally committed to me and to my country – she has said so.'

Chomin shook his head in sorrowing disbelief and shuffled out.

Watanabe, who had been drinking heavily for some time, handed Kenjiro a brimming cup. 'Come on – tell me about your barbarian wench now the old man's gone.'

'She's not a wench, she's a well-born young lady.'

'Oh, I do beg your pardon! So – your foreign princess with hair the colour of bleached rope, who has stolen your heart away.'

Kenjiro stood still, the cup trembling in his hand. 'Leave him be, Watanabe,' muttered Ando uneasily.

'Ah, but you really must tell me about her.' Watanabe raised a flushed face. 'I'm all ears. What's the colour of a barbarian's love-fuzz, Kenjiro? And the cunt? Is it the same as a good Japanese wench's – dark red and juicy as pomegranates to suck? Or does it have a distinctly foreign flavour? Like ice-cream perhaps? Or does it bubble like French champagne?' He giggled lewdly. 'Oh I wish I could taste it! You are lucky, old boy – free champagne any time you like from now on!'

Kenjiro threw the *saké* in his face and Watanabe leaped up to cuff him, but Ando grabbed his arm. 'Stop it, you fools. You're drunk, Watanabe – leave the poor sod alone. He's enough to worry about.'

Kenjiro hesitated, furiously ready to fight, but sober enough to realise the foolhardiness of doing so.

Ando threw Watanabe back on the floor. 'Get away to bed, Miyata. What's the point of creating a disturbance over such a trivial matter? If Mr Komatsu heard, he'd be furious.'

Kenjiro nodded unhappily and went out, leaving Ando and Watanabe to finish the *saké* and, as the night wore on, embroider further on the nature of foreign female anatomy.

Chomin Komatsu refused to attend the wedding; but his absence was more than compensated for when, just before the ceremony, Ryo arrived without warning at Bay View House. Her decision to come had been a last-minute one, she told Elinor, and she had been finally persuaded by Mrs Hubbard. After Kenjiro's departure, Ryo had been homeless until Mrs Hubbard offered her accommodation in return for her teaching in the mission school. 'It's very difficult for her to understand, as it is for me,' Ryo explained. 'But she's willing to forgive you and hopes you will both be happy. She prays constantly that − through you − my brother and I will be converted to the true faith.'

Elinor sighed. 'Oh, forgiveness − for eloping, I suppose? Why do I require forgiveness for marrying the man I love most? As for Christianity, that is a matter I must leave for Kenjiro's own conscience, at least for a while. But you − how do you feel about it?' She looked at Ryo keenly.

'Mrs Hubbard has been very kind to me and is such a good woman. When I listen to her teaching the girls about Christianity I am drawn towards it, just a little.'

'Then I am very pleased for you, for there are no finer people in this world than genuine and devout believers like Mrs Hubbard.'

'Mr Coburn wouldn't agree with you,' Ryo said softly.

'Felix? I suppose not − he worships at the shrine of Science, believing it holds the answer to all our problems. Have you been discussing such weighty topics with him, then?' Elinor teased, thinking it most unlikely.

'Yes, we talk often about the differences between our two countries and what he calls the tyranny of blind Christian dogma. He's writing scholarly articles about our country for English magazines, and asks me to help him sometimes. I'm very honoured to be of use to such a clever man.'

'Oh, pooh! I don't think Felix is as clever as he pretends. He just loves to play the professor. Still,' she added, seeing Ryo's crestfallen look, 'I'm sure such articles are very valuable. Most English people are dreadfully ignorant about Japan. Anyway, what does Professor Coburn think of my marrying your brother?'

'He thinks you are both very right and brave to do it.'

'Then he has risen in my estimation. But talking of brothers – what about my own? You haven't mentioned his name yet?'

Ryo plucked agitatedly at her sleeve. 'He is usually in Edo now, I've hardly seen him.'

'But he's not coming to our wedding?'

'I think not, though it was not my business to ask him directly.'

Elinor sighed. 'No . . . oh well, blow him! Your arrival is joy enough. It's the icing on our wedding cake, dear, and I shall always be grateful to you – so, I know, will Kenjiro.'

There was, of course, a cake; it was decorated with white icing and silver bells and cut during the small reception held at the Bellevue Hotel after the two marriage ceremonies. A hired photographer grouped the wedding party on the hotel lawn – Kenjiro and Elinor, flanked by Ando, Ryo, and Desmond Hand, who had given Elinor away. Elinor's dress of white satin was fringed with finest Portuguese lace. Kenjiro looked most uncomfortable in a single-breasted frock coat that was too tight at the shoulders and cuffs, while his trouser legs drooped baggily over his patent leather shoes. Elinor, when she saw him that day, formed her first wifely intent – to find him a good European tailor. The resulting photographs of the stiff-looking, solemn bride and groom gave no hint of their feelings, as they stood, sharing the joyous tingling of their closeness. It was mixed with a certain apprehension – of the unknown on Elinor's part and, on Kenjiro's, of how he was ever going to manage the removal of western clothes, with all their mysterious loops, buttons, fastenings, the layers and the casings.

In the evening after the guests had gone, they strolled across the lawn of the hotel where they were staying the night. Side by side they stood on the grassy slope at the garden's edge gazing at the bright stars and the darkness of the sea. They were self-conscious, tongue-tied, tensely excited as two children, gripping each other's hands; then Kenjiro touched his wife's cheek and they went to their bedroom. As he moved over her, erect and sure, he murmured, as if in surprise, 'Why, I had my weapon ready for you the first time we met. Do you remember, my Elinor?'

She closed her eyes, seeing with vivid intensity the handsome, unknown, alarmed young Japanese standing by the courtyard well with his sword drawn. 'Oh, Kenjiro, oh yes, I remember, darling,' she murmured as he opened her wide to receive into her virginity the first of his gentle thrusts.

The next day the newly married pair moved into a small bungalow that had just been built in the grounds of Bay View House to accommodate the increasing number of Desmond Hand's visitors. Such visitors were both foreign and Japanese, for Hand, now the acknowledged doyen of Nagasaki's mercantile community, had his fingers in even more pies: schemes for building a steam-saw mill and a dockyard; agencies for marine insurance and banking; the export of sugar and silk from the interior; and the import of weapons and machinery. He could easily afford to be generous to the Miyatas and he was well aware also how useful it was to have a fluent and trustworthy linguist on hand − especially one belonging to the clan with whom he had most business dealings. So Kenjiro found himself kept very busy as usual, while Elinor simply idled the days away, in a happy dream that was like a prolonged honeymoon.

During it, she found herself beginning to appreciate more of the natural world, as if through Japanese eyes − the beauty of a single feathery reed reflected in water, the clean lines of grey rocks on mossed banks, the single, flowing stroke of black ink on white paper. She often smiled to herself at what, she now realised, had been there all the time waiting to be seen, and when Kenjiro was there he took pleasure in her serene smiling.

In tune with her mood, the spring, which always came early to Nagasaki, seemed to begin on her wedding day that year. In the gardens of the foreign settlements on the hill, camellia and jonquils opened, plum, almond, cherry, and peach trees bloomed, and close-trimmed shrubs of unknown name flowered dusk-pink, violet, and transparent ivory in the sun. From her verandah, sweet with gardenias and potted fuchsias, Elinor could see the white-sailed fishing boats scudding like butterflies over the blue waters of the bay, and the distant hill-terraces greening with the first crops. In the foreground, the servants' children, bundled in scarlet and orange jackets, ran along the garden paths flying coloured paper kites, also shaped like butterflies.

The pillars of their little bungalow were entwined with creepers, its windows overlooked a grove of ornamental bamboo, palm trees stood sentinel at its side, their spiky tops outlined black against the southern sunsets. During the warm nights of early summer when roses were in bloom, it became a magical setting for their love, for their growing delight as they learned to move sweetly in unison with each other. Desmond Hand, noticing how often they lightly touched and held each other's gaze in the daylight hours, guessed the passion of their nightly communion and was pleased. They were auspicious first guests for his new bungalow, he felt; and ever after he called it the little honeymoon-hut, though he seldom explained why.

With Misako, Elinor had little in common, but the shared experience of inter-racial marriage was a sufficient bond for the time. Misako was obedient, adoring and humble, catering to her husband's every need as a good Japanese wife should. She took great pleasure in laying out Desmond's formal clothes for his evening excursions (though she seldom accompanied him), scrubbing his back in the bath-tub, massaging his legs when he came home tired. But she was also shrewd, and quickly learned how to cook and serve foreign dishes and entertain his foreign friends. Elinor marvelled at her capacity for so much selfless, thoughtful caring and knew she could not and would not emulate it. Aware that this was what a Japanese male was brought up to expect from a wife, however, she felt occasional twinges of doubt about the future; but Kenjiro, she told herself, was a modern young man, much more so than Desmond Hand, who seemed thoroughly to enjoy his wife's traditional ministrations.

In early July, Misako gave birth to a daughter, and on the

seventh day after the birth a naming celebration was held for her in accordance with Japanese custom. The baby was given the very English name of Dorothy in memory of Desmond's mother, and two godparents – Elinor and Kenjiro. It was a happy occasion and at the time Elinor contentedly assumed she would live long enough in Nagasaki to see little Dorothy toddling about the lawn with her brother. But this was not to be, for, soon afterwards, Kenjiro received a letter from Taneo Takahashi.

Though Taneo began by politely congratulating Kenjiro on his marriage to such a charming and intelligent foreign lady, his tone was gently censorious. How long did an able fellow like Miyata intend frittering away his days in a backwater like Nagasaki? Was he allowing himself to become just another frog-in-the-well provincial? In Edo and Kyoto momentous upheavals were about to take place that would change the entire face of the nation. Taneo knew for a fact that the Bureau of Foreign Affairs would take him on now that the Shogunate had belatedly decided to initiate cautious reforms and develop international trade. Moreover, Taneo had recently rented a large residential compound where he ran a school for western studies. Why didn't Kenjiro and his new wife come and stay and make themselves really useful?'

The letter was a revelation to Kenjiro; possessed of quick wits, energy, and ambition, he lacked the foresight and confidence of maturity and found definite next-steps difficult to take without guidance. This was why he had remained an interpreter for the British for so long. Now the way ahead had been shown him and, that very evening, in the manner of Japanese husbands, he simply told his wife that they would soon be going to Edo to live with Mr Takahashi. Elinor was sad at the prospect of leaving lovely, lazy Nagasaki, but as long as she was with Kenjiro nothing else really mattered; and so it would be, she told herself, for the rest of her life.

CHAPTER TWELVE

The Miyatas, approaching Edo along the Tokaido highway on a fine autumn day, saw first the high land on which stood the ancient castle of the Shogun surrounded by miles of wooded grounds and two wide moats bordered by steep embankments and by stone walls surmounted by watch-towers. Between the outer and inner moats were several of the principal *yashiki* – the private residences of the clan-leaders, each in its turn enclosed within spacious gardens, imposing gate-ways, and cordons of barrack-like buildings where their retainers lived. This was Edo's High City – powerful, aloof, aristocratic, its wealth and splendour carefully secluded from the common gaze of all who dwelt below.

The half million or so ordinary townsfolk who did were proud to call themselves Eddoku – children of Edo, inhabitants of the Low City, which was flanked by the outer moat to the west and, to the east, the River Sumida and Edo Bay. The land here was flattish, intersected by numerous canals and crowded with buildings: shops, restaurants, merchants' houses, shrines and temples, rows of closely packed, two-roomed dwellings of artisans and tradesmen, innumerable canal-clustering back-alley shacks of the poor. The hub of the Low City was Nihombashi, and its nucleus was the famous Japan Bridge that gave the district its name and from which all distances in the country were measured. Parallel and south of Nihombashi was the Low City's other principal quarter, Kyobashi, where Taneo Takahashi had managed to rent cheaply the walled compound of a well-to-do merchant who, fearing the present disturbances, had fled the capital with his money and family.

The Miyatas were extremely glad to reach it, for the journey had been long and bothersome. Elinor had travelled little previously, and always accompanied and protected by her own kind. Now she was at the mercy of the country, a lone foreign woman in a man's company. The people they met on route usually took her for a harlot, a Dutch strumpet, a trollop from the stews of San Francisco; it was fortunate, Kenjiro realised, that her Japanese was not colloquial enough to understand much of what they said. He in his turn had been horrified both by their ignorant crudity and by the many difficulties he had encountered while trying to behave like a proud samurai on the one hand and, on the other, like the courteous husband of an English lady.

The house they were offered in Takahashi's family compound had four rooms and a verandah with a little garden plot; but it was quite good enough, and their first real home, as Elinor announced, standing in the sparsely furnished interior surrounded by their luggage and wondering where everything could be put.

'Here you are at last – delighted!' Taneo Takahashi came bounding in, bowing and shaking hands. 'My servant will help you unpack later. Please come and take some refreshment after the journey. And how did you find it, Mrs Miyata, travelling in the Japanese style?'

She smiled faintly at his keen look. 'Well . . . most interesting, but not very easy, I must admit. I'm sure I'll get used to it though.'

'That's the spirit. Come now, my wife wants to meet you.'

Over tea, during which Mrs Takahashi waited on them more like a servant than a hostess, Taneo regaled Kenjiro with what he termed the latest buzzes in the capital.

'The situation is coming inevitably towards a crisis and we scholars dread the prospect of bloodshed in the land.' He knocked his head rapidly with clenched fist in a characteristically worried gesture. 'Agitators are roaming the city, holding meetings, looting, starting fires; every good-for-nothing swaggers about spoiling for a fight, and I've even seen priests carrying long swords.'

'The proposed opening of Kobe and Osaka to foreign trade is increasing tension?' Kenjiro suggested.

'Of course, and there's a rumour that the Shogun might resign before then, which could help the situation. But the latest thing is the dancing; have you heard about that?' He chuckled warmly as they shook their heads. 'Yes, and it's a sign that the common people have been affected by the political upheavals at last. Began in Nagoya and has now spread here – groups of people massing in the streets, singing, dancing, men dressing up as women, women as boys or demons. But sometimes it gets ugly – houses have been attacked, stones thrown. And, "What is the good of all that?" they keep chanting again and again. I've heard them. It's quite wonderful and awe-inspiring: our docile, down-trodden commoners who humbly licked the feet of their so-called superiors for centuries like pet dogs are suddenly getting up on their hind legs – and dancing!' He chuckled again, then added seriously, 'And once ordinary people start asking themselves what is the good of traditional law and custom the spirit of liberation must really be stirring in their souls.'

'Don't the authorities do anything to prevent it?' Elinor asked timidly.

'Oh, the high-and-mighty wring their wrists and wonder what to do.' He jerked his head scornfully to westward. 'And the *bakafu* are trying to strengthen their militia. But men are very wary of allying themselves with the Shogun, who may well lose the day soon.'

'And my south-western clansmen, are they active here?' Kenjiro asked eagerly.

'Oh, gangs calling themselves the advance guard of the Imperial Army go pushing about, quarrelsome as the rest.'

In the glum silence Elinor looked at the two men in growing alarm. 'Wouldn't it be dreadful if there were full-scale civil war?' she whispered.

Kenjiro smiled. 'Oh, I don't suppose it will come to that. You mustn't worry, Elinor.'

So she tried not to, and at first there seemed no need.

Kenjiro was soon gainfully employed translating documents that passed through the Bureau of Foreign Affairs. He and Elinor also taught in Taneo's western studies school. There the curriculum was as usual – English, history, geography, economics – for Taneo refused to be deflected from his long-term aims by the current political turmoils.

'I've never been much of a clansman,' he lectured his students. 'And I won't risk my head in this stupid internal strife. My loyalty is to a united Japan, no more, no less.'

At this, some students left in disgust, and returned to their native provinces, determined to fight to the death for their clan whichever side it was on. Others stayed, and were labelled as lazy, cowardly, long-sleeved scholars.

For Kenjiro too there was conflict. His clan was in the very forefront of the struggle for power and mustering its forces to march to Kyoto, where the pro-Imperial clans were gathering. He might have made his mark there, but was restrained, both by Taneo's opinions and by the plight of his young wife, who was very isolated in this disturbed, alien city. Although her brother now resided at the Edo Legation quite close by, she adamantly refused to contact him or any of her English friends. He respected her proud decision; yet secretly chafed a little at the bit of marriage, for the first time.

In November, Edo was startled by the news that the Shogun, Keike, had resigned his political authority to the young Emperor. But this, which initially seemed a step towards a peaceful resolution of the crisis, only aggravated it, for the Shogun, like the Emperor, was little more than a figurehead, and his supporters continued to struggle for supremacy. Taneo, who often visited Edo Castle in the course of his work, reported that, following the resignation, the place was reduced to near chaos.

'Those ancient walls haven't seen the like for centuries,' he told Kenjiro, vacillating as usual between delight in the spectacle of oppressive authority's decline and dismay at the disorder and violence that followed. 'The grand waiting rooms with their beautiful paintings – of the Geese and of the Willows – are disfigured with ruffians who sprawl about loose-legged, drinking and quarrelling about what should be done. Everyone argues all day, all night; I'm tired of hearing it. So much wasted energy, mad schemes . . .'

He knocked his forehead and Kenjiro said gently, 'You will soon make holes in your head, *sensei*, forever beating at your brains like that! Please let's take one evening off. It happens to be my birthday and I'm to tell you that my wife is expecting our first child.'

'Why, double-double congratulations, Miyata! And, oh, how refreshing it is to hear something jolly after all this mix and muddle. Of course we'll celebrate − bring some of your clan-cronies along and we'll hire a boat and go to feast with the Yoshiwara girls.'

Kenjiro hesitated. 'But my wife will want to come too; it would hurt her very much to be left out of such an occasion. Western women expect to be included, as you know.'

Taneo grimaced wryly. '*Ah-so*, I forgot. The actual business of emancipating women from their oppression is very hard for us men to accept, is it not? But you are right, I suppose. The Yoshiwara must wait and tonight we three will go quietly to a very respectable restaurant.'

'And *your* wife, *sensei*?' Kenjiro needled him.

'Oh, my wife is traditional and knows her place in the home, my dear young man. And for me it would be most uncomfortable to fill her little head with too many modern ideas at this stage.' He grinned impenitently.

And so, on that December evening, just the three of them went out. It was an excursion Elinor long remembered, for she had been out very little since her arrival and, though she did not realise it at the time, so much of what she then saw was rapidly passing away. They went by hired boat propelled by a single oarsman. The quiet canals they moved along were overhung with close-packed houses and spanned by high-arched bridges; a cold mist hung about, blurring the coloured lanterns on shore and the moon above into mysterious, fuzzy circles. Passing through pools of blackness under the bridges, they heard the echoing clatter of footsteps above, the lap and suck of water below. A thin boat glided out of and back into the mist with a thin man at its prow rhythmically beating a drum; a larger vessel surged by, strung with lights and full of painted singing-girls, chattering and calling out like caged birds. Along the narrower stretches, drooping willows cast spindly shadows and steam came clouding out from the nearby house-kitchens. Elinor, sitting chilled and quiet, was oddly moved by it all – the drifting from melancholy to gaiety, the familiarity of much that seemed, in the misty dark, to be suddenly strange, the throb and pulse of thousands of people, invisible yet almost palpable.

Upon landing they passed along a brightly lit street thronged with very visible people. Men in padded overcloaks were hurrying to the pleasure-quarters, for the night was still young; muffled-up children were bouncing beside their mothers, who were dressed in their evening kimonos, their coiled hair glittering with ornaments. It was the hour when whims were most often satisfied, and street-hawkers did their best business, offering for sale prawns, paper flowers, barley-paste men, painted tops, dried grasses, lamp-wicks, caged crows, or bean-cheese, well cooked or partly fried.

They did not linger, for Elinor's foreignness was very conspicuous and every head turned as she passed by, the children tittering at her strange clothes and light hair. As they sat in the restaurant Taneo recalled his own impressions of the Washington he had visited with his country's delegation five years before and tried to imagine the Edo of 1867 through a foreigner's eyes. But all he could produce was a string of dispiriting negatives: no imposing public buildings, meeting halls or libraries, no post offices or banks, no trains or horse-driven carriages, no newspapers, gas-lights, opera houses, telegraph wires . . . He felt a disgusted impatience at his country's shortcomings and began covertly watching Elinor for any sign of disdain or disappointment. But she seemed starry-eyed with enthusiasm at the passing scene. Solemnly he raised his *saké* cup and drank a toast to the brave, lioness-haired lady from across the ocean, and then they drank to Kenjiro's birthday and the fortune of the coming child. At Taneo's insistence, they returned early; and he was glad when they got safely back, for, as he told Kenjiro in confidence, it had been madness for a foreign woman to be abroad at such a tricky time even with male escorts. This Kenjiro explained to her and for a while afterwards she had to live as cloistered within the house as any Japanese wife.

She saw little of Kenjiro, for he was intensely involved in the national crisis, which by now was so serious that armed conflict was unavoidable. The New Year opened to the noise of guns – fired from foreign ships to mark the opening of Osaka and Kobe to international trade and residence. The sound was peaceful, but peace did not last much longer. On January 3rd the south-western clans staged a *coup d'état* in Kyoto; their leaders began setting up a provisional government; and the Emperor announced that complete authority to rule was restored to him. Four days later the Shogun Keike, officially deprived of his office, and his loyal troops from the northern clans, now called 'rebels', retreated towards Osaka.

Though these dramatic upheavals were to determine the country's direction for the next half-century, they were contained within the vicinity of the Imperial capital and those not on the spot had neither time nor opportunity to participate. Official circles in Edo were naturally agog for the latest news, which, being brought by hard-riding couriers of different factions, was often contradictory and incomplete, and Kenjiro, like many of his fellows, spent much time in his clan *yashiki* in a state of perpetual suspense and anxiety. Such was the nerve-racking state of things when, one wintry afternoon, Elinor heard a familiar voice in the outer courtyard asking for her. She jumped up, paling slightly, and hurried to the door.

'Arnold!' Her brother looked even larger and fatter than she remembered, in his double-breasted Chesterfield overcoat and top-hat.

He smiled hesitantly, holding out his hand. 'Elinor . . . May I come in?'

'Please do.' As he stepped inside in his heavy boots she pushed a pair of Japanese slippers at him. 'We have *tatami* here, no foreign carpets.' He grunted reluctantly, unlaced his boots and put on the slippers, which were far too small, then shuffled inelegantly into the little sitting-room. There seemed nowhere big enough to hang his coat and hat; Japanese homes were like that. He looked with scarcely disguised disapproval at the loose, native-style robe she habitually wore around the house.

'I'm glad to see you looking so well, Elinor.' His tone implied that he had expected otherwise.

'I'm extremely well, thank you. Please sit down. I'll order tea. And you are well too, I hope?'

He nodded, trying to fit his bulk into one of the only small armchairs. 'Oh yes, thanks. Just back from Osaka – went down with the Chief for the opening, of course. It was rather jolly to be so near the scenes of action.'

She drew a little breath and said deliberately. 'Really? Then I'm sure my husband would be most interested to hear about it. He has remained here, partly on my account, as things are so unsettled.'

'Well, I'm glad to hear that. I've been extremely worried about you – here alone at such a chaotic time; that's really why I've come.'

'I'm perfectly all right,' she cut in proudly. 'In fact I'm to have a child in the summer, Arnold.'

'Oh, my dear . . .' He leaned forward eagerly, then checked himself. 'Please accept my congratulations, Elinor.'

'Ah, tea . . . thank you.' She took the tray from a servant, and he shifted uncomfortably in his chair, watching her pour, her head with its thick fair braids bent over the pot. He had always liked to see her hair so arranged; sensible Ellie, his young sis. She came over with a cup and a plate of nasty green and pink sweetmeats, and he took one gingerly. 'Elinor, I've come to say that I think we should be reconciled, you and I. We are brother and sister alone in an alien land and it is absurd that we should remain estranged. What is done is done, and can't be helped now.' He heard her quick breath of annoyance and hurried on. 'I feel that for your sake, and more especially now I hear a child is coming, you should be able to count on my help and protection as a brother if and when you need it. It has saddened me to think of you cut off from us all recently. And your friends in Yokohama are also willing to . . . well . . . accept that matters can't be changed now.' He paused, but she remained silent. 'Well? What do you say, Elinor? Surely, when I've actually come here . . .'

She put down the sweetmeat she had been nibbling and looked at him. 'I'm glad you've come, believe me, Arnold. And certainly I'd like us to be friends again. Only, frankly, I don't like your tone. You sound as if you – and everyone else – are magnanimously prepared to forgive me for some misdeed. But I must point out that I've done nothing of which I'm in the least ashamed and am in no need of forgiveness. I've simply married the man of my choice and our conduct before the wedding was just as it should have been. May I say also that Kenjiro is now legally your brother-in-law, and unless you're going to accept him as such, you and I won't get on for long, I fear.'

He blinked; the 'brother-in-law' jarred; he had not encompassed it before. He met her eyes; her chin was raised, just as when a child she used to face her father in some small act of defiance. He thought of a child growing inside her; he had a suspicion he would officially remain a bachelor for life; but the idea of unclehood appealed to him. She was waiting for his reply, not giving an inch.

He looked away and shrugged. 'So be it, my little sis. As you say, I must accept your choice with good grace – or not at all. Well, I accept; we will all be friends, a family together.' He went over and kissed her hair, 'There, is that all right now?'

'Yes, of course, Arnold, and I'm so pleased.' She touched her cheek. 'I too have hated our quarrelling. Now drink your tea and I'll fetch Kenjiro to join us. He's here today, fortunately, helping Taneo with some translating.'

She went out and he had a chance to look round. The room was as scantily furnished as a native's and extremely chilly to boot. Ellie should be kept warm and comfortable in her condition. He sighed, strolling over to the only piece of furniture – a bookcase with English books and oddments along the top shelf. There he saw a small framed watercolour of the parental home; the front lawn bordered with hectically blooming rhododendrons; it had been painted by his elder sister and it was not good.

He decided not to tell Elinor about the intemperately furious letter he had received from their father about the marriage. The news that Elinor was wedded to a 'yellow-skinned nigger' had almost killed her mother, Mills senior had written, and she was still in a state of utter prostration. A 'yellow-skinned nigger'; Arnold winced at the blind, illogical fury behind such words. Certainly, whatever the term was supposed to mean, it hardly fitted Miyata as he came in now beside his wife, dressed in a well-cut striped suit and braid-edged waistcoat. Arnold greeted him over-effusively and Kenjiro bowed his head and shook hands, looking embarrassed but not in the least apologetic.

Elinor fussed about getting fresh tea while the men chatted politely. 'Elinor tells me you were at Osaka for the opening and saw something of what went on?' Kenjiro asked after a while, settling back in the other chair, while Elinor sat on a cushion beside him.

'Yes, it was all rather a rum do – all sorts of wild rumours flying about, messengers and troops running hither and yon, difficult to find out what was really happening. But then on January 7th we actually saw the Shogun returning to Osaka Castle from Kyoto. It was what you might call a dramatic spectacle. The drilled troops came first, bugles blaring, followed by such a motley collection of warriors as you never could imagine. Some wore helmets with wigs of long black hair attached, others those basin-shaped war-hats, dressed in coats of many colours and carrying swords, muskets, long and short spears. All good medieval stuff! Then a silence fell – quite spine-tingling it was. And people watching fell on their knees as a group of horsemen approached. In the middle was the ex-Shogun, Keike himself, muffled in a black hood, looking quite worn out and sad. "Take off your hat to fallen majesty," said Percival, so I did. Then we ran to see the whole procession file across the bridge over the moat into the castle. Everyone dismounted except the Shogun himself. It was all quite moving somehow – momentous – watching history in the making.'

Kenjiro smiled. 'Thank you for telling me that. It will be a scene to describe to my children one day, even my grand-children perhaps. Has Elinor told you?' He looked proudly at his wife.

'Yes, and I'm quite delighted, of course. And that brings me to . . . well, I must say, Kenjiro, that I came here partly because I've been so worried about Elinor's welfare. This city is a powder-keg at the moment, as you well know; and there's every likelihood that fighting will begin soon, probably centred on the castle, only a couple of miles yonder. So I beg of you – Ellie – go and stay in the protected settlement of Yokohama until things settle down. For your own sake and the child's.'

'Oh, but Arnold, I . . .'

Kenjiro patted her head protectively. 'Your brother is right, Elinor. Taneo and I have also worried about you. Foreign women are too conspicuous here, and there are still mad anti-barbarian fanatics about. I want you to take his advice; for a while, anyway.'

'And leave you here, Kenjiro? No, please – isn't a wife's place beside her husband if there's any danger?'

'Only if there's no alternative and her husband wishes it,' he replied rather pompously.

She looked sulkily from one to the other. 'But I don't want to go.'

'Please don't sound childish, Elinor.' Arnold stood up. 'I must get back to the Legation. I'm not at all keen at being abroad myself in the dark, I can tell you, and we've orders to be very much on guard. There's no immediate urgency; but the sooner the better I think, Kenjiro.' He glanced at his sister, who sat pouting while the men discussed the arrange-ments for her removal to Yokohama.

Shortly after Arnold's visit, hand-to-hand fights occurred in the capital between government police and bands of south-western clansmen who went about robbing the wealthy to pay

243

for their military expenses. In reprisal, the main Satsuma *yashiki* was burnt down by rebel sympathisers and, on hearing that bad news, Kenjiro overrode Elinor's protests and took her to the British Legation nearby. That same day, January 27th, in the villages of Toba and Fushimi, east of Kyoto, armed clashes broke out between the Imperialists and the ex-Shogun's forces. After several days' fighting the former, though numerically the weaker, emerged victorious, and the latter began retreating towards Edo, where they intended to make a decisive stand.

By this time Elinor had been escorted by her brother to the greater safety of Yokohama, where she stayed with Ryo in somewhat cramped and noisy rooms adjoining the Hubbards' school. Socially, Elinor found her return easier than expected, for the shock caused by her elopement had been almost forgotten and the scandal attached to it much diminished by her subsequent marriage. Moreover, one or two other alliances between foreigners and Japanese had since occurred, so even its rarity value was at a discount. And, as Mrs Fortescue said to Mrs Marshall, it was utterly incomprehensible to her that an attractive young lady like Elinor Mills, who had had practically the whole of the dashing XXth Regiment to choose from, should have wed a native, but it was done and one could not cast her out forever in consequence.

So Mary Fortescue was the first of the settlement's ladies to call on Elinor, congratulate her on her pregnancy and bring her up to date with the Yokohama scene. The settlement had become very smart since the '66 fire, with a noble road now dividing the foreign and native towns, and new buildings, even including a proper post-office. Yet more exciting, settlers had been allowed to purchase land on the Bluff from the Japanese authorities and were in the process of building sturdy residences thereon at last. 'We're just moving into our hill-top house, and you must come and visit immediately,' Mary commanded. 'Perfectly charming, with a splendid view of the bay and we can watch the Pacific Mail ships come and go. You've heard of them, of course? On the regular new run between San Francisco and Hong Kong. Their biggest vessel, the *Colorado*, is positively a floating hotel for five hundred passengers, and such marvellous parties they have in port! Makes one feel much more linked to the outside world and brings lots more visitors. So we've all become terribly respectable. Did you hear of the notification recently ordering our boatmen and carters to cover themselves up instead of "appearing publicly in a state bordering on nudity"? Too funny! And the old mixed bath-houses have been screened from sight – no more "indiscriminate tubbing"! Still it's all for the best, I suppose; though I must admit to a truant affection for the old pioneering days.'

Elinor smiled. 'Me too . . . One didn't realise how short-lived they were and now they've vanished forever, I suppose.'

Ryo, who had been sharing tea with the more talkative foreign ladies, now murmured mildly, 'But that is always so, is it not? The changing, the passing away of so many beautiful things and days before one realises?'

Elinor grimaced. 'Oh, I suppose it is – and you Japanese revel in it, I do believe! Kenjiro is the same – blossoms always falling, moons always waning, noons the birth of every midnight. After all, I tell him, there'll be new blooms, moons, and noons. You make everything sound so melancholy.'

Ryo smiled. 'I suppose we're taught to think like that – our poets express it so. And the melancholy becomes part of the beauty. And every blossoming leaves us older, fewer springs to see in a life-time. The blossoms outlive us and we are saddened.'

'Oh, come, Ryo,' Mary protested. 'We carry on too – look at dear Elinor, near her first blooming. Anyway, I much prefer to think of human life as a definite progression towards the good. We British usually do.'

'Perhaps you are fortunate, and that is one reason why you are such a strong nation,' Ryo acknowledged.

'Well, I'm sure it helps,' Mary agreed complacently, turning to Elinor and pressing her to come to the Bluff the very next day.

As soon as Mary left, Ryo excused herself, saying she had to prepare for the arrival of Mr Coburn. Elinor had soon realised that, for Ryo, part of the attraction of Yokohama was Felix, who, in her view, simply exploited the Japanese girl's knowledge for his own purposes. But Ryo was thrilled and honoured to be of service; and to see some of her own phrases actually printed in the foreign magazines for which he wrote was sufficient reward. Moreover, Felix actually discussed points with her, chatted and joked informally in a manner no Japanese man, except her brother, ever had; in response she too was blossoming, her confidence growing, her mind sharpening.

Felix was currently working on an article about Shintoism, which seemed to him most remarkable for its deficiencies – having no idols, few rituals or formal services, no moral teachings, and primitive architecture. Felix likened it to a Japanese living-room, which, to western eyes, looked very spartan without carpets, armchairs, sideboards, or curtains. Pleased with his metaphor, he read it aloud to Ryo that evening and she thought it profound, though not readily understandable.

'Shintoists do go on long pilgrimages,' she remarked, feeling the need to say something positive in their favour.

'Ah yes, I'll mention that – to sacred mountains and shrines. And what do the pilgrims do when they arrive?'

'Oh, just wash in the font, strike bells, throw coins in the prayer-box, clap their hands, buy charms.'

He made notes. 'I think that should come after the first part about the race of heavenly beings from which the first Japanese Emperor was descended etc . . .' He put down his pen. 'Now the social aspects – you and your family are Buddhists, isn't that so?' She nodded uncertainly. 'Because you are of the samurai class, Shinto being more for the peasants?'

'Not exactly, it's more mixed up. People of all classes can be Shintoists and Buddhists at different times for different reasons.'

'Really? What a nuisance! But when you were a child you went to Buddhist temples to worship?'

'Yes, we went to my grandfather's temple for festivals and

fairs. There was a large iron pot outside, I remember, with sticks of incense burning in it. We used to pass our hands through the smoke and dab our hair with it so good things would happen to us.'

'Did you believe in that?'

'Of course – people still do, just the same. And we believe in Shinto too; it isn't contradictory. Indeed when I was a child I think I was more of a Shintoist.'

'How was that, tell me.'

She hesitated, then began speaking softly. 'There was a little Shinto shrine in the wooded hills above our house and I used to go there often. I went up a lot of stone steps all mossy and overgrown and along a stone path that ran between thirty red *torii* arches. Beside each pillar stood long banners on bamboo poles and at the end of the path stood the shrine, with a bronze fox on either side of the entrance, one with a paw on a ball, the other baring its teeth menacingly. It always scared me, remembering childish tales of ghosts and foxes. I used to imagine that one day it would come alive and bite me and, as the place was nearly always deserted, no one would have come to my rescue. I often had nightmares about that fox.' She smiled shyly.

'But you still went. Why?'

'Because it was such a beautiful and isolated place. I liked pulling the bell-rope, looking at the shrine offerings. And there were always offerings – oranges, eggs, flowers – though I never saw people bring them and I thought that was very mysterious too. And the bell's tone was mysterious when I rang it, the sound drifted up and away into the trees. Birds were always singing there and the wind always rustling the leaves and making the bamboo poles creak and the banners flap. I used to imagine the souls of our Satsuma warriors who carried their banners into battle were resting there, protecting me; so I was both afraid and not afraid, always. I daresay I'd still feel like that if I went back.'

As she lifted her face to him, he had a vision of the solitary, serious child in her country kimono, kerchief, sandals, small and alone between the arches of that mysterious pathway.

Perhaps it was a good idea to mix up Shintoism, Buddhism, and all the other 'isms' too, that worshippers might feel the presence of the spirits in any religious place? Assuming of course there were spirits . . . He pulled his thoughts back. 'What a charming memory, but I don't think I can use it in my article, Ryo; it's a little . . . well . . . pointless.'

'Oh no, I just told you so you should know.' She looked at him intensely, hardly concealing her adoration, then went to fetch some refreshments.

But Felix was unaware of Ryo's feelings; for his own emotions still centred on Honoria, though they had been deeply frustrated in the past year. Indeed, the occasion of their last meeting had been worse than none at all. She passed through Yokohama briefly with her husband and son on a local leave spent in Shanghai. And it had been very like torture to see her out walking on Harold's arm, returning to the hotel with him at night. They had met at parties, exchanged surreptitious kisses, spent just one stolen hour alone together, when she had talked most of Oliver and how like Felix he was growing in looks and intelligence. She missed him desperately, she told him, but could not face the scandal of marital separation, at least not yet. And he missed her desperately, he vowed with equal passion, and was willing to wait. So they parted again, their bodies sick and hollow with unsatisfied lust, made the more urgent by that fleeting, painful proximity. Felix thought of her again now as he heard the familiar sound of a ship's siren in the harbour. Soon the first mail steamer of the season would arrive from Hakodate and would surely bring news of her.

He shook himself from his lovelorn reverie as Ryo returned bearing a tray, followed by Elinor Miyata. They greeted each other coolly, for they had never really become friends, and, in answer to his question, Elinor explained that her husband had been summoned to Kyoto by the leaders of his clan.

'So what's going to come of it all, does he think?' Felix asked as Ryo poured tea.

'Oh, he's confident the Emperor will reign supreme eventually, but there's a great deal of loyalty to the ex-Shogun still.'

'So there could be more bloodshed?'

'Alas yes, if the Tokugawa loyalists fight on to the bitter end – which we pray they won't. Kenjiro hopes the Imperialists will show clemency and make terms for an honourable surrender.'

'Well, at least up to now it seems a fairly civilised civil war,' Felix commented. 'Most people hardly know it's going on.'

'Oh, I hope it remains so,' she agreed, thinking anxiously of her absent husband.

For the next three months the country teetered on various brinks, 'an egg-shell balanced on a fingertip,' as the *Japan Herald* put it. The Imperial forces, distinguished by pieces of material pinned to their left shoulders, giving them the name 'strips of brocade', were now in full control of Kyoto. In February they began marching towards Edo and, as they advanced, peace talks between the two sides became ever more urgent. For Kenjiro it was all very exciting, even though his personal involvement was confined to the often-fraught consultations between the Satsuma leaders and the foreign representatives; and Sir Harry Parkes and Percival Storey were in their element – offering secret advice to their Imperialist friends while maintaining a pose of diplomatic neutrality.

In April the Emperor issued his famous Charter Oath, which promised the country a form of democratic government. Shortly after, as a result of peace negotiations, the main body of the Tokugawa forces agreed to surrender and their ruler, Keike, left Edo for voluntary exile. The Imperialists moved into the capital without any serious fighting; but their victory was not yet complete, for some contingents of the rebel forces fled north to organise further resistance, while others remained, organising themselves into guerrilla bands of '*shogitai*' – the loyalty-exhibiting ones.

The majority of the country's commoners were shielded from any direct involvement in these skirmishes and so were the foreign residents, who were forbidden to travel outside the treaty ports. Yokohama was heavily guarded and when Kenjiro Miyata arrived there he had great difficulty in gaining admittance, and reached the Hubbards' compound in some considerable agitation as a result.

'The guards simply wouldn't believe I'd come to see my wife,' he said, still flushed with anger. 'They laughed in my face . . . Oh, it's all so difficult and stupid sometimes!'

Elinor, almost crying with relief at his safe return, said gently, 'Oh, my dear, it's been so difficult for me too. Only snippets of news about you. You at negotiations – in Osaka, Kyoto, Edo . . . You might have sent more messages – only three in three months!'

He hugged her in silence; he had been so thoroughly engrossed in the political situation that it had not occurred to him to keep her informed of his movements or his continuing devotion; Japanese wives did not expect it. 'My activities were all secret,' he explained. 'You'd have heard if there was anything wrong with me.'

'But I wanted to know all was right with you, dearest. You are my beloved husband.'

'Yes, and I thought of you often – especially at night!' He pinched her cheek affectionately, patting her bulging stomach. 'And our soon to be born son – is he doing well? Your brother is looking after you?'

'Arnold does what he can but he works in Edo now and has his hands full with wounded Imperial officers. He suggests I go and stay at the Legation where he can keep an eye on me and deliver me. I think it would be best, don't you?'

Kenjiro frowned. 'Well, probably, but the capital isn't quiet yet. The *shogitai*, about three thousand strong, have barricaded themselves inside the temples at Ueno and make forays in the northern suburbs, looting and killing our soldiers. They'll have to be dislodged soon, which will mean another fight.'

'But surely the Imperialists can defeat them quite easily?'

'Not easily. We too have problems – shortage of money and arms and dissension in our ranks. Some want to kill every Tokugawa supporter in the land; others, like myself, want to

250

show clemency in victory. After all these enemies are our own countrymen, not barbarian outsiders.' He chuckled. 'But my own little barbarian-outsider – yes, if you and your brother think it best, then go to the Legation hospital for the birth. Certainly no one of either side would dare attack that.'

A day or so later Elinor went to Edo in a closed palanquin with a mounted escort and stayed there quietly, moving into hospital on July 3rd, as the birth was imminent. As it happened the timing was dramatic. The very next morning the hill in Ueno where the *shogitai* were holding out was encircled by Imperial troops and the final battle for command of the capital began. Fierce fighting continued throughout the day; several magnificent temples were gutted by fire. In the intervals between her labour pains, Elinor heard the distant boom of cannon, the rattle of Armstrong guns, and felt as if she too were on the battlefield. Desperately she strugggled, sure that in such circumstances she must bring forth a boy-child, a son for her samurai husband, a loyalist for the Emperor. In the late afternoon, as the last of the *shogitai* were routed, she gave birth. It was a girl, and Elinor cried weakly with relief and a certain sense of disappointment as she held her in her arms for the first time.

Though the birth was without complications Elinor was laid low afterwards with mild recurring fevers, lassitude, and depression. Arnold wanted her to recuperate in Yokohama, but she adamantly refused to be parted from her husband again; so when she left hospital she returned to their home in Taneo's compound and Ryo came to look after her and the baby. Expecting a boy, the parents had no female name in mind and compromised on Hannah as it sounded very similar to the Japanese 'Hana', meaning flower. Hannah's eyes were too wide, her nose-bridge too high for a true-bred Japanese flower; but to Ryo of the kinky hair this made her the more endearing and, during the heat of the late summer, she quietly but fiercely took possession of the baby as if by right. All the pent-up love that had long sought an outlet was directed towards her niece, and Elinor seemed scarcely to notice, saving her weakened resources for her husband, who, she felt, had slipped away from her a little during the recent troubled times.

Though most of the country was at peace, all the momentous decisions about its future had still to be made. 'Will Japan really progress towards prosperity and greatness, or will it sink back into the mire of feudal oppression?' as Taneo put it on more than one occasion. He was in the habit of making such sonorous statements to Elinor, sitting on her verandah steps in the late afternoons and unashamedly practising on her his ability to express abstract ideas in English. And she was quite flattered to listen, imagining he had her further education at heart. 'For centuries clans have fought each other for power and territory, but we have no concept of men fighting each other bloodlessly for political authority. That is the leap we have to make, from the feudal to the modern. Is that clearly put?'

'Excellently, Taneo.'

'Ah, good — for that too is the point. To convey these ideas so that everyone may understand — peasant bumpkins, women, hotheaded youngsters; not only educated men.'

She turned on him irritably. 'I must say, Taneo, I think there's something very feudal about the slighting way you categorise the minds of women along with bumpkins.'

'Ah — a hit! You have me . . .' His skinny arm shot out in mock self-defence. 'I wasn't thinking of your clever little head, Mrs Miyata. But for centuries the minds, the spirits, the whole lives of Japanese women have been stunted, hacked into shape to suit the needs and desires of men — like bonsai trees. They have to be taught to grow naturally, express themselves, learn new ways and new rights. And for our ordinary people that will be a long and difficult process.'

'Well, I shall make certain that my daughter is no bonsai tree, Taneo. But what about yours, I sometimes wonder?' She glanced at him slyly, for Taneo treated his daughter, like his wife, in a conventionally traditional fashion.

'She receives some western-style education,' he replied sulkily.

'But not so much as your sons, for whom she is a kind of

252

unpaid servant, as is Ryo to my husband. I cannot make Kenjiro see that, though. Do you know, we received a letter from a friend of his recently consoling us for the birth of a girl with the thought that at least we'd have a nurse-maid to carry the first-born son? Is it any wonder that my husband considers it his right to be waited on like a prince by the women of the house?'

She bit her lip, for the conversation had hit a raw nerve, she and Kenjiro having had their first real quarrel since marriage over just such an issue a few evenings previously. He had been invited to a banquet in the recently formed Ministry of Foreign Affairs and had suddenly asked her to brush and lay out his best silks for the occasion.

'I think that's a job for Bimyo,' she had replied. 'He's always acted as your valet and now he's returned to our service.'

'Normally we consider it is the honourable wife's task. It is something she enjoys doing for her husband,' he had replied stiffly.

'But, my dear, I don't even know exactly what you require – all those ties and tassels, matching belts . . .' She tried to make light of it.

'You can learn, Elinor.'

'It's really Bimyo's job in my view.'

'Elinor, I make many concessions to you in public – perhaps you don't realise that every time we walk out together passers-by are amazed to see us so, side by side, you even holding my arm. They laugh at me, often, thinking I am humiliating myself to you. But surely when we are here alone at home . . .'

'But even at home I won't behave like your servant, Kenjiro.'

'I do not see it like that – the honourable wife enjoys laying out her husband's clothes,' he repeated with an obstinacy that infuriated her.

'It is a valet's job and I, an Englishwoman, will not be your valet.' Her voice rose and he faced her just as angrily. 'You are far too argumentative for a woman, Elinor. It is a great fault in you. Again and again I hear it. I was little more than your brother's servant-interpreter for several years, and it was a role I accepted as a duty and without complaint. You are my wife, and you have duties towards me now. And they should be performed uncomplainingly.'

'My brother! But that was a job. Do you hold that against him – or against me?' She looked distraught.

'No, no, I don't think so, at least I didn't until the matter of these clothes. But we will say no more about it.'

He had left quickly and she had spent a miserable evening alone. They had made up the quarrel that night when he had returned late, a little flushed with *saké*, looking magnificent in the silks that Bimyo had earlier laid out for him. When he had disrobed and moved gently over her she felt it mattered not at all to what extent she was his slave, his valet, his mistress, his consort, and his queen; but she knew also that only in the intimate recesses of the marital bed could she allow this to be so.

Taneo, taking her silence as reproof, stood up to leave. 'I think these changes must come gradually, Elinor. My daughter must not grow so modern that no Japanese man would marry her. The same applies to your little Hannah. It will not be easy for her in any case.'

Elinor nodded wearily, overtaken again by the lassitude that plagued her. The future was bound to be difficult sometimes and she was beginning to realise that all its problems had not been solved by a happy marriage to the man of her heart, especially as he was Japanese. She watched Taneo walk towards his own house – his spindly frame in its usual hurry, his faded jacket flapping. He was a kind, original man and she was fortunate to know him, she thought, reminding herself of the benefits as well as the drawbacks of the life she had chosen.

Autumn invigorated Elinor at last and she started taking her baby to enjoy the cool sunshine in the grounds of a nearby temple. Arnold's first avuncular present, ordered from Shanghai, was a perambulator the like of which had never been seen before in that neighbourhood. Women and children came running from afar to look at it, touch its wheels and hood, coo at its tiny occupant. It must be a rich man's baby to ride in such princely state, they decided, and with a smart-looking foreign nurse (for so they imagined Elinor to be). But the baby was not quite right looking for a proper Japanese, they said, and its poor little head was not close-shaven; so it would soon get lice, even if it was rich. Sometimes, as a surprise, Elinor entered into their conversation; at others she simply sailed past, smiling to herself, absorbed in the peaceful tranquillity of the surrounding scene.

Bright yellow and red chestnut leaves swirled along the paved paths in the breeze, like laughing lemmings towards the bonfires; silver fronds of pampas grass shone in golden shafts of sun wherein blue-grey smoke curled from the fires lit by the garden sweepers. And every park and thoroughfare was swept especially clean that autumn, every bridge repaired, every gate re-painted, for the city was proudly living up to its new glory. In September it was re-named Tokyo, the eastern capital, and, a month later, the young Emperor, given the reign-title Meiji, left Kyoto to take up his residence there. He eventually reached Tokyo on November 26th, and, on that day, the Miyatas joined Arnold and Percival Storey near the temporary Foreign Office, where they had a good view of the proceedings.

As the notes of a pipe band signalled the procession's approach, the crowds lining the streets bowed their heads respectfully. In Elinor's eyes, however, the vanguard was rather disappointing, consisting as it did of ranks of shambling soldiers each sporting the obligatory strip of brocade, but in a diversity of uniforms and headgear gleaned from both East and West. Behind them, however, the procession took on a purely oriental dignity as lines of bearers in yellow silks appeared carrying ornamented chests containing the Imperial possessions and followed by the nobility of the court riding on horseback in robes of coloured brocade and high ceremonial hats.

Kenjiro nudged Elinor and muttered reverentially, 'You see that fine-looking pale-faced man on the white charger? That's Count Iwada, one of the Emperor's most trusted advisers. He was wounded and left for dead at the Battle of Fushimi; but you wouldn't think so to see him today, would you? How stern and aristocratic he looks!'

Behind the nobles the palanquin of the Emperor was borne aloft, steadied by thick, red silk ropes held taut at each corner, its lacquered roof ornamented with the golden Imperial chrysanthemum. As it passed by on its way to the castle the people fell into total silence, which, Elinor thought, was far more effective than cheering. 'Take off your hat to risen Majesty,' she heard Percival whisper to Arnold, and the two men did so.

She glanced at her husband, who stood with head bowed, hands clenched, and face screwed tight with emotion. For Kenjiro, this solemn, silent passing was a joyous, inspiring, momentous culmination of a long struggle, the presage of a glorious future. Half understanding, Elinor squeezed his arm.

'The Emperor is here — he's really here,' he murmured.

She nodded, smiling at him. 'Yes. You and yours have really won.'

For a moment he looked up at the bright sky, seeming to revel in the knowledge; then he said solemnly, 'But also I must remember, Elinor, the words of the great Shogun Ieyasu, "After victory tighten the strings of your helmet." Come — let us go.'

CHAPTER THIRTEEN

The Imperialists were now in complete control of the main centres of population, but elsewhere resistance to them was not yet fully crushed. Tokugawa supporters throughout the northern provinces continued fighting against the new regime until the year's end and a two-thousand-strong force, led by one Captain Enomoto and including a number of French officers, arrived at Hakodate in eight ships of the former Shogun's navy and took possession of it. News of this last reckless stand percolated south slowly and was generally regarded as no more than a rather amusing epilogue to the drama of the Imperial Restoration, except by those with some personal involvement.

Among them was Felix Coburn, who had received one letter from Honoria during the summer saying she had been unwell but hoped to come to Yokohama when things settled down. It seemed too cruel that, now the rest of the country was at peace, Hokkaido was suffering more disturbances than before. He imagined his beloved lying ill and helpless in that cold Consulate at the mercy of rebel soldiers, perhaps held captive, perhaps even dead. Personally he could do nothing, but in January, when it became clear that the Imperialists would not attempt to oust the rebel troops until spring, Sir Harry Parkes instructed a British warship, the *Serpent*, commanded by Captain Mayhew, to sail to Hakodate to reconnoitre. Felix had no respectable reason for going, but, considering the bleakness of the destination and the inclemency of the weather, there was plenty of room aboard and so − in the capacity of freelance reporter for the *Japan Herald* − he went.

257

The voyage was as rigorous as forecast and, clinging to his berth listening to the savage north-westerlies whistling through the rigging, Felix could no longer solace himself with the notion that he was suffering in the cause of Science. It was love, lust, compassion, affection, obsession that drove him, and his awareness of this did nothing to help his bouts of sea-sickness. After a dreadful day spent riding out a storm near their destination, the *Serpent* glided into Hakodate's sheltered bay on a calm tide.

Never imposing, the port had now almost vanished under the snow; every roof was freighted with it, every eave chained with icicles. Harold Rayne was waiting on the jetty, arms outstretched to welcome Captain Mayhew and his officers.

'My dear fellows – what a surprise. How grand to see you! I could scarcely believe my eyes when I spotted you through the glasses.'

As Felix stepped ashore Harold halted, staring at him in obvious dismay. 'Why – if it isn't . . . Felix Coburn. What on earth . . .?'

'Good morning, Harold. I'm glad to see you looking so well.' Felix peered at him cautiously.

'Certainly didn't expect to see you here,' Harold mumbled accusingly.

'Oh, I just took a chance to come up and report on things for the *Herald*,' Felix said airily. 'There's been considerable concern about Hakodate's beleaguered foreign residents. I hope your family is well?'

'Oh, that's it, then. We're surviving; mustn't grumble, I suppose. Not been easy, but surviving.'

He turned away hastily and, taking the Captain's arm, suggested they all go to his office out of the cold for a little nip that cheers, though, he added, supplies in that department were lamentably low and he hoped the Captain might be able to help him out. Felix, trailing behind the others, was puzzled. Obviously Harold had not been pleased to see him, but neither had he shown the overt hostility he surely would have, had he known the full truth. He hesitated, longing to go immediately in search of Honoria, but decided it would be

258

prudent to find out a little more first. The familiar quayside office was crowded when he arrived, a bottle was circulating and Harold had just launched into the tale of what had been going on.

'This Enomoto fellow has set up his headquarters in the Fort Goryaku and wants to rule Hokkaido as a separate colony or some damn fool thing. And the Froggie officers are egging him on – trying to make another Napoleon of him, I shouldn't wonder.'

'But how did the rebels take over so easily?' Mayhew asked.

'There was some fighting, but all we foreigners were placed under house arrest for safety, so we didn't see much. Bit of firing round about, then the Governor of Hakodate skedaddled apparently and next thing we were summoned to meet this bandit-chief and his merry men. The Froggies promised we should be protected, and I must say we have been – no violence, no casualties, but it's a damn tricky situation for all that. Surely the Imperialists won't let this lot get away with it?'

'Oh no, they'll come and rout them out when the weather improves,' Mayhew assured him, and, as the bottle circulated again, Felix slipped away unobserved.

Rebel soldiers were wandering aimlessly about the streets in uniforms even more motley and tattered than their opponents, further south. They looked cold, disheartened, ill-fed; and Felix, who had not considered their plight before, felt rather sorry for them. Clouds leaden with unreleased snow hung over the Consulate hill and monstrous drifts reared on either side of the narrow path cleared between the gate and the front steps. Felix hurried along it, his heart pounding with anticipation, anxiety, and the freezing air. When a servant answered his knock, he pushed past into the cold dining room. Honoria sat at the table feeding – he paused and stared – a baby on her lap; Oliver beside her was spooning gruel.

'Honoria.' He took off his hat and stood there trembling.

'Felix – you . . . Can it be? But however did you get here?' She started to rise; the baby screamed. She sat down again, saying in low, sullen tones, 'This is Letitia, my new-born.'

'Yes, I see. Congratulations, Mrs Rayne.' He twisted his hat, not looking at her.

'And Oliver you remember, of course?' Her voice was fragile. 'Say hello to Mr Coburn, Oliver.'

'Herro,' the child mumbled without looking up.

Honoria tutted. 'He can't say his "l's" properly – just like the Japanese. He spends too much time with the servants.'

Felix nodded; he had scarcely given a thought to this child who could be his son. And now another child; certainly not his. He began to wish he had not come.

'But this is such a surprise; please sit down and tell me how you got here,' Honoria prattled nervously.

He did not move. 'You wrote saying you were unwell; and I was very worried about you in these disturbed times, so I took the chance to come up with Captain Mayhew on a reconnaissance trip. We've just landed.'

'Are we to be evacuated?' she asked eagerly.

'No, I fear not – as you're safe and all seems well.'

She got up, dumping the baby, who wailed again, and gestured round the bleak room.

'Everything's absolutely splendid, as you can see!' She looked almost slatternly in a way he had never seen her before, her velvet dress front discoloured with milk stains, her hair in loose half-coils round her pale face. 'Please go into the parlour and I'll order tea. Is Harold bringing the officers here? Oh dear . . . I really must change . . .'

'I expect so, later. I slipped away to see you first; I had to.'

She paused, irresolute, then called a servant to see to the children before following him into the parlour.

He stared round the familiar room; the iron stove was barely glowing; the piano he had sent stood against the wall looking very cheap and ordinary compared to the ebony Broadwood that had vanished. One gold summer afternoon, greatly daring, they had enjoyed passionate love on the fur rug that still covered the floor; he remembered the soft caress of the fur, of her on his bare skin. He reached for her chilly hand. 'Honoria, I had to see you. Of course I didn't know about . . . you should have told me.'

She averted her face. 'That's why I didn't come to you. She was born in May, it was impossible to leave then. The Russian doctor said it was safer to stay here in the circumstances. It was dreadful – I didn't want her – the baby. I didn't want her, Felix.' Her face crumpled a little. 'It's been worse than I thought possible this year.' He touched her shoulder, feeling her shrink away. 'No, no, it's no use now, not after Harold. When we came back from that holiday in Shanghai he wouldn't leave me alone, beseeching me, he . . . Oh, God . . .' She covered her eyes. 'It went on – the quarrels, sulks, his marital rights.' She shuddered. 'Then he started coming home drunk from that horrible place in town and he . . . he forced me . . . several times.' Her voice was a low, cold whisper, remembering the indignity of it. How revolting sex was; she remembered the animal stink of the Ainu hut, the hairy rapist of her earlier fantasies, and was sickened by Felix's touch.

'I'm very sorry,' he muttered.

'I hate him now, hate him. He gets worse, drinking more, spending more stupidly. Doesn't care about anything.'

'His behaviour towards me this morning was very odd. Do you think he suspects us?'

She shrugged, pulling her stained robe round her thin shoulders and shivering. 'I don't think so, but I don't care anyway. In fact now you've come unexpectedly like this, I've a good mind to tell him . . . today.' She looked wistfully at Felix, but he did not reply. 'Oh, I look such a fright! How could I let myself slop about like this? It's the place, the winter, everything. I feel utterly locked up inside, Felix, like a lump of solid ice – no love or warmth left, not even for my children.'

He reached for her hand but she pulled away. 'And for me?'

'I don't think so, Felix; your coming is too sudden. I've been in a cold stupor for months. I can't thaw in a moment.'

'But I could thaw you,' he said confidently.

'Oh, it's no use, I've nothing left to give. Oliver – your son – is my only comfort.'

'But you're not sure that . . .' he began hesitantly.

261

She snorted angrily. 'Oh, but I am! There's nothing of Harold in him, thank goodness. Let me fetch him – you'll see . . .' She moved towards the door, then gave a cry of alarm. 'Oh, my goodness – yes, here they come! Harold, the Captain and . . .'

He looked out, saw the dark, burly figures filing up the narrow white path, their breath steaming, their cheeks red with cold and drink.

'You mustn't be found here – not in front of them all. And I'm such a mess. Oh, I must put on something decent . . . go, Felix, please.' He was already grabbing his coat. 'Quick – out through the back door and down that little path, remember? I must change.' She bundled him towards the kitchen, then, as Harold opened the front door, fled to her bedroom.

For Felix the remainder of that day dwindled into bored, melancholy irresolution. He stamped miserably about the streets near the quay, remembering the occasion Honoria had first shown him the sights of Hakodate, the ironic humour of her smile, that smart navy outfit. Darkness fell early and with it more snow. He ate a bad meal in a cheap restaurant and retired early to his cabin. Much later he heard the officers returning, but he did not have the heart to inquire how they had spent the time.

He was awakened next morning by a loud knocking at the cabin door. 'Hello, who's there?'

There was no reply. Thinking he knew, Felix draped a robe over his night-shirt and opened the door, smiling. Harold marched in.

'You!' Felix retreated. Harold slammed the door; he was purplish-coloured, breathing harshly. 'Yes, me – the cuckolded husband. You bloody swine, Coburn! You bloody swine! A whole summer you spent in my home enjoying my hospitality, taking advantage of my friendship, making love to my wife . . . You bleeding sod!' He thumped his large fist against the bunk-rail. 'I've a good mind to smash your clever-clever face in.'

Felix pulled himself together, wishing he were properly dressed. 'I . . . what can I say? Yes, it's true . . . You obviously know. I'm desperately sorry, Harold. She told you last night?'

'Yes – probably wouldn't have, but the kid blabbed, didn't he? Clever little Oliver, who she now says is your bastard, which I don't believe for a second. Anyway, as he was going to bye-byes, he starts telling me about the gent who came earlier and rushed away through the kitchen. So then I began to put two and two together – at long last – and a pretty tale I got out of her eventually. My lovely lady, my elegant Honoria, coupling like a savage in an Ainu hut . . . Pah!' His mouth twisted with the sourness of it and he spat deliberately on the floor. 'That's what I think of you, Coburn, and that's what I'd like to do to you.' He ground the spittle into the carpet with his boot.

Felix shuddered. 'There's not much I can say, Harold. I've behaved like a heel. I confess it. I can only say that I loved Honoria, still love her. And she me – I think . . . or at least thought. I'll take her away now if you wish, and if she wants to come. I'll behave decently, marry her, do anything you want.'

Harold slumped on the bunk and ground his wrists into his eyes. 'Take the faithless whore if she wants to go. I don't give a tinker's cuss. But you're not taking my children, Coburn; I'll kill you first – and her too. Those children are mine, both of them, mine – that's what I told her. She's not taking Oliver from me . . . do you understand?'

'And what did she say to that?'

'God knows – first one thing, then t'other. She doesn't know what to do. Left her crying in a heap on the floor. Devil of a night we've had, I can tell you . . . not a wink of sleep.' He groaned, burying his face back in his hands. Felix stared down at a bald patch on Harold's skull that he had not noticed before. A heel, yes he had been a heel. He said, 'Shall I go and see her? We sail early tomorrow.'

'You're not setting your blasted eyes on her again in my house.' Harold jumped up. 'She's mine – my wife, you young bleeder . . . Oh, I don't care, let her come to you if she wants. But if you set foot over my threshold again, I'll kill you.' He stuck his face close to Felix's, his breath rancid with alcohol and sleeplessness.

Felix nodded again. 'But you'll let her come if she wants?'

'Yes, you can have her — for what she's worth. But alone . . .'

They stared at each other. 'Goddamn it,' Harold mumbled. 'If only I'd known this before . . . The fret I've wasted over you.'

'Fret? What do you mean?'

'Oh nothing, bloody nothing . . .' Harold suddenly let fly, cuffing Felix hard across the face, then punching him in the stomach several times. Felix doubled up defensively, not hitting back. Harold thumped him twice more about the head, then threw him back on the bunk and slammed out.

Felix crawled under the bedclothes and lay there for a long time, trembling, dabbing a cut above his eye. He deserved it, and more. But what could he do now? What did he want to do? He did not know and could not think, and spent the rest of the day in a dreary ache of physical discomfort and mental uncertainty, not daring to go to Honoria, wondering, dreading, dreaming, hoping, fearing that she would now come to him.

Again the dusk brought snow. Leaning over the deck-rail, Felix watched the flakes swirling through the rays of lanterns hung at the corners of the Customs shed. So much snow — surely the whole port would be smothered, totally collapse under its deadening weight? He wondered if Honoria had left the Consulate to come to him and had lost her way, was lying submerged in some soft, shrouding drift?

Captain Mayhew joined him. 'Hell of a hole, isn't it? Well, with luck we'll be out of it tomorrow. Got the inf. you wanted for your paper?'

'Oh, I suppose I'll rustle up something. Not much going on to report, is there?'

'Nope. And won't be till spring. I feel sorry for the Raynes stuck here, I must say.'

'Couldn't you possibly evacuate them — the wife and children anyway?'

'I was to do so only if the situation seemed dangerous. It

isn't and as far as I can see this Enomoto fellow is quite well disposed towards the foreigners here, and his French cohorts wouldn't let anything unpleasant happen to damage their cause.'

Felix gnawed his lip. 'So we leave tomorrow?'

'At dawn, unless another gale blows up.'

Snow fell at night from a still, black sky, a thick blanket of despair that muffled the heart. Felix, dozing fitfully, heard the engines throb into life while it was still dark. He dressed and went on deck, peering into the half-light, imagining her wrapped in a cloak, long hair flying loose, running out of the snow towards him, like a figure in a dramatic painting. Anchors were weighed and the *Serpent* sailed out of the bay on a calm tide. She had not come; it was over.

In retrospect, Felix felt he should have foreseen the immediate future and, when he returned to Yokohama, wound up his business and left the country. But he did not because the omens still seemed propitious; his textile exports were doing well and the general opinion among the settlers was that the new Meiji era would bring peace and prosperity to the country, from which those foreigners already established would be first to benefit. And so he lingered, reasonably content, except for the space left in his life by Honoria's withdrawal from it. For months he had remained celibate, imagining an eventual reunion with his beloved; now he was footloose and vaguely questing, and Arnold, guessing his plight, goodnaturedly introduced him to a friend of his own Yasu's. But she, like Yasu, was a commonplace woman in Felix's eyes, whose only resource was a coquettish, indiscriminate flattering of the male kind that was not to his taste. As he told Arnold, a woman must have a certain dignity, intelligence, even mystery to appeal to him. In retrospect, therefore, Arnold, too, felt he should have foreseen disaster, but he had not.

Ryo Miyata returned to Mrs Hubbard's school in the spring to help with the growing number of pupils; and was soon also helping Felix with his current article, entitled 'Topsy-Turvy Japan'. The subject did not inspire him, but as it was his first to be actually commissioned, he determined to do his best. 'Japanese books begin at the back instead of the front,' he had listed. 'The best rooms of the house are at the rear'; 'the Japanese stir their tea anti-clockwise' . . .

He turned to Ryo. 'Oh Lord, this is boring. Now what about the behaviour of Japanese men towards women — always adds a spice. Men go through doors in front of women, don't they, and are served first at table?'

She nodded. 'And men always get the cleanest water in the communal bath-tubs and the warmest seat by the stove.'

He looked at her curiously. 'Do you mind all this?'

'I never think of minding. It is the custom. You foreign men are courteous to women of a certain class. But it is only pretence. You still think of us as inferior.'

'Oh no, surely not! Well, some men may, but I don't.' He put down his pen. 'I have a very, very high regard for womankind, Ryo. My mother was the most important person in my life till she died. I worship women for their beauty, their sweet sensitivity of spirit, their . . . well . . . hiddenness . . . Really I do.'

She blushed and lowered her eyes and as she did so he seemed to notice for the first time the lovely coiled upsweep of her hair, the soft white nape below, the gently sloping shoulders under her kimono patterned with plum blossom and slender green willow leaves. He drew a sharp breath of delight — why, she had been here all the time and until this moment of her blushing he had not noticed! It was a thunderclap, a falling star, a miracle — this first surge of excited recognition of another person's sexuality. He jumped up and went across to touch her shoulders tenderly, caress the white nape. 'Ryo,' he murmured. 'Ryo . . . of course.'

She raised her head, eyes shining, and he kissed her gently on the cheek, astonished and pleased by her glowing response. Outside they heard the school's pupils leaving class and he whispered, 'Will you come back to my lodgings, Miss Miyata? We have much serious translating to do and the children's noise is disruptive, is it not?'

She blushed red, flustered.

'Is it not?' he persisted, stroking her neck again. 'You have such beautiful hair, I have often thought so.' He stared at the lustrous jet of it, wondering why he had not so thought.

She hesitated, feeling her scalp tingle. 'But I . . . it's dangerous . . .'

'We will be very careful; it's all in the cause of education, you know.' He had such a teasing, tender smile.

'I'll go and tell Mrs Hubbard — only for an hour or two, of course.'

'Of course,' he agreed, gathering up the books from the table.

On that occasion Ryo did stay with Felix for only two hours, though it was long enough for her to lose her virginity. She went again the following week, and then, at Felix's prompting, invented an Aunt Omasa, who, she told Mrs Hubbard, was a widow living in the native town quite close to Mr Coburn's lodgings. Aunt Omasa suffered poor health and was pleased to have Ryo stay overnight sometimes. Mrs Hubbard, coping with her fourth baby and fifth pregnancy, running the school, and looking after her husband, whose endeavours were confined to the elevated planes of preaching and compiling a Japanese–English dictionary, was far too busy to question Ryo's story. Indeed, she felt it was the manifestation of a growing Christian spirit in her.

So when, one summer morning, Elinor and Kenjiro appeared at the Mission unexpectedly to see Ryo, Mrs Hubbard told them without hesitation that she had not yet arrived as she had been spending the night with her Aunt Omasa.

'Her who?' Kenjiro stared.

'Her aunt . . . why, of course, you'd know, wouldn't you?' Mrs Hubbard blinked at him. 'The invalid who . . .'

'She hasn't got an Aunt Omasa, here or anywhere else,' Kenjiro interrupted flatly.

'Oh dearie me! I wonder if . . .' Elinor wailed.

'Wonder what?' Kenjiro wheeled on her.

'Well, I've suspected that . . . Is she still translating for Felix Coburn?'

'Why yes, Elinor, she usually goes to his lodgings to work

first and then goes to her aunt . . . You mean?' Mrs Hubbard faltered. 'Oh my, oh, surely not? Not your sweet sister, Mr Miyata? Why, I never thought to inquire . . . You're sure you've no such aunt?'

'People usually know if they have aunts or not, Mrs Hubbard.'

'Yes, silly of me. But this is most upsetting. And Mr Coburn . . . such a clever and charming man.' She looked at Kenjiro appealingly.

'Let us not get in a tizz yet, Mrs Hubbard. Perhaps there's a perfectly innocent explanation,' Elinor said. 'We'll wait in the parlour if we may. And perhaps you'd send Ryo to us when she arrives?'

'And don't tell her who's here – it was supposed to be a pleasant surprise,' Kenjiro added.

They knew the truth as soon as Ryo walked into the parlour and stopped still, her cheeks a-flame. 'Why you! Kenjiro . . . Ellie . . . how delightful . . . when did you arrive? I wish I'd known . . .'

She did not raise her eyes as her brother said, 'I expect you do wish.' He switched to their own tongue. 'You wouldn't have been away at Aunt Omasa's last night then, probably?' He reached and grabbed her shoulder. 'Where were you, sister? What have you been doing? Have you been behaving sinfully? Ellie suspects it is . . . tell me, woman. The truth, now.' He shook her and she cringed.

'Don't hurt her, Kenjiro,' Ellie commanded.

'Well then, let us hear. Have you been spending your nights with a man? My purest, proudest sister.'

Her voice broke in distress as she fell on her knees.

'Oh, what can I say – I should have thought of this. The shame of it!'

'Who is it? By heaven, I . . . Who?'

She turned to Elinor for help and Elinor said softly, 'It's Felix Coburn, isn't it? I often wondered.'

Ryo covered her face with her sleeves as Kenjiro stared down at her, his face twisted. 'Coupling with a foreigner!'

'You couple with one often,' Elinor said furiously.

'We are married, yes,' he threw back at her. 'And this foreigner, this trader in silkworms and corsets – you are married to him secretly?'

Ryo sniffed. 'No, brother.'

'But he intends to marry you, Ryo?' Elinor prompted.

'We haven't discussed it,' she whispered.

'Faugh! Oh, faugh! What can have possessed you – my well-brought-up, unblemished sister? Telling me the tale of a loose woman.'

Elinor tugged his sleeve. 'Kenjiro, please . . . not so harsh. She's been led astray by that man. He's a charmer and something of a philanderer. There were rumours about him earlier – and that hoity-toity Mrs Rayne from Hakodate.'

Ryo raised her head at the name. 'Is she the woman I saw him dancing with at the Marshalls' once?'

'Never mind that now,' Elinor cut in. 'Does anyone know of this, Ryo?'

'No one. We've been very discreet and . . . occasional. Mrs Hubbard doesn't suspect.'

'She certainly didn't. Aunt Omasa indeed!' Kenjiro snorted.

'Then you must leave here at once, Ryo.' Elinor was firm. 'We're moving into our proper home any day now and we hoped you'd come and live with us in Tokyo; that's why we've come today. There's a nice little room for you, overlooking the pond.' She paused, glancing at her husband.

'That damnable fellow,' he was still fuming. 'Sister, however could you bring yourself to . . .?'

Ryo got up and stared at him, suddenly defiant. 'But you did nothing for me, did you, brother? You were my self-appointed guardian after Uncle Gengoro disowned us but you never exerted yourself to find a suitable husband for me, did you? If you had, this wouldn't have happened. I kept waiting, thinking about it. But you'd obviously decided no one would have me anyway.'

He groaned. 'Oh, it wasn't that. There's been so much happening I didn't stop to think – I ask you, what chance has there been, with Elinor, the war-trouble, the baby, all these changes . . .? When we settled in the new house I intended to

. . . but now, I don't know, what man of rank would have you if this liaison with a foreigner becomes common knowledge?'

'But it simply mustn't,' Elinor cut in firmly. 'Ryo must come back with us now.'

Ryo glared at her. 'No, I won't just go away from him – the first man who has wanted me. Oh, love is a fine thing for you two, isn't it! Love was all that mattered when you defied the conventions. But for me you think it is nothing. And you'd take me back on sufferance only – a soiled woman no decent man would marry, as you say, brother. Well, I won't come on those terms. I'll go and live with Felix openly, and I'll enjoy it. Where else would I go? Mrs Hubbard won't have me anymore – a fallen woman.'

Elinor grasped her arm. 'Then Felix must marry you honourably. Tell him that. He knows full well you are not the class of woman who lives as a kept mistress.'

Ryo shook off her hand. 'I shall decide for myself what to do for once. You've been no help to me.' She gave a strangled sob and rushed from the room.

Kenjiro beat his fists against his temple as he strode about. 'My only sister living openly with a foreigner – that will be the last straw!'

'What do you mean?'

He hesitated. 'Well, I've been told in confidence that I'm being considered for an important post in the Ministry of Foreign Affairs. But being actually married to a foreigner doesn't help my chances. And now if this comes out about Ryo I might as well resign myself to a clerk's stool for life.'

'Oh, my dear.' She stroked his angry back. 'Why didn't you tell me? It's not fair, we are properly married and it is right for us, isn't it?'

He turned to her with a brilliantly warm smile of agreement and she rubbed his cheek as he continued, 'But this – why didn't you tell me of your suspicions? Why didn't Ryo remind me about herself? She never complained, seemed content.'

'But she'd be too proud, after her earlier rebuffs, so she just bottled everything up until along came romantic Mr Felix, who listened to her, brought her out of her shell, seemed so clever and interesting. Don't you see?'

He shook her off. 'Oh, you women always stick together.'

'Kenjiro, I'm only explaining.'

'Oh, don't let us quarrel over it. But what do we do?' he asked helplessly.

She stared back, equally helpless. 'I honestly don't know.'

There turned out to be nothing they could do short of kidnapping Ryo and removing her to Tokyo. She moved out of Mrs Hubbard's school that very day and into Felix's lodgings. The new arrangement did not entirely please him, for he realised that it was fraught with problems. But he put a good face on it for Ryo's sake, thinking too that her constant presence might eventually compensate for Honoria's continuing absence. For Ryo, the brief period of their living together that followed was almost painfully happy. The frustrations of her youth fell away from her, and she began to grow and expand like a formerly stunted tree. Felix treated her with an affectionate regard that she had never before experienced, and in return she worshipped him, waited on him, hung on his words, flowered into passion under his tender caresses.

His lodgings, that had remained spartan during his occupancy – tables still rickety, the even damper Scottish glen still on the wall – brightened under her loving care. She sewed cushions, arranged flowers, surprised him with western-style supper dishes, dreaming of the day when he would suggest marriage, convinced that one so kind and chivalrous would not fail her. But it was against all her upbringing to broach the subject herself, and, in the way of oppressed women, she simply tried to make herself indispensable to his comfort, and hoped for the best.

In this state of quiet, undemanding separateness they sat together one summer evening, she sewing, he reading the *Herald*. The sun's last rays streamed through open screens leading to a small verandah bright with flowering plants; in a suspended wicker cage a black mynah bird named Minnie jabbered contentedly; a street musician passed, playing a plaintive tune on a bamboo flute. Felix, having read the latest news about the situation in Hokkaido, where the Imperial troops were now routing out the last of the Tokugawa rebels, raised his head and grinned.

'I think I should go into rabbit importing, listen to this. "The Japanese have developed a mad craze for keeping Australian rabbits as pets. White ones are fetching specially high prices". I don't suppose you've read *Alice in Wonderland*? It's a charming story about a little girl who fell down a rabbit-hole and . . .'

They heard a loud knock on the outer door, the sound of a woman's voice. Felix dropped the paper and jumped up as Honoria came in. She stood for a moment on the edge of the tranquil scene, then cried sharply, 'Felix who is this? Who are you?' She glared at Ryo, putting a hand to her head. 'Oh, Felix, you cannot guess what's happened. It's like a nightmare, and now this . . .'

She swayed, holding on to the door frame and Felix ran to her with arms outstretched. 'Honoria, come in and sit down, please. What is it, my love? I'm so relieved to see you safely away from all the fighting.'

He helped her to his chair, she sank down, pinning back stray wisps of hair, still staring at Ryo. 'But who is she, this . . . this . . .?'

'I am Miss Ryo Miyata and I understand quite well what you are saying, Mrs Rayne.' Ryo stared at her coldly.

'Oh, I see. Well, it hardly matters now.' She pressed a hand to her head. 'Get me a brandy, Felix, and please send this person away. I've something too dreadful to tell you, I can scarcely believe it even now.'

Ryo walked to the door, saying with dignity, 'This is my home, Mrs Rayne. So I won't go away, but I certainly don't want to stay in this room with you.'

Felix rushed to the drink cabinet, saying agitatedly, 'Ryo, I'm sorry, I'll explain later.' Ryo closed the door and Felix, groaning, poured two large brandies. As Honoria began drinking greedily, he murmured, 'But I didn't expect to see you again. I thought you'd decided to stay with him. You didn't come to me.'

'Oh, how I wish I had now!' she sighed. 'But he vowed to keep the children there with him. How could I abandon them in such a place with a drunken sot of a father? And not only that, as I know now,' her tone was venomous, 'but a double-crossing swindler, a common criminal, at present in the custody of Her Majesty's Legation police.'

'Harold? Oh surely not? Whatever's happened, Honoria, for pity's sake . . .?'

'And it all began with you,' she spat at him. 'With your seductive charms and your damnable scientific enthusiasms.'

'Honoria, please, what are you saying? I love you dearest, still. Don't look on me so harshly. What is this all about?'

'You have ruined our lives, and I will tell you how,' she said tonelessly. 'Here,' she handed him her silk cloak, 'please hang this up while I collect myself.' She took another long drink, then, staring at him coldly with her wide blue eyes, began. 'Harold and I stayed there the rest of the winter, scarcely speaking. He was drinking heavily and I often wondered where he got the money for so much imported French brandy. We'd agreed to stay together at least until his term of duty was over, this coming autumn. So things just drifted on until, about a week ago, we heard that the Imperial fleet was coming north, and all foreign residents were to be evacuated before the fighting. Then everything happened quickly. We awoke one morning to see the *Pearl* in the bay and we had orders to be aboard before dark. So there was a great rush. Young Robert Enslie from the Legation, who Sir Harry had sent to help us, was packing up the quayside office, which Harold had left in complete chaos, and it was there that he found it. Do you know what I'm talking about?' she shot at him.

He blinked. 'I've no earthly idea.'

'A box file that he found in the back of a cupboard with a picture of a skeleton pasted on the front.' Felix shivered, though he still did not understand. 'Young Enslie took the file aboard and locked it away, which meant that Harold was in a frightful state when we sailed that evening, though I didn't know why at the time. Enslie read the file, took it to the captain and they hauled Harold in. Faced with such damning evidence, he confessed on the spot.'

'Honoria, will you please explain exactly what all this is about,' he moaned.

'You know – don't you?' she challenged him over the rim of her glass. 'So you can tell me how *much* you know.'

He shrugged. 'I . . . skeletons, you say. Well, all right. When I first met you – five years ago, wasn't it? – I had a harebrained idea that the Ainu would provide clues to Darwin's missing link. So, we – Harold and I – dug up a handful of skeletal remains and I sent them home for investigation. Unfortunately they proved to be scientifically value-less. No links, nothing.'

'And you told Harold so?'

'Why yes, I wrote and told him at once.'

She took a quick breath. 'Then let's hope your letter is on that file. You see, he's been doing it ever since – sending bits and bobs of dead Ainu to learned societies in various countries, claiming they were missing links. It's paid quite well, apparently – all the brandy bills, sheet music, and dresses for me. Fraudulent grave-robbing; quite an unusual crime, I must say. Though of course the original idea was yours – far too clever for Harold.'

'Oh, my darling – believe me, I hadn't the remotest idea . . .'

She waved her glass. 'Get me a drink.' He stumbled to obey, asking, 'But why did Enslie latch on to it so fast?'

'The Ainu had told the Japanese authorities some time ago that a large foreign devil was robbing their graves. They passed it on to Harold, who pooh-poohed the suggestion, naturally. A second report came in, though, and went directly to Sir Harry who instructed Enslie to keep an eye open when he was in Hakodate. Which he did – quite a sharp young cub. After Harold's confinement to his cabin, on the *Pearl*, I managed to get Enslie sufficiently drunk – and intimidated – to tell me the full story. Officially I'm still not supposed to know, but Enslie has promised to arrange a passage out on the first ship for me and the children, before the scandal breaks.' She put down her glass with a shrug of despair. 'I had a stupid notion you might come with me, or join me later. But I see now you've made other arrangements. In any case, I don't suppose you'd want to associate with the wife of a man of Harold's stamp. Oh, the shame of it — the humiliation! How I loathe and detest him in the uttermost depth of my being!'

She buried her face in her hands and he watched tears trickle through her shapely ringed fingers. He thought of the piano in the Consulate parlour, the moments of passion fulfilled. 'Honoria, what can I do to help?' he murmured wretchedly.

'Come away with me — and your son.'

'But you don't know that . . .'

'Oh, I know nothing — though I was sure you'd desert me, too. But I didn't expect to find a native woman in residence, I must say.' Her voice was high and slightly slurred.

'But you *chose* to leave me alone and —'

She jumped up. Reaching for her handbag she swung it hard into his face, and the clasp cracked against his cheek.

He put up a shielding hand. 'Do I deserve that? Honoria, listen to me; how could I have known things would turn out like this? I never wished you anything but good, and love. Even Harold I quite liked and felt guilty about . . .'

She sniffed, her head buzzing with drink and tension. 'Well, he certainly doesn't like *you*, Mr Coburn. And at his trial he'll do his best to incriminate you too. I suppose any cuckolded husband would.'

'But Honoria — I knew nothing whatever about his fraudulent dealings. Come, you know I didn't . . .'

She looked at him disdainfully. 'You're just a self-indulgent, weak-kneed puppy, Felix. That's what Harold called you and he was right. I was a fool not to see it sooner. I honestly don't care whether you were involved or not. You and Harold can work out your own salvations between you, and good riddance. I shan't be here to witness it. I feel I've only one mission left in life and that's to keep my children free and ignorant of the dreadful stain of dishonour that is their only inheritance from this loathsome country.'

Her voice was again under control as she walked past him, picked up her cloak, and went out, shutting the door quietly.

275

Felix sat for a long while in the chair she had vacated, sipping brandy; Ryo tiptoed in; she had been crying; he sent her away; the musician passed by again in the outside dark, piping the same melancholy tune. He wished himself back to the moment of first hearing it that evening – the golden sun setting, Ryo sewing, Minnie the mynah chattering. Another dream crumbled away; like Honoria, he could not wait to leave this loathsome country.

Honoria left with the children two days later and Felix saw them off, though afterwards he wished he had not, for Honoria did not spare him, pointing out how Oliver was so very like his father in looks. But, even had he wished, Felix could not have accompanied her, for, that very morning, he had received notice that he would be called as witness in the trial of Mr Harold Rayne, to be held a few weeks hence.

Obliged to stay, Felix resolved to use the interim to wind up both his business and his household so that he could leave immediately the trial was over. He said nothing to Ryo of his decision, but, as a first step, sent a note to Arnold Mills asking to meet him at his convenience. He had seen little of Arnold recently and was surprised by the apparently curt tone of the reply, suggesting they meet at the military hospital after his consultation there the following Thursday.

The curtness was obviously deliberate, as Felix realised when Arnold, coming into the hospital waiting-room, gave Felix a cool nod and informed him he was very busy and would he come immediately to the point. Taken aback, Felix asked instead after Elinor, remarked on the pleasantness of the weather. Arnold replied briefly, and waited.

Felix coughed. 'Well, old man, it's not easy to come straight to the point – two points, actually. Separate, though connected . . .'

'You simply start with the first and go on to the second.'

'You're very cool, I must say, Arnold.'

'Does that surprise you – after the way you've behaved to a woman who is, in a manner of speaking, related to me?'

'Yes . . . well, that's one of the points actually. Fact of the matter is, you see, and this relates to the second point also, I

276

intend leaving Japan for good as soon as the Rayne trial is over.'

'Running out on her, hey? We always guessed you would.'

Felix bridled. 'Put it like that if you wish, but I must point out that she ran *in* on me. I didn't ask her to come and live with me. She simply arrived, saying she'd left the Hubbards' school after a row with your sister and her husband. And I swear I never promised her anything – the subject simply wasn't discussed.'

Arnold scowled. 'Oh, I grant you she's behaved damn stupidly. I'd never have believed it of her – she always seemed so reserved and biddable. But you must have known how serious the social consequences would be for a woman of her class?'

Felix looked away. 'I didn't give it much thought. Anyway, all I hope now is to see Ryo decently settled before I leave, which is why I've come to you. What do you feel? Have her relatives totally disowned her? Would they overlook this little . . . misdemeanour – and offer her a home?'

Arnold frowned. 'Hard to say. My sister's still very fond of Ryo and so is Kenjiro, I imagine.'

'So will you see what you can do? I want to pack up my place and I can't push Ryo out on the streets. Such a reconciliation would surely please your sister?'

'Perhaps – Kenjiro is deeply shocked and outraged, but the sooner Ryo is away from you the better – he must see that.'

'And our little . . . idyll . . . was of short duration. People will soon forget,' Felix added persuasively.

'Hmm. Proud Satsumas don't easily forget, or forgive. Still, I'll try, and let you know shortly.' He looked pointedly at his watch.

'Here – wait a jiff – there's something else.'

'Well?' Arnold paused on his way to the door.

Felix took a sharp breath. 'It's about the Rayne business – that's why I'm leaving. It's such an appalling mess. Did you know I'm to be called as a witness?'

'Rumour has it so.'

'Rumour has run riot over the whole business. Well, I just

wanted to say − in spite of your disapproval of my conduct − I hope you won't make me out to be more of a renegade than I am? You may be called to the box too, you see.'

Arnold shrugged. 'Let's leave it to the lawyers to get to the bottom of it, shall we? If I'm asked I shall simply say what little I know − of your involvement, or anyone else's.'

'Fair enough. I was afraid you might be tempted to . . .'

Arnold turned at the door. '. . . brand you a criminal? No I don't think that of you, Coburn. But you're a damnably selfish, silly sort of cove in my view. And you haven't done anyone much good here as far as I can see. So the sooner you leave the country the better for all concerned.'

'Thanks for that final diagnosis, Doctor. Makes me feel much better! Ironic, you must admit, that I came out here filled with hopes of making a grand scientific discovery and, perhaps, finding the romantic passion of my life. And what's happened? Dreams crumbled to dust and all I've succeeded in is making money. Coburns' corsets go from strength to strength. You may even be able to buy them in Tokyo's shops, one day!'

Arnold shuddered. 'Hope you're not expecting our dainty little Japanese ladies to strap themselves into your horrible contraptions?'

'Some of 'em may, Arnold, you wait and see. And if so you can say that even the bounder Felix got something right!' He gave Arnold a grin of bravado as he went out.

Two days later Felix received a note from Arnold saying that the Miyatas had agreed to offer Ryo a home and that he would take her away with him on his next visit to Yokohama. The speed and finality of this was dismaying, but Felix braced himself to tell Ryo of his decision to leave Japan that same evening. She wasn't really surprised, for nothing had been the same between them since Honoria's visit. Ryo had felt herself shrivel up inside at the very sight of the Englishwoman's beauty, and her imperious demeanour; and all the Japanese woman's earlier feelings of inferiority had returned in double measure. It seemed to her then that Honoria and Felix existed on a plane of sophisticated intimacy to which she could never

278

aspire, and she even sympathised with Felix in his hardly disguised misery at Honoria's departure. For what could she, the unmarried, untutored, kinky-haired daughter of a provincial samurai, offer to Felix? And in competition with the dramatic Honoria?

Thus, when Felix broke the news, she bowed low, accepting the sentence of banishment with resignation, feeling it was almost deserved. For in her heart she had guessed that this one defiant gesture against the oppression of her sex, class, and upbringing was doomed and she would suffer for it. The choice of freedom would never be hers; it was already too late. 'A nail that sticks up from the wood will inevitably be knocked on the head,' as her mother used to say. She did not even blame Felix till much later; she simply accepted the sorrow, though her very limbs became heavy with it, weighing down the silken sleeves of her kimono like the stones women often put inside them before jumping into wells to escape the injustices, frustrations, griefs of their lives.

When Arnold arrived to collect her in his phaeton, she summoned all her proud resources and made no whimper as the two men loaded her cloth-wrapped bundles under the canopy. In one of them was her wooden pillow; on its base she had carved Felix's name several times. Felix touched her hand, wished her good luck, and she climbed aboard, clutching the mynah's cage in her arms.

'You'll like the new house,' Arnold said kindly, as Sam cracked the whip. 'It's absolutely top-hole and very spacious.'

The residence into which the Miyatas had moved had formerly belonged to members of the northern Aidzu clan, supporters of the Shogun, who had fled the city during the Restoration. Several neighbouring establishments had been similarly vacated and, as they were well-appointed with park-like grounds and situated in the hillier, less populated area to the west of the castle, were now much sought after by Imperialists from Kyoto and the southern provinces.

The place allotted to the Miyatas was not on the grandest scale, though it seemed a mansion to Elinor, compared with Taneo's bungalow. An arched gate led into a pebbled courtyard flanked with servants' quarters; the main house had two outstanding features: an entrance porch with upswept tiled gables, and a wooden fire tower on the roof-ridge, in which hung a carved bronze bell. From the pillared reception hall, sliding screens opened into suites of small apartments, the paintings on their walls blanched by the years into shadows of flowers, reeds, and birds that seemed about to fade totally into some other world. The most secluded apartments, now occupied by Kenjiro and Elinor, overlooked a spacious garden landscaped with rockeries, a sloping shrubbery, and a flagged terrace beside an oval pond, from which a stream flowed to a boundary fence of split bamboo. It had fallen into temporary neglect during the recent troubles and outdoor servants were now busy pruning, tidying and replanting, while workmen put finishing touches to the room overlooking the pond, which had been converted to 'western-style' with glass windows, carpet, and bookshelves.

Elinor, standing on the pond's far side, looked towards the room wondering whether to order the curtains that were indispensable in a western house, yet quite inappropriate in a Japanese. Perhaps blinds would be the answer? She wandered restlessly along the paved path to the shrubbery. It was extremely hot; crickets whirred in the bushes; dragonflies skimmed over the sun-white glare of water; their recently acquired Pekinese lay panting under a maple. Elinor had named the pup 'Duke' in honour of the Duke of Edinburgh, who was arriving shortly on a state visit. The occasion would cause great excitement, for it was the first time in Japanese history that a foreign prince would be personally received by the Emperor. Such a departure from time-honoured customs that used to govern the seclusion of the heavenly-descended Japanese royalty was considered both a compliment to the British and, as Kenjiro said, 'a way of putting Japan on the map of the modern world'.

Elinor smiled fondly, thinking of the optimistic determination of young men like her husband to 'make the country go forward', even though the Restoration had not smoothed away all the difficulties and there was still considerable

280

confusion and discontent in the land. Many clans had recently relinquished their territorial rights to rule to the Emperor, but it had not yet been settled how their former domains should be governed. The Satsuma leaders, with whom Kenjiro's fortunes were closely linked, had become dissatisfied with the share of power so far allotted to them and had recently retreated to Kyushu in some dudgeon. In consequence, Kenjiro's future was still uncertain, and political bargaining and rivalry were rife, as Elinor knew. Kenjiro told her little of all this, however, for wives were not supposed to know about such matters. She sighed now, aware that their continued occupation of this pleasant residence depended on factors she did not understand or was not privy to. But Kenjiro had hinted that some decision regarding his future was imminent and so, each evening, she waited impatiently for his return in the hope of news.

As she moved towards the house, she saw Ryo go into the nursery to look at Hannah. Her sister-in-law was also tense that afternoon, for in Yokohama it was the final day of what everyone called 'The Skeleton Trial'. It was rumoured that Felix Coburn, who had been called to the witness-box, might face a charge of desecration of graves after Harold Rayne had been sentenced, and Arnold had promised to bring them news of the verdict as soon as possible.

'She's still asleep.' Ryo came on to the terrace. 'You should come inside, Ellie; the hot sun isn't good for you.'

Elinor was again pregnant and, as both Kenjiro and Ryo were convinced it would be a boy, they were specially solicitous for her health. She moved into the verandah's shade and picked up her sewing, and the two women sat in companionable silence. Ryo's recent return to her relatives had been tranquil, for they were greatly relieved to have her back and, realising her hurt, did not add to it with fresh recriminations. The best course, Kenjiro said to his wife, was to pretend that the disgraceful episode had never happened; and next year, by which time people should have forgotten, he would find a husband for his errant sister.

Ryo looked up from her embroidery. 'Isn't it time for the

Doctor to arrive?'

'By tea-time, he hoped; yes. Why don't you order tea, perhaps that will bring him,' Elinor replied; and indeed just as Ryo returned from the kitchen quarters she heard Arnold's wheels in the courtyard. She put her hand to her mouth. 'Here he is. Shall I leave you together?'

'No – stay. I'll ask him for you,' Elinor whispered as he came towards them.

'Good afternoon, ladies. How are you faring in these dog-days? Phew! Am I too late for tea?'

'Just coming, Arnold; and your Big-san chair is here in the shade. But come – we must have the news. The verdict – tell us all.'

He lowered himself into his chair. 'Ah, that.' He mopped his brow; then began in stately, sonorous tones. 'Speaking before a packed, silent court-room, the Chief Justice of the Yokohama Judiciary stated that Mr Harold Rayne, formerly Consul in Hakodate, had been found guilty of the wilful desecration of native graves on six separate occasions, and of fraud perpetrated in relation to the contents thereof. He was therefore sentenced to a term of twelve years' imprisonment in accordance with . . .'

'Twelve years, that's very harsh, isn't it?' Elinor exclaimed.

'No mitigating conditions could be permitted having regard to the fact that at the time of his crimes Mr Rayne was an appointed official of Her Majesty's Government, and had thus brought into disrepute the entire British Consular Service in Japan,' he continued in the same tones.

'Poor Harold!'

'Oh come, Elinor, the evidence in the Skeleton File didn't leave him a bone to stand on. The man's a proven criminal and criminals have to be punished.'

'Yes, but . . . considering the circumstances . . . Anyway, what about Felix Coburn?'

'Ah – tea, I'm gasping for it; thank you,' he smiled at the maid. 'No charge against him.' He carefully did not look at Ryo. 'I had to speak in his defence, as you know. Luckily for him, his letter to Harold saying that the Ainu remains were

282

valueless was still in the file – which made Harold's wild accusations about Felix inciting him into fraud look rather silly. Of course, we all know why he made them, but this didn't give them any credibility in court. So Coburn got off quite lightly. A very odd case altogether – one for the legal annals, I'll warrant.'

Ryo rose. 'Please excuse me for a few minutes; I think I hear Hannah.'

'Has she settled down?' Arnold asked as she disappeared.

'I think so; we simply don't speak of it.'

'Best thing. Thanks.' He took more tea.

'But I do feel sorry for Harold – twelve years and a career utterly ruined. Where will he serve it?'

'Hong Kong, but he's being held in custody here until the High Court in Shanghai confirms the sentence, I believe.'

'So I could go and visit him?'

'What on earth's the point? Come, Ellie – you must give up your lame dogs. You've got much better things to do. Like the party, for instance – the Fortescues were asking about it.'

'Ah yes, the party. We've decided to have it on September 14th, when the Duke will be attending that state banquet and we shall have our own little housewarming celebration. We shan't aim as high as Count Iwada, who seems to be something of a hero to Kenjiro, but we'll ask some of the lesser lights. Oh, and Arnold – dear Arnold . . .' She leaned forward, pleading, 'I want to serve ice-cream.'

'Ice-cream? Here – with the dairy and ice-making plant in Yokohama?'

'Ah, but I have a most obliging brother, do I not? And he has a very fast phaeton and a ready supply of those lined containers for chilling medicines.'

'So I'm to be the ice-cream man, hey?'

'Please, dear. Some of our Japanese guests won't have tasted it yet and they'll love it. You know how sweet-toothed they are. I want it to be quite a memorable party, if not exactly a royal banquet. And we'll be about thirty, so you'll need to collect several containers . . . Please?'

'I'll do my best,' he chuckled, and strolled over the terrace to look at the pond.

The sun's rays were slanting now, making the surface a scramble of white, grey, and pink shadow. The Japanese, for all their sweet teeth and fiddle-faddle enthusiasms, knew all about reflections, he suddenly thought – in water, in life. Reflected lanterns and grasses, upside-down images, cherry blossoms and stars. 'Topsy-turvydom' was the silly foreign term. He had never begun to suspect how complicated life could be until he came to this country, even though most of his time was spent trying to make things simple for himself. He shook his head, watching his pregnant sister stroll along the verandah, and he chuckled again. An ice-cream party, hey? Quite a jolly frolic!

A drizzle of rain fell during the night before the Miyata's party, but the morning brought clear sun that sparkled on the damp mosses and rocks in the garden, where a refreshment tent was erected. While Elinor checked supplies on the serving-tables inside, Kenjiro agonised in their bedroom over what he should wear for the occasion. Usually the matter was clear-cut: western-style for work and official functions involving foreigners; native apparel at other times. But this gathering had no precedent in his experience – a buffet tea for foreigners and Japanese and his own housewarming. Moreover, his appointment to a higher office in the Ministry of Foreign Affairs had just been confirmed, and it was that which made him reach, albeit reluctantly, for his high-collar shirt and stiff-limbed suit. But, at the last minute, he could not bear the additional constriction of patent leather shoes and hurried to meet the first guests shod in comfortable thonged sandals.

Among the early comers were several of his own clansmen now serving, like himself, in the recently created government departments – Civil Affairs, Finance, War, Foreign Affairs, Justice. The times being politically delicate, they clustered together warily, at first, commenting politely on the beauty of the garden and the success of the Duke of Edinburgh's royal audience in the Waterfall Pavilion, at which the

Emperor had been presented with a golden snuff-box from Queen Victoria. None of these men had brought their wives, and Elinor, standing beside Kenjiro, was relieved to hear the voices of her own kind in the courtyard. The Hubbards had come with their two eldest, and the Fortescues with their daughters, and their son Edgar, who was about to go into banking like his father. A gangly, earnest youth, he stood on the fringes of every group and enjoyed only the throwing of sticks for Duke in the shrubbery.

Taneo Takahashi and his staff arrived next; and Elinor, knowing of his recent pamphlet urging Japanese men and women to mix socially as westerners did, had shamed them into bringing their wives. The women, radiantly dressed, stood in a tight alarmed cluster in the tent's shade and talked only to Ryo. At this juncture, with the guests gathered in separate circles according to race and sex, Elinor began to despair of her party's success – when the sound of a hunting horn heralded the arrival of Arnold, Percival, and the phaeton filled with containers of ice-cream. Giggling servants rushed to carry them into the tent, where the guests crowded round delightedly, spooning up the fast-melting strawberry and vanilla, accompanied by cakes and pastries, cordials and champagne.

'How very sweet of you both – just what was needed as a conversation-piece.' Elinor went to thank the ice-cream carriers.

Percival grinned. 'Look at those two fellows from the back-woods – you can tell they've never tasted the stuff before.' He adopted his Japanese-speaking-English voice. 'It's made from real cows' milk – what a filthy idea! I know I shall loathe it – but one has to be so polite to foreigners these days . . . Hmm . . . Very cool on the tongue . . . Let's see . . . *Ah-so*, better than I thought, I must say. Maybe a little more? Why, a lot more . . . Amazingly toothsome, this funny western grub, isn't it?'

Elinor giggled as they watched the two, in their flowing silks, bend their top-knots eagerly over the bowls to scrape up every last morsel. As they themselves went for second helpings, Mary Fortescue joined them.

'The ice-cream is a wonderful wheeze, Ellie! I'm sure the Emperor and the Duke aren't enjoying their banquet half so much.'

'Oh, we didn't set ourselves up in deliberate competition, Mary . . . But did the Duke make a good impression in Yokohama, too?'

'Oh yes, my dear. He danced twice with Mrs Marshall of Windsor Castle at the Club Ball. She was over the moon for days; though she thought it no more than her due, living where she does. But apart from that little flurry we've been dreadfully flat since the trial ended. Did you see the local press reports? There never was such a collection of terrible puns committed to print about skeletons rattling in and falling out of cupboards.'

She lowered her voice, glancing towards Ryo. 'And Felix Coburn sailed for home yesterday. Just as well, don't you think? Now what else can I report to you sophisticated city-dwellers? Oh, the lighthouses are in full working glow; we're going to have our streets properly drained at last; and you know of course of the plans to lay the first rails for the proposed Yokohama to Tokyo line? The awfully sad thing is that we probably shan't be here for the grand opening. Or don't you know our news?'

'Why no – what's happening, Mary?'

'Claud's got a promotion. We have to go and live in Shanghai.'

'Oh Mary, no – how dreadful!' Elinor wailed, as Claud Fortescue approached.

'Come now, Elinor, please don't join the common chorus of woe. No one congratulates me on my promotion, they simply lament at the thought of losing Mary. One great advantage of the move in my opinion is that it will stop her spending my entire salary buying those wishy-washy Japanese prints.'

'And in my opinion you'll eat your words one day, Claud, as they become increasingly valuable.' She wagged a finger at him.

'But I'm desolate at the news – Yokohama without Mary. . .

oh dear; but here I am doing just what I don't want my guests to do — talking only to their own kind. Come now, Mary, meet Mr Takahashi, he's a dear — you must have heard of him.'

Elinor led Mary across to Taneo, who was talking to Percival on the terrace while consuming his third dish of ice-cream. 'Most delicious, Elinor!' he greeted her. 'I'm quite converted to your dairy products, as you see, especially when washed down with champagne.'

'I saw one or two traditionalists quietly tip the vanilla into the bushes; but, generally, a huge success, Elinor,' Percival added.

'Mr Takahashi is famous for explaining the complexities of western things to his people, Mary,' Elinor said, introducing them.

'Ah — but things are easy to explain. We are hungry to understand your ideas as well. Some of your abstract terms simply have no equals for us, you know, we have no mental pegs to hang them on.' Taneo cornered Mary, eager for a new convert.

'Such as "democracy", I believe, Mr Takahashi?' Mary murmured.

'Indeed yes, madam. And "benevolent polity", "public interest", "constitutional rights". This is what makes the present so exciting — the very beginning of a new era, the Meiji era of enlightenment. Even our new leaders haven't a true understanding of these abstractions, nor the faintest notion of how to put them into practice. So many changes to be accomplished so quickly. Take other words — like "individual initiative" and "responsibility". We must learn their meaning at once, now that the earlier privileges of birth and inheritance are being abolished and men must earn their own way to wealth and power.'

'It will fall rather harshly on some, surely?' Mary looked a little hunted.

'Changes of such magnitude always do, Mrs Fortescue,' Taneo replied, launching into another of his favourite themes on the relationship between a nation's adaptability to change and its capacity for progress.

Elinor, leaving Mary to extricate herself as best she might, went in search of her husband, whom she discovered on the verandah steps talking with some clansmen. Tongues having been loosened, they were spiritedly discussing the volatile politics of the day, particularly the strong stand of Saigo Takamori, who was pressing for drastic monetary reforms, which were not popular with all those present. They nodded perfunctorily at Elinor and continued their conversation, probably imagining she couldn't understand it. Kenjiro, flushed with wine like the others and in sparkling, teasing mood, was saying how glad he was that, at least, he would never again have to depend on paltry pittances handed out by his clan-superiors. Elinor smiled, thinking he richly deserved these small triumphs, and was about to move on when Arnold tapped her on the back.

'Shall I open the last of the champers? All the men have developed the dickens of a thirst, but the servants hate popping the corks.'

'Oh, please do – and ask Kenjiro to help you. He rather enjoys it.'

As Arnold strolled to the refreshment tent with his brother-in-law, he remarked casually, 'Odd coincidence, Percival was just telling me. He was chatting to one of your clansmen and they realised it was exactly seven years ago today – on September 14th, 1862 – that he was riding along the Tokaido road in that procession of Lord Shimazu's which set upon old Charlie Richardson. Amazing when you think about it, isn't it? That then – and now, look at all this . . .' He waved about the champagne bottle that Kenjiro had just handed him.

Kenjiro straightened and stood still, clutching another bottle in his hand. 'Can that really be so? Just seven years ago? Today?' He gulped, then impulsively revealed a secret he had long kept. 'That was the day I first set eyes on you.'

'Me? But I didn't know you then.'

'And I didn't exactly know you; but I was the man delegated to stay behind in Namamugi to report back on the barbarians' reaction when they found Richardson. I was watching from that tea-house when you went to examine the body. When you

288

stood up you seemed to look straight at me.' Kenjiro stared intently at Arnold, trying to see again with the unknowing, youthful eyes of that distant time. He murmured, 'I thought your hair was the colour of wet sand and your eyes like grey pebbles. An ocean-crossing man from a far country who must be very skilful and wise.'

Arnold chuckled uncomfortably. 'Well, you know better now, Kenjiro.'

'Ah, but now you are my brother-in-law. I have seen you laugh and rage, work hard and play well. We have quarrelled and become friends again because of Elinor, and now we are here in this tent, popping champagne corks together. Seven years only — to me it seems a lifetime, several lifetimes.' He began pulling the bottle's cork. 'Come — we'll share a toast, to you the ocean-crossing man whose sister I married against your wishes, and to me, the yellow-skinned native interpreter who promises to make her happy all the days of her life. And you will love me for that eventually, I promise you, Arnold-san.'

As the cork flew out Arnold grabbed glasses and they downed the amber liquid. 'To us,' Arnold agreed, and slapped Kenjiro on the shoulder. 'Funny old world, isn't it, Kenjiro?'

'Funny old world,' Kenjiro echoed, as, a little drunkenly, they refilled their glasses and went to serve the waiting guests.

Glasses were refilled all round, but the occasion had passed its bubbly peak and people began drifting away, complimenting their hosts on the successful holding of Tokyo's very first ice-cream party, which would certainly go down in the social annals. By the time the last guests had departed, golden shafts from the setting sun were slanting across the pond, where Elinor, holding Hannah in her arms, stood beside Ryo.

'I'm very pleased that Mrs Hubbard talked to me,' Ryo said timidly. 'It shows her true Christian spirit.'

'She's a fine woman. I think she suspects the seeds of a convert in you, Ryo, and is anxious to nurture them. I hope

289

she's right – but you won't desert us for her school again yet, will you?'

'Oh no, not with Hannah – and the boy coming.'

'What if she's a girl?'

'No, no, speak of him as a boy, it all helps.'

'Oh, you Japanese and the inborn superiority of the male!' Elinor sighed as her husband joined them. 'One has to fight so hard for a place here. Even your friends paid no attention to me, Kenjiro, and they are supposed to be aware of western social customs.'

'It will take a long time, as Taneo says – two or three generations. So I shall be all right!' he grinned, draining his last glass while Elinor tutted and slapped him on the wrist.

'Anyway, it was a most successful party, wasn't it, dear?'

'Wonderful – and the ice-cream was "a winner", as you'd say. What a clever wife I have!' He squeezed her waist. 'Give the baby to Ryo and we'll take a stroll round our little domain. Probably now I have the promotion, we shall be allowed to buy it, if I can raise the capital. And we can live here for years and years. You'd like that, wouldn't you?' She smiled into his eyes for answer.

Ryo took the baby to its cradle on the verandah and sat watching her brother and sister-in-law walking together along the paved path.

'Do you know a very funny thing, Elinor?' Kenjiro whispered in a kind of wonderment. 'It was exactly seven years ago today that our men killed Mr Richardson at Namamugi.'

Elinor yawned, beginning to sink into after-party weariness. 'So it was! And I arrived the following day. Isn't that worthy of record too?'

'But I hadn't even met you then.' He stopped at the shrubbery edge and looked at her, wanting to explain how monstrously, incredibly, improbably funny it all was – that stupid killing; the years between; their standing here now, man and wife in their own garden where Japanese and foreigners had just passed an afternoon drinking champagne and eating ice-cream together. But words failed him; his mind, like the sun, was becoming soft-gold and fuzzy at the edges.

So instead he reached for his wife, took her in his arms, gave her a close, tender hug and a long, deep, lover's kiss.

Ryo, on the verandah, thought it was a most unusual thing for her brother to do out in the open where the servants could see. A very *western* thing, she decided with a wry smile, as she picked up the baby and took her inside to bed.

PART TWO

1888—1895

CHAPTER FOURTEEN

The party of globetrotters from the P. & O. passenger liner
Chusan clambered from their rickshaws at the gates of the
foreign cemetery on Yokohama's Bluff. It was their first
experience of such quaint, comical vehicles, for they had
reached Japan only that morning after a fourteen-day
crossing from San Francisco and were in a state of rapturous
enchantment about everything they saw in this fairy-like
oriental wonderland. Considering that they had already
visited a Buddhist temple, a Shinto shrine, and the Curio
Street shops, and that more hectic sightseeing awaited them
on the morrow, they could easily have foregone the cemetery,
which was neither quaint nor oriental, as Daphne Draper
whispered to her sister Fay. But, Fay replied, the funny little
Japanese guide was trying so hard to please that they had to
pretend an interest.

With deferential efficiency, the guide marshalled them
through the gates for a brief tour of the main historical
attractions. In the lowest, oldest section was the grave of an
Englishman, Charles Richardson, murdered by Satsuma
clansmen in September 1862; a lofty stone obelisk nearby
was dedicated to the officers and men of USS *Oneida*,
accidentally sunk by a steamship in 1870; under a spreading
yew were the graves of two other military men, Major Beale
and Lieutenant Bradshaw, assassinated in the autumn of 1865.

As the group hurried on, Daphne conscientiously read her
Murray's Guide. 'Those two poor officers were murdered
near a statue called the Diabutsu, in Kamakura, Fay. That's
where we go tomorrow, isn't it? Just think, less than twenty-

295

five years ago the Japs were running around with swords, killing people for being foreigners and calling them – us – barbarians. It's hard to believe, isn't it?'

Fay, who found history boring, nudged her sister. 'Oh, look, Daph. There's our artistic Mr Rayne. How melancholy and lonesome he looks! I wonder what he's doing here?'

Daphne glanced. 'The same as us, I guess. Sightseeing . . .'

'But he's going to stay here, not rush about on a mad tour like us. Why should he come to the cemetery immediately? I bet you someone he loved is buried here. He never would say much about himself, would he?'

'Not to you and I don't blame him. You ask far too many impertinent questions and Englishmen don't like it.'

'Oh, hoity-toity! But he's rather mysterious and handsome, you must admit. Just what I like. I shall go and speak to him.'

'Fay, you'll do no such thing. Come along now, the others are way over there.'

Oliver Rayne, overhearing, deliberately moved off down the slope without turning his head, and the sisters went to join the tour group. The high-pitched tones of the guide carried to him for a while as he waited unobtrusively in a tree's shadow; but then he heard the iron gates clang, and he was alone. He shivered, pulling his silk muffler tight, for the day, which had sparkled earlier, was dwindling to grey twilight and a chill autumn wind stirred the trees between the graves. He had looked at lots of graves that afternoon, several dated earlier than the one he sought. He had not found it. Yet his father must be buried here somewhere, for he had suddenly died of a heart attack in Yokohama in the autumn of '69, just before he was due to sail home.

This much his mother had told him, though she spoke rarely of her husband or the years they had spent in Japan. The comments she had made were always unfavourable: it was a loathsome country, cold, primitive, dirty; and he and Letitia were neither to believe a word of the globetrotters' glowing tales about the place nor ever set foot there. He wandered disconsolately towards the cemetery's lowest level, remembering the drawn, sallow face of his formerly beautiful mother in the last stages of the wasting disease that had eventually killed her a few months ago. The last cemetery he had been in before today was in Brighton, where they had settled after Honoria's return from Japan and where she was now buried.

While his mother lived he would not have come here, of course; nor had he ever admitted his desire to do so — prompted by a vague sense of a mystery in his parents' past and his admiration for Japanese art. Oliver had early shown artistic promise and his mother had fostered it sedulously, paying for his private tuition, and encouraging him to mix with other artists, among whom the works of Whistler, and oriental paintings, were the rage. Oliver's standing had been enhanced simply because he had spent his infancy in Japan, and he had tended to embroider upon his small store of childish memories. In fact he remembered very little except snowfalls and the tonal lilt of Japanese speech, which he had been delighted to find so familiar when he had heard it again that day.

Still, Oliver might never have returned to Japan, but for ecstatic letters from his artistic friend, Walter Munro, who had been living in Tokyo for about a year. Honoria had left him a little money, which Oliver, who did not believe in saving, was spending on this, his first real adventure. But, as he stood in the dusky, chill cemetery, he began wishing he had never embarked upon it.

For solace, Oliver lit his curved-horn pipe, and the match's flare revealed a small headstone half-buried in the undergrowth across the path. He bent over it, lighting matches to read the faded inscription, which said simply, 'Harold James Rayne: 1824 – 1869'. Why so cruelly curt? His father had been a respected member of Her Majesty's Consular Service and had served on the China coast and in Hakodate. He frowned, running his fingers over the rest of the stone's surface, which was, and always had been, blank. As he did so he tried to recall his father — a man of large bulk, surely, with reddened cheeks, timid eyes, and a loud voice?

He straightened, for the cemetery was about to close, and

went back uphill, shutting its gates behind him. He wandered along the Bluff road, past elegant residences built in the Anglo-Oriental style, and the Gaiety Theatre, lit up in readiness for the evening's performance by Yokohama's Amateur Dramatic Society of *To Oblige Benson*. At the hill's edge he paused to view the scene below: carriage lights and rickshaw lanterns were jogging along the main thoroughfares and beyond the low, jumbled roofs of the native quarter. To his right, passenger and trading vessels rode at anchor, masts and portholes twinkling.

He shivered in the wind, his uneasy sense of being alone in an alien land made more acute by the discovery of his father's blank, neglected tomb. Perhaps his mother was right and he should never have come here? Staring at the scene, he had a sudden eerie sense of her closeness to him, her slender, ringed fingers on his shoulder, pulling him back from the brink. Was she protecting him or punishing him for disobeying her wishes? He could not be sure. Shaking himself impatiently from the imagined grip, he hurried downhill to the secure warmth of the Oriental Hotel on Main Street.

Oliver, awakening into a morning of such soft, limpid light as he had never seen before, felt his spirits soar. After breakfast, he strolled along the Bund, then dashed off a few lines to his sister before leaving the hotel. Japan was like a fairyland, he wrote, full of dainty, doll-like little people who smiled and bowed most charmingly; the streets were so clean, the wee shops so packed with beautiful things, the weather so sparkling that he was beginning to think Mother had not lived here at all but in some other Asian outpost. After all, she had never been much good at geography! He hesitated, then decided not to mention Father's grave. Letty, probably, was not having much fun anyway, living with Aunt Lydia in Lymington; and it was she who had suffered most from their lack of a father, for Mother had not concealed her preference for him – her artistic son. Letty, unfortunately, showed no special talent for anything, which was not surprising, Honoria used to say caustically and without explanation; and her role during Mother's last years had been household drudge and nurse. Feeling an upsurge of guilt, Oliver abandoned the letter and called for his luggage to be collected.

He soon forgot the melancholy of the past in the joy of his first train ride to Tokyo — inside a neat little carriage that rushed past irregularly shaped paddy-fields linked by networks of raised causeways where white egrets stalked and pecked. In the far distance rose a range of hills, crowned by snow-tipped Mount Fuji, its well-known shape an exciting confirmation that he had truly arrived. The train stopped at Kawagawa, Kawasaki, and Shinagawa, where orderly passengers filed in and out. Travellers' accounts of the 'seventies which Oliver had read expressed much mirth at the country-bumpkin Japanese who left their shoes on the platform as they boarded a train, as they would have outside a house, expecting them to be miraculously delivered to their destination. Nothing like that happened now. The passengers were very composed, tucking themselves up tight on the narrow seats and seeming thoroughly to enjoy the journey.

At the terminus a score of competing rickshaw-pullers offered Oliver the cheapest, most comfortable ride to Walter's house — which turned out to be a bungalow of unpainted wood on a quiet back street. Walter clattered down the verandah steps to meet him, his stocky, hairy frame wrapped in a loose native robe of quilted grey. Walter rented the place from the Japanese principal of a nearby school, he explained, where he taught English occasionally in order to conform to regulations, for foreigners were expected to live in the Foreign Concession on the banks of the nearby River Sumida unless they were in native employ. It was an awful bore, he told Oliver, as they squatted on cushions near the charcoal stove waiting for tea, and he was a rotten teacher, but any foreigner — butcher, baker, candlestick maker, even artist — could teach English these days, so great was the demand.

'But mainly you're painting?' Oliver asked eagerly. 'Everything in sight looks so eminently paintable I can't wait to begin.'

Walter grinned. 'Oh, that'll soon wear off, then you won't know how to begin. Certainly it seems to be a perfect paradise for artists at first — beautiful arrangements of pleasing shapes, subtle textures and colours. But then it rather disintegrates somehow into an endless, if charming, series of odds and ends. There's no statement to make, no Grand Design as we Europeans think of it . . . But I'm bone-lazy; always was. For you things might be different. Ah, here's Mademoiselle Hyacinth come to welcome you!'

He rose, turning to her with a flamboyant bow that was almost an insult. Walter had told Oliver about Hyacinth, his very own little Japanese *mousmé*, a captivating creature with alluring ways whose sole aim in life was apparently to please her foreign lord and master. Envious, Oliver had imagined a graceful and exotic maiden like a picture on a fan, but Hyacinth was short and stubby with no expression he could fathom in her narrow, deep-set eyes.

Hyacinth served the food that evening and there was much joking at Oliver's expense as he tried to manipulate unfamiliar chopsticks and finish his first flask of warm *saké*.

'You must get used to the native fodder and avoid expensive foreign fripperies,' Walter advised. 'I teach, sell a few paintings, get a small allowance from the Pater, and all's well, isn't it, dear?' He squeezed Hyacinth's flaccid hand. Walter, Oliver remembered, had always been an easy-come, easy-go chap, son of a wealthy Scottish shipbuilder and five years older than Oliver, though he looked more, with his walrus mustachios, balding hair, and budding paunch.

He reached for more *saké*. 'It's keeping up with the gilded youth that costs the money, I find.'

'And who would they be when they're at home?'

'Offspring of the old aristocracy who used to live in Kyoto before the Emperor's restoration, and of politicians and high-ups in the government, most of them former samurai. They live in the High City west of the royal palace. A Nobs' Hill sort of district. They're full of hare-brained ideas, faddish, fashionable, and fun. The only people I've met who are, really. Yokohama's full of stuffed-shirt merchants, bankers, and their tittle-tattle wives. And here in the capital foreigners are either diplomats — who seldom deign to mix with the likes of us – or frighteningly worthy teachers and missionaries who infest the Tsukiji settlement down the road – you hear their confounded church bells ringing day and night.'

'So most of your friends are Japanese? How exotic of you, Walt!'

'Well, except for one or two – like the great Panjandrum Professor Fantani, an American of Italian extraction and number one expert on oriental art, at whose feet we all bow.'

Hyacinth, who had been nodding vigorously and partly understanding, added proudly, 'Relatives of Viscount Mori he know. He is a big man in the government.'

Walter grinned. 'The Minister of Education, no less! Oh – and don't forget the "mixed-ups", as you crudely call them, Hyacinth. The Miyatas – Joey and his sister Hannah.'

'Why mixed up?'

'English mother. Jap father.'

Hyacinth wrinkled her nose in distaste and Walter slapped her knee heartily. 'Did you know the Japanese secretly despise everyone who isn't a hundred and one per cent of their own race? They're worse than us white men.'

'But when do I meet all these rich, fashionable, and fascinating people?' Oliver's flippancy concealed his eagerness to do so.

'All in good time. We just drift about together sometimes, not much now, it's too cold . . .' Walter yawned pointedly. 'How about burrowing under the bed-quilts, Oliver? We've put you in the little holy room at the feet of Buddha; there's nowhere else. But I'm sure he'll protect you as if you were one of his own. He's a much more accommodating deity than ours, I'm beginning to realise.'

And so for that night and many thereafter Oliver curled up in his bed-quilts on the floor staring at the Buddha in the alcove. The dimmed night-light glowed magically on its gilded breast and cheeks; behind, the paper-screen walls were translucent silver in the same light. He smelled the unfamiliar odours of the house – long-fermented pickles, hair-oil, bad drains, incense – and heard strange sounds – the clack of the night-watchman's rattle, the plaintive call of the blind shampooer on his late-night rounds, the tinny tip-tap of Hyacinth's pipe as she knocked the ashes out against the edge of her smoking-box before retiring.

The box had fascinated Oliver that evening. It was made of red lacquered wood and contained a blue and white tobacco jar shaped like an obese toad, a tiny porcelain stove filled with glowing embers, a bamboo pot, and two long-stemmed pipes. Hyacinth had sucked at them briefly but frequently, and Walter, happily puffing cigars, had not seemed to mind. But Oliver decided there and then that he never wanted to share a bed with a pipe-smoking lady, even if her name was Hyacinth. With that thought he closed his eyes reluctantly on the exotic scene. This was truly the mysterious Orient; yet it felt rather as if he had come home.

Oliver's sense of delighted recognition persisted and, following Walter's advice, he did not attempt to paint immediately, but spent the days walking about and looking around – as he had never really looked in his life before. Even the most commonplace Japanese objects seemed exquisite and admirable: cherrywood chopsticks wrapped in patterned magenta paper and tied with thinnest gold thread; the skimpy towel with a flowing design of pine trees and mountains that the rickshaw-man used to mop his brow after wheeling a heavy foreigner about; stripped spruce-fir wall-pillars glossy as the finest grey silk.

The main avenues of the city, lined with stone, plaster, and brick buildings and shops with English signboards where assistants wore pinstripe suits, pleased him not at all; but he never tired of the narrow back streets. Here, painted and gilded signs of elegant incomprehensibility swung among rows of tiny, grey-brown dwellings with tin chimneys and kerchief-sized gardens. From them, housewives sometimes emerged and trotted off pigeon-toed to the fishmongers and vegetable-sellers; ragpickers shuffled by with large baskets of rubbish bumping against their skinny rumps; workmen jumped nimbly about on flimsy scaffolds repairing roof-tiles; children clustered round the itinerant vendors who sold dabs of sweet paste quick-cooked over hot plates into intricate shapes of letters, animals, and birds. The vendors' instinctive touch moulded even the humble paste into a pleasing arrangement – the formation of harmonious balances between objects, lines, and spaces which he saw on every side and recognised, with a thrill, as something for which he had long been searching.

Returning late one afternoon from one such pleasurable wandering, Oliver found that they had a visitor, whom he first took for a Japanese. He was sprawled carelessly on a cushion close to the stove and over his fashionable belted Norfolk jacket was draped a plaid blanket, which he shrugged off as he rose to be introduced, saying in faultless English, 'Joey Miyata; how do you do? Please forgive my blanket, I must look like an Indian squaw. But I find the native houses infernally cold at this season; they're strictly for summers and earthquakes.' His brilliant smile lit up a pale, handsome face which, Oliver realised, was not entirely Japanese with its high-bridged nose and wide eyes flecked with a hint of amber. 'You've recently arrived and are quite overcome with rapture at picturesque Japan, Walt tells me? A touch of the dollywobbles, hey?'

Oliver smiled in polite incomprehension as they all huddled round the stove, Joey carefully re-arranging his blanket. 'The . . .?'

'A family joke, excuse me – about the ubiquitous globe-trotters who write home saying that Japan is a fairyland full of doll-like little people. One gent was positively wobbling with delight as he described some tea-house girls to my mother. She coined the phrase, actually.'

Oliver winced, remembering his first letter to his sister. 'And does one soon recover from the state? It's rather pleasant.'

'Oh, if one stays long enough reality obtrudes, doesn't it, Walt?'

'You sound disenchanted?'

Joey shrugged. 'We are very picturesque here, of course, but much else besides. In any case, I can't see through globe-trotters' rosy specs. I've always lived here, except for a

303

spell of schooling in England. My mother's English, you see.'

Oliver nodded; the 'mixed-ups', of course. 'And did you like England?'

'Very picturesque. Full of the quaintest people – large, clumsy, grossly overdressed, living on slabs of beef and brown ale. The cricket and rowing were splendid, but I'm taking up *kendo* now. I was telling Walt that it's about time to return to the traditional pastimes after all the billiards and ballroom dancing.'

Oliver, unsure how much of this was mockery, took refuge in the straight question. 'Forgive my newcomer's ignorance, but what is *kendo?*'

'A kind of ritual fencing. My father, who was a samurai, learned it in his youth, along with wrestling, jousting, archery – the martial arts of feudalism.'

'And now he wants you to learn them?'

Joey pulled irritably at the fringes of his blanket. 'Oh, father wants me to learn simply everything! He'd like me to study by the light of the firefly and the glare of the snow, as the Chinese say. But most of the things he has in mind – economics, maths, and so on – I can't seem to develop a taste for.'

'More tea, Joey?' Walter interrupted. 'Mr Miyata feels Joey is frittering away his precious youth in idle pursuits with dissolute Bohemians like us, Oliver. Why, when he was Joey's age . . .'

'. . . he was up at dawn studying English for eighteen if not twenty hours a day. Not to mench living on a perfectly beastly diet of beancurd and barley gruel.' Joey uncoiled himself in a single graceful movement. 'No more, thanks, Walt. *Kendo* calls. May I hold fast to this comforter till Hyacinth produces my overcoat? So you'd like to take it on then?'

'Delighted – thanks.' Walter turned to Oliver. 'A commission to paint young Arisuke, a relative of the Viscount Mori. *A la* western in oils, of course.'

'Our beloved Viscount is more western than any cowboy, Oliver,' Joey added. 'Went west when he was quite young and has remained there in spirit ever since. He's a friend of my father's, which is how I heard about the commission and suggested Walter. Quite lucrative, and I shall expect a very fat rake-off.' He winked as Hyacinth brought his coat and he bundled into it, handing her the blanket with a mock-gallant bow.

Walter snorted. 'Oh you do, do you – a night in the sinks of iniquity then, I promise. And we must find a little painting pitch for you, Oliver. But you're not muscling in on my exclusive Japanese clientèle. You see, there aren't many of them with the right sort of walls to hang western pictures.'

Joey grinned. 'I know – how about the lovely foreign ladies of Yokohama? They'd positively adore to be painted *en kimono* posing under cherry blossoms – while Master Arisuke will undoubtedly wear his tweediest knickerbockers for the occasion.'

'A capital idea, Joey. I'll see what I can do. I have connections in that quarter.'

'And I shall start an agency for indigent artists. I was born to be a go-between.'

Easing into his shoes at the outer door, Joey asked casually, 'And what are you doing for Christmas, Walt? You came to us last year.'

'Hadn't given it a thought, actually. But if you're asking me again, I'd be delighted to come.'

'Please do – and you too, Oliver. Just the family, plus a few. Mother blossoms into extravagant Englishness – silver coins in the pudd. and hymns of praise to the Christmas tree.'

'And I shall pay my usual homage to your beautiful sister.'

'You won't – sorry. She and Aunt Ryo have gone to Europe. They'll be away for months.'

'Really? Don't you worry that some rich English stuffed-shirt will steal her heart away?'

'Oh, no; Hannah hasn't got a heart except in the purely mechanical sense of a pump . . . Well, we'll see you both on Christmas Day, then? We usually feast about six, but come earlier if you like.'

'Clever lad,' Walter remarked as Joey disappeared through the gate. 'Only nineteen but sharp as a whippet. Can't settle to anything, though. He's supposed to be studying for university at the moment.'

'His father sounds quite a Tartar.'

'Oh, Joey exaggerates — the Miyatas are very pleasant and quite easy-going for their class.'

'And the daughter . . . is she a heartless beauty?'

'Stunning certainly . . . but heartless? I don't really know. Keeps her feelings very much to herself, unlike Joey, who's all over the place. She's very attached to her spinster aunt Ryo, who's a Christian convert and rather formidable.'

'I was rather hoping to forget all about Christmas for once. What on earth's the point of it out here?'

'I thought the same last year — having just arrived. But when the actual day came I was glad to spend it somewhere home-like. I bet you'll feel the same. If not, you needn't go.'

Walter was right, for even in the 'heathen' Orient, Christmas could not be quite overlooked. Joyous bells pealed in full strength from the Foreign Concession's churches, and groups of Christian converts came singing carols. When the familiar notes of 'Hark the Herald Angels Sing' seeped through their closed shutters on Christmas Eve, Oliver was reminded only too clearly of his childhood, when Mother, Letty, and he created a sparse, forced jollity together. 'I'll come with you tomorrow if I may, Walt? Here alone I'd be haunted by the ghosts of Christmasses past.'

'You didn't enjoy them?'

'No. You met my mother. She had a great sense of occasion and desperately wanted Christmas to be lavish and lovely for our sakes, poor dear. But we never had enough money, nor enough friends, so it was always a little pathetic and make-do — a ghost of what it could, and should, have been.'

'Then you'll find Christmas at the Miyatas a welcome change.'

'Happy Christmas, dear.' Elinor Miyata kissed her husband's forehead lightly as she got out of bed, taking over to the window the cup of morning tea the maid had brought. She drew back the thick velvet curtains. 'Oh good — it's a glorious morning!'

The Miyatas' bedroom, spacious in the western style, was on the second storey of a substantial brick extension that had been built on extra land they had bought several years before. It somewhat resembled the residence of an English doctor in a country town, with its fireplaces of imported marble, tiled bathrooms with cavernous baths, drawing-room with brocade-covered sofas, and a wainscotted hall. Attached to it was the house in which they had first lived, now used mainly for Japanese New Year functions, and the accommodation of visitors. The room that Ryo had used was still kept for her. But the family's pulse beat in the newer building and the older part had a rather melancholy air, its painted screens further faded, its wooden floors lacking the lustre bestowed by constant care and use. The decision to 'go western' had been taken at a time when it was most fashionable to do so; it was also more practical for bringing up children, Elinor had said. Recently, however, she felt they had gone rather far, and was re-introducing Japanese-style lamps, wall-hangings, and fabrics in the main rooms. Kenjiro expressed no opinion either way, for he did not feel it was his province.

The upper storey commanded a fine view of the fast-growing capital, and their bedroom, facing north-west, over-looked tiled blue and grey roofs set among garden shrubberies; the open space of the military parade ground; and, beyond, crests of conifers breaking towards distant hills. Beyond again, above a skein of cloud, the snow-capped summit of Mount Fuji floated in the cold blue like a lily on a lake.

Elinor threw back her head and gave a small stretch of contentment. 'Fuji-san is very clear.' That was always an auspicious omen – the sacred and powerful one displaying a benign dominance over the land below. Opening the window a crack, Elinor heard the morning bugles on the parade ground, and St Andrew's church bells proclaiming the day's importance.

'Don't forget it's morning service,' she murmured as she went to her dressing room.

Kenjiro buried his head under the bedclothes without replying. Unlike his sister, he had never become a Christian

307

convert, and this Elinor had been sadly forced to accept. At her insistence, their two younger children, Tomi and Umé, attended church regularly; but Kenjiro and Joey wore their Christianity very occasionally – like a charm amulet, interchangeable with those of Buddhism or Shintoism. They would wear it today and attend morning service at St Andrew's for Elinor's sake.

Going downstairs, Elinor heard the squeals of the youngsters as they opened the joke-presents hung in white socks on their bed-posts, and told them to hurry and dress properly for church. The tall Christmas tree in the drawing room was decorated with painted toys, bells, paper streamers, glitter beads, pink rice-paste balls, gold and silver flowers, red candles, and long glass chopsticks hung among the dark branches like frozen icicles. 'Doesn't it look perfectly lovely, Ohisa?'

The maid, who was drawing back the night shutters, nodded. 'There!' The women smiled as the sun flowed into the room and the tree shone in the light. 'Shall I throw this away, madam?' Ohisa indicated a heart-shaped plaque stuck with a few dried grasses, the remains of Kenjiro's present to her on the last day of November. He never forgot the 'heart-drawing' – annual reminder of their pledge to each other long ago in Yokohama's Consular library. Seeing him note 'the heart-thing' in his diary each year with family birthdays and festivals, Elinor was no longer quite sure what it meant to him. The previous year, when he had been more than usually preoccupied and absent from home, she had said pettishly, 'Wouldn't it be easier for you to move it to Valentine's Day when hearts and such are about everywhere?'

'But that wouldn't be the same thing at all.' He had sounded quite shocked.

'No, but I was just wondering if you remembered what it was about.'

'But of course I remember, Elinor. I always shall.' He had come to her, then, clutching her quite fiercely. 'Whatever makes you say such a thing?'

'Oh . . . I don't know . . . You're always so busy elsewhere these days, and gestures like this can become empty rituals – the sort you Japanese specialise in.'

'But this is not one of them. I'm a sentimentalist, as you've often said. And when I'm elsewhere you're still my heart-drawing. That is what I tell you each year.'

She had rubbed against him, then, laughing and saying she was glad he was a Japanese sentimentalist and not a stiff-necked Englishman who would not dream of such delightful presents. Following that conversation this year's 'heart-drawing' had been an especially elaborate concoction of expensive flowers, and she had been reluctant to throw it away. But it was now thoroughly faded, and she said, 'Yes, take it, Ohisa. And sound the gong for breakfast, please.'

After breakfast and the prescribed visit to St Andrew's, Kenjiro and Joey began setting up a magic lantern for the younger children, who were holding an afternoon party; and while they were doing so Arnold arrived, flourishing a silver-topped walking cane which was his present to himself.

'It will be most useful when your gout's bad,' his sister said, admiring it after they had exchanged the season's greetings.

'Gout! My dear Ellie, that's an old man's disease and I only feel the merest twinge, occasionally. I'm giving one to Joey too. *Not* for his gout, but for the young-man-about-town to twirl.'

'Just the thing, dear. He'll love it,' Elinor soothed quickly, for she had not meant to raise a sensitive topic. Nevertheless, Arnold was looking older, his heavy frame showing the strain after years of eating and drinking too much. It was a consequence of having only himself to please, as he freely admitted; for, though he had flirted energetically with several eligible Englishwomen over the years, he had never actually married – officially. What he did unofficially Elinor had never again inquired, though she had her suspicions.

'You've managed to make the tree just as splendid this year even without Hannah's help,' he remarked as they went into the drawing room.

'Joey helped me. He's got the same national knack for decorating. There's a letter from Hannah, by the way; I'll show it to you later. She and Ryo will be in Harrogate now. I keep wondering how she'll enjoy her first English Christmas. It's hard to imagine her reaction — you know how she is.'

In fact he had very little idea and thought it simpler to change the subject. 'And I had a letter from Percival Storey. He and Edith are back in Bangkok and have a daughter at last. Called Lilian — he always like the name. I think he'd have married you if it had been yours.'

Elinor sniffed. 'Except I never had the slightest inclination to be his wife. He was always so opinionated — and a bit of a cold fish, in my view. Presumably he's become an expert on Siamese politics now he's First Secretary there? But I must go and see to the youngsters. Make yourself at home — there's loads of food laid out in the dining room.'

'Righto; thanks.' Arnold strolled off to fetch his presents from the hall. Elinor was getting French perfumes as usual and Kenjiro a tooled-leather, made-in-England briefcase. For among businessmen and higher civil servants in the capital, briefcases had become as much a badge of rank as two swords had once been. Arnold spent lavishly on the Miyatas at Christmas, for their home was open to him all the year and he could afford to be generous. He had set himself up in private practice several years before and he and a German, Dr Baelz, were now the men most often called upon by citizens of means who had been persuaded of the superiority of western medical techniques. As Arnold arranged his presents beside others under the tree, his niece Umé darted in and tugged his sleeve.

'Happy Christmas, Uncle. Father wants you to come quick and help with the lantern. It's all gone stuck.'

'And Happy Christmas to you, little Umé. Would you like to be a fairy on a Christmas tree?' He swung her high towards the topmost branches while she struggled and giggled. She and her brother Tomi were pink-skinned, sturdy, with brownish hair but none of the exotic grace of their older siblings; and the early death from influenza of a middle child served to emphasise the divisions in looks and age between the older and younger Miyatas. Arnold set his niece down gently. 'All right, I'll come. But what do doctors know about magic?'

Between them, though, they managed to get the lantern working just as the juvenile guests arrived; and after the show came tea, and games that were still in progress when Joey's friends appeared.

'Ah yes . . . Merry Christmas . . . Walter . . . er, Munro, isn't it?' Elinor held out her hand, flushed slightly, for of course she ought to have remembered the name. But there were so many names in her head these days, each with its label: Deputy Secretary, Ministry of Justice; Anglican Bishop and wife from Shanghai; owner of new textile factory from Osaka; female journalist from Boston; third son of Count Iwada; headmistress of St Hilda's Mission College; assistant secretary, Public Works Department, Member of Parliament, Far East fact-finding mission; lecturer, Imperial College of Engineering . . . and now artist Walter Munro and his friend, Mr Ray, was it?

'How do you do?' She gave her bright party smile. 'Please make yourselves at home. It's a home-like day, I hope Joey explained. The small fry will be leaving soon, then we will be able to hear ourselves speak. Joey, please rustle up some mulled wine for your friends in the drawing-room.'

Oliver, following Walter, thought it surprising that this open-faced, brisk Englishwoman was Joey's mother; how odd for them both. He wandered to look out at the garden, which was beautiful in the fading wintry dusk with its perfectly trimmed shrubs, and irregularly paved paths leading to an oval pond edged with bulrushes. The branches and trunks of the ornamental trees were carefully swaddled in straw – a protection from the cold, Walter had explained. An elderly man pottered slowly into view poking at the straw with a stick. How lucky young Miyata was, he thought wistfully, even if he was a 'mixed-up'; to live with his family in this rather grand house, waited on by servants, no money worries, and a promising future when he chose to pursue it.

'Wine?' Joey came up behind him.

'Thank you. I was admiring your garden. Whatever is that

311

old man doing?'

'Oh, that's old Yoshida, father of our cook. He's a wee bit simple, likes to tuck the trees up for the night. Servants come in families here, you know − right down to the second rickshaw-man's third grand-daughter.'

'It must be rather expensive for you?'

'It's the system, and they live very cheaply. Mother won't turn any away, however far removed from the working source. The season's greetings!' He raised his glass, ' 'Fraid this must seem awfully dull for you? I did warn you it was mainly a family gathering.'

'But I'm thrilled to be here, Joey.'

'Are you honestly? A few more friends are coming, and we'll sneak off somewhere more jolly after dinner . . . Ah, there's father; come and meet him.' Joey led him towards a tall, handsome Japanese, impeccably dressed in morning coat and striped trousers, a single-breasted, braid-trimmed waistcoat, patent leather buttoned boots. 'So you're going to paint young Arisuke?' he was saying to Walter. 'After which we might arrange for you to paint our youngest daughter, if you'd care to?'

'I'd be delighted, Mr Miyata, and perhaps I might then have the honour of trying to capture the fabled beauty of your older daughter on canvas? A challenge that might elude me but . . .'

'We'll see . . . one thing at a time. And you are also an artist, I believe?' He turned to Oliver.

'Yes, sir. A watercolourist. But I also do portraits.'

'*Ah-so* . . . It's quite astonishing how many artists come here these days. They seem to find us quite exquisite − the quality of light . . . shadows on paper screens . . . Art is in the very atmosphere, I'm told.'

'It doesn't sound as if you agree, sir?'

'Being Japanese I've never made such an analysis. I suppose these things are part of my inmost eye. And now there's a College of Art here in Tokyo to teach these imponderables to our young in the western fashion. Is that an improvement? What do you think, Arnold?' He turned to his brother-in-law, who had just come in.

'Blessed if I know. Certainly the College of Western Medicine is a fine institution . . . but art? A mixed blessing in my view. Is there wine perchance?'

Kenjiro went in search of some while Arnold lowered his bulk into an armchair, sweeping off the red-paper hat he had been wearing for the children. 'Well, that's my Uncle Christmas role over for another year! More years than I care to count, in fact.'

'You've lived here for a long time, Doctor?' Oliver drew up a chair.

'Over a quarter of a century. A working life-time . . .'

As they sipped wine, Oliver was tempted to ask about his parents, whom the doctor had probably known; but, feeling unsure, asked instead, 'So you'll have seen many changes here, sir?'

'I certainly have, and many for the better. But some things have got quite out of hand recently. Feminine fashions, for instance – Look at that perfectly ghastly purple outfit she's laced herself into.'

He gestured at a newly arrived Japanese girl in a tight-waisted, high-necked dress of plush velvet, its draped over-skirt protruding into a shelf of bustle; her hair was swept into the fashionable Pompadour style, her small feet encased in laced black boots.

Oliver chuckled. 'That's not purple, that's heliotrope, sir. All the rage just now; and trimmed with white muskrat, just as it should be.'

Arnold scowled. 'And underneath she'll have hideous bloomers and corsets, I'll be bound. There was a chap out here years ago in the corsetry line who vowed that Japanese women would come to this. But I never thought I'd live to see the day.'

Oliver, hiding his amusement, asked earnestly, 'So the fashion for western dress is quite recent, is it?'

'Among the ladies, yes. But now it's a rampant plague in the wealthier classes and sad to say the Empress herself is partly to blame. Berlin gowns became *de rigueur* at court last year, and how fearsomely uncomfortable the dainty little ladies look, weighed down with flounces, furbelows, feathered hats, velvet ribbons, bugles . . . tottering in high-heeled shoes . . . Ugh! All their naturally elegant simplicity of line and colour sacrificed . . . to what?' He drained his glass gloomily, handing it for a re-fill as Joey approached. 'But my smart nephew here will tell you it's romantic nonsense to want the good old days back . . . Still, the Japanese will go overboard for novelty, that's their trouble. Take the Rokumeikan, for instance . . .'

'The . . .?' Oliver queried.

'Explain to your young friend, Joey, while I see if your mother wants me to help with the carving. It must be grub-time.'

Joey rolled his eyes teasingly. 'But I'm far too young and innocent to know about such giddy goings-on, Uncle. You have more experience, surely? In any case, the rumour is that it's quick-fading-away.'

'And a good thing too, say I.' Arnold heaved himself up and wandered off and Joey curled up in the vacant chair. 'And I think it's rather a shame. The poor Rokumeikan . . . "quick-fading-away" is a Japanese term for describing so many things that have come and gone, by the way, the Rokumeikan being one. It opened about five years ago as a centre for "social intercourse between the peoples of all nations". German beer, American cocktails, English roast beef, Dutch cigars, and French pastries are dispensed to members who play billiards while their poor wives learn to polka. They held a grand masquerade ball there over a year ago, and everyone who was anyone attended. Count Ido, the then head of government, was there with his "Dancing Cabinet".' He giggled. 'Apparently quite a lot of . . . er . . . social intercourse went on then, and on similar occasions, and scandals blossomed. There were pictures in the papers showing our revered national leaders dressed up as pirates, Roman soldiers and French troubadours. Their elders and betters disapproved, said it was all going too far, just like Uncle. But he's wrong – halts are sometimes called; and I'll wager the heyday of the dear old Deer Cry Pavilion – that's the English translation — is about over.' He rose as a gong sounded from the dining-room. 'At last! Let us gather round the festive board.'

For the traditionally lavish Christmas dinner, Oliver found himself next to the young lady in heliotrope. She introduced herself in excellent English as Miss Emiko Hattori, who had studied in America. She was related to Viscount Mori, the Minister of Education, who was currently introducing English studies into all elementary schools, and she was a great admirer of his, she explained earnestly, because he wanted to improve the legal and social conditions of Japanese women.

Oliver raised his eyebrows quizzically. 'But do you honestly consider that the clothes you are wearing constitute an improvement on the native dress? Are they not vastly more restricting and cumbersome?'

She bridled. 'Oh, that might be your romantic way of looking, as a foreign man. But for me any discomfort is well worth it, for I'm treated with a great deal more consideration and respect by my own countrymen when I'm dressed like this. Why, they even open doors for me and let me enter a room first!'

'But surely any man would pay attention to you whatever you wear?' Oliver exclaimed lightly, feeling the whole question of female apparel beyond him. 'Here, let's pull a cracker instead and we'll see if your modern attire makes you strong as a man.'

Gallantly he let her win, at which she took the tin whistle from inside and blew it fiercely in his ear just as they were all asked to rise and propose a toast to the Emperor, in his nearby palace, and her distant majesty, Queen Victoria. After that the flaming Christmas pudding was borne in by Mr Yoshida the cook, who was wearing a velvet coat and pinstriped trousers to mark the occasion; then port was circulated among the gentlemen. At the first decent opportunity Joey whisked his friends away to some secret, jollier destination, leaving the others to settle quietly in the drawing room.

'Thank you very much indeed for this, Arnold.' Kenjiro stroked the briefcase appreciatively.

'For the future Minister with Portfolio perhaps?' Arnold asked genially.

'Oh, I'll never make a minister, with or without one.' He said it matter-of-factly, having long accepted that the basic reason was his marriage. Other similar alliances had occurred since, but he and Elinor had married at a time when the forces of reaction were very strong, and, secretly, many of Kenjiro's contemporaries still distrusted him for his too intimate contact with a foreigner. He had reached the important position he now held in the Ministry of Foreign Affairs through intelligence, drive, and membership of one of the south-western clans in whose hands power was still concentrated. With such advantages Kenjiro might well have risen further – but for Elinor; it was something he never voiced, even on the several occasions when divisions and disagreements between them were deep and bitter.

Elinor, searching in her handbag, remarked casually. 'Oh, you never know; there'll be new opportunities in the first Parliament, surely? Ah, here's Hannah's letter, which came on Christmas Eve, and I don't think you've read it yet? Written from New York as they were leaving for England; and she's having a thoroughly enjoyable time, except that men will stare at her, and it's annoying!'

Kenjiro hissed his irritation. 'I told you they would.'

'And I told you that we're not keeping her in seclusion on that account.'

'Men here don't stare at her in that rude way.'

'Because it isn't the done thing and she doesn't conform to their extremely conventional ideas of feminine beauty. Foreigners admire her looks more, as you well know.'

Hannah's opportunity for the journey had arisen when Ryo, now a mistress in an Anglican girls' school, was invited to attend a conference in London, and Hannah, protesting that Joey, though her junior, had spent more time abroad, begged to accompany her. Kenjiro had initially opposed the plan, for he loved his daughter protectively and unreservedly – both for herself and her strong attachment to his sister, whose single life he considered to be unfortunate and unhappy. But Elinor had over-ridden his fears that she might be. wooed from the home nest and, reading the letter, was now able to placate him further.

'I really don't think you need worry about her. It sounds as if the young men she's meeting all wear dog-collars, and I doubt that they will turn her head.'

'I certainly hope not.' Kenjiro shuddered, crossing to the tree and idly flicking the glass chopsticks sparkling in the candlelight. 'A good day as usual, don't you think? Another drink, Arnold?'

'An excellent day, but no more. Ample sufficiency all round.' He stirred, reluctant to leave the home-like atmosphere for his own well-ordered but empty house. 'Has Joey settled yet?'

'Not really; he's having private tuition in maths and physics and we're hoping he'll get into university.'

'He doesn't seem the scientific type?' Arnold ventured.

Elinor sighed. 'Oh, he could study the humanities if he wished, but he won't make up his mind to anything.'

'And the political hot-heads and artistic globetrotters he mixes with only confuse him further,' Kenjiro added disapprovingly.

Elinor smothered a yawn. 'That young fellow with Walter Munro — Oliver Ray was it? Did he remind you of someone?'

'I don't think so . . .' Kenjiro smothered another yawn and Arnold, taking the hint, rose and kissed his sister goodnight. 'Must go. Will you be on holiday till after the New Year, Kenjiro?'

'I'm afraid not; the thorny matters of foreign treaty revision and the promulgation of the constitution keeps the department at full stretch.'

'But exactly what the constitution contains is a closely guarded secret, I believe?'

'Yes . . . modelled on the Bavarian apparently . . . the Germanic influence in the ascendant again . . .' Kenjiro explained as they went out.

Elinor wandered about gathering gift-wrappings and ribbons from the carpet. Portentous, jarring words like 'promulgation' and 'constitution' aroused in her a sneaking nostalgia for the old days when such concepts were almost unknown in Japan. But one had to keep moving with the times; everyone said so. She glanced at the clock; not very late, but she and her husband were alone at the end of Christmas. It had not happened before, but as the children grew older it was inevitable; and she straightened her back in a characteristic gesture, expressive of her customary determination to face facts. She picked up the cane Arnold had given Joey, its handle carved into an impudently grinning monkey's head. An excellent present for her son's young-man-about-town role. It was one Kenjiro had had scant opportunity ever to play – and that was one of the rubs between them.

She blew out the last of the tree candles and went upstairs, recalling with some satisfaction that, in the early years of their marriage, Christmas had been a considerable strain, a time that emphasised the differences between themselves and friends and neighbours, who either celebrated it whole-heartedly or not at all. But now the differences had blurred; the Miyatas had found their own compromise and people had learned to accept and enjoy it.

CHAPTER FIFTEEN

The parties of that New Year merged into those given to celebrate the first constitution in the nation's history. A public holiday was declared, the streets of the capital were decorated with floral arches and banners; Rising Sun flags flew from balconies and rooftops. On the morning of February 11th, Joey rushed to the breakfast table waving a flag, jumping up and down and chanting in his long-perfected parody of Japanese-style English.

'Now we have constitution like great West country. Next year we have election and after we have proper Parliament with house peer and house representative. What does constitution? What does Parliament? It doesn't matter what does . . . we have and now are grown-up important peoples like West peoples . . .'

He paused for breath, and Kenjiro, swallowing his tea, shouted, 'Be quiet, you stupid young cub! You know nothing whatever about it! Doesn't it mean anything to you that our revered Emperor is actually giving us − his people − a constitution, limiting his own power for the sake of his country's standing in the world. It's just a silly charade to you, isn't it? Well, it's about time to realise the trials and struggles we older men have been through to get as far as this! The bigotry, the ignorance and fear of the West we were up against . . . You know, I sometimes wish you'd met Uncle Gengoro before he was killed. There was a reactionary for you! I should think he's turning in his grave this very day to hear all the talk of elections and people's rights.'

He paused to drink more tea while Joey carefully, silently,

buttered toast, and Kenjiro continued in a more moderate tone, 'I once shouted at him that he didn't know anything, nor did he. Contemptuous he was, and blinkered like you, but for quite the opposite reason. Isn't that so, Elinor?'

'I never had the pleasure of making the gentleman's acquaintance, remember. But Joey's just a young man trying to work things out for himself and no generation has a monopoly of wisdom, not even yours.'

'Oh, I'm well aware of that. Why, they're already starting to call us the "old men of Tempo" – young men like Joey who can't wait to thrust us aside.'

'Nonsense, you're not old . . . And what does it mean exactly?'

'Born in the Tempo period of '30 to '43, as I was.' He scowled, quoting bitterly, ' "If the rooted and withered old men of Tempo were to be blown down in a typhoon tomorrow like ancient trees from a hill-top, then the young shoots could spring up that would rise loftily to new heights. This age is one of youth and hope etc . . ." I read that in one of your radical pamphlets recently.'

Joey mumbled unhappily, 'I didn't mean any harm, father; it was just a joke.'

'Not in very good taste,' Elinor reproved briskly. 'We don't want you to be too solemn, Joey, but you seem to think everything in the world is just a joke. There are serious matters and this constitution is one of them.'

Joey shrugged sulkily. 'Oh, it's just quick-fading-away like everything else.'

'You're always throwing that silly phrase about! Now please let's all enjoy the day and you can wave your flag to your heart's content this afternoon when the Emperor and Empress ride by.'

Kenjiro snorted. 'Oh, he wouldn't do it then, that would be far too ordinary and simple-minded for him and his sophisticated friends.'

Nevertheless, later that day, Joey, like everyone else, did get caught up in the spirit of the thing. Every quarter of the city was garlanded with streamers, lanterns, evergreen arches,

320

while bands played, bells rang, and festal floats rolled through the streets displaying tableaux of dancing girls, masked clowns, and armed warriors. In the throne room of his newly built palace the Emperor Meiji read the speech of promulgation to the assembled nobility and dignitaries of the Empire and afterwards rode in triumphal procession through the streets in a handsome gilded carriage escorted by mounted guards, just like the royalty of Europe. The spectacle was wondrous and awesome to the citizenry, for whom the Emperor was a sacred, divinely descended figure; and equally astonishing was the sight of the Empress riding beside him instead of in a smaller carriage behind, as had formerly been the custom. It was symbolic of the new dignity of Japanese womanhood, Elinor remarked; but Kenjiro mischievously informed her that the Empress would not be allowed to get above herself, for he had heard that the dais in the throne room had been built of unequal heights, the Emperor's being the higher!

For three days the city was in carnival, but for some the rejoicings were soon marred by the news that Viscount Mori, whose extremely pro-western policies and attitudes had made him many enemies, had been assassinated as he was preparing to attend the throne ceremony. It came as a great shock to the public and a personal grief to the Miyatas, who had known him quite well. Kenjiro felt it most keenly, for he had been in sympathy with many of Mori's views, including his belief in self-discipline and making one's own way in the world − as both of them had. Mori had also been a fervent supporter of women's rights, denouncing the widespread custom of keeping mistresses, and, when in his company, Kenjiro had been forced intellectually to agree; but in such a half-hearted guilty fashion that, he thought, his dead friend had probably guessed the truth.

The afternoon of Mori's funeral was drear and cold; after it Kenjiro told Elinor he was dining with some of Mori's friends, but went instead to a certain house in a narrow street near the Yoshiwara. The red and white pear-shaped lanterns outside announced it was the House of Gold, where one Koyuki

321

lived. Female attendants welcomed him with soft cries of delight as was their custom, bringing slippers, a padded robe, hot towels. Koyuki appeared, looking exactly as she always did, her face heavily powdered, lips gilded, hair arranged in oiled, scented coils festooned with dangling ornaments and combs. While she soothed him with her *koto*-playing, maids fed him with delicacies and warm *saké*.

Kenjiro had first sought out Koyuki several years ago, when Elinor withdrew from him in sorrow after the death of their third child. Since then, he had visited her fairly regularly, titillated by her coquetry and flattery, her music and singing, her knowing skill between the bed-quilts. For him she represented security, and reassurance that the old Japan of his ancestors had not quite vanished after all, that even here, in many hidden corners of this rapidly modernising city, it was still inviolate. Everything in the House of Gold affirmed it – the antique-style lamps, elegant arrangements of flowers and scrolls, Koyuki's plaintive songs, the demure ministerings of her attendants who teased and cossetted him so that he felt protected and potent, childish and superior all at once.

'I've just come from the Viscount's funeral,' he said, accepting more *saké*. 'Thousands were there in procession, many students among them.'

Koyuki tutted sympathetically. 'The poor Viscount was known to you?'

'A friend, of a sort, though he always kept his own counsel. He was a Satsuma man and our families knew each other. I used to play billiards with him occasionally. He swung his cue like a walking stick, I remember. Wasn't afraid of anything – except earthquakes. They terrified him and he always felt he'd die in one. Better that than this – cut through the belly by a mad-dog fanatic priest . . . I'll eat,' he added abruptly, feeling depression swamp him.

But the meal did not lighten his mood and as the evening wore on, he began to wonder why on earth he had come here, when he was filled with bitter sadness that a man like Mori, who had done so much for the country, should have been branded by wrong-headed zealots as unpatriotic because of his ideas. For Kenjiro, Mori's murder seemed to cast in temporary doubt the validity of his beliefs – his devout Christianity, his fearless advocacy of equality, modernity, and common justice. So Kenjiro's coming to Koyuki this evening was an act of defiance and betrayal, a deliberate reversion to hide-bound, anciently rooted customs which Mori had spent his life trying to banish from the land.

Sprawled negligently on the *tatami*, he remembered Mori's claim that such low-level lying about encouraged the oriental towards self-indulgence and inferiority, and should be discarded in favour of upright chairs. He was ashamed, confused, yet in desperate need of the respite and refuge this house afforded him. His beloved wife could not have provided as much, though he knew she would be deeply wounded and outraged if she had known where he was. Remembering this, he consulted his watch, resisted Koyuki's blandishments to stay the night, and called for a rickshaw.

Elinor was sleeping unsuspectingly when he returned; but sleep eluded him as he lay pondering the full implications of the murder. It had been announced that the priest-assassin (killed in turn by a guard) had acted in reprisal for a presumed act of disrespect by Mori at a Shinto shrine. But it was strongly rumoured that the real motive had been his part in the negotiations for treaty revision with foreigners. Kenjiro, involved in the same negotiations, felt extremely uneasy and for several weeks thereafter was prey to his own long-buried fears of violent attack.

His tension and irritability were directed particularly towards his eldest son, whose light-hearted raillery on the day of Mori's assassination seemed even more misplaced and foolish in retrospect. For his part, Joey was subdued, applying himself diligently to his studies in one of his sporadic attempts to please his parents. Until, on a day when spring breezes were humming against the strings of a thousand children's kites, restlessness overcame him and he impulsively sought out Walter and Oliver. According to the newspapers, the cherry trees along the banks of the River Sumida in the district of Mukojima were at their pinnacle of pink perfection, he told them – a spectacle not be missed by natives, much less two artistic foreigners, whom he insisted on whisking off there forthwith.

The scene was as colourful as Joey had promised as they strolled along the tree-lined left bank of the broad river. Its waters were crowded with rowing boats full of students, ferries, and pleasure-boats with lantern-fringed awnings, from which came shouts of laughter and snatches of song. Genial sunshine filtered through the laden arches of blossom overhead and petals flurried about in the breeze-blusters like unmelted snowflakes, settling on the heads and shoulders of upstaring admirers, tossing about in the river-wash from passing boat-loads of sightseers. Families with small children passed them as they strolled by the banks, the girls sedate in their holiday-best kimonos, the boys leaping about blowing whistles. An elderly grandfather suddenly detached himself from one such group and tottered over to tie a piece of paper to an overhanging branch of blossom.

'What *is* he doing?' Oliver asked.

'It's a poem, I expect . . . we'll find out.' Joey winked and as the man disappeared, pulled the branch down and read, ' "When I see the lovely flowers o'er the water, I think of sixteen-year-old girls" . . . Ho-ho, they say the itch never dies till death! Here's another . . . in a more classical vein, "And so the spring buds burst and so I gaze, And so blossoms fall and so my days." ' He let the branches go. 'I've a queasy feeling there are just too many blossoms and too many poems about today. A strawberry, raspberry, and cherry jam sandwich; ugh!'

But Oliver, gazing ardently upward, breathed, 'But you must admit they're the loveliest cherries in the whole world . . .'

'Only because we make such a fuss about them! Come, let's go and get a nice cup of bitter tea.'

They went into a tea-house with a wide verandah overlooking the river; it was packed with people, including a noisy group waving flags and chanting. 'Let's not stay here.' Joey turned away. 'I don't want to get involved with that bunch today.'

'What are they shouting about?' Oliver asked as they retreated.

'They're student agitators demanding treaty revision and an end to extra-territoriality that has given foreigners certain legal and trading privileges here for years. The government is weak-kneed on the issue in their view and we "young men of Meiji" must fight for people's rights, freedom of the press, socialism for all, etcetera . . .'

'And you don't agree, by the sound of it?' Walter quizzed as they strolled on.

'When I'm with them I do, but I find so much fervour tedious. I just can't seem to stick at . . . Here, I know,' he clutched their arms, 'Enough of all this sugary pinkness; let's go to the Yoshiwara and view the "cherries of the night" instead. It will be a haven of peace compared to this place today.'

'The famous courtesan quarter?' Oliver sounded dubious.

'You've not taken him there yet, Walt? Shame on you! It's an essential part of every young man's education . . . Come, I'll teach you.'

It was only verging on twilight when they reached the Yoshiwara; but its lanterns were already lit, for shielding, tempting night was always welcome there. Joey capered ahead through the imposing stone gateway to one of the 'introducing tea-houses', where he signed their names in the register with the knowing flourish of an habitué, though he had only been twice before.

'See that tree at the gate?' he pointed. 'It's called the "Gazing Back Willow" because fellows are apt to look at it longingly when they have to leave . . . Ah, just on cue, there's the curfew bell of Iriya temple, the time to "see the flowers of the Yoshiwara coming into blossom . . .".'

The deep-toned notes reverberated sadly along the wide main avenues that were flanked by pretentious buildings with colonnaded façades and vaulted entranceways, suggesting business of some official nature. But, passing close, Oliver caught an occasional glimpse of a bright robe on a balcony,

325

heard the plangent thrum of a *samisen*. In the streets behind, the narrow front rooms of the brothels were fitted with rows of cage-like iron bars behind which the women sat on cushions or benches, often pretending to ignore the men who were beginning to gather round to appraise them. In their stiffly embroidered kimonos and high-piled coiffures they looked like displays of waxwork dolls to Oliver, who felt no surge of desire to intrude upon the pitiful barriers between them.

Pausing near one cage, Oliver stared intently at the older woman seated in the back row who seemed to be in charge. She wore a kimono of starched black silk with a white collar, a golden *obi*, and her long pallid face was immobilised into a mask of disdain, bitterness, and despair. Unwillingly Oliver was reminded of his dead mother in her last years – that trapped beauty, that unbending endurance pared down to contempt. He shuddered, feeling the woman's empty, dark eyes on him, and turned away.

'Yes, let's move on. These are the lower-class wenches, the poor lotuses-in-the-mud. We don't consort with them; come . . .' Joey led the way to a large corner house with a façade of shuttered windows. Its reception room was furnished in western style with plush sofas, gilt-edged mirrors, pictures, and French clocks that reminded Oliver, to his disappointment, of the Brighton brothel where he had first lost his virginity. It was, however, run along oriental lines: serving girls brought *saké* and delicacies while others showed the house-album containing photographs of the girls available. They looked as indistinguishably doll-like as those in the cages, and Oliver eventually chose Little Wisteria, who was at least smiling. She turned out to be soft and coquettish as a kitten, rubbing against him and popping bonbons in his mouth whenever he opened it.

'Ask her if she minds – my being a foreigner, Joey.' Oliver stared at her uncomfortably.

Joey did so, and translated, 'She's very honoured to arouse the interest of an honourable Englishman.'

'Oh, try and get something truthful from her . . . Where

she comes from, why she's here.'

'Oh, truth is far too unpalatable for her pretty lips; but I'll tell you. The girls are usually sold into the life young by their parents, who've fallen on hard times. Brothel-keepers rush like locusts to any scene of disaster – fire, flood, earthquakes – and buy up the female pickings cheap. If you worry about such matters you won't enjoy yourself and Little Wisteria will feel slighted. So drink up your *saké*.'

When the three men were thoroughly relaxed by wine, food, and feminine wiles, attendants conducted each to a separate chamber. 'Don't worry about a thing,' Walter whispered, seeing Oliver's apprehension. 'These ladies are well trained in what's called the Forty-Eight Ways of Pleasuring a Man. They won't let you down, as it were.'

And so it proved. Oliver sprawled naked on piled damask and velvet bedding while Little Wisteria, looking pretty in the dim lantern-light, caressed and stimulated him with gentle knowingness, seeming to anticipate his every need and acquiesce gladly in his every whim. All too soon came a discreet scratch on the door-screen and she rose to sponge herself unselfconsciously at a wash-bowl in the corner while a maid appeared bearing Oliver's garments folded on a lacquer tray. Their mouths had not met, nor their eyes, he thought as he fumbled clumsily with his buttons, feeling the onset of a post-orgasmic depression that was further increased when he and his companions were presented at the 'introducing house' with a two-foot-long, very substantial bill.

The Yoshiwara gates were still brightly lit and crowds of rickshaw-men were clamouring to carry men back to their families. The blind shampooers, beancurd vendors, flute players, fortune tellers, and street-singers were also leaving, while stray dogs and beggars of the night-watches were just arriving – to rummage through the backyard-buckets for left-overs from the evening's feasts. The budding branches of the 'Gazing Back Willow' drooped gracefully in the moonlight, but Oliver did not regard them with longing. He yearned for a sexual encounter with an oriental woman much more romantic and mysterious than poor Little Wisteria, whose face he had already half-forgotten. But the ravaged face of the old woman in her black silks stayed in his memory for a long while.

Oliver and Walter did not become spendthrift habitués of the Yoshiwara, but other bills of varying length and size kept appearing nonetheless and even Walter became concerned. His commission to paint Viscount Mori's nephew having been postponed during the family's mourning period, he suggested to Oliver they speculate in some Japanese prints, which they could sell to foreigners at handsome profits.

'Nothing venture nothing lose, as Pa says,' Walter grinned. 'Now, there's a coterie of ladies in Yokohama who simply adore the native culture and discourse mightily on the oriental harmonies between Art and Nature which we over-sophisticated westerners have lost. What they lack in judgement they make up with enthusiasm, not to mention ready cash! So let's try a visit to Mrs Fortescue, who's a leading light and quite the most agreeable.'

Edgar and Sylvia Fortescue lived in a two-storey brick and stucco house built near the site that Edgar's parents had bought over twenty years before, but on a much larger scale. Edgar, like his father, had followed a banking career and, after several years in Singapore, was now manager of Yokohama's Hongkong & Shanghai Bank, which gave him a prestigious position in the community. He had married young, and his wife Sylvia was blonde and blue-eyed like his mother, though also built on a larger scale. They had four children: Lawrence, the eldest, at school in England; then nine-year-old Grace, Rodney, and 'Johnathan-Baby-Dumpling'. Sylvia wore dresses of large floral design with wide-brimmed hats to shade her fair skin from the eastern suns and had a rather loud laugh that made her mother-in-law wince.

The late May afternoon on which Walter and Oliver came to see her was the first in the year that she and the baby had retreated indoors because of the heat, she told them; but now she had company they would all go out again for tea under the walnut tree's shade. So Jonathan-Baby-Dumpling lay and gurgled in his cot, pointing pudgy fists up at the sun-dappled leaves, while servants arranged basket chairs and footstools for their comfort. Oliver glanced round enviously as he had at the Miyatas'; if only he could find a way of making money in this congenial country he would never leave – for he had little to pull him homeward. Smiling in impish, boyish eagerness, he drew a chair close to Sylvia's. 'I hear you're a patroness of the arts, Mrs Fortescue? What a blessing it is for us struggling artists that such divinities exist!'

Sylvia fanned herself vigorously. 'Oh, someone's been exaggerating again, Mr Rayne. Probably wicked Walter over there. I'm quite ignorant of the finer points still, and my husband prevents me from being as generous as I'd like.' She turned innocent-looking blue eyes on him, thinking he was really rather a handsome young man; such a romantic pallor and lovely dark hair, and he smiled with winsome diffidence, asking, 'But what first roused your enthusiasm for Japanese art? I know it's all the rage in certain circles, but the – er – ordinary run of foreigners here give it short shrift, I'm told.'

She settled back, waving a freckled plump arm to direct the maids approaching with tea-trays. 'I've had a notion for things Japanese since I was a girl . . . well, since I first met my husband, to be exact. He was just a schoolboy then, but he used to tell me about his parents living here and made it sound so mysterious and picturesque. They had a bungalow on this very spot in the 'sixties and my mother-in-law never tires of telling me how easy life is here nowadays by comparison.' She pulled a wry face. 'Put the sponge cakes here, thank you.'

'Really? I wonder if they knew my parents, Mr and Mrs Harold Rayne, who were here at that time? I was very young and don't remember much.'

'How exciting! You must ask my husband about it, he'll be home soon . . . Ah, Walter . . . come and have tea. I was telling Mr Rayne about my mother-in-law. She and her new husband visited us last year. I don't think you met them? Edgar's father Claud dropped dead suddenly several years ago, you see, and Mary upped and married a handsome Indian Army officer, Major Greenwood, very quickly. Their

Shanghai home, Fairlawns, is quite beautiful, though, I must admit. Mary has a collection of Japanese paintings which she picked up here quite cheaply and that are now worth a small fortune. Walter, that reminds me – do show me the picture you've brought before Edgar arrives. He's so disapproving of my little hobby.'

Walter took a print from his portfolio with a flourish. 'There, a Kuniyoshi; Utagawa Kuniyoshi, to be precise, who died about twenty-five years ago. "Kuo Chiu finds the pot of gold", it's called. Isn't it splendid? There's a story behind it, of course, and I've brought a translation.'

Sylvia clapped her hands. 'Walter, it's divine, quite divine. A pot of gold – how we could all do with one! Perhaps this will be mine. And there's that little fellow on the right fishing quietly beside the river as if nothing exciting were happening . . . Just in the way of things! Oh, I simply adore it. But, Walter dear, how much? Dare I ask?'

'Dates from his best period and not cheap. But I'm sure Kuniyoshis will increase in value, because they have a popular narrative appeal . . . And there are distinct traces of European draughtsmanship in the woman's pose and the lines of the robe . . . See?'

'Yes, yes, oh, absolutely. Isn't it superb, Mr Rayne? My mother-in-law has some really famous prints by – let's see . . . Katsukawa Shuncho, Torii Kiyonaga, Masanobu . . . er . . . someone . . .' She recited the names carefully, counting them on her fingers, and Oliver chuckled, suddenly reminded of Joey's student friends listing the names of European intellectuals with similar precise reverence: 'Herbert Spencer, Adam Smith, Jean Jacques Rousseau . . .' 'And I'm hoping,' she continued, ' – Ah, there's Edgar. Put it away for the moment, Walter, and we'll have a private confab. before you go. I don't want to spring it on him. Edgar hates being sprung upon. Ah, there you are dear! This is Walter's friend, Mr Rayne, a fellow artist . . .'

Edgar shook hands stiffly; like his father he was highly suspicious of artists and their works and it caused him some chagrin that his mother seemed to have done so well out of them, as his wife often reminded him. He collapsed in a chair. 'Hottest day of the year so far and hotter to come.'

'Yes, I had to take Jonathan-B.D. out of the sun. Tea, dear? I was just talking about your mother and her golden days of yore here.'

'There's a letter from her today, in my briefcase. She's worried about Lilian as usual.'

Sylvia explained that Lilian was Edgar's youngest sister, who had insisted on becoming a medical missionary, '. . . which is quite beyond the pale in mother-in-law's eyes, though I honestly don't see why, considering her own new husband comes from a missionary family. His father was actually killed for it by the Chinese, wasn't he, Edgar?'

'Yep. Caught up in some massacre in Tientsin years ago. Ah, tea, thank you.'

'Anyway, Edgar's mother is terrified lest Lilian remain a spinster or perhaps worse, marry some quite unsuitable missionary – like a blacksmith.' She chuckled and got up, 'Now please entertain Mr Rayne for a few minutes, Edgar, while Walter casts his eye over a picture of mine.'

She winked, and as Walter followed her across the lawn indulged one of her favourite fantasies, which was that Edgar's sister did indeed marry a blacksmith and an uncouth one at that. For Sylvia had never forgotten a remark of Mary's she'd overheard soon after she and Edgar were engaged. Coming to join her and a friend in the sitting-room, she'd overheard Mary saying, '. . . a Suffolk greengrocer's daughter, my dear! Captivated poor Edgar over the cabbages. Claud and I are rather appalled, I confess, but what . . .' Mary stopped as Sylvia came in, smiling valiantly. Sylvia was humiliated, for her parents, the Catchpoles, were indeed owners of the market-square greengrocers in Beccles, where Edgar Fortescue had sometimes stayed with a friend during the school holidays, his parents being in the East. As she had seen him approaching in his smart school uniform to buy fruit she used to brighten her lips with cherry juice.

Nowadays Sylvia's parents were seldom mentioned by the Fortescues; but in distant Beccles Mr and Mrs Catchpole never tired of telling customers about their daughter's life in Japan with her servants, rickshaws, and grand house on the Bluff. Mary made the best of her son's unfortunate choice, as she did of most things, for Sylvia was a good wife and mother and knew the price of everything – as she should, considering . . . Secretly Sylvia longed to make a name for herself as a connoisseur of the arts so that she could quite eclipse her mother-in-law's reputation. With this in mind she handed Walter a considerable sum of money, hoarded from her monthly allowance, and bought the Kuniyoshi print.

Stranded on the lawn with Edgar, Oliver nibbled sponge cake, commented on the pleasantness of the view, then asked, tentatively, 'Your wife tells me your parents lived here years ago, Mr Fortescue? I wonder if you remember them mentioning my father, Mr Harold Rayne. He was Consul at Hakodate in the 'sixties.'

Edgar frowned, teased by a vague recollection of a party – a fuss about ice-cream, wasn't there? – and some very odd story about a Mr Rayne? He glanced warily at Oliver, who saw the wariness. 'Can't say I do, but I was seldom here in those days. My mother might know, of course . . .' and he trailed off gladly as Sylvia returned with Walter saying, 'Oh, Mr Rayne, Walter has been telling me what a good portraitist you are and I was wondering if I might persuade you to paint my daughter Grace? She's really quite pretty, though I say so myself . . .?'

'Really, Sylvia, I'm sure Mr Rayne didn't come all this way to paint little English roses.' Edgar sniffed in annoyance; Sylvia seemed to think he actually manufactured banknotes instead of simply handling other people's.

'Oh, but we'll have her *en kimono* holding a fan in the garden somewhere, so she won't look in the least English-rosy . . . Would you consider it, Mr Rayne?'

'I'd be delighted, madam.' He glanced at Mr Fortescue. 'Artists can usually adapt themselves to circumstances. Perhaps I could meet the young lady?'

'Unfortunately she's out at a birthday party today. But you must come again quite soon, Mr Rayne, and I'll show her to you.'

Before they left Sylvia insisted on a tour of the garden to select a suitable backdrop for little Gracie, and Oliver joined in with enthusiasm, guessing he had made his first catch. At the gate, Oliver decided, on impulse, to take another look at his father's grave, promising to join Walter in a harbour restaurant later. It was a mild, bright evening and the cemetery looked much less forbidding than on his earlier visit; but Harold's grave, almost hidden by the season's new growth, was just as unmarked and abandoned.

He strolled among the headstones, many dating from the same period yet all inscribed with the occupations, family connections, and worthy virtues of the deceased. He recalled Mr Fortescue's evasiveness, and his earlier uneasiness returned, mixed with resentment towards this almost unknown father of his – for dying out here so inconveniently, for leaving nothing to his son but this bare, neglected tomb, this hint of mystery. Oliver wished he could let the matter lie like a dead dog under the green bushes; but he knew that one day he would have to find out more.

CHAPTER SIXTEEN

The high, proud, sun-swept prow of the *Empress of the Pacific* edged into Yokohama's dock. Tug whistles blew, bells rang, passengers hanging over the rails waved and called, and Elinor, standing on the quayside, waved back at her daughter and sister-in-law, then strolled to the tea-room to wait until they disembarked. She seldom went to Yokohama these days, for it was so greatly changed from the flimsy, spartan, jolly little port she had first seen. It was twenty-five years ago, of course, but it seemed longer. Now its main streets were lined with bulky European-style buildings – government and Customs offices, consulates, banks, hotels and silk, tea, and marine agencies.

From the tea-room verandah she could just see the Bluff hill, one of the few familiar lineaments remaining. Incredible to imagine there had once been regiments of British and French troops camped there to protect foreign settlers from native attack! Poor Reggie Bradshaw . . . she could scarcely remember what he had looked like; or even the Kenjiro she had first known, wearing that ridiculous topknot. Treating herself to a moment of nostalgia for the arrogant, black-lacquer-like upsweep of it, she realised there was not one topknot to be seen along the busy street below.

Her tea finished, she went to watch passengers bumping down the ship's gangplanks, their becalmed, sea-borne psyches harassed by the sudden onslaught of unfamiliar faces on shore. When Ryo eventually appeared Elinor felt a surge of affection for one who did indeed remember Kenjiro with his topknot, his horse, and his samurai swords, and had never made the slightest concession of her own to western fashions. Her kimono and over-jackets were always of the finest materials and nowadays of such subdued hues as widows habitually wore – deep mauves and maroons, twilit greys and quiet browns. Hannah, on the contrary, had bought her travelling outfit in Paris – a flounced skirt, a wide-collared, tight-waisted jacket, a lace-trimmed hat. She carried a parasol, handbag, and white gloves and looked rather self-consciously grown-up after her first long stay away from home.

They greeted each other affectionately and, as Ryo beckoned a rickshaw-man, Hannah exclaimed, 'But first you must meet our new friend, Mother. She's come to teach at the American Presbyterian school and we met her on board . . . Miss Pilcher, here we are!'

A short, dumpling-shaped lady of some thirty-five summers bustled over and shook hands vigorously. Her face was also round, her brown hair scraped up in a tight bun that suggested a determination not to make the most of its limited attractions. 'Delighted to make your acquaintance, Mrs Miyata. I've heard a lot about you and your family and I'm so thrilled to be here in your beautiful country at last.'

Elinor grimaced. 'There's not much beauty left in Yokohama, I'm afraid, so please don't judge by first appearances. Shall we get another rickshaw and take you to the station with us? Visitors always love their first rickshaw ride; they say it feels like being a baby in a perambulator again.'

Rickshaws were soon assembled and Miss Pilcher did indeed squeal with joy as the runner, who looked wonderfully picturesque in blue and white cottons and a comical straw hat, picked up the shafts and wheeled her away. In the train, Ryo sat next to Miss Pilcher to point out the sights while Hannah, next to her mother, gave a contented sigh as she watched the familiar scene. The passing rows of low wooden houses looked very humble and insubstantial compared to the edifices she had seen, but she was pleased by them nevertheless, and by the uniformly black hair and eyes of her fellow passengers, and the chatter of two nearby girls, whose 'women's language' reminded her of her own schooldays.

During them she had often felt an outcast, due to her mixed blood, and, in defiance, had adopted a pose of proud detachment, verging on disdain. Her recent discovery of just how 'mixed-up' the wider world was had excited her, yet, in a contradictory sort of way, had made her long for home, where she knew the rules.

Elinor interrupted her thoughts with an anxious, 'You really did enjoy yourself, Hannah?'

'Oh, it was wonderful, Mother. Though I must admit it's a great relief not to be an object of such curiosity any more. Not just silly men ogling; but in Harrogate everyone stared at Aunt and me wherever we went *en kimono*. They positively twitched the curtains aside and rushed from shops to look. And I heard them whispering, "Are they Chinks? No, no pigtails! Must be Nips from Nippon . . ." '

She imitated the local accent well and Elinor winced. 'Well, now you know how I felt when Father and I used to go out walking together side by side in a manner quite improper!'

'Hmm . . .' Hannah relapsed back into a silence that was fairly habitual to her and which always suggested she could say more if she so wished.

Elinor, who preferred pursuing matters to a conclusion, added, 'You must remember, Hannah, that we British are islanders too, and rather insular in our attitudes. Those who stay at home aren't used to many different races and cultures, any more than the Japanese.'

'Yes, Mother, which makes it particularly strange that you and Father married really, doesn't it? I never thought much about it before, but being with your family made me realise how odd it was. I don't think *they* quite believe it, even now!'

Elinor sighed. Her two visits home since her marriage had been painful and uncomfortable, especially the first, of fifteen years before, when her parents were still alive. Her mother, who could not be persuaded from her conviction that the Japanese were a primitive tribe who worshipped snakes and the sun and ate boiled monkeys, had retreated to her bedroom for days pleading what Kenjiro called, bitterly, 'a severe case of diplomatic sickness'. 'As for marriage,' she continued defensively, 'one doesn't always know how or why it happens as it does . . . Not that I've regretted mine for a single minute.' She glanced almost shyly at her daughter, for they had never discussed such topics before; but before Hannah had been a girl of small experience. She smiled. 'We've such a nice surprise for you, dear. But you must wait to see Father; he wants to tell you himself.'

Hannah's dark eyes opened wide with alarm and she whispered urgently, 'Not someone else he wants me to marry, is it, Mother? Not yet . . .?'

Elinor patted her hand. 'Of course not, dear. No man will be allowed to marry you unless you've grown to know and like him. We've already promised that we aren't as oriental as that!'

Hannah's friends from schooldays were already married, several were mothers, and, before she had gone abroad, Kenjiro had proposed an alliance for her with the son of a wealthy business friend. She had rejected it fiercely, saying she would rather remain single like Aunt Ryo than marry a man she hardly knew, and Kenjiro had reluctantly shelved the matter. It had caused considerable dissension, however, for he firmly believed that the female's principal role in life was as an obedient wife and devoted mother and it was her parents' duty to select a husband of appropriate rank and prospects. Education, an unmitigated good for boys, could therefore spoil girls by making them discontented, argumentative, as was his wife, and diminish their femininity, which, he feared, might happen to his daughter.

On this trip abroad, Hannah had encountered for the first time the bold gallantry of young western men, whose behaviour seemed to her extremely forward. At dances and dinner-parties she had coquetted a little in return, but without much skill or conviction, for she had not been taught the western ways of social flirtation. Indeed, the combined influences of her disciplined schooldays, her resolute spinster aunt, and her recent experiences had left her with a nagging fear that she would never enjoy courtship and love in the western fashion, while the oriental arranging of alliances appealed to her even less.

It was partly with the aim of introducing Hannah to various eligible young men that Kenjiro and Elinor had planned her surprise – a large party to celebrate her twenty-first birthday on July 4th. Hannah, reading the guest list, recognised the stratagem at once but said nothing, simply adding a few names of her own, including, to Elinor's surprise, Miss Millicent Pilcher.

'You're sure, Hannah? Teachers in mission schools don't usually enjoy parties.'

'Oh, Miss Pilcher isn't strait-laced and is longing to meet more Japanese. She and Aunt are quite friendly, you know; they're going to a conference in Kyoto next week and then Aunt's taking her to visit the relatives in Kyushu.'

'So she told me. I think it's a mistake.'

Relations between the two branches of the Miyatas had been coolly courteous since Gengoro's death, but there was little understanding on either side. Elinor felt that Millicent Pilcher's presence in Kentaro's household would do little to help matters. But Ryo set her own course these days and had not heeded her warning. To invite Miss Pilcher to the party could do no harm, however, and Elinor added her name to the guest list.

July 4th was sunny but with a hint of sultry oppressiveness in the morning air that suggested a later storm. The gardeners said so to each other while sprinkling the ornamental rocks and mosses to make them glitter for the grand occasion. By noon, clouds were massing in the north-west, and Millicent Pilcher wondered, as she rode to the party, if she should have brought a brolly instead of a parasol. It did not much matter; one could buy oiled-paper brollies for next to nothing, though they probably would not last long. Millicent hailed from Maine and it was natural for her to prize things that were durable and worth their price, however minuscule. The frailty and disposability of many Japanese objects rather disturbed her, suggesting an insouciant light-mindedness in the people she had not expected. This party, for instance; would the men drink too much, would those immoral women called geisha be there? As her rickshaw passed under the Miyata's front entranceway she gripped the parasol handle tightly, feeling beleaguered.

Many guests had already arrived and were standing chatting in the garden, where Ryo greeted her. 'It's so hot, you must be thirsty. Orange or lemon juice? I'll introduce you to . . . ah, there's my brother, whom you haven't yet met. Kenjiro . . . my friend Miss Pilcher, who's going to Kentaro's with me.'

He was by far the most distinguished-looking Japanese she had yet encountered, Millicent thought, as they shook hands, and she smiled warmly. But Kenjiro's greeting was distant, for he was not partial to mission teachers. 'How do you do? I hope you are enjoying your stay in our little country? Far be it from me to interfere, but I must warn you that our old family home is very humble and inconvenient, with none of the modern comforts you are used to in America.'

'Oh, I didn't come to Japan to be comfortable, I assure you, Mr Miyata! That won't worry me a scrap and you can't imagine how much I'm dying to see the "real Japan" outside these big cities.'

He inclined his head resignedly, and as he made an excuse to leave, Ryo took her arm. 'Come, you must meet my nephew before he gets too carried away by the party spirit.'

She began steering Millicent in the direction of Joey, who was welcoming an Englishman near the gate; then suddenly halted with a gasp, putting a hand to her head.

'Is anything wrong, Miss Miyata?'

'I . . . yes . . . I'm afraid . . . I'm sorry, please excuse me for a minute. I feel quite giddy . . . I can't think why. If you care to wait for me in the refreshment marquee . . .?'

She bowed perfunctorily and hurried off, glancing over her shoulder not at Millicent, but at Joey's companion. Elinor was introducing guests on the terrace when Ryo drew her aside. 'A word in your ear, dear, please. That young man talking to Joey . . . who is he?'

Elinor shaded her eyes. 'Oh, that's Oliver someone . . . an artist friend of Walter Munro's.'

'Oliver! But doesn't he remind you very strongly of someone, Elinor; can't you see? Surely I'm not imagining . . .'

'No, I can't say . . . he was here at Christmas and seemed amiable enough.'

'Oh, Ellie, use your eyes! I shall simply have to go and make sure.' Ryo tossed her head angrily and positively flounced over to her nephew. 'Ah, Joey . . . I wanted to introduce Miss Pilcher to you . . . But I don't think I've met your friend?'

'My aunt, Miss Miyata . . . Mr Rayne.'

'How do you do, Mr . . . er what is the name exactly?'

Oliver smiled, spelling it out, 'People often think I'm called after the wet stuff that falls from the sky.'

'Ah yes . . . the name is familiar. Were your parents out here years ago, by chance?'

'Why yes, my father was Consul in Hakodate. Did you know him?' He sounded eager.

'Not really, but I did meet your mother. Just once. Is she here with you now?'

'Alas, no. She died last year, Miss Miyata.'

'Oh . . . I see.' Her eyes as she looked at him were narrow black stones. Then, with the barest inclination of the head, she walked away. Oliver stared after her; surely the absence of even a token murmur of regret at his mother's death was unusually impolite for a Japanese?

'Did I offend your aunt, Joey? I didn't mean to.'

'I don't see why. She's rather more brusque than most ladies. It's being a teacher that does it. Let's get you a drink before she bears down again with that missionary woman.'

But for the moment Ryo had quite forgotten Millicent as she slipped unobtrusively into the Japanese wing of the house, where she leaned against a pillar, wiping her spectacles agitatedly. The years had blurred the vision of Felix Coburn from consciousness, though during her recent stay in England she had wondered occasionally where he was living and with whom. She had accepted long ago that he had never loved her because he loved Honoria Rayne; but it had never occurred to her that Honoria's son was his until she had seen Oliver. The same soft pallor, dark curls, and impish grin had jolted her inmost being like a well-aimed punch. She shuddered,

341

feeling suddenly young again – vulnerable, lost, betrayed – recalling her hopeless, frightened defiance during that brief and only sexual liaison of her life. A *shoji* drew back and Elinor hurried to her. 'Ryo . . . I watched you come in . . . whatever is the matter? Tell me, please.'

Ryo averted her face, whispering. 'It's that boy, Oliver Rayne he calls himself; Oliver Coburn he is. Can't you see the likeness, Elinor? It's unmistakable.'

'Oh dear . . . yes, I suppose I can now you mention it. But I've only met him once before and didn't make the connection. Ryo, I *am* sorry. But you mustn't let it upset you after so long.' She laid a hand on Ryo's wrist, but Ryo shook it free, blinked, and put her spectacles back on. Elinor hesitated; Felix Coburn's name had not been mentioned for years; both Ryo and Kenjiro seemed to prefer it so. Elinor had almost forgotten the entire episode; but clearly Ryo had not.

'He should never have been allowed to come here,' Ryo muttered sulkily.

'But he's just one of Joey's chums and was only a child when Mrs Rayne . . .'

'She's dead, he told me.' Elinor did not know what to say. 'I wanted to ask about Felix, but how could I? I wonder how much he knows? Probably Felix deserted her as he did me.'

'Probably.' Elinor was increasingly aware of the party outside, demanding her attention.

'He mustn't come here again.'

'No dear, I'll see to it. But possibly the boy doesn't even know about . . . a lot of things. He may be quite innocent.'

'We're all innocents, at first . . .' Her tone was venomous, and Elinor sighed, 'Ryo, I'm sorry, but I really must . . .'

'Yes, of course. I'll come out again shortly.'

She walked off along the passage and Elinor, returning to the terrace, saw her daughter talking to Yukio Iwada and thought how pleased her husband would be. Yukio was the youngest son of Count Iwada, a member of the old Kyoto aristocracy whose title had recently been revived. Kenjiro, despite his enthusiasm for western-style democracy, was still impressed by titles, and by Count Iwada in particular because he had fought bravely for the Emperor during the civil war of Restoration.

Yukio, a cadet at the Imperial Military College, was wearing its dark blue, brass-buttoned uniform, which hung stiffly on his stocky frame, reminding Elinor of prints she had seen of sixteenth-century samurai clad in Portuguese armour which did not fit quite naturally. He was ill-at-ease, standing almost to parade-ground attention, for, though he had learned during a visit to America that casual chat of this sort between the sexes was acceptable, he had no idea what to say. Hannah, inhibited by his shyness, was also finding conversation difficult. They turned from each other in mutual relief when Oliver Rayne approached, introducing himself with a charming smile. '. . . I've heard so much about you from your brother, Miss Miyata,' he continued, 'so I hope you'll allow me to say how admirable I think you look in your kimono – its beautiful simplicity of design and pattern quite puts to shame all the tasteless flounces and frills I see elsewhere.' He had been practising that little speech, watching her intently, ever since he had learned who she was.

'Thank you, Mr Rayne.' Her voice had a warm lilt, her smile was both sweet and grave. 'But I must tell you that I sometimes enjoy wearing those frills and flounces you so dislike. It depends on the occasion . . . and my mood.'

Yukio, whose English was not fluent, felt himself at an immediate disadvantage compared to this suave English fellow and moved away with a mumbled excuse as Oliver pressed on.

'Oh, how I should adore to paint your portrait on just this occasion and in your present mood, Miss Miyata . . . that delightful garment, the red flowers in your hair – I believe I would be truly inspired. Would it not be possible? I am an artist, you realise, and . . .'

'Yes, yes.' She guessed from his flushed sparkling that he had been drinking quantities of champagne. 'Perhaps some time, Mr Rayne; but not just as present . . .'

She turned as Miss Pilcher plucked her sleeve. 'Hannah, excuse me, but have you seen your aunt? She wasn't feeling well and asked me to wait in the marquee. She went indoors but hasn't returned and I'm a bit worried . . .'

'Oh dear, what could be the matter? We had better go and see. Please excuse me, Mr Rayne.'

As they moved away, the clouds that had long threatened the sun began moving heavily across it, and Oliver, instantly aware of the light's dimming, felt his happiness drain from him. For was not she, Hannah Miyata, Joey's sister, the most wonderful creature he had ever seen; and what was the use of the day without her?

On their way indoors Hannah murmured, 'Europeans are so fawning and the Japanese so totally opposite that it's funny. I was talking to Count Iwada's son Yukio earlier — that fellow with hair like a bottle-brush. He expects any mere woman to fawn on him.'

'Which is far worse, surely?' Millicent asked severely.

'I suppose so. But they don't mean to be rude. It's the way boys are brought up.'

'Yet outward appearances have changed even more drastically than I realised. I was talking to an old gentleman in the marquee who told me that in his youth all men wore native dress, even in the cities.'

'They still do in the rural areas, Miss Pilcher, you'll see. There's a priceless photograph of my father as a young man . . . Ah, let's see if Aunt's here.' Hannah knocked gently on Ryo's bedroom door and, receiving no reply, peeped in. Ryo wasn't there but had left a note explaining that she felt poorly and had returned to the mission school for a rest.

Hannah frowned. 'That's most unlike her. She gets tired of young men; I expect that's why she left . . . She'd have that photo somewhere . . .' She opened a drawer tentatively.

'But not on display, I suppose?' Millicent glanced round the room. Although Ryo had spent the previous night there, it looked permanently untenanted, its only decorative objects being two calligraphy scrolls and an enamelled vase on a shelf. She picked up the object next to it.

'What's this?'

'Oh, that's an old-style wooden pillow. Aunt still uses it sometimes when she doesn't want to muss up her hair at night. We call them "execution blocks" nowadays.'

'They look mighty uncomfortable to sleep on.' Millicent prodded the thin pad on top, opened a drawer near the base containing hairpins, then reached to put it back. 'Why, there's a name scratched on the bottom. It's rather faint . . . but English surely . . . Yes . . . Felix Coburn.' She traced the letters with her finger.

Hannah came over, 'Fancy! Yes, that's the name . . . It's translated into Japanese too.'

'Have you heard of him?'

She shook her head. 'He must have meant something to her once. It's a sweetheart sort of thing to do . . . I'll pump her about it.' She giggled. 'Who would have guessed? Aunt Ryo with a man's name under her pillow!'

'Better be careful, it's probably a delicate subject, and could hardly have had a happy outcome.'

'I suppose not . . . Look, here's Father's photo; doesn't he look quaint with his Satsuma crests and his two swords? It was taken soon after he started working for the British as an interpreter . . .'

Millicent stared at the sepia picture: Mr Miyata was certainly handsome even then and very determined-looking . . . No wonder that Hannah's mother . . . But it must have made quite a stir at the time . . . a romantic one, though – marrying a samurai. She handed the picture back with a sigh, for romance had never figured much in her life. 'I suppose he used an "execution block" in those days to keep that topknot in place?'

'Presumably. I wonder if he ever carved Mother's name underneath? Felix Coburn . . . I'll have to investigate . . . But we'd better go.'

As they emerged rain began plummeting from the sky and thunder reverberated in the distance. Guests ran for cover laughing as servants, also laughing, rushed out with umbrellas to shield them. It was too late in the day for the party to re-establish itself indoors and people soon began leaving, the girls, in their bright party clothes, folding themselves inside black-hooded rickshaws like butterflies returning to their chrysalises.

'It was a truly marvellous party, Mother and Father. Thank you very much.' Hannah, feeling a formal statement was required, bowed to them as the family gathered in the drawing room for a rest.

Kenjiro patted her head. 'Well, I've never had a child become an adult before.'

'So will I get a party when it's my turn, Father?' Joey wheedled.

'We'll see . . . If you deserve it.'

'But what's Hannah done to deserve it?'

'Girls don't have to deserve, they just are; and she's the loveliest, sweetest daughter in the world and that's enough.' Hannah laughed in embarrassment, 'Oh Father, you sound like one of the flattering young men!'

'The foreign ones you mean? I can't imagine someone like Yukio Iwada flattering!'

'Oh no, he's far too proud and full of himself. He said he intends to be commander-in-chief of Japan's modern army one day. Just like that. It must be rather wonderful to be so sure of oneself. I've no idea what I want to do or be now I'm an adult.'

Joey grinned slyly. 'Girls don't have to know. They just are.'

'But women can *do* a lot of things too, if they're given the chance and the education,' she rounded on him fiercely. 'Yet all the higher education is offered to you – and you don't want to learn . . . It's not fair!'

'I agree totally, Hannah. Father, why not let my sister study economics and politics and I'll take the "bridal subjects" like flower-arranging? I'm sure I'd be good at it.'

He struck a flamboyant pose, but Kenjiro, knowing he was being baited, simply walked away to the window, looking out on the damp debris of the party. What would not he have given for Joey's chances at his age? And how well he had used those he had by comparison! The well-tried samurai virtues of discipline, perseverance, and self-control seemed non-existent in his son. Joey's face was wide-open to the world, his body relaxed and sprawling as a puppy dog's. From babyhood he had had an air of expectancy, of waiting for good things to fall out of the sky. But Hannah was his true samurai daughter, tight-lipped and self-contained; only, she being a girl, her sense of purpose was, as she had just said, undirected. Rain was falling heavily and, hearing water gush along the stream towards the pond, he was reminded of the family home in the Imamura valley and of her who had shared it with him and knew his heart best. 'Where's Ryo? I barely saw her at the party.'

Elinor, looking through the presents guests had brought, replied, 'She felt rather poorly and left a note saying she'd gone home.'

'Not like her – and on Hannah's birthday. She introduced me to that odd little missionary, whom I suspect of supporting more rights for women.'

'So she does, Father, and none the worse for that.' Hannah flushed. 'But what made you think so, may I ask?'

'Oh, the plain face and her manner, I suppose. No alluring feminine charms about her.'

'But it isn't . . .' Hannah was wondering how much she dare say when Ryo hurried in, her eyes sparkling with an animation that quite alarmed Elinor. 'Ryo dear, we were just talking about you. Are you feeling better?'

'Perfectly, thank you. Just a slight headache. And I found a letter waiting for me – a piece of good news that I thought you would like to hear?' She glanced half-timidly at her brother. 'I've been offered the post of headmistress, Kenjiro, at the mission's elementary school for girls.'

'Ryo, how marvellous!' 'Congratulations, Aunt . . .!' They clustered round her and Kenjiro sent for more champagne, though Ryo would have only tea, protesting the appointment was of no importance.

'Don't be so modest! There are only two other women heads in the country as far as I know, and it's a great honour.' Elinor raised her glass. 'And will you be allotted that pretty bungalow next to the school?'

'Yes . . . In fact I'm to move in at once before we leave for Kyoto. So I thought I'd take your presents for the family away now, brother. I mayn't have time to collect them before we leave.'

Draining his glass, Kenjiro took Ryo to fetch the presents, which had been carefully wrapped in readiness for the journey. 'There's a book about new farming methods for Kentaro and for Fumio a kerosene lamp. A pocket watch for Koichi and brocade for his wife. Satchels, toys, lead pencils for the children. They're all labelled.'

'My, my, such extravagances . . . Fumio will thoroughly disapprove.'

'She'd disapprove anyway. If I sent cheap things she'd think me mean.'

Ryo nodded. 'Yes, we'll never please Fumio.' Yet she herself was not entirely pleased with this evidence of her brother's liberality; they had been brought up to respect thrift and frugality; she, at least, continued to do so.

'And that's a widow's *obi* for poor Ofuku.' Ofuku's husband, whose bed-place Kenjiro had once envied, had died a few months before and she now lived in somewhat straitened circumstances with her eldest son. 'Tell Ohisa to put them in the waterproof baskets, it's still pouring; listen . . . You know I rather wish I could join you there . . . just to hear the stream running and see the crops high on the terraces . . .' He clicked his tongue. 'Odd, isn't it? I'm sometimes reminded of that poem by the great Saigo — about the clamour in the cities that alarms one's soul, the dust that soils one's clothes . . .'

'The great Saigo never indulged in the modern trappings of our city life,' she agreed, and for a moment they fell reverentially silent, for Saigo Takamori had died twelve years before. 'But I have only a short holiday and I'll spend it with the family,' Kenjiro concluded briskly.

'You work hard, brother.'

'I always have. And you'll have to work in your illustrious new position, sister.'

'I shan't mind that.'

He shook his head, thinking that she should be married instead. After they had settled in Tokyo years ago he had tried to arrange an alliance for her with a man of suitable age and rank, but Ryo had been coldly uncooperative, putting her worst face forward to every suitor. Admittedly the selection had not been very choice, for Ryo was nearing thirty by then and her reputation was clouded by rumours of a vague scandal. Eventually, at Elinor's insistence, he had abandoned the attempt; and now here was his formerly docile younger sister – a headmistress in her own right, working outside the home for a salary. It was not truly proper for a lady of her kind and in his heart he could not rejoice. But Ryo was proud and happy at her promotion; and as the news had reached her on the very day that she had been so painfully and unexpectedly reminded of the past's bitter sorrow, it seemed a personal benison from the Lord, an assurance that she had chosen the right direction for her life.

CHAPTER SEVENTEEN

Ryo Miyata, Millicent Pilcher, and others of similar persuasion travelled by train to Kyoto for the Mission Conference the following week. There, they listened attentively to lectures delivered by English and American churchmen on such topics as 'The Counfounding of Confucius' and 'How the Superstitions of Buddhism and Shintoism are being exposed by the Strong Light of Modern Science'. Then they spent a few days sightseeing in the old capital, before continuing to Nagasaki and from there by coastal steamer to Kagoshima, which they reached on the evening of August 12th.

To Millicent, leaning over the ship's rail, the scene looked magical – the rugged flanks of the Sakurajima volcano gashed by deep violet shadows in the setting sun; reflections of protruding fishing stakes rippling like thin snakes in the glossy pink and turquoise waters of the bay.

'So that's your home town . . .' Millicent stared towards the shore, where soft lamplights were appearing in the houses. 'It looks wonderfully quiet and peaceful, as if nothing ever happens here.'

Ryo smiled gently. 'And we are often told how deceptive appearances can be! Our first Christian missionary, Francis Xavier, landed here in the sixteenth century and caused a lot of turmoil, remember. Things were fairly quiet during most of the Tokugawa period, I think; but the British bombarded the place in the 'sixties and it was partly destroyed again only twelve years ago at the end of the Satsuma Rebellion – the last uprising of the old feudal order against the Meiji government.'

'Honest! My land, who would have thought it.'

'My Uncle Gengoro was killed fighting with Saigo Takamori, who led about twelve thousand Satsuma clansmen against the Imperial forces. They say that, at the last ditch, some samurai threw away their modern weapons and rushed full-tilt into the enemy fire waving their swords. If it's true, Gengoro would certainly have been among them; he was that sort of man. I rather hope he did, really.'

'You were fond of him, in spite of his views?'

'No, I was terrified of him as a child. He was a bullying tyrant who wouldn't listen to anyone. Only, in retrospect, I have to admire him just a little – and what he stood for. People are beginning to feel the same about the great Saigo, who committed *hara-kiri* at the end. He'll probably be rehabilitated as a national hero one day.'

'Japan is a very complicated country,' Millicent said solemnly, 'but I didn't think it was until I came here.'

'All ancient countries are complicated, that's their curse.' Ryo moved away, disinclined to chat with this comparative stranger at such a moment. She was thinking of her nephew, Eitaro, Kentaro's eldest son, whom Gengoro had enrolled in Saigo's military academy; he too had been killed in the Rebellion, aged seventeen. So much for not listening to anyone; she couldn't forgive her uncle for that. She looked down into the dark waters, which were glittering now with dense masses of phosphorescence. Ghost-pale outlines of large fish nudged the ship's side, and smaller marine creatures darted through the black depths with the speed of shooting stars. The first heaven-held stars illuminated the water's surface and she stared upwards, rejoicing in the harmonious mirror of sea and sky. She bestirred herself to polite conversation as Millicent rejoined her.

'The local people believe their hero Saigo went to Mars and you can see him there when it shines brightly.'

'So many silly superstitions, folk tales, primitive beliefs you must have heard in your childhood, Ryo; and yet there must have been a still small voice telling you they weren't true.'

'Was there? I'm not sure. I believed in many different things when I was a child, but they didn't seem to conflict.' Ryo was talking so softly, looking so dreamily from sea to sky, that Millicent didn't dare to interrupt. 'When I was a child it all seemed so simple – the very complexities of our ancient land held me safe in a huge net, that you call superstition, idolatry. We had little, needed little, expected nothing to change. So much we didn't know about and didn't want, even in the realm of material things . . . No bread, beef, beer, or butter; no watches, trains, or newspapers, or rickshaws, or . . .'

'No rickshaws, even? I thought you'd had them, at least, for centuries.'

'No, they were invented just after the Restoration and didn't reach these remote parts for years.'

'So what did you go about in?'

'Palanquins, litters, carts. People seldom travelled far, especially women. My sister-in-law Fumio, whom you'll meet tomorrow, has never been more than fifty miles from home. Kenjiro and I have asked her to come to Tokyo, but she refuses. Kentaro came once and hated it. They're very set in their country ways.'

'But the next generation will move ahead, surely?'

'I doubt it. Kiochi, the second son, is taking over the reins, their married daughter lives near, and then there's young Junji . . . You'll see . . . it's very old Japan still. That's why I wanted you to come.'

'And I thank you from my heart for the chance, Ryo. Perhaps this is an occasion for an oriental bow of gratitude?'

'No. You can save that for tomorrow when you meet my elder brother, the head of the house. Well, I'm off to bed. We want to get ashore quite early tomorrow.'

As it turned out they were considerably delayed the next morning by an officious inspector who examined all their luggage, incredulous that two women could own so much. But at last they were under way, bouncing over the rutted tracks towards the Imamura valley in a double rickshaw pulled by two skinny men and pushed by two more, with the luggage in a cart behind. It was extremely hot; men and women working in the terraced fields were bare to the waist; the pullers, who stopped frequently to mop the sweat from their bodies, wore nothing but very scanty loin-cloths. Turning away from the offensive sight, Millicent asked, 'What are those white sticks in the rice paddies over there, Ryo? They look like feathered arrows.'

Ryo shaded her eyes. 'Oh my goodness . . . it's Bon Odori! I quite forgot . . . Oh dear, why ever didn't I think . . .?'

'Bono . . . what?'

'Our annual festival for the dead. It's still held in mid-August according to the old calendar in these parts. The sticks are Shinto charms – with messages to the gods written on bits of paper and stuck in the tops. There'll be dancing in the temple courtyards tonight.'

'How interesting! I like to watch dancing.'

'But it's sacred dancing to entertain the spirits of the dead who return to their former homes for three days at this time of year.'

'You sound almost as if you believe such twaddle, Ryo.'

'No – of course not. But one can't just ride roughshod over long-held beliefs. It would be most rude.' She sighed in vexation. What an unfortunate time to bring an unknown and very Christian foreigner to her brother's home! Again she wished, as she had on the ship the previous evening, that she had heeded Elinor's warning and not brought Millicent.

The men were anxious to get on; but when they started, a cart-wheel buckled under the weight of luggage, causing further delay, and it was mid-afternoon before they arrived. Kentaro and his family, who had moved into Gengoro's house on his death, were waiting, arrayed in their best garments, politely concealing their annoyance at their lateness under a flurry of welcome. Fumio, whom Ryo had not seen for a long time, looked much older than her fifty years; her back was bent, her hair greying and wispy, several of her marriage-blackened teeth were missing, her skin wrinkled to walnut by southern suns. But her voice had not lost its habitual edge of hostile resentment, nor her eyes their keenness as they flicked

354

disapprovingly over Ryo's expensive silk kimono and the ridiculous starched frills on Millicent's blouse-front. Kentaro, ever a mumbler, introduced the family to the foreigner — twenty-six year old Koichi; the last, late child, Junji; and Koichi's pregnant wife, Fusako, who seemed cowed and tired, which was not surprising, as her main duty in life was to wait upon and try to please her mother-in-law. Shyly she showed Ryo her first-born daughter, a healthy, well-fed baby and evidence that conditions had in fact improved for the family, though Fumio would never admit it.

The rooms were spruce with new screens and mats, and a guest wing had been added, to which Kentaro conducted them, pointing out proudly that the larger room, reserved for Millicent, had been fitted with western-style glass windows. He stared at the strange suitcases with shiny metal fittings stacked on the verandah.

'You have many things.'

'Well, we left a month ago, remember, and came here directly from the Conference in Kyoto.'

'Conference?'

'For missionaries and teachers in Christian schools.'

'Christians gathered in Kyoto, the old imperial capital!' he frowned in amazement, having never come to terms with the fact that his sister was a true Christian.

Skirting trouble, she indicated the luggage. 'And there are presents for you all from Kenjiro. Shall I unpack them?'

'Oh, not now. Wife is anxious to serve the meal. It's getting late and we are to attend the temple-dancing this evening.'

'The Bon Odori, yes . . . I fear it's a rather inconvenient time to arrive, Kentaro. I'm sorry.'

He muttered something inarticulate; at least, she thought, he would never guess that she had actually forgotten the date of the ancient and well-beloved festival. A chair had been procured specially for Millicent, borrowed from Junji's school, Fumio explained, for the teachers sat at desks nowadays and the pupils used new-fangled slates, pencils, and bound textbooks. Such things were far too expensive for them, in Fumio's opinion, and she could not see the good of it all.

Ryo gulped the soup, her mouth dry with heat and tension. 'But, Fumio, the young have so many new ways to learn.' She looked up defiantly. 'I may as well tell you that I've just been made the head of a school in Tokyo and I feel it an honour and responsibility to teach the young of Meiji about the modern world.'

'You . . . a woman . . . head of a school; but that's a man's job!' Fumio glared at her, horrified.

'But it's a girls' school.'

'Run by Christians?' Kentaro interrupted.

'Yes . . . a mission school.'

In the ensuing cold pause Fusako and the maid cleared the bowls and Millicent, perched uncomfortably on her chair, murmured, 'Are they disapproving of me, Ryo?'

'No, no, of me. I just told them of my new post – but only men should be heads, they tell me.'

'Oh stuff and nonsense . . . They must be made to understand . . .'

'Millicent, not now; we've only just arrived.'

Fusako brought the next course, apologising for the lack of meat or fish because it was Bon Odori, when only the spirits of the ancestors could be offered such luxuries. 'Perhaps you'll explain that to your foreign friend,' Fumio said maliciously. 'She may not know our Buddhist laws and I wouldn't like her to think we're being inhospitable, serving such poor food.'

'I'll explain it later,' Ryo gulped, watching Millicent picking dismally at her plate.

'Fusako and I visited the graves yesterday in the correct manner with flowers and offerings for Uncle Gengoro, his wife, young Eitaro,' Fumio continued, clearly reproaching Ryo, for it was well known that Christian converts failed to pay proper reverence to their ancestors. But Ryo pretended not to notice, saying after a decent interval, 'Now tell me about the living family, Kentaro. Married daughter is well, I hope? And Ofuku, how is she bearing her loss?'

Her brother, also anxious to avoid trouble, answered at unusual length for him and the meal finished peaceably.

By the time they set out to see the dancing, a just-rising

356

moon was casting slant shadows on the uptilted gables of the country farmhouses, most of whose inhabitants had already gone to the village. As they reached its main street they heard ahead the intermittent clap of many hands accompanied by a sonorous, muffled drum-beat. The temple courtyard was fringed with people; in its centre stood a high frame from which swung the great drum. A long line of female dancers was slowly swaying and gliding round it, gracefully extending their arms on either side and holding their palms outward as they did so. The loose, droopy sleeves of their summer robes lifted, hovered and fell rhythmically like silken wings beating in the moonlight, and their sandalled feet slid in unison over the dry dust in long, soft swishes. During the intervals between drum-beat and hand-clap, that was the only sound, save for the shrill of crickets from the graveyard behind where white lanterns were lit among the dark tombs and bushes in honour of the dead.

The villagers made way for the Miyatas, ushering them to benches near the front and gasping with amazement at the sight of a foreign woman in their midst. Then they quietened and all fell under the spell of the evening's magic – the gentle glow of moonlight and lanterns; the girls' slender bodies weaving and circling; the mesmerising clap, beat, and glide. Ryo felt herself to be almost bewitched, turned back to half-remembered times of childhood, or perhaps further yet to the unconscious awareness of long-dead generations buried nearby who had once seen and heard these ancient rites. Her spine and scalp prickled at the awesome mystery of these changeless, undulating patterns of movement and sound that seemed to whisper like a dark, beautiful wave through her every sense, drawing her down and back into itself, enveloping her like a mother or like a shroud. She tilted forward, her whole body yearning to join the dancers, pay homage at their shrine – though she was far too old for that now, and their shrine was no longer hers. Then she straightened, glancing guiltily at Millicent as if she might divine her truant thoughts.

Had she done so, Millicent would have felt even more besieged by the forces of heathenism that were hemming her in. She held tightly to the bench with both hands, back straight, thick thighs firmly together, and stared at the pagan rite without really seeing it, only longing for it to end. At long last the dancers' monotonous bowing and scraping was broken and two young peasants bounded into the circle, their bronzed bodies naked to the waist, their movements bold and free. They led the procession round the drum again in a quickened rhythm, chanting as they went,

> *'Whether brought forth in mountain or in field,*
> *It matters nothing,*
> *More than treasure of one hundred gold pieces*
> *Is a baby precious.'*

Millicent shuddered, clutching the bench harder as Ryo whispered the translation to her. 'Is it going on much longer?'

'But it's beautiful — don't you think?'

'I don't really find it so,' Millicent said, staring in alarm at the two young men, who were now capering with such joyous abandon that she greatly feared what might happen next.

Then quite suddenly, to her immense relief, the performance ended on a final drum crescendo; a sigh of appreciation passed through the spectators; the dancers, bowed, dispersed, chatting and giggling together, transformed within the space of a few minutes from arcane votaries to ordinary village lasses. As their varying emotions drained, both Ryo and Millicent were overcome by immense weariness and simply sat in numbed silence until Kentaro led them away, back over the dark hill-tracks to the house.

They slept late, waking to the sounds of servants clattering and chattering and cicadas thrumming in the bushes. After the midday meal — again of such frugality that Ryo rightly suspected her sister-in-law of taking gastronomic revenge on them for coming during Bon Odori — the gifts from Tokyo were ceremoniously presented. Her own offerings, being small souvenirs from her foreign travels, were quite acceptable; but, as she had feared, Kenjiro's generosity was interpreted as an ostentatious display of his wealth and sophistication.

'One of those newfangled kerosene lamps with a glass chimney, isn't it?' Fumio examined the present suspiciously. 'Junji's teacher has one. I've been told they smell terribly. We'll have to save it for festivals, the oil is far too expensive for every day.'

Ryo murmured defensively, 'But as more people use them the oil will get cheaper.'

'Doesn't she like it?' Millicent asked curiously. 'Explain how well one can read by them at night.'

Ryo sighed. 'Oh, she's so conservative. And to think how dear Kenjiro could have benefited from one of these when he was studying here! But he had to manage with dim little pith-wick lamps . . . I was just explaining . . .' she began, but fell silent, for Fusako, at Fumio's bidding, was already wrapping the lamp with great care, which meant it was destined for the family storehouse and would probably remain there for years.

When everything had been presented, they moved to the shaded verandah, where Koichi kept pulling out his pocket watch, saying it made him feel like a town swell, while Junji ran off outside, delighted at his present – an Honourable Monkey dressed in scarlet and blue that ran up a stick when he pulled its tail. Fusako, diplomatically concealing her pleasure in her length of brocade, showed it diffidently to Fumio. 'Very good quality. You are very very fortunate, Fusako,' she fingered it enviously. 'There's not much of good quality about these days. Pedlars come with made-up cottons imported from heaven knows where. Terrible vulgar stuff it is, but so cheap that there's no point in dyeing and hand-spinning your own garments anymore. It's sad. You must take great care of it, Fusako; you won't see its like again.'

Fusako bowed meekly and, as she went to fetch more tea, nearly bumped into Junji. 'Look what I caught near the pond, Mother! Isn't it a beauty?' He held up a tiny wicker cage in which fluttered a large dragonfly, its gauzy purple-black-green wings beating helplessly against the bars.

Fumio jumped up with an alarmed cry. 'Let him go, child, let him go at once . . . Out . . . shoo!'

'But, Mother . . .'

She grabbed the cage. 'Silly boy. May the august dead forgive your young ignorance. Don't you remember my telling you? Dragonflies carry the spirits of our revered ancestors back to their homes at this Bon Odori time. We must never capture them then. We don't know whose messenger this beautiful creature is. Come now, careful, don't harm it and let him go . . .'

She hurried the child down the verandah steps and opened the cage, but the insect seemed reluctant to leave, alighting first on its top, then circling slowly back over their heads, glinting in the sunlight.

'Shoo . . . shoo!' Fumio cowered, moving her lips in silent prayer till at last the dragonfly dipped and soared back towards the pond.

'Whatever was that all about?' Millicent asked. She had been dozing, listening vaguely to the pleasant rural sounds, till Fumio's cry roused her.

Ryo explained a little apologetically, concluding, 'It's just a country folk tale. Rather poetic, don't you think?'

'Poetic! But these people are weighed down with such superstitious nonsense. Why, your sister-in-law is quite frightened, look at her! Oh Ryo . . .' she clasped her hands, 'I know one cannot rush matters, but we are in a very stronghold of Buddhism and surely now is the time to say something about the true light of the Word that casts out all heathen fear and ignorance. Or I'll do so and you can simply translate, if that's easier . . .'

Ryo rubbed her knuckles nervously. 'Millicent, you must understand. It would only antagonise her further and there's so much misunderstanding and disagreement between us already. And, after all, I'm not a missionary . . .'

'Granted, but as a devout Christian . . .'

Ryo turned her head away as Fumio, hot and bothered, sank down on the matting. 'I was trying to remember the names we used to give dragonflies when we were young, Fumio,' Ryo soothed. 'Barley Straw, Lamp-wick, Lady of the Willow . . . And we learned poems about them too, didn't we?'

Fumio's face brightened. 'Ah, yes . . . let me see now . . .

> *Much more red*
> *seems the dragonfly*
> *as it hovers over the pond.*

And,

> *One of the fencing posts*
> *is higher than the rest,*
> *But no — a dragonfly*
> *sits on it.'*

She gave a rare cackle, showing her gapped black teeth. 'I loved learning poems when I was a child. I used to dream of becoming the lady of some grand lord, sitting on a silk cushion all day composing poetry and doing embroidery.'

'Did you? I wouldn't have guessed.' Ryo stared at her.

'Fat use . . . idle girlish fancies! I made sure my daughter didn't harbour the like, nor Fusako either — who'd be a lazy minx if I let her . . . Where's that tea?' she called peremptorily, and Fusako came hurrying in with it, looking scared.

As they slowly sipped, the sun's white glare faded to pale amber and at twilight Fumio lit the lamps on either side of the Buddha shelf with extra care, placing before it fresh offerings of rice-balls and cakes while Millicent watched, her lips tight-pursed. After the evening meal they retired early for, though the festival lasted another day, the menfolk would be up at dawn for normal work.

But Ryo, having risen late, was now wide awake, and lay on her quilt under the bluey-green mosquito net in the guestwing's smaller bedroom thinking over the events of the day and listening to the familiar sounds of the frogs in the dykes and a nightingale in the woods. Restlessly she rose and drew back the screens; a mist floated in layers over the flowers on the pond and up into the trees on the hill beyond, whitewispy as summer ghosts that roam on warm nights. She shivered, closed the screens, and lay down again, sensing some alien element in the room — a vibration of the still shadows that lurked beyond the tiny flicker of the night-light. She stared into that netted dark, aware of every creak as the house cooled after the day's heat — for that was what it surely was, she told herself. She buried her head under the thin quilt and lay for a long time tensed and curled up like a fearful child.

The night drifted warmly on, the mists swirled closer, the flutterings in the air seemed to draw nearer. It was the black-winged dragonfly. 'Only silly superstition, of course,' she murmured, or thought she was murmuring . . . 'and forgive us our trespasses as we forgive them . . .'

Then he was there, standing just within the circle of light, glaring right through his eyes at her with a ferocity that was more evil and terrible than it had ever been in life. 'Uncle Gengoro, Uncle Gengoro . . . forgive me,' she was whimpering. 'Forgive all my trespasses as . . .' His face puckered into a vicious snarl of fury. He raised his arm, thick and huge in the light that was stronger now, and his sword flashed above his head. As he lunged at her with a belly-shaking roar she saw that his head was covered with blood, only his eyes glowing black and bulgy like those of demon-guards at the temple gates, like those of a monstrous dragonfly that was falling on her, smothering her inside its beautiful, baleful wings . . . She woke with a loud scream, hearing a mad fluttering in the darkness and the crash of heavy steps outside, and screamed again, jumping off the bed.

'Aunt Ryo, Aunt . . . what's the matter?' Hands fumbled with the shutters and were drawn back to reveal Koichi staring at her.

'Oh, it's you . . . I'm so sorry, nephew; I had a bad dream. I must have cried out.'

'You screamed so loud I thought you were being murdered.'

She shuddered. 'Oh, it was nothing, really.' She looked round in the half light. 'Look — how silly of me. A dragonfly has got in. That probably disturbed me. Catch him and put him outside, please, Koichi . . . quickly.'

The young man took off his shoes, stepped in and began chasing the elusive insect. As he swiped at it, Ryo cried, 'Oh,

362

don't kill it please! Just shoo it out.'

He gave an odd, lopsided grin and gently fanned the dragon-fly towards the open screen; for a minute it skittered tantalisingly on the threshold, then sailed off into the dawn.

Ryo watched it go, a hand on her forehead. 'Thank you, Koichi. I think I'll sleep a little longer. You're up so early.'

'We always are at this time of year,' he replied stolidly. 'I was on my way to the toilet when I heard you screaming.' He closed the screens and Ryo lay down again, feeling exhausted, melancholy, and rather ashamed of herself, until the rising sun dissolved the terror of her nightmare and she slept dreamlessly and late.

The workaday rhythms were well underway when Ryo eventually sought out Fumio in the back courtyard, where she and an aged servant were pressing nuts for hair-oil. Hens scratched in the warm grit; washing hung up on bamboo poles was already dried stiff by sunlight. She turned on Ryo fiercely. 'Your foreign woman has gone to market with Fusako. There was nothing for her to do here except show her disapproval of our primitive, country-bumpkin ways. That's why you brought her, I suppose?'

'Oh, Fumio, it wasn't meant like that at all.' They moved out of the servant's hearing. 'I simply wanted to show my new friend part of rural Japan – the "real" Japan, I sometimes think, that hasn't changed so radically. I realise now it was probably a mistake to bring her, especially at Bon Odori; but my intentions were good. Fumio, if only you'd try to understand . . .' She put a hand on her sleeve, but Fumio shook it off, saying. 'This is no time for talking. I'm busy and someone has come to see you – Genzo Yamaguchi, Ofuku's second son. I told him it's city hours you keep and were still asleep. So he's gone to the fields with Koichi. He'll be back soon.'

'I get up quite early in Tokyo,' Ryo said defensively. 'But I didn't sleep well last night.'

Fumio glanced slyly. 'You were screaming, Koichi told me, because there was a black dragonfly in your room.'

'Oh, it wasn't entirely due to that! But why has Genzo

363

come, exactly?'

'He'll tell you himself. He's taken with what he reads about city ways in the newspapers, like lots of the young men in these parts. Country life isn't good enough for them any more.'

'I think that's a shame,' Ryo murmured.

'But you're fond enough of the city yourself, so why shouldn't others be?'

'But I'm not always. I often feel drawn back to the life here, and so does Kenji. We're proud of our ancestral roots here, and one doesn't break from them without pain.'

Fumio sniffed. 'Nothing to be proud of here, nothing worth coming back for. Our lives are just a long, monotonous struggle against troubles and higher prices, and we know how luxuriously you live in Tokyo by comparison, I assure you. And being still unmarried you'll have no one to spend on but yourself, I suppose. As for Kenjiro's presents, I wonder he didn't think them altogether too good for the likes of us.'

'But you are our dear relatives; he wanted to give you things that you can't get easily in these parts.'

'And can't afford either. Nor can we afford to send presents anywhere near as costly in return – there's the rub.'

'Oh, sister-in-law, they don't want anything similar in return. Please explain to Kentaro that in these special circumstances . . .'

'Oh, Kentaro . . . he'll say nothing and do nothing. He never does. It always comes back on me – the burdens and responsibilities.'

As she moved towards the kitchen, bent shoulders stiff with rage, Ryo made a last plea. 'Fumio, please don't feel so aggrieved. If only you and Kentaro would come to Tokyo for a holiday and get to know Kenjiro's family properly I'm sure you'd begin to see things differently.'

'We've no time or money for such jaunts, Ryo, and we wouldn't feel at all comfortable with his foreign wife and newfangled ways. I'll have food sent in. You've missed the midday meal.'

Ryo wandered on to the verandah, her head throbbing

from a variety of unpleasant causes, and ate the food list-lessly, then fell into a half-doze of dispirited lethargy. She was roused by the sound of footsteps on the verandah and opened her eyes to see a sturdy young man approaching, bowing as he came.

'Miss Miyata, I think?'

'Why, it's Genzo Yamaguchi, of course. Please come in and sit down. I must apologise for not being ready when you arrived.'

He grinned slyly. 'City people sleep later, don't they?'

'Not always. But I feel I'm on holiday here. Now please tell me about yourself, Genzo; and how is your poor mother bearing her sad loss?'

'She is well enough and sends warm wishes to you and your brother, but didn't feel able to travel in this time of great heat.'

'And you are a married man yourself now, Genzo? It's hard to believe.'

He leaned forward and began speaking with an intensity that surprised her. 'Wife Akiko also sends regards. We have a baby girl and a boy very soon, I hope. Many mouths to feed; but now my older brother is head of the main house and there is little for me. I don't complain, but I see no way forward for myself here where folk live cramped like shellfish, thinking all is well and safe forever. Till one day they'll poke their heads out only to find themselves on the chopping board in a fish market! I'm not like them. I keep asking myself how the future will be in a few years when the railways arrive and there'll be telegraph poles marching across our valleys. My sons will wear school-caps like soldiers and learn scientific things and foreign tongues. They won't remain in these provincial backwaters even if I do. So why should I live out my time here like a frog in a paddy ditch seeing nothing but mud and one strip of sky? Many times I say all this to my mother until she's weary of my restless talking. "Oh, go and ask cousin Ryo if her brother can find work for you in the big capital, then," she said yesterday. I have some education. Perhaps I could become a salary-man in an office, sitting at a desk?' He stared at her with an expression of suppressed energetic rage against the world that reminded her of his grandfather . . . Gengoro's grandson. Perhaps this was the way to make amends and lay the ghosts forever?

'Genzo, I'm sure Kenjiro will try to help and so will I. But is it really what you want? The big city isn't a paradise. Millions struggle for survival there. Things are very costly; there's noise, dirt, and a closed-in feeling. You mightn't like it after all and you'd have to work very hard to succeed.'

He glared truculently. 'I work hard now, and for next to nothing; and I shall like it well enough.'

'And Akiko – does she want to move so far from home?'

'She's my wife and comes with me.'

Ryo nodded, wishing that Ofuku had accompanied this prickly, jumpy fellow who obviously disliked seeking advice from a mere woman. 'Then when I get back I'll . . .'

The door rattled clumsily and Millicent came padding heavily in.

'Phew, what heat! It's like the tropics . . . oh, sorry . . .'

Genzo stared at her in horrified curiosity and Ryo, introducing them, realised he had probably never engaged in conversation with a foreign woman before, and certainly did not intend doing so now, for he began backing off down the steps.

'Excuse me, I must get home before dark. No lights in the streets here, you know. Gas-lamps, they have in Tokyo, don't they? I read about them in the papers. Goodbye, cousin . . .'

'Oh, Genzo, need you . . .? Here wait, you must take Ofuku's present.'

While a servant fetched it, she promised that Kenjiro would contact him soon about work prospects, and with that assurance and the present under his arm he fled from the compound as if pursued by demons.

'Why ever did he rush off like that the moment I arrived?' Millicent asked peevishly. 'Really I'm beginning to think I have the plague, the way people . . .'

'Oh, please don't take it personally. It's just that young men like him are overcome with embarrassment when they find themselves alone with ladies – most especially foreign ones – because they aren't taught to converse with women at all outside their close family. It's a great failing in our society and perhaps if Genzo gets to Tokyo he'll learn better. That's what he came to see me about. Ironic, isn't it? The visit here has made me feel quite nostalgic for the peace and beauty of the countryside, while he's itching to get away, sit at a desk, and cut a dash under the gas-lamps.'

'Well, the grass is always greener, I suppose . . . I thought perhaps Fumio had warned him against me. I'm afraid I made her real angry this morning, though I didn't mean to . . .' She peered at Ryo anxiously.

'What happened? I should have been up to translate for you.'

'She was prettying up the god-shelf again, bobbing about, offering slices of fruit. It seemed so pathetic, Ryo. I just felt deeply sorry for her, living out her days in heathen darkness. So I fetched my Bible and showed her some pictures. She was quite polite at first, but then I tried to explain that the Bible is the Book of Truth and Salvation while her so-called god is nothing more than a meaningless gilded idol. Anyway, she grew angry and I couldn't make her understand. I'm sorry, Ryo. I know your relationship with your sister-in-law is difficult but I got carried away . . .'

'She's quite a devout Buddhist, Millicent, and I can't honestly blame her for being annoyed. You wouldn't like a guest in your house to try and convert you to another faith, would you?'

'But there's no comparison. Ours is the true faith and . . .'

Ryo rose, desperately wanting this protesting, penetrating foreign voice to cease. 'I know you didn't mean to offend.'

'No, I certainly didn't . . . Well, I guess I'll go and rest for a while; it was such a hot trudge back.' Millicent gathered up a clutter of souvenirs she had bought and went out, allowing Ryo to escape outside.

Ryo strolled across the compound, then, glancing round to make sure she was unobserved, slipped quickly through the outer gate and up the hill-track into the wood. The warm earth smelt fusty-moist as it always had and the leaf-shadows were dancing. The Shinto shrine of her childhood stood just as she remembered it, the stones a little more worn perhaps, grey-green lichens spread a little further over their rain-streaked surfaces. The banners beside the red *torii* arches hung limp on their poles; no flapping of cloth, no birdsong broke the late afternoon stillness. The shrine tables were bright with Bon Odori offerings – lotus flowers, sweetmeats, slices of melon – and the guardian foxes crouched much smaller than she remembered, quaint rather than sinister.

She perched on the pillar beside the one with a ball under its paw and stroked its nose gently as if it were a beloved dog. The bronze was still warm from the day's heat and the warmth flooded through her fingertips to her heart like a benison. It seemed as if the old gods, the spirits of the ancient warriors that dwelt there, had not quite cast her out after all, and neither had she them. But even as she stroked, the metal began to cool, the silence to become more oppressive as if it welled from the depths of nature itself – a neutral, infinite emptiness. Hot tears of memory scalded her eyes as she visualised the child she had once been, running along that path between the red arches in her faded country cottons and wooden pattens, half fearful and half joyous, something of a solitary outcast even then.

As she rose to leave, the image of Ryo as child dissolved into her adult self, who was now an alien in this once-familiar setting that she had discarded for a more intrusive and personal creed. Gingerly she touched the nose of the snarling fox, and it did not bite her; daring, challenging, she gave the bell-rope a quick tug, and the sound drifted away from her as sweetly as it always did. A faint breeze had risen as she walked back along the path, making the banners and poles flap and creak in mocking farewell. As she emerged from the woods she saw the first blazing of distant fires that were lit at the end of Bon Odori to guide the spirits on their return journey to the Land of the Dead, and she felt as if a portion of her own spirit had also gone away and been lost.

To mark the end of Bon Odori and their visit, Fumio served

a banquet that evening: garnished sea bream and lobsters, prawns with almonds, lotus roots and baked sweet potatoes. Kentaro drank flasks of *saké* and reminisced about long-ago days when he used to ride and wrestle with the other samurai lads. It was a great pity, he claimed, that nothing of the kind went on nowadays; the loyal spirit of the clan had vanished; boys crouched at school desks all day trying to outwit each other.

'Even our young women are told not to blacken their teeth when they marry because it's unhealthy,' he added gloomily.

'Unhealthy, huh! Look at me – nothing wrong with me, is there?' Fumio interrupted her husband, who continued unnoticing, 'The government won't leave us alone, sending out inspectors telling us to do this and not that. Why, they even sent a man round recently to explain how we should grow our rice!'

'Better strains of rice,' Koichi added, 'with fertilisers and new kinds of ploughshares to till the ground.'

Ryo nodded non-committally, determined not to quarrel with her brother on this last evening. So harmony was maintained and, as they retired, Kentaro, flushed with drink, bowed elaborately, saying what an honour it had been to accommodate a foreign lady and a headmistress from the great capital in their humble abode, while Fumio sniffed her disapproval in the background.

They left quite early the next morning in hired rickshaws loaded with their remarkable quantity of luggage and the 'poor' presents pressed upon them – packets of locally grown tea and tobacco, jars of camphor oil and gingko nuts, pieces of Korean pottery and a framed photograph of Junji in his peaked school-cap. Millicent and Ryo sat in preoccupied silence as the rickshaw runners, near-nude and sweaty as before, trundled them through the valleys.

The visit, more stressful than either had foreseen, had particularly disturbed Ryo. Her usual equilibrium, based on the Christian faith, which had seemed so rock-firm at the recent conference in Kyoto, had been badly shaken – and by what? Temple-dancing, a Shinto shrine in a wood, a black dragonfly? It was embarrassing, shaming, and frightening. At a time when she needed all her reserves of strength, she had been made to feel insecure, as vulnerable as the country girl who, in her imagination, ran again and again along that stone path between the *torii* arches as if trying to catch up with dignified Miss Miyata of the spectacles and neatly coiled hair, a headmistress in the nation's capital. Her spirit quailed at the thought of what lay ahead and she sat rigid, hands tight-clenched in her lap, staring at, but not really seeing, the familiar landscape.

Millicent, watching, partly understood the reasons for her tension. She too had been shocked from her usual calm by the very fervour and prevalence of what it pleased her to call 'primitive superstitions' and their hold on the family. Until she had come to Japan the 'heathen world' had been to her but a dark wilderness waiting to be conquered by the light of Christianity. But now she had witnessed its own matter-of-fact, deep-rooted reality she began to comprehend for the first time what drastic steps Ryo had taken in her life.

As they neared Kagoshima, Millicent ventured, 'You mustn't worry Ryo. He will show you the way. You have only to put your trust in Him.'

Ryo stared back glassily, then muttered, 'But do I deserve His trust in me, I wonder?'

'Why of course, of course. You are being very brave, have already been very brave. I see that more clearly now.'

'I don't feel in the least brave at the moment. And I'm not sure I even want to be.'

Millicent patted her clenched fist. 'We all feel like that sometimes, dear. We do, you know – every single struggling soul of us.'

Ryo stiffened her back, staring ahead at the sparkling bay in which the Nagasaki-bound steamer rode at anchor. She could not say any more. So much was inexplicable.

CHAPTER EIGHTEEN

Ryo Miyata sat at her desk wondering which of her staff would be the least incompetent to teach her young pupils the rudiments of English poetry. None of them was sufficiently fluent in the language, but several parents had written to request it. The recitation of foreign verse was considered something of a social asset for girls, whether or not its meaning was understood. Within strictly defined limits female education had become fashionable among the upper-middle classes, and the Empress Haraku herself, a patroness of Japan's first women's college, had expressed pleasure in Ryo's appointment. This had been a proud highlight during the first difficult months in her new post.

One of her greatest difficulties was the making of decisions and now, as on several past occasions, she postponed doing so, re-reading instead a letter from an irate father vigorously opposing a recent suggestion that western-style uniforms be adopted by the pupils. The dress of foreign females was unbecoming and vulgar, he wrote, and allowed girls to move about in such an indecorous and immodest manner that they no longer learned the correct, lady-like control of their limbs. This letter also put Ryo in a quandary, for she had a sneaking sympathy with the writer's viewpoint, though she also wanted her girls to look and feel 'modern'. She was trying to draft a tactful reply when a maid announced the arrival of Mrs Miyata.

'My dear, how very commanding you look behind that desk. Quite the captain on the bridge – when everyone else has gone home, too.'

371

Ryo smiled faintly, knowing Elinor was trying to be kind. 'It's my job. Let me send for tea?'

'Please, it's freezing . . . Winter's really here.' She sat down, loosening her fur collar.

'And how are the hospital plans progressing?'

'Well, I think. Arnold and I had a meeting with the architects the other day.' She and her brother had initiated a fundraising campaign for a Red Cross hospital with a training section for female nursing aides; it was the sort of thing they were good at. 'And how have you been? We haven't seen you for ages. I've come to invite you to stay for the weekend; we all want to see you.'

'Oh, I've been so busy, tackling various prickly problems . . . The question of etiquette classes, for instance. How much time should be spent these days teaching girls how to close a sliding screen in the most decorous manner, I wonder? But thank you, I'd love to come.'

As they sipped tea, Elinor broached the real object of her visit. 'There's a slight difficulty about Hannah. It's bound to come up at the weekend and I wanted to talk to you first. You see, she's getting rather restless and wants to do something useful, but the Red Cross fund doesn't much appeal, unfortunately. She wonders if she could do some English teaching – here or in one of the other girls' schools?'

'But Ellie, how amazing! The answer to my fervent prayer. I'm desperately searching for someone capable of taking poetry classes and she'd be absolutely perfect. I can employ her every day if she wishes. The salary won't be large, but something . . .'

'And her own money! She'd love that, and I can well understand how she feels. The trouble is, Kenjiro's set against it. She's had quite a good education, a world tour, and now the next obvious step is definitely marriage and the sooner the better in his view. Men – fathers especially – are so one-track about such matters, aren't they? As I pointed out, I was twenty-five when I married him, and made an independent choice against all the odds, which I've never regretted. I'll never forget either how uneasy I felt when I was engaged to

372

poor Reggie Bradshaw – the wrong man – and secretly I knew it. But he was socially acceptable, everyone approved . . . Thank goodness it never happened! But now we must allow our own daughter an equal amount of leeway and not put too much pressure on her; I'm sure you agree?'

'And he would deny it her?'

'Well, he wouldn't put it that way, but yes . . . Looking back, I can see that when we decided to marry he was so involved in what he was giving up for me, his own leap into the foreign dark, and I was equally self-absorbed. So now, when I try to explain Hannah's situation, it doesn't awaken any echoes for him, though it does for me. He simply wants his beautiful, beloved, and – we have to acknowledge it – racially mixed daughter to make a good match. Before the best of the pickings are snapped up, to put it crudely. He sees eligible young men getting married to her friends and worries on her behalf. But if he mentions the matter to Hannah she simply withdraws, in her fashion. I believe she's suggested teaching partly to escape the strain. Ryo, Kenjiro is your dearest brother and my dearest husband, and I hope you don't think I'm being disloyal; but I felt I had to explain this confidentially. He may well put obstacles in her way, and I think you should know that it's not because he's against you or the school. It's just that, being Japanese, he can't actually visualise Hannah as having any kind of half-independent life, even for a short time.'

Ryo turned down her lips. 'Oh, I understand dear, only too well! Has he ever been able to accept my independence? No. I'm a freak in his eyes and in society's generally, and I'm sure his worst fear is that his daughter could end up an "old miss" like her aunt.'

Elinor paused; for that was exactly how Kenjiro had often expressed it. 'Oh, Ryo, it's not that bad, and in any case I'm not for a moment suggesting Hannah should never marry; indeed I devoutly hope she will.'

'But, as you say, she should have breathing space, and coming here to teach might give it her – if that's what she wants.'

Elinor stood up. 'She certainly does and between us we'll see she gets it, won't we?' She smiled at her sister-in-law. 'Must dash — another formal dinner tonight. I get so wearied by them — the people one has to meet but never know.'

'I can imagine, or can I? It's quite lonely being a head, I'm finding out, so it will be splendid to have Hannah for company. She'll stay in the bungalow with me, of course?'

'During the week, perhaps, though I shall miss her.' Elinor sighed. In the past she had been jealous of Hannah's attachment to her aunt, yet had encouraged it, as compensation to Ryo for her unmarried state, about which she had always felt guilty. Now she seemed to be encouraging it afresh, but it had to be done for Hannah's future good. 'Then that's agreed. Can she come back with you after the weekend? It's best to settle such things quickly. By the way, Kenjiro's just heard from that young Genzo Yamaguchi whom you met. He and his wife Akiko are coming to Tokyo in a few months, after the birth of the next child. Kenjiro's promised to find him an office desk somewhere.'

Ryo stared glumly at her own paper-covered one. 'Trappings of a little brief authority — it's what he desperately wants; but I don't think I ever did, not really.'

Elinor squeezed her arm. 'My dear, I know; but think what good you can accomplish with it. See you for lunch on Saturday.'

That weekend Kenjiro reluctantly capitulated to the arguments advanced by the women of the family, but Hannah's move to Ryo's school had a disadvantage none of them had foreseen; Walter Munro and Oliver Rayne lived near by and immediately inveigled her more closely into their circle. Nor was Hannah averse to being so inveigled, glad of an occasional escape from the school's earnest missionary ambience. Their favourite haunt was the entertainment quarter of Asakusa, and Oliver whisked her off there one evening to join Joey and some friends at a restaurant.

Townspeople were milling aimlessly about the streets, content just to be out and about with others of their kind, and groups of pilgrims were also there to view the famous temples and spit 'lucky' paper pellets at the huge red and green guardians of the gates. Stalls, propped against the temple's outer walls, sold trinkets, roast chestnuts, toys, and boiled red beans, and the neighbouring alleys were lined with show booths behind whose purple curtains you could, for a price, see performing snakes, monkeys or dogs, masked dancers, jugglers, transvestites chanting recitatives, and men running up ladders with naked swords for rungs. Outside one, a brown-faced hunchback dressed in gold brocade was imitating bird noises to attract custom; next door, giggling, painted girls in an archery gallery beckoned to Oliver, calling, 'Come on, hairy-chested foreigner, come and shoot your big arrows into me . . .'

Oliver smiled back, uncomprehending, won over by the light-hearted, bubbling mood of the place. Often he envied these people their joyous community of spirit, longing to be carried away on its tide; but he was ever an outsider among them, and the cautious tug of his upbringing held him back. 'What are they saying?' he asked Hannah, who blushed.

'I'd rather not tell you. It wasn't very polite . . .'

He squeezed her hand. 'Sorry . . . Look, what's happening there?'

'Oh, they're building the Twelve-Storey Tower of Asakusa; it will be the highest in the city.'

'But what's it for?'

'Just for the view – isn't that enough?'

They left the temple area for quieter ways, where firemen, barbers, grocers, cooks and their families lived in small houses with low picket fences, and hawkers were shuffling about trying to sell them fried eels and brown-sugar cakes. Here the rickshawman lost his way and it was late before they reached the Fisherman's Lantern Restaurant, a modest establishment from outside, but with a clientèle of discriminating gourmets inside feasting in a honeycomb of tiny matted rooms. In one, Joey and his guests – Walter and Hyacinth, Emiko Hattori and her brother Ogai – were already eating. As Hannah and Oliver came in, Ogai, a student at the Imperial University, was in full rhetorical flood.

'. . . the government is simply holding on, not wanting the

375

boat rocked as usual. What do they care about more rights for the people, who might then threaten their authority? Unless we get a true socialist movement here with the masses behind it, nothing will really change, not even when we get our so-called democratically elected Parliament . . . you'll see . . .' He turned briskly to Oliver. 'I've read there are terrible slum districts in English cities where the down-trodden live, Mr Rayne . . . Is this so, may I ask?'

Oliver dabbed his face with a warm towel, a little flummoxed by the sudden challenge. 'Well yes, there are . . . though I can't say that I . . . In any case, that doesn't necessarily mean . . .'

'It means similar districts will soon exist here. They've started already, and we too will have cities full of oppressed millions slaving for the new capitalists. Your so-called western liberalism is a sham, Mr Rayne, and is based on nothing but brute force. It's force that keeps the poor and weak under the heel of the strong and wealthy, just as it keeps the countries of Asia under the tyranny of the rich and powerful West.'

'May we eat something, I'm hungry,' Hannah murmured plaintively, and Joey signalled the waiter, whispering to Oliver, 'The trouble is that Ogai's older brother usually keeps him under control with his own brand of political diatribe. But he's gone down with influenza. Why not see what you can do?'

'Well I'm no political theorist, but . . .' He downed two cups of *saké* quickly and, in the hope of impressing Hannah, challenged, 'It seems to me, Ogai, that if you Japanese want western goods you have to raise the money to pay for them. And how better than by manufacturing things in your own factories that the world wants?'

Ogai turned on him fiercely. 'The most obvious capitalist trap – creating more expensive needs and tastes among the people so they compete with each other like fighting cocks in a ring for every miserable penny, instead of uniting to fight the privileged few who sit on the side-lines quiet and tight with the real wealth in their pockets. But just because your society works like that, it doesn't mean ours has to. It's a cruel, heartless system, Mr Rayne, and not nearly as civilised as you westerners would have us believe. Why, your own Mr Disraeli has spelled out the dangers. You in Britain have two nations – the rich and the poor – as a result of your industrial revolution. And he calls on you, the youth of England, to change these evils and inequalities, and we young men of Meiji must make sure they don't develop here.'

Walter spluttered through mouthfuls of fried prawns, 'So what are we doing here? Why aren't we at home fighting for the causes of righteousness?'

'Because I believe your father is a ship-owner, Mr Munro? So it wouldn't be in your personal interest for those who actually build his ships to earn decent money for their labours, would it? You're one of the privileged.'

'May be so now,' Walter retorted languidly. 'But in the first place my father wasn't born with a silver spoon. He earned his money through enterprise and the hard work you admire, and others can do the same. At any rate, what makes you think that, if the poor of today became rich, they'd behave any differently? Oppression is as much a part of basic human nature as altruism – and greed – in my view.'

'No, sir. The accumulation of too much wealth corrupts, I grant you, but . . .'

'Oh, do be quiet a minute, Ogai,' Joey interrupted crossly. 'Exercise your jaws on these delicious sticky dumplings instead. I'm giving this supper, which is supposed to celebrate my election to the Quill and Inkstone Society, and I've hardly had a chance to say a word!'

'The *what* Society?' Hannah asked.

'You heard. I've written two stories for their magazine which have been accepted, so now I can join.' He raised his cup to his sister with a defiant grin. 'You see, I've found my destiny at last! I'm going to be a novelist. Not your tedious Disraeli type, puffed up with abstract theories and Utopian dreams. The real job of the novelist is to explore the crevasses of the individual heart, the absurdities of passion, the mysteries of the soul. And that's what I intend to do.' He drank with a flourish.

'Well, that sounds like a lifetime's work, and good luck.'
Walter saluted affably. 'But will you find a publisher, I
wonder?'

'Oh, there's a vogue for such stories just now, especially
about the passionate, sensitive nature of Japanese women,
which is my next subject. It's a pity you can't read Japanese,
Walt.'

'Why only Japanese? Aren't the natures of women everywhere more passionate and sensitive in their understanding
of humankind than those of men?' Oliver glanced adoringly
at Hannah, who pulled a face. 'You're a romantic idealist,
Oliver, and so is my brother, I suspect. Men like you want to
believe that women possess such qualities — from the safe
distance of your masculinity, of course, while we women get
all the hurt of the condition.'

Joey chortled. 'I told you my sister was heartless! But what
is life without love and passion, oh beautiful Hannah? "He
who has not experienced love is like a tree before Spring
comes, a chick in a shell, a . . ." '

'Oh, Joey, what do you know about it, anyway? You're
simply describing yourself,' Emiko protested quietly while
Joey continued, heedless, 'But I don't intend to fall in love. I
shall merely observe others doing so and describe their toils
and tribulations. And I shall be supported by a wealthy
heiress who will find my many charms irresistible.'

Ogai finished the last of the *saké* and rose unsteadily.
'What a useless sort of life you plan for yourself, Joey!
Writing books about kissing and cuddling — horrible sticky
western habits . . . Honestly, I don't know why I waste my
time with such as you.'

Joey flushed angrily. 'It's not a waste of time to search out
what really matters to people and alters their lives — and
that's seldom political theories. And we have enough of those
around just now to float several battleships — and battleships
will probably be floated on them, what's more. But we haven't
nearly enough insight into our own hearts and minds.'

'Oh, hearts, hearts . . . well, you stick to your last and I to mine and we'll see who comes out on top.' Ogai bowed, thanking him for the meal. 'Now if you'll excuse me, I must return to my useless studies.'

'What a bore he can be!' Joey exclaimed when he had disappeared. Nevertheless, Ogai's combative presence had been the leaven of the evening and; after a final toast to Joey, the party broke up.

To his chagrin, Oliver could not find a double rickshaw to hire for the return journey and had to trundle in a separate one, jumping out to bid Hannah good night at the school gate.

'I do hope you enjoyed the evening? It's hard to know what pleases you, sometimes.' He glanced at her shyly.

'Oh, it was all right. But I get tired of you men arguing while we women are supposed to just listen politely.'

'But I didn't argue much.' He caught her hand. 'You were the one I really wanted to talk to and be with . . . Just the two of us, I mean. I think we have a lot in common, you and I – a sort of seriousness, an underlying reserve, which is partly why I'm so attracted to you.'

She stroked his fingers. 'Are you serious, Oliver? You don't often give that impression.'

'Oh, impressions, impressions – sketchy lines on a sheet of paper for people to recognise us by. So I draw the frivolous, talented young Bohemian. But I'm not. At least, I hope I'm talented; I am serious about that. Only I need time to find out.' He frowned at her. 'And you need time to find out what you can do and be, don't you? I love your . . . hesitations.' She looked into his eyes as he drew her to him. 'Darling Hannah, let me try to paint you when spring comes. Not that I'd be able to capture an iota of your radiant loveliness, but . . .'

She rubbed her cheek against his. 'Oh, Oliver, don't spoil it! That sounds like a line from one of Joey's unpublished and unpublishable novels. No – you must draw my hesitations so the world can recognise them.'

He nodded, clutching her more urgently against him. 'Oh, Hannah, but you *are* lovely too. And if you would just agree to . . .'

A trifle breathlessly she disengaged herself. 'But I'm not

379

ready to agree to anything, and that is what you say you like.'
She kissed him lightly on the cheek. 'There! Good night,
Oliver, and thank you for the evening.' He managed only to
brush her lips with his warm mouth as she slipped away.

After he left Hannah that evening Oliver's spirits were
high – on *saké* and Joey's praise of passion, that nurtured his
secret dream of winning Hannah's love. But next day he fell
victim to the prevailing influenza epidemic and was perfunctorily looked after by Hyacinth, whose only remedy was to
heat water on the stove and tell him to inhale the steam. For
days he lay inert, dozily watching the white wraiths swirl
from the spout of the bronze kettle, with its inlaid design of
dragons disporting themselves among clouds, and coil round
the gilded Buddha on the god-shelf. The whole world had
become wraith-like and insubstantial, and he resigned his
low-fallen spirits to the final Nirvana, haunted not by visions
of the lovely Hannah, but by memories of his dead mother.

Distanced by time and place, he perceived far more clearly
the unhappy bleakness of Honoria's life while he and Letty
were growing up. Sadly he mourned the long waste of her
elegant beauty, intelligence, and occasional sly wit. What a
dazzling hostess she would have made for the right husband;
how graciously she could have queened it over a circle of
friends with musical taste! But instead she had eked out her
days in that cramped terrace house, which was always chilly,
as if incurably pervaded by that Hakodate cold which, she
used to claim, had frozen up her soul for ever.

Oliver's melancholy reveries were interrupted one morning
by Hyacinth, who came in with a bag of dried peas, which
she proceeded to scatter in the room's corners. It was the
feast of Setsubin, she explained, which marked the end of
winter, the year's darkest period, when demons lurked close.
But demons, for some unfathomable reason, had a strong aver-
sion to dried peas and, as spring began, would flee the house
at the sight of one. Illnesses also vanished miraculously at
this season, she assured him, and he would soon feel better.
Oliver chuckled at the absurdity of it and felt his spirits rising
almost immediately. Why shackle himself in the sad past when

he should be using the best qualities inherited from his mother to his own advantage, as she would have wished? He determined to be as charming, stylish, artistically successful as she should have been and, with a boldness all his own, vowed also to pry out the mystery of his father's death, that its shadows might flee from him like demons from a dried pea.

In purely practical terms, he needed a supply of ready cash to carry out his grand ideas, and so, once he had recovered sufficient strength, he went to visit Sylvia Fortescue. She was delighted to see him again, for he and Walter were the only 'real' artists of her acquaintance and her artistic circle had languished somewhat recently, without their inspiration. To encourage him, several of its members commissioned Oliver to paint 'Japanese' portraits of servants dressed up in the garb of beggars, rickshaw-pullers, samurai, or geisha girls, and for Sylvia he painted Grace, dressed in a kimono, holding a fan, posed behind a vase of carefully arranged plum blossom in the conservatory – it was still too chilly to pose outdoors. The portrait required three sittings and Oliver was secretly bored and displeased with it long before he finally put down his brush with a sigh of relief.

'There – I'm afraid it's the best I can do, Sylvia. I'm not satisfied with it, but then artists never are.' He held up the canvas proudly nevertheless and Grace rushed to inspect it closely.

'Oooh, isn't it lovely, Mummy? Don't I look pretty? That's winter me, isn't it? Mr Rayne can paint spring me under the cherry trees and summer me under . . . what do you think?' She pirouetted, her fine blonde hair shining in the light, displaying her blossoming nubility to give him fresh inspiration for these further endeavours.

Sylvia clucked indulgently. 'You're a vain little minx, Gracie. What a coquette she'll be one day, Oliver!'

'I expect so,' he agreed without enthusiasm, for he was not inspired by Grace's charm nor by the more mature version possessed by her mother, who now stood very close to him admiring the painting. Even on a cool day Sylvia seemed over-warm, the dimpled flesh dampish to the touch. He moved away, slightly but unobtrusively, for he guessed that she rather fancied herself as his artistic inspiration and even as an object of his youthful ardour. It would be foolish, in the circumstances, to disillusion her.

'Now go and take off that pretty kimono, Gracie, before you get it dirty. Mr Rayne has many other subjects worthy of his brush, you know.'

Indeed he had, Oliver thought, flopping into a basket chair and staring through the conservatory glass at the grey-blue sky. He had no desire whatever to paint solid pink-and-white Englishness, aspiring rather to capture the fleeting beauty of bamboos fading into twilit hillsides, birds into pale horizons, fish into limpid waters – that subtle suggestion of space beyond and harmony within which seemed to him the essence of the oriental genius.

Sylvia returned with a tray. 'I've assumed you'd like coffee, Oliver? And please give me your account for the picture. Oh, it must be absolutely marvellous to paint! I've always longed to do something creative; but what a hope!' She plumped into the opposite chair, wishing, as she often did, that she had sprung from less common clay. 'Was your mother artistic?'

'She was very musical and encouraged me towards art. She didn't want me to become "just an ordinary sort of fellow".' He grimaced painfully, remembering his mother's voice, and reached to tap a purple and scarlet fuchsia flower that swung like a bell at his touch. 'My mother was very fond of fuchsias and grew them in our conservatory . . .' No larger than a greenhouse, he realised suddenly, just room for that tattered wicker chair and the round table marked with stains of flower-pots and watering cans. Fuggy in summer, draughty in winter, but she had loved it. 'She used to cut the plants back very hard, disciplining them. It was amazing they survived, I used to think.' Inside his head that firm chip-chop of secateurs cutting off jaunty shoots that had looked so promising; Letty used to stroke the amputated stems afterwards to make them feel better. He glanced round admiringly. 'Your plants are positively profuse by comparison.'

'They wouldn't be if the gardener had his way. The Japs

will lop off, cut back . . . those poor crippled bonsai. But I insist on something rather wilder . . . I love things that trail a little, don't you?' She glowed cosily at him, smoothing a wayward tendril of pink fuchsia against her pink cheek.

'Oh, I'm all in favour of trailing!' He smiled back uneasily, thinking it was time to leave.

'Your poor mother! It must have been very difficult for her, bringing up two children alone. My mother-in-law apparently met her a few times in the 'sixties; a striking-looking woman, she wrote.'

'She was, yes. At least until near the end. She stopped cutting the plants back. That was what made me realise she was ill. A wasting disease. Quite a jungle, our little conservatory was by the time she died . . . Well, I really must go.' He got up, handing her his bill. 'I hate to do this, Sylvia, when you're so helpful and hospitable. But even artists have to eat.'

'Think nothing of it, dear boy. And I shall think of the large profits I'll make when the works of Oliver Rayne are world famous and everyone will realise at last what discriminating taste I have.'

He shuddered in the knowledge that people's opinion of her 'taste' was her prime consideration, then stared without scruple at the bill in her hand.

She followed his gaze. 'Could you bear to wait for the money till we next meet? Which will be very soon, I hope. There's the cherry blossoms next, as Grace says.'

'Quite honestly, Sylvia, I don't see cherries and Grace as an ideal combination. A little too much pink and white – verging on the sugary? The cherry is best suited to glossy black hair, an olive pallor of skin, a hint of the oriental dark . . .'

'Ah, young man, how wistful and warm you suddenly sound! You can't fool me, you know . . .' She tweaked his ear sharply as he moved towards the door. 'So who is she, this cherry-blossom divinity?'

He looked charmingly rueful. 'Well, I confess – Miss Hannah Miyata. You know her, of course? An unusual kind of beauty – not my personal type, you understand; but my artistic eye is intrigued. And . . . to confess further, I have your cherry-tree arbour in mind as a perfect backdrop. That dragon aunt of hers keeps her on a close rein, but if she were to come here, then I . . .'

Sylvia pouted, for this go-between role was not how she envisaged their growing relationship. 'But does the young lady want her portrait painted?'

'She's willing, but stipulates that no one must be told till it's finished so, if it's too dreadful, she can cut it into a thousand pieces.'

'That sounds rather cruel.'

'Oh, she is – quite dreadfully heartless. Her brother says so and I shall depict her thus – cruelty under the cherry blossoms.' He laughed lightly, thinking that his real desire was to touch rather than paint Hannah's flesh, explore her, burrow into the very core of that cruelty, if it existed. 'Dear Sylvia, I must go. Your worthy husband will be home shortly and he doesn't much like your Bohemian friends, does he?'

'Oh, he's just jealous of your *insouciance*.' She pronounced the word carefully, in the French manner. 'But he does like that Kuniyoshi print Walter got for me. Can't you possibly find me some more? Everyone admires it.'

'I'll see what I can do, but they're hard to come by and going up in price . . . Now about Hannah Miyata; if you'd prefer not, then would you mind frightfully sending me the money before too long?'

'Oh, you shall have your cherry-bower assignment, you naughty boy.' She slapped his sleeve as he touched her cheek.

'Sylvia, it's not like that at all. But thank you most awfully. And I'll be in touch about the how and when . . .'

It was a cold spring; the cherries bloomed late and were torn early from the trees by chill winds that sent shoals of petals drifting along the River Sumida in Tokyo. One more high wind and there would not have been a petal left to pose under, as Sylvia said to Hannah when she arrived on the first warm afternoon for the portrait painting. She was wearing a leaf-and-water-patterned kimono and looked, as Sylvia generously said, as pretty as a picture already.

'How kind of you, Mrs Fortescue. As to the picture, I don't

really know why I agreed; but Oliver was so persistent.'

'He can be – when he's set his heart on something.' She rolled her eyes roguishly. 'I'm surprised he didn't come with you.'

'He'd business in the town and promised to meet me here – by now, in fact.'

'Then we'll sit indoors until he comes. And how is your mother? I seldom see her these days.'

'She had a trying winter, I'm afraid. The youngsters went down with that 'flu and she was terribly worried because she lost a baby son of it years ago. They've recovered, but she's taking them to our country cottage soon to get thoroughly fit.'

'And your handsome father?'

'Even busier than usual, with the elections coming in July. He's concerned that our present rulers will lose control; but my brother Joey supports the more radical parties, so they have frightful arguments. I find it so hard to actually believe in politicians; do you, Mrs Fortescue?'

'Oh, I simply leave the whole business to the men, my dear. They won't let us have any say, after all.'

'No, and that's what's so unfair and wrong. Miss Pilcher, an American friend of my aunt's, declares herself a suffragist and has opened my eyes a lot. Why shouldn't we vote for our leaders as men do? We are just as able to think for ourselves and often more sensibly than they. But there's simply no question of women citizens voting in the coming elections.'

Sylvia blinked in amazement. 'My dear young lady, why on earth bother about such matters? We women are not mentally capable or physically constituted to cope with the hurly-burly of public life. Why, I was reading an article in some English magazine recently which said as much. It was signed by that famous woman novelist, Mrs Humphrey Ward, too.'

Hannah snorted. 'Oh, she's a traitor to her sex! But in America, Miss Pilcher says, brave women travel round lecturing in the cause of women's rights and . . .'

'Ah, here he is at last!' Sylvia jumped up. 'Did you know your cherry-blossom damsel is something of a suffragist, Oliver? I don't think that fits very well into your ideal picture.'

Oliver paused on the threshold. 'Oh . . . that . . . Yes, I've heard some of her strange ideas. Good afternoon, Hannah, sorry I'm late. Shall we go straight into the garden while the light's still good?'

He stalked out and Sylvia shrugged at Hannah as they followed him. Oliver set up his easel and opened his box in silence, waving Hannah towards the cherry trees round the belvedere on a knoll overlooking the bay.

'But where exactly do you want me to stand?' She prowled restlessly.

'Under that trailing branch on the left or . . .' He sorted through his brushes.

'Or? . . . Please get on and tell me, Oliver. I don't much like posing anyway.' Irritably she began plucking petals, throwing them upwards, watching them swirl and float against the blue sky. Their very beauty lightened her mood and she swayed into a graceful dance as she plucked and tossed, singing in Japanese,

> *'I am a cherry child, goddess of the cherry tree*
> *spirit of the Cherry River.*
> *The blossoms, flowers, snow and waves —*
> *I see them all and scoop them up.'*

'What are you singing?' He was still fiddling aimlessly with his brushes.

'It's the song of some mad unhappy woman in a Noh play. But come on, Oliver! You're the one who was so eager to get me here and now I obviously don't inspire you in the least. My heartless hesitations are supposed to, if nothing else. Paint me with my fangs showing if you wish, but please start something.'

He hunched over the canvas and Sylvia came up, touching his shoulder.

'Oliver, aren't you well? I thought you looked rather pale when you arrived.'

He groaned and threw his brushes on the grass, burying his head in his hands. 'I'm sorry, Sylvia, sorry, Hannah . . . I simply can't today . . . You see, I've just discovered something so terrible . . .'

Hannah hurried over to him. 'Oliver, what is it?'

For answer he took from his pocket a yellowed piece of paper and handed it to her. She read aloud, 'Mr Harold Rayne, formerly British Consul at Hakodate and recently sentenced to twelve years' imprisonment by the Yokohama Court of Justice on charges of fraud and desecration of native graves, was found hanging in his prison cell in the early hours of this morning. Foul play is not suspected.' Above the notice, which he had torn surreptitiously from the files, Oliver had written: '*Japan Herald*, Sept. 25th, 1869.'

'Oh, dear heaven . . . your father comm . . .' Sylvia laid her arm over his bent shoulders. 'My poor dear boy.'

He straightened, shaking her off, twisting his mouth. 'It explains why there's nothing but his name on his grave. That had nagged at me for months. This morning I finally decided to search the old newspapers before coming here. I rather wish I hadn't, now.'

Hannah re-read the notice. 'And did you discover anything else?'

'A lot . . . too much. I read reports of his trial held a few weeks previously. Apparently he'd been robbing Ainu graves and selling the bones to various scientific societies. "A most bizarre felony," someone said in court. I could hardly believe it at first . . . My father.' He bit his knuckles.

'And your mother never told you anything?'

'Not a word. Which explains too why she hated this country and forbade me to come here.'

'Your poor, poor mother!'

'Yes . . . but she went away and left him, didn't she? To face it all alone. She didn't stand by him; and I should think that's why he killed himself. And she must have felt guilty ever after.' He looked from one to the other, agonised.

'Yes, she must, and yet − she had two children to think about. Perhaps that's why . . . Oh, what a terrible situation . . . Why, I'm nearly in tears just imagining it.' Sylvia dabbed her eyes. 'Come inside and let's have a nice cup of tea, Oliver.'

He gathered up his scattered brushes. 'No thank you, Sylvia. I just want to go away alone and think. I'm sorry; I thought I could pretend nothing had happened, but it was too much . . .'

'My dear, of course, you couldn't and shouldn't. We're friends and it's right for you to tell us.'

'But I don't want a lot of people to know. Not after all these years.'

'I shan't breathe a word,' Sylvia promised fervently and Hannah added her assurance, asking, 'Your poor father though; didn't he even defend himself?'

'Not much. He did claim that the first instigator of the whole sordid business was another man, an amateur scientist called Felix Coburn.'

'What name did you say?' Hannah halted as they were crossing the lawn.

'Felix Coburn. Father obviously loathed him for some reason and kept trying to implicate him. But he couldn't make the charges stick. Coburn was just a silly young man with science on the brain, one lawyer said. He sounded quite a decent sort, in fact. Have you heard of him then?'

'The name sounded vaguely familiar,' Hannah muttered. 'But poor Oliver! What a terrible shock . . . perhaps a brandy instead of tea?'

'No thanks; I'd really rather disappear for a while, and leave the canvas here for a happier day if I may, Sylvia?'

'Why, of course, dear. We'll get you a jinricky . . .'

The fussing women escorted him to the little vehicle and Oliver curled up inside, not wanting to be seen. As it was a Friday afternoon, several of the offices closed early and a number of fresh-faced young men of about Oliver's age were hurrying to cricket and rowing practices. Oliver gazed at them, thinking they looked just the 'ordinary sort of fellows' his mother had hoped he would never become . . . But, oh, how grand just then to have been an ordinary fellow bowling off to sports practice on a warm spring evening, with nice, ordinary, loving and law-abiding parents somewhere in the background!

Shaking himself free of self-pity, he began to consider Letty, who depended on him for comfort. Should he tell her the truth about their father, who had swung in a prison cell in this very port over twenty years ago? They had said some terrible things about Harold Rayne in that courtroom and Oliver shuddered as he thought of them and the burden of silence his mother had borne for so long. Now it was his turn to bear it and he, the elder brother, would continue to shield Letty from the shaming truth. It was, he felt, the least he could do.

CHAPTER NINETEEN

After the cherry blossoms came the wisteria, followed by June's irises. The best times and places for flower-viewing were printed in the capital's newspapers, as usual. But in that summer of 1890 the papers were most unusually lively with debates about 'people's rights' and the holding of the nation's first ever general election, on July 1st. Only one person in a hundred was actually eligible to vote and the government was still controlled by men of the Satsuma, Choshiu, and Tosa clans, who had seized power after the Restoration. Nevertheless, Japan now had its Parliament, and to those of the Tempo generation this was a triumph in itself, proof of a developing democracy, of progress beyond the 'backward feudalism' of neighbouring countries.

Kenjiro, sitting in his drawing-room a few days after the election and reading press commentaries on the final results, felt proud and pleased that it had all gone off smoothly, even though – with ten parties in the new House of Representatives – he foresaw that the opening sessions would be stormy. He wandered restlessly about, feeling hot and uncomfortable, for, as he was expecting visitors, he had not changed into his customary cool *yukata*. His older children were out; the younger ones away with Elinor at their cottage. He stretched his tired back and massaged his aching limbs, promising them a treat later. The thought pleased him and, summoning a maid, he ordered a box of the best chocolates to be sent up from the German confectioners to take out with him after his visitors had gone.

'I think they've just arrived, sir.' She bowed. 'They came in through the kitchen courtyard by mistake – a Mr and Mrs Yamaguchi.'

'Yes; please show them in.'

He straightened his collar and smoothed his hair, turning to greet Genzo and Akiko. They entered hesitantly, much flustered by the sight of him, in his impeccably tailored suit, standing by the marbled fireplace in the spacious, thickly carpeted, well-furnished room. Genzo had grown into manhood since Kenjiro had last seen him and his stocky frame was stuffed into a cheap, ill-fitting check jacket and black trousers; only his feet were comfortable, for he had left his shoes outside. His wife's skinny frame, draped in a garish, factory-made kimono, was bent almost double in embarrassed timidity. The visible skins of both were roughened and tanned to a shade that smacked of southern suns, and their country accents sounded quite odd in their present surroundings. Tea and cakes were served, pleasantries exchanged about the family, and Kenjiro, seeing Genzo's expression of truculent awe, asked jocularly, 'Well, well; I wonder what your grandfather Gengoro would have made of all this, hey? He loathed everything foreign up to the day of his death. You remember him, don't you, Genzo?'

'Yes, though I was only a lad when he died in the Rebellion. Just before it I do remember him raging against the sword edict and telling us how he'd followed the great Saigo back to Kagoshima carrying his swords in a white cotton bag because samurai weren't allowed to wear them any more. He said then it would soon be the death of him, and it was.'

'That sounds like Uncle Gengoro! He was certainly an all-in-one-piece man.' Kenjiro sighed, betrayed by the wistful thought that he, by contrast, was made up of multiple pieces that formed different patterns every few years. 'Anyway, in spite of your grandfather, you want to come and live in the new capital, work in a modern office, hey? So sister told me and I've done what I can to get you started; but it won't be easy, because you've no experience. I've found you a clerk's post in a textile factory across the river. I've never seen it but I know the owner and he'll keep a weather eye on you and you'll get promoted if you show your mettle. A bout of good hard work never does a young man any harm while he's learning the ropes.'

Genzo jumped up and bowed low, hissing his gratitude while Akiko mumbled inarticulate thanks behind her hand. 'Your main problem will be finding a place to live,' Kenjiro continued. 'Rents are high because of demand – hundreds of young hopefuls like you coming in from the provinces. You're at the lodgings I suggested at present? . . . Good.' He turned to Akiko for the first time. 'So you have two little ones now, wife?'

'Two girl babies, yes,' she whispered.

'Never mind . . . two nursemaids for the sons to come, hey?' Kenjiro spoke the conventional words jovially, then flinched; he would not have dared utter them in the presence of his womenfolk. 'You must look after them carefully in the big city; it's not so healthy for children . . . Not plain sailing for anyone, I warn you. More of the dog eat dog than in the country.'

'But people here have money in their pockets and eat well – or so I've heard say?' Genzo challenged.

'Well, some do, but you have to work very hard to become successful.'

'Well, I can do that right enough.' He squared his shoulders, glaring defiantly.

'Why, you have your grandfather's bushy eyebrows growing on you!' Kenjiro smiled. 'But not too much of his pepper-hot temper, I hope?'

'I know what I want, sir, that's all.'

'Then good for you. I wish another young man of my acquaintance could say as much. But that's enough for now.' He consulted his pocket watch. 'Here are letters of introduction to the office manager and so on. Report for work tomorrow to show your eagerness. If I hear of any suitable accommodation in the vicinity I'll let you know. Contact me again once you've settled and if you have any particular difficulties, don't hesitate to let me know.'

They rose instantly and started backing and bowing out of

the room. Akiko, unused to such quantities of furniture, knocked against an occasional table, from which a china ornament fell and chipped. She fell on her knees trying to fit the piece back, apologising in profuse agitation until her husband led her cowering away. Looking round after their departure, Kenjiro tried to imagine his surroundings through their eyes – or his own of twenty-five years ago. He should have received them in the Japanese wing to put them more at ease; but he had taken a sneaking pleasure in their confused awe and hoped moreover that Genzo would tell Ofuku about the grandeur of his western-style room. Anyway, Genzo seemed to be made of the right stuff and might even achieve a little grandeur of his own eventually, Kenjiro thought as he wrapped the box of German chocolates in a kerchief and called for a house rickshaw.

It was a sultry evening of purple-massed clouds on far horizons and mosquitoes humming over stagnant drains. Bowling north near the banks of the Sumida, Kenjiro could see the straight, still masts of junks waiting for a wind and hear shouts of boys bathing in its murky waters. Shopkeepers, reclining in loose cotton robes on tiny house-verandahs, were trying to fan a breeze around themselves and there were queues at the chipped-ice stalls. As he neared Koyuki's House of Gold he longingly imagined the cool mountain airs of the town of Karuizawa, where he would soon be spending his holiday with the family. Then he sealed off the thought, anticipating instead his enjoyment of the time-honoured, familiar rituals ahead.

Koyuki and her attendants were always ready, as if waiting only for him, presenting cold or hot face-towels according to the season. His first need that evening was for a bath, and after it a pretty maid massaged his legs, shoulders, and back with soothing unguents while Koyuki plucked her *koto* and chanted well-known songs about the passing of life and love, and the heroic deeds performed during various clan wars of the past. 'Why don't they put fine samurai-men like you into this new Parliament place instead of old greybeards who've had their day?' she flattered him, wrapping him in cool silks and clapping her hands for *saké*.

Kenjiro stretched luxuriously. 'Ah, those greybeards have got in the habit of power and won't give it up easily . . . As for me, I'm not so young, sugar-blossom; this is my fiftieth year under heaven.'

'No! I'm amazed. Why you're as smooth-skinned and tight-muscled and upstanding as a man half your age.' Her soft fingers stole between his legs, cupping his genitals gently.

He tweaked her ear. 'Still, it's true, and I should start conserving my male essence instead of spending it freely inside your silver chamber in the golden house of Koyuki. A man of fifty years should have but one emission every twenty days; that's what the Chinese sage tells us.'

'Hoo-paah! That may do for the sapless jellyfish of China but not for a potent Japanese man. Why, see how your godly cock begins to swell at my tiny pitty-patty and don't tell me it should ration its rising. Why, such suppression would lead to outbreaks of boils all over your fair body!'

'Then I shall retain my seed but not curb my desire, as the sage also advises. And that will please us both, will it not?'

'Indeed it will, handsome Kenji. And when you come to spend you will be like a hawk soaring in the sky, like a wild horse leaping.'

She purred against him and he pushed away her fondling fingers. 'But bring me food first, woman. A man cannot perform his best on an empty belly.' He chuckled, relapsing naturally into terms appropriate to the occasion. She went out and he sprawled negligently on the padded cushions, lifting his *saké* cup to the porcelain statuette that stood in a flower-decked alcove. It was the traditional symbol of the geisha – a beckoning kitten, teasing, cuddlesome, skittish, and with hidden claws.

'By the way,' he said, as Koyuki and her attendants returned with food, 'do you happen to know of any respectable, inexpensive lodgings to rent round here? A distant relative has just arrived from Kyushu and I've found him a clerk's job in a textile factory. He's got a wife and two babies, but not much money for a start.'

'Why yes, as it happens. An old friend of mine who's become very respectable since her patron died and left her a tidy sum has bought a couple of houses to rent out, and was asking me just the other day if I knew of any honest, reliable tenants.'

'Then give me her address and I'll pass it on. No need to mention any connection with me.'

'Of course not.' She bowed, plucking a *samisen* as he settled to his food, and crooning in a low chant,

> *'A full cup of wine taken*
> *Into the black jug pour it,*
> *Into the white jug pour it . . .*
> *Together with my lover, giving, taking.*
> *How does it feel?'*

After his meal Koyuki suggested they play the forfeit game, 'Fox, Man, Gun', at which she was much the more adept, but chose not to win, for when she lost he demanded, as forfeit, pieces of her outer apparel.

'And I'll have this now, fox-woman.' Playfully he grabbed at her long satin sash tied with a bow in front.

She partly unwound it, then rolled skittishly away, whispering, 'And you shall see my brush in the bedroom, sir, but not here; for I'll play no more before the maids.'

Eagerly he followed her into the back chamber, where lamplight glowed upon straw-gold mats, and quilts of damask and crepe, edged with red velvet, were laid out in readiness for his pleasure. That night Kenjiro did not preserve his essence, but spent it copiously inside her silver chamber; after all, he thought, before eventually drifting into sleep. he was not quite fifty yet and would be soon restored by the invigorating airs of Karuizawa.

The mountain town of Karuizawa was accessible from Tokyo in a long day's journey by train, horse-drawn tram, and rickshaw. It had been discovered only a few years before by foreigners seeking relief from the noise, summer heat, and what was known as 'high-collar entertaining' of the capital.

The idea of having a cottage there had been entirely Elinor's for Kenjiro could not at first see the point of a rural retreat. The countryside was associated in his mind with all that was backward and unfashionable, from which he had escaped once already. But the charm of the place had won him over. It was cool and shaded on the hottest day; its furniture made locally from bent saplings, cut bamboo, and stripped pine. The smell of wood, of fresh grass blinds and mats wafted through it. The verandah overlooked an immaculate moss-garden with a stream and a miniature waterfall, and beyond its fences ranks of conifers rose into the hills.

The accommodation being limited, visitors came in relays, and the first to arrive to see Elinor that summer were Ryo, Hannah, and Millicent Pilcher. The American missionary, Elinor feared, would prove a tiresome guest in this tranquil place, where the only pastimes were walking, reading, and riding. But she seemed to find them congenial enough and, to celebrate Hannah's birthday, which occurred soon after their arrival, they decided on a riding picnic to the famous viewing spot for Mount Asama Yama. The route being long and rather precipitous, the youngsters were left behind, and the four women set off early, riding along shady paths bordered by bushes where insects rattled and clacked their summer songs. The fragrance of mountain pines hung in the warm air, mingled with the scent of mulched leaves, wild flowers, and ferns. Rivulets trickled downhill over weedy rocks, and the only other sounds were the occasional squawk of a magpie or the rustle of unseen woodland creatures. High up on a ridge where the trees thinned, they stood in silence to survey the panorama of peaks, plains, and rivers glinting green and silver in the sunlight below.

'It's indescribably magnificent, don't you think?' Elinor murmured at length, then turned to where the servants were unpacking the picnic baskets and the grooms watering the horses. 'I brought a bottle of champagne . . . after all, it is Hannah's birthday, and a very quiet one for her. I hope you'll all partake? We'll put it in the stream to cool.'

Millicent said resolutely, 'I really don't care for it, Mrs

Miyata. Excuse me.'

'Please yourself, of course.' Elinor sauntered off with the bottle, and Hannah walked beside her. Millicent bit her lip; she knew Elinor did not much care for her, and she had a missionary's desire to convert her, if not to liking then at least to understanding. Perhaps Hannah would help, and it occurred to her then that the three older women were engaged in a covert struggle for Hannah's allegiance, each sure that they knew what was best for her.

Elinor's only wish just then was that her daughter should enjoy her birthday and she murmured, 'You should have brought one of your own friends, Hannah; Emiko, for instance. More fun for you.'

'Oh, she's much too infatuated to leave Tokyo. She's met a gentleman who was educated in Paris and opens every door for her with a gallant gesture. She seems to think the battle for equality has been won, and can't wait to marry him.'

Elinor laughed. 'Oh, you young people! I hope she finds he has other good qualities too.'

'I doubt it. Appearances are all with Emiko. Perhaps she'll enjoy life more that way.'

'More than you, you mean?'

'I suppose I do, yes.'

'But why shouldn't you enjoy life, Hannah? You have so many advantages.'

'I know, I know . . .' She drifted languidly along the path beside the stream, her slender fingers trailing over the grass-heads, and her mother thought how exotic she looked – oval face almost expressionless, framed by her dark hair, which she had let down, to fan over the shoulders of her dusky pink and turquoise robe. A woodland nymph, almost – elusive, always just out of reach.

Returning to the picnic place, Elinor arranged dishes of melons and prawns, cold chickens, salads and pickles, then summoned them to the feast. The maids and grooms had retired into the deep shade and she could hear their cheery banter as they munched their much humbler fare. The servants seemed to be having a happier time than their masters, she thought irritably, for between the picnickers she sensed underlying tension. She popped a champagne cork and Hannah handed a brimming glass to Ryo, who hesitated.

'Oh come on, Aunt, please . . . It *is* my birthday!'

Ryo grimaced but took it and they all toasted Hannah's fortune, Millicent with fruit juice.

'And it's also a year ago that you came back after the party to tell us of your new appointment, Ryo, remember? Another cause for celebration. Doesn't seem that long, I must say.'

'Doesn't it to you, Ellie? It seems forever to me – an endless, difficult forever.'

Elinor sought the right words. 'But it's bound to get easier as people become more accustomed to having you as a Head.'

'Will they ever?' Ryo swallowed her champagne with sudden vehemence. 'It's against all the grains. Mine as well as theirs. It simply isn't a woman's place to give orders outside her home. I can't get used to it and certainly the music teacher, Mr Sato, hates me for it. His nose positively twitches with fury if I dare to make a suggestion and I've heard that his own mother is ashamed of him because his superior is a woman. He finds it demeaning, and how can I blame him, considering how he, and all of us, were brought up?'

'I've told Ryo many times that she simply has to assert her authority,' Millicent interjected, '. . . prove to everyone that she's absolutely capable and ignore their old-fashioned prejudices. Unless there are pioneers to break the old moulds of behaviour here, the upbringing of the young will never change and the same patterns of authority and submission will continue.'

'Millicent, I know you are right, but I can't feel that I was born to be a mould-breaker, I'm afraid,' said Ryo.

'The greatness was thrust upon you,' Elinor murmured, re-filling the glasses and wishing they could just drink quietly and admire the view.

'I'm afraid I can't find it a jesting matter,' Millicent retorted, finishing her juice and looking longingly at the food.

'I'm not jesting, Miss Pilcher. I feel every sympathy for

Ryo and for the general battle of improving women's position. But, if I may say so, I do think one of the troubles with the suffragists is that they always appear so dreadfully earnest and . . . well, joyless. I'd like to think they and their kind enjoyed themselves occasionally, and then perhaps intelligent girls like my daughter might be more inclined to ally themselves with them.' She drained her glass and whispered to Hannah, 'There's another bottle in the hamper. Let's have it . . . Now could you explain, for instance,' she turned back to Millicent, 'why a stand for women's rights should be associated with drinking fruit juice or scraping one's hair in a bun and wearing drab, mousy colours as Ryo does, as if she were ashamed of her femininity?'

'But I can't feel that authority becomes a woman, Elinor; my very position makes me feel unfeminine, that's the trouble. So it's easier to look . . . well . . . sexless, I suppose.' Ryo stared unhappily into her empty glass. 'Remember I was brought up a samurai's daughter, trained to self-abnegation and sacrifice from childhood. Any kind of expressive behaviour, even talking and laughing loudly, was greatly disapproved in a girl. I dared not say boo to a goose when I was in my twenties. You must remember that, Ellie? After years of being terrified of my uncle and at the beck and call of my brothers . . . And what an ordeal it was later when Kenjiro kept trying to marry me off to various unattractive men and I would squirm and prevaricate, run away and hide rather than refuse directly.'

'But you did stick to your convictions, Ryo — that you wanted something different from life.'

Ryo averted her gaze. 'But what I really wanted I couldn't have, could I?'

There was an awkward pause and Hannah, who had returned, looked at them curiously. Elinor took the second bottle from her and, as the liquid bubbled out, Hannah mischievously held up Millicent's glass for filling and handed it to her. 'Just try! It's not poison you know. Why not enjoy yourself a little sometimes, Miss Pilcher? As mother says, the supporters of women's rights don't seem to have much fun.'

Millicent looked at the drink suspiciously. 'But there are many kinds of so-called fun, Hannah, and I have a great deal of pleasure in my life, I assure you – as I often tell my two sisters. They're both married with lots of children and are very much inclined to pity me. "Poor Millicent" – they've even said it to my face, as if I were a dumb invalid. They think because I'm short and plain I couldn't find a husband. But I have always had other plans for myself and besides, I never much liked babies, to tell you the truth. I have no desire whatever to be like them, but I can't make them believe that. And I just couldn't bear their pity; it's partly why I came abroad.'

She had spoken in a rush of angry honesty, as if she had downed a whole bottle of champagne, though her glass was untouched. She swirled its stem forcefully, 'Women should have opportunities to live in different ways according to what they can do best and without being blamed or pitied for being a little unusual – like men do. At least, that's what I think!'

'That's what the woman writer Kishida says, Miss Pilcher,' Hannah agreed. 'She gives a lecture entitled, "Daughters confined in Boxes", about middle-class girls who are restricted and oppressed by the old educational traditions – how to entertain guests and open doors graciously, arrange flowers, play music, just like apprentice geisha, as she points out. And it's true, as Aunt said, that girls are taught to subdue their natural personalities while boys are encouraged to go forward and be what they want.' She looked at Elinor and quoted, ' "Parents must give their daughters as well as their sons the right tools for managing their own lives." '

Elinor blinked. 'Surely you're not suggesting your parents have confined *you* in a box?'

'Not exactly, but all Father wants for me now is to marry some well-off man from a good family, doesn't he? He doesn't want me to do anything exciting or interesting by myself, does he, Mother? Look at the fuss he made about my trip abroad! Well, maybe I don't want to stay here forever and lead your sort of life, which is what you both have in mind for me.'

Elinor winced, reminded suddenly of Taneo Takahashi, a fervent advocate of women's rights till the day of his death a few years before, but who had married off his own daughter in the traditional fashion. She pushed the thought aside and said mildly, 'But I'm quite happy, Hannah, and that's all we want for you.'

'But when you were young you hated the prospect of leading a dull life in Harrogate like your mother. You told me that once.'

Ryo, helping herself to more champagne, giggled. '*Touché*, Elinor. I remember that too. So why shouldn't Hannah want something different again? Perhaps she'll be a mould-breaker for the new generation?'

'And remain an "old miss" into the bargain? I confess I don't like the idea of that, Ryo,' said Elinor.

Hannah nodded. 'In a way it seems more fun, being married. But to whom? All the young men I know are no better than little boys, puppy dogs, like my own brother.'

'But he is younger and . . .'

'Not by much, and he'll take years to grow up at the rate he's going. Perhaps a few years in the army would make a man of him.'

Elinor stared at her. 'Whoever put that curious idea in your head?'

'Oh, nobody special. I can think for myself.' Carelessly she tossed back her glass and then poured more all round while Elinor brushed flies off the food. 'Come now, it's time we began to eat . . .'

But Millicent, who had been waiting her chance, interrupted, 'Certainly, Mrs Miyata, I can understand why you, or any mother, wants to see her daughter happily married with children of her own. But the personal sacrifice demanded is very heavy as things now stand for a woman married to a Japanese. She has hardly any legal or property rights – why, just recently we learn that women have been more or less written out of the new constitution. And as for their private lives – it is surely well known, though seldom talked about publicly, that many Japanese wives have to resign themselves to the humiliation of their husbands keeping concubines or mistresses? Please excuse me for mentioning such a disgusting subject, but Hannah . . .'

'Well, that certainly won't be allowed to happen to Hannah any more than it has to me,' Elinor said decisively. 'I wouldn't countenance such a situation for a single second.'

'My dear Mrs Miyata, I wasn't talking about you personally. You are an Englishwoman, with an Englishwoman's rights, and your husband is a highly moral and exceptional man, if I may say so. But Hannah was talking generally about the pro's and con's of marriage in this society as it's at present constituted, and I was just pointing out the difficulties and dangers for an attractive, educated, rather strong-minded young lady like her.'

'Thank you, Miss Pilcher.' Hannah dipped her head in mock humility, 'But I assure you . . .'

Ryo, who had been sitting silent for several minutes staring into her empty glass, suddenly jumped up with a horrified exclamation. 'I'm sorry; excuse me, but I don't feel well . . .' and went scurrying off into the trees, from which they soon heard the sound of retching.

Ostentatiously, Millicent tipped her champagne on the grass, and Elinor said with asperity, 'No, it isn't poison, Miss Pilcher. But Ryo drank too much too fast and she's not in the least used to it. We should have eaten sooner instead of getting carried away by arguments that lead nowhere. Are you all right, Ryo?' she called and, hearing a tremulous affirmative, they began picking half-heartedly at their lunch.

Eventually Ryo emerged wan and shame-faced to say she had a splitting headache, and it was decided that Millicent would keep her company while Elinor and Hannah rode home and sent a rickshaw back for her. They trotted down through the woods in silence, their earlier high spirits dwindling. As they neared the cottage, Elinor said, 'I'm afraid it turned out to be a rather sorry birthday picnic, Hannah. I shouldn't have opened that second bottle; it loosened tongues, and who would have thought that Ryo . . .'

'But I rather enjoyed the loosened tongues, Mother, with

403

all of you arguing honestly. Usually you're so wary and polite with each other.'

'Oh well, if you enjoyed it . . . Miss Pilcher is certainly opinionated and strait-laced, though I feel rather sorry for her now – that story about her sisters . . . Of course pity is just what she doesn't want. And I can well understand your aunt's difficulties.'

'By the way, who was Felix Coburn, Mother?' Hannah asked suddenly.

'Who?'

'Felix Coburn. Didn't you know him once?'

'How did you hear about him?' Elinor's tone was steely and Hannah prevaricated. 'Oh . . . I think Mrs Fortescue mentioned him in connection with some old Yokohama scandal.' She glanced inquisitively at Elinor, sure she must know the circumstances surrounding Oliver's father's death. She considered telling her of the surprising place she had first come across Felix's name, but sensed it was dangerous ground.

'He was on the fringes of a scandal, yes,' Elinor replied briskly. 'One of those young fly-by-nights who came out here in the old days seeking their fortune. A bit shallow and weak. Thought he knew it all . . . but didn't.' She spurred her horse into a quick trot, definitely closing the subject.

Hannah had hoped to satisfy her curiosity on that and other subjects further; but, shortly after, Elinor received news that Kenjiro and Joey were fleeing a heat-wave in the capital and arriving at the weekend, which meant that Ryo and Millicent had to leave. Though father and son travelled up together, they spoke little and it was not until the family were gathered on the verandah on the evening of their arrival that Joey announced without preamble and in a loud voice that he had failed his college entrance examinations 'quite abysmally'. There was an uncomfortable silence; Kenjiro hissed painfully, for he had desperately wanted his son to have the higher education he had been denied.

Elinor said carefully, looking at her husband, 'Oh Joey, we are sorry . . . and you did try, didn't you? Towards the end at least . . .'

'Not for long enough, Mother, and I'm afraid I just don't have the brains for it.' He too was watching Kenjiro anxiously, tensed for an outburst, but Kenjiro merely said, 'So what now, young man? I must find you some kind of suitable post, I suppose.'

'That's not what I want, Father. You see, my ambition is to write for a living.'

'You mean become a journalist, Joey?' Elinor was determined to make light of her own disappointment, knowing that Kenjiro's was greater.

'No, none of your gutter-press snippets. I mean a proper writer − a novelist.' He looked round fiercely, daring them to laugh. But there was another stunned pause; and Joey rushed to a cupboard, pulling out a number of books he had brought with him. 'See . . . look at these! *Floating Clouds, Love Confessions of Two Nuns, Immaculate Drewdrops* . . . I don't suppose you've ever heard of any of them? But these novels are in the great European tradition of real literature that delves into the hearts of men and women. Up till now our so-called writers have produced mere social commentaries, comedies of manners, political tracts; nothing to awaken the soul and the senses, nothing to depict man in his actual condition of spiritual torment.'

'We aren't an audience of your Pen and Inkstone Society, Joey,' Hannah interrupted tartly.

'Oh you! − Hannah, the aloof and stony-hearted. I doubt that even Shakespeare's sonnets could move you. Well, he does me and I don't mind admitting it, and if I could only write the truth about life and love and move others . . .'

'Don't you think you're a mite young and inexperienced for all these moving torments?' Kenjiro began heavily.

'But one can imagine, Father, share vicariously in one's own soul with the sufferings of others. I know I can. Why, all these writers are quite young and . . .'

'Perhaps that's why their books sound a trifle airy-fairy?'

Elinor smiled. 'Joey, we don't want to trample on your dreams and ambitions, but you have to be practical, too. You're not a rich man's son and you simply can't afford to be a dilettante. It takes years to earn a decent living from writing and many never succeed in doing so.'

'Oh, he'll starve in a garret, won't you, Joey?' said Hannah. 'Like the Bohemians in Paris. You'll enjoy the role for a while, but I can't see you as a hand-to-mouth man for long – too fond of life's little luxuries, aren't you, little brother?'

He turned on her, blazing with anger. 'You wait – I'll show you! I'll be a world-famous author one day. You're so cold and calculating and cautious; but you'll never do anything worthwhile, for all that.'

Hannah wrinkled her nose derisively. 'You know nothing whatsoever about me – boy!'

Elinor rose and rang the supper bell. 'Stop it, you two. We're supposed to be on a family holiday and if you're going to quarrel you can both go away and leave Father and me in peace. Isn't that so, Kenjiro?'

He nodded. 'It's amazing to me how you dare insult each other so in front of us. Anyway, Joey is going to be a novelist, for which you don't have to pass exams. Maybe that's why you've chosen it, hey? No, I'm not listening to any more impertinence now, but I expect to see you with a pen in your hand every day diligently practising your craft. This is surely an ideal spot for studying human torments from a safe distance? So let's see what you can do.'

Joey spluttered, on the verge of protest at his father's tone, then smiled with the same brilliance. 'The rest of his family were hopelessly helpless when he made up his immovable strong will.' He quoted one of his familiar Japanese-English parodies; and they all laughed in relief.

The next two weeks were harmonious: Elinor and Hannah took the youngsters on riding and sightseeing excursions; Kenjiro followed a careful regimen of exercise, hot baths, and massage he had worked out for himself in order to combat any symptoms of ageing; Joey went off into the woods or huddled in house-corners writing, muttering, frowning, biting off the ends of several pens.

'But you can't expect me to have finished a novel in this short time,' he exploded when, just before returning to the capital, Kenjiro enquired how he was progressing.

'I don't, and I don't really want to know how you're getting on,' Kenjiro replied evenly. They were strolling through the woods near the cottage and could hear ahead the delighted squeals of Tomi and Umé on their ponies. 'Your mother suggests that we continue to give you an allowance for up to a year. You'll have plenty of time to write, but I insist that you also study something practical – engineering, economics, politics – just in case you don't produce a great novel in the time. I hope you consider that fair?'

'Yes, Father, and thank you. I'll try hard, really I will.'

'Then you'd better return to Tokyo with me and we'll fix up some courses for you.'

'Yes, Father.'

As Kenjiro was wondering whether such docility indicated success or failure in Joey's recent literary endeavours, a young man swinging a cane passed by with a quick greeting. 'You know him?' Kenjiro queried.

'I'm trying to know him better.' Joey grinned. 'A son of Nishi, the power behind the successful electrical company of that name.'

'Ah . . . the development of electrical equipment is a field well worth studying for interest and profit.'

'I was thinking of studying the eldest unmarried daughter from the same motives.'

Kenjiro grunted. 'As a great author you'll surely be much too intellectual to care about heiresses?'

'But one must have enough money *not* to care about it . . . Perhaps my trouble, Father, is that I'm really cast in the samurai mould of my revered ancestors. I'd have made quite a good samurai . . . living on a regular stipend provided by my lord and master, cutting a dash in crested silks, with two swords at the ready, not having to think too hard about anything and then – wham! Rush bravely into battle and die young for the honour of the clan. It might have suited me very well. I'm sure I could be brave, given the chance. But there aren't any battles left to fight, it seems.'

'What romantic twaddle you do talk! I suppose you think

407

I've never fought for anything since I ceased to be a samurai? But I tell you, son, I've fought for myself and my family for years and years. It's the long hard pull that counts, not the quick blaze of glory.'

'Yes, Father. I remember you telling me many times when I was a boy that it took Mr Stephenson fifteen years to perfect the invention of the railway engine. Fifteen years of slow, steady perseverance, just puff-puff-puffing along. That's the way isn't it, Father?'

Kenjiro gasped; Joey's audacious breaking of every rule of the respect due from son to father literally took his breath away, infuriating him the more because he considered himself a thoroughly modern parent. Pushing Joey almost off the path he strode on ahead. 'It's no use talking to you! You've learned just enough to make you thoroughly big-headed but not enough to understand the true value of anything – or anyone. As you enjoy clowning so much, why not go and be a mountebank actor? Write your own plays with yourself as chief fool! But don't expect me to support you while you're doing it . . . As far as I'm concerned, this offer is your last chance. You understand me?'

'Yes, Father,' Joey called after him, in a mood of immediate contrition, which he sustained during the return journey to the capital, but which Kenjiro suspected as simply another piece of play-acting.

Hannah left the cottage soon after, while Elinor lingered to close it up, relishing the excuse for a few more tranquil days before the bustle of the autumn season. Under her direction, the little dwelling and its garden were sealed, protected, covered over with matting and straw – a polished brown nut preserved in its shell that she could dig out like a squirrel for her later enjoyment, she thought, watching the gardener carry away the porcelain plant-pots for winter storage. And how fortunate she was to have such a rich store of life's pleasures and treasures to draw upon – a loving husband, four fine children, the house in Tokyo, this mountain retreat. She had her share of irritations and perplexities like everyone else, of course, but essentially she felt happy and confident of the future. Indeed she wondered fleetingly if she was perhaps too sanguine. Were there dangers ahead that she could not even imagine? But why should there be? Never a self-deceiver, she had surely earned her present measure of contentment? Satisfied with that, she went to finish the packing ready for the return journey to Tokyo on the morrow.

CHAPTER TWENTY

Joey Miyata took up politics that autumn, though not quite in the way his father expected. It was a highly political season. In November the Imperial princes, in their regalia, and the recently elected members of Parliament, in formal evening dress, took their seats for the first time in the new Houses of Peers and Representatives inside the new Parliament building, which was decorated in pale terracotta, dark green, and dusky gold and lit by electricity. In the course of his opening address the Emperor Meiji claimed that the administration of his Empire had been brought to a 'state approaching completeness and regular arrangement' during the twenty years of his reign and that its relations with other nations were 'on a footing of constantly growing amity and intimacy'. Tranquillity and security must be preserved and the glory of the country and the enterprise of its people be made manifest through the proper working of the constitution and the endeavours of the men there gathered to usher in Japan's modern epoch of democratic government.

The picture, as rosy as those invariably presented by rulers to their subjects, was taken on trust by the majority of law-abiding citizens; but there were dissident voices – mainly young men of reforming zeal who had come into contact with foreign socialist movements. They were bitterly opposed to Japan's headlong pursuit of western-style capitalism, urging instead that the country formulate and pursue its own goals in its own eastern fashion and act as a bulwark against the tyrannies of foreign colonialism in Asia.

Their radical opinions attracted Joey and he determined to

write the first political romance of the period. Its hero was a young, reckless dissident doomed to fall hopelessly in love with the daughter of an old-world aristocrat and be killed while attempting to assassinate a stubbornly reactionary leader. After his death, his inamorata would kill herself from grief in a scene reminiscent of Romeo and Juliet. In an enthusiastic moment, Joey outlined the plot to his sister, who thought it quite promising – though why didn't the heroine commit herself instead to the cause of oppressed Japanese womanhood? Joey promised to consider the alternative and, in the meantime, unbeknown to their parents, they went to a course of political lectures together, he to gain background colour, she from a vague desire to make her own mind up about the world.

At one of these lectures Hannah again saw Oliver Rayne, who had gone there expressly to find her. After the disclosures about his father's past, they had met only a few times, for the painting of Hannah's portrait, completed long after the cherry blossoms had fallen. It was not one of Oliver's best; and indeed he seemed unable to produce good work any more, and had spent the recent months in a mood of melancholy withdrawal, wondering how it was that so many people contrived to make their lives sufficiently interesting to want to live them.

In this condition he had fallen prey to self-pity, telling himself that his several misfortunes were none of his making but due to his parents' misdemeanours and failures. Believing the Miyatas disliked him on that same account, he had resolved to see no more of Hannah and was contemplating leaving the country when another blow struck – the house he and Walter shared burned down. Such calamities were quite common among the tight-packed, wood-and-paper dwellings of the back streets, with their kerosene cooking stoves and charcoal fires. It only needed a small earthquake to start a large blaze, and one occurred during the New Year festivities, when the lights were at their brightest and many firemen, usually renowned for their heroic fire-fighting feats, were on holiday. In the resulting conflagration Oliver's possessions went up in smoke along with much else of more value. Workmen arrived within days to begin the erection of an equally combustible dwelling on the same site, and Walter accepted the incident as no more than a minor set-back; but to Oliver it seemed a final, bitterly unfair punch from a malignantly disposed Fate.

It was at this nadir of his life that an idea came to him, which, once rooted, would not be dislodged. It seemed to follow with dreadful, inevitable logic from all that had happened to him − and his father before him. On the first day of the new month he and Walter moved into their resurrected house and the carpenter's, tile-layer's and furniture-maker's bills arrived, together with the usual ones from the laundryman, the fishmonger, and the oil and charcoal sellers.

Oliver, surveying the beautiful but menacing pieces of paper, said carefully, 'What we need is a few more Kuniyoshi prints, old man.'

Walter nodded glumly, for he too was feeling a temporary pinch. 'But there aren't any more, not for sale anyway. Snapped up by collectors, you know that.'

'Perhaps we should . . . er . . . have a few made, to satisfy continuing demand . . . among Sylvia Fortescue and her artistic ladies, for instance.'

Walter chuckled. 'What a capital wheeze!'

'I'm serious − partly.'

'But that's called forgery.'

'It seems to run in my family, but I only mean to dabble.'

'Well, it doesn't run in mine.' Walter backed away firmly.

'Oh, it would just be a bit of a joke − against Sylvia Fortescue, I thought. She's becoming rather a pest, you know. She flirts with me quite shamelessly sometimes and gives herself such airs about her discriminating "taste" as the well-known Patroness of the Finer Arts. I'd rather like to take her down a peg, I must say − sell her a couple of . . . er . . . Kuniyoshis that she could show off at her next "salon". You won't split, will you?'

'No, but I won't help, either. If you're found out . . .'

'Oh, I'll tell her myself after I've recouped my resources − and pay her back for the forgeries.' He chuckled. 'Just a temporary expedient. She'd probably lend me some money if I asked, but that wouldn't be so much fun . . . and, good Lord, man, I'm tired of living in this rotten down-at-heel fashion. I simply haven't got enough of the ready to buy any decent togs or paint brushes, nor to pay my fare home . . . If I wanted to go, which I don't.'

'You could teach English for a while.'

'And end up like my mother – bitter, thwarted, caught in a trap, hating every sodding pupil? No thanks! I'd rather play a little joke and take the risk, just for once.'

Walter shrugged. 'Do what you like; but your father wasn't exactly successful at a similar game, remember?'

'One should sometimes tempt the gods . . . But would it at all worry you if I tempted the divine Mrs Fortescue with my counterfeit wares?'

'Not specially. She's got a bit above herself, I agree, and I daresay her husband can afford it.'

Forgery of many kinds flourished in the capital's back streets; holy and secular artefacts took on the patina of centuries after being buried in the earth, exposed on rooftops, steeped in tea, and begrimed with incense smoke. Ivories were spuriously darkened to the sere and yellow; scrolls and brocades carefully faded into distant antiquity by present sunlight. Oliver soon found an engraver willing to try his hand at a couple of lesser-known Kuniyoshis. The results were of such verisimilitude that he would certainly have been fooled by them himself. The much less expert Sylvia bought both for a considerable sum and showed them proudly to all her friends.

With the money Oliver replaced the necessities he had lost in the fire and felt no compunction on that score – for hadn't he made all concerned happier? In this mood of renewed buoyancy he again sought out Hannah, installing himself in the role of her escort – amusing, just sufficiently outrageous, a constant worshipper at the shrine of her beauty. Yet it was not only her physical charms that captivated him, for he responded at a deeper level to her quiet perceptions, her uncertainties and vulnerabilities that resulted from being branded as a 'mixed-up' by a thoroughly homogeneous society. Oliver too felt rather on the social fringes, though from different causes, and, for their mutual comfort, he would sometimes conjure visions of a more unconventional Bohemian way of life abroad where they would both feel quite at home. On such occasions, tempted and entertained, she would allow him to fondle and kiss her; then send him away – elated, frustrated, dreaming of eventually making love to her, in some artist's garret perhaps, with the roof-tops of Paris for backdrop.

Hannah's attraction to Oliver was heightened because it was an act of deliberate defiance against her mother and aunt, who evinced quite irrational animosity towards him. At first, she had pleaded his cause with them in vain, but then, feeling protective towards him, she simply refrained from mentioning their meetings. However, on a wet evening in late spring, when she returned to the school-bungalow after one such unexplained absence, she found Ryo waiting for her, seated beside the brazier, patiently piling tiny pieces of charcoal into a pyramid atop a cone of ashes.

'I think you've been seeing Oliver Rayne?' she challenged in a quiet, deliberate tone that Hannah knew well.

'And why not? And how did you know, if I may ask, Aunt?'

'Joey mentioned it casually, not meaning to tell tales.'

'But why should it be a matter of tale-telling?' Hannah remained huddled in her cloak, holding her fingers to the fire. 'Isn't it chilly for the time of year?'

Ryo pushed some embers about to encourage a flame. 'I wouldn't like to see you ensnared by one of his ilk – a rich dilettante posing as a creative artist – which he thinks gives him licence to behave as badly as he likes.'

'I can't understand why you and Mother dislike him so, and he's neither rich nor dilettantish.'

'He always seems to have money, so I assumed his mother must have left him well off. Does he ever talk about her, or anyone connected with her?'

'Not much. He has a younger sister, Letitia, and I gather they lived in rather straitened circumstances.'

'Just the three of them?'

'As far as I know, and now he earns his living by painting portraits.'

'Better than the one he did of you, I trust?' Ryo sniffed, adding abruptly, 'Are you really fond of him? I'd rather you told me the truth.'

Hannah swivelled, her pleated brocade skirt and fur-edged cloak twirling round her ankles. 'No. He's amusing, quite sensitive for a man, and happens to be a little infatuated with me . . . that's all.'

'So far so good, then. Indeed, as you haven't fallen captive to his manly charms it might be quite fun to practise your feminine wiles on him a little, and then drop him when it suits you.'

Hannah frowned. 'That doesn't sound very Christian of you, Aunt.'

'It's the way many so-called Christian men behave, nonetheless. You see dear, your mother and I want you to be happy above all things, and there are so many possible traps. I want you to learn how not to fall into anything you could regret later.'

'You might show him more sympathy, considering his history, which you and Mother won't discuss.'

'There's nothing to discuss, Hannah. But you shouldn't waste your sympathy on him. Young men of his sort always take very good care of themselves, I assure you.' She rose stiffly. 'The fire's beyond saving. I'm going to bed. By the way, your mother called in to suggest we go with the rest of the family to that delightful inn near Enoshima Island during the Boys' Festival next week. Personally I don't consider boys a cause for celebration, and anyway I have work to do. But I said you'd go.'

'I'd love to – only I hope it's warmer than this.'

The weather did improve in its unpredictable spring fashion, and by the time they had settled into the inn the following week it was mild and sunny. Ideal, they all agreed, for an excursion to Enoshima Island itself, except Joey, who dashed off for a *kendo* practice, promising to join them later.

The island, approached by a flimsy bridge with waves

splashing just beneath its planks, was sacred to Benten, goddess of love and good fortune, and crowds of holidaymakers were toiling up the steep village street to her temples. There were parties of pilgrims, with staves, white mushroom-shaped hats, and cloth-wrapped bundles of offerings, and hordes of high-spirited boys waving miniature war-banners and toy swords, for this was their festival day. The Buddhist temples on the summit, hidden among groves of trees, had a neglected air, Elinor thought, as she watched her husband make brief, seemingly automatic obeisance there before the altars. Was he really showing reverence to the goddess Benten? Did he truly believe in her divine existence? But she had long since ceased to ask him such blunt questions on a variety of topics – religion being one of them. His native preference for evasion and ambiguity had taken her years to accept; but now she seldom searched her own mind for answers either, caught up and acclimatised to what Joey once defined as 'the fuzzy Japanese drift'. Dear Joey – he was so perceptive, yet so uncoordinated in his mind and habits.

'Don't you think it's rather sad, allowing these lovely buildings to fall into decay?' she asked Kenjiro as he joined her.

'A result of the new reform movement, I suppose; Shintoism as the official national religion, the "purification" of Buddhist deities.'

'Why don't the Buddhists protest?'

'Not the Buddhist way. We aren't persecuted. People can still worship as they choose,' he replied casually, leading Tomi off to the far side of the grove to see the steps that led down to sea-caves wherein dwelt the fiercest dragon and the largest turtle in the world. While she waited, Elinor perched beside an old stone lantern, idly picking ochre lichen from its surface and remembering a discussion she had overheard at a dinner party of Arnold's recently about the upsurge of Shintoism being an ominous portent. Several foreigners present, who had been arguing against any revision of the treaties currently in force, which gave them many rights and few obligations, were of the opinion that it was another symptom of the Japanese getting above themselves – building up their armed forces and redeifying their Emperor were other unfortunate signs. Such discussions always made Elinor feel uncertain; for she was increasingly comfortable in the 'fuzzy Japanese drift' of things, yet knew herself to be forever excluded from any real participation in the national life.

'Has there ever been a *foreign* Shintoist?' she asked as her husband reappeared.

He grinned. 'I should suppose such a phenomenon to be impossible.'

'But why?'

'Because Shintoism is an exclusively Japanese religion, of course.'

'But I can be a Shinto man or a Christian one, can't I?' Tomi asked proudly.

'Oh, I suppose so. Come on, my lad, let's go down and buy some fried eels.' Kenjiro grabbed his son's hair playfully and they went jogging off together, leaving the others to follow.

Enoshima's village street was lined with tiny shops selling sea-shells, milky-white and sky-blue sprays of them, furled and doubled rosy-pink whorls, iridescent twists of grey-turquoise mother-of-pearl. Elinor and Hannah slipped into one shop, as softly luminous in the sunlight as a shell itself, and delved among trays of shell-ornamented hairpins, boxes, combs, mirrors, miniature glass globes containing wisps of seaweed, and postcards of Mount Fuji and of foreigners in dark suits perched on the huge, accepting hands of the bronze Diabutsu at nearby Kamakura. They heard Joey's voice before they saw him and Hannah nudged her mother to keep quiet, for he was entertaining someone with one of his funnier parodies.

'See, look at Fuji mountain, sacred Peak of White Lotus. She is most benevolently standing high for many thousand year. But only few old master paint her with proper. Especially western-school student in this grand modern era measure size and shape of Fuji-san, make her like photographic, so she has no life . . .'

Hannah pounced out at him. 'How little Japanese man twaddle talk . . . oh . . .' She paused, seeing that his companion was Yukio Iwada, who was looking uneasy, for his own English was not sufficiently good for these nuances. He exchanged stiff greetings with her and Elinor, but soon edged away, plucking Joey's sleeve and obviously uncomfortable in their female presence.

'You'll find my husband and Tomi ahead, probably at the eel-stall.' Elinor released him and they dashed off.

Finding his brother at the stall, Joey joined the queue while Yukio strolled on towards the bridge with Kenjiro. 'So you'll be a fully-fledged cavalry officer soon, Yukio?'

'Yes, sir . . . Final exams and passing out next month.'

'A good time to be in the army.'

'Yes, sir.' Yukio glanced at him, wondering how much he dared ask.

'We have to be militarily on the alert considering the threat from the Chinese dogs in Korea, wouldn't you agree, sir?'

'Yes. It's a tricky situation.'

'Do you think the Korean rebels who are trying to overthrow the old regime will succeed, sir?'

'Difficult to say.' Kenjiro knew full well that he was being pumped.

'And if they do, there'll be a civil war, surely?'

'I imagine so.'

'But if they don't there could still be war?'

'Perhaps . . . later.'

'Next year? The year after?'

'I couldn't say, but I'm no expert in this area.'

'No, sir. I beg your pardon.' Yukio was silenced by the slight reproof, wondering nonetheless how he could find out more. He yearned for war; he wanted it to be against the Chinese; he was certain the Empire of the Rising Sun would win.

As they reached the mainland end of the bridge, a man standing on the sands with two companions shouted loudly and hurried up waving a *saké* flask, which he handed to Kenjiro with a flourish. 'Mr Miyata, please drink. Your most excellent health, kind sir! You'll remember me? Genzo Yamaguchi at your service.' He bowed low.

'Ah yes, good day to you.' Kenjiro took the flask in some

embarrassment, for Genzo looked exactly what he was; a somewhat dishevelled, inebriated rural-born office worker on a day's spree.

'I have you to thank for this occasion, Mr Miyata. For I'm here to celebrate my recent promotion, which is entirely due to your help. I was saying as much to my friends only a minute ago, wasn't I?' They nodded solemnly. 'And now here is Mr Miyata himself! Come, you must have a drink with me at the stall, I insist.'

As he tugged Kenjiro's sleeve, Elinor came up. 'Who is this man?' she spoke in quiet English.

'My cousin Ofuku's son, Yamaguchi. I told you about him.'

Genzo dipped in another, lesser bow. 'Ah, it must be Mrs Miyata – the foreign wife. I am honoured.'

Resignedly, Kenjiro introduced everyone, and Elinor asked, 'And is your wife with you, Mr Yamaguchi?'

'No, no. She has the babies to look after. Two girls, and a boy coming soon, I'm sure.'

Elinor nodded frostily. 'And I hope she's keeping well in the big city?'

'Oh, she's all right. Now you'll drink . . . come, come!'

He capered towards the stall and Kenjiro hesitated; but Joey, laughing, ran after him, 'Why not? Come, Yukio, let's drink with my hayseed-relation.'

As Kenjiro followed, Elinor called in irritation, 'We'll see you at the Inn of the Silver Turtle. Don't be too long.'

The Silver Turtle Inn was perched atop steps on a shady cliff, where Elinor and her companions were ushered into a balconied room overlooking the wide, sparkling bay. Its matted floor was awash with sea-glints and leaf-shadows, its azure screens sprinkled with patterns of silver pine-needles; in the single alcove hung a single scroll framed by slender boughs of ash-wood and bearing a motto appropriate to the gastronomic speciality of the place, 'The crab digs a hole exactly the size of its back.' Beside the alcove, a slim vase held an arrangement of three sword-upright irises and another, decorated with a shrimp leaping over a wave, contained three fans embossed with the Inn's poetic name. It was no more, and no less beautiful than many other inns Elinor had visited, but its subtle harmonies of line and texture soon dissolved her slight irritation at the encounter with Mr Yamaguchi. She relaxed on the cushions, pleased that, in honour of the Boys' Festival, she was appropriately dressed in a kimono. Tomi, however, feeling people were not paying sufficient deference to his boyhood, prowled about in a pout, and suddenly called from the balcony, 'Come and look! There's a fight!'

Leaning over the rail, they saw a small crowd had gathered near the *saké* stall on the beach below, watching two men locked in combat.

'I can't quite see who . . .? Not Joey, surely?'

'I'm going to see . . . Come on, Hannah.' Tomi crammed on his pattens and scurried down the steps, Hannah behind him; Elinor hesitated, then followed with Umé.

Ringed by spectators, Yukio and Genzo, both stripped to the waist, with white towels bound round their foreheads to keep sweat from their eyes, were circling cautiously, sizing each other up. On first sight they looked evenly matched, being stocky, with tight-muscled shoulders and chests and trim waists, their thick, bare, brown feet splayed firmly in the warm sand. A second round was about to begin and Joey, self-appointed umpire, clicked two bits of wood together, then pointed a fan at each, calling in a high formal chant, 'Yamaguchi, Genzo to the east. Iwada, Yukio to the west.' As he lowered the fan the combatants rushed together, each trying to overthrow the other.

'However did this start?' Elinor whispered to Kenjiro, who was leaning against the stall sipping beer and watching intently.

'It was that fool Genzo. Began bragging about having been a champion wrestler in his youth and saying the namby-pamby cadets of today aren't properly trained in the old-style martial arts. Sheer jealously, of course! Yukio got annoyed, I don't blame him; and challenged him to a bout. He'll show him. He's in much better fettle than Genzo, who's out of practice and fairly tipsy to boot!'

As Kenjiro was speaking, the two men closed, panting and

heaving against each other until Yukio gave a mighty shove, his fingers slipping on Genzo's damp flesh, as he threw him down. The onlookers bellowed approval and Hannah cried impulsively, 'Oh bravo!' Her eyes were shining and she stood with hands tightly clasped, watching Yukio's every move as he towelled his face then squared up to his adversary again. Once more they circled, pawing the sand like young bulls, then locked again, their muscles bulging high in arms, neck, chest, and legs; but Genzo was clearly losing ground and slipped down clumsily. As Yukio stood back and lowered his guard, he leaped up suddenly and charged, ramming his head into the other man's body.

'Foul, foul,' shouted the crowd, and Elinor saw Yukio carefully control his anger, walling his stomach against the blow and moulding his face into impassivity. Sullenly Genzo gathered himself together and they sprang at each other immediately, with hostile snorts and thuds of hard flesh. Within seconds Yukio heaved Genzo clean off his feet, let him dangle helplessly for a moment, then turned and threw him hard towards his companions, where he lay inert, his mouth in the sand.

'The victor, the victor!' cried Joey, and Hannah, smiling broadly, handed Yukio a clean towel. 'I'm glad you won,' she whispered.

He took it from her with a shy, crooked grin, then went to drink a beer. Genzo rose unsteadily, brushed himself down, buttoned on his shirt and was led away by his friends.

'Now the conquering hero will come and feast!' Kenjiro slapped Yukio on the shoulders.

'No no, please excuse me. I'm far too dirty. I need a bath. Thank you for your support.' He bowed jerkily in their general direction and hurried away, swaggering just a little, his crumpled shirt under his arm.

'You rather like Yukio, don't you?' Elinor asked her daughter as they returned to the Inn.

'Oh, he's just a wild young animal like the rest, I suppose.' She shrugged casually, but in a manner that wasn't quite convincing.

On the day following the wrestling bout Kenjiro took ship for Nagasaki, where a party of officials were assembling to greet the Cesarevitch, the Russian heir apparent, who was coming for a tour of the country. Elaborate preparations had been made for his reception and he and his companion, Prince George of Greece, were enthusiastically and royally entertained in Kagoshima by leading members of the Shimadzu family – an occasion at which Kenjiro was proud to be present.

A week later the royal party reached Kyoto, where disaster struck. An elderly police-guard, appointed to control the welcoming crowds, attacked the Cesarevitch with his long sword, inflicting severe head-wounds from which he nearly died. The country, which had but recently managed to acquire a reputation for hospitality and warmth towards foreign visitors, reacted with anger and consternation. The Emperor and members of the court went at once to offer condolences and the Russian ship in Kobe harbour, where the prince lay ill, was positively weighed down with gifts.

Throughout this distressing episode Kenjiro and other officials worked frantically behind the scenes to put the best possible face on it before the world, and when, after a prolonged period of anxiety, the Prince was pronounced out of danger, Kenjiro was utterly exhausted. He did not admit as much to himself or anyone else, however, and continued with his usual routine, until the afternoon Elinor received word that her husband had been taken ill at his desk and was in hospital. A severe case of nervous prostration brought on by strain and over-work was diagnosed and a long period of quiet convalescence recommended.

So it was that Elinor went to re-open the Karuizawa cottage in a far less sanguine mood than when she had left it the previous year. Kenjiro's illness had shocked her deeply with its intimations of his age, his mortality, and perhaps of secret strains and sorrows he had concealed from her. Long accustomed to her exclusion from his working and much of his social life, she now felt she should have tried harder to share some of his burdens. But that was not his view of the matter, for, after they had settled quietly in the cottage and she tried to elicit some explanation for his breakdown, she only provoked a storm.

'Explain, explain . . . spell everything out, be precise, put all your cards on the table! That's all you foreigners ever want,' he moaned pettishly. 'I think that's been one of the troubles in itself. I've been expected to provide logical explanations for so much that is inexplicable. Things that never should or can be explained in precise words. The times I've been misinterpreted, misunderstood; and I've done the same myself − getting the wrong end of the stick, as you lot kindly put it. It's a dog's life, I tell you, being involved in these "foreign affairs palavers"! Real mutual understanding is as rare now as when I was a humble interpreter twenty-five years ago. So please don't *you* ask me to explain anything, Elinor; there's nothing to explain. I'm kept working too hard, people depend on me to produce results, it's my job. That's all there is to it.'

She said mildly, 'But you mustn't let it go on, Kenjiro. You got so dreadfully distraught over that Cesarevitch business, one would almost think you were personally responsible; but people don't blame you individually when things go wrong in these "foreign affairs palavers"; you simply take them too much to heart.'

He snorted, moving discontentedly about the small room. Monsoon-like summer rains were falling, the grey-green trees dripping moisture. Elinor wished Joey were there to lighten the mood.

'Am I not a foreign expert?' he barked at her suddenly. 'Men with my experience are still thin on the ground, so we have to take a crisis like this recent one seriously. It's important that the government receives the right advice. I don't expect you, a foreigner, to understand, but please don't keep asking me to explain.'

'A foreigner − that's the second time you've called me that, as if I were a distant stranger instead of your wife of many years' standing.' She turned her head from him in hurt, but he only hissed loudly through his teeth − a national habit that had always irritated her. 'Will you say nothing to that?'

she asked eventually. 'No word of mitigation? Am I indeed such a stranger to you?'

'Explain yourself, Kenjiro . . . spell it out; there you go again! I love you very much, and we've been long married; but sometimes you seem a stranger. We all do to each other.' He paused, knowing the words sounded rather harsh, then exclaimed with relief as the door opened, 'Ah, here's Ohisa with the post. I wonder what the latest news is on the Budget crisis?'

He sorted through his several letters, reading first one written in an unfamiliar hand. 'Why, here's a thing! You remember Genzo Yamaguchi, the wrestler on the beach?'

'Of course . . . what of him?'

'He was killed that same day on the train returning to Tokyo. This is from Ofuku, who says he tried to challenge the ticket collector to a wrestling match – couldn't stomach his defeat, I suppose. Apparently he kicked up the deuce of a rumpus and when the guard tried to restrain him, threw himself against a door, which gave way. Fell out on the track and was killed instantly by another train. What a stupid, stupid fool!'

'Oh, dear me . . . and only a young man. How very sad. No one else to blame?'

'No. At the enquiry he was judged to have been drunk and bellicose. Poor Ofuku! The fates are definitely set in their paths against her. She says she can only lie very low and hope for better times.'

'And his young wife, what of her?'

'Let's see . . . oh yes, she gave birth soon after, prematurely, and the baby died.'

'Can we do anything to help her?'

'Not really. Ofuku says she'll be returning home with the children as soon as she's fit to travel . . . Gengoro's grandson, hey? A prickly, fierce young cove, wasn't he? The samurai strain strong in him. And to be killed by a train, legless from drink, trying to practise the old martial arts . . . Poor, silly devil! Not born to be a salary-man after all . . .' Kenjiro gave a snort somewhere between mirth and sorrow, as he

contemplated the letter again. 'Odd . . . when you think of it
. . . and I remember his grandfather . . . but what's the use?
No explanation really, not in so many words at any rate . . .
And poor little Ofuku. She was a pretty maiden once and I was
expecting to marry her, only Gengoro gave her to Yamaguchi,
a man of much more substance, then.'

'Did you want to marry her?'

'Oh yes, desperately. I got very drunk and morose at her
wedding, I remember, watching her leave for Yamaguchi's
house . . .'

'You never told me this before!'

'Why should I? It's long dead and gone. And here I am
over fifty in a state of nervous prostration, and there she is –
a widow grieving for her son killed by a "snorting iron
monster". When she was married neither of us had ever seen
the likes of it.'

'I wonder how it would have fared with you if you'd married
her instead of me? Perhaps you wouldn't be spending your
life in bothersome foreign affairs palavers?'

'Perhaps not.' He grinned impishly. 'And if Bradshaw
hadn't been murdered you'd be enjoying the carefree life of a
memsahib instead of cooped up here with a sick man!'

She came and stroked his hair. 'You're just playing for
sympathy, my dear! And I'm glad things turned out as they
did. No Reggie for me, no Ofuku for you.' He took her hand,
pressing it against his cheek in a way that sealed their
marriage bond without verbal explanation.

'Who is your letter from?' was all he said.

'Arnold. He's coming up at the end of next week, but staying
at the local inn. He's far too large to squeeze into this
nutshell with us already here, he says.'

'I suppose you asked him to come and check on my health?'

'Not at all,' she lied. 'He's come up like this before.'

'Well, it will be good to see him anyway. But I must write
to Ofuku . . .' He went out, re-reading her letter.

By the time Arnold arrived Kenjiro was feeling much
better and was taking regular exercise. 'He's out walking
now. A little further each day, and nothing will deflect him.

You know how he is,' Elinor explained to her brother when he first came to call. 'Do you think he's doing too much too soon?'

'He'll be all right. I had a word with his doctors before leaving, and there's nothing to worry about.' He flopped into a chair. 'Oh, the dedicated intensity of these Japanese; makes me tired just to watch sometimes! Typically over-dramatised rumours flying about the capital now by the way, fanned by the Cesarevitch business. The assailant was a Satsuma man, you know; and now they're saying the great Saigo Takamori didn't commit suicide at the end of the rebellion of '77 after all, but went into hiding and is about to re-appear, clean the Augean stables of Meiji corruption, and lead the nation to victory against the Chinese in Korea!'

'What a lot of rubbish! But Arnold, will there be war?'

'Quite probably. The country isn't flexing all these martial muscles for fun. But Saigo certainly won't be C.-in-C. of the army. Another year or so of peace is my guess. May I have a b. and s.? Long enough to see me out of here.' He stretched and yawned.

'Whatever do you mean?' She paused on her way to the drink cabinet.

'Well . . . let's have the drink first.'

She got out bottles and poured in silence.

'Cheers! Well, the fact is I'm a middle-aged man rising fifty-seven, Ellie, and I've been in this country thirty years.'

'It doesn't seem possible.'

'Quite . . . You know, patients have said to me sometimes it seemed absolutely incredible that they'd actually lived as long as seventy-five or eighty years. Used to think them short-sighted, or dim-witted. But now I begin to understand – a sign of age itself perhaps. Anyway, Ellie, I've more or less made up my mind to go home.'

She jerked her head. 'You mean for good?'

'Er . . . yes. Well, I'll call on you during my grand world tours, of course.' He chuckled unconvincingly. 'Fact is, I've amassed enough capital through investments and such for a reasonably comfortable retirement. And I honestly don't see

427

the point of working myself into the grave here for another decade.'

She said nothing, twisting her sherry glass as if trying to screw it into the drinks tray. He too was silent, and at last she murmured, 'But won't you feel a little lonely? There's the relatives in Harrogate, of course, but . . .'

'Oh, I shan't settle there. We've nothing in common with them any more, have we? No, I'll put down a few roots of my own before it's too late. In Bath perhaps, a pleasant spa, and I shall court every wealthy widow in the place!'

She tried to smile but said, 'Oh dear, I shall miss you terribly.'

'And I you, Elinor.' He wandered towards the verandah to avoid her look of desolation. 'But it's very different for you – all your close family and friends are here now. And while I love you all dearly, I'm only the visiting uncle, likely to get more boring and crotchety as time goes by.'

'Nonsense, Arnold! You're very much a part of this close family.'

He changed tack. 'And besides, there's a lot here I like less than I used to. The uglification of the cities, all these monstrous brick offices and factories, gas-lamps coming in and pretty paper lanterns going out . . . Telegraph poles along the highways where the majestic cryptomerias used to stand. The needless rush into everything modern . . . And I detect a growing chauvinism too, a decline of the earlier ideals . . . Oh, I don't know. A mixture of things really, but it all adds up to a feeling of distaste, disillusion, even boredom . . . You know that charmingly old-fashioned inn we've sometimes stopped at on the way up here? I had lunch there yesterday. They've added a European-style dining-room with hideous cut-glass cruets on every rickety table. Soy sauce in the vinegar bottles, of course.'

'But the same sort of thing is happening at home,' she countered. 'More ugly factories and telegraph poles there too.'

'Oh, I know. Probably just the cynicism of old age creeping on . . .' He went to replenish his glass.

'So when do you intend to go?' she asked at length.

'Next year. I'm sorry, Elinor. I know it's a bit of a blow for you. But you're my only real tie here . . .'

'Am I really? Your only tie, Arnold? Aren't there others, of which we never speak?'

'What are you talking about?'

'You know perfectly well – your Japanese *mousmé*. Do you deny her existence?'

'I'll see she's well provided for.'

'And the children?'

'And the children.' He drank again quickly.

'There are children, then?'

'I'm simply not prepared to discuss it with you, Elinor. It is, and always has been, entirely my private business and I'll see to it that matters are arranged properly before I leave.'

'But leave them, nevertheless?'

He slammed down his glass. 'That's all I'm prepared to say, and unless you want to cause real unpleasantness between us, please drop the subject now – once and for all.'

He got up and went stamping off across the verandah and into the garden, his big boots trampling indignantly over the tender mosses.

Resolved that harmony should be maintained, for Kenjiro's sake, Elinor did not again refer to her brother's impending retirement during his short visit, though the prospect rather clouded the rest of her summer. Arnold was her only remaining link with home, reassuring evidence of her own roots, a bulwark against occasional loneliness and isolation. She had made many friends over the years, but few were close, mainly because of her own anomalous position between two communities. Arnold had always helped to bridge that gap, and now he was leaving. It seemed like the end of an era and made her, too, feel very middle-aged.

CHAPTER TWENTY-ONE

The Miyatas left Karuizawa before the summer's end, for Kenjiro had fully recovered and was eager to return to work. Once settled down again in the capital, Elinor went to see Ryo, who had recently returned from a trip to America with Millicent Pilcher. It had been a great success, she reported, and Elinor marvelled at her sister-in-law's growing self-confidence, a sense of purpose and drive almost equal to her brother's. Japanese men were reputedly terrified of her and some of their women scornful and shocked; but Ryo no longer cared.

'I gave talks to several women's groups during the trip,' she told Elinor proudly. 'Our lack of women's rights appalled them, though some think we're still living entirely in feudal times.'

'Ryo, I really do admire you for speaking up like this.'

'It's partly due to Millicent. You remember when I took her to see Kentaro and Fumio soon after she came? We thought at the time it had been a mistake; but it helped her to understand my position, and why we women are as we are. Now she introduces me to Americans as the "daughter of a samurai who's stepped into the modern world alone". She's become a true friend.'

'And we need those as we grow older and families disperse in different directions.' Elinor sounded a trifle forlorn.

'But you had yours with you this summer, surely?'

'On and off. Joey was often away. He loves to be with a crowd the whole time. Very Japanese of him, but not conducive to novel-writing, I tell him. Hannah spent weeks at the

431

Hattori villa in Hakone, much smarter than our cottage.'

'I think she still sees Oliver Rayne, but she's very secretive about it. Does she know the truth about him, do you know?'

'She knows the scandal surrounding his father.'

'I mean who his real father was.'

'Some dogs are best left sleeping after so many years, Ryo. Anyway, I wasn't thinking so much of the children growing away as of Arnold. He plans to return home next year.'

'But he's not that old, surely?'

'Rising fifty-seven, and comfortably off.'

'You'll miss him sorely, Elinor.'

'Yes . . . Ryo, do you know anything about his Japanese mistress and her children? He admits they exist, but simply won't talk about them.'

'Oh, but that's scandalous! I've heard occasional rumours . . . Elinor, you can't allow him to just disappear, leaving them high and dry. You must find out how they're situated at least . . . in all humanity. Women's humanity.'

'I've thought of that. But how can I find out if he won't . . .?'

'The Yoshidas, of course.'

Mr Yoshida was head cook in Elinor's household and when Arnold moved to a larger home a branch of the family went into his service; it was a standing joke that the quickest way for Elinor to discover her brother's whereabouts was to ask the cook. She nodded unhappily.

'Yes . . . of course.'

'Leave it to me,' Ryo said in such a grim tone that Elinor began to wish she had not broached the subject.

A considerable interval elapsed before Ryo raised the matter again, and Elinor had lulled herself into believing all was well. However, Ryo explained, she had been very busy after her absence abroad, and then she had decided to take the matter further on her own initiative.

'The servants told me what I needed to know, and I went to see the woman, Yasu, who lives in the poorer part of Kyobashi. She has three children there, all Arnold's. Two boys and a girl, ages fifteen, twelve, and ten.'

Elinor groaned. 'What sort of a person is she?'

'Perfectly ordinary middle-aged shopkeeper type. A good housekeeper, rather garrulous, not in very good health, so she says. She seemed very fond of your brother. He's treated her well, she said – as a dog might say of its master. There are photographs of him standing about. I said you were generally concerned about her, but apparently Arnold hasn't yet told her he's leaving, so I didn't either. But there's something else – much worse.'

Elinor felt that Ryo was rather enjoying herself, but couldn't imagine why.

'The eldest girl, Taki . . . I don't know how to put this . . . She's a common prostitute in the Yoshiwara and has been for years. Arnold's daughter – your niece.'

Elinor shivered. 'Oh, surely not! He'd never allow that . . .'

'He doesn't actually know. Yasu's never dared tell him and he never asks about her. But I bullied the truth out of her. It seems that when he was away on that very long leave about nine years ago, he left her with very little except three small children – and Taki. They fell on hard times and Yasu sold Taki off – for money, a contract-bond with a brothel-keeper. Didn't fetch a very good price apparently because she's got an ugly scar on her face from the Yokohama fire of 'sixty-six when she was a few months old.'

'So it *has* been the same woman all along! I wondered.'

Ryo nodded. 'Ironic, isn't it? And you're a member of the Women's Reform Society, campaigning for the abolition of legalised prostitution.'

'Ryo, you don't have to turn the knife.'

'I'm sorry. I suppose I was so outraged.'

'And you've never much liked Arnold, have you?'

She paused. 'Well, no . . . I have to admit it.' Arnold – so secure in his confident, masculine professional world; easy to be affable and generous with so much on his side. 'He's always patronised me . . . a mere oriental female. And this is proof of how he regards us.'

Elinor could think of no defence and Ryo continued, 'But the point is that Taki must be removed from that abominable place, and I've found out how it's done. The original contract money has to be returned to the brothel-keeper, and the girl has to sign a form saying she wants to leave, in the presence of an independent witness.'

'You haven't been letting the grass grow.'

'I've spent far too much of my life doing that already, Elinor! I suggest we go first and find out if the girl wishes to leave. If she doesn't there's nothing we can do.'

'But surely she will?'

Ryo shrugged. 'After years of corruption, defilement, indolence, their natural feelings crushed, some choose to stay there, I'm told.'

Elinor and Ryo Miyata went to the Yoshiwara on a grey winter's afternoon when it was at its dreariest. They were accompanied by a lawyer's clerk and an attendant from the introducing-house, who led them to the House of the Seven Red Moons, where Taki lived. Unlit lanterns, and blowsy heads of the season's last chrysanthemums in the street flowerbeds, were swaying in the chill wind and the empty rooms where the women would later sit on display looked like dark animal cages. Visits of this kind had to be made without warning so the girl in question couldn't be bribed or bullied; and the brothel's madam was obliged to admit them and send immediately for Taki. The house-signs announced that its specialities were foreign girls and exotic 'mixed-ups', and the reception hall in which they waited was lined with photographs to prove it.

Elinor resisted the temptation to guess which of the fleshy, gaudily dressed females might be Arnold's daughter, staring instead at the hideous magenta and pink carpet, thinking deliberately of nothing.

The girl who entered, and was introduced as 'Big Orchid', bore no obvious resemblance to her brother except for sandy tints in her frizzed hair and a clumsy lumpishness of movement which, allied to her pale flat face, was so unappealing that Elinor's first, quickly suppressed reaction was wonderment that men paid good money to have intercourse with her. She sat in silence while the clerk, in a pompous monotone, explained the procedure and that the two good women present had come to free her from a life of shame if she so wished.

When he had finished she stared around in blank bewilderment, then muttered, 'But what would I do outside? Mother doesn't want me back. I've no man of my own . . .'

'You can come and live in my mission school for girls,' Ryo replied briskly. 'There's lots you can do to help earn your keep and we'll try to improve your education.'

Taki seemed hardly to understand and Elinor added gently, 'You can come and go as you please. You won't be a virtual prisoner as you are here.'

The brothel's madam, a buxom woman with dyed-blonde curls, said sharply, 'But you needn't think you can come back here if that mission place doesn't suit you, Big Orchid. You're not that much in demand, I can tell you! Once you go, you go.'

Taki blinked at her. 'But it would be a nice change not to have to mess around with men every night.'

Elinor shuddered. 'Do come, dear. I promise we'll look after you. Just sign the paper as the clerk explained and you'll be free.'

In the uncertain pause that ensued, Elinor heard women chatting and giggling in distant rooms, presumably preparing themselves for the night ahead – sponging, painting, rouging, bedizening their bodies ready to be obliging. Smells of scent, powder, hair-oil, and the cloying under-whiff of stale sex that hung in the atmosphere made her feel slightly sick; she wanted desperately to escape, and shifted in her chair.

Taki said slowly, 'All right, I'll come and see what it's like outside. I can always come back to somewhere like this if I want to.'

She glowered at the madam, who tossed her curls. 'Please yourself, I always say in cases like this. If you think you can do better outside – you just try!'

The clerk handed Taki the form and she signed it unread; he and the madam also signed. As Elinor moved to the door, Ryo handed Taki a card. 'This is my address. When the clerk brings the bond money you must go there. I'll have a place ready for you.'

Taki nodded, showing no sign of gratitude. But what had she to be grateful for, Elinor thought, as she hurried out, breathing great gulps of cold, relatively pure air. As they reached the willow tree near the entrance, the name of which was unknown to them, Elinor said firmly, 'I'm going to see Arnold at once. While the horror of all this is uppermost.'

'Excellent, Ellie. Here, take the lawyer's letter and persuade him to pay the bond money through him to the brothel, then we needn't be closely involved any more.'

Elinor put it in her handbag. 'Yes . . . thank you. You're being very kind . . . and efficient, if I may say so.'

'That's part of my stock in trade now. And let's hope you can bring off the next stage without too much unpleasantness.'

On the way to Arnold's home Elinor tried rehearsing her lines, carefully suppressing her usual feelings towards him, which were affection, trust, and the remnants of admiring regard for an older brother. He was still at work when she arrived and she had then to suppress a cowardly impulse simply to leave the letter with an explanatory note. However when he came into the sitting room, hurrying to greet her with his customary warmth, she faced him boldly with her opening line.

'Do you know where your eldest daughter is living at present, Arnold?'

He hesitated in genuine astonishment. 'Who?'

'The eldest of Yasu's children. I imagine that's how you regard them.'

Slowly he unbuttoned his overcoat. 'So you've been prying into . . .?'

'Well, do you know where Taki is now?'

'Taki? I haven't seen her for years and I've no idea and I couldn't give a tinker's cuss, to be honest.' He threw his overcoat over a chairback. 'And I'd trouble you to stop interfering.'

'She's an inmate of a Yoshiwara brothel that specialises in foreign harlots and "mixed-ups".'

'Good Lord! But Elinor, I'd no earthly idea and I don't . . .'

'Your daughter, who's also my niece, was sold into prosti-

436

tution nine years ago by your mistress when she was desperate for money and you were gallivanting round Europe. Not a very pretty picture, is it?'

'Now, hold hard! I simply won't be blamed for this. When I returned from Europe, Yasu said the girl was in domestic service and I didn't inquire further. I never much liked that one, I will admit.'

'She probably held some unpleasant past associations for you, hey? And now she's come between us again. Odd, isn't it?'

'Oh . . . that. Ellie, whatever do you expect me to do about it after all this time? I really can't . . .'

'Be held responsible, you're going to say. But to a considerable extent you are, Arnold. And the least you can do is make amends by paying her bond money back to the brothel, which will release her from it. Here's a lawyer's letter – you can deal with it yourself in the way he proposes.' He took the paper unwillingly and she continued, 'Ryo and I went to the place this afternoon and . . .'

'Ryo! What damn business has she poking her long nose into this?'

'She's as outraged as I am at the defilement of these poor women, and even more that someone so closely connected with our family should be a victim.'

He threw the letter on a chair. 'Ryo's getting very much above herself these days.'

'Isn't she just – in your masculine view. An oriental woman in a post of authority who dares assert her own rights, be independent, even criticise men like you. It's no wonder you yearn for the days of old Japan, as you were saying in Karuizawa. Things were arranged very pleasantly for bachelors of your sort, weren't they? Well, it won't be like that in future. Ryo and her sort will see to that.'

'And thank heavens I shan't be here to witness it . . . . A Japan ruined by socialist enthusiasts and holier-than-thou, prudish spinsters.'

'How dare you insult her so, Arnold! Why, I . . . Oh, I'm simply too exhausted to quarrel any more after what I've just seen. Are you going to pay this money without fuss or not?'

She brandished the letter at him again.

He scowled. 'The devil take it; pay him his dues for the sins of the past, hey? I suppose I will, just to keep peace with you. And what's the poor creature to do when she's freed from her bondage, as you call it, into a life of blameless virtue? If you expect me to introduce her at my dinner table as a long-lost daughter, you're sorely mistaken.'

'No, we shan't trust her to your tender mercies. She's going to help in Ryo's school for a while, and then we'll see.'

'Much joy she'll have there.'

'Much joy she's had anywhere in her blighted young life, Arnold.'

He ignored that evident truth and went to ring the bell. 'All right, all right; now let's drop the subject. Have a drink . . .'

She followed him to the door. 'No thanks, I really don't feel like one. All I want is a long hot bath after seeing inside that dreadful place . . . ugh! Will you fetch my coat, please?' she said, as a servant appeared.

Arnold shrugged, and muttered, 'She was never pretty, that Taki, with that scar. How does she look now?'

'The scar is practically hidden under powder; but she's a lumpish creature, crushed and sullen-looking. What else can you expect? The money is due for payment within a week and the sooner the better. Goodbye, Arnold.' Taking her coat she went out before he could think of what to say next.

Arnold kept his word and within a week Taki was installed at Ryo's school, where she found herself able at last to enjoy her favourite pursuit, which was sleeping. Deprived of a normal night's rest for years, her greatest luxury in life outside the Yoshiwara was going early to bed and rising late, while, even in her waking hours, she scuffed about somnolently in heel-less woolly slippers, yawning. She evinced no interest in learning anything new, and no talent, except for cooking. So after a few weeks, Ryo, who could scarcely endure the sight of the slippers, put her in the school's kitchen, where she seemed reasonably content.

To Hannah and the other staff Taki was simply one of several pathetic women redeemed from unmentionable horrors to a useful life by the efforts of the Women's Reform Society. They did not question her presence there and Arnold, who refused to see her, contributed a small amount to her upkeep. The matter seemed closed and Elinor, relieved, closed her mind too against the memory of the House of Seven Red Moons – the vulgar photographs, inane chatter, that sickly-scented, coarsely sweet, intimately human, grossly animal smell. Throwing herself with greater fervour into the activities of the Reform Society and the organisation of a training wing in the new hospital, she refused to worry about the future, telling herself that even Arnold's departure was a bridge she would manage to cross when it came.

A few days before February 11th the post brought an invitation for Mr and Mrs Miyata to the annual reception at the Japanese Embassy in commemoration of Constitution Day. It also brought another letter from Ofuku, which made Kenjiro hiss in annoyance.

'Listen to this . . .' He glanced at Elinor across the breakfast table. 'This silly young wife of Genzo Yamaguchi's is causing anxiety now, as if Ofuku didn't have enough trouble. Apparently she fell ill for a time – shock and the miscarriage – then wrote to say she'd moved to rented rooms and was working in a spinning mill to earn money to take her and the children back to Kyushu. But no one's heard from her for two months and Ofuku asks if I could possibly look into it on her behalf. She sends the name of the mill, the Rising Sun Cotton Works, which is their only clue to the wretched woman's whereabouts. What a nuisance . . . and just when I'm so busy!'

'You're always so busy, Kenjiro, and she is a relative.'

'A very remote in-law only. Anyway, I'll just have to go to the mill some time and give her the money to take herself off.'

'But soon – she and children could be ill.'

'After this is over.' He tapped the invitation card. 'Oh no! I'm going to Nagasaki for a week for discussions with some foreign ship-owners . . .'

'Then you must see to it before you go, and I'll come with

you. If Akiko is in difficulties I may be of more help than you.'

Kenjiro evaded the issue; but on the afternoon before the reception Elinor finally persuaded him to leave work early and they set off in house-rickshaws for the east bank of the River Sumida. It was an area she had never before had occasion to visit, a working-class district inhabited by artisans: carpenters, roofers, carters, stone-cutters, screen-fitters and, more recently, by employees of the newly built factories where bricks, tiles, and matches were made, glass was blown and cotton spun. It had rained heavily the previous night and their vehicle wheels slushed along deep furrows of evil-smelling street mud, flanked on either side by dingy, box-like dwellings. The Rising Sun factory was a ramshackle, almost window-less building down a back-alley and as Elinor's runners put down the shafts, Kenjiro called, 'You must wait outside. It's no place for you. I shouldn't have let you come,' he added, over-ruling her protest and ordering the factory's gatekeeper to fetch a chair so the lady could sit in his hut while he went inside. She waited a long time. From the factory came the discordant clatter and hum of machinery; the air that gushed from its ventilators was dust-clogged and steaming; occasionally ragged boys with heavy bundles staggered across the filthy yard.

'Do those boys work here all the time?' she eventually asked the gatekeeper, who was standing in the doorway noisily sucking a pipe, much discomposed by her intrusive foreign presence.

''Course they do,' he growled.

'But they're only children.'

'Ten or eleven, many of 'em. Poor little sods don't have much childhood.'

'And girls of that age work here too?'

'They do. In the mill sweeping up the filth and fibres. Some of 'em get chest diseases and die before they're twenty.' He was obviously relishing this opportunity to give her some facts of life from the other side of the fence.

'And how long do they work each day?'

'Ten- to twelve-hour shifts, night and day. The factory doesn't close. It's a hard life.'

'It certainly is. I'd no idea.'

He snorted. 'They don't tell rich foreign visitors like you about such things.'

'But I live here and I ought to know,' she murmured, thinking that Kenjiro ought to know more than he seemed to, also.

'Like some tea?' He was warming to her genuine interest and she nodded gratefully.

It was brought in cracked cups by a weedy female waif with a dirty rag wound round her head. Elinor thanked her profusely and tipped her generously, feeling wretched. As she was drinking, Kenjiro returned followed by a boy.

'They don't seem to know about her, but their record-keeping is disgraceful,' he reported. 'She's not working at the moment, but she may be sleeping in the women's dormitory for the night shift. This boy is taking me to it. You wait here.'

'No. I'm coming with you.' She stood up.

'You are not.'

'I am.' Even though they had reverted to English, the gate-keeper was grinning broadly, enchanted by the spectacle of a foreign woman answering a man back in such a bold fashion. He had heard rumours they behaved so, but had never believed it until now. Kenjiro stalked away behind the boy and she followed, thinking that, if the factory looked like a run-down barracks, the women's dormitory seemed a penal institution, enclosed inside a barbed wire fence and with metal-screened windows. The boy led them across a yard where wan-faced women were drawing dirty water from a communal well, and through a bare, cold room where others huddled on benches scooping up bowls of gruel. The supervisor, in a small office at the far end, told Kenjiro she had a vague recollection of the woman he sought, but believed she had left the mill.

Striding to the door, she yelled at the nearest worker, 'Go and find out if there's a Mrs Yamaguchi anywhere about and bring her here.' She sat down again, grumbling, 'They lie abed till the last moment before the shift instead of eating their grub. Can't blame them really, it's only the left-over slops from the army mess hard by. But if they don't eat they fall ill and I get blamed.'

'Do many of them fall ill?' Elinor asked.

'Oh yes. The air in the factory is filthy and it's always too hot or too cold. They get tuberculosis, influenza, dysentery, and Lord knows what else.'

'And then you send them home?'

'If they've homes to go to. Flat-faced peasant girls with their toes turned out, most of them, and parents in the backs-of-beyond who can't afford to keep them any more.'

'But it can't be much of a life here, either . . . So I suppose they leave for better things when they can?'

'Not much better going, lady. And we keep them on a tight rein. They're locked in every night so they can't go gallivanting and it keeps the men out. But some decide they'd rather be birds in a Yoshiwara cage than work here and they usually manage to fly away. They can please themselves about that.'

Elinor glanced at Kenjiro, who was standing in the doorway drumming his fingers impatiently. She tried again. 'But if they work hard they can surely earn enough money to leave?'

'They're left with a pittance by the time they pay back their contract money here and their board and lodgings.'

'But can't they . . .'

'That's enough, Elinor,' Kenjiro ordered in English. She glared at him but relapsed into silence until a woman returned to report that Akiko Yamaguchi had fallen ill and left the mill several weeks before. One worker knew her address, which she handed to the supervisor, who passed it on to Kenjiro. 'Better try there, sir. I can't help you any more.'

As they left the building they heard men shouting and whistles blowing from the mill; time for the next shift.

'Where's that address?' Elinor asked as they reached their rickshaw.

'Too late to go now, it's a mile or so away and we're going out this evening, remember.'

'But then you'll be away and . . .'

'I'll deal with it when I come back. I can't disrupt my

442

entire life for this wretched woman, Elinor.'

On their return journey the main thoroughfares were crowded with rickshaws, carriages, and horse-drawn buses carrying people from work, and it was indeed late when they reached home and hurried upstairs, where their clothes were laid out in readiness for the reception at the Embassy. They dressed quickly and silently, both aware that the evening had been ruined in advance by their visit to the Rising Sun Cotton Works.

CHAPTER TWENTY-TWO

Elinor woke late the next morning and lingered in bed, reviewing the previous day's events with some displeasure. Kenjiro had left early for Nagasaki, so she had had no chance to ask how he felt about them. At the reception, he and his Satsuma cronies had not behaved well; withdrawing into a side-room, they had lapsed into maudlin lament, feeling the occasion to be more the anniversary of Viscount Mori's assassination than a celebration of Constitution Day. Would the country have been a better place today if he had lived and his views prevailed, they asked themselves rhetorically? In their bones, they felt it would have been, and drank copiously to that.

Elinor, islanded as always among the ladies, had acted as valiant linguistic intermediary between Japanese and British; but instead of thanks, Lady Hawton, the Ambassador's wife, had lightly bemoaned the fact that she was not equally and usefully fluent in French and Italian. Lady Hawton herself was well versed in the tongues and cultures of most European countries, where, she confessed, her heart remained. She expressed great admiration for Japanese civilisation nonetheless and had accumulated an exquisite collection of oriental porcelains. But with orientals personally one had to draw a tighter line, she often said, and made it quite clear to Elinor that the line she drew excluded, by several miles, any white woman who had actually married one of them. The other diplomatic wives, following her lead, were extremely gracious, but none ever offered real friendship, and to none could Elinor confide her distress at what she had seen earlier that day.

She got up languidly, still irritated with Kenjiro for leaving without making any further effort to trace Mrs Yamaguchi. Reluctantly, she went to his wardrobe and found the note of her address in his suit pocket. Why should she not go herself to see if she could help the poor woman, who had actually worked in that dreadful factory and might now be lying ill in some poverty-stricken slum with her babies? Having made up her mind, Elinor bathed, dressed, and breakfasted quickly and was soon bowling back across the city and over the river, where the branches of the cherry-tree avenues were bare-brown against a neutral sky.

The tenement in which Akiko lived was as bad as Elinor's worst imaginings, a warren of half-derelict apartments in a filthy alley. The pallid woman who answered Elinor's knock shrank back at the sight of her.

'Mrs Yamaguchi?'

'Ye . . . es . . .'

'I'm Mrs Miyata. You've met my husband, Mr Kenjiro Miyata, I believe?'

Akiko nodded. 'Oh . . . you are the foreign wife?'

'You could say that, yes,' she agreed reluctantly, guessing it was the term used in his family.

'Come in, please. We are very poor here. It is very humble; I am so sorry. I have been ill, and the babies also.'

The tiny room was ice cold, its floor bare except for a thin quilt in a corner on which sat two babies who stared at Elinor in alarm. A tattered screen in another corner partly concealed a bench on which stood a wash-bowl, a blackened rice-pot, and a tea-kettle. The room smelt of drains, kerosene oil, stale food, and babies' vomit.

'I'm so sorry, I have no chair.' Akiko darted about breathing shallowly and finally produced a torn red cushion. 'This is all . . .'

'Oh pray, don't concern yourself on my account, Mrs Yamaguchi. It's you we are concerned about. I've come on behalf of my husband, who's away on business. Just before leaving he heard from his cousin Ofuku, your mother-in-law, that she was most anxious about you. They haven't heard from you for a while and she and your own family want you to go home now your husband is dead. They asked us to find out how you are faring . . . and it looks as if you need a little help?' Elinor paused, but the woman simply hung her head. In the silence a baby whimpered. 'Why didn't you come to us? I do wish you had instead of going to work in that dreadful factory.'

She touched Akiko's sleeve and the woman shivered, turning her face away, near to tears. 'But your house is a long way off somewhere. A grand place, on a hill. I didn't want to trouble you. When I went before I broke an ornament. It was so stupidly clumsy of me . . .'

'Oh, good gracious, what does that matter? You should have come . . . But never mind, I've come to you now and we'll see what can be done. You don't look at all well, my dear, nor do the little girls.'

'They've had dysentery and I . . . I may have tuberculosis, the doctor said. So they sent me away from the factory.' She shivered again.

'But surely it would have been wiser to go straight home where it's healthier and you have relatives?'

'I hadn't the fare and . . .' she looked up sulkily, 'besides it's better in the city if you can work — the liveliness in the streets and the shops full of pretty things. As Genzo used to say, it's much more exciting than our dull old village. What would I do there but endless boring housework? And everyone would despise me for having worked in a mill like a low-born slut.'

Elinor chewed her lip; she had not foreseen this.

'I'll make some tea, Mrs Miyata. It's very kind of you to come all this way.' Akiko moved to the screen. 'I'll be all right once I feel better, and I've a good friend who's helping me.'

'Oh, I'm glad you have someone.'

'Yes, she's very kind. Your husband knows her, of course, but perhaps you don't?' She relapsed into a coughing fit.

'My husband . . . really!'

'She's promised to come along today with soup for the babies. She has a job for me, but it's not the sort of thing I want to do . . .'

447

'What kind of job? And I wonder how . . .?' Behind the screen Akiko clattered about the stove and Elinor, puzzled but unperturbed, inspected the infants, who shrank from her like frightened animals, hiding their spotty faces with spotty hands. Elinor tutted; she could not leave matters like this; but Akiko, for all her shyness, had a stubborn streak, as Ofuku had warned, and should be handled carefully. She re-appeared, apologising profusely for the cracked cups, rusty tray, small teapot.

'This friend my husband knows . . . is she a neighbour?' Elinor squatted uncomfortably on the cushion.

'Not now. She lives near where we first stayed. We moved when Genzo saved more money, but we kept in touch.'

'I see. And she can afford to help you with food and things?'

'She has since Genzo was killed, yes.' Akiko kept her face averted, obviously unwilling to say more.

'Your babies have dreadful colds and skin troubles, Mrs Yamaguchi; it's the surroundings. You must let us help you to something better, for their sakes. Will you not come and stay with us for a while, and when you're restored to good health we can decide on the best course?'

'Your husband will send me back to Kyushu,' she mumbled.

'Not if you really don't want to go, but . . .'

'Akiko, it's me.' The door slip open and a woman stepped in, carrying a cloth-covered bundle. 'I've brought the soup . . . oh, excuse me . . .'

Akiko jumped up and took the bundle from her . . . 'It's . . . It's . . .'

Elinor smiled. 'I'm Mrs Miyata, and you must be the kind friend Akiko was telling me about?'

The woman's narrow eyes seemed to disappear entirely into the flesh of her powdered face and she made an odd sound, between a snort and a cackle. 'Mrs Miyata, hey? The foreign wife.'

Elinor rose. 'So Akiko calls me, I gather.'

'And not only Akiko; many's the time I've heard your own husband call you that.'

Even then Elinor did not understand. She berated herself afterwards for her stupidity. '*My husband* calls me that? You must be mistaken in his identity, Mrs . . . er . . . Or perhaps you're distantly related to his family?'

The woman unfastened her cloak, handing it imperiously to Akiko, who stood shivering violently between them. Her kimono, patterned in bright reds and violets, shone like a warning beacon in these dingy surroundings, and Elinor suddenly sensed it.

'Not exactly a relative, though I know a lot about your family – your son Joey, daughter Hannah. My name is Koyuki and I live in the House of Gold, which your husband often used to visit when he grew tired of his foreign wife and her foreign ways.'

Elinor gave a cry of pain, recoiling from the sudden onslaught.

'No . . . oh, no . . .' She stared in horror at what now looked like a mask of powder and rouge framed by stiff coils of oiled hair, its cloying perfume mingling unpleasantly with the room's odours. She had seen many such faces on the streets of the city's entertainment quarters; it was extraordinary she had not recognised the type immediately – but she had been expecting Akiko's kind friend. 'He visited you often?' she repeated in a whisper.

'Quite often. It's no more than the custom of the country; you surely know that, Mrs Miyata. No real harm in it.' Her face cracked into a furtive smile. 'For a handsome, virile man like him.'

'Get out, get out of here at once. Why, you're a harlot!'

Koyuki's eyes positively twinkled. 'And who are you to order me out of the home of a friend I've been helping in her time of trouble? Akiko told me about you, but for all your wealth you did nothing.'

'We didn't know she was in trouble till the other day . . . oh, get out, woman . . . I won't bandy words with you. The House of Gold, you call it? He *often* went there?'

'Yes. Until about three months ago, when he said he wasn't coming any more, and hasn't. No reason given, left me high

449

and dry. But that's how brave men behave, you must know *that*. I expect he's found some younger doll to fondle . . . So I'd nothing to lose by telling you, had I, Mrs Miyata? I must say I'm surprised that a sophisticated foreign lady like yourself has been so completely fooled for so many years. Eh . . . eh . . . many's the rollicking times we've had, Kenji and me, in the House of Gold . . . You better heat up the soup, Akiko. Would you like some, Mrs Miyata? I'm a generous woman, always have been, and I've carried on helping Akiko out of the kindness of my heart in spite of the way your husband's treated me. But I don't bear any ill-will, so let's . . .'

'Oh, for God's sake, go away, go away . . . I can't bear it.' Elinor covered her face. 'No . . . I'll go, of course.' She dived for her coat, bundled it on with shaking hands. 'But Akiko . . . the babies. You must come with me now, this minute. Get your things together. I can't possibly leave you in this sink of filth with this depraved woman.'

Koyuki reared her coiled head and shouted, 'You hold your tongue about me, Mrs mighty Miyata! No wonder Kenji came to me for some fun! Choc-a-bloc with righteousness, aren't you?' Alarmed by the noise, the babies, who had been watching wide-eyed, burst into squeals of fright and their mother rushed to calm them. Koyuki looked over at them compassionately, saying more quietly, 'I'll be the one to go and you can look after them now, Mrs Miyata — you and your precious husband. Why the hell should I scrimp to bring them soup when you can well afford to keep them in luxury?' Furiously she threw her cloak round her shoulders. 'That will make you feel even more virtuous, won't it, foreign wife? How bored Kenji must be with you! You better look out — he's found another pretty wench, I'll warrant, and may leave you in the lurch soon as he did me.' She giggled. 'Goodbye, Akiko; be sure to screw what you can out of this hoity-toity madam. And good riddance to the lot of you . . . And I'll have my soup back.' She grabbed the basin and stalked out with a swagger which suggested that she, at least, had thoroughly enjoyed the encounter.

Elinor stood rigid, listening to Koyuki's footsteps clattering down the bare passage, while the babies whimpered afresh at the disappearance of the promised soup and Akiko coughed and cringed in apology. She wanted to run after the woman, to make certain there had been no mistake, to find out more, to hold her, shake her . . . But what more did she need to know? There was no mistake.

She said, 'Akiko, pack your things quickly and I'll take you home with me. Please don't apologise, it's not in the least your fault. Just do as I ask.'

Trembling, Akiko wrapped scraps of clothing inside cloth bundles; as she reached for the black tea-kettle, Elinor said gently, 'Don't bother with the utensils, leave them for the next tenants. Come – we'll look after you.' So saying, she picked up the larger child and carried it out to her rickshaw; an extra one was hired and they jogged back through the city. Passing the park-space outside the grounds of the Palace, Elinor noticed that an old woman in a faded grey tunic who had been cleaning mosses from a flagstone path when she had passed earlier was still bent over the same task. She could hardly believe it was the same day, the same path, the same woman . . . She installed her visitors in the Japanese wing, supplied food and clothing, sent for a doctor and then for the medicines he prescribed. It was evening before she could escape to her own bedroom. There she sat at her dressing table brushing her hair mechanically, pretending, for just another few minutes, that nothing exceptional had happened. Then she clenched her fists tight in front of her and stared into the mirror, facing the pain.

Kenjiro with a woman of the entertainment quarter – a common harlot with a painted mask-face indistinguishable from hundreds of her kind. Why her especially? And if her how many others? The supply was unlimited, his desires perhaps insatiable? She touched her cheek to feel its reality, remembering a much younger Elinor who had once looked into her mirror at the Yokohama Consulate facing the fact that she loved Kenjiro Miyata and could not bear to leave Japan without finding out if her love was reciprocated.

Throughout the years since, the strains, quarrels, gulfs of

mutual incomprehension, she had kept tight hold of that love. She had learned that his prolonged absences, his frequent failure to confide in her was what she must accept as the wife of a Japanese, whose place in society was subordinate and separate. But she had always trusted the one inviolable meeting place of their marital bed, their intimate, pleasurable knowing of each other, her delight in his handsome virility, his continuing desire for her body, where the marks of years were more evident. But for him it had been a mere pretence, apparently, the mechanical act of a man with his heart elsewhere.

When had it begun? she wondered miserably; for the woman had spoken of years of intimacy. Perhaps after their first visit to Europe, where he had suffered many slights and humiliations and withdrawn for months into a shell of hurt? Or after the death of their third child, when she had removed herself from him, grieving and lonely with a sense that he was not truly sharing her grief? Or later, when he began staying away for longer periods, 'on business' he always said, and she had always believed him implicitly, without the shadow of a doubt. Her body shook with fury and humiliation and she began to cry at last from a profound sense of loss and pity for that young, innocent Elinor who had once stared into her mirror and declared undying love, for a man who had betrayed her.

Elinor spent the next week in an ache of despair, haunted by visions of Kenjiro's past infidelities, his present shameless cavortings in the brothels of Nagasaki. Fortunately much of her time was occupied in nursing Akiko and the babies, who seemed at first to sicken rather than recuperate in their healthier surroundings. Obsessively she rehearsed what she would say and do when Kenjiro returned, but the cool trenchancy that had seen her through other crises had quite deserted her. She pictured packing her bags and leaving the country with the younger children, denouncing him to her older children and the wider world; even killing herself so he would be the one to find her corpse.

But, when he did return, quite late on the expected evening,

452

she simply shut herself in their bedroom, instructing Ohisa to inform him of Akiko's presence in the house. Accordingly he went to see her first, and eventually came upstairs, loosening his collar, yawning, quite unsuspecting.

'Elinor, are you there? Are you all right?'

The very casualness of his enquiry infuriated her. 'All right? Oh, marvellous, perfectly marvellous.'

'What's the matter?' He closed the door quietly.

'You're late! I suppose you've been rollicking with Koyuki in the House of Gold?'

He stared at her; with his tie dangling and his collar unbuttoned he looked, she thought, suitably dissolute. 'Koyuki? I haven't seen her for months.'

'So that makes it all right, does it? But you used to see her regularly, didn't you – whenever you got bored with your tiresome foreign wife?'

'But how did you find . . . Oh, lord; Akiko, I suppose?' He clenched his jaw on the words, then added, 'It was never important. She never mattered in the least, and it's all over now.'

'Because you've found some younger, prettier wench, I'm told.'

'No, there's no one else . . . no.' He came to where she sat huddled deep in a bedroom chair and touched her shoulder. 'I'm very sorry, Elinor. I realised, after the episode with Arnold and his woman, how much it would wound you, so I stopped visiting her. But I forgot to cover my old tracks, unfortunately.'

'So . . . you're sorry. Just an unfortunate little mistake; say no more about it, shall we?' She rose suddenly and slashed at his face with her hand as hard as she could, watching his stunned recoil with a certain pleasure. 'Who do you think I am? Just another down-trodden, helpless oriental wife who snatches at any little crumb of her husband's affection, asks no questions, puts up with his unexplained absences? Oh, I've known it's happened to other women, that's the terrible thing, but I always believed we were unique, that we loved each other in a truly different way. Stupid, credulous fool that I was! As Koyuki had the wit to point out.'

'Damn her, Ellie. It's not true. We are and always have been different.'

'Not true, either, that you used to call me your foreign wife? Oh, everything she said was true. I'm certain of that. How could you describe me in such a way, Kenjiro, betray me to her so utterly, be so intimate with her?'

He stood rubbing where she had hit him, twisting his face in a desperate effort to make her understand his version of truth. 'Elinor, it wasn't a betrayal of our love. That has always been the most important thing in my life – I swear it. But yes, I admit to the "foreign wife". There is a foreignness between us from which we can't escape because of our separate race and culture. Is it not part of our love? Wasn't it so from the start? And don't I sometimes seem foreign to you, in spite of our long intimacy?'

'Never more so than at this moment. Indeed you have gone completely beyond my understanding. You are quite alien to me and I've never felt such a stranger in this country as I have this past week.'

He sighed, summoning reserves of patience, though he found discussions of this kind acutely embarrassing and distasteful; with a wife of his own race he would never have countenanced them.

She continued, as if composed, 'So I'm seriously considering returning to my own people in England and taking Umé with me. I see no future for her or myself in this primitive land where men are permitted to behave so monstrously. I hope Hannah will join us. I dread the thought of her marrying a man of your race after this and . . .'

'Stop it, stop it! What are you saying?' He came and shook her shoulders. 'Go away to England? For such a trivial matter as this! And it's ended anyway. Elinor, for pity's sake, how can you even contemplate it? You are my heart's drawing, you always have been. I tell you so every year and I mean it, always . . .' He clung to her in angry fear. 'Leave? With Umé? With Hannah? Destroy our family, our lives and our love on account of some silly painted woman? Have you lost your senses?'

She tried to shake free from him. 'Not my senses, just my spirits – and taste for living. I feel totally desolated. This week has been hell for me . . . hell. The shock of her – a painted woman, as you say – her mocking, cruel words, that were yet true! How could you consort with her, Kenjiro, instead of me?'

'Listen to me, listen.' He put a gentle hand over her mouth. 'It was never instead of you. It was . . . I will try and explain honestly . . . just listen. It was – the house she kept, the old-fashioned way of things there. It was so thoroughly, familiarly Japanese. Everything that we men are expected to enjoy. It was a little corner of the past that's slipping away forever and I indulged myself in it now and then, that's all. It had nothing to do with our love. Can't you understand that, Elinor? After all, I gave up a great deal when I married you. We live in this western-style house, my life is that of a modern city man, and our children are educated in partly foreign ways. I accept it, we have made this home of ours together, but occasionally it still feels strange, and I am awkward and uneasy in myself. At such times I used to go there, that was it, and that was all. When I realised how it would hurt you if you knew, I stopped going, as I said, and I promise you here and now that nothing of the sort will happen again, never ever.'

He stood back, giving her a brilliant, confident smile, certain that his very honesty – of explanation and intent – would melt her anger and pain.

'You – how dare you plead what you gave up to marry me! What about me? How much have I given up for you? Living for thirty years in a foreign land among people to whom I'm forever an outsider, cut off entirely from my own roots and even from my own compatriots here, who think me contemptible for marrying "a native". Oh, *I've* felt lonely and isolated often enough! Of course, I should have taken some thoroughly typical English lover to make me feel comfortable and at home . . . That would have been quite permissible in the circumstances, surely? Perhaps he'd have loved me truly and

455

I could have gone home with him and been happy, instead of being stuck here in this state now, my life in ruins . . .'

She started to sob noisily and he looked on in shocked silence. He would go no further to help her. He had already pleaded to the very boundary of his self-respect. It was said that Japanese men who spent too much time abroad became women-worshippers like western men, and perhaps he had lived so long with Elinor that he was in danger of falling into the same trap, succumbing to the same weakness. Yet his heart was wrung by their dissonance and the sight of her misery. He went to the window, running his fingers over the glass – foreign glass, foreign house, foreign wife. In his country divorce was called a broken mirror, a shaming tragedy for all concerned. The thought of it appalled him and he made a last appeal. 'Elinor, I beg of you to put this incident behind you for everyone's sake – ours and the children's. I've told you the place you hold in my heart and my life. I've asked your forgiveness, promised you fidelity in future. Elinor, this is no use . . . You're upset and I'm tired after the journey and I'm going to sleep in another room. I can't and won't say any more. I've already humbled myself, conceded far far more than most men like me would, I might add. And now I'd rather you didn't refer to the matter again. Ever. What is done, is done and it is over.' He went briskly to the door, closing it on her last words.

'Is that all you . . .?'

It took Elinor weeks to accept that in her husband's mind the matter was indeed closed. Still racked with misery, humiliation, and anger, she tried raising it again, but he simply refused to be drawn. One night, returning late from a social gathering, he came into her bed and made love to her with gentle determination, in spite of her lack of response. Afterwards she sobbed a little and he ignored the sound, though troubled by it. However, he knew he held the key to her desire and was confident she would eventually open herself gladly to him again, even though her closing against him was more than physical, her sense of betrayal deep.

In the meantime they were occupied as usual in their very

separate spheres. Akiko fell extremely ill and Elinor helped care for her and the babies until they were well enough to make the journey back to Kyushu. Kenjiro was promoted to higher office in the Ministry of Foreign Affairs, where the main preoccupation was the increasing tension between Japan and China over the buffer state of Korea. With a view to sounding out the attitude of the powerful western nations on the issue, the government dispatched a delegation to Europe; Kenjiro was one of their number and Elinor, in consequence, spent the summer season at the Karuizawa cottage with the younger children for company. Joey, Hannah, and their friends came for brief jolly visits and only Ryo, the last to arrive, sensed the hollow of misery that lurked beneath Elinor's usual calm.

'I'm afraid you're depressed about your brother's departure?' she ventured as they sat sewing on the verandah one warm afternoon.

'Arnold? Yes, it is a blow, but he isn't going till the New Year, after all. The government have persuaded him to accept a short contract to help a training scheme for army doctors.'

Ryo nodded, still puzzled. 'And has he made proper arrangements for his family, do you know?'

'I haven't broached the matter again. He'll never regard it as we do.' She unreeled a length of cotton and bit off the end savagely. 'Has Taki settled in well with you? One tends to forget her – she makes so little impression.'

'That's the trouble. She's docile enough, but nothing seems to interest her, except Hannah, whom she follows around like a pet dog.'

'Really? How unfortunate!'

'Perhaps it's because she's everything poor Taki isn't. Pretty, intelligent, and virtuous.'

'Thank goodness Hannah doesn't suspect who she is.'

Ryo nodded, stitched quietly for a minute, then tried again. 'But I do feel there's something troubling you, Ellie. Of course, Kenjiro being away for the whole summer is . . .'

'Oh, I don't bother on that score. Why should I? He's away

457

so frequently. He's just written to say his return is delayed for another two weeks because the delegation have been instructed to stop at Hong Kong for discussions with the Governor about China's policy in Korea. I wonder if that's the truth . . . not that it matters.' She plied her needle energetically and Ryo stared at her bent head.

'But why shouldn't it be true?'

'Oh, it sounds plausible, your brother always does. But I don't necessarily believe what he says anymore. He's probably staying on to sample the local bordellos.'

'Elinor! What on earth makes you say such a thing?'

'Oh, I . . . I . . .' She threw down her embroidery and went to hunch over the verandah rail. She had blurted the bitter words without considering their full impact, but she was feeling desperately alone with her trouble and Ryo was the only one in whom she could confide.

'Please tell me,' Ryo said softly.

So Elinor told her, standing looking out towards the trees and speaking so faintly that Ryo could barely catch all the words, that gradually fell away to a silence.

'Oh, dear . . . oh, dear me.' Ryo took off her spectacles and wiped them agitatedly. 'But it is all over now? He's promised you?'

'But surely *you* don't think that makes everything all right? As he seems to?'

'Well, no . . . but . . .'

Elinor turned to face her angrily. 'Well, what do you think? Don't you find his behaviour absolutely outrageous?' . . . sitting there so untouched and spinsterly, she almost added.

'Yes, of course I do. Only I'm not so totally surprised. I suppose I'm almost as surprised at your state of outrage. Occasional visits to houses of that sort in the entertainment quarter go on all the time here at every social level and wives have to turn a blind eye. You must know that?'

'Oh, blind I was . . . blinded by love, after all these years! Of course I knew, but I still believed Kenjiro and I were different and had been from the very beginning of our reckless, unconventional alliance. When I think now of how supremely confident I was as recently as that birthday picnic, remember? Oh, it would never happen to me, I wouldn't countenance it for a moment . . . and so on. But already, to an extent, I have, because I haven't any weapons to fight with – as you, a supporter of women's rights, well know. The weight of law and custom is on his side, even though he's committed the offence.'

'Offence yes, and yet very much part of oriental custom, as you say, and for the men only.'

'Fine old oriental customs, hey?' Elinor rubbed her hand angrily along the verandah rail. 'Inevitable consequence of marrying an "oriental gentleman", as my mother used to call him with a sneer. Are you suggesting it's my fault for not seeing through his tatty veneer of "westernisation" earlier, or for making a fuss about it when I did? Aren't you a campaigner for the abolition of prostitution and more rights for women? But now it's your brother at fault all that goes for nothing, I suppose? As you reminded me over the matter of Arnold's woman . . . Men, men, oh why do we ever love and trust them, Ryo?'

She bent miserably over the rail and Ryo moved to stroke her back soothingly. 'Ellie, of course I'm ashamed, and very angry with Kenjiro. He should have appreciated and respected your difference, as you say. And our customs in this regard are a vile, cruel insult to womankind, but they simply won't be changed overnight and I beg you not to let this one wrong ruin all the rights in your married life.'

Elinor straightened. 'It's too late to go away. I've faced that. Too much of me is invested here and I'll just have to stay on and endure.'

'Is that the best attitude, Ellie – only endure?'

'I feel capable of nothing else. I'm hollowed out, raining inside day after day.'

Ryo returned slowly to her chair. 'Dear Ellie, try and remember what your life with Kenjiro has been, as a whole. You can't wish it all undone, surely you can't.'

'I don't know, Ryo. Certainly when we married so innocently in Nagasaki all those years ago I didn't dream of how much I was taking on – the heart-woes, rebuffs, the clashes of our differing backgrounds. It took me years to face the truth; that one can't do much to change a Japanese. You – women included – are surely the most intransigent people in the world? You conceal it quite carefully, as a courtesy to strangers, but you are unalterable, inexorable. Fads, fancies, and fashions wash over you, but you drop down into the same sand always, hard as pebbles, unchanged at the core.'

Her calm, considered tone brooked no dissent and Ryo whispered only, 'It's a mixed blessing for us.'

Elinor nodded and continued, 'One thing is certain. I intend encouraging Hannah to marry an Englishman. These vile oriental practices won't vanish yet awhile as you say, and I don't want her to suffer from them as I do.'

'Elinor, come – that's ridiculous! Are you suggesting all white men are pure as snow? How about your own brother, for example?'

'He isn't legally married . . .'

'Legally, no . . . but . . .' They glared at each other till Ryo lowered her eyes. 'We must let Hannah marry the man of her choice of whatever race and creed, as you did, and as we agreed she should.'

'I think she has chosen, only we've been doing our best to discourage her for reasons of our own.'

'Oliver Rayne? No, surely not. That cannot, must not be . . .'

'But I don't think we've ever judged him fairly because . . . well, you know why. Anyway, let's see how things develop. I found him quite personable and charming when he came here for a weekend recently.'

Ryo yelped indignantly, 'Came *here*?'

'Yes. It is my prerogative to select who comes here, Ryo.'

'He's a mere poseur. He'll never stick to anything or anyone, just like his father.'

'But he seems to be doing quite well nowadays.'

'I wonder how he manages to have so much money; there can't have been much in the background?'

'He paints and sells pictures, as you know.'

'Yes . . . I suppose that's it . . .' Ryo gathered up her sewing.

'I'm glad I told you, Ryo, though it's not been pleasant for you to hear. I suppose you are right. There's nothing to be done and I have to learn to forgive, if not forget.'

'I think so, dear. And please do both if you can.'

She went inside; Elinor continued to stare out at the trees, their straight, imperturbable stillnesses an ease to her troubled mind. After a while her thoughts, that had centred obsessively on herself and Kenjiro, circled out to include her daughter and Oliver Rayne, and she began increasingly to doubt Ryo's harsh judgement of him. After all, Oliver was talented, and both amusing and serious which seemed a good combination, and she was sure he loved Hannah. But did she love him sufficiently to take to the insecure, rootless 'artistic' existence which was quite alien to most Japanese but which Oliver would probably expect her to lead? Yet wasn't Hannah's alternative a strictly conventional marriage to a man who, on account of her mixed blood, would not be her equal in rank or intellect? Again Elinor rubbed hard at the verandah rail, remembering the conversation she had just had with Ryo, and hoped above all else that her beloved daughter might find some easy way to happiness.

CHAPTER TWENTY-THREE

Early in the capital's autumn 'season' the Miyatas, including Ryo, were invited to a large gathering held at the Fortescues in Yokohama. It was a happy occasion for Oliver in his dual role as Hannah's escort and promising young artist and his pleasure was increased because Mrs Miyata, at least, seemed less hostile towards him. He and Walter were holding a joint exhibition later in the year, he told her, and he believed the water-colours he was painting for it were better than anything he had yet done.

He had rented an attic above a rice-warehouse near Walter's house which he called his studio and dabbled about in it contentedly every day. Dressed in a paint-daubed workman's tunic and baggy trousers, with a wide-brimmed felt hat and wooden pattens, he was becoming known in the neighbourhood as the foreign artist, which pleased him well enough. Pictures for the exhibition were propped against the studio walls and he was currently working on a composition called *Bat's Wings*, the Japanese sobriquet for a western-style umbrella. In his picture, two large, black, slightly menacing ones were prominently visible among a crowd of bright, flimsy, native umbrellas along a Tokyo back street. The quality of the light was a misty-mauve early-evening raininess and this he was still trying to perfect one dry, grey autumn afternoon when there came a loud thudding on the studio door. As he moved to open it, Sylvia Fortescue burst in, the heels of her smart button-boots digging sharply into the worn floor-mats.

'Sylvia!' he exclaimed, with a semblance of pleasure that he

463

guessed was misplaced.

She came right up to him, pressing her face close to his. 'Oliver – those Kuniyoshi prints you sold me; they're fakes, aren't they? I want the truth . . . now.'

He shuddered away. 'Fakes! Why . . . whatever makes you think that?'

'They are, aren't they? I can see the guilt written all over you . . . you young swine.' She raised an arm as if to strike him, then dropped it hopelessly, tossing her bag and gloves on a cushion and simply glaring at him. 'You've ruined me, Oliver Rayne! My reputation, my marriage, not to mention my finances . . . And I trusted you as my friend, gave you hospitality, paid good money for your rotten portraits and your trashy fakes.' She came close again, and again he recoiled, trying to break her flow, but her voice was louder. 'Well, I'll get my own back; I'll make you pay for this somehow, you'll see! Like father, like son you are, aren't you? I should have guessed. Instead I even felt sorry for you . . . ugh!' She kicked the cushion and prowled up and down as if wanting to tear the room apart with her large hands. 'So this is where you cook up your artistic muck, is it?' Without warning, she grabbed an empty paint pot and threw it wildly, hitting him below the belt. He cried out in surprise. 'I hope it hurt! You and your flirting and flattery, leading me on. You must have taken me for a real nincompoop. That's what Edgar called me when he came home last evening in a towering rage.'

Oliver, doubled over, managed to interpolate, 'Would you mind telling me how he . . . er . . . found out?'

'Oh, you have your precious Hannah's spinster aunt to thank for that. Edgar was proudly showing her my collection of rare Kuniyoshi prints at that garden party last month and she sowed little seeds of doubt in his mind about two of them. So he sent them off to Professor Fantani for his expert opinion. Quite clever forgeries, the Professor conceded; but not clever enough, Oliver . . .' She collapsed on the cushion, burying her face in her arms and sobbing noisily. 'Oh you rat! What a fool you've made me look before my friends, my

464

husband, my mother-in-law. Do you know what Edgar shouted at me last night? "Got above yourself, didn't you Sylvia? . . . 'A greengrocer's daughter with ambitions above her station. She'll get you into trouble one day' – that's what my mother said about you before we married. And right she was indeed! Trying to take a leaf out of her book, weren't you?" he said, "But without an ounce of her artistic savvy." ' Sylvia's voice broke and she fumbled for a handkerchief. Oliver handed her a towel and she wiped her cheeks, continuing, 'So I asked him if he wished he'd taken his mother's advice and not married me. And he said he did, because then we wouldn't be in this sorry mess – the laughing stock of the community. Arty Sylvia gets her comeuppance and hubby has to foot the bills!'

Oliver leaned against his bench, horrified and shamed by the extent of her distress. 'Sylvia, please – I'm not really wicked. I just didn't think. I never meant to hurt you or cause trouble between you and your husband. I like you, truly I do, and it was a cruel joke to play, I realise that now. Only I was hard up and bitter at the time – and you did carry on rather about your cultural taste and patronage of the arts!'

'You mean I didn't have the proper savvy to carry it off, I suppose? Just as Edgar said. And that made it all right to cheat me and do me down?'

'No, no, it didn't, and I never intended to cheat you, honestly. I fully intended to blow the gaff and pay you back after my exhibition, where I'm sure to sell a lot of paintings.'

She snorted. 'You think Edgar will wear that? Not him! He's threatening to go to a lawyer tomorrow and file a suit against you for dealing in forgeries. You'll be hauled into court and convicted and end up in a prison cell just like your precious father, and serve you right!'

'Oh, no . . . not that . . . It was just a silly prank.' He stared at her appalled, then hauled a box from beneath the bench, produced a bottle and poured two brandies. For a minute they drank in silence while he stared miserably round the studio he had grown to love. 'Please believe me,' he ventured. 'I just stumbled into those forgeries. It was no more than a tease, I only did it twice and . . .'

'Oh, what's the use of excuses, Oliver? You've ruined yourself and done me down so that my so-called friends and my wretched mother-in-law can gloat! I always hated her snobbish chit-chat and now she can say "I told you so, Edgar" for the rest of her days.'

'Perhaps he won't tell her?'

'He's writing today to ask her advice about what to do.'

'So he is still uncertain? Sylvia, can't you persuade him to keep it out of court? I'm a man of straw and you won't get anything from me except the price of these.' He gestured round the studio. 'Give me a chance. I'll sell them all now instead of having an exhibition and pay you back with the proceeds. Then I suppose I'll have to leave the country. I'd never be able to hold my head up again anyway, now the great Panjandrum Fantani knows I've been selling forgeries. But not everyone need know.' As she hesitated between her desire for revenge and hope of salvaging at least part of her artistic reputation, he pressed his point. 'I'll say my sister is ill and I have to go home . . . Oh, what a stupid mess I've made for both of us! Please, Sylvia, please . . .'

'I'll never do another thing to please you, Mr Tricky Rayne.' She heaved herself up, thumping her empty glass on the bench. '. . . But to please myself and save face I might. I'll see if Edgar will wear it, and let you know.'

'Do you know why Mrs Miyata and the aunt dislike me so?' he asked dispiritedly.

'They're simply a lot more clear-sighted than I was, I suppose, and didn't want to see their lovely Hannah trust herself to the likes of you . . . Talking of trust, how do I know you won't do a bunk and get away scot-free once my back's turned?'

'But I won't. I promise.'

'Ha . . . promises!' She marched heavily round the room, picking out three paintings which she held out to him. 'Wrap those, I'm taking them with me. Hostages to fortune, you might say . . . And this . . .' she grabbed the painting on the easel.

'Oh, not that one, it's my favourite!'

'Then I'll definitely take it.'

He wrapped them in a clumsy bundle. 'But how can I sell them if you . . .?'

'Sell the rest first and bring me the proceeds, then we'll see about these. If I can persuade Edgar to keep quiet, we'll give you two weeks . . . Do you understand? And if you get off this lightly you should thank your lucky stars!' she concluded, slamming out.

As Oliver made the rounds of the capital's art galleries with his pictures it seemed to him that no one's stars could be unluckier. He was doomed like the rest of his luckless family, and the worst was that the blow should fall now, just as he thought his stars were rising. The pictures sold well, at least, and he duly sent the proceeds to Sylvia, who wrote a curt note to say she was keeping the other paintings and the matter was closed as far as they were concerned. In conclusion, she advised him to leave the country at once, for the outraged Professor Fantani was still considering legal action.

Accordingly, in a state of numb despair, he gave up his beloved studio, booked a second-class passage to Southampton on the *Princess Royal*, and wrote briefly to Hannah saying he had to return home urgently because of his sister's illness. That evening, his last in the city he had grown to love, he took Walter and Hyacinth out to supper, though neither of them, knowing the facts of the case, offered much sympathy for his predicament.

Late the following afternoon Oliver took the train to Yokohama and a rickshaw to the Oriental Hotel, having decided to spend his last sad night in Japan at the same establishment as he had spent his first joyous one. He supped in an almost deserted dining room, for the tourist season was over, staring at the menu with its excellent examples of Japanese-English: 'Mary Widow crab coktale'; 'Delice Florida creme-pie'. He thought of Joey, and even more miserably of his sister, and cursed himself for his folly.

Back in his room, he made straight for the bottle of brandy in his overnight bag, for only alcohol could get him through the remainder of that night. A half-formed plan was skimming about his head which he dared not confront, but could not banish. He wandered out onto the tiny balcony; the street below was almost deserted; on the right he glimpsed the dark cold sea where swaying vessels rode at anchor. He drank deeply without pleasure. He would reach England in the first week of 1894; Letitia, in robust health as far as he knew, would be delighted to see him. But what else? What next?

The more he drank the more he became obsessed by thoughts of his father — a weak-willed, unprincipled man, they had said in court, a trickster who had committed suicide in this very town because, obviously, he had nothing left to live for. The parallels, though not exact, were certainly too close for comfort.

He looked at his watch; the nearby ships' chandlers would be closing soon, but there was still time to go and buy a rope, have it here, just in case . . . It was absurd, of course, to have to go and buy a rope to . . . well, nothing was decided. 'In his room at the Oriental Hotel . . . Foul play is not suspected.' He poured another drink, thinking it was not merely suspected but evident, everywhere. His own ineffectual life to date riddled by it and ruined by an unkind practical joke. As he glanced again at the time there came a knock on the door. He stood stock still, heart beating fast. Fate had come to him then; the police were outside; Professor Fantani had . . . His suicide would be in a prison cell, just as it should be. The knock was repeated; he moved quietly towards the balcony . . . was it high enough from the ground to . . .?

'Oliver,' the woman outside called, 'you are there, aren't you?'

'Hannah . . .' He rushed to open the door and pulled her inside, clutching at her desperately.

'Steady on.' She pushed him away, put down the parcel she was carrying, took off her gloves and hat.

'Oh, Hannah, Hannah, darling . . .' He hugged her again and she noticed the brandy on his breath, the glitter in his eyes. 'But how ever did you know I was here?'

'I got your letter by the first post. It wasn't hard to guess you'd be sailing on the *Princess Royal*; I checked the passenger list in Tokyo.'

'Oh, Hannah, you can't imagine how delighted I am to see you. Have you come to rescue me?'

'Rescue? No . . . I've come to tell you something, bring you something . . . and to say goodbye.'

'I know I should have come and said my farewells to you personally. But for me it would have been so painful that I funked it. And my sister . . .'

She dropped her coat over a chair, looking at him gravely. 'No, Oliver, not your sister.'

'You know why I have to leave?'

'Yes.'

His cheeks burned. 'I've been a damnable fool. How did you find out?'

'That letter of yours didn't ring true for a start. I was sure there was more to it. So I decided to come and see you before you sailed. We've been friends for quite a time, after all . . .'

'Oh, yes; good friends, haven't we? And if it hadn't been for my stupidity . . .' He trailed off desolately.

'I came here first, thinking you'd be bound to spend your last night where, you once told me, you spent your first. It would be like you.'

'A taste for self-dramatisation, hey? Yes, I've just been indulging it.' He grimaced.

'What do you mean?'

'Never mind. You're here, now.'

'But I came first before lunch, and the hotel clerk said you weren't booked in till about six; so having hours to wait, I went to call on Sylvia Fortescue to see if she could throw any light.'

'And she did . . . Cheers!' He drank another brandy with bravado.

'You treated her extremely badly, Oliver.'

'Yes, I see that now, though at the time I hardly considered it from her point of view, which was shameful and I fully deserved her fury.'

'Oh, she's cooled down, now she's got most of the money

back. And . . . another thing . . . she showed me a letter that stuffy husband of hers received yesterday from his mother – Mrs Robert Greenwood as she now is . . . Well, she wrote that . . . oh, dear . . .' Hannah began walking restlessly about the room, fingering the shabby velveteen curtains and staring outside. 'What a second-rate hostelry this has become! It used to be called the Hotel de l'Europe and was one of the best in town, Mother told me.'

'For heaven's sake, Hannah, what is it? Do you have more dreadful skeletons to rattle from my father's cupboard? I've followed quite nicely in his footsteps, haven't I?'

'No, that's just what you haven't done; but I knew you'd be thinking it, so I decided . . .' She began fumbling in her handbag.

'Hannah, please stop tantalising me.'

'Incidentally, Mrs Greenwood didn't read the riot act at Sylvia for being taken in by your selling her the forgeries. Could happen to anyone, put it down to experience, she wrote, and Edgar wasn't to make such a fuss about it. That made Sylvia feel much better, the nicest thing her mother-in-law had ever done, she said . . . Anyway, Mrs Greenwood also sent this . . .' She handed Oliver a page of photographs torn from the *Far East Magazine* of 1866, headed 'Some of Yokohama's Foreign Merchants'. Against one, Mary had scribbled, 'Is there a family likeness to your artistic friend?'

Oliver stared at the man in the smart, high-buttoned jacket, whose face was startlingly similar to his own; the name below was Felix Coburn. 'Well . . . I can see a strong resemblance, certainly . . .'

Hannah's voice was neutral. 'There was a scandalous rumour about it in Yokohama at the time, Mrs Greenwood wrote.'

'You mean my mother and . . .?'

'Yes. So you see you haven't exactly followed in your *father's* footsteps after all. I felt you should know that before you sailed. It might help alter your view of things for the better. And there's yet more . . .' She sipped the brandy Oliver had poured her, while he sat staring at the carpet.

'Sylvia told me it was Aunt Ryo who first raised doubts about the authenticity of the Kuniyoshis.'

'Yes. She always hated me, I don't understand why.'

'Well, I do, now. You remember that twenty-first birthday of mine when she first set eyes on you?'

He groaned. 'Lord, how young and happy and innocent I was then!'

'You're not exactly old yet! Anyway, during that afternoon I took Miss Pilcher, galumphing Millie, as you called her, to Aunt's bedroom and she happened to pick up her old wooden pillow. There was a name scratched underneath – which is a sweetheart sort of thing to do. Guess whose it was?' She took hold of Oliver's dark curls, raising his head to look at her.

'Sweetheart? Hers? . . . My dear, I'm utterly foxed . . . You don't mean Felix Coburn's?'

'Yes. She actually went to live with him for a brief, unhappy period. My mother told me.'

'Your *mother*!'

'Oh, I didn't explain. I left Sylvia's with these things buzzing about my head that I had to sort out. So I hurried back home and confronted Mother. She was having tea in the drawing-room – alone, luckily. "Tell me the whole truth about Mr Felix Coburn," I began. I was quite proud of myself. But it seems Mr fly-by-night Coburn didn't really love poor Aunt and soon left her in the lurch. It rather ruined her life, Mother said. She was broken-hearted and very ashamed of herself and never wanted to marry afterwards. Of course, it was a scandalous thing for a woman of her rank to do. So she hated you from the moment she saw you – recognising you as Felix's son.'

'Good Lord, Hannah! This is all . . . I just don't know what to think . . .' Oliver rubbed his cheeks and laughed noisily. 'What it boils down to is that instead of a committed felon and suicide for a father, I have a womanising cad. And I'm a bastard.'

Hannah put a hand on his wrist. 'At least you needn't have any more nightmares about prisons and men swinging in them. And there's another point. Mr Coburn is probably still alive and kicking; he'd be about my parents' age, and quite rich.'

'Why should he be?'

'Well Coburn's corsets sell remarkably well even here nowadays.'

'Corsets! What a joke! Yes, it was mentioned in the court case.'

'And Mother heard later, though she's never told Aunt, that he met a wealthy heiress on the ship going home from here and married her.'

'Quite a ladies' man, hey? I suppose we should drink to his continued health and strength. Another, Hannah?'

'Just a drop before I go.'

He came behind her, touching her sleek hair. 'Do you really have to go?'

'Yes, Oliver, really.'

He returned to his seat on the bed without further protest. 'So you're suggesting I move from fraud to blackmail? I suppose there's a connection.'

'Don't be facetious. But you might decide to try and contact Mr Coburn. It seems he never helped your poor mother, but he might help you.'

'I doubt it; anyway, I don't need help. I am determined to make my own way as a painter.'

'Oh, splendid, Oliver – you've a lot of good qualities and talents. Sylvia and I were saying so only today . . . oh, that reminds me.' She fetched the parcel she'd left at the door. 'This is for you from her.'

He unwrapped it eagerly, laughing with delight. 'Oh, just what I hoped for – my favourite painting; the *Bat's Wings*!'

'She said it was your favourite and you can have it back – for nothing.'

'Oh, thank you; please thank her . . . it's extremely generous of her in the circumstances.' His eyes misted as he gazed at the picture. 'If only I'd not been such a fool . . . I wanted to stay so desperately, and I'd no money, and she was such a pretentious ass – I longed to be able to take you out and about, move in your circle. I kept hoping that if I was persistent enough you would . . . but you haven't, have you?'

'What can you mean?'

He put down his glass and came close. 'You know what I mean – start to love me a little. I've dreamed you might for ages because I love you a great deal. Oh, Hannah – sail away with me tomorrow. We could start again together. I'm sure now that I do have some talent and with you beside me I could . . .' He caught her hand, pressed it to his lips. 'I can scarcely bear the thought of leaving you. Oh, Hannah, we could go to Paris, where there are artists, writers, people like us who don't quite fit into the ordinary grooves. It would be blissful . . .'

He trailed off, for she was shaking her head, prising her hand free. 'I'm sorry, Oliver, but I'm not sure enough of you or myself. Besides, it would break my parents' hearts.'

'But they once had the courage to defy the conventions for love. You told me so, and that you admired them for it. They didn't worry about their parents' hearts.'

'They must have been much more certain than I am. After all, you've not behaved in a very kind or trustworthy fashion, have you? And another thing – there's going to be a war soon between ourselves and the Chinese.'

He was astonished. 'A war? So I've heard, but what difference does that make to you . . . to us?'

'I couldn't leave at such a time of crisis, and Joey will be involved. He's just joined the army. Yukio has persuaded him.'

'Oh, I don't understand this at all.' He thrust his hands in his pockets and moved away. 'Such an abstract sort of reason, such loyalty to a country that doesn't truly accept you! You'll always be a "mixed-up" here, Hannah, whereas in Europe . . .'

She shook her head slowly. 'One has to make oneself Japanese to live here happily – even if one isn't quite. There's no other way for me. I was born and brought up here and I'm part of the tribe, even though it doesn't fully accept me. But I can't leave it, probably I never will; it's too deeply ingrained already. No, I can't go, certainly not just now.' She stood up, drawing on her gloves. 'There's a house-servant outside with a rickshaw and I'm booked on the late train. I arranged that in advance.'

'Thinking I might suggest alternatives?'

'Perhaps, yes, and knowing I might be tempted by them, and knowing it would be wrong.'

'Wrong . . . wrong . . . oh why?' He made a last appeal, holding on to her coat as she reached for it.

'Because I'm not sure enough and you're not grown-up enough, to be frank. You visualise a romantic Bohemian life for us in Paris, but I can't believe in it. I've a sneaking suspicion we'd be poor and miserable and I'd be homesick.' He relinquished her coat and she put it on. 'I'm very sorry, Oliver.'

'Oh, I fully deserve it. I've behaved irresponsibly, why should you believe anything I say?'

'But there's no need to follow an irresponsible path further. Things must look a little more promising now. At least I hope so; that's why I wanted you to know the whole truth.'

Oliver gazed at her, agonised. 'Do you think Felix Coburn really loved my mother?'

'I'm certain he did; for a while at least, and she him. It must have been very painful for them both and I feel quite sorry for them. But you mustn't feel sorry for yourself any more . . . A kind of love-child . . .' Her cool lips brushed his cheek. 'Goodbye, Oliver, and good luck, whatever you do. Write and let me know . . .'

'Dearest Hannah, I will. I'll come down . . .'

'No, please . . . I'd rather just slip away.'

She did so quietly and quickly and he leant for support against the door, staring after her. When she had gone he went back inside and poured a last drink, gazing solemnly at the picture propped on the table. It was quite good, he knew, for he had at last managed to capture the atmosphere of an oriental street at dusk – low-lying, narrow, congested, a little mysterious, dream-like, and beautiful. Now he had to leave behind all that beauty and mystery and his heart ached for it. But perhaps Japan had taught him how to paint; certainly it had taught him much else. He drew back the curtains and went out on to the balcony for the last time, his earlier desperation muted to a mood of quiet melancholy. He thought with distant pity of his parents, from whose past toils Hannah's visit had helped to free him. He was his own man now and the prospect of the coming voyage filled him with new, though fragile, hope. He would work hard, look after Letty, and make a name for himself as an artist.

CHAPTER TWENTY-FOUR

In retrospect Hannah believed she had truly grown up on the eventful day which ended with her farewell to Oliver Rayne. She had been more tempted to go away with him than she had allowed him to guess; but was restrained by a stronger sense of duty, uncertainty, and a fugitive imagining of some sweeter alternative to which she would not quite admit. Once he had sailed she was glad she had stayed behind, though she found herself viewing others more critically, as if from a small distance. Forbidden by Elinor to discuss with anyone, especially Ryo, her discoveries of the scandals of the past, she still pondered secretly upon the stormy scenes that must have occurred, the long-buried hurt and bitterness. To Hannah, Aunt had always seemed an admirable and dignified woman in complete command of herself; but now she knew that she had once been recklessly, deeply, vulnerably in love with a foreigner. The knowledge increased her sympathy, but suggested that even familiar people were not always what they appeared to be — not Oliver, not Ryo, nor, she now discovered, Uncle Arnold.

Arnold's government contract ended with the year and he was free to leave Japan. Accordingly he attended a number of farewell parties held in his honour and began to dismantle his household. But the accumulation of the years was not easily or painlessly disposed of, and by late February he had made such small headway that he called Elinor in to help.

'Take what you want of that lot and the rest can go to Red Cross jumble sales,' he told her, waving his hand despairingly round an upstairs room filled with half-emptied cupboards and half-filled packing cases.

'But surely you're taking what's already packed?' She pointed to two tea sets lying in straw.

'Oh, what's the use of tiny cups like those, in Bath?'

'Perhaps the rich widows you intend courting will sip tea very daintily from them.'

'That's not very funny.'

'Well, it's no good being miserable about it. You've decided to go so all this has to be cleared up.' She began bustling about decisively, though her heart was not in the task either and she was relieved when Arnold suggested a break.

'But it will take months to finish at this rate. You'll have to be more ruthless . . .'

'I'm not in a ruthless mood, unfortunately. Come on, let's have a drink and quick bite of sup., then try again.'

In the sitting-room two over-full bureau drawers stood on a table.

'I'm taking that lot, definitely,' he gestured on the way to the drinks cabinet. 'But there's a few souvenirs I thought you might like to see before I pack them.'

She went to rummage. '. . . My goodness, an old silver *ichibu*; I'd forgotten they existed! Remember the rows about currency values in the old days?'

'We could have made our fortunes if we'd bought gold with silver at the right moment − or was it t'other way round? Cheers − here's to the good old days.'

'They weren't all good.'

'No, but there was more light-hearted, informal fun about, surely? Look at this . . .' He held up a faded photograph. 'Muffin the mad pony, who used to scamper along to Mississippi Bay in the phaeton.'

'And what's this? The inscription is too small to read.'

'Ha . . . miniature replica of the Shanghai Racing Cup presented by officers and men of the XXth. Blighters took it back when they went, leaving me this . . .' He chuckled, polishing it with his sleeve. 'Swore it was genuine silver underneath − a long way under! There's a photo of you somewhere looking sweet and maidenly with your golden locks tightly braided . . . Ah . . . there.'

'Rather prim and prudish, more like . . . And what's this?' She unfolded a piece of paper pinned on the back. 'Good heavens . . . how horrible!' She held up a newspaper sketch of a man's head impaled on an iron spike, the mouth distended in a savage grimace of rage and pain.

'Oh, that was . . . what's-his-name? Killer of poor old Beale and Bradshaw.'

She stared at her photo and the head. 'Have you ever thought what a difference that man made to my life?'

'Probably I did when I fastened them together years ago. Come, let's eat. Very simple fare. Yoshida junior's lost his culinary heart now I'm leaving.'

She lingered over the pile, reluctant to leave the past behind.

'Why, here's a whole envelope full of praise for the works and talents of Dr Arnold Mills! A citation for the part he played at the Battle of Kagoshima − wherein we British reduced Kenjiro's grandfather's temple to rubble, I believe? A bronze medal for devoted tending of the wounded of the Imperial forces during the civil war of Restoration. And . . . how funny . . . a letter of thanks from the attaché of the French Legation for advice on "health preservation of a most helpful nature offered to members of a game-shooting expedition to North China . . ." Here's more devotion to duty − during the rebellion in the south led by Saigo Takamori against the Emperor. And now the great Saigo is rehabilitated as a hero . . . History in the making we've witnessed, hey, Arnold?' She joined him at the table 'And more soon to be made, I fear? War is inevitable now, isn't it? More devotion to duty, wounded to tend. Volunteers are flocking to our hospital, begging to train as nursing aides. Hannah wants to be one, though we're trying to dissuade her.'

'Don't blame you; Joey's commitment is enough surely? He's still determined on the artillery?'

'Absolutely, though he could get exemption, being the eldest son.'

They ate in silence for a while, each wondering anxiously what the near future held for them in their separate ways. As the plates were cleared, Arnold stared morosely into the wineglass, 'That's the trouble about retiring home from somewhere like Japan. No one will give a tinker's cuss about what's been going on here for the past thirty years. No one for me to exchange reminiscences with; whereas the country's stuffed with old fogeys gossiping about the doings of the scandalously rich maharajahs and who-was-who at the Calcutta race-meets of the 'eighties. I could look up Percival Storey, I suppose. He and Edith are retiring next year. Never took to Edith — much too thin.'

'Hardly her fault and many would consider it an asset,' Elinor murmured, amused, then raised her head. 'Why, that sounds like Hannah outside . . . I wonder what . . .?'

She rose as her daughter came in. 'Hello, Mother, I didn't expect to find you here too. But maybe it's as well. Good evening, Uncle.' She paused just inside the room, glaring.

'Good evening, dear. Would you like some supper?'

'No, thank you.' She hesitated for a second only. 'I'm not sure I want to eat at your table again.'

He wiped his mouth carefully. 'Now, Hannah, what's all this about?'

His tone of uneasy jocularity incensed her further and she shivered. Elinor, guessing, poured a glass of wine. 'Now, dear, please calm down.'

'Well, well, what have I done to deserve . . .?' Arnold resumed feebly as Hannah marched to the mantel, warming her hands over the flame. 'I visited Taki's home this afternoon, Uncle. She wanted me to meet her mother, Yasu.'

He grunted and turned away, glancing at his sister.

Hannah caught the look. 'Oh yes, nothing new to you in this, is there, Mother? But I think it's absolutely shameful and disgusting.'

'Hannah, why did you have to pry . . .?'

'I didn't pry. But for some absurd reason, Taki's quite fond of me, and confided recently that her mother had received a fairly large sum of money from a "big foreign gentleman" with which she wants to open a cookshop near the Yoshiwara. So Taki wants to leave the school to help her mother with the

480

shop. After all, she has lots of experience in what customers want there, hasn't she?' She glanced angrily at them both and continued into their glum silence, 'But she didn't dare ask Aunt's permission. So she took me to see her mother, thinking that when I heard from her what a good idea it was I'd intercede with Aunt on Taki's behalf. So I went . . . I hardly need say whose photograph I saw on a shelf the moment I walked in. "Why, that's my uncle," I blurted out, before I'd time to think. Then I forced Yasu to tell me everything. I wonder if you knew that most of the money you gave her for the children's education after you've skipped the country is going into a Yoshiwara cookshop, Uncle? From Yasu's point of view it's a much better investment.'

'No, I didn't know that, Hannah. It's not what I intended.'

'And Taki has no idea of the connection?' Elinor queried.

'No, she's not in the least to blame, nor is anyone else. Yasu had kept the secret. You two – three, Aunt Ryo also – have been most careful to protect the untarnished reputation of the esteemed Dr Arnold Mills. Taki was quite happy at the news. "It makes us almost like cousins, doesn't it, Hannah?" she said. And so it does.' She sniffed in distaste.

'And how did Yasu take it?' Arnold muttered.

'She was most upset, afraid you'd be angry with her, though it's none of her doing. Such a good, kind, generous Big Foreigner you've been over the years, apparently. She's actually very sad that you're leaving for good. Did you know *that*, Uncle? But she doesn't blame you, couldn't stand in your way. Oh no, not in the least! Big foreign gentlemen come here and make use of native woman like her all the time, don't they? Take over their lives, have children by them, swan off when it suits them – without, in many cases, leaving enough money for a cookshop behind. She seemed quite grateful, actually.' Hannah sniffed again. 'May I have a glass of wine?'

They both hurried to pour her one. 'I'm very sorry you've inadvertently discovered all this, Hannah. I don't see what good it's done,' Arnold said heavily.

'The truth doesn't always do good, does it, Uncle? I'm

481

finding out that people aren't always as "good" as they seem, especially older ones whom I used to rather admire.'

He sighed and Elinor interrupted, 'I don't think you should be too harsh, Hannah. I know wrong has been done, but according to his lights your uncle has behaved fairly decently.'

'What about your lights, Mother? I don't think you and Aunt have behaved decently at all — covering up for him, doing nothing beyond removing Taki from the Yoshiwara. And you're both active members of the Women's Reform Society! It's rank hypocrisy . . . I've been thinking it over ever since I left Yasu's and that's my considered opinion.'

Elinor looked vaguely round the table, moving pieces of cutlery about. 'Doesn't this remind you of something, Arnold? A quarrel between us, a long time ago?'

'Hey? Oh . . . ah . . . yes, I suppose there is a resemblance,' he laughed dully. 'Hypocrites both, now, hey?'

'What are you talking about?' Hannah asked irritably.

'Nothing whatever to do with you,' her mother replied, so firmly that she didn't press the matter, gesturing round instead. 'So you're helping your brother to pack up the souvenirs, Mother? And there wouldn't have been a single mention of Yasu, Taki, and the other children, would there, if I hadn't appeared, to spoil your nostalgic evening?'

Arnold wandered over to the bureau, pulling out another drawer. 'There's something here that I put out of sight before your mother came, Hannah. Ah . . .' he took out a cherry-wood box with a stork of longevity inlaid on its lid. 'I always keep it locked and can't quite remember where I've put the key. I was thinking about it earlier, wondering whether to take it home or . . . burn it, I suppose. It contains a few mementoes of what you might call my family life. Photographs of Yasu and me, and the children at various stages — the girl dressed up for a Dolls' Festival, the boys wearing their first school uniforms. Shell-trinkets . . . I took them all on a seaside holiday once. It was a happy time. Yasu's quite a cheery soul . . .' He fell silent, standing there, holding the box in both hands with an appealing expression, as if asking them what to do with it.

Hannah lowered her eyes and Elinor said quietly, 'Why don't you stay, Arnold? For a few more years, anyway? Till the children are older, better able to fend for themselves?'

Hannah drew a sharp breath; Arnold put the box carefully back in the drawer and stared at the pile of things he and Elinor had been musing over. 'Yes, I think you're right, Ellie. I think I shall stay. My heart hasn't been in this packing up and leaving business, to be honest. So perhaps you came at just the right moment, Hannah. Instead of spoiling things maybe it was a blessing in disguise that you found out and came to confront me at once. Not easy to do. I see you have your mother's courage in such situations. Don't you agree, Ellie?'

She nodded, touching her daughter's shoulder. 'You know, I'm quite proud of you for this. Really I am.'

Hannah stared at them both in astonishment, then buried her head on Elinor's shoulder with a little sob. 'Oh, Mother, I never thought I'd change my mind! I felt so angry and miserable after seeing Yasu. About life in general as well as her in particular. It seemed that so many people are hypocritical . . . But now I'm glad I came . . . You really will stay on, Uncle?'

'Oh yes, I really will.' He began throwing things back in the drawers.

'You might have a bit of a sort out while you're at it, Arnold.' Elinor smiled happily. Hannah, pulling herself together, said, 'Oh dear, I suddenly feel awfully tired. It's been a strange sort of day. I'm going to leave you two to talk things over.'

'But we've more or less said it all . . . So won't you stay for coffee?'

She shook her head, moving to the door, where she paused. 'Can Yasu start her cookshop anyway, Uncle? I'm sure she'll do well and Taki would be much happier helping her than at the mission school. Especially after I've left.'

'Yes, yes . . . if that's what they want.'

'What do you mean, left?' Elinor asked sharply.

'I'm going to train as a nursing aide, Mother. I told you I

wanted to, and now I've decided.' She went out quickly.

'I don't think you'll change her mind on that score, Elinor.'

'No. But she's made of the right stuff, isn't she?'

He nodded, ringing the bell for coffee. 'It was brave of her to come, though perhaps only a last straw from my point of view.'

'Well, let her think it more; t'will help restore her faith in human nature. She's almost too serious sometimes.'

'Quite, and in any event, it doesn't matter exactly why – but I'll stay, do my bit, rise or fall with the Rising Sun . . . I was beginning to feel rather a heel about leaving. All these honours showered on foreigners for very little, while the natives have to be thrice as brave and worthy for half as much. They judge themselves by stricter standards, of course. Ah . . . coffee . . . So let's sit down by the fire and talk over old times as we were doing, Ellie. One doesn't know what the coming year will hold for any of us. But at least I shan't be so far removed from the scenes of action.'

She handed sugar. 'You're content? We haven't made you change your mind against your true inclination?'

He stretched his long legs towards the flames, smiling at her tenderly. 'I'm happy as Arnold, my dear, whatever may befall . . . happy as Arnold.'

Not only Elinor was pleased at her brother's decision; the Japanese medical authorities were quite delighted, welcoming him back into their fold with acclaim, touched that he should, as he said, have found himself incapable of leaving the country at this critical juncture in its history. And, during the spring, the sense of crisis intensified. Orderly groups of conscripted soldiers in spruce western-style uniforms marched about the streets, where children chanted rhymes about cutting off a thousand Chinese pigtails with a single sword stroke; on the parade ground near the Miyatas' house, military bands practised patriotic songs such as 'Though Ten Thousand Strong the Enemy Is', which was intended to reassure the populace that, though numerically the weaker, they had the edge in terms of dedicated loyalty and fighting spirit. But the world at large was not convinced of this and the Japanese were branded as vainglorious, power-hungry upstarts who would quickly be vanquished if they dared to intrude upon China's long-established suzerainty over Korea.

In May a rebellious group called the Tonghaks tried to overthrow the Korean government, and the Japanese sent in a division, ostensibly to help the King quell the revolt, but actually to establish a military foothold there. Alarmed by this strategy, the Chinese also sent in forces, and from then on war was inevitable. The Japanese, whose plans had long been laid, set up military headquarters in Nagasaki and Hiroshima and detachments of troops were moved south in readiness for embarkation to the scene of conflict. A naval engagement was won by the Japanese before war was officially declared and, five days after its declaration, on August 1st, their advance regiments marched victoriously into the Korean capital of Seoul with guns firing and banners waving, proclaiming themselves liberators of the kingdom from the Chinese yoke. It was their martial debut on the world scene, and the first time for over two hundred and fifty years that the nation had fought beyond its own boundaries; and the civilian population was delirious with delight at this initial victory.

During the triumphal celebrations, Joey paid a brief visit to his parents before leaving for the battle-front. They hadn't seen him for several months and in that interval he had quickly and truly grown up. He strode firmly instead of darting about, a full moustache gave his face authority, and his eyes shone with a new look of purposeful happiness. Elinor could not imagine him ever again sporting a straw boater or a silver-topped cane. Now, he belonged to the masculine Japanese tribe, wore its uniform, obeyed its stern disciplines, was unquestionably devoted to its immediate goals. Perhaps that was what he had most wanted all along, she thought wryly. She and Kenjiro raised glasses of champagne with heartfelt wishes for his safe return while he stood between them, obviously restive to be off – to adventure, action, destiny.

'You're a lucky young man', Kenjiro said enviously. 'I

never fought in battle, as you once reminded me. So now you must be brave enough for us both.'

'And careful!' Elinor added quickly.

'Carefully brave not bravely careful is the way of the samurai, Mother.'

'Samurai – pooh! Most of them were reckless, stupid daredevils; for heaven's sake don't try to emulate them.'

'Like Great-Uncle Gengoro, you mean?' He rolled his eyes teasingly, for Gengoro's fierce, obstinate courage was a family legend.

'That reminds me . . .' Kenjiro muttered, hurrying out, as Elinor replied, 'Exactly, not like Gengoro. You are our beloved eldest son, Joey, don't forget that in all your martial fervour, please – my handsome soldier-boy.' She stroked his sleeve.

'No, Mother, I won't.' He raised his glass, smiling at her brilliantly. 'And thank you – for all the Christmas trees, the frolics, and the fun.'

'Oh, Joey, don't say things like that, you make it sound so . . . final.'

'I just meant that I really *was* a boy then, whereas now I'm an officer and a gentleman.' He grinned, setting down the glass. 'I must say farewell to the younger ones and the Yoshidas before I go.'

'And Hannah, of course. She was sorry not to be here, but she's taking her second proficiency exam at the hospital today, did I tell you?'

'I never thought hard-hearted Hannah would take to nursing.'

'Joey, she never was hard-hearted and you know it.'

'I know it now and I'm glad. Anyway, I shall see her this evening. She's joining Yukio Iwada and me for a brief raising of glasses. He's off to join the First Army, by the way, but he wanted to see her before leaving.'

'Yukio wanted . . . Do you think perhaps . . .?' She left the question unfinished as Kenjiro returned with a long object wrapped in gold and red silk, which he handed to his son with a slight bow.

486

'The sword of my father, Joey. I want you to take it with you, even though it's unlikely to be of any practical use.'

'Oh, Father!' Joey said. 'Oh, Father!' They looked at each other and Joey bowed in his turn. 'Thank you. I shall treasure it with my life.'

Elinor walked aside to hide her emotion, thinking how deeply she loved her son and her husband – for their warm passions, their efforts to control them, and so much else besides. It seemed absurd now that, not so long ago, she had seriously considered breaking the bonds that united her and Kenjiro, for what had been little more than a trivial, almost a ritual offence. And her eyes swam with tears of love as she looked back at them, still standing together rather formally, playing the correct parts the occasion demanded, but not coldly. They were quietly discussing the merits of the weapons Joey was more likely to use than his ancestral sword – the modern Murata rifles, and field guns, with breech action calibre 2.95 inches and projectile weights of nine pounds five ounces. That weight, hurtling at high speed, would kill a man, Elinor thought, suddenly wanting to scream, go down on her knees, beseech her son not to go. Then she straightened her back, half-teasing herself with the reminder that she was, after all, the beloved wife of a samurai and must behave as such.

Completing his round of household farewells with a show of cheerful nonchalance, Joey collected his sister from the hospital and they drove to a quiet garden-restaurant in the suburbs, where Yukio was already seated at a terrace table drinking the expensive Scotch whisky he had specially ordered for the occasion. The evening was warm and he was wearing loose, dark blue silks that suited him much better than his usual tightly creased uniform. After the warmth of their initial greetings an uncomfortable silence fell, for they were all aware that this meeting would be the last for a considerable time and that the future was uncertain. Yukio pulled out cigarettes, threw one at Joey, lit one himself, then gazed intently at the packet. It was emblazoned with the brand name 'Hero' and a Japanese soldier in a peaked cap with a modern rifle slung over his shoulder striding before a rising sun.

'Studying for your new role?' Joey quizzed.

Yukio chuckled. 'I do not presume so much! No, I was looking at that rifle and remembering the "airing days" we used to have in the old Kyoto home. The servants would bring everything out from the store-rooms to hang up in the spring sunshine. They would brush, polish, beat the dust from the torn banners and battle-curtains, suits of leather armour, horned helmets, cloth horse-covers, quivers of arrows – arrows, I ask you! And in my childishness I imagined wars would always be fought in such a fashion; and that was barely twenty years ago . . . .'

'Eh-hey, Kyoto folk are always half a century behind the times!' Joey teased, referring to the ancient rivalry between the old capital and the new.

Yukio puffed smoke at him. 'Who'd want to be born an upstart Tokyo-man – "glittering brief and shallow like a summer sunbeam in a dusty street"? I quote from one of your own poetasters.'

'Nothing amiss with the brief and shallow, the quick-fading-away,' Joey retorted, and Hannah broke in, 'Oh, I wish you'd drop that silly phrase, brother!'

'You sound just like Mother!' He squinted and raised his glass to her, but she ignored him and changed the subject. 'But didn't you leave Kyoto when you were quite young, to visit America, Yukio?'

He nodded. 'And what a surprise that was to a growing lad! I was sorting through some of the first letters I wrote from San Francisco, when I went home last week – just in case, you know . . . They were quite funny. A top-man in our party started picking his teeth with a fork during a formal dinner and then an American lady in a low-cut dress treated us to an operatic air at the piano . . . When she trilled to a high note we lads nearly exploded with laughter . . . Well, I still think it's the most ridiculous noise!'

Hannah grinned. 'I rather agree – and I suppose the low-cut gown shocked you?'

'I was so appalled I daren't look at her — though I certainly wanted to.'

'Well, Mother was just as shocked, when she first came here, by the old men who used to scrub women's backs in the public baths. So it's simply a question of custom, you see!'

'And now the old men have lost their jobs, while even our own ladies show off their bare shoulders . . .'

'. . . and go out into society much more, which is surely a good thing?'

Earlier he had evaded her attempts to elicit his views on 'the woman question', but tonight he was more forthcoming. 'Yes, I do see it as a good thing, Hannah. Women should mix socially with men, and countries that keep them totally segregated are primitive and uncivilised.'

Joey poured more whisky for them both. 'Bravo, Yukio! That's the way to my sister's heart. She has got one after all, you know.'

'I never doubted it.' Yukio smiled at her. 'And I'm sure she'll make an excellent nurse because of it. Why, I quite envy the soldiers whom she will be tending . . .'

It was the first overt compliment he had ever paid her and she lowered her eyes in sudden embarrassment, saying only, 'Well I certainly hope neither of you will need my ministrations.'

'So do I. To be killed outright is nothing, but to be maimed . . .' He shuddered as he drank, while Joey lit another cigarette and prowled restlessly about the terrace, saying, 'At least no one will expect me — a budding novelist — to perform any heroics in the course of military duty; but a few medals wouldn't go amiss for you, Yukio.'

'I'll see what I can manage, now I have the right inspiration,' he murmured, again looking at Hannah.

In the sweet, melancholy pause that followed they heard frogs croaking beside the pond below the terrace. Darkness had fallen and moonlight shone on the still water and the damp lily-pads.

'My, what a romantic summer night it is! And here we have very civilised mixing of men and women!' Joey bounded

489

to them, putting a hand on each of their shoulders, and ducking his head at a nearby tree,

> *'The Moonlight on the pine,*
> *I keep hanging it, taking it off,*
> *— and gazing each time.'*

'So we must poetise now?' Yukio drained his glass and recited,

> *'The octopus, while summer moonshine streams*
> *into the trap, enjoys its fleeting dreams.'*

They looked expectantly at Hannah, who rose, 'It's not fair; you've appropriated the best ones. So now,

> *Leading me along,*
> *My shadow goes back home*
> *from looking at the moon.'*

Joey sighed, consulting his watch. 'Yes, we must go. Hannah's on duty later.'

Yukio hesitated, scrubbing his head with his wrist to keep his thoughts inside, then he too rose, bowing formally. 'Then we must say goodbye. May the spirits of the ancestors protect you, Joey.'

They bowed in return and expressed similar prayers for Yukio, who was bound for Korea. At the gate, Joey turned and gave his friend an exaggerated military salute which Yukio returned in good measure. Then Yukio sat down again to finish the last of the whisky and gaze at the moon alone.

Joey left Tokyo the next day to join his artillery regiment, proudly carrying with him his grandfather Aritomo's sword. His regiment was attached to the Second Army, commanded by Marshall Oyama, but at that stage of the conflict the military initiative was with the First Army in Korea, which was pressing steadily north towards Manchuria. The Chinese soldiers sent to resist its advances were ill-equipped, poorly trained, and old-fashioned; Japanese newspaper cartoons showed them dropping their ancient rifles and running to hold umbrellas over the heads of their superior officers when it began to rain during the Battle of Pyong-yang. Not surprisingly, the Japanese were the victors; still they suffered casualties and the wounded were sent to the port of Chemulpo for transportation home in hospital ships waiting in the Yellow Sea.

Rather to Elinor's consternation, Arnold volunteered for duty on one of these ships, following the Battle of Pyong-yang, and was immediately posted south. It was not in the least dangerous, he assured his sister when she protested that he was carrying his determination to 'nail his colours to the Rising Sun' altogether too far. Korean coastal waters were already under Japanese control and the hospital ships well protected, but by being on hand when the wounded came aboard, he might help to save more lives. Thinking of Joey, she could hardly gainsay that argument and sent him off in a happy bustle, sniffing the air of adventure again like a twenty-year-old.

But within a month his ship was crammed with men wounded during the next battle of the River Yalu at Hushon, a strategic crossing point into Manchuria. Medical resources aboard were badly over-stretched; infections spread in the overcrowded, unhygenic conditions. Arnold contracted a virulent fever, died after a brief illness, and was buried at sea.

Elinor, whose anxieties and fears had all centred on Joey, found the news almost unbelievable. Her brother had gone away so breezily and casually, and the poignancy of his death was intensified by the thought that if the women of the family had not interfered with his plans he might even now be courting rich widows in Bath. Yet they simply must not blame themselves on that score, Ryo insisted, for they had acted from the best of motives and Arnold had made his own final decisions. He had simply gone to his predestined fate; Christian though she was, Ryo had no doubt on that score. But were their motives so pure, Elinor wondered? Had not Ryo been spurred partly by a deep resentment towards any foreign male who used a Japanese woman for his pleasure, as she had once been used? And had not she herself been moved partly by a desire to keep Arnold near her? She could find no answer to these disquieting questions, but they lingered for a while, clouding her grief with a taint of remorseful guilt.

Before leaving, Arnold had made a meticulous will, with bequests to his sister and her family and the bulk of his estate going to Yasu and her children. His resolution was correct, Elinor knew; but she still couldn't bring herself to share her sense of loss with the one other person who probably felt it most. Yasu first read of Arnold's death in the newspapers, then received letters from lawyers. Thanks to her and Ryo, she would have enough capital to open a whole chain of cook-shops, Elinor thought sardonically, leaving the woman forever unvisited even while berating herself for her lack of Christian charity.

CHAPTER TWENTY-FIVE

In the weeks following the tragic news of Arnold's death Elinor threw herself wholeheartedly into the civilian war effort; the Chinese became her enemy too and she felt totally at one with the Japanese cause. Throughout the country societies were formed to raise money to provide the front-line soldiery with flannel clothing, fur coats, and soft red blankets; and the Red Cross hospital was inundated with bandages, socks, and home-made salves for the wounded. Troops travelling to the embarkation ports were showered with gifts of food, tobacco, and lucky charms at every railway station, and at the news of every victory, huge processions bearing lanterns and banners flocked to the temples of the war-gods to give thanks.

While the First Army was pushing across Manchuria towards Mukden, the Second landed on the Liaotung Peninsula, the eastern-most spur of Chinese territory and closest to Korea. There too the Japanese advanced rapidly, crushing the enemy defences in every town.

'It's as easy as swallowing oysters,' wrote Joey in his first letter from the front. 'The Sons of the Celestials usually turn pigtail at the very sight of us – most irritating, for it leaves us nothing but rabbits to fire at. (Rabbit stew is much tastier than I imagined.)'

By November the Second Army had pushed down the peninsula as far as Port Arthur on its extreme tip, a fortified Chinese base that had to be captured. A squadron of Japanese warships converged on it from the south, while land-forces pincered in from the north. On November 21st, after a brief, violent invasion, the port fell into the invaders' hands. Again Tokyo's streets rang with joy and hawkers did a roaring trade in coloured pictures showing 'Our Heroic Soldiers capturing Port Arthur', which had been confidently printed before the battle took place.

The greatest joy for the Miyatas was another letter from Joey, which Elinor described to Ryo as they sat together in her tiny office at the hospital.

'He's made it all sound rather jolly until now,' she began, 'but Port Arthur was obviously dreadful. A horrid place, he says, squalid streets lined with dirty hovels, a range of stoney hills behind and, bordering the sea, ugly dockyards and a depot full of torpedoes which the Chinese didn't know how to use . . . Listen, this part makes exciting reading, now we know he's safely through . . . "We crept towards the town under cover of darkness and positioned the Krupp field guns within range of their forts on the hill-tops and began firing after dawn. The enemy pounded back with their old-fashioned mortars but our men simply pressed forward and about noon were able to blow up the magazine of their largest fort on Pine Tree Hill. It made an almighty racket, I can tell you, and when the smoke cleared I saw, through the field-glasses, soldiers flying for their lives, tearing off cartridge belts and tattered bits of uniform as they ran. Their officers waved fiery-dragon banners to rally them for another stand, but they weren't having it — and one can't blame them. They had neither good discipline nor decent weapons.

"After that we just kept going and by evening the town and most of the forts were in our hands. What happened next was terrible, though I doubt you'll hear much about it in the official reports. Apparently a division of our men under Yamagi had seen bodies of some captured comrades strung up on poles as they entered the town from the north-west, and later they simply ran amuck in revenge. I've never witnessed such slaughter and hope never to again; our men swathing down, bayonetting and chopping up hundreds of innocent civilians till the streets ran with blood. It had nothing to do with honourable warfare, or the glory of our ancestors. Some of our officers were stabbing people with their swords, but I didn't unsheath mine. I'm sure you wouldn't have wished it in such circumstances, Father.

"For the first time since this little fracas began I loathed it, but I didn't do anything because I was paralysed with a kind of sick horror, to tell you the truth. Captain Hirata tried to stop the butchery at first . . . Have I told you about him? He speaks quite good English and appreciates the finer points of my occasional little burlesques, so we've become quite chums. He's a devout Christian and makes the faith sound more persuasive than anything I've ever heard in St Andrew's, Mother! He always wears his grandfather's sword as I wear mine and also sports snow-white gloves. The men think he's a bit of a sissy-lily, but I admire him as a man of great rectitude. He couldn't do much about the goings-on that night though, and we eventually left them to it. The men had calmed down by the morning and hundreds of Chinese corpses were shovelled into the sea. So that was the end of it. And now we're stuck in this hole till the top brass decide where we push on to next. I'm passing the time by trying to write in a new way, my previous literary efforts are so much folderol. At this rate of advance we'll all be home in a few months, and I'm beginning to think that will be very pleasant . . . War is such a stupid muddle, don't you know?" He goes on a bit, messages to friends, love to you . . .'

Ryo breathed a sigh of relief. 'How very sensible he sounds now! Maybe he will become a writer one day; wouldn't that be marvellous?'

Elinor nodded energetically, trying to banish the unspoken fear between them, as Ryo continued. 'And isn't it encouraging about that Captain Hirata? Perhaps he'll be the instrument of Joey's true conversion. I shall pray for it, Elinor. But now I'd better go. You're always so busy these days, while I'm quite on the side-lines. No one bothers about girls' education or women's rights any more.'

'War puts things in a different perspective for a while, that's all,' Elinor replied, rising.

'And one that men dominate. Is that why they enjoy it? So

it makes a hero of Joey and of Hannah a devoted nurse . . .'

'I see nothing very wrong in that, anything if it helps us to a quick victory. Kenjiro thinks Joey's regiment will be sent north again to join up with the First Army and if that goes according to plan the Chinese might surrender . . .'

'A consummation devoutly to be wished . . . And meanwhile I won't keep you a moment longer from your labours . . .'

Elinor continued to work hard in the course of her chosen duty, partly to keep her anxiety about Joey at bay. The main battlefront was now concentrated in the wintry spaces of Manchuria, and in his next letter Joey gave grim accounts of soldiers with frost-blackened feet, tents submerged under snow-drifts, Chinese forced-labour gangs freezing to death on the mountain roads. Icicles festooned his moustache every morning, he joked, but he hesitated to shave it off because it kept his upper lip the one warm spot on him for the rest of the day. They were on the move again, he concluded, into the teeth of the gales; destination secret.

Elinor, having tea by the fire late one January afternoon after her hospital shift, could not forget her son's wintry tales. She reached out her hands to feel the flames' congenial heat, then withdrew them guiltily. How could one endure such implacable icy freezing, she wondered, staring intensely into the glow, hoping to make her son feel warmer thereby. The door opened quietly and Kenjiro came in, leaning against its inside. His face was carved blank-white like a Noh mask, his eyes narrow black slits looking out from behind it.

She jumped up, gasping, 'Kenjiro . . . what's happened . . . Is it . . .? Is he . . .?'

'Killed. Yes. At the battle for Kaiping on January 10th. No other details yet.' He tottered towards her and they fell against each other, clinging together shaking, both, after a while, mercifully able to weep. She gripped his jacket-collar in agony. 'And I was just thinking about him . . . the dreadful cold he must be suffering.'

'He's not suffering anything now.' He stroked her hair mechanically.

'But oh, Joey . . . Joey . . . the fun, the youth, all that spirit

496

'. . . cut off.'

'He and many others too.'

'That doesn't help.' She sobbed again and after a while asked in a kind of helpless rage, 'No details at all?'

'None. Just the bare telegram.'

'Where is this Kaiping then? I've never even heard of it.'

He moved slowly to find an atlas, showing her carefully, as if the very pinpointing of that fateful place could make some sense of what had happened there. 'They were pushing up here to meet the First Army, as I thought they would. You see? It's on a strategic junction between the Liaotung Peninsula and Manchuria.' Tears slid down his cheeks on to the map but he did not shut it. He wanted them to stain the page permanently.

She too kept studying it. 'I wonder where he was when he wrote his last letter?' She rasped painfully, 'His *last* letter, forever and ever.' She leaned against Kenjiro's chest and wept more as he stared over her head into the flames that shivered beautifully before his damp eyes.

At length he disengaged her gently and she collapsed back into the chair. 'People must be told. The news came an hour or so ago, but it will be in the papers by tomorrow.' Savagely he kicked a live coal into the fire. 'Quick-fading-away, quick-fading-away . . . Perhaps in his bones he knew?'

'Oh, I pray he didn't.' She rocked to and fro, holding her stomach, which had turned to a large, hard lump of ice. 'Because he was happy in his short life, wasn't he? Often? His sparkle, the irreverence . . . if only we hadn't kept trying to make him grow up and be serious, Kenjiro.'

'We simply weren't to know. And he was a man by the time he died.' He stood silent for a few minutes more, gripping the marble mantel to get full control of himself, then looked up at the clock. 'I must get a telegram off to Hannah before the wires close. She must come at once. We must be together. And then I'll go to Ryo . . . and there's the younger ones to tell.'

'Not so young any more that they won't understand,' she whispered desolately. 'But I'll try and break it to them . . .

497

soon.' She rose to dab his moist face with a sodden handkerchief. 'We had a lovely son, Kenjiro, a lovely son. We
mustn't forget that.'

He grunted agreement and shuffled to the door. 'Shall I tell
the servants?'

'No, the children first. I'll manage it. Don't be too long,
please, dear.'

After his departure an uncanny silence settled over the
house. She wandered to the window, drew back the curtains;
snowflakes were whirling out of the darkness into the beams
of the lanterns hung at the gable-ends and back into the dark.
'Oh, my darling Joey, my hero-soldier boy . . . Quick-faded-
away, quick-faded-away . . .' she murmured with stiff lips
over which the tears still fell. Then she went to prepare her
face for the children.

Snow continued to fall for several days, muffling them in a
cocoon of grief. Kenjiro, staring at its sharp morning glitter,
remembered his own youthful joy in its beauty and mourned
that his son would never see it again. Hannah arrived after a
storm-delayed journey from Hiroshima and retired to bed,
suffering from grief, a chill, and exhaustion. Ryo became the
strongest and ministered to them all. Newspapers hailed the
latest victory – the capture of Kaiping with a loss of only
forty-six men and three officers, who were named. Tributes
and letters of sympathy flooded in and Kenjiro sat long hours
at his desk meticulously answering each one, for he had taken
leave from work and could think of nothing else to do.

Shortly after the news reached them, a Shinto service in
honour of the dead killed in recent battles was held in the
Great Imperial Hall near the palace. Only close relatives were
invited and Elinor was the sole foreigner among rows of
bowed black heads. After the service, mourners with tears in
their eyes came up and whispered that she had now made the
greatest sacrifice for the Empire of the Rising Sun that a
woman could ever make. They stroked her sleeves, patted her
hands gently, promised her that heroic Joey was safely
gathered into the folds of the illustrious ancestors. She and
Kenjiro drove home in a black carriage, silent and dry-eyed.

Dusk was falling, the gutters, running with melted snow; from the parade ground came the usual sound of the evening bugles, and close by the whistle of the noodle-vendor trundling his steaming hand-cart to the servants' quarters of the big houses.

They ate supper quietly alone together and towards its end, Elinor said, 'Yukio Iwada was badly wounded in the battle for the River Yalu last October. Did Hannah tell you? He caught a severe infection from his injuries and his life was despaired of. But now he's recovering in her hospital. He hopes the war will continue long enough for him to get back into it.'

'Still as a cavalry officer?'

'He's learning to ride again already. Hannah says he was extremely upset about Joey.'

He poked his dessert dish wherein lay a mushy slab of pink and yellow pudding. 'What's this concoction?'

'I don't know. I think Yoshida is trying to cheer us up with what he imagines to be French cuisine.'

'Well, he's wasting his time. All food tastes the same – of nothing very much.' He rose and poured a stiff brandy instead, rolling the first sip vigorously round his mouth to activate his taste-buds.

'It's the sorrow,' she said. 'I feel the same.'

'I read somewhere once that "as the dried sponge absorbs water slowly and slowly, as my heart fills with sorrow gradually". So . . . that has happened, yes, and it is more than that too. A general sense of disillusion that has been filling me – like water into a sponge – even before his death. I keep harking back to the years just before and after the Emperor's Restoration . . . our certainty of vision and purpose, our dedication to the goals of ending feudalism and modernising the country, our talk of progress and taking our place among the great nations of the world. But what has happened now, Elinor, I ask you? The strict disciplines and grand ideals are dying away and we're becoming a nation of fashion-seekers and easy livers. Those whom the Restoration brought into power are obsessed only with holding onto it at all costs as if the heroism and enterprise of their youth entitled them to rule ever after. There's greed, corruption, and cynicism in high places just as there always was, and the exploitation of the poor and lowly by the rich and powerful, which I used to think we could banish from the land, still goes on. Only now the wealthy men of industry and commerce are oppressing the common workers, cities grow bigger and uglier at the expense of our beautiful countryside. You remember the Rising Sun Cotton Works, don't you? One of hundreds – symptom of the future.'

He took a long drink, but moodily, not enjoying it. She considered him; because of what had followed from that visit to the works they had never mentioned it again till now. But he, she realised, had quite forgotten the connection, and to her it was no longer of any importance, overtaken, engulfed by the recent tragic events that had yet left them united. 'But things have been accomplished, steps forward taken,' she said, wanting to lift his spirits.

'Yes, yes I know. I suppose we expected too much too soon, in the way of youth. I remember when I was young all the talk about the great Saigo Takamori and his ideas, which I thought old-fashioned. He was a hero even then, though always an inconsistent one. But he believed in the peasants – the body-workers – and in the Confucian virtues of stoicism and frugality. Too much materialism would be our ruination, he wrote, and that is what I'm afraid of now. We think we need more and more for our pleasure . . . Look at this house, compared to the one in which I grew up!' He flung his arms about in disgust.

'With its earth-closets and pith-wick lamps to read by? Is that what you hanker after?'

He glared back defiantly. 'Sometimes I do. But that's not my main point, which is that we didn't foresee all this, did we, when we started out with such enthusiasm along the great highway to westernisation and progress? That's all I'm saying . . . It's turned rather sour, hasn't it?' He grimaced as if his brandy were bitter gall.

'It is both sour and sweet, but you only taste the sour now

because of our loss. Yet only consider what your children have learned and will learn, think of your achievements and your brave sister's. Think of how far you have travelled, what you have understood, and compare that with how it would have been for you and Ryo living out your feudal lives in a thatched cottage near Kagoshima, following the footsteps of your ancestors from one Bon Odori to the next. You, and thousands like you, have gained much more than you've lost, Kenjiro . . . And for those wise words you can pour me a brandy too!'

He smiled brilliantly at her for the first time since the news of Joey's death. 'And I, personally, have gained you, Elinor, my heart-drawing.' He drew her to him. 'Thank the gods I still have you. We still have each other, don't we?'

'For as long as we live,' she agreed, nestling against him. He stroked her thick hair, thinking that too would be quick-fading-away, but he minded less than he used to about that, for he was in his fifty-fifth year under heaven and had enjoyed a fair measure of cherry blossoms and snowflakes already. 'Yes, yes, sensible Ellie . . . And for tomorrow, tomorrow's wind will blow . . .'

He went to pour her a drink and she wandered to the mantel, staring into the bright flames. It was still cold outside and in distant Manchuria the Japanese armies were still tramping to victory in the teeth of the wintry gales. And here in their own comfortable home she and Kenjiro were as united as they had been when they eloped together twenty-eight years ago.

Shortly after taking Kaiping, the Japanese consolidated their position further with the capture of Wei-hei-wei in the Chinese province of Shantung, from which point they were poised to march towards Peking itself. The Chinese, their morale broken, their forces decimated, sued desperately for a cessation of hostilities, and a peace treaty was signed in the town of Shimonoseki on April 17th, 1895. The war, lasting but eight months, had proved an absolute triumph for the victors. No eastern country for centuries had given such a strong, convincing display of military expertise, and the western world was amazed, not to say a little perturbed. Japan's international status was certainly enhanced, however, and, conscious of both this and a new sense of national unity, the people rejoiced, while their rulers proclaimed glowing confidence in the future.

Shortly after the victory celebrations, Hannah returned home, where her parents lived in an aura of subdued mourning. Respecting their feelings, she at first forebore to tell them her own news, which, though joyous, heralded another parting. But one morning she found a letter beside her breakfast place which she read with such evident eagerness and delight that Elinor eventually had to ask, as if casually, 'Is it from anyone we know?'

She looked up shyly. 'From Yukio Iwada.'

'Poor fellow, badly wounded, I believe?' Kenjiro's query was genuinely casual.

'Yes. He says his wounds are still causing discomfort, but he's persevering . . .' There was a pause; Elinor was staring at her pointedly and Hannah stumbled, 'Father . . . Mother . . . you should know . . . Yukio and I are engaged to be married.'

'Engaged! Without even asking or consulting us in any way!'

'Father, please . . . it was war-time and the circumstances unusual. My nursing him in hospital, both of us separated from our families. Yukio said we couldn't marry till after the war anyway, in case he was killed. Then, because of his wounds, he simply couldn't believe that I wanted to marry him – though it didn't make the least bit of difference. He showed great bravery at the Battle of Yalu and has been awarded the Order of the Falcon. But secretly I loved him well before that, ever since the wrestling match on the beach. Do you remember, Mother? Only I didn't want to be in love with anyone then. The war, and Joey's death, made me realise how foolish that was – one has to take the opportunities, the people that life offers . . . Don't you agree? I mean, you two did. So I hope very much that you will give us your blessing, Father.' She stopped abruptly, eyes glinting ready for defiance.

'Well, I still think we might have been consulted at least,

instead of springing it on us like this.' Kenjiro was injured.

'But we are adults, Father. I know you like Yukio, and I've heard you express admiration for the part his father played in the wars of Restoration. And surely it isn't such a very great surprise?'

Elinor broke in. 'No, it isn't, and I think we should give our assent and offer congratulations, Kenjiro. Hannah has chosen the man freely and he her, which is how we always hoped the matter would be arranged, is it not? And he was Joey's friend.'

Kenjiro nodded; he was happy, even proud, and ready to be mollified. 'Yes, yes, your mother is right as usual, Hannah. And what does the Count think of it? You know, I remember seeing him riding with the Choshiu men in the entourage of the young Emperor when he first came to this city. A dignified aristocrat, but ill-looking at the time from the wounds he'd received on the battlefields near Kyoto.'

'And Yukio says he's pleased because he has always admired your devotion to the Imperial cause and the government, Father.' She read from the letter. 'Also, he welcomes the formation of new bonds between Satsuma and Choshiu.'

Elinor laughed. 'How the old clan spirit does cling on! So have you gone as far as discussing a wedding date, dear?'

'We want it to be soon, before my next birthday. The Count requests that the main ceremony be Buddhist and held in Kyoto, where he's lived for several years past. He's a little infirm these days and dislikes the vulgar noise and bustle of the new capital, Yukio explains.'

'He is a cultured man and his requests should present no difficulty,' Kenjiro murmured.

'And what about a Christian service? I trust you'll have both, as Father and I did?'

'Yes, Mother. We thought there could be a service at St Andrew's if you wish and Yukio says here that his eldest brother will represent his family. He wants to come and see you soon, of course, to discuss details.'

'He has two older brothers, does he not?'

'Yes. The elder came to the hospital to see Yukio. He looks

503

very like his father, apparently; but Yukio doesn't . . .' She hesitated, resuming in an edgier tone, 'You see, Yukio's mother was the Count's concubine, who lived in the household for years in the old-fashioned style. She died when Yukio was a boy and he was then brought up as the youngest son; only he isn't entirely, not in terms of inheritance and so on. I thought you should know, though it doesn't make a scrap of difference, does it?'

'A concubine's son!' Elinor laughed shortly, thinking it explained only too clearly why a family of the Iwadas' distinguished lineage were not objecting to Yukio's marriage to a 'mixed-up'. Kenjiro also understood and his pride in the alliance was momentarily diminished. But what could he say, he – who had chosen to marry outside his race?

'If it makes no difference to you then it mustn't to us, Hannah,' he replied eventually. 'And Yukio has a fine record on his own account. He's to be decorated, you say?'

'Yes, Father. Moreover, he's determined to become C.-in-C. of the Japanese army one day.'

Elinor stared at the cold toast on her plate. How was it that this perceptive daughter of hers had chosen to marry a military man? The role of soldier's wife was hardly what she would have chosen for her. But, if Hannah was aware of this, it made no dent in her own certainty. She was radiantly happy, accepting the whole world without reservation or withdrawal because it included her lover, and she waited impatiently for his arrival to make her complete.

Tomi and Umé were the first to respond to their older sister's bubbling gladness, which soon lightened the gloom of the entire household; though Elinor and Ryo shared very mixed feelings about the alliance. Was it their over-solicitude that had pushed Hannah in this unforeseen direction? More likely, they agreed, it was the war itself, which had reduced all other causes to insignificance, united Hannah totally with the land of her birth, and confirmed her earlier attraction to Yukio – now a hero-figure and a man of action. To Ryo, Hannah's choice was a betrayal from which she withdrew, injured; while Elinor, who understood better, found herself

504

defending her daughter and anticipating Yukio's arrival eagerly too, that she might view him in this new light.

As soon as he reached Tokyo, Yukio was invited to luncheon, and at exactly the appointed hour his carriage drove into the front courtyard. The family, including Ryo and the head servants, were gathered in the entrance-way to greet him formally; but to their surprise, not one but two army officers climbed out. Yukio, bowing in his usual stiff, brisk fashion, introduced his companion as Captain Hirata, who had served in the same artillery regiment as Joey.

'How very good of you to come. Joey wrote to us about you.' Elinor shook his hand, from which he had removed an immaculate white glove.

The Captain smiled. 'And he spoke to me often about you – all of you – his beloved family.'

'Did he really? I'm glad to hear that,' she gulped painfully.

As they settled in the drawing room, where sherry and biscuits were served, Yukio explained that he had met Captain Hirata, who had been wounded during the last battle of the war, in the Hiroshima hospital. The captain had been intending to visit the Miyatas in any case, so they had decided to come together. 'I thought it might please you,' he added, bowing to Kenjiro. Yukio's formerly sturdy frame was gaunt from his war ordeals and he moved with care, his wounds still torturing him. But his hair was as wiry, his narrow eyes as deep-set, his skin as sallow – typically, totally oriental, Elinor thought, trying not to wish it slightly otherwise.

'We are indeed pleased to make your acquaintance. You were, I presume, at Kaiping?' Kenjiro was saying to the Captain carefully.

'Yes, I expect you've heard the details of the engagement?'

'Not really. Rather a minor skirmish, wasn't it? We've heard no first-hand accounts, so anything you could tell us would be welcome.'

The Captain glanced worriedly at the women present. 'I would be sorry to upset anyone, especially on an occasion like this. Perhaps later?'

'No, Captain, the children will be joining us for luncheon,

so it's preferable that we hear now,' Elinor interrupted, in that authoritative tone which always surprised Japanese men. He looked for guidance to Kenjiro, who nodded.

'Then . . . just a moment . . .' He went to the door, whispering instructions to a servant and saying, as he returned, 'There's not a lot to tell. It was a short, swift victory. Kaiping is a walled town with a river running round its south side. The Chinese had fortified it quite well and even contrived to break up great blocks of ice on the frozen waters, making it difficult for us to cross. Quite a brilliant stratagem by their pathetic standards! Gales of snow were blowing and so everything was against us really – the weather, the fortified town, the river with open fields between it and the walls. But none of us doubted we would win.' He looked anxiously at the women again, then resumed with an effort, 'When we were getting ready to attack just before dawn, Joey seemed especially happy – you know how he enjoyed his parody-English jokes. And that morning he said to me as we were watching the men load the field-guns, "I have a Mikado-worshipping intimation which I have inherited *from* generations. It seems to me that is the highest form of etiquettes, yes!" ' Hannah gave a painful gasp, but the others remained silent.

'At first light the order came to advance and we started across the river, slipping and stumbling over the ice-blocks with the guns and ammunition. The enemy were firing from the forts, and lines of them faced us across the fields. We simply went ploughing on into a line of heavy fire and your son, Mr Miyata, was right in the forefront of the first charge. He should have received a posthumous decoration, in my humble opinion. As we neared, the Chinese turned and fled in their usual cowardly fashion, and just then a soldier came to tell me Lieutenant Miyata had fallen. I ran back to find him lying in the snow. He'd been killed almost instantly, the field doctor told me later, and didn't suffer long. I wanted you to know that, and I wanted . . .' He went to the servant waiting at the door and returned with a parcel, '. . . to give you this, Mr Miyata.'

Kenjiro took it with a low bow, unwrapping it slowly. They all knew what it was. He unsheathed the bright sword, holding its jewelled hilt very tightly. 'Thank you, Captain. It belonged to my father before me.'

'So Joey said.'

'It looks quite undamaged.'

'He treated it with great care. I took it from his body on the field there and then.'

Hannah dabbed her eyes and Kenjiro sheathed the sword in silence, then looked at her tenderly. 'And now we will raise our glasses — first to the departed soul of our brave and beloved son, then to celebrate the betrothal of our dearest daughter.'

After their second toast, Yukio produced a betrothal ring, slipping it on Hannah's willing finger as they were going into luncheon. At the table, the betrothed pair sat together, glancing at and away from each other self-consciously while Yukio told his fiancée that Count Iwada would be presenting her with a family heirloom, a bridal *obi* beautifully embroidered with a design of phoenix and paulownia blossoms. It was of great length to signify his hope for their long and fruitful union; and to the promise of the *obi* they also drank. When the fish course appeared, it became apparent that Yukio, whose right hand was still stiff, could not manage a knife and fork, and Elinor, cursing her thoughtlessness, sent for the best ivory chopsticks.

He grimaced. 'I will learn — this hand will mend and be able to do anything; but like a good horse it needs training.'

'Quite so, and Hannah tells me it isn't going to deflect you from your military ambitions?'

'Why should it? After all, your Admiral Nelson managed well enough with one eye.'

She laughed. 'You have studied British history, then?'

'Certainly. You are a small island that has prospered exceedingly and now rules a considerable proportion of the globe. It is an admirable example for us Japanese.'

'I suppose so, yet I'm not altogether convinced. Our colonial policies also cause conflict and suffering.'

'War, you mean? I think it's inevitable there will be more fighting for us to do, which is why I intend staying in the army.'

'But why must it always entail war?'

Kenjiro interrupted mildly, 'You know perfectly well, Elinor – because nations with power don't take kindly to ambitious upstarts. Already there are hostile rumblings from the west about our overwhelming victory against the Chinese, and we may lose on the tables of diplomacy what we won on the battlefields. But that won't be the end of it either, for we shall then have to prove ourselves again – and again if necessary – and our strength has to be partly military.'

Hannah giggled. 'Oh, you make the future sound so gloomy and difficult; but Yukio and I think it's going to be very exciting, and quite easy – compared to the past!'

'So you should. But I'm become an old man of Tempo, as Joey used to say, and am growing cynical in my later years.'

Elinor clucked exasperatedly. 'Well I don't feel the least like an old woman of Tempo, nor do you, I'm sure, Ryo?'

'Certainly not. There's a great deal for us to do yet. But then, many women come into their own later in life after spending many years in the service of others.'

She looked keenly at Yukio, who bobbed his head in her direction. 'Hannah has often mentioned the subject, Miss Miyata. She hasn't quite capitulated, you know.'

'I'm glad to hear it, Yukio. Perhaps your marriage can be more of a partnership than a battleground?'

'I think we acknowledge the possibility, Miss Miyata,' he replied, but in a tone of quiet mockery that left her unsure of his true meaning; and she returned to her conversation with Captain Hirata as they waited for the next of several courses.

It being a warm afternoon, they moved on to the terrace for dessert; servants brought dishes of fruits, jelly-moulds, and ice-creams, and Tomi came scampering after, carrying the ancestral sword that he was forbidden to unsheath.

'Oh, Father, Captain Hirata was telling me about this. Please show it to me!'

'Wait a minute, lad, eat up your ice-cream first.'

Obediently Tomi squatted on a step for a few minutes spooning the cool, strawberry-flavoured stuff and thinking sorrowfully of his fun-loving elder brother. Then he jumped up, holding out the sword again. 'Now . . . please!'

Kenjiro rose and drew the sword from its scabbard, twirling it about his head, the blade glittering in the sunlight. 'Huh-uh!' he gave a warlike grunt and jumped into an aggressive posture, pointing the weapon at Tomi, who giggled, 'You don't look very frightening, Father.'

'I'm not much of a swordsman. Your Great-Uncle Gengoro was the last of that line in our family.'

He lowered the blade and Tomi touched the bright metal lovingly. 'Is it still very sharp?'

For answer Kenjiro walked down the steps to the pond, whirled the blade in the air again and with one powerful cut slashed down heads from a whole clump of irises.

'Oh what wanton destruction!' Ryo cried irritably.

'You can use them for a flower arrangement, sister,' he replied, sheathing the sword and leaving it on a table beside her. 'Come, Hannah, let's show Yukio the new rose-garden. I intend to cultivate English roses in my later years as I did in my youth.' He smiled in his wife's direction, then led the way round the pond, leaving Captain Hirata with the ladies. 'I think Captain Iwada and your daughter will be happy together, Mrs Miyata,' he ventured.

'Oh, I'm sure of it. They seem very much in love, which is the main thing. You are a married man, Captain?'

'Yes, and my wife is also a Christian. I was telling your sister-in-law during luncheon that we are bringing up our children in the faith.'

Ryo, gathering up the iris-heads, added, 'And I was telling the Captain what Joey said in one of his last letters, Ellie, about learning more about Christianity from him than ever in a church. Had he lived, I think he might have been a convert eventually.'

'Alas, we shall never know, Miss Miyata, but there is one more small thing on that subject . . .' He hesitated, wondering if he should again shadow the sunny day with talk

509

of death.

'Please go on,' Elinor urged.

'Well, the day after the battle Joey was buried along with the other dead; and it so happened that an aged missionary of the China Inland Mission, a Mr Edward Blake, had died in the town two days before. His wife and daughter − I assume she was − who had courageously remained by his side to the end, wanted a Christian burial for him, which I was able to arrange that same day in the mission's cemetery. It was freezing cold, I remember, and Chinese coolies had to break the ground with pick-axes. As the old missionary was laid to rest, I said a Christian prayer on behalf of Joey. I felt strongly at the time that part of him was being buried there too. I thought you might like to know that . . .' He glanced tentatively at them both and they inclined their heads in agreement, hearing in the sad pause the chatter of voices returning from the rose-garden. The Captain consulted his watch and rose with the air of one who has satisfactorily discharged all his duties at last. 'And now I fear I must go, Mrs Miyata; I'm catching a late train home.'

'Must you really, Captain? Then I can only thank you again for coming.'

'It has been a great pleasure to meet Joey's parents, I assure you. I doubted the wisdom of it on such a day, for fear I might be something of a skeleton at the feast, but Yukio insisted. He too was very fond of Joey and wanted his presence to be remembered.'

Elinor smiled gratefully at Yukio as he approached with the others. 'Captain Hirata has to catch his train; I wonder about your carriage . . .?'

'Of course, I'm taking him to the station.'

The two officers bowed and shook hands all round, returning, in departure, to the correct formality of their arrival, even though, as Hannah protested, they would meet again shortly, for Yukio was staying several days in the capital, and Captain Hirata was to be best man at the St Andrew's wedding.

Hannah went to see the carriage off and, when she returned,

510

stood for a moment on the threshold of the terrace gazing out. Ryo was still sipping tea in the shade while Elinor and Kenjiro were strolling along the paved path by the pond. It occurred to Hannah then that, as a married woman, she would be bound to move away from the family and the house in which she had grown up. Regret tugged her at the thought, and at the sight of her aunt, sitting very upright, a little severe and solitary as was her wont. Across the pond, Elinor suddenly laughed, and Kenjiro touched her cheek in an affectionate gesture as she looked up at him. Hannah smiled at them both and slipped away to examine her betrothal ring. Ryo, meanwhile, sat staring solemnly at the jewelled hilt of her father's sword glinting in the sunlight, remembering that once, long years ago, she had stood with her mother at the gate of the thatched farmhouse in the Imamura valley and watched her brother go riding away on his horse wearing it.

THE END

A SELECTED LIST OF FINE NOVELS
AVAILABLE FROM CORGI BOOKS

☐	12281 5	JADE	Pat Barr	£2.95
☐	12142 8	A WOMAN OF TWO CONTINENTS	Pixie Burger	£2.50
☐	12637 3	PROUD MARY	Iris Gower	£2.50
☐	12387 0	COPPER KINGDOM	Iris Gower	£1.95
☐	12503 2	THREE GIRLS	Frances Paige	£1.95
☐	12641 1	THE SUMMER OF THE BARSHINSKEYS	Diane Pearson	£2.95
☐	10375 6	CSARDAS	Diane Pearson	£2.95
☐	09140 5	SARAH WHITMAN	Diane Pearson	£2.50
☐	10271 7	THE MARIGOLD FIELD	Diane Pearson	£2.50
☐	10249 0	BRIDE OF TANCRED	Diane Pearson	£1.75
☐	12689 6	IN THE SHADOW OF THE CASTLE	Erin Pizzey	£2.50
☐	12462 1	THE WATERSHED	Erin Pizzey	£2.95
☐	11596 7	FEET IN CHAINS	Kate Roberts	£1.95
☐	11685 8	THE LIVING SLEEP	Kate Roberts	£2.50
☐	12607 1	DOCTOR ROSE	Elvi Rhodes	£1.95
☐	12579 2	THE DAFFODILS OF NEWENT	Susan Sallis	£1.75
☐	12375 7	A SCATTERING OF DAISIES	Susan Sallis	£2.50
☐	12880 5	BLUEBELL WINDOWS	Susan Sallis	£2.50
☐	12636 5	THE MOVIE SET	June Flaum Singer	£2.95
☐	12609 8	STAR DREAMS	June Flaum Singer	£2.50
☐	12118 5	THE DEBUTANTES	June Flaum Singer	£2.50
☐	12700 0	LIGHT AND DARK	Margaret Thomson Davis	£2.95
☐	11575 4	A NECESSARY WOMAN	Helen Van Slyke	£2.50
☐	12240 8	PUBLIC SMILES, PRIVATE TEARS	Helen Van Slyke	£2.50
☐	11321 2	SISTERS AND STRANGERS	Helen Van Slyke	£2.50
☐	11779 X	NO LOVE LOST	Helen Van Slyke	£2.50
☐	12676 4	GRACE PENSILVA	Michael Weston	£2.95